FROM THE BATTLEFIELD TO THE BEDCHAMBER . . . FROM THE MARKETPLACE TO THE TEMPLE . . . A TUMULTUOUS TIME OF INTRIGUE AND CRUELTY, PASSIONS AND DREAMS . . .

TIGLATH—Destined to become a legendary warrior, his fate is the torment of a blinding love, a crushing hatred, and a terrible vengeance on an entire land. . . .

ESARHADDON—Chosen as heir of King Sennacherib, he does not wish the power given him or the deed he must perform: to destroy the brother—the rival—he loves. . . .

ESHARHAMAT—Born to be consort to Assyria's king, her seductive beauty and passionate desires will drive one man mad with hunger, another with murder and revenge. . . .

THE ASSYRIAN
AN EXPLOSIVE SAGA OF LEGENDARY COURAGE AND UNFORGETTABLE LOVE

"ASSYRIA IS ALL HERE, VIVID, ALIVE, ENGAGING FOR ALL THE SENSES."
—Robert Shea, author of
All Things Are Lights

"THE STORY OF A PASSIONATELY MORAL MAN TORN AMONG AMOROUS LONGINGS, THE SEDUCTIVENESS OF POWER, FRATERNAL EMOTION, AND COGNIZANCE OF HIS NATION'S WELFARE."
—*Publishers Weekly*

THE
ASSYRIAN

NICHOLAS
GUILD

A DELL BOOK

Published by
Dell Publishing
a division of
The Bantam Doubleday Dell Publishing Group, Inc.
666 Fifth Avenue
New York, New York 10103

ISBN: 0-440-20197-7

Reprinted by arrangement with Macmillan Publishing Company on behalf of Atheneum Publishers

Printed in the United States of America

Published simultaneously in Canada

October 1988

10 9 8 7 6 5 4 3 2 1

OPM

For Mikey and his Mom

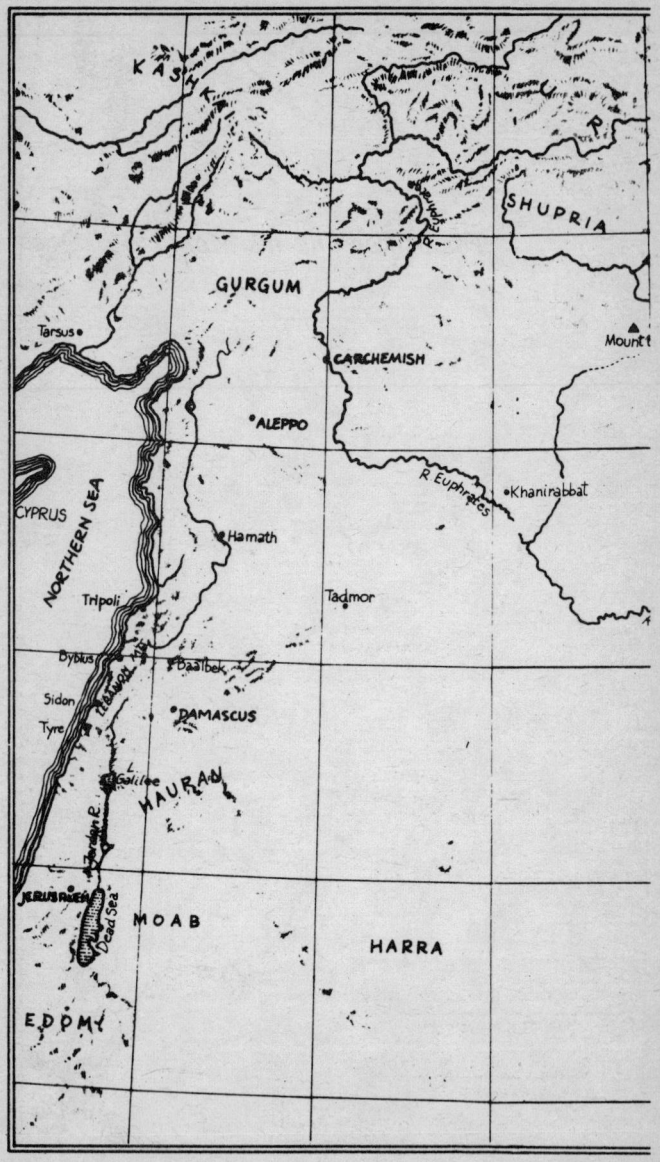

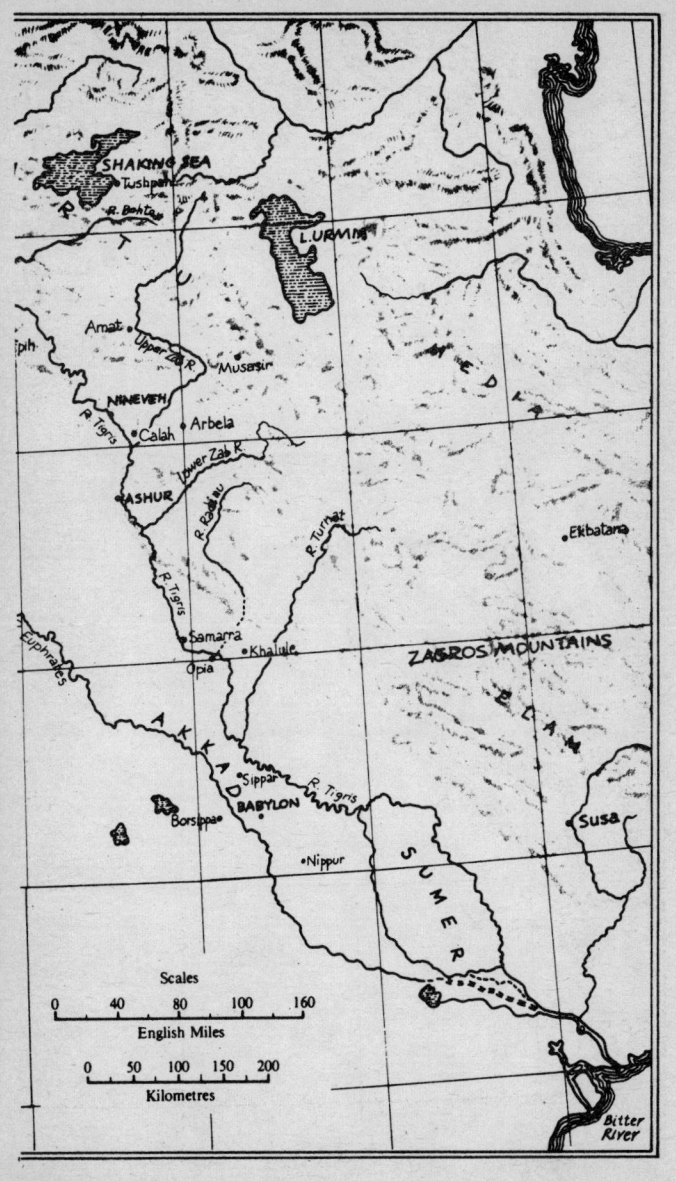

SHAKING SEA

Tushpan

R. Bohta

L. URMIA

R. Tigris

Amat

Upper Zab R.

Musasir

NINEVEH

Calah Arbela

Lower Zab R.

ASHUR

R. Radanu

R. Turnat

Ekbatana

R. Tigris

Samarra

ZAGROS MOUNTAINS

Opia Khalule

ELAM

Euphrates

AKKAD

Sippar

R. Tigris

Borsippa BABYLON

Susa

Nippur

SUMER

Scales

0   40   80   100   160

English Miles

0   50   100   150   200

Kilometres

Bitter River

1

At night outside my sleeping chamber the wind moans in the trees. The great firs, as old as the foundations of the world, high above us their needled branches are pulled about by storms that rise as the day perishes. I turn on my sleeping mat, awake and listening, for an old man finds little rest. Others hear only the wind, but I the speechless words of the Lord Ashur, King of Heaven. The wind is his messenger and in it I hear the voices of the dying.

Even here, at the edge of the world, the smell of corpses is in my nostrils. Among these people who know not the flint-hard sun of my birthplace, no one speaks of omens, and yet I know. In the east the earth in which my fathers lie buried is soft with blood. The gods are carried off into slavery and their cities burn at their backs. The rich fields of barley, the swaying grass, all are waste. I see all this. I have only to close my eyes.

Yet are these phantoms only restless dreams? Are they nothing more? As a man's life decays, day by day, sometimes his mind fills with shadows.

I believe it is more. Even while I was still a boy the god Ashur thought fit to open the future to my sight. He has not deserted me now. The walls of Nineveh are broken, and her people perish by the swords of foreigners. It was all foretold, a secret I have carried in my breast these many years, a black vision of what must be. That which I see with the soul's eyes has happened —or will.

And if the end has come, if the throne of empire is cast down and the mighty are dust, then who but I, who have made my home among strangers, whose grandchildren speak with a borrowed tongue, can recall its beginning?

So let me open my tale, for the god, who rules in this life and the next, sets our feet upon strange paths. I am Tiglath Ashur, son of Sennacherib the Glorious, Terror of Nations, and my words ring with truth like silver coins.

My mother was Merope, a woman whom one of the seven kings of Cyprus had given to the King of the Earth's Four Corners as an article of tribute. The king, being already in the afternoon of life, sent her to his son, whose two lawful wives had yet given him but few male children such as the gods did favor. Thus it was that this foreign woman, this stranger to the king's city of Dur-Sharrukin, carried me in her womb through the halls of the house of women in the palace of the heir and prince, the Lord Sennacherib. She waited there, big with her burden, while the god perfected his design.

And as my mother approached her time, the great king, Sargon, Lord of the World, my father's father, was making war in the land of the Kullumite, fighting against a people who lived in tents, wandering from one watering place to the next. In the mountains of the east, Sargon led the armies of Ashur so that these nomads would taste of our might and be sent limping back into the wilderness, never again to trouble the rich lands of Akkad and of Sumer, of the swift-flowing Tigris.

It is a bitter place where the Kullumite dwells. Scarcely a blade of grass can force its way between the sharp stones. There is no comfort, neither for men nor beasts. It is a land of mountains, where the king's chariot must be carried on the backs of his soldiers and he himself must abandon the saddled war horse for his own legs and climb the hard, rock-strewn trails like any goat. And the Lord Sargon was already old.

On the twentieth day after his armies had last wet their sandals in the great Turnat River, the king ordered that a camp be struck in a plain beneath the nameless cliffs of shale and limestone, near a spring of living water that forced its way up through the ground like blood from a fresh wound. He decreed that all should rest there through two nights to refresh their spirits and find strength. The king pitched his tent and sat down before it, his hands resting on his knees, while the host of Ashur made themselves easy in his mighty shadow. The cooking pots were found and men who had forgotten the faces of their wives and the taste of fresh-killed lamb stripped off their armor and washed the sweat from their faces, dancing in the cold, clear pools like children. A soldier is pleased with little and takes comfort when and where he can, and the king smiled upon them like a father remembering his age.

The Lord Sargon had ruled the wide world for seven years and ten. The kings of Tyre and of Sidon at the edge of the Northern Sea, the rich cities of Carchemish, Aleppo, and Damascus, all wore his yoke. He had taken the hands of Marduk and made himself king in Babylonia. As far away as Egypt and Lydia and the wastes of the Arab desert, men sent him rich gifts and trembled at his word, for he was mighty and his anger had a long reach. The Land of Ashur had seen many great kings, restless conquerors who had made the earth quake under the feet of their armies, but Sargon was far the greatest. On his hard old body were the scars of many wounds, for his campaigns reached back to the days of his beardless youth. He was brave as the wild boar and cunning as an adder, and his soldiers loved and worshiped him as though he were the bright god in his own person.

And yet he was old and tired, and the joy of war had left him. Death circled around his head like a black bird.

That night he feasted with his officers, sharing out bread and dark beer, listening to the storytellers and waiting for the time to close his eyes and sleep. The campfires of the army burned while men played at lots and laughed and forgot the hardships of campaign. But in the mountains the Kullumite watched, numbering the hours.

I cannot account for all that followed. The annals, which in any case are always full of lies, are silent here, and memories had grown clouded with the years before I knew to ask. The survivors of that terrible night were few and—who can say?—perhaps reluctant to talk of such things. Who, after all, would speak ill of the Great Sargon, and to the king his son's own son? But men who have not seen the enemy in many days grow careless—this I have seen myself—and it is easy for the army of a great nation, at war with savages, to imagine itself invincible. Whatever the reasons, there were no scouts sent out to search in the mountains and the sentries of the king's mighty host were deaf and blind.

And in that dark hour just before the dawn's first stirring the Kullumite riders came, carrying fire. They had painted their faces black as they rode through the camp, trampling down the tents where our soldiers lay sleeping and setting them to blaze with their torches. Men rushed into the darkness, fresh from their sleeping blankets, blinking like owls, and were killed with their hands empty. They hardly knew what was happening around them before they were struck to the ground, their breasts torn open and their brains scattered. Many a brave soldier of Ashur fell before the long spear with its copper point and the curved sword that knows no pity. The horses screamed as if they were devils and beat the hard earth with their hoofs so that it trembled like a drumhead. There were battle cries and shrieks of panic and the groans of the dying. There was blood for the ground to drink. The cruel goddess Ereshkigal, Queen of the Dead, grew sated with carrion.

"And then it was over. As swiftly as they had come, the enemy withdrew, riding back into their mountains, the spoils they had captured slung across their saddles, happy in their riches and glory. We few left alive looked about us, our minds clouded with confusion and fear. We understood nothing except that we had come within a whisper of death. We could think of nothing except that—it was almost like being dead, that panicked helplessness. The brain and the senses throb like a wound. The world in its solid shape seemed almost to vanish, as if we had become ghosts. And then we found that which brought us back to life, for behind them, lying in the dust, his night clothes spattered with gore, they had left the corpse of Great Sargon, hacked like a joint of meat and run through the body with a spear, his death the work of many hands. For one blow, Prince, could never have killed him."

So the story was told to me, many years later. So it was that there, in the mountains, he died. He fell in battle, cut down by bandits whose highest arts were thievery and the herding of goats. His son, my father, had to buy back his body from his murderers.

I will not trouble myself to recount how the remnants of the king's grand army found their way home, how they were harried by raiders, how they starved and suffered and died. Theirs is not my story. It was many weeks before those in the Land of Ashur knew of their fate, and of the death of the Lord Sargon. They did not know, the subjects of the king, but they guessed, for the gods from whom nothing is hidden had sent them a sign. On the night of Sargon's death a star was seen in the east, hanging low over the mountains. When men saw it they trembled and hid themselves inside their houses, muttering prayers to turn away evil from the land, for it was a star of ill portent and as red as blood.

On that night, in the house of women in the palace of Sennacherib, the *marsarru,* the heir, who was king now without knowing it, my mother brought me wailing into the world, and thus my birth cries were the first lamentation for the dead lord.

"See, my little Lathikadas, you can do it. You can do all things. All mysteries are open to you. See how easy, my sweet little prince? . . ."

My mother's voice, as she taught me to walk on my hands over the cool brick floor of the arcade around our garden—I speak of it as ours and remember it so, but it was common to all who dwelt in the house of women, all the wives and concubines and the king's children. She had to hold my feet to keep me from toppling over, but I could support my own weight and walk in a straight line until we drew abreast of the great fountain whose falling waters seemed to laugh. She wanted me to have strong arms. She said the god had set his mark upon me and I would need them. I was perhaps four or five years old.

"The star is the token of Ishtar, Goddess of Lust, Queen of Battles, and red is the color of mourning. It is a bad omen your little boy carries in that birthmark of his."

Naq'ia smiled, narrowing her eyes as if to measure me for my grave. She sat at the fountain's edge, resting her hands on her elbows like a man and watching us. She was one of the king's two legal wives and his favorite by all accounts, though not yet lady of the palace—the mother of the heir yet lived. It was said that beauty such as Naq'ia's could melt the bowels within a stone idol, but a child does not see this, so I was merely frightened of her. She was ambitious for her own son and hated me and Merope for bearing me. Little Esarhaddon stared at us from behind his mother's skirt. I stuck out my tongue at him and he hid his eyes.

"Let the child down, woman. See how the blood rushes to his face?"

My mother released my legs and I tucked my head under and rolled, just as she had taught me. I sprang to my feet like a trap snapping shut.

"Anyone can see he is an Ionian, woman. A foreigner, like

yourself. He will end his days making mud bricks for the city walls."

"A slave, like all of your family, *Zakutu*?"

Because, of course, everyone knew that Naq'ia was a Babylonian freedwoman whom the great king Sennacherib had purchased from a tavernmaster in Borsippa. In the days of her glory it was not safe to speak of such things, nor to remember that the Akkadian name the king had given her meant "the freed one," but they were no less true for that.

The smile faded from Naq'ia's lips like melting frost.

"My son, *Zakutu,* will be a great man in the land of Ashur," Merope said, picking me up in her arms and holding me to her. She took my hand, covering the star-shaped birthmark, red as fire, that glowed on the soft white flesh of my palm. "This is prophecy. This is written in the hour of his birth, for the god favors him."

I always loved my mother, but I knew even then she was not always wise.

And Naq'ia, whose mind was ever turning on dark things, sat quietly by the fountain's edge, smoothing with her fingertips the hem of her black linen veil. With my mind's eye I see her there, so many lifetimes ago, not as she was then but as I remember her from my young manhood, still beautiful but with gray in her shining black hair, her mouth lined with years of cunning. She must have been yet almost a girl that morning in the garden at Nineveh, but was she ever young? It is unimaginable. Those who would be the mothers of kings are never young.

"Lathikadas, go and play with the little prince your brother," my mother said, letting me down so that my sandals scraped against the brick floor.

"And mind how you treat the next king, my great man of Ashur."

As I drew close, Naq'ia touched my hair, as if she never ceased to marvel at the color of it. I looked up into her eyes, fascinated by the nearness of my danger. Little Esarhaddon came out from behind his mother's skirt. He was but a few weeks younger than I but smaller, as were most such of the king's sons who counted as my fellows in the house of women. I held out my hand to him, as I had been bidden, and he took it and smiled. For all that he was his mother's child, Esarhaddon was even then beginning to think of himself as my friend.

"Yes—it is all right, my son." Naq'ia leaned forward, taking us each by the shoulder as if she would push us away like boats from their moorings. "Run and play with the god's little darling, for all that his mother is only a concubine. Learn all the ways of the great men who will be as slaves beneath your feet in a few years' time."

Turning my mind back to those times, I can see now what was hidden from me then, that the house of women was a strange, unnatural, unhappy place. It was always crowded—young girls, mothers with their children, old crones who had been the pillow mates of long-dead kings and who had nowhere else to go—but what I remember best is the quiet. We spoke in soft voices, even the little children, as if afraid of breaking some spell. It was the place to which the king my father came to take his pleasure, but no one else found any joy there.

The house of women was a prison, a cage with golden bars, for none might leave or enter without the great king's order. But a child knows nothing of such things, and our garden, walled around on four sides by the dwellings of wives and concubines, was to me a place of enchantment. The tiled pools were filled with fish that glistened in the water like flashes of lightning, always just out of reach, and the king kept a tame gazelle, raised from a baby and without fear, who would come to lick the salt from our sweating arms.

There was also a linden tree, considered a great rarity. I was forbidden to swing from its low-hanging branches for fear of breaking them, but I did anyway. It was to the linden tree that I took Esarhaddon, that I might astonish him with my daring in this matter of swinging, but all he wanted was to learn the secret of walking upside down.

"Show me, show me, show me," he chanted, his black eyes glistening, dancing without much agility on his thick legs. Esarhaddon was no more dexterous than the generality of little boys, but to the hour of his death he was solid and unmovable as a wall. "Show me how—teach me, Laf'kos."

I was not pleased, so I turned away from him with a shrug.

"I am Tiglath," I said coldly. A child brought up in the house of women learns early to stand on his dignity, and it had the desired effect. Esarhaddon stared at me with wonder.

"Your mother called you 'Laf'kos.' I heard her."

"She calls me 'La*thī*kadas'—*she* does, no one else. It is a word in her tongue."

Esarhaddon, who at that age hardly knew even his own tongue, cocked his head to one side as if trying to shake something loose.

"What does it mean?" he asked finally. In the presence of this mystery he had forgotten all about walking upside down.

"It means my name is Tiglath. You will call me Tiglath, nothing else. Can you remember as much as that?"

And the little boy smiled and said "yes," apparently unaware that we had been settling a point of honor, and a door in my heart opened to him, one that would never close. Not even death could close it. Even now my eyes fill with tears as I remember when we were children together. Esarhaddon, my brother, my friend, whom I wronged, who wronged me in his turn, but whom I always loved. Whom I love now as he is dust.

"Teach me the trick," he said, sticking his arms straight in the air. "Show me, Tiglath."

"All right. But I am not to blame if you break your neck."

"What does it mean?" My brother Esarhaddon might well ask, for the name by which Merope called me was then a riddle, even to me, even as I was a riddle to myself.

We were strangers, she and I, beings set apart. Even as a child I was conscious of this. The ladies of the king's house would come to look at me, to confirm for themselves the story of "the child whose eyes stayed blue." The men of Ashur are thickset, black-headed men, and I am tall and slender and in my youth had light-brown hair. Since Shamash, God of Destiny, has made me a wanderer through all the lands of this world, I have learned that there is nothing monstrous in this, that the men beyond the Northern Sea, and even the Nile dwellers in the Land of Kem, though they are browner, are not so different. The broad earth holds a great multitude of peoples, but I was not to learn this for many years. All I knew was that my mother had blue eyes and hair the color of bronze, that she spoke a tongue that none save myself could understand, and that I was her son and different from all around me. Children dread the mockery of others, and I felt my strangeness as a curse. And I at least had been born there beside the swift-flowing Tigris—what must my mother have suffered, a foreigner in the house of women?

My mother was what the men of Ashur called an Ionian, or as she would have expressed it, a Greek, since she had been born on the mainland, in a city called Athens. Her father, so she told me, was a shoemaker given to speculating among the merchant ships that went forth over the dark sea. I understood nothing of this—I had never seen a ship nor heard of such a race as "merchants"—but she made it plain to me that he had fallen upon hard times and had been forced to sell his eldest daughter as a slave. He was a sentimental man and had wept as he led her from his house that last day, and she bore him no ill will. Thus, at thirteen, she found herself on a ship bound for Cyprus, where lighthaired women fetched a better price. From there, by what accident I know not, she made up part of the tribute the kings of that island sent in their fear to the Lord Sargon. She never saw the land of her birth again.

Lathikadas, "he who banishes grief." The great king my father chose for me the name Tiglath Ashur, thus to honor at once his grandfather and his god, but my mother, in her life of sorrow, called me Lathikadas. I only hope it could have been in some small measure true.

But little brother Esarhaddon, the color and shape of a mud brick, that black-haired boy knew nothing of these things as he asked his harmless question. Naq'ia might intrigue to put him on his father's throne, but his heart was all innocence. He meant harm to no one save the enemies of Ashur, and in those days little enough even to them.

And while Naq'ia dreamed of his glory, no one, least of all Esarhaddon himself, imagined any destiny for him except that of a soldier. He wanted to be a *rab shaqe,* a leader of the king's armies. He would cry if one of the royal pigeons died, but that sweet little boy, like all the rest of us, dreamed of his sword dripping with the blood of Elamites and Medes.

"I hate writing," he would whisper to me as we hunched over our tablets, copying out the characters of an incantation to the god Nabu we were to learn by rote. "This is for scribes and priests, not for men of valor. It is hopeless. I will never remember the tenth part of all this."

It was true that the mystery of which Nabu was the patron was no simple business but an art of the highest refinement. We

wrote on tablets of wet clay that when baked would last, they told
us, until the end of the world, so we must be wonderfully careful
to scratch in the long tapering lines that made up a character, the
least part of a word, so they would not form unsightly ridges in
the smooth surface. And characters there were in their hundreds
beyond counting, and a true scribe wrote not in the Akkadian of
common men but in an old dialect not spoken in the Land of
Ashur since the days of the heroes. And then there was Sumerian
to learn, the sacred tongue, written with the same characters but
with different meanings and sounds, a tongue to tie one's brains
into knots, such as no men could ever have spoken with comfort,
not even in the most ancient times, but such as was pleasing to the
gods' ears.

Esarhaddon held the flat-sided stylus in his thick fingers,
copying out the daggerlike strokes of our text, hating each one of
them as they passed through his mind like water through a sieve,
hating the old scribe who taught us, with his white hair and his
beardless face and his mighty fear of the king's wrath. All this was
for Esarhaddon the torment of his youth, for his mother, who
could not form the symbols even of her own name, was most
anxious about his progress. And Naq'ia, it seemed, had eyes everywhere.

"Mother, can you write?"

Merope looked at me as if she expected the gods to turn me
to salt for my impertinence, and sighed, and ran her hand through
her bronze-colored hair.

"In the city of Athens everyone can write who is not a sucking babe or a fool. It is only the country people with dung stuffed
into their ears who cannot write."

In fact, she could only form some ten or twelve signs, enough
to spell her name and the name of her city's patron goddess and a
few other trifles, but she taught me these.

Writing is a strange, unnatural affair. I have heard it said that
the god Nabu in pity gave men the daggerlike script that they
might remember his preserving prayers, but I do not believe this.
The Greeks can spell any word they wish with four and twenty
signs, which they call "letters," so why should Nabu have burdened the people of Akkad and Sumer with hundreds of symbols,
as difficult to form as to remember? The writing of the Nile people, which I never learned, is even worse. Only men could produce a thing of such perversity. The gods had no hand in it.

"The gods have blessed you with good ears," old Bag Teshub would tell me, his voice quavering like a reed flute as he wiped the sweat from his beardless face. "As a scholar you have few rivals among your royal brothers—even Nabusharusur, who is your elder by a quarter of a year, lacks your refinement of understanding. If the lord king your father decides to make a priest of you, you will be a fine omen reader."

One day our text was the story of Ashur's victory over Tiamat the Chaos Monster, how he used the winds to keep her mouth open while he shot an arrow into her heart, how he cut her body in half, making the sky with one part and the earth with the other, and thus became lord over all the other gods, who gave him fifty great names. It was an easy text, except for the fifty names.

"Prince Esarhaddon, recite for us the lines from the second tablet in which Ea fails to subdue the monster. Here—take it."

My brother, poor soul, accepted the delicate little clay rectangle, its edges made smooth and round by the caressing hands of generations of scribes, and he glanced back over his shoulder at me, begging my pity with his eyes.

" '. . . terror . . . jaws . . .' " He dug the point of his writing stylus into his cheek, as if to prick himself awake. " 'The terror of her . . .' something 'jaws.' "

Nabusharusur, my only rival in our little schoolroom, a bright, lively boy and my closest friend after Esarhaddon, glanced at me and smiled with mischief. Yes, it was only human to feel a certain self-satisfaction in our brother's misery. I was probably smiling myself.

"What *some*thing, Prince?"

And Esarhaddon, who never in his life feared any living thing except his mother, let his face grow dark with anger at the aged scribe.

"I'll *some*thing you, you flabby old gelding—the purse between your legs is empty as a boatman's belly!"

The clay tablet flew across the room like a weapon of war, shattering against the wall not a hand's span from Bag Teshub's head.

I think Esarhaddon was even glad to receive his thrashing, as if each stroke of the old man's oxhide lash—which he used only lightly, as these were the king's sons and might one day grow up to nail his wrinkled old skin to the city wall—were a mark of honor. Almost anything was more to Esarhaddon's taste than recitation, and when we were released from our labors that day, he was as cheerful as a sparrow. In an hour, when by some mysterious but no less inevitable process word of what had happened reached the Lady Naq'ia, then he would know sorrow in all its rich variety, but for the moment, as we sat under the linden tree, unknotting the napkins in which we carried our lunches, he was pleased enough with himself.

"You shouldn't do such things to Bag Teshub," I announced grandly, and then my glance met Esarhaddon's and we grew helpless with little boys' laughter. "And you shouldn't say such things."

"Well—isn't it true?" Esarhaddon's mouth was crammed with dried dates, full of sweetness but as difficult to chew as saddle leather. Finally, because he desired to say more, he swallowed so hard that tears started in his eyes. "Have you never seen the old fool make water? His stick is so shriveled up the dead skin sloughs off like the husk of an onion. And the rest of him is just gone! There is nothing there except a shiny scar, as if someone scoured away his pouch with its two little pellets like dried food from the inside of a cooking pot!"

Esarhaddon laughed, as if at a joke he was hearing for the first time, but I was shocked—I could not have said precisely why. Of course, we all knew there was something different about Bag Teshub. For one thing, he was admitted to the house of women, which it was death for another to enter. And, of course, he had no beard.

We were of an age, Esarhaddon and I, that on rare occasions we were let out of our golden prison to witness some solemn public ritual or watch the New Year revels from a safe distance. It did not happen often—we were too young—but it was felt that we should begin to understand that there was a life beyond the house of women and that someday we would find our place in it.

So we knew that men grew hair on their faces, great shining black beards, oiled and curling. The nobles of our father's court looked like gods, an impression no doubt strengthened by the fact that we saw them only from a distance.

Yet Bag Teshub looked nothing like them.

"How did he get that way?" I heard myself asking. I was almost afraid to hear the answer.

"My mother says . . ." Esarhaddon leaned toward me, clearly conscious that he was imparting a great secret. "My mother says that it was done to him, that the priests took a knife and cut away his manhood when he was a child. You know, don't you, that he is one of the lesser brothers of the old king who is dead."

With my heart pounding inside my breast, I shook my head. It was as if I were looking into a dark future.

"If he is the old king's brother, who would dare do such a thing? Who would wish it done?"

Esarhaddon, in the innocence of his heart, offered me one of his dates, and I took it, hardly knowing that I did.

"What a silly question, Tiglath. You surprise me. Do you not know why? A king has many sons, and he knows that once he is dead not all of them will live forever on terms of love. He must wish his heir to succeed him without dissension, and a gelding may not aspire to the throne."

For a few nights the castrator's knife haunted my dreams—after all, was I not myself one of the lesser sons of the king? The lady of the palace, the Lady Tashmetum-sharrat, had two sons, almost grown men, and then there was Esarhaddon himself. And my mother was a mere concubine, and a foreigner in the bargain. Did I not have reason to be frightened? But a child does not stay frightened long. Only a present danger is real to him, so I soon forgot.

Besides, I had other thoughts with which to occupy my mind, for the gardens of the house of women had received another prisoner. At the age of eight, and already the master of the daggerlike writing, which I took to be all the wisdom the world had to offer me, I discovered what it was to fall in love.

What can I write of Esharhamat—Esharhamat, fair to look upon, whose memory softens my liver like damp clay beneath the potter's hand—what can I put in words that could convey the least particle of her shining beauty? Those who have known this childhood love of another, all tenderness and sweet pain, have no need of my words. And those who have not could never be brought to understand. I have heard it said that time heals every hurt, but it is not so. Some wounds, received early enough, will always ache in cold weather. Such was my love for Esharhamat.

We were cousins, since Esharhamat also claimed the Lord Sargon for an ancestor. Esharhamat's father was a Babylonian, of noble family, whose grandmother had kept company in the princely bed while the fifth Shalmaneser still ruled. But the great king Sargon had scattered his seed widely in the lands of Akkad and Sumer, so it was not out of respect for her slight connection to the ruling house that she had been brought to Nineveh to be raised among the children of Sennacherib, Ruler of the Wide World. The gods had elected that my little maid from Nippur should have no insignificant hand in kneading the destiny of nations.

In the place of my birth the god rules. Ashur gave his name to our ancient capital and to the land itself. We are all his slaves, born to serve him, even the king. No one more than the king. On the day he assumes his office, the crowds follow him from the temple shouting "Ashur is King! Ashur is King!" and this is no more than the truth. And Ashur had proclaimed it his will that a maid born in Nippur and of the Lord Sargon's blood should be the mother of kings in this land until Nineveh and Calah and Ashur itself were merely words in the mouths of strangers.

So Esharhamat was not for the whelp of a Greek slave woman. She would be the wife of Sennacherib's heir when she was grown to an age for bearing sons. This was written. This was the law and the god's pleasure, before which all men are helpless.

But a child, who knows neither the passion of the body nor the law's weight, a child who loves only with his eyes and ears and the touch of his hand takes no account of the god's pleasure. Esharhamat would one day be queen, the consort, I assumed, of the *marsarru* Ashurnadinshum, who was many years older and had long been received into the house of succession, where he was as distant from us as the king himself. What was this to me? A child knows no impediment to love. He simply loves. I loved Esharhamat.

And what should I care about Ashurnadinshum? Was I not lord of the wide world? Was I not old Bag Teshub's best student, master of the daggerlike writing and able to speak the tongue of Sumer? Was I not half a head taller than any of my brothers? Could I not walk upon my hands, and now without my mother's steadying assistance? And was I not all that was beautiful and perfect in Esharhamat's great black eyes?

"Oouuh, Tiglapf," she would say in her lisping southern, child's voice when I would kiss her on the palm of the hand—it was a game of our own invention—"you are *su-u-uch* a bad boy!"

And then she would hold out the other hand, palm up, and I would kiss that, and she would giggle madly, first hiding her face in the hem of her pink linen shawl and then peeking out at me.

I loved her. She ruled my heart more firmly than any king ever ruled in the Land of Ashur. I wanted nothing more from life than to sit with her beneath the linden tree, sharing out dates and smiling together over this wonderful secret that was somehow ours and no one else's. We could not imagine a future when this would not be so.

And Naq'ia watched us and smiled her own smile, which was perhaps not so harmless as ours.

"You see? Before he lives through his ninth year, Ishtar has him snared in her net. If it was the gods who gave him that mark upon his palm, they did not intend it for a happy destiny."

But my mother dismissed Naq'ia's words with a shrug of her shoulders.

"They are children," she said. "What harm can come to them from such as this?"

Oh, Merope, how ill you spoke in that hour. I was but a child, with a child's eye, but could you not have seen the evil circling above your son's head?

But she would not see, and I could not. To me the house of women was still paradise, although I was beginning to grow restless in my happiness. I knew that soon I would be leaving that place to enter the world of men, and I was all impatience.

At the end of his ninth year, during the festival days that mark the end of the summer planting, each of the king's sons comes out of the garden and takes up his work as a servant of the god. After that day, whether he becomes a scribe or a soldier or one of the king's companions, those few chosen to stand by their lord's right hand and assist in the direction of the state, he is a child no longer. There is no turning back—the door to the house of women is closed for him. I knew all that, and yet I did not understand why my mother looked upon me with such hungry eyes, why she wept in the darkness of our room at night. I could not fathom that we were about to lose one another, perhaps forever. This she kept from me.

And, of course, on that day I would lose Esharhamat as well, but that too she kept from me.

For Esarhaddon and myself the one reality was that we would soon enter the house of war, there to prepare for the only

life fitting for men, that certain path to glory, the life of the soldier. We took this for granted. Such was to be our *simtu,* our
destiny. It was our pleasure and therefore, of course, the god's.
Nothing else was possible.

"However, it may be that such things are no longer to your
taste," Esarhaddon said, smiling with mischief as he sat on the
ground and watched me swing by my arms from the forbidden
linden tree. "Perhaps that girl has turned your wits and you long
to stay here, supporting yourself upon a pillow and dreaming
about her eyes."

I let go the tree limb and, dropping down to the earth, aimed
a kick at Esarhaddon's chest with my bare foot. I missed, of
course; he had seen it coming and dodged out of the way. He
grabbed my foot and twisted it so that I came crashing down
beside him. He was always a splendid wrestler—not quick but
strong, and at close quarters that was all that mattered. He had
me pinned on my back in a matter of seconds.

"Admit it!" he shouted, laughing straight into my face as he
held me down. "Admit it—she's made you soft as spring mud.
Before she came you wouldn't have been so stupid, even in wrestling, at which you are not gifted. You would have kept your
distance and worn me down until you could toss me over on my
face with one of your fine Ionian tricks. Girls—paugh!"

It was all a splendid joke, and I laughed with him. I had no
objection to admitting to Esarhaddon that, yes, there was something ever so slightly ludicrous about this passion I had conceived
for our little cousin, who could not fight with a wooden sword or
stand on her hands or even wrestle, who cried when the lightning
frightened her, who could only smile and admire and bewitch.

"You are a foreigner, of course—if you were a real man of
Ashur you would know better than to melt like beeswax just because she looks at you."

"I am no more a foreigner than you, you son of a Babylonian!"

This time he was not quick enough to avoid the foot I placed
behind his knee to tumble him over backward.

A quarter of an hour later, when we had both washed the
dirt from our faces in the fish pond, it was still a splendid joke.

"Well, you will be cured fast enough. When she is the wife of
Ashurnadinshum, and that will be sooner than you think, you will
have to get over this folly of yours."

"I don't see why," I answered back, perhaps a little too loudly—for part of me knew even then that there was something dangerous about my feelings for Esharhamat. "Just because she is queen, I don't see why we can't go on loving each other. What should it matter to Ashurnadinshum?"

"Tiglath, my brother, for all that you are a clever Ionian, by the gods' will there never was born so great a fool."

As with the approach of a thunderstorm, as the time for parting drew nearer, the air in the house of women seemed to grow heavy and hard to breathe. Bag Teshub became ever more anxious and seemed to whirl with business as he prepared us for our final recitations, and those of the king's wives and concubines who had sons of leaving age withdrew into the silence of their own hearts. And Naq'ia, as she watched me from the fountain's edge, smiled as if she knew all the secrets of my future life.

At last, when my mother could no longer restrain her tears in front of me, she gathered me in her arms, covering my head with the heavy bronze curtain of her hair, and wept as if she were to lose me to death. It was the first time I tasted fear.

"You will see, my little prince," she said in between her sobbing. "You will see how the god of this land protects you from your enemies. The god's mark upon you will see you through every danger—you will see. You will see."

"What enemies could I have in my father's house?" I asked. It seemed suddenly an important question.

"None from whom the greatness of your destiny cannot protect you. You need be afraid of no one."

And when I looked into her eyes, flooded with tears, I knew at once that she did not credit her own brave words and my heart quailed within me.

"We will not be parted long, Merope. When I am a great general and high in the king's favor, I will win you out of this place."

My mother smiled, as if she believed me.

When I left my mother's arms my one thought was to find Esharhamat, for my mind was troubled. She was sitting beneath the linden tree, as if waiting there, but there was no comfort to be gained from her because the contagion of dread had found its way even to little Esharhamat.

"I will never see you again," she said in a voice that was no more than a whisper. "I will be walled up in Ashurnadinshum's house of women and you will forget me. When you leave this garden you will no longer love me."

They were strange words—I could not imagine what she meant, nor, I suspect, could she. But some foreboding had reached her, child that she was, and she was filled with helpless terror. I was but nine years old, she even less, and we sat there together beneath the great tree's spreading branches as the future appeared before us like the iron bars of a cage.

The next day, in the presence of the Lord Sinahiusur, the king's brother who served at his right hand as *turtanu*, commander of the royal army and the crown's most trusted and powerful servant, stood four of us: myself, Esarhaddon, Nabusharusur, and a boy named Belushezib, the child of a concubine despised even more than my own mother, since she was the half-wild wife of one of the mountain men of the east, captured by the Lord Sennacherib on the field of battle, where her man lay slaughtered—it was not even certain whose child he was, the king's or the dead Mede's. There we all waited before old Bag Teshub to be heard as we each read aloud the daggerlike writing from the clay tablets. It was the last moment we would be schoolboys together. Today, for good or ill, we became men.

Bag Teshub, I suspect to display his prowess as a teacher, gave me a tablet in the tongue of Sumer—it was a simple prayer to Enlil, an ancient god, the guardian of the nether world. I read it haltingly, but the *turtanu* Sinahiusur, resplendent in his tunic embroidered with blue and green and shot through with silver, nodded his head as he stroked his black beard in approval. Of the others' recitations I remember nothing, except Esarhaddon's remark as we were dismissed.

"I read well enough to make sense of a dispatch," he said. "And what more does a soldier need? It will do."

We four little boys, our tasks as children behind us, were led away by Bag Teshub and the Lord Sinahiusur, down a corridor we had never walked before, through a door that I had never seen open, and into the hard light of the outside. This was the moment of parting. The *turtanu* stood with his hands on Esarhaddon's shoulders, for Esarhaddon was the son of the king's second lawful wife—not like me, whose mother was merely one more among the royal women—and thus he had already been selected from among us. But as the Lord Sinahiusur held my brother under his hands, his eyes were all the time on my face. He seemed intent upon carrying away in his mind my indelible image. What his thoughts might have been I had no notion. He never spoke.

"Come, my children," Bag Teshub murmured, looking away from Esarhaddon as if the sight of him troubled his conscience. "Come now—you are all to be scribes. Your lives will be here in the palace of the king. Great things perhaps await you."

My disappointment in that moment was the sharpest emotion I had yet experienced. So I was not to be a soldier after all. For me there were to be no conquests, no glory. I would pass my days copying tablets. In my heart I cursed the old eunuch for distinguishing me before the king's *turtanu*— I was naïve enough to imagine that was the cause of my unhappy fate. I had forgotten the half-smiles of the Lady Naq'ia.

"Come this way," he went on, his voice piping. "The moment has come for your—your initiation."

While the *turtanu* led my brother Esarhaddon away, we three were conducted to a vast courtyard far off from the house of women. There four men in the vestments of priests awaited us, their sleeves rolled up to reveal the heavy bulging muscles of their arms and their faces set as if they cherished some special anger against boys of our age. I will remember the expression on their faces all of my life. I have seen it many times since, but that was the first.

We hung back, we three. We were afraid and tried to hide ourselves behind Bag Teshub's skirts. But even he, in this place, was not our friend.

"Start with this one," he said, his voice strangely altered. He grabbed Belushezib by the shoulder and thrust him forward. Belushezib did not stand on his dignity as a king's son—he let out a scream of terror as two of the priests grasped his arms, twisting them cruelly as they marched him to a low stone altar in the center of the courtyard.

In late summer we children wore nothing except thin linen robes and loincloths. These the priests removed from Belushezib's body as roughly as they might have ripped the skin from a rabbit. The boy kept screaming the whole time, as if he really were being flayed alive.

At first I understood very little of what was taking place. I saw two of the priests holding Belushezib down upon the altar

stone by his arms and legs while another, carrying a leather cord
in his hands, stepped forward and made a loop with it around
Belushezib's private parts, choking off the scrotum as he pulled
the cord tight. It was all done in the calmest, most workmanlike
manner, as if they were cooks in the king's kitchen dressing a
sheep for the night's banquet. Nabusharusur and I watched in
horror as the fourth priest produced a knife with a curved blade
and sliced open the scrotum, letting its bloody contents spill out
over Belushezib's legs. I thought the air would shatter with his
shriek of terror and pain.

And then, of course, everything was plain to me.

"How dare they?" I thought. "How dare they do such a
thing?" But they did dare, and as I felt Bag Teshub's hand on my
shoulder I knew that I was next.

I looked up into his beardless face—he was smiling at me.
The skin around his neck was loose and jiggled when he moved.
He was fat and strengthless, and he had been the old king's
brother.

Suddenly I understood why my mother had been so afraid,
and why Naq'ia had smiled.

Yes, of course. Esarhaddon was not here. He was safe, should
the throne come to him. And I was here, about to have my manhood stripped away from me before it had even begun.

And Bag Teshub could smile.

"No—not to me."

Whether I actually spoke these words I know not, but they
filled my mind. My father was the king, and they would not do
this to me.

They had finished with Belushezib. One of them took a
torch, dripping with burning pitch, and seared closed his wound.
He screamed yet once more, but no one paid any heed. They were
already turning their eyes to me.

"Go on, Tiglath," Bag Teshub whispered. "It is over in a
moment. Show them what a brave boy you are."

He gave me a gentle push forward. The priests were content
to wait for me. The one with the curved knife balanced it in the
palm of his hand, almost playfully. I took a step, then another,
then another. I hardly knew what I was doing.

I would have been a warrior, and a warrior tells himself he is
not afraid of suffering and death. I was not afraid of the pain—

and I hardly knew what death was. But this shameful dishonor
. . . No, it must not be allowed to happen.

I knew what I had to do.

They were far from expecting resistance. I approached them
meekly, my eyes upon the ground, like the boy that they thought
me to be. The one with the knife was closest to me, his back to the
altar stone. He was so sure he had me in his power it was almost
like an invitation.

I was only a boy, but my mother had taught me to be agile
and quick. I shuffled my feet as I approached him. I kept my eyes
down.

Then, at the last moment, when he began to reach out his
hand to me, I rushed at him with all the sudden force I could
command. It was enough—I hit him just above the knees, striking
hard with the palms of my hands, and he rocked back, losing his
balance. He fell backward over the altar and, as I had expected,
allowed the knife to slip from his grasp.

It fell clattering to the stone floor. While they all recovered
from their surprise I had just time to scoop it up as I ran to one of
the pillars that supported the arcade around the far end of the
courtyard. I ran like a deer, my heart pounding within me. I did
not stop until I had that massive granite pillar at my back. I
turned, the knife in my hand, to face my tormentors.

"I am Tiglath Ashur!" I shouted. I was half mad with fear,
but it was mingled with a strange exultation such as I had never
known. "My father is Sennacherib, Lord of the Earth, King of
Kings! Come near me at your peril!"

For an instant there was only silence. I could even hear the
faint whispering of the wind overhead. For that instant I thought
I might really have won.

But then I was answered with laughter, laughter that
boomed like thunder, like the laughter of the god Ashur himself.
How dare they? I was so filled with wrath that I wished to shed
tears until I saw that it was not the priests who were laughing.
They had forgotten my existence. They were on their knees, their
faces pressed against the dusty stones.

And then I saw them, across the courtyard, in the shadow of
the arcade, two men. I strained my eyes to see clearly and, as if to
oblige me, they stepped out into the sunlight.

One of them I knew. He was the *turtanu* Sinahiusur, the

king's brother; he stood silent and majestic as before, wise and
heroic.

But I hardly had eyes for him. I was looking at his companion, he who had dared to laugh at me, who laughed still. His tunic
was covered with gold. I thought I was in the presence of a god.

He gestured toward me with his arm, his lips still smiling.

"Bag Teshub—Uncle," he said. "This is but a boy, though he
roars like a lion, eh? Take the knife from him."

Bag Teshub picked himself up from the stones and came
toward me, bowing even as he walked.

"Give me the knife, Tiglath. We are not in the schoolroom
now. This is the—augh!"

He had come too close. The knife struck out and cut him
across the hand so that red blood spattered his arm and rolled to
the ground. I waved my little weapon threateningly and he
jumped back and out of danger. And the thundering laughter
sounded again.

"He is as he styles himself, eh, brother?" the golden man
said, turning a little toward Sinahiusur. "This one has the bowels
of a prince, eh?—yes? I am convinced, so let it be as you think
best. He shall be spared the knife."

Sinahiusur said nothing. He merely placed his right hand
upon his breast and bowed. And then he turned his eyes to me.

"Bow down, Tiglath Ashur," he said, in a voice like the
stroke of an ax. "Bow down before the king thy father."

My knees became as water and I fell to the stone floor,
touching it with my forehead. I was in the presence of the god's
chosen one, and my mind was clouded with awe. It was Sennacherib who stood before me, whom I myself had named Lord of the
Earth.

"Come to me, boy," he said, his voice all gentleness. "Come
and let me see you."

In all my life I had never yet seen the king my father, and
now I stood before him. He rested his hands upon my shoulders
and my eyes clouded with tears.

"Do not be afraid, my son. Have a lion's heart and I will
make you great in the land of Ashur. How is that, eh? Better?"

There was a slight sound. It was Bag Teshub, his bleeding
hand wrapped in a scrap of linen, clearing his throat.

"Yes—what is it, Uncle?"

"What of the other, Dread Lord?"

Because, of course, we had forgotten all about Nabusharu-sur. He stood in the shadow of a pillar as if he wished to disappear altogether. I do not know what I felt for him in that moment; perhaps my heart was too glutted to feel anything more.

"Yes, of course." The king's face went hard, though his hand still rested lightly enough on my shoulders. "I think one lion is enough for this day, eh? Fulfill your task, Uncle."

The priests were quick this time. They gave Nabusharusur no chance to resist but lifted him from the ground by his arms and legs. He screamed, he filled the air with his shrill voice, but in an instant he was upon the altar stone and the cruel knife had begun its work.

"No, do not turn away, my son," the king said, laying his hand upon my cheek so that I could not. "Learn to be a man and shrink not from pain and blood."

And so it was that in my ninth year I learned what it meant to become a man of Ashur.

2

Sinahiusur was a pious man, a respecter of omens. He had remembered the child who was born the night the great Sargon died, and thus it was that the god's mark which I bore was my deliverance, as my mother had said it would be. So I was sent to the house of war after all, and the king my father's eyes were upon me. "I will make you great in the Land of Ashur," he had said. I was to have all the world could offer, it seemed.

And in the house of war I found Esarhaddon.

His eyes met mine at the door of the royal barrack, whither I had been conducted after receiving the king's blessing and parting from him. It was evening and Esarhaddon was still in his leather breastplate, polishing his new sword as he sat on his sleeping roll. He glanced up at the sound of footsteps and, even in the flickering yellow light of the oil lamp that rested on the floor, I could see the mingling of surprise and joy in his face.

"By the sixty great gods, is it really you, Tiglath?"

He sprang to his feet and came rushing toward me, the sword still in his hand as if he planned to run me through merely as a friendly demonstration. In an instant our arms were around each other's necks, and I will never know how he kept from cutting off my head.

"So it is you, in your own flesh, and not some deceiving *gallu* called up by Zaqar, Lord of Dreams? I thought you were going to the tablet house to be a mud scratcher with the others."

"I was very nearly rendered fit for nothing else," I said, and then I told him of what had happened. He did not seem surprised, and the fate of Belushezib and Nabusharusur moved him not at all. Would he have felt the same had it been my *simtu* to go under the gelding knife? Would he have smiled smugly then and spoken bland words about the god's will? I will never know. But when I described how I had sliced open old Bag Teshub's hand he threw back his head and laughed.

"Did you really do it, Tiglath? By Adad's thunder, I wish I had been there to hear him howl! Tiglath, my brave brother, I will love you onto death for every drop you spilled of the old maiden's blood. And so you really saw the king?"

"Yes, and he put his hands upon me and called me 'my son.' "

"Then you are blessed. Remember your poor brother when the king has made you *shaknu* of Babylonia and the black-headed people feel your foot upon their necks like Sargon come back to life."

This made him laugh all over again—it was mere excess of good spirits, for Esarhaddon was possessed of a loving heart.

"What is it like in this place?" I asked, looking around me with a curiosity I did not trouble to disguise, for the royal barrack had been my dream no less than my brother's.

"What is it like in this place?" Esarhaddon put his arm over my shoulder and led me inside the tiny room we were to share for the next four years. " 'This place,' as you call it, brother, is the temple of glory."

How shall I speak of the house of war, in which Esarhaddon and I filled such exalted stations? In my time there I learned how to ride a horse and drive a chariot, how to fight with the sword, the dagger, the bow, and the javelin. I learned the forms of military courtesy. I learned tactics. I learned discipline and the leadership of men. And, most important of all, I learned arrogance.

I learned that I was a prince of Ashur, that all the peoples of the world were but dust under the feet of the unconquerable armies I was destined to lead. I learned that I had every right to be pleased with myself and contemptuous of all others because I would be a soldier and my father was the king. This was a most necessary lesson, since arrogance is the sole parent of both daring and cruelty, and without these no wars have been won since the first turning of the sky.

We men of Ashur are farmers. We harvest our barley and our

vines. Our lives are bound up with the soil and the life-giving water which are both gifts of the great Tigris River. But our land is flat and offers us no protection from the marauders of the eastern mountains, and it is poor in metal. Gold is from Egypt. Silver is from the Bulghar Maden, north of the Cilician Gates. A nation may manage without these but not without copper, which must come from Haldia, and even Cyprus. Our tin is mined in the north, beyond Lake Urumia, and our iron from the southern shore of the Black Sea. All of these places lie outside the plains where our first fathers set up their brick huts and worshiped the god from whom we took our name. Thus, because men envied us our rich harvest and because weapons are not made from mud and river reeds, we became warriors and spread the glory of Ashur to the four corners of the world.

And our rule brought the blessing of peace. This, I know, is no more than is claimed by every conqueror, but it is still the truth. The tiny western kingdoms that called us a den of lions and cried after their lost freedom had bled each other to exhaustion for a thousand years before we came. Each would be a tyrant over the others and cursed us only because we were in the place they would have had for themselves. Thus the merchants and artisans and the common farmers, who cared nothing for the ambitions of princes, such humble folk might complain because we taxed them, but they would not have rejoiced to see us overthrown. The trade routes were open and men might lie in peace. And these are not small things.

Thus was I taught in the house of war.

But such matters mean little in youth. What I loved were the horses and the bronze-tipped arrows and the growing strength of my own body. I would be great in the Land of Ashur. I had for this the word of the king my father. Happy is that boy, yearning after manhood, whose hand has been filled with a sword.

On the first morning after my arrival at the royal barrack, I awoke with a violent shudder of astonishment and found myself dangling by my sleeping tunic, my toes reaching in vain for the rush mat beneath me.

"You are not in the house of women now, Prince," said a voice very close to my ear. I twisted around and with my small surprise beheld the sun-blackened face of a man in the green uniform of a *rab kisir*. His hair and beard were streaked with gray. He looked inexpressibly old to me, but he might have been forty.

He seemed angry. He was holding me up by the scruff of the neck with one hand. The other hand was missing—there was only a stump sticking out of the sleeve.

"I am Tabshar Sin, Prince Tiglath, your servant. In the army of your grandfather the Lord Sargon, I led a hundred men against the Nairians. We won a great victory that day. I lost my left hand, as you see, but I spilled much blood and the great king was pleased to provide for me by giving his grandsons into my charge to be trained up as soldiers. And soldiers, Prince, do not sleep till noon like tavern harlots. Dress yourself and wash your face. There is no one here to perform that office for you."

I was dropped to the ground like a broken water pot. Two minutes later I had performed my toilet and was standing outside in the gray light of morning. Tabshar Sin was waiting for me. We were alone on the dusty parade ground.

"What a great pity, Prince—it would seem you have missed breakfast!" He grinned at me, showing strong white teeth. I felt like the rabbit under the paw of a lion. "Nevertheless, we will hit upon something to keep you occupied."

This was my introduction to the life of glory. From first light to dusk, out of everyone's sight and with an empty belly, I studied the art of foddering the royal war horses.

The king's stables boasted over a hundred horses, great stallions, each more skittish and fierce than the last, with flaring nostrils and stonehardened hoofs that could have taken a man's head from his shoulders as neatly as the executioner's ax. Among these I made my way through the narrow stalls, carrying huge bundles of hay and sacks of barley. I felt myself ill used, and more than once I sat down on an empty grain jar to weep for the sad fate that had taken me from my mother and put me among such cruel strangers There was no noon meal in the royal barrack—a soldier has to learn to work all the day on his breakfast—but I did not know this and was sure all had forgotten me.

But at nightfall, when I was quite convinced I had been given over to starvation and despair, Tabshar Sin returned, looked about him, and seemed pleased to see that I had performed the tasks assigned to me.

"This, Prince, is a soldier's lot," he said, putting his hand upon my shoulder as if he understood everything of my sorrow. "Most of his time is filled with drudgery and boredom. The rest is fear, pain and, finally, death. Glory awaits but few, and only those

who have accepted all the rest. Come. It is time to eat, and then to
sleep. Tomorrow will be better."

We dined that night on bread and goat cheese and strong
brown beer. I sat among the royal princes and at Tabshar Sin's
right—indeed, his only—hand. This was meant, it seemed, as a
singular honor. Tabshar Sin told stories of his campaigns, and I
and my brothers listened with attention and admiration. Never
had I tasted such fine food nor known such splendid company. I
had forgotten all about the king's stables. It was the most glorious
evening of my life.

Esarhaddon was not there. When I asked after him I was met
at first with an embarrassed silence and then informed that he had
been sent to sleep under the stars, a bitter punishment indeed
because the nights were cold. He had been caught fighting. I had
only to look around me to discover with whom—at the end of the
table was a boy with a blackened eye. His name was Arad Malik
and I knew him slightly, since he had been removed from the
house of women only the year before. He had a wide, stupid face
and he stared at me with hatred all evening, for he knew Esarhaddon was my friend.

The only other one of my royal brothers whom I knew by
sight was Arad Ninlil, the second son of the Lady Tashmetum-
sharrat. He was a thin, sickly-looking boy of about fourteen, with
blue shadows under his eyes. He never spoke or smiled and hardly
seemed to be listening to Tabshar Sin, as if his mind were occupied with the contemplation of some private sorrow. His training
was nearly finished, and in a few months he would leave to join
the army in the north. After his brother Ashurnadinshum, he was
heir to the throne.

When the meal was over I managed to steal half a loaf of
bread and one of the small sealed jugs of beer. It would not surprise me to discover that Tabshar Sin was aware of my theft, but
if he was he said nothing. I returned to the barrack, rolled up my
blanket and that of Esarhaddon, and went looking for him. I
found him on the roof, his hands clasped behind his head, watching the stars. He was happy to see me but happier, I think, for the
bread and beer.

"Why did you blacken Arad Malik's eye?" I asked him.

His mouth full of bread, Esarhaddon smiled in recollection
as his heavy fingers broke through the seal of the beer jug.

"He gave me no choice," he answered. "He would fight, and

only because I said his mother's breasts were as round as summer melons and just as green. It's quite true, you know—I saw them once when I was but a child of six. They aren't a sight to be forgotten."

We both laughed. We couldn't help ourselves. Arad Malik's mother was from Hamath, a gift of their king from his own harem, and the men of Hamath are famous for their sharp trading. It did not surprise me to learn the Lord Sennacherib had received less than full value.

"Nevertheless, it is a fool who makes enemies needlessly, my brother." I accepted the jug from Esarhaddon's hand and took a swallow, I was unused to beer and suspect I had grown a trifle drunk at dinner. "Learn caution. Arad Malik is a stupid lout, but one day he may do you an injury."

"To make enemies is the business of a warrior's life, and besides, the day I have aught to fear from that son of a cow . . ."

And we laughed yet again and passed the beer jug until it was well and truly empty and our heads were buzzing like the inside of a termite mound. And then the empty jug rolled over the edge of the roof and smashed to pieces on the ground and we laughed then even more. We were laughing still while we wrapped ourselves in our blankets.

At last Esarhaddon stared up at the bright stars and smiled.

"Would that there were other worlds to conquer besides just this one," he said dreamily. "Would that they were as many as the stars."

"One is enough, brother. You and I will have our fill of battles before we are done."

There was no answer. Esarhaddon lay there beside me with his eyes closed, already dreaming of the glory of war.

We slept together that night under the dome of night, content in our lot and in each other, for we were brothers and shared a brother's love, and we believed it would always be so between us, that there was safety in the heart. To the eye of a child the world is simplicity itself.

The following day I was issued a bronze helmet and a corselet made of leather, and Tabshar Sin began to teach me the elements of swordsmanship. He worked me until I could no longer raise my right hand higher than my shoulder, and then he strapped a small round shield to my other arm, drew his own sword, and told me to defend myself or begin collecting scars. In the end I collected no scars, but I fancy that was due more to Tabshar Sin's restraint than to any skill of my own. By the middle of the afternoon everything above the navel felt as stiff as wood and I was quite sure I would be crippled for the rest of my life. Finally Tabshar Sin led me to the shade of a wall, sat me down, and poured water over my head and body until I covered my face with my arms and begged him to stop.

" 'I am Tiglath Ashur, son of Sennacherib!' Yes, boy, I heard about your skill with a knife. It would seem, though, that you are only fierce in front of priests and eunuchs."

I swore at him, calling him all the worst names I could remember, but he only laughed. He was an old campaigner. Nothing shocked him and he was without pity. Tabshar Sin had decided I had the makings of a soldier.

A boy's body hardens quickly, and it was not many days before I could train from sunrise to sunset, feast and make jokes all the evening, and then stagger off to bed to rise the next morning as fresh and cheerful as a maiden on her bridal day. I loved the house of war.

The royal barrack, of course, was only one part of that vast complex, which had been intended originally to provide the king with his bodyguard and the city of Nineveh with its garrison. The princes of the blood mixed on friendly terms with officers and common soldiers alike, for the men of Ashur are a proud race and only the king himself is sacred. Although still a boy, I lived a man's life among men, and I was profoundly happy.

My time there passed quickly. I learned all the arts of siege and pitched battle and became proficient in some of them. Esarhaddon, with whom I maintained a fierce competition, was always a better swordsman, but I was better with the bow and, most particularly, the javelin. I had no equal for managing a chariot, but he was my superior as a rider. Esarhaddon was a fine wrestler, as I have had occasion to mention already, but I was more agile and could run great distances without tiring. We never grew weary of this rivalry. We never grew weary of each other's company, or of thinking of ourselves as the most amiable, the most accomplished, the most blessed of boys. So passed each hour of each day of each month in the tranquil violence of camp life.

The one variation came after I had been in the royal barrack for about half a year, and it took the form of an unexpected gift from my uncle the Lord Sinahiusur.

It was only the middle of the afternoon when a runner came to fetch me from the parade ground, saying only that I had a visitor whose presence would excuse me from my exercises. I was not sorry to leave, being tired and dirty and having had my backside scraped raw from waist to neck by falling off a horse. My foot had caught in the stirrup and the broken-winded old mare, who knew all about little boys who fancied themselves masters of the king's cavalry and had evidently decided she would teach me to respect my elders, dragged me perhaps as many as twenty paces before Tabshar Sin could overcome his paralysis of laughter enough to disentangle me. It had not been one of my better days, and I welcomed any excuse to quit the scene of such a humiliation. I didn't care who wanted me, or for what.

"Go to the dwelling of the camp commander," I was told. The thought entered my mind that perhaps I had disgraced myself enough to warrant dismissal, but it was all one to me.

But it was not the camp commander whom I found sitting on a stool beneath the vine arbor in his garden, drinking beer from a brightly glazed jar, but the Lord Sinahiusur.

The king's *turtanu* had lost none of his majesty of bearing since the last time I had seen him, nearly seven months before, when he had saved me from the gelding knife. His tunic, the color of the hot summer sun, blazed with silver threads, and his beard was as black as pitch. He sat calmly, impassive as a monument, seeming to notice nothing, the jar held delicately in his right hand, as if he were considering if he should let it drop to the ground. I approached him to kneel and place my hands upon his knee in token of respect. There was no servant to attend him, so we were quite alone. At last the Lord Sinahiusur touched my head and bid me rise.

"What happened to you?" he asked, bidding me turn around that he might examine the scratches on the backs of my arms.

"I fell from a horse, my lord."

It was not a subject for which I had much enthusiasm, and I was just as happy when I was allowed to hide my injuries from his sight. They were painful enough, for the winter sun had dried them until they were as cracked as mud, but I felt the injury most deeply in my pride.

"And dragged, from the looks of things."

"Yes, my lord."

"So you are not yet ready to lead a charge?" He searched my

face and smiled, though there was that in his smile to suggest it
was more to put me at my ease than because his liver was quiet.
"Nevertheless, I hear good reports of your progress, Tiglath
Ashur. So you get on well here? The life pleases you?"

"Yes, my lord."

"And do you fancy you will make a good soldier for our
master the king?"

"I hope so, my lord."

"Well, and there is more to the soldier's craft than can be
taught in the house of war—or learned from the back of a horse.
You would be wise to remember that, Tiglath Ashur."

I did not know what answer to make, so I made none. Instead, I let his wise old eyes hold me and I waited, for the *turtanu*
had not come to this garden merely to exchange pleasantries with
a boy—I did not need Tabshar Sin to tell me that.

And he, it seemed, waited too. I do not know what sign he
expected, but perhaps, finally, he saw it because he smiled once
more, this time with something like real pleasure, and his hand
settled upon my shoulder.

"You will live in a troubled world, Tiglath Ashur. You will
need many friends. I wonder if you will count me among them.
What do you think? Shall we be friends, boy?"

He tilted his head to one side, still holding my shoulder in his
strong brown fingers.

"What do I not owe you, Lord?" I asked—I hardly know
where I found the courage to speak, for my heart was in great
confusion and I understood nothing. "All that I am is yours to
command, and if you wish the friendship of one so insignificant . . ."

"Good, then, we are agreed," he barked, shaking me as his
grip tightened and then relaxed. "You speak well for a boy, but
sometimes it is best to say nothing. You will learn that. I think
you may have learned it already. Come."

He rose from his seat and we walked out to the front of the
camp commander's house, where the Lord Sinahiusur's chair was
waiting for him. His bearers, their naked bodies blackened by the
sun, crouched on the ground like dogs, staring up at us with eyes
that seemed to measure us only as weight.

"I think it possible, my friend Tiglath Ashur, you may grow
up to be of some small use to your king, whose servants we both
are. And thus I wish to be of use to you—is that not the truest

meaning of friendship? Yes, of course it is. So I have brought you a gift. Where is he?"

I looked about me as if the question had been addressed to myself, but the *turtanu*'s eyes were fixed on his head bearer, a huge fellow with a captive's ring through his nose, who used his thumb to point back toward the curtained chair.

"Get out of there, you cursed rascal!"

The Lord Sinahiusur's face went suddenly black with rage. A few quick steps took him to the chair, and he pushed back the curtain with an impatient gesture to reveal the cursed rascal, only just awakened from his comfortable nap. Never had I seen such a ridiculous mixture of surprise and slinking guilt as when the *turtanu* grasped him by the collar of his slave's tunic and pulled him out with a yank that sent him sprawling in the dust some four or five paces distant. The bearers roared with approving laughter at the sight, and I laughed with them. Even the fellow himself smiled foolishly as he knelt in the dust, his hands raised in supplication as if to ward off the beating he must have expected.

But the *turtanu* did not strike. His whip stayed in his belt as he studied the slave with obvious distaste.

"You must think it a poor gift I bring you," he said at last. "But perhaps, Tiglath Ashur, you will find him of more use than I ever did. He has certain talents and he is cunning—make of him what you can.

"And, you there, see to the boy's back lest you shame me utterly."

The slave ducked his head in eager compliance, his hands still raised to shield his face though he would have known he was safe enough now. The Lord Sinahiusur glared at him, as the cat glares after the rat that has escaped his jaws.

He spoke no more, but held out his hand that I might touch my forehead against it, stepped into his chair, so recently vacated, and pulled the curtain shut. As he was carried away, I turned to the slave who was still kneeling in the dust, wondering what I was to do with this curious new possession.

I regarded him with puzzlement. Finally the slave stood up and looked about him. He was perhaps twenty-five years of age, though he did not exhibit the bearing of a young man. He had a fair complexion which, in our part of the world, suggested he had spent most of his life within doors, and there was something almost of insolence in his manner, as if he did not greatly fancy the idea of being slave to a boy not yet ten. This in itself irritated me greatly, for I had had enough reminders already that day that I was still less than a man grown.

He was waiting, it seemed, as uncertain of his position as I was of mine.

"I am a soldier," I said finally. "I have no need of a body servant and, in any case, such a thing would not be permitted in the royal barrack. Perhaps the *rab kisir* can find a use for you somewhere."

He registered no reaction at first, and then the words seemed to take hold in his mind.

"My lord, you must not judge me too harshly from that . . ." He made a gesture toward the spot where the *turtanu*'s chair had stood and let his pale, mobile face widen into a rather doltish grin. "You will find I am an excellent servant, and . . ."

He had rehearsed the speech and now, it seemed, had run out of words. The words did not come easily, for this was a foreigner whose Akkadian rasped on the ear as coarsely as a grinding stone on an ax blade—a stranger in the Land of Ashur. And he had been made to look a fool. Well, I knew exactly how he felt on both of these accounts and could feel sorry for him.

"I will do what I can for you," I answered, in Aramaic. It was the language used by many of the soldiers and probably half the city of Nineveh, and one always assumed any foreigner would speak it. "What would you have of me?"

My back was bothering me as we stood there in the cold wind. I would have liked to finish this business so I could go indoors to bathe and change, but the slave merely stared at me with a look of what had become helpless appeal. It was not very long before I grasped that he had understood not a single word.

I peered into his face, with its light eyes and its sharp, almost delicate features, so different from the faces I saw around me each day, and suddenly I understood.

"What would you have of me?" I repeated, but this time in my mother's language. The change in him was immediate and unmistakable.

"Gentle master!" Before I could stop him he had thrown himself to the ground and was embracing my feet. "Little did I expect, in this place . . ."

And thus it was that Kephalos attached himself to my destiny.

"I was not born a slave, master," he said as, in the dim coolness of my barrack room, using a basin of water and a soft cloth, he washed the dirt out of the scratches in my back. His touch was as gentle as a woman's. "I am a prisoner of war."

He said it with great pride, but I had already gathered as much from the notch which had been cut in his left ear—a runaway slave who is recaptured and found to bear that mark is put to death at once. This is the law.

Most prisoners of war, however, are forced to labor digging in the canals or carrying stone for one of the king's building projects. They are worked without mercy and quickly die, and this slave did not have the hands of one who had endured hard toil or even the rigors of parade drill. It was difficult to credit that my new possession had ever been a soldier.

"What war?" I asked him. I was frankly curious and I wanted to hear what lies he would concoct to make himself a hero. "How did you happen to be taken?"

But the Greek merely shrugged his shoulders, as if in regret over some lost opportunity. It was perhaps a quarter of a minute before he could bring himself to answer.

"Five years ago I was on my way home from Aleppo and had the misfortune to be in Tyre when the Assyrians came. Only two days before I had been set upon and robbed outside a tavern and thus, unfortunately, in the ensuing panic was without means of purchasing my escape by sea. The Tyrians impressed me into their army, so I spent the siege on top of the walls playing dice while we waited for the city elders to negotiate a surrender. I won a great deal of money and perhaps this caused some resentment—a foreigner in a city under attack, master, is always in an awkward position. In any case, when the moment came to deliver up prisoners, I found myself in chains, prodded along with the point of a spear toward the Assyrian encampment. And that is the whole history of my military career."

He sighed and opened a small wooden box that rested beside him on my pallet, taking out a tiny clay pot filled with a gray ointment which, as soon as it touched the raw skin, took the sting from my back and made me feel much better.

I discovered that my bad temper had left me, that I was disarmed of my amused contempt for this man, and that I would have liked to do him some service before parting, since it seemed unlikely I would be allowed to keep him.

"What are you trained to do?" I asked him, glancing down at the wooden box as he helped me back on with my tunic. "How have you thus far avoided the labor gangs?"

A sly smile flickered for just an instant at the corners of the slave's mouth, disappearing almost at once.

"Ah, master," he exclaimed, casting his eyes toward the ceiling, "always beware to waste your youth in profitless follies. Had I drunk less that night I was robbed in Tyre I would not be a slave today. Had I been less indolent I would instead be home in Naxos, growing rich as a physician—such, indeed, has been the calling in my family for uncountable generations.

"Nevertheless, I am the son of a physician, and I did not walk through my father's house with my eyes quite closed. I have learned a few things, and the *turtanu*'s principal wife, as perhaps you did not know, suffers from complaints connected with her monthly bleeding, the precise nature of which you are too young to understand but which have been a source of great inconvenience to her husband. I have managed, with the aid of a few little tricks I picked up in my travels . . ."

He stood back as if to consider what more could be done in the arrangement of my tunic, and the subject of the *turtanu*'s lady seemed to pass from his mind like a wandering shadow.

"And now the *turtanu* gives you to me?" I asked, unwilling to lose this highly interesting narrative.

He smiled, as one awakened from a trance.

"Who am I, master, to unravel the secrets of the marriage bed? The lady is past her first youth, so perhaps the difficulties have ceased of their own. Perhaps the *turtanu* has grown impatient with her and has hit upon this means of—no, no, young master, do not seem so shocked. When the gods see fit to afflict you with a wife you will understand how trying they can be. I myself have never taken a woman to wed, but every man has a mother and I could tell you stories of mine . . . But enough of this. It is time, Lord, for you to go to dinner, where you must plead my case before the *rab kisir,* for if I must be a slave among the Assyrians the gods grant at least that my master be a Greek."

I opened my mouth to remind him that I was no foreigner

here like himself but the king's own son, but the expression on his face made me think better of it. The Land of Ashur might be my home, but I knew how it felt to be a stranger in it and thus understood what was in Kephalos' heart. I was no more than a boy but not so young as I might otherwise have been.

"This slave, Prince, he is a gift from the *turtanu*?" Tabshar Sin rubbed his cheek with the fingers of his one hand as he leaned toward me, his elbow nearly knocking over his beer pot.

He picked up his knife and began tapping the blade against the edge of the table, a sure sign that his mind was troubled. He had drunk deeply that evening and, at any time, a matter such as this would have filled him with misgivings. He was responsible for good discipline in the royal barrack, but the *turtanu* was second only to the king as commander of the army.

I nodded, without smiling. Kephalos, who I sensed was less than happy about entrusting his fate to a child, had rehearsed me with great care.

"It is my impression that the Lord Sinahiusur wishes me to have opportunities for practicing the Ionian language, that I may not lose what might be of practical value in years to come. The Ionians are an ambitious people, Tabshar Sin, and who knows but that one day . . ."

It required no more than an equivocal shrug to crease the *rab kisir's* brow with anxiety. I had little enough idea what my own words meant, for Kephalos had stuffed them into my head like straw into a cushion, but it seemed that Tabshar Sin's grasp of these matters was less certain even than mine. He was a soldier with a soldier's virtues. He was brave, he was good at his craft, and he followed orders with blind fidelity. Questions of state, as mysterious as necromancy, were the king's province and the god's.

So if the *turtanu,* who spoke with the king's voice, wished that Tiglath Ashur should be possessed of a slave from some unheard-of corner of the world, that was enough for Tabshar Sin.

"But mind, Prince, that this soft little Ionian of yours does not make a nuisance of himself," he said finally, gesturing at me with his knife, the point of which was almost dancing against my breast. "And see to it that he doesn't teach you any of his foreign laziness. None but a fool whom the gods have forsaken would

trust the tools of his trade to a slave, so mind you keep your own
sword bright and find other things with which to occupy the rascal. Mind, Prince."

His expression was so fierce, and the point of his knife so
close to my heart, that I ducked my head rapidly and agreed to
everything.

"The gods know," I said quickly, "that I have little enough
need of a servant, but the fellow does seem to have some knowledge of healing wounds, so . . ."

"Good, then. That's settled."

As abruptly as if the idea had just come to him, Tabshar Sin
stood up from the table and shuffled outside to relieve himself
against the barrack wall. It was late, and he would find his bed
now, and in the morning it would be as if the slave Kephalos had
been his own inspiration from the first.

I never had the opportunity properly to thank the Lord
Sinahiusur for his gift, for I saw him little after that day, and then
only from a distance and in the awesome state of his office, which
did not allow for communications of a personal nature. In truth,
the king and his companions were as remote as gods. For all that
the Lord Sennacherib had placed his hands upon me and called
me "son," I beheld him only twice over the next two years and
heard his voice but once.

The first of these was at a military parade held as the king set
out upon campaign. I stood at attention with the other boys from
the royal barrack as he rode by in his chariot, resplendent in his
robes of gold and silver that shone in the sunlight like dancing
fire. He looked neither to the right nor to the left as he passed—he
might have been an idol of stone. But this is the way of kings. It is
how they demonstrate their majesty.

The second was on the occasion of his return and, although it
began well enough, will always endure in my memory as among
the most painful nights of my life.

There was a great banquet to celebrate the triumph of our
arms over the hill tribes who gathered like locusts east of the
Tigris River. It was held in one of the palace's great halls, where
the walls are covered with carved stone panels showing how
Ashur's mighty sovereign subdued his enemies. Torches dipped in
wax burned in the wall sconces and there were the sounds of
many voices and of the musicians from the earth's four quarters
whom the king had brought as spoil to Nineveh. Women in gold

and fine linen danced, their bodies swaying to the rhythm of cymbals and drums, and the smells of spices hung heavy in the air.

I served as a page, for on such occasions the Lord Sennacherib liked to have his sons about him that they might behold his glory. I waited beside an entranceway, in the clean uniform of a royal cadet but without my sword, since none might carry a weapon into the king's presence. I watched my father as he sat at table with his two eldest sons, the Lord Sinahiusur, and some dozen or so of his most eminent courtiers whose names I have long since forgotten.

I felt invisible there—in such noise and confusion these splendid nobles, as they concentrated on their own pleasures, would never notice one such as me. It was to be my education in the character of greatness, for these, I thought, were the men who would rule in the land of Ashur for the length of my life.

The king and the *turtanu* were blinding in their majesty. The greatness of their power surrounded them like a living aura and I felt as if the sight of them would burn my eyes out. These were not flesh and blood like myself, but almost gods.

The *marsarru* Ashurnadinshum, whom I had never seen before, I found less impressive—and this in spite of the fact that he was already by his father's grace king of Babylonia. He was up from the south for his wedding, I had heard, but the prospect seemed to give him little enough joy. He had a thin, dissatisfied face and appeared most unwilling to speak. He sat by the king's right hand, his fingers drumming against the sides of a golden wine goblet, silent, almost absent.

And this, I thought to myself, this is the man who will wed Esharhamat and take her from me forever—since I knew by then that my brother Esarhaddon had spoken truly and that that separation would be final—and in my jealous despair I cursed Ashurnadinshum, for I was young and the sight of him tore at my liver. I wished him misery and ruin. I asked the gods to strip him of his life. If they listened, may his wandering ghost forgive me.

But I was not suffered to stand there invisible forever. At last the king glanced in my direction, and then, when he was almost ready to look away, something about me seemed to attract his attention. He turned to the *turtanu,* murmured a word, and then nodded gravely at the answer. The next instant he raised his hand and beckoned me toward him. I came and knelt, clasping his knee in token of submission, and with his own hand he raised me up.

"So this is what has become of the mighty Tiglath Ashur, eh?
'My father is Sennacherib, King of Kings,' is that not right? Yes?
Hah, hah, hah!"

I was not abashed, for I had heard that laughter before and
now it echoed from many throats. The king put his hand upon my
arm and brought me closer, as if he would look at me.

"In a few years' time this one will pile many heads before my
lord's feet."

I do not know who spoke, but in answer the king laughed
once more, and his laughter seemed to beat against me like a fist.
He struck me a joking blow with the backs of his fingers and
feigned astonishment that I could stand my ground. Once more
his laughter filled the great hall, for the Lord Sennacherib was
pleased with both himself and me.

I brought my eyes up to see into his face, for it seemed to me
unworthy that the king's son should stare dumbly at the ground
like any plowboy, and I was surprised to behold that his gaze
turned aside at once. He would not look at me straight, so I found
I had a moment—just a moment, for the great are averse to being
stared at—in which to study his face.

Yes, I had not been mistaken. I could read it in his eyes, what
I had sensed with a child's quickness of insight but could not have
put into words. The Dread King, the Chosen One of Ashur, the
Lord of the Universe was afraid, weary and afraid. Not of me, for
who fears a boy?—but of life. He was but a man after all, and his
burden weighed upon him. And in my heart in pity I called him
"father."

It was the thing of an instant. It was over in the time it takes
to draw a breath, and he was the king again. He smiled at me and
I felt the pressure of his hand upon my arm and his dark, lined
face resumed its majesty, but the impression stayed with me all
my life.

"I have a surprise for you," he said. "Who do you imagine
waits to see you tonight, boy? Eh? Yes?" He raised his arm and
pointed into the shadowy corner of the room. I tried, but I could
see nothing except a doorway standing half open. "Your mother,
boy! Eh? Yes, you are excused. Run to her!"

The great king, the Giver of Gifts, could not more have won
me to him had he cast half of Asia at my feet. In my confusion of
mind I did not even bow myself out of his holy presence. The

blood pounded in my veins and I flew to that shadowed corner like a hawk falling upon its prey.

She was there, my beautiful bronze-haired mother, and she knelt in the murky light to open her arms to me and crush my body against her. I could feel my heart pounding with a joy that was almost like the agony of death as she dug her fingers into my back. And she wept—she rocked me in her spasms of weeping and I felt her tears upon my back. I had not known, until that moment, how much I had longed for her. What was glory, what was the favor of kings compared to the sweet embrace of my mother, whom these things had stolen from me? Where else but here in her arms could I feel any happiness? For a great time we did not speak. We could not speak. Our tongue were frozen.

"My Lathikadas, my fine boy, you have grown," she said at last. She held me a little away from her that she might see that it was true, and yes, I was her fine boy—I could see it in her eyes, blue like my own. Her fine boy. Better that, I felt, than *rab shaqe*. I straightened up and smiled and let her fill her sight with me.

"You have grown, yes. You are almost a man now." She smiled back, but there was a misery in her smile, as if she were measuring the distance that yawned between us. "Tell me, tell me everything that has happened to you. Do you like being a soldier? Is it all that you dreamed it would be in the house of war?"

What was it that I read in her face in that instant? Did she dread to hear me say that I loved my barrack and my horses and all the cruel implements of battle? Did she fear that that new idol might have replaced her in my heart? Or did she long to know of my happiness there, that she might believe the sacrifice of losing me had been worth all that she had to pay for it in anguish and loneliness? I did not know. A child cannot know these things, for he understands no happiness or misery but his own, and yet I sensed in that moment that mine was not the power to ease her sufferings but only, if I spoke the wrong word, to burden her with more.

"Oh, Merope," I said, holding her face between my hands, "would that you could see the glory of it, that you could see me there! You would not be ashamed to call me your son."

I told her everything, about Tabshar Sin, who had but one hand, and my Greek slave, about my prowess with the javelin, about Esarhaddon's skill in wrestling, and the chariots that threw up curtains of dust behind their burning wheels and the sunlight flashing off the weapons during sword practice. I wearied my tongue now. The words poured out of me like water at floodtime, and she was content to listen and admire and be still. It was not wrong to speak of these things. It was of these that she seemed most eager to hear, for she understood that she had not lost me to them. That I was free set her free as well, for she was still in my heart.

But when I asked after her and the house of women, she was silent and evasive.

"Oh, my son—it is much the same." Her eyes turned aside from me. "The fountain waters still laugh like naughty children. Do you remember the fountain, Lathikadas? And the little gazelle? He is grown now, and they took him away. . . ."

"And what of Esharhamat, Mother? Is she still so pretty? Does she ever ask about me?"

It was an innocent enough question, but my mother covered my mouth with her hands as if I had uttered some terrible curse that would come back to fall upon my head.

"You must never speak of her, my son. You must forget her. You must forget that she exists."

She held me to her again and, although she did not weep, I knew she was wretched. Young as I was, I could not guess why.

"Forget us both, and go on to be a great man.

"Now go," she said suddenly, releasing me with a push. "You are mine no longer, my Lathikadas. Go back to your father —you are his now. You belong to him and his god. Forget me and be happy."

I did not think I could bear it. The moment of parting was almost upon us, and this time I understood how completely I was to lose her. The tears started in my eyes. I thought my heart would crack within my breast.

"I will ransom you free from the house of women, Mother," I said, hardly able to speak. I held her arms as if without them I might sink into the earth. "You will see. The king is pleased with me. I will win you away from this. I will never forget you."

The door behind us opened a little wider, and I saw the eunuch who was waiting to take my mother back to her golden cage. The sobbing rose in my throat as if through its own will.

But Merope was already on her feet, fading into the shadows. I would have rushed to embrace her once more, but she held out her hands to prevent me. I could see, even in that dim light, the tears that wet her face.

"Good-bye, my Lathikadas, my son," she murmured. "I cannot help you with my love now. Forget me, my son. Only remember that I love you more than life."

And then she was gone. The door closed. I was alone.

3

I do not know how I found my way back to the royal barrack that night. I remember that I lay on my bed, that I thought I would die of misery, that my tears choked me and made my throat burn. I was but a boy and nothing cuts as deep as a boy's sorrow.

My mother had hurt me more deeply than she could have imagined, for she had made me feel all over again the sharp pain of losing her. For many days I was thus. While the sun shone I did my work, the work of learning the soldier's craft, and none saw any difference in me, but at night I was overwhelmed with grief. Only Esarhaddon was my witness, and Esarhaddon said nothing. I was grateful to him for that.

And then, at last, the torment subsided into a certain moroseness that was with me always but left me free to think of other things. I was unhappy, but I had not lost interest in life. I was thus when Kephalos came to me one day.

I had been speaking no more than the truth when I told Tabshar Sin I had little enough need of a servant. I was merely a boy, I had few possessions to trouble about, my needs for food, clothing, and shelter were met by the royal barrack, and I spent the greater part of my time in military training. True, Kephalos did teach me what remained of the Greek alphabet, but that was quickly done and there was, in any case, nothing to read in that tongue. For the rest, he seemed to spend most of his day loafing around the parade ground, idle and useless. He was never an energetic fellow, but in time even he began to grow restless.

"Master," he said to me at last, "is it not the case that in this country slaves are sometimes allowed to go out and find occupation in the city, to enrich both themselves and their owners? Is this not the custom?"

I was sitting on my sleeping mat, unstrapping the greaves from my shins, and I looked up at where he was standing in the doorway. It was almost evening. I had had a strenuous day and was tired and hungry, but not unpleasantly so—in a quarter of an hour I would come out of the steam baths, sweated and clean and ready for dinner. So I listened to his talk as I might have to the good-natured growling of a camp dog, without much understanding or interest but willingly enough.

"Yes, of course, Kephalos, that is indeed the custom."

"Then, I was wondering . . ."

"Yes, Kephalos?"

He showed his teeth in a nervous smile, an admission that we both understood he had gotten himself into some difficulty. I was even then accustomed to this.

"Master, I am of little use here, as you know. And the atmosphere of a barrack is not much to my taste. I wonder if I might have your indulgence to follow my old profession . . ."

"And what profession is that, Kephalos?"

The smile grew a shade more tightly drawn across his face, for he was aware I was baiting him.

"I would, with your permission, young master, set up as a physician."

I kicked off my sandals and he swooped down to gather them from the floor, hugging them to his breast as if he had some idea of forcing me to ransom them.

"Master, you must understand I . . ."

"Have you read the law codes, Kephalos? Do you understand how the king punishes a physician who is negligent or even merely inept? If you make a man blind in one eye, the king will send a soldier to your house, where he will gouge out one of your eyes with the point of a dagger. I was under the impression that you had not yet completed your apprenticeship at the time of your capture. Was I mistaken?"

"Master, you are young—let me explain something to you," he said, and knelt beside me, placing the sandals neatly by my sleeping mat. "Master, you must know that one does not grow rich as a physician by treating the sick . . ."

The program Kephalos outlined to me was simplicity itself.

"You see, my young lord who knows nothing of the world, I have what is more than learning—I have the prestige that comes with great patrons. I am the slave of a royal prince and have served as physician to the wife of the *turtanu* himself. With such credentials, wealthy patients will flock to my door, if only that they may have the pleasure of speaking of it to their friends and acquaintances—'Of course our physician is the clever Ionian Kephalos, who treats the king's own family!'—and from these I will take as patients only such women as have nothing to occupy them except their imaginary illnesses, and of such, let me assure you, no city has ever known the lack. The rest, those who are truly sick, I will refer to my Assyrian colleagues, that there should be no jealousy among them. Thus I will undertake to make us both rich within the space of a year."

He peered at me speculatively, tilting his head to one side as if he were considering some weighty matter.

"Because of course, master, I would divide the profits with you justly. I understand the natural order of things, and you are entitled to a reasonable return on your investment. Shall we say, one part in four? My lord is a soldier and his father is the king, so his needs in days to come will not be as pressing as mine. One in three, then?"

"Kephalos, a person needs money to start out as a physician. Boy that I am, I know as much as that. You will require a house, and instruments, and drugs. I have no money to give you, for all that you style me as a royal prince. Where will you get it?"

He held his lower lip between his teeth, and I understood at once there was more to this sudden inspiration than he had so far been willing to confide to me. I picked up my sword and balanced the point against his soft throat.

"Kephalos . . ."

"Master, you need not concern yourself with these sordid details. Leave all to me, and . . ."

"Kephalos, you have been dicing with the soldiers again! How much have you robbed them of this time? Tell me the truth."

"Master, I . . . Well, truly I have been lucky just recently and . . ."

"And therefore someone has offered yet once more to cut out your entrails and hang you in them?"

"To be honest, master, it would be better if I could take

myself off from here for a term—you understand. Shall we say, then, equal shares?"

That very night Kephalos removed his belongings and disappeared into the city.

When I next saw him, ten days later, I hardly thought he was the same man, so richly was he dressed. His wool robe was embroidered in blues and yellow and red. It was a marvelous transformation. And he had a house and a servant of his own, and he gave me twelve shekels of silver as my share of his first fees.

"It is beyond anything I could have imagined, master. The fact that I am a foreigner is a great asset, for it gives me the advantage of novelty—women love novelty above all things, as you will no doubt discover in time—and the learning of distant lands is held in high esteem among the merchant classes. We will prosper greatly, master! I have had the most astonishing success with a certain aphrodisiac, the recipe for which I happened upon quite by chance once in Aleppo. I sell it as fast as I can compound it, although one ought to feel some compassion for the poor husbands—if that is who they are—for it has a dreadful odor and lingers upon the tongue for hours. . . ."

I told Kephalos to take back my share of the profits and invest it for me. I had two reasons for this. One was that I had no immediate need for money, and the other was a growing respect for my slave's cunning. I felt he might indeed make us both rich, and in the shadowy places in my mind there was some idea of buying my mother out of the house of women. It was an absurd notion I knew even then—the king my father did not trade in flesh like a merchant and, in any case, a handful of silver shekels was unlikely to impress him—but it gave me hope. It was at least something to do against my loneliness and dark rage.

And life went on within the royal barrack. Tabshar Sin was well pleased with me. I was growing taller and stronger with each day. I was almost a man, as my mother had said, and almost a soldier. And there was Esarhaddon, to whom I could confide my feelings, who understood but little yet was my friend.

"You care too much," he said, using the point of his sword to open yet another jar of beer, for he had learned to love beer almost as much as fighting. He settled back on his sleeping mat, his eyes half closed, a picture of drowsy contentment. "My mother is in the house of women too, and I hope she stays there forever. By the sixty great gods, I would rather face a thousand

Medes with nothing to defend me but a copper pruning knife than live with her under the same roof again."

He smiled at me, quite pleased with himself. It was ever my brother's special gift to see life in terms of solid, simple, personal reality, as if by his own will a man's needs and desires could be raised to a law of nature.

"Mothers—they are worse than all the devils in all the hated places of the earth," he went on, waving his beer jar in the air to indicate the cosmic character of this new wisdom of his. "You should have had a mother like Naq'ia, Tiglath, and then you would know how to be happy now."

It was not long after, in the month of Ab that burns like a furnace, that I was crouched by the doorway of my quarters—it was the hottest part of the day, when man and beast alike sought only shade and quiet—my attention absorbed in an attempt to repair a sandal strap, when a boy of perhaps seven or eight presented himself to me, bowed very low, and asked if he had "the honor of addressing the Lord Tiglath Ashur." He was as pretty and delicate as a girl, this child, with large brown eyes and long lashes. When I nodded, he bowed again and presented me with a folded piece of leather. The writing inside was Greek, so I did not have to guess the identity of the sender. The boy had apparently been instructed to wait for an answer, for he stood at something like attention while I read.

"His humble slave, the physician Kephalos of Naxos, begs that the Dread Lord, the Prince Tiglath Ashur, Son of Sennacherib, King of Kings, King of Assyria, would honor him by attending his poor table this evening, at his house by the Gate of Adad. The presence of the Prince Esarhaddon would be an added felicity."

"You may tell the physician Kephalos that we should be happy to accept," I said, "but that we are soldiers and must ask for leave."

The boy bowed a third time, lower still if such a thing were possible, and withdrew.

I did not trouble myself with consulting Esarhaddon, since I knew he would fall like a starving jackal upon any chance to escape the barracks for an evening, so I went directly to Tabshar Sin, who also had taken refuge from the summer heat and was lying on his sleeping mat, squeezing water onto his face and beard from a cloth he dipped now and then into a large clay jug. Like every good soldier, he had learned long since to take full advantage of his hours of rest, and he scowled in irritation when my shadow fell across his doorway.

"What is it you want, Prince?" he asked, in a tone that said I might go to Arallu, which the Greeks call "Hades," for all of him.

"Permission to be absent this evening, *Rab Kisir*. I have received an invitation to dinner."

I showed him the scrap of leather, but he only glanced at it before letting it drop to the floor. "That effeminate, dice-playing slave of yours, I take it. So he issues invitations now, does he? He has grown quite prosperous, I am told."

"But may I go, *Rab Kisir*?"

"Is your kit prepared against tomorrow's field exercises?"

"Yes, *Rab Kisir*."

"Then you may go. I expect you will be served a better meal than the royal mess could offer."

"And Esarhaddon?"

"Him too?" Tabshar Sin turned his head a few degrees in my direction, as if to underline his astonishment. "Yes, very well. But don't allow him to drink too much beer. And come straight back when your dinner party is finished. You are royal princes, but these days Nineveh is full of foreigners."

The shadows were already lengthening when Esarhaddon and I set out. It was a glorious adventure. The camp and the palace, that had been our world, and to us the great city of Nineveh, where we had lived all our lives, was as unfamiliar as the wilds of Judah.

"Read it to me again."

I took the scrap of leather from my pouch yet once more and for Esarhaddon's amusement translated its contents into Akkadian.

"Why does he call our father king of 'Assyria'? What sort of a place is this 'Assyria'?"

"The Ionians have no *sh* sound in their language, so 'Ashur' becomes 'Assur.' It is simply their word for the Land of Ashur."

"This slave of yours is a funny fellow, Tiglath. 'Assyria.' By the gods, he is a funny fellow."

The palace and all that is attached to it rests on a great platform of bricks and is thus many cubits higher than the surrounding city. We had to walk down a long flight of stairs before we reached the streets, and it was like descending from a mountain into a forest. Suddenly a crowded, noisy humanity closed around us, people brushing each other with their shoulders as they walked past, the cries of vendors, the smells of food and human sweat and decaying garbage. I have been in many great cities since then, but none has stayed in my memory like Nineveh.

There were women on the streets, a thing I had not expected, and they wore the brightly colored costumes of many lands— green, blue, yellow, even red, which no woman of Ashur would wear except in mourning—their veils drawn over their faces so that there was nothing to see except their large black eyes. Some did not wear veils, which meant they were concubines, and some did not even cover their hair.

Among the men I heard more Aramaic than Akkadian, and many times I could not have said what language was being spoken. Some I could recognize by their dress as Hittites or Hebrews or, by their pleated linen and their shaved faces, Egyptians.

We passed a spot where three men were squatted on the pavement drinking beer from a common pot. They sucked through hollow straws, for among the common people it is not the custom first to strain out the husks—something I had not realized before then. One of the men, I noticed, had had the tip of his nose cut off, no doubt as a punishment for lying under oath.

Esarhaddon insisted we stop at a stall where an old woman with no veil and a series of waving lines tattooed over her nose and left cheek was selling fruits preserved in sugar. There were flies swarming over the fruit, but Esarhaddon would not be pleased until we bought some. We paid for it with a couple of copper half-shekel pieces, most of the money we had, and it turned out to be a bad purchase. As soon as we bit into the fruit and pierced the sugar that coated it, the smell was dreadful and there was black rot at the core. We threw the rest into the gutter.

Here and there we heard the sounds of music and sometimes of women's high-pitched laughter. Open doorways invited one inside buildings made of yellow mud-brick.

The people in the streets, citizens and foreigners alike, stared at us and stood out of our way, for we were dressed in the uniform of the royal barrack. Boys that we were, no man would have dared to raise his hand against us.

There were no beggars on the streets, as I have seen in other places, for the king punishes begging. Nineveh is a rich city and there is work for all who want it. A bankrupt may always sell himself as a slave, which is considered more honorable than begging because one may buy oneself out of slavery, but begging is a stain upon the soul.

At last, after asking directions many times, we found our way to the Gate of Adad. It was a district that offered constant tribute to that god, patron of war and storms, called "the thunderer," for everywhere there was the sound of hammer upon anvil and the heat from the furnaces made a scorching wind. The men there went about bare-chested and they all carried many scars from old burns. When we asked for the house of Kephalos the physician, we were directed to follow a street somewhat wider than most, and when we reached his door we could no longer hear the clanging of hammers. Kephalos, who must have had spies out to bring him word of our coming, was there to greet us, resplendent in a tunic of blue wool with sleeves embroidered in yellow. He had grown a beard, which was brown as Tigris mud and added to his dignity of bearing. He went down on his knees before us, opening his arms to embrace my feet.

"Young master, welcome, many times welcome to the house of your servant Kephalos. And you, Prince Esarhaddon, welcome as my master's royal brother and in your own right as well. I am honored beyond words to think . . ."

"Obviously not beyond words, Kephalos. Come, up on your feet again, honored physician, or you will soil your robes."

This consideration seemed to carry some weight and we were finally able to persuade him to rise and finish his effusive greeting inside.

His face was shining with oil and his prosperity was everywhere evident as he took us into the private rooms of his house. There were carpets on the floors and the chests that seemed to stand against every wall had been left open to show forth linens of many colors and richly embroidered wools. Even before we sat down at his table the smell of spiced lamb had reached us from the kitchen. My slave, without doubt, had grown rich.

"Half of all this is yours, young master, pursuant to our agreement." Kephalos waved his hand so that the lantern light flashed from his ringed fingers. "And I have invested sums with the Aramaean traders—wisely, of course, for I am careful of my lord's wealth—and we can expect good returns next year, when

the caravans return from the Northern Sea. Yes, come here, my
sweet boy."

It was the child who had brought me Kephalos's invitation
that morning. He sat down beside his master, close enough to
touch his side, and Kephalos put his arm over the boy's shoulder
as if their intimacy were of long standing. Esarhaddon and I exchanged a glance, but we said nothing and Kephalos went on
talking as before, apparently quite comfortable in the usages of his
own house. He spoke of the metal trade, and in a way that would
have convinced anyone he had been born to commerce. He drank
a great deal of wine as he talked, and the more he drank the more
openly he caressed the slave child, who accepted it all without any
self-consciousness, like a baby in its mother's lap. Matters had
proceeded almost to the point of indecency by the time a fat little
woman with the broad brown face of a Phrygian and gold bangles
on her ankles and wrists brought in the first course of our dinner
and set it down before us. As she left, she swept the child up in
her arms with the practiced motion of a boatman loading cargo.
Kephalos smiled after her with indulgent lechery.

"Mother and son," he said, after she had gone back to her
kitchen. "Arrived in the land two years ago. The boy is young,
and Philinna, though sweet as a fig, is a simple creature and
speaks hardly a word of Akkadian. She understands Greek well
enough, but who else does in this part of the world? I picked them
both up for I am embarrassed to tell you how little. The boy's
name is Ernos. Try these, my young lords—honeyed locusts,
which I would not be ashamed to serve to the king your father
himself. Philinna has a loving touch with such delicacies. . . ."

After dinner, Kephalos took us out to his garden and we sat
under a vine arbor and drank wine mixed with water at three
parts to two, as strong as any I had ever tasted. It was not very
long until I felt as stunned as a man who has just fallen from his
horse, and Esarhaddon was drunk almost to incoherence.

"We cannot allow the prince to go back to your barrack in
such a condition," Kephalos said finally, shaking his head as he
looked at the way Esarhaddon sagged against the arbor. "I have
something to bring him back to life."

He stepped back inside his house and in a moment returned
with a small flask which he emptied into the wine that remained
in Esarhaddon's cup.

"In an hour he will be fresh as dew."

While we waited for Kephalos' potion to do its magic, he and I listened to the crickets and enjoyed the relief of cool night breezes. It was as pleasant an evening as I have ever known.

Eventually Esarhaddon got up, staggered to a corner of the garden, and retched loudly. When he came back he was smiling and talkative and asked for more wine.

The night was black before Kephalos allowed us to say our farewells, and as a parting gesture he gave me a pouch bulging with silver coins.

"You are reaching the age, master, when you will find uses for ready money," he said, holding my hands in his own and cupping them around the pouch. "And the night is still fresh and it is a long way yet back to the royal barrack."

Then, once more, at the threshold of his grand house, he went down on his knees before me and clasped my ankles.

"I am your servant," he said. "And though I was born a free man I could not want a better master. Always remember, in this life I and my home and all that I have is yours, my prince."

He, too, had drunk more than was good for him, but I knew that he meant what he said and there were tears shining in his eyes as he rose from the ground. A rascal and worse was this slave of mine, but for some reason he had decided to be my friend as well and I could not help but love him. He waved after us as Esarhaddon and I walked away down the street to the Gate of Adad.

In the light from the doorway to a tailor's shop—Nineveh never sleeps, so the tailor was still at his needle and glanced up to watch us, perhaps thinking we meant him some mischief—I divided the contents of the money pouch with Esarhaddon. We always divided everything, bread, beer, work, so why not this? It was more silver than either of us had seen before in our lives.

"I wonder which of them he is bedding with," he said after we had resumed our journey—more slowly now, and watchfully, because Esarhaddon had settled with himself that we were to make proper use of our sudden good fortune. "The mother or the son, or possibly both, do you think? Perhaps both together?"

He was grinning because he knew he had shocked me, although there was no reason why I should have been shocked. We were both aware, in the rather abstract way of boys just on the threshold of their manhood, that women were useful for other things besides preparing honeyed locusts, and no one who has

lived any time in an army encampment, even if it be the royal
barrack, can escape the knowledge that there are those who prefer
a boy to any woman, even if she be sweet as a fig. Still, I was
shocked. The meaning of Kephalos's behavior at dinner, which I
had found more puzzling than anything else, was suddenly clear
to me. Then, all at once, as if I had just seen the joke, I broke out
into loud laughter.

"Yes," I said, laughing still—we were both laughing now.
"Yes, knowing Kephalos, I would say both together."

With our arms about each other's shoulders and money in
our belts, Esarhaddon and I went off in search of adventure and
pleasure and all else that silver coins could buy in the streets of
Nineveh.

In the end what we found was a wineshop, not a hundred
paces from the palace walls.

I have since been in a thousand such places, for they are to be
found everywhere in the world, but of course the first time for
everything is what one remembers. It was only a few tiny rooms,
and its mud walls had never felt the stroke of a brush. There were
tables and benches about, all of rough dark wood, and everywhere
men in plain wool tunics and with their heads bare sat drinking
with sullen concentration. The air smelled sour and was itself
almost thick enough to drink. Huddled in one corner were three
men with musical instruments, and in front of them danced what
at first sight I fancied the most enchanting beauty I had ever
beheld, for her breasts were as round and brown as apples, and
her belly, as she swayed to the music, seemed possessed of its own
independent life. My mother excepted, it was the first time I had
ever seen a woman naked.

There were other women there, carrying wine to the tables
and sometimes leaning over the men they served, and they—it
suddenly struck me—were naked too. One of them turned as Esarhaddon allowed the curtain over the doorway to drop back into
place, and she smiled at us with a smile that seemed to promise all
the delights of this earth.

"By the sixty great gods, Tiglath my brother, I think we have
found what we were seeking."

Yes, indeed we had.

Everyone stared at us as we approached an empty table and
sat down. It did not seem a place much frequented by the cadets
of the royal barrack, but that did not, it appeared, count to our

disadvantage. The girl who had smiled at us came by with a jug of wine and a pair of pottery cups, and as she set them down we could smell the perfume of her bare body. I do not know how Esarhaddon felt, but I was mortally frightened. Much as I longed to, sooner than touch her brown flanks I would have put my hand into the armorer's furnace. She, however, was not so reluctant.

"Lords," she murmured, letting the fingers of one hand trail down the side of Esarhaddon's face. "You do us honor by your presence." She poured the wine, and as she did one of her breasts, which were by no means undersized, brushed against the sleeve of my tunic. For a moment I thought I would choke with sheer excess of pleasure. "Anything you wish you may command. Food, wine, a woman to help you drink it—a woman to help you forget your cares. All you need do is speak."

We could not have spoken. Our tongues were glued to our palates and we dared not risk so much as a syllable. It was then that I noticed Esarhaddon's face had turned as red as fire.

"Later perhaps?" She looked from one to the other, but we were both equally helpless. "I will come again—or if you wish anything, you need but raise the smallest of your fingers."

She took my little finger, hooking it with her own, and brought it up to her mouth and pretended to bite it with her white teeth. *My life has been wasted,* I thought. *Until this moment I have learned nothing, done nothing of the slightest importance.* Under my loincloth, my member was as rigid as a tent peg.

She went away, and I lifted the wine cup to my lips and the sour taste of it brought me back to earth with a jolt.

The woman who had danced began again, and all the time, as her body undulated to the rhythm of the flute and the drum's beat, she never seemed to take her eyes from us. She would tilt her shoulders and her breasts would swing out to one side, and her hips twitched back and forth and the heavy mat of hair between her legs strained up and back.

"By the sixty great gods," Esarhaddon breathed, his voice hardly more than a whisper. "For just half a quarter of an hour alone with her, what I wouldn't give. What I wouldn't give."

It seemed, however, that many were not so fastidious as my brother, for as soon as the woman had finished her dance, a man in the costume of an Amorite approached her, gave her a drink of wine from the goblet he carried, and began to engage her in a discussion the subject of which was more than obvious. At last he reached into a pocket and counted out a few copper coins for her. She rested her back against the unpainted wall and placed one foot upon a stool she might have kept there for the purpose, and the Amorite lifted up the front of his tunic and pressed himself against her.

I have seen such things many times, for the people who live beside the two great rivers feel no shame about satisfying themselves. In all the great cities of the East one can walk down the streets in broad day and behold men rutting on women. They do this as casually as a Greek or an Egyptian might empty his bladder against a temple wall. Perhaps it is only because I am half a foreigner that I have always turned my eyes away with a feeling of unease, as if I had chanced to witness a profane thing. It is a prejudice of mine, something I have never overcome.

But I must confess that I watched that Amorite and his dancer with something like awe. I could not have looked away if I had wanted to, and I did not want to. All I could see of her from behind the screen of his green-and-white tunic was one leg, the foot of which rested on her stool, but it took no great labor of the imagination to understand what was taking place. His tunic, the only curtain he allowed his modesty, trembled and shook like a fishing boat's sail in a squall. When it was over—for the whole act occupied no more than a minute or two—and he shuddered and was at last quiet, he sagged away from her as if somehow she had squeezed him dry. The woman, when she stepped out from in front of him, was of course unchanged. It might never have happened. She went back to her musicians and sat down and sipped a cup of water. Nothing had touched her.

"I have a room upstairs—perhaps you would prefer that, Lord?"

The serving girl returned. She was leaning over us, closer to Esarhaddon than to myself, and it was difficult to know which of us she addressed.

"Yes, I would . . . ." The words died in Esarhaddon's throat. I do not think I could have spoken at all.

She turned her eyes to me, but I could only look down and shake my head. All desire, if such it was, had deserted me. She put her arm across Esarhaddon's shoulder, dismissing me with a tight smile.

"Then come, Lord, and share my sleeping mat for a time. You will see that we know the difference between a greasy caravan merchant and a cadet of the royal barrack. Come now, Lord . . ."

Esarhaddon glanced at me, and I could see he was almost as frightened as I had been, but he rose and went away with her. I was left behind to consider my failure in solitude.

She made short work of him, for not a quarter of an hour later he was down again and we were back out on the street. We had had enough of reveling and it was time to turn our steps back to the palace and our quiet beds.

"Well—did you?"

I felt myself entitled to as much curiosity as that.

"I'm not sure—I *think* so." Esarhaddon shook his head in perplexity. "She lay down and told me I could do as I liked and wanted to know if I preferred her on her back or her belly. At last she grabbed me—you know—and it was over in a second. I couldn't tell whether I was actually inside her or not."

"How did it feel?"

"It is difficult to put into words. At any rate, for two pieces of silver, I think I made a bad bargain."

He threw back his head and laughed and, arm in arm, we went home.

As soon as we were within the barrack compound we could sense the change—lights were on everywhere, and the only sound was the hum of voices. We had not been in our room long enough to remove our sandals when the doorway darkened and we heard Tabshar Sin's voice.

"Where have you been?" he asked. He did not sound pleased.

"We went to the Ionian's house for dinner. Tiglath asked permission—don't you recall?"

Tabshar Sin stared at us in the gray darkness, almost as if he couldn't understand what the words meant.

"Be ready for arms inspection in five minutes," he answered. "There will be no sleep for anyone tonight. We are on alert until the palace sends word to the contrary."

"Why? What has happened?" I do not know which of us spoke.

"You mean you have not heard?"

Tabshar Sin turned back toward us from the threshold, and his astonishment seemed genuine.

"Nothing—what is it?"

"The rider came an hour ago. The Elamites have crossed the

Tigris with a great army. Babylon has fallen, it would seem without much resistance, and the *marsarru* Ashurnadinshum was captured. Whether he is alive or dead . . ."

"Then it is war," I said. It was a conclusion at once obvious and stunningly important. The Elamites had ridden in and taken the king's heir. Ashurnadinshum might even be dead already, and I would not envy him the manner of his dying.

The Land of Ashur was to fight, and not for a day or a month or even a year. There would be many campaigns, for it was no small thing to snatch the king's son from the throne of Babylon and the Elamites were not old women. If it went on long enough, even Esarhaddon and I might see battle. With a shock I realized that this night was probably the last moment of my boyhood.

"Yes, Prince—it is war."

4

Nergalushezib, for a few months at least, had felt the throne of Babylon under his haunches. Now his kingdom was an iron cage hanging by a chain from the Great Gate of Nineveh. Naked and filthy, the crown he had usurped from Ashurnadinshum fixed to his head with copper nails, on his hands and knees he roamed back and forth, back and forth, while the citizens pelted him with mud, excrement, and curses. I saw him on the third day of his exposure, and already then hunger, the merciless sun, the anguish of his own heart, and perhaps the copper nails driven through the skull and into his brain had deprived him of reason. He howled like an animal, praying for death through his cracked and bloody lips. The gods must truly have scorned him, for he lived to the sixth day.

Thus did the Lord Sennacherib, the Servant of Ashur, avenge himself for the butchering of his eldest son.

That day and all the days while Nergalushezib lived were like a time of festival in the city. Fortunetellers and prostitutes, sellers of beer, fruit, honey cakes, and roasted meat all followed their trades under his eyes. All the delights of this life, all just beyond his reach, all were there for him to witness as, a finger's width at a time, his life ebbed away through the mire-coated bars of his iron cage. As he raved and howled and begged for the pity of men and gods, the people of Nineveh laughed at him with many voices. Most of them were foreigners—this wasn't their quarrel. They were merely there to watch, and the war was good for trade.

And the war, it seemed, would never end but would go on and on, for Nergalushezib had not been taken in some decisive

battle but sold by a traitor, to whom Sennacherib gave as his
reward the man's measured weight in silver. The Elamites and
their Chaldean allies could always find a new wax doll to reign for
them in Babylon, and it was at Susa, in the dungeons of the
Elamite king Hallutush-Inshushinak, that Ashurnadinshum,
strangled with a bowstring, had met his death. Then that king in
his turn had perished, slain by his own people after Sennacherib's
victory at Nippur. But now his son reigned, and Kudur-Nahhunte, as all men knew, was as poisonous as a coiled serpent.

It had been almost two years since the night the royal barrack had stood at alert. The beginnings of a beard grew on my
chin, and to my intense embarrassment the hairs were straight
rather than curly, declaring once again my mixed blood. I was
almost a man and my military training, greatly accelerated since
the war's beginning, was nearly over. All these things weighed on
my mind as I stood in the crowd that had collected outside the
city walls to witness the usurper's agony.

The sight of him, his nakedness and his mad, glittering eyes,
troubled my mind and I did not know why. He had connived with
the Elamites to bring the *marsarru* to ruin and a shameful death.
He had insulted the majesty of Ashur. It was fitting and proper
that his own death should be a mocking agony. And yet I could
find no satisfaction in the spectacle. I watched for a while, for
Tabshar Sin had said it was wholesome for a soldier to witness
these public shows of the king's wrath, telling me that the sufferings of one's enemy were sweet, but I could not enjoy them as I
had expected. Of this softness I was ashamed.

The walls of Nineveh rose to such a great height that they
seemed almost more the work of Great Mother Earth or of the
younger gods than of men's hands. They shut out the city and its
noise so that one might almost fancy these had never existed.
Beyond them were fields of barley that stretched out endlessly
and, always, the great Tigris, queen of rivers. Sometimes, at night,
if a solitary man came outside the gates for the refreshment of his
soul, the only sound he heard would be her rushing waters.

But there was no solitude now. The chatter of ten thousand
voices stilled the river's urgent whisper. The confused, swirling
movement of ten thousand bodies screened the earth from my
eyes. It would be so until the usurper's cries had ceased to be
diverting to the multitudes of Nineveh.

It was the sixth hour of the morning, when the sun had

nearly reached its height. I stood near Nergalushezib's cage in the uniform of a *quradu*, a member of the king's personal bodyguard, holding the javelin I carried everywhere. It would have been the work of an instant to raise my weapon and strike. The distance was no more than twenty paces; it would have been an easy matter to split his heart like a wineskin left out in the sun, and then the crowd would have had nothing left to grin at. I felt a strong impulse to do this—I did not consider that I would be punished for the act, for I was high in the royal favor and disdained to think of punishment—but a *quradu* is above all else loyal to the king's will and it was the king's will that Nergalushezib should live through the extremity of his suffering. So I stayed my hand.

"Tiglath, is it really you?"

I felt a hesitant touch upon my shoulder and turned around to see a woman standing behind me. Her face was covered with a marriage veil, but there was something about her eyes that stirred my memory.

She was richly dressed, after the fashion of court women— the fringes of her shawl were decorated with tiny gold and silver coins, and the red weave of her widow's tunic was shot through with silver thread. She was a great lady, and behind her, when I had the presence of mind to look, I saw three other women in attendance, also richly dressed, and a tall eunuch carrying the staff of the royal household.

But this great lady was in stature hardly more than a child. She did not seem old enough to have known a husband, let alone to have lost one, and her eyes, luminous and black, said that she was still waiting for the man who would make the blood quicken in her veins.

I peered into those eyes, which seemed as familiar to me as the reflection of my own image, but I could not speak her name. At last, and with a glance behind her to make certain none would take note of her boldness, she unfastened the corner of her veil and let me see her face. Yes—the truth my heart had known was answered. She was Esharhamat.

"Don't you know me, Tiglath?" In her voice was the faint quaver of a sob.

But she need not have feared I would forget her. In the years since I had departed from the house of women I had tried with all my might to blot her image from my memory. *"When you leave this garden you will no longer love me,"* she had said, but I had carried my love away and it had never left me. Would for both our sakes it had been otherwise.

"Yes, I know you, Esharamat," I answered, my voice nothing but a thick whisper. "I would know you in the dark, with the eyes plucked from my head."

"But not, it seems, until I had taken away my veil."

She smiled, for her confidence in her power had returned, and with her white hand she returned the veil to its place.

And then, for a long moment, we were both too overcome with shyness to speak.

It was still Esharhamat, but the child was almost gone. In her place was the woman she would be, and very soon. She had always been beautiful to look upon—her skin was still wondrously clear, pale almost to transparency, and her features possessed a delicacy hardly known among the river people—but now she was all of that and bewitching as well. Her eyes, so deep a man could lose himself in them, held me with a magic I could neither understand nor resist. I could only stare helplessly. She was so familiar, and yet I felt as if I had never really seen her before.

Then the damned soul over whose wretchedness we had all come to rejoice screamed through the bars of his iron cage, and the crowd laughed again and surged around us, and the spell was broken. We both turned to look at him, and my heart almost died within me when I heard his incoherent supplication and saw that he was pointing down with his arm at the two of us.

No, it was only at Esharhamat.

"He seems to recognize you," I said. "Why would that be, I wonder."

"I was here yesterday and the day before." Esharhamat lowered her eyes, as if confessing to some terrible frailty. "It is the king's wish, since Ashurnadinshum was my husband. I must come each day until . . . Perhaps he knows, and somehow blames me for . . ."

Yes, of course. I had known of her marriage to the *marsarru,* which had been celebrated here in Nineveh only a few months before the Elamites crossed over into Babylonia. It had been judged, it seemed, that she was still too young to enter into the duties of a wife, and her husband had left her behind when he returned to be lord once more over the black-headed people—otherwise she might have followed him into captivity and death.

But no—Nergalushezib could not have known the identity of the child-woman in her mourning tunic. It was vain to speculate about what might have attracted his attention to her, about what could have been going through that tormented, crippled mind. I turned away and, putting my hand upon Esharhamat's arm, drew her eyes back to me.

"He cannot blame you," I said. "What he suffers is done by the king's will, who revenges himself upon one whom he numbers among his son's murderers. That wretch is beyond blaming anyone now."

"Thank you, Tiglath," she murmured as she allowed the tips of her fingers just to brush the back of my hand. "Have you ever felt that . . . shame? To have done nothing, and still . . . ?"

"Yes. But we cannot help what we feel."

"No—we cannot."

She turned, as if to go. It seemed I had not had time even to catch my breath.

"Will you return again tomorrow then?" I asked. Surrounded by strangers, I could not speak my heart. I could but hope she still loved me a little and would hear all I left unsaid.

And did she? Was what I saw in her face no more than my own entreaty being mirrored back to me, or did the way the light changed in her black eyes mean that she too hoped that, having found one another again, we would not now remain forever parted?

"Yes. Tomorrow."

"At this hour?"

"Yes."

Once more her hand reached out to me. For an instant we almost touched, but perhaps we were already too far apart, for she caught back her arm, hiding it beneath her widow's shawl as if its very existence were some guilty secret. She turned away again.

"Tomorrow," I said, but if she heard me she gave no sign. In an instant the crowd swallowed her up and she was gone.

I hardly knew what I should do. It was as if some part of my soul, long dead, had suddenly returned to life. It flooded back upon me, all the love I had kept dammed up in my heart, and I thought it possible I might drown. Among the Greeks there are many who sing of love's sweetness, of its mad joy, but they are merely singers. For those who truly love, to whom love comes early in life and lingers through the years like a ghost that will not be driven out, it is an agony tearing at the liver. Love is a sharp knife in the hands of a child—it cuts to the bone and leaves a scar that time can never rub away.

Esharhamat was still a maiden—her virginity was something I would prove for myself in time—but she was also a widow, one whose husband had been swallowed by the earth, and therefore free in the law's eyes. I knew that as soon as her period of mourning was finished the king would give her to Arad Ninlil, his second son by the Lady Tashmetum-sharrat and the new *marsarru,* but I did not care. As a widow she had her own establishment—she was not shut up in the house of women—and she could come and go as she liked. She was within reach.

I did not care about Arad Ninlil, whom everybody knew for a languid, cruel brute and half an idiot. The prospect of his being Esharhamat's husband was repulsive enough—he was not such as any maiden would relish taking to her bed—but he was a future evil, and the future beyond tomorrow did not exist for me. There was only this moment. I felt a longing that seemed to fill me, leaving room for nothing else, as if my skin were merely a thing to contain it. I knew I was about to throw my life away like the rind of an empty melon, and I did not care.

Suddenly I wanted nothing so much as to be alone. The crowd of strangers was an oppression, and I wanted to breathe cool air and listen to nothing except my own thoughts. I decided I would follow the wall south until I came to the river, for I had a great longing for the sound of its rushing waters that it might wash over my mind and cleanse me of this torment.

As I walked along I stabbed lightly at the ground with the point of my javelin. It was my favored weapon and I was never without it. I could hit a mark the size of my open hand at seventy paces, and in close combat a skilled fighter can empty a man's guts from his belly with a single stroke of its copper tip, but I had never used it except in hunting. I would be brave and terrible in war, and I would joy to lay down my life for my king, but this was all in the abstract. At the moment I was plotting how I could cheat him of his heir's intended bride.

I loved Esharhamat, and that was not abstract. The shyness that had undone me on the night of Kephalos's dinner party was far in the past, for it was an easy thing to become a man in the city of Nineveh. Almost as soon as my voice had changed I went to the temple of Ishtar, dropped a silver coin into the lap of one of her sacred harlots, and the thing was done.

Once in her life, each woman owes this duty to the goddess— she waits beside the temple door until a man comes, and he gives her a silver coin, which thus becomes sacred and is never spent. This she does that the goddess may smile upon her and make her marriage fruitful. For a pretty woman it is the business of a single evening, but some must wait for months, even years. And some decide never to leave and consecrate themselves to the goddess's service. These become skilled in all the ways of fleshly love and are honored wherever they go.

I confined myself to such, although their price was higher, and as a matter of routine and for the sake of my health, like all the young men of the royal barrack, I visited them once every week. They did not touch my liver—that was not their concern— but my visits to the temple allowed me to be quiet in my mind.

That was all finished now. I loved Esharhamat. If it happened that I never put my hand upon her in the whole of my life I still would not find peace in any other woman's arms. In an instant, with a smile as guileless as when she was a child, she had ended all of that for me. I could not regret it.

There is a place where the city wall appears to step to one side to avoid getting its robes wet. The river hurries by, Nineveh seeming to rise from its banks. In the season of floods its waters almost touch the wall, but that time was past now. I seated myself on the bluff, letting my feet hang down almost to the river's surface, and balanced the javelin across my thighs. I had only to remember the moment Esharhamat had undone her veil that I might see her face, and I was filled with a wretchedness that was itself more profoundly joyous than anything I had ever known. I did not know what I felt. I had become a stranger to myself.

That I was a condemned man I had not a moment's doubt. The king's favor did not extend to tampering with the destiny of his house, so when he knew that I had raised my eyes to her who must be the mother of all the kings to follow, he would strip the skin from my body and nail it to the city gates. This seemed right and just to me—I did not question it. That I must love Esharhamat, this too seemed beyond my power to prevent. Thus I regarded myself as a dead man. Perhaps not this year, or the next, but soon enough. I had found my *simtu,* my fate, the end the gods had selected for me. How could it be otherwise? Where else could it lead, this love that had begun against the background of a public execution? Somehow I could not bring myself to care.

But that I should involve Esharhamat in my disgrace, this tormented me. For if I loved her more than my life, how could I wish her to be otherwise than happy and safe? But could she be happy parted from me when I was thus wretched away from her? It seemed a knot that would never be untied. I almost wished that the priest's knife had not been stayed, that I were now a gelding in the tablet house, my mind untroubled and Esharhamat safe.

And at the same time I was profoundly happy. I had seen her again—I would see her tomorrow. What was this not worth?

How long I continued thus I cannot say. All at once I looked up and saw my shadow lengthening across the ground and realized it was nearly night. If I did not return to the royal barrack in the next hour, Tabshar Sin would make me spend tomorrow cleaning out the stable and then Esharhamat would think I had deserted her. I sprang up as if the river had suddenly turned to boiling.

"Have I startled you, Prince?"

I saw him and heard his voice in the same instant. He was standing at the edge of the bluff, seven or eight paces distant, and in his right hand he held the staff of a pilgrim. He was an old man —his hair and beard were whiter than a pigeon's wing and the sun had burned his face to the color of harness leather. He stood with his head uncovered and wore the yellow robes of a priest, although I had never seen a priest wear anything so threadbare— the garment looked as if he could have been born in it, and it and he had grown old together.

Moreover, I had never seen a priest who was not smooth-skinned and fat, for priests are great lovers of luxury, and this man was as gaunt as a corpse dug out of the hot sand. His collar-bone was clearly visible under his thin tunic, and the ridges of his brow were so prominent that his eyes seemed buried deep in his face.

He smiled, but he appeared to be looking through rather than at me. And then, of course, I understood—the old man was blind.

"No, you have not startled me," I replied. His hand moved slightly on the staff—a small thing but eloquent in its way, enough to suggest that he knew I was lying. "I simply remembered that I have to be somewhere else. The hour is late."

"Is it?" The old man turned his dead eyes to the sky, as if he wished that they might at least feel the dying day's heat. "Not for you, Prince. Your day has hardly even begun."

We stood on the bluff facing each other, a breeze from the distant mountains beginning to stir around us, and I was overcome with a sense of dreamy unreality. The setting sun at the old man's back cast an aura about him, like the *melammu,* which the Greeks call "nimbus," said to signify the presence of a god.

"You know me, then?" I asked. I was not at all sure I wished to hear the answer.

"Yes, I know you. You are Tiglath Ashur, are you not? And you have the mark of the blood star upon the palm of your right hand."

"But—you are blind! How . . . ?"

"Am I?" He shook his head, as if in pity, and he smiled. "Am I blind or are you, whom the sight of this world dazzles so that you cannot see what the god would show you? No, you needn't be frightened. I am no more than a man, and it is not I whose shoulders the god surrounds with his divine light. Your soul is troubled, Prince? Do not fear. All will unfold by design. All this has been foreseen, and the sin will not be yours."

"You speak of sin?" I asked, for I understood now that I was in the presence of a *maxxu,* a holy man, one who speaks with the god's voice.

"Yes."

I approached, quietly, as if stalking a deer through the high grass. He knew I came near but made no sign. His blind eyes never left my face—I might have thought he could see except the pupils were misted over like the river on a cold morning. He was blind and a stranger, yet my life seemed open to him.

"I come from Mount Epih—do you know it?"

I stopped. I shook my head. "It is sacred to Ashur. Few have ever been there."

"Few have, yes. But you will one day. Until then listen to the promptings of your heart, for the god Ashur has entrusted your footsteps to a *sedu.* All is by the god's design. The sin will not be yours."

"What sin, old man?" I reached out my hand, but I had not the will to touch him. It was not in my power to touch him. "What sin? Speak!"

"Do you wish to know? Truly, Prince?" The smile said once

more that he pitied me my ignorance. He raised his arm and
pointed toward the city wall.

"Look to Nineveh, Tiglath Ashur. Its streets will become the
hunting ground of foxes, and owls will make their nests in the
palace of the great king. Do not think that happiness and glory
await you here, Prince, for the god reserves you to another way.
Here all things will be bitter—love, power, friendship. Sweet at
first, but, in the end, bitter. The *sedu* protects your footsteps.
Listen to your heart."

"My *sedu*? What . . . ?"

"You bear his mark, Tiglath Ashur. We will meet again."

He turned, as if dismissing me from existence, and walked
away—away from me and from the city he had cursed with his
prophecy. My mind was full of words, but I could not speak
them. I could only watch helplessly as his figure contracted in the
distance.

"Then it is not your *simtu* to have your hide nailed to the
city gate. By the sixty great gods, I imagine it comes as a relief,
brother."

Esarhaddon sat on his sleeping mat, his head supported in
the palm of his hand. He had been much impressed by what I told
him of my two meetings outside the walls, for Esarhaddon put
great trust in omens of every kind.

"And if the god has granted you a *sedu*, then your life will be
full of glory."

"He says not." I shook my head—except for the prophecy of
Nineveh's fall, which it would have been treason to repeat, I had
told Esarhaddon everything. But I had not told him that.

"But a *sedu*, Tiglath . . ."

"Perhaps he was merely a crazy old man."

"But he knew you, though you say he was blind—he knew of
your birthmark."

"Perhaps someone pointed me out to him. Perhaps someone
told him about the mark—I do not keep it hidden."

I shrugged my shoulders, wishing I had said nothing. I did
not want to believe anymore.

But Esarhaddon was not to be dissuaded. Blind holy men
who journey from sacred mountains, guardian spirits, birthmarks
that foretell a man's destiny—it was all very much to his taste.

That my visitor had been a *maxxu* sent from the god was to him a settled matter.

"A *sedu* . . ." Esarhaddon lay back on his sleeping mat, his hands clasped behind his head as he stared dreamily at the ceiling. "If such a thing were to befall me . . ."

Perhaps, once again, it was only my mixed blood that made me doubt, for the Greeks do not place such reliance on the favor of their gods, who, in any case, seem an indolent lot, loving most those men who have least need of them. In my mother's language there is no word for *sedu*, for in the western lands the dead, if they have been properly covered with the ritual three handfuls of earth, do not return. The gods, from whose sight they have been cut off, have no commerce with them and thus do not send them to protect and guide the living. And, in any case, who among the great—and the god always chooses a *sedu* from among the souls of fallen heroes—who would come back into the world for the sake of one such as me?

Esarhaddon, of course, had an answer.

"The blood star," he said, nodding gravely. "You were born in the hour that sent him to Arallu—who could it be but the king who is dead? The great Sargon is your *sedu*."

He was mightily awed at this, was my brother. For the next hour, until we went to sleep, he treated me with profound respect. By the time the sun rose, fortunately, he had forgotten all about it.

In the morning I returned to the Great Gate. The crowd was much thinned—Nergalushezib was silent and listless, hanging on to the bars of his cage, clearly not long for this life and thus a considerably less entertaining spectacle. It was hardly dawn when I came, and impatience was eating away at my entrails like ants in the carcass of a dead pig.

She will not come, I thought. *She does not love me and thinks of her own safety, and so she will not come. It is better thus.*

Yet I was not so unselfish that life did not seem a bitterness to me. In the dim gray light of morning Nergalushezib and I stared at one another, and I was young enough and fool enough almost to envy him.

And then she did come, her light little feet parting the still-wet grass, and the blackness lifted from my mind.

We could speak no more than a few words that morning. The crowd was around us, and Esharhamat had her attendants with

her. But the widow of the *marsarru* had her own apartments
within the king's new palace. She lived under the protection of her
mother-in-law, the Lady Tashmetum-sharrat, who, as lady of the
palace, was not walled up within the house of women, but that
stricken soul, old now, forgotten by the king, and bereft of her
eldest son, had withdrawn into a seclusion deeper than any there
had known.

It was not wholly improper that I should visit my childhood
friend in her own rooms. We were never alone together, and I did
not allow myself to call too often. We were safe enough, provided
it went no further, and we were both happy. Under the vacant,
grieving eyes of the Lady Tashmetum-sharrat, we sat together
beside the fountain in her garden, so like the fountain of our
shared childhood, and we talked and played with her pet cats—
Esharhamat had a great love for overfed cats with long white fur
and sharp claws—and sometimes I would bring her some pretty
trinket I had bought for the purpose among the bazaars.

"What is it?" she would ask, smiling with her dark eyes and
holding it up to the sun's light.

"It is a brooch for your veil—see how cleverly the pin is
concealed? It comes from Tyre."

She would laugh and clap her hands as clumsily I tried to
open it. While we were together in the privacy of her garden she
did not wear her veil, which I took as a token of her trust in me.

"But what are the figures? Cats? Really, are they cats?"

"Yes. You see? This one looks exactly like Lamashtu."

"Oh, Tiglath—you mustn't call her that."

"Why not? Is she not the most frightful of your demons? Did
you see what she did to my fingers the last time I tried to take her
from your lap . . . ?"

We never spoke of love. It was sufficient for me if I could but
see her from time to time. I believed—I believe still—that I
wanted nothing more. My liver was easy, and I went no more to
the temple of Ishtar.

And while Esharhamat and I followed our innocent love, the
Land of Ashur was at war. I felt strangely divided—or perhaps
not so strangely, since war quickens the hearts in men. Esharhamat was the breath of life in my nostrils, but I lived only for the
moment when I might do battle against the Elamites. My training
had been greatly accelerated, and I knew that when the next army
marched south, I would be with it. I wanted only to love Esharha-

mat, and I wanted only glory. The day I had my final orders was one of the happiest of my life.

"And I," lamented Esarhaddon, "I, your superior in every way—I, Esarhaddon the mighty, the valiant, I am to be sent off to garrison duty in the west."

"They know which of us is the true warrior, brother," I said, dodging out of the way to avoid the sandal aimed straight at my head. "You would only disgrace yourself, making water in your loincloth the first time an Elamite sneezed at you."

That was too much for him and he charged at me from across our room, head first like a bull. When finally he had pinned me to the floor and we were both laughing too hard to fight anymore, he relented and we went out into the city to celebrate my glory over a pot of beer.

"But I see my mother's hand in this," he said—he was deep in drink, but he may have been right. "That bitch among women. She is ever plotting, spinning webs like a spider. If I die of the gout at the age of one hundred, it will be her doing. That Babylonian she-cat. By the sixty great gods, why does she torment me so?"

"That she can make you a great man and rule the Land of Ashur through you," I answered him. I was drunk too, and at the time it sounded like a harmless enough joke.

Esarhaddon nodded, as if the idea were his own and had just flown into his head.

"I shouldn't doubt it. The she-cat among women."

And thus did we both enter into the estate of manhood.

Let me now say something of the land and people of Elam, for the story I tell is about more than my own little life and they were once among the mighty nations of the earth, though now their memory is dim even where before they were feared. When I am dead, it may be that only these few words still remain as their memorial. It is cruel that men's names should perish without a trace, so let them live a little longer in this the chronicle of an old enemy.

Elam, like the Land of Ashur, was nourished by the waters of the Tigris. It lay many days downstream and to the east, facing Babylonia across the river. It was a rich nation—as its inheritors ever will be, since the land abides forever. The soil is deep and blessed by the Tigris, the Uqnu, and the Idide, whose floodings keep it fertile.

Beyond the plains there are the mountains, yielding copper, lead, silver, tin, basalt, stone, timber, iron, and horses. All that the men of Ashur had had to gain by conquest, the Elamites were given as a birthright.

It is said that the summers there are like a furnace, that a dog left out of doors at midday will go mad in an hour and a lizard cannot cross the road in Susa without being roasted alive. I have never been closer to their borders than the Turnat River, and that in the month of Siwan, after the floods have subsided but before the season when the sun beats down like a hammer, but even there the people had cellars dug into the earth, where they could find some relief from the terrible heat.

There are three races of men who call themselves Elamites: the plains are inhabited by dark-haired, white-skinned people who are no different from the Babylonians; the mountains produce men with brown skin and of great height; and from the plateaus beyond the mountains come men whose skins are black but who are nothing like the black-skinned men I have seen in Egypt, who come from the place where the river Nile finds its source. But all the Elamites, of whatever color, are regarded with great suspicion by their neighbors, who call them brutal, humorless, weak, grasping, and untrustworthy. The Sumerians had a proverb: "An Elamite is unhappy with nothing but a house to live in." The Babylonians speak of Elam as a land of witches, magicians, and all manner of evil spirits. Of my own knowledge I can only say that they are not weak—I have stood against them in battle, and they are brave to the point of rashness.

Of their customs I can report little. I never learned their language, nor have I ever met anyone who has, for it is of a fearful complexity. Their writing is clearly based on the daggerlike script, although I was never able to read it, and they witness documents by impressing their fingernails into the soft clay of the tablets. The common people worship snakes, which are plentiful in that country, and a goddess called Pinikir, whose clay image they wear about their necks—I know nothing of her except that she is always depicted naked and holding up her great breasts with her hands. The priests enjoy vast influence among great and humble alike, and they go naked even when they follow their armies into battle. Whether this might be to honor their goddess, I know not.

But of the many remarkable things in the land of Elam, the most remarkable are the customs of their ruling house. Like all civilized nations they have a king placed over them, but the king's power is divided among himself, his next eldest brother, who is called the lesser king, and the king's son, who is governor of Susa, their capital city. When the king dies he is succeeded not by his son but by his brother, who does not then appoint his own son governor of Susa but leaves his brother's son in that office. Brother succeeds brother until they are all exhausted, and only then does the eldest brother's son come to the throne. This system has the obvious disadvantage that a younger brother is more susceptible to jealousy than a son, and the history of the Elamite royal family has been filled with bitter quarrels. Indeed, Hallutush-Inshushinak, who began the war with the Lord Sennacherib, came to power by overthrowing his brother.

Complicating all of this is the king's custom, dating from the most ancient times, of marrying his own sister. At the king's death his brother marries the widow, who is of course his sister as well, and it is the order of her male children and not the identities of their fathers that settles the succession. This practice of incest raises the women of the royal house to great prominence, which is a misfortune for any country, and also, as any cattle breeder could tell you, weakens the vitality of the line. Sons die young and their loins are not fruitful, and for as long as men can remember the kings of Elam have gone mad, one after the other, their minds shaking apart like a reed fence in the wind. Elam is a rich land and her people were brave and gifted, but a nation cannot prosper while her kings rage and stagger and foam at the mouth like a dog with the water-hating sickness. Thus were the Elamites a burden to their neighbors and hated accordingly.

But for myself I hardly thought of them as men—they were simply the enemies of Ashur, the proper objects of my cruel valor. For I had no doubt I would be terrible in war. I spent the pocket money I had from Kephalos on polished bronze mirrors and pieces of carved ivory to give to Esharhamat, but I would be a demon of destruction when I fought the Elamites.

Thus did the year slip by us, and soon the time approached for the summer campaign. There was the camp and the final frenzied days of preparation, and there was Esharhamat. Nothing else stands out in my memory of that time, except a single chance encounter the significance of which I did not grasp for many years.

The week before our departure, after the day's arms drill was finished and while I waited under the shade of a reed lean-to for my turn to enter the sweating house and clean my body before dinner, Tabshar Sin came to me. He squatted on the ground beside me, and his face was set and grim.

"You will go to war as a member of the *quradu*," he began, shifting his weight uncomfortably, as if the interview was not pleasing to him. "The *quradu* always take many losses, for they fight in the vanguard around the king's own person. Further, you are both daring and inexperienced, which is a dangerous combination. A little fear is a good thing, Prince—I make no complaint against your courage, for courage is a soldier's chief virtue, but I could wish you had more respect for the terrors of death. Remember that you are soon to lead men into war, and you will have their lives to think of as well as your own. But that is not what I wished to speak of."

I said nothing. I waited in silence, for Tabshar Sin was a serious man and a brave soldier, deserving of respect. If I lived through the first rush of battle, I knew it would be a blessing I owed to him.

"Prince, it is always a prudent soldier who settles his affairs before the start of a new campaign. That lazy Ionian I know has made you rich, and you have a mother in the house of women. Go to the tablet house and write a will."

He left me, and already I could hear the sound of wings fluttering over my head, as if the Lady Ereshkigal, Queen of Arallu, were even then circling above, ready to swoop down and carry off my life.

So the next day, with Esarhaddon along to act as my witness, I went to the tablet house. The air there was damp and smelled like a riverbank after the floods have gone. We were shown through room after tiny room, the walls crammed with shelf upon shelf of small clay slabs, and I was reminded how close I had come to living out my days in this place. The thought made me shudder. At last we came to a room somewhat larger, like the schoolroom of my childhood, and there, sitting at a desk, the palms of his hands stained from years of contact with the damp clay, sat a scribe in a white linen tunic. He was young, perhaps the same age as ourselves, and his face was beardless and ever would be. His eyes were dark and filled with smothered anger, almost as if he had settled with himself that we were responsible for whatever clouded his life. Esarhaddon and I took our places on a bench opposite, and for a moment the three of us regarded each other without speaking.

"What is it you wish here, Tiglath Ashur?" the scribe said at last in his reedy eunuch's voice. I could not have been more astonished.

"You know me then?" I asked. "We are—acquainted?"

"You have not changed so very much, either you or Esarhaddon. Perhaps the difficulty is that I have changed hardly at all."

It was almost an invitation to examine him more closely, but it did not take much time to solve the riddle. Yes, of course. I wondered how I had missed it before.

"Nabusharusur! By the Lord Ashur—is it really you?"

I began rising, as if to embrace him, but Nabusharusur rather pointedly kept his seat. He seemed less pleased with the meeting than I was. His black, hating eyes never left my face.

"Yes, it is I," he answered, his hands folded together in his lap. "You, it is obvious, have fulfilled your ambitions, while I have become . . . I have grown to be what you see before you."

He shrugged his thin shoulders. It was the gesture of a woman, of one who knows he has become an object of contempt and, still more clearly, that it was through no will or fault of his own that this was so. In these moments he was alone, as if, under the burden of his blameless misery, he had forgotten our existence, and then he came to himself again and his eyes fixed on Esarhaddon. I understood why at once—Esarhaddon was grinning at him.

"I have come to have my will registered," I said quickly, for Esarhaddon could be a stupid enough brute at times. I would gladly have kicked him but that Nabusharusur would have seen me do it. "The war, you understand—I leave for the south this week."

"Yes." Esarhaddon was still grinning, as if he found the joke delightful. "That is at least one hazard you have been spared, Nabusharusur."

Esarhaddon, who was my royal brother, and Nabusharusur, who was no less, exchanged a look that told me more about both of them than I cared to know.

"Yes, Esarhaddon," Nabusharusur said, almost between his

teeth. "There are many hazards awaiting the unwary in this
world."

One who lives in a barrack, where men are packed in together and the business of life is violence, cannot help but acquire
an intimate knowledge of all the shadings of anger and hatred. I
had seen fights over a jug of beer or the winnings of a dice game
where men would have killed one another had they not been kept
apart by their comrades—I once saw an infantryman from Edom
use his thumb to take out another soldier's eye, and all because of
the hot sun and a cup of spilled water. But I had never seen
anything like the cold wrath in Nabusharusur's face. It never even
broke the surface of his patient, contemptuous calm, but it seemed
all the deadlier for that. This was not the fury of a moment, to be
forgotten before dinner or, perhaps, regretted for the rest of one's
days. This was a hatred that seemed ready to last out the span of a
man's life.

And then, as if to say that he was accustomed to such insults
and counted them as nothing, Nabusharusur turned to me. When
he spoke his voice was as level as a pool of rainwater after a
storm.

"How do you wish to dispose of your property, Tiglath?"

The hour approached. The day before the army's departure,
I put on my new green uniform—I was a *rab kisir* now, although,
I must confess, this was because my father was the king and not
through any merit of my own—and went to spend one last hour
with Esharhamat. She received me, as had grown our custom, in
her garden. I found her sitting at the fountain's edge, and as I
approached she raised her gaze to my face. In all the months I
had been going there, this was the first time I had ever seen her
cry.

"What is it?" I asked—it was a foolish question to which I
desperately wanted to hear the answer I knew already. I took my
place beside her and recklessly took her hands in my own. She did
not withdraw them. "What has made you unhappy, Esharhamat?
Tell me."

"What is to become of me if you are killed, Tiglath?"

I had only to look into her eyes, glistening with tears, to
know what she meant. The time of childhood was over, she was
saying, and of this woman I was the beloved.

"I wonder what will become of you if I am not."

Together we looked across the garden to the spot of shade where the Lady Tashmetum-sharrat lay on a wicker couch, fanned by one of her women while she stared at nothing.

"I will not be her son's wife," Esharhamat murmured in an icy voice. "I am a widow—soon I will have control over Ashurnadinshum's estate, and then I will be free. No one can compel me to marry Arad Ninlil, who makes the flesh crawl up my back like a serpent. I may choose whom I like, and I choose you!"

I smiled, partly at her still childish confidence that she could have whatever pleased her—I speak only of her power of choice, for it was not the child but the woman who knew I would risk any fearful death for her sake—and partly because no man could hear such words from those lips and not be happy. I smiled, but I knew it was impossible.

"We are the king's servants," I said—I had never felt the truth of it so deeply as I did that moment. "It is your *simtu* to be the mother of kings. You cannot avoid that, no more than I can choose to take the crown upon my head. You will marry whom the king my father commands, as I follow him into battle now."

"You are suddenly very noble, Tiglath. I think I liked you better when you were impudent."

She withdrew her hands from mine. The tears had already dried on her cheeks, and when I looked at her I saw someone I did not know. The woman had put aside the child's softness, and her unsmiling mouth mirrored a will as hard as flint.

"This war will not quickly end," she went on, almost as if she were telling these things to herself. "More than one of the king's sons may die in it. You told me once you have a *sedu*—or was that simply more of your impudence?"

"I think perhaps it was nothing more than the fantasy of a crazy old man."

"Mind you come back from the war alive, Tiglath."

She smiled at me, and the smile was also one I had not seen before.

"I have every intention . . ."

"I believe you will come back." This time it was she who took my hand. "He was not a crazy old man—I believe in your *sedu,* Tiglath. Make the king love you, as the god does—as I do. I will not marry Arad Ninlil, and if I must be the mother of kings, you must be their father."

When I returned to the royal barrack I found I had a visitor of my own. Kephalos was waiting for me, sitting on a stool outside my door, looking very important and out of patience as the boy Ernos held a fan of ostrich feathers over him to keep off the sun. He rose when he saw me, and I was at some trouble to keep him from going down on all fours to embrace my knees.

"Master, come—let us go inside out of this heat." He took a large leather pouch and an even larger pottery jug from the boy and then waved him away. "As you see, I have brought my lord the finest wine from Lebanon that we may refresh ourselves."

"Then come inside," I said, placing my hand upon his shoulder and pushing open the door. "For the sight of you is always welcome, Kephalos, my friend, even without the finest wine, and from Lebanon at that."

I really was glad to see him, for it had been my intention to call upon him at his house that very evening and now I was saved the trouble. I took two goblets made of blue glass from a shelf under the room's only window and, while my slave made himself quite comfortable on my rolled-up sleeping mat, I broke the seal of the wine jug and filled them both to the rim.

Kephalos was as impressive a sight as ever. He had grown stout in his prosperity and his beard, which had reached vast proportions over the last few years, was combed and curled and smelled of pomegranate oil, and he wore more rings and bracelets than the most expensive harlot in Nineveh. His tunic was of blue wool, shot through with silver thread like one of the king's own nobles and embroidered richly with yellow and green. The turban on his head was set off with a silver clasp the size of a war shield. No one looking at him would ever have taken him for a soldier's slave.

When we had both gladdened our hearts with wine and Kephalos had entertained me with stories of his many successes as a physician—which to him was merely a pretext for robbing selfish and witless women—he lifted the leather pouch onto his lap and opened the string.

"I bring you gifts, master—having been a warrior myself and knowing you for a thoughtless and improvident youth, I thought to supply a few items against this mad campaign. No, no, my young lord—all wars are madness and enrich only the crows and the jackals, but since you have set your heart upon this one . . ."

From the pouch he took two small enameled jars, green and red, their mouths sealed with clay.

"In this," he said, holding the green one in his left hand, "you will find a salve of great benefit in treating all manner of wounds, but be sure you use it at once lest the wound come to fester." He lifted the other jar between first finger and thumb, as if he wished to assess its weight. "And this, this is the one sovereign remedy against the infections carried by unclean women. Remember, Lord, that a soldier going into strange lands . . ."

"Thank you, my friend," I answered, making a solemn show of refilling his goblet, for had I been compelled to look him in the face I should have burst out in laughter and I had no desire to offend him. Kephalos saw all men as no less wicked than himself, but in his way he was an honest soul and I loved him.

"And I, for my part, have a gift for you."

I rose and went to my kit bag, from which I took an object folded carefully in leather. When I sat down again I placed it before Kephalos and unwrapped it.

"I have made my will," I said. "In the event I should not return from his war, what I own—the silver you have gained for me with your industry—I would wish put into my mother's hands, and I ask you, as a favor to a friend, to see to it."

"This I will, master, but yours is a melancholy subject. I would as soon . . ."

"I have but one other item of property, and that is yourself." He began to make a gesture of obedience, placing his hands and forehead against my knees, but I held him back. "I do not know what might befall you if I die, so you also are among my heirs. Should my *simtu* come to me in the south, this tablet, of which there is a copy in the royal archives, will attest that you have been given your freedom."

I could not restrain him now for he threw himself to the floor, burying his face in his arms and clasping me by the feet. He wept, and I wept—we were both, I suspect, a trifle drunk, for the wines of Lebanon are notoriously strong.

"As you know, master, I was born a free man," he said, when he had regained his composure. "And I feel sure that I am destined to die one. But know, Lord, that I would not purchase liberty at the price of your life. Come back from your war no worse than you are this moment—and mind about those filthy southern women!"

At last, when he had risen to leave, he placed his hand upon my shoulder.

"And, Lord, when you have used all that the jars contain, be careful that you do not throw them away."

The door closed on him. I poured myself the dregs of the wine, puzzling over what he could have meant. Finally I picked up one of the jars and was surprised by it heaviness. Then I took my sword and with the edge scraped away a little of the enamel on the bottom of the red one. The metal underneath was the color of old honey and as soft as wax.

"Solid gold," I whispered. I balanced them again in my hands—each, discounting its contents, must have weighed close to seventy shekels. "Kephalos, you clever rogue, may you live forever."

5

The world holds many fine things to look upon, but I have always believed that the finest sight which can fill a young man's eyes is that of an army on its way to war. A young man's heart swells with dreams of glory, and while kings wage wars for revenge or profit and common men to escape their debts or their wives or the reach of the law—or because they have been conscripted—the dreamy youth shoulders his arms and marches to the drum of greatness, fame, adventure. The army of Sennacherib was a magic carpet stretching far, far into the distance, and it would carry me . . . I hardly knew where, but surely to some shining triumph. This impression stayed with me for many weeks —indeed, up to the morning of my first battle.

On the day of our departure from Nineveh I almost envied the crowds that lined the southern road, for I was a great way back in the parade, looking after my baggage and my company of a hundred men, some of them old campaigners but some of whom knew less about being a soldier even than I did myself. I did not see the king in his war chariot, and the sound of the trumpets was but a distant murmur. By the time we passed through the city gates, the people had stopped cheering hours before. The only witnesses to our going were a few glum shopkeepers and the poorest among the harlots, those who served travelers with the dust of their journeys still clinging to them, and they merely laughed at us, shouting obscene jokes and lifting up their tunics that we might know what we were leaving behind, perhaps forever.

I held the rank of *rab kisir*, with authority over a hundred

men, but this was purely a matter of courtesy. The armies of
Ashur had not conquered most of the world because they were led
by fools and raw boys, and I had been made to understand quite
clearly that, until I proved my worth, I was to regard myself as no
more than another soldier. The man who had been set at my
elbow as *ekalli*—the word means nothing more than "messenger"
—was in actual command. His name was Nargi Adad, and he had
campaigned with Tabshar Sin in the wars of the great Sargon.
Indeed, he had been part of the army that had had to fight its way
home after the king's death, and it was from him that I heard the
story of that final battle.

Nargi Adad had a quick laugh and a sunny temper. He was
always hungry and never tired, and he was as fine a soldier as ever
lived. In appearance he was a short, thick man and as hairy as a
goat. He had almost no forehead at all and his beard seemed to
begin just below his eyes. His hands and even his feet were matted
with black hair, and when he took off his tunic he looked like the
animals called bears which I have seen in the mountains of the
east. What another man might have cursed as a disfigurement was
to him a source of immense pride, and he claimed the harlots of
all nations found him irresistible, a thing I doubted not since, as
Kephalos was always fond of pointing out, women are great lovers of novelty.

Under conditions of forced march, traveling during the
whole six hours of daylight, an army could cover in four days the
distance between Nineveh and the disputed territories that lay in
Akkad east of the Tigris, but they would arrive in no fit condition
to fight. We were more leisurely, since we knew that the Elamites
and their Chaldean allies were already in the field, and, as pious
men, on all unlucky days, of which each month carries five, we
kept to our tents, wearing ragged clothes and eating no food
cooked in a pot. Thus we did not wet our sandals in the Radanu
River until the twelfth day.

"Well, Prince, when once we are across this dribble of ox piss
we will have to look about us, for between here and the Turnat
surely we will meet the enemy."

Nargi Adad laughed and clapped me on the shoulder, for like
most of the soldiers of Ashur he was no respecter of birth. The
uniform of a *rab kisir* makes no man a warrior and I took some
small pride in the fact that my own *ekalli,* who had fought by the
side of mighty Sargon, treated me quite as if I were neither his

officer nor the king's son but a comrade in arms of long standing. I knew this was no more than his whim, but it meant that Tabshar Sin, who was his friend, had given a good report of me.

"How many, do you think?"

"An army, Prince, and a big one." He nodded at the flat brown shoreline beyond the river, no longer smiling. "These men are not cowards and they know it is past a joke with the king your father, that they must stop him here or he will march us straight on to Susa to couch with Kudur-Nahhunte's women and dig up the bones of his ancestors. They will be fighting for their homes and fields, as we might be ourselves before long—if we don't stop them."

"But we will stop them."

Nargi Adad turned the head on his short neck and looked at me out of the corner of his eye. He was on the verge of making some remark but then stopped and laughed.

"Yes, Prince—with Ashur's help, we will stop them. Their bones will be stretched from here to the Bitter River so that a man could walk there stepping on the faces of dead Elamites. Come. Let us feed the men and be off. Tomorrow night we will camp within sight of the Turnat River, and the next morning there will be a battle which, should somehow you chance to survive it, will provide you with tavern stories for the rest of your days."

And so we crossed the Radanu, and the next day, near a wretched little cluster of mud huts called Khalule—may its name disappear from the lips of men and the fields there be plowed with salt—the army made camp.

Nargi Adad and I decided to see for ourselves how the land lay, and together we went into the village. The inhabitants had fled, since they knew there was about to be a great battle and that, no matter who won, the pillaging and slaughter to follow would be terrible. As we walked among the deserted houses, the only sound we heard was the barking of a dog unfortunate enough to have been left behind. The place made a dismal enough impression. We climbed to the roof of the highest building there and looked about us that we might know the terrain.

I do not like the southern lands. This is in greater part because my memories of them are a chronicle of destruction—no one who took part in the wars in Babylon longs ever to look upon that slaughtering ground again—but also, to some degree, because I was born in the Land of Ashur and love the sight of distant

mountains. The plains of the south are flat as a drumhead, with
nothing to distract the eye except, perhaps, the sight of a mud-
filled river or a clump of date palms—as all men know, the ugliest
tree the gods ever made. From that rooftop in Khalule the land
seemed to stretch without a ripple into misty infinity.

"See how they come?" Nargi Adad murmured, almost as if
afraid that Elamites might hear him. He pointed with his furred
arm toward the distant glimmering ribbon of water that was the
Turnat. Already its surface was half covered with the round little
boats made with pitched reeds and called *gufas.* "They are crossing in force. In two hours we shall be able to see their cooking
fires, and in the morning . . . They mean to make a fight of it,
Prince. They have no thought of retreat. As you see, they will
have their backs to the river."

By the time we returned to camp we could already hear their
war drums, like the brooding of distant thunder.

"They will keep that up all night. No doubt they mean to
frighten us to death." My *ekalli* grinned, showing his large
stained teeth. "I don't know how well they will sleep, but for
myself I find the sound quite restful."

That night, after I had had my dinner and the half jug of
strong Babylonian beer Nargi Adad forced down me, I took off
my sandals and wrapped myself in a blanket, letting it cover my
ears to keep out the booming of the Elamite drums. It was a hot
night, so I cannot claim that I was trembling with anything except
a great fear of death. My head buzzed from the beer, but still I
was tingling in all my limbs, feeling alive as those who have not
known battle rarely do—fear does that to a man.

Tomorrow, as early as first light, I thought to myself, *tomorrow I may be dead. An arrow, perhaps, or I may be trampled to
death under a chariot. And afterward when the battle is finished,
they may mutilate my corpse. Some Chaldean, it might be, will go
back to his wife and children with my private parts dangling from
his quiver.* I had forgotten all about my *sedu* and my dreams of
glory. All I wanted was to rise from my bed, choose a direction
away from the river Turnat, and run until I dropped. If I slept at
all that night, it was only for seconds at a time, but I do not
believe I did sleep.

I was a *rab kisir* and deeply ashamed to be afraid, but I have
fought many battles since then and yet never lost that stark terror
in the darkness before, so I have learned not to think so badly of

myself for it. Fear is as natural as breathing. How a man copes with it is the only question.

The next morning I had a breakfast of bread and grapes, put on my greaves, my leather corselet, and helmet of bronze and, as I stood with my javelin in my hand, discovered with surprise and relief that my fear had deserted me. I would not turn tail and flee, at least, and that was almost the same thing. I found I was actually looking forward to the battle. It is thus, I think, with most soldiers.

I will not speak of the ordering of troops, of which forces were held in reserve and which not, of the weight of cavalry or the tactical disposition of the chariots, for if there was any grand strategy at work that day, I did not see it. In any case, the schemes of both commanders must have been hopelessly inept to go so wrong, for a well-planned battle does not end in so general a slaughter. The object in war is to kill one's enemies, and this at as little cost as possible. On that day at Khalule it was not kings and generals who fought, but men. The armies were like two giants locked in combat, their hands about each other's throats, and when at last they separated it was not because one had vanquished the other but because both were too weary and wounded to go on. That was how it was.

So I have no story to tell of that day except my own, which I think is as close to the general truth as any. In other times, when I was myself a commander of armies, I would stand on a bluff overlooking the field and watch the battle unfold according to the plans I had hatched in my brain, and I believe my plans saved the lives of many soldiers on both sides, for a clear victory is always cheaper for everyone. But at Khalule that was not the way of it.

In the dim gray light of morning the smoke from the cooking fires hugged the ground like mist. Men did not speak. There was no sound except the clink of weapons and the snorting of horses. Even the drums of the Elamites had stopped, for they too knew that time was short and everyone was too occupied with the practical business of shield straps and bowstrings for the luxury of some nameless dread.

"Come, Prince. Let us see that the men are ready."

In his armor and helmet, Nargi Adad looked as round and impregnable as a stone, making me think that all we needed to do was to roll him toward the enemy lines and he would crash through as if they were a row of reeds. He put his thick, hairy hand on the muscle of my right arm and squeezed it.

"Tabshar Sin tells me that you have a mighty skill with the javelin," he said, grinning like a dragon. "He claims you can take the eye out of a mouse at a hundred paces. I pray it is not too much less than the truth, Prince."

My men were a company of archers and throwers, the backbone of any army. They fought in units of two men, one to wield the bow or the javelin and the other to protect them both behind a huge woven leather shield. We were to fight in the first line, arranging ourselves in an arrowhead pattern, and we would be opposed by cavalry, who would try to ride us down, to break up our formation and scatter us like chaff. But they had to reach us first, and they would be riding straight into the points of our weapons. If they did not reach us, or if we did not break after their first charge, then we would advance on the Elamite lines where, at last, it would all be close fighting with sword and dagger. Of the great armored chariots, which could cut down men's bodies like standing wheat, we tried not to think at all.

I shall not soon forget my first sight of the Elamite lines. They, of course, had many allies among the small southern states —the men of Anzan and Lakabra, the Chaldeans, the tribes of Iazan and Harzunu, the Pasheru, peoples and races beyond counting—but the Elamites were in the center. Without them the others were no more than buzzing flies. We were of the *quradu* and thus formed the vanguard around the king's own person. We would take the full force of the Elamite advance.

As I stood on that dusty, windless plain, shaded from the morning sun by a leather shield, I could watch their war horses digging at the air with hoofs that would cut like daggers. The soldiers wore bronze armor and helmets with horns like a bull. Their shields were without number and their weapons flashed in the dim light like the glinting of water as they raised their spears and swords in taunting challenge. Their drums were silent now and they did not waste their breath on war cries. Their very silence was enough.

"All right, men!" It was the voice of Nargi Adad, breaking the quiet air like a hammer. "Remember—it is the brave man who lives to fight again. Panic, and they will trample you down like grapes in a wine vat. The only way to keep them from killing you is to kill them, so have hearts of snow and aim true. We are the *quradu,* the strong ones, and we have the king's life in our keeping. Remember that as well. And tonight we see how the beer tastes in Elam!"

Every man's voice rang with cheering, and mine not least. If ever I believed in the glory of war—if ever there was glory in it—it was in that moment.

Suddenly, somehow, we were moving forward, one step at a time as we kept our formation, as we listened for the pounding of hoofs of the Elamite cavalry and readied our weapons. My bearer carried our shield on his left arm, and with his right he held in a leather sling perhaps five and twenty of my thin, copper-pointed javelins. Another was in my right hand, balanced and ready. I was even then looking for a mark.

The javelin thrower must be quick, for his is the most dangerous of arts. The bowman may stay behind his leather shield, but the thrower needs more room and thus must step out and into plain sight to make his toss. He must take the time to be accurate or he risks his life for nothing, but he must be fast or an arrow will find his belly and he will not throw again. The Elamite cavalry were coming now—I could see the flash of their long curved swords. I waited for them to come near enough. At all but the closest range one aims for the horse, for a cavalryman will run like a rabbit as soon as he loses his mount, and the horse is bigger and carries less armor and can tear a formation to shreds even without its rider. I waited for the horse—it was my enemy, and the man whose knees clutched its shoulders was a mere shadow. I waited, for my arm trembled with eagerness and my javelin was thirsty for blood.

At last—at last—the lead rider was close enough. I did not see him, only the horse, only a patch of brown. I stepped out from behind the shield, yanked back my arm, waited that fraction of an instant that allowed me to be sure, and threw. Everything, every fragment of my strength went into that throw. The javelin arched through the air like a bird of prey and I stood and watched it, bewitched, unable to move. Higher and higher it rose, and then it swooped down and buried itself in the base of the horse's neck. The beast rolled straight over like a cartwheel, and its rider did a quick acrobat's flip in the air and fell beneath his dead mount. He must have been either crippled or killed, because he did not even try to crawl away. It was a beautiful sight. I could not take my eyes from it.

An arrow buried itself in the dust at my feet, and I remembered that I too was mortal and ducked behind the shield. Even as
my hand reached out, my bearer thrust another javelin into it. I
searched the field for another mark.

Over and over again I threw. Sometimes I missed, but for the
most part I found my target. I killed I know not how many men
and horses, and the sight of their deaths filled me like the breath
of the gods. Arrows dropped around me like hailstones, but I
hardly noticed for they could do me no harm. Once, and once
only, the point of one touched the edge of my thigh, but I could
not be bothered to remark it—I did not even trouble to wipe the
blood away. I was in ecstasy. Men who say that war is the greatest
joy under the bright sun are not fools and only lie a little, for the
pleasure of danger and death are great and wash the mind clean. I
think I must have been a little mad.

When the cavalry were almost upon us, we aimed for the
riders. As my men died around me, dropping on their faces without a word, I could think only of the next throw, and the next.
Once a man on horseback rushed directly upon me, and as he
swung down with his sword to take my head off, my point went in
under his corselet and lifted him straight back over his mount's
tail and he hit the ground with a thud. I didn't even glance at his
face. I merely pulled the javelin free and looked about me for
another target.

They did not break our lines, and the cavalry are good for
one charge only and then fall to looting the baggage train—their
battle is a short one. When they had passed, the chariots came.

We were lucky—we had but two venture our way, and we
killed the horses of one of these before it reached us. The other,
though, swept over a corner of our formation, crushing men under its wheels like dates.

By then we had almost closed with the Elamite line, and the
time for javelin and arrow was past. I drew my sword and my
bearer threw down our shield, for now it was each man fighting
his way through alone.

I had come to myself by then, at least enough to know that
these men meant to kill me and that my skin was not made of
iron. I was afraid now, but the fear only made me feel more alive.
It was almost a pleasure, a joy of the senses, to be afraid like that.

There was noise all around me, shouting and the screams of
the wounded and dying and the clash of weapons. Those of my

men who still lived clustered together like bees swarming on a tree limb. We acted in a kind of concert but by instinct rather than plan. There was no discipline, only the will to live and the knowledge that we needed each other. But the final truth was that each of us fought alone and for himself.

I am blessed with long arms, so I had that advantage to compensate for my lack of experience, but I still collected two wounds that vexed and weakened me. Once a spear struck me above the elbow, almost causing me to drop my small round shield. The pain was great but only the matter of an instant and, in any case, not so great as the danger, for I nearly died a score of deaths before I could pause long enough to reach down and retrieve the shield.

It was the great black Elamite with the scarred face who came closest to giving my body to the crows.

The fighting, which had aimlessly wandered this way and that like an ant crawling over a stone, seemed to have moved away from me, and for the first time in what felt like hours I had a moment to stop and catch my breath. That moment almost cost me my life, for when I leaned forward, sucking a little air into my lungs as I rested my hands upon my knees, I suddenly felt something scrape against the side of my shield—I wasn't even conscious of having raised it, but the soldier who lives fights by instinct and perhaps I had had a glimpse of what was coming. I looked down and was appalled. The leather was torn open like the belly of a butchered ox, and I had just time to dance out of the way as the sword that had done it swung around for a second try at finding my entrails. I hadn't even noticed the man.

It wasn't very long before he forced himself upon me, though —all at once I was foot-to-foot with a black giant, the sweat streaming down his arms and his eyes rolling with that ecstasy of fury that marks the born warrior. His taut face gleamed, as if it might have been hacked out of obsidian with an ax, and he showed his teeth in a fierce grin. It was a face that had felt the stroke of more than one sword, for across the bridge of the nose and down the side of his jaw were two great scars, ridged and shining and thick as sandal cords. When he lunged at me again, his war cry alone, like the scream of some great bird of prey, almost unstrung my sinews. How it was he did not kill me in those first few seconds, I will never know.

We seemed to be alone in that raging battle—there was no

one to offer help, and this devil was bearing down on me as if he
thought to trample me underfoot like standing barley. His was the
initiative. Slashing wildly so that my blade made the air hiss like
an adder, I was somehow able to keep him at sword's length, but
that was all. I could hardly breathe, and my heart beat within my
breast as if it wanted out. Again and again my shield felt the
impact of his thrust, until I was certain the next would tear
through and find my bowels. Surely he would kill me, I thought.
This is it, this is the moment of my death. Over and over his
sword point darted at me, seeking my life, and each time I managed to fend it off, and each time it came closer. A thrust, and his
blade slides by against mine, just missing my shoulder. Another,
and his point scrapes against my leather corselet. The sound of
sword rasping against sword filled my ears. I was the goat, almost
ready for sacrifice, and the augur was sharpening his knife. The
next lunge and he would kill me—the suspense itself was a torture.

And then, at a distance, above the clamor of battle, I heard
the voice of Nargi Adad.

"Hey! You there, you bastard!"

I did not turn to look, for to turn would have been inviting
death, and I knew he was too far away to save me. The Elamite
would have me spitted like a roasting duck—already I could see
the muscles in his great neck tensing to deliver the mortal stroke.
I was already a corpse in that instant.

But he too had heard Nargi Adad's shout and he must have
thought to make short work of me before that great hairy millstone had a chance to roll over him. That is the only way I can
explain how I survived, for the great black one pulled his stroke
and somehow I was able this one last time to turn it aside.

But not enough. It cut through my leather corselet and
bounced over my ribs so that I thought the man had killed me. I
was dead—I knew it.

Yet the black one had stepped in just close enough that I had
the chance to avenge myself. With what I thought might be my
dying strength, I lunged. My sword entered just under his ribs,
and I drove it home. He cried out—more with surprise than pain,
I think—and then, as with a quick yank I pulled the sword free,
he sank to his knees, his eyes holding mine the whole time, and
fell over onto his face.

And somehow I was not dead. The wound in my side stung

like an adder bite—this was a good sign, really—and I was not dead. I reached inside my corselet, and my hand came away smeared with blood, but I was alive. I did not even feel weak, merely sore. I looked around for Nargi Adad, but he had already vanished into that chaos of fighting. Yes—I was all right. The Elamite was dead by my feet and I was alive. I lived and fought on. In a moment I had even forgotten that I was wounded and that was just as well, for the battle did not end with the death of one enemy.

Time and again we threw ourselves against the Elamite line, but it would not break. Neither would we break, for to break was to invite death. And so the battle went on and on, without end or hope of it. Sometimes, as if by common consent, the two great masses of men would fall away from each other, for the moment too weary to go on. Then there would be a rush and a shout, and shields striking together would echo like cymbals. And each of us had eyes only for the men to the right and to the left and for the enemy in front. If a man died, be he friend or foe, we stepped over his corpse as if it were a rock, for there was neither time nor breath for anything more. Thus did the plain at Khalule grow clogged with dead bodies.

At last the gods, who must hate men for their folly, took pity even on such as we and let the light of day fade from among us. We needed only this, it seemed, for the two great armies—slowly, and with many thrusts and some hesitation—drew apart from each other, each flowing back toward its own camp like the tide ebbing away from the sandy shore. No one had won or lost. It was simply that we could not fight on. Mere flesh would not stand it.

At last we sat down on the ground to rest, and as I looked about me I grasped for the first time the true character of war. Men whose arms and faces were streaked with smoke, blood, and dust stared out at nothing through eyes that had grown old in the space of a single day. The smell of corpses hung thick in the air like fog. There was no heroic grandeur here, only an appalled horror at what they had done and seen and suffered. None of these men would ever again know the world in its innocence—life had changed for them, forever. That was what I saw. I expect they saw the same in me.

"Where is Nargi Adad?" I asked finally, when I could find the breath.

"Only the great gods know, *Rab Kisir*. Probably dead."

They watched me through their weary eyes, and suddenly I understood that they were waiting for me to issue orders. I was the *rab kisir*. It seemed time I remembered that.

"Go back to your tents then. Eat and rest. The fighting is over for this day."

Slowly they pushed themselves to their feet. I counted them as they collected their armor and weapons—there were only two and thirty men left. Some of them might have run away or become separated somehow, but we had begun the day with a hundred men and now there were but two and thirty.

"Are you coming, *Rab Kisir*?"

"Not now—later."

I wanted to find Nargi Adad.

The battlefield at Khalule had become a scene out of a nightmare. This had not been war but mutual slaughter—dead and dying men lay on the ground everywhere, their limbs tangled together like driftwood. Crippled horses screamed and thrashed about, trying to stand up again. Crows perched on the faces of corpses, picking out the eyes with their long beaks. Discarded weapons, dead men and animals, the cries of the wounded, the stink of carnage. The ground was slippery with blood. Everywhere, as far as sight could probe, it was the same. I have not words to describe it, but I will carry the vision of that place with me into the dark earth.

But I found Nargi Adad, and he was alive, if not by much.

He was lying on his side, alert enough but with pain glistening in his eyes, a great hole torn in his belly, which he tried to keep closed with his hairy fingers, and they had grown crusted with dried blood. He smiled when he saw me—I have never known a braver man.

"You fought well today," he said. "You fought like a raging devil. That great black one . . . And you killed him, did you? I wish I could live to tell Tabshar Sin how well you fought."

"You will tell him." My face was wet with tears, for I knew there was no hope. "We will find a physician . . ."

"No, Prince—you see, I can't even feel my legs. I think the villain must have cut my spine before I spilled out his life. That's him over there."

Almost at Nargi Adad's feet lay the dead body of an Elamite, his eyes still open, the sword still in his hand. There would be no more wars for him either.

"Does it hurt much?"

"Yes, Prince. It hurts like a bellyful of nettles. What of the battle? Have they quit the field yet? There's an overturned chariot yonder—climb up on that and have a look around for me."

I went and looked and came back.

"They are crossing back over the river. The water is black with boats."

"Good. Then at least we've stopped them. And now be a good lad and kill me, would you?"

"I couldn't—I—"

"Do it, Prince. As a favor." He smiled still, but his eyes begged me. "It isn't pleasant work, dying, and I don't want to take all night over it. One quick thrust, and you'll finish me. As a favor, Prince."

Before he had time to see the stroke, or I to lose my nerve, I drew the dagger from my belt and pierced his heart. He died without making a sound.

I left him there, and wandered without direction. My mind was throbbing as if from too much wine, and there was nothing left inside me, no courage, no will. If an enemy soldier had come upon me and drawn his weapon, I would have fallen on my knees and begged for life like a woman. There is only so much any man can bear.

How long I walked aimlessly over that vast killing ground I do not know. Darkness had long since closed over the earth; there was only the light of torches from the camp. I must have been drawn to them.

It was at the edge of the camp that I found the king. He was alone, sitting on the back of his chariot, his head in his hands. He looked as if he had been weeping.

Many years later I read of this battle in the annals, of the king's glorious anger and his victory over the Elamites, whose knees trembled like reeds in the wind. It was all lies. The histories of nations are usually lies, their own or their enemies'. The king was not glorious that night when I found him weeping in his chariot. I touched his arm and knelt beside him, for it was easy to forget that he was Lord of the Earth's Four Corners. He looked up at me, and at first his eyes shone with fear before he recognized me.

"And is it you, Tiglath, my son? You are still alive in all this, eh? It must be the gods have granted you a *sedu*."

I started at the word, but he did not notice. He was lost to
anything so insignificant as my small shudder of despair.

"Yes, Lord, it is I."

"And are they gone? Eh? Yes?"

"They are gone back over the river, Lord. I do not think they
will soon return."

The king my father put his hands upon my shoulders, this
time not to save me from the gelding knife but to support his
weary heart. He was old and frightened and so he rested in his
son's arms, for all men must trust someone. Thus it was that we
found each other on the blood-soaked plains of Khalule.

6

The next day, and the next, we gathered our dead from the plain at Khalule and buried them with offerings of food and wine. The corpses of the enemy we looted and left to the crows; their wounded, those who had survived the night, we put to the sword. We took their hands and heads for trophies, for there was no mercy in our bowels. When we had finished, we nursed our own wounded and rested, waiting for the king to issue commands. The Elamites had withdrawn—not even our outriders could find them—so we were free to call the battle ours if we wished, but I remember no talk of victory.

So we waited for the king my father to tell us what he wished of us, praying in our hearts that he would not order us across the Turnat and into the Land of Elam, for we had no more heart for war. The ground on which we had fought was covered with the stinking carcasses of men and animals and the fresh-turned earth of graves. Our losses were close on to two men in five, and the enemy must have suffered even worse. If we pursued them into their own kingdom, they would be driven to the limits of desperation, and no foe is so deadly as he who has abandoned the hope of life.

But for three days the king kept to his tent, refusing all food, seeing no one. None were admitted into his presence, not even the *turtanu*. And thus we waited, measuring the bitterness of our suffering against what was left of our manly courage. None thought of rebellion against the Servant of Ashur, the Lord of the Earth's Four Corners, for the king was sacred and the soldiers of the god were pious men, but the mood in the camp was dark. We waited, for there was nothing else.

The death of Nargi Adad had made me *rab kisir* in fact as well as name, for there was no one else to lead. The men in my company were only common soldiers, lost without someone to give them their orders—it was then I first understood that for a warrior orders are the breath of life, all that stands between him and what he fears more even than the enemy, that terrible chaos of his own ungoverned will.

And thus it was my place to argue with the supply officers for bread and beer, to see that the physicians attended to my soldiers' wounds, and, more than all else, to keep them occupied with work. I was not quiet in my own mind—the wound along my rib cage pained me constantly, and I had used up all of the ointment in Kephalos's green jar to help those among the men who might have died without it. Besides, from one day to the next, my memory had grown clogged with unspeakable recollections, so I was glad to be busy in the management of others. Authority and the endless business that follows in its wake are the best vehicles of escape from oneself. Each day, as my soldiers grew to depend on me more and more, my command over their loyalty became ever more firm, and each night as I lay down upon my bedroll, too tired even for dreams, I put yet a little more healing time between myself and the horror of that one long day.

On the third evening after the battle, as I sat with my men around a campfire, waiting for the cooking pot to boil so that we could be done with eating and find our rest, I glanced up and saw standing at the edge of the firelight a man carrying the white javelin of a royal messenger. Fluttering from the shaft of the javelin was a silver ribbon, a sign that he carried words to a prince of the blood. I did not at once grasp the implications of this.

"*Rab Kisir*—direct me to the Lord Tiglath Ashur," he said. Like all such court officials in all nations, he was a fine-looking young fellow and obviously very taken with himself. His beard glistened with oil and his hands, showing white as ivory against his beautifully embroidered blue uniform, were well tended and as expressive as a woman's. I would have wagered much that to this one his weapon was no more than a badge of office, a thing to be carried about like a walking stick, but I was dirty and tired and out of temper with the world. Also, I did not care for his manner of addressing me.

"Your search is over," I answered, hardly looking at him while I used the point of my sword to stir the fire. My men, I was aware, found the exchange rather comical—they were already nudging one another and exchanging sly little winks. It would seem the royal messenger was not greatly to their taste either. "What do you want?"

"You . . . ?"

"I. State your business—or am I required to guess?"

He might actually have said something, but if he did I could not hear it in the ensuing laughter. The messenger, when he had recovered from his confusion—clearly a royal prince lying around a campfire with a pack of dirty sweat-streaked soldiers was not something he saw every day—he bowed from the waist, touching his right hand to his brow in token of respect. It was a gesture to which no true warrior would have condescended before any man not the king, and I despised him for it.

"I have been sent by the Lord Sennacherib, Prince. He sends you his prayers for a long life and bids you attend him."

"Now?"

"Now, Prince."

It was not a summons that could be ignored, so I rose to go, cursing only in the privacy of my heart. Someone handed me a jar of beer, and I rinsed my mouth out with a swallow and spat the rest into the fire, making it hiss like a witch.

"Never fear, My Lord Prince," said Lushakin, my new *ekalli.* "I will keep something from the pot for you should the king your father not invite you to stay for dinner."

The remark was greeted with renewed laughter, for Lushakin was regarded as a great joker, natural enough in the son of a boatman, quick-tongued rogues and fine storytellers in all the nations.

"Do not trouble yourself, My Lord *Ekalli.* Remember that the king has prayed that I might live until breakfast."

As I followed the royal messenger away I could hear them laughing still, even until the sound was swallowed up by the general buzz of camp noise.

And as we walked I had only to look around me to see that the stricken weariness of my own soldiers, the fear that had sunk bone-deep in each of them, was common to all those in the king's army. The cooking fires lit up their faces as men sat with their arms slumped over their knees, staring out into the darkness as if

they could see their own deaths there. Their voices were muffled
and hollow, their movements slow. They had the look of men
only just recovering from sickness, except that their sickness was
not of the body but of the will and spirit. All of this I could see in
the firelight that flickered against the black night.

I did not ask myself why the king should send for me. My
mind was not clear enough even to frame the question—I could
only look out at the things about me and see what was plain to
everyone. I had not even the wit to be surprised.

The king's tent was in the camp's very center, surrounded by
those of his principal officers. It was of heavy purple linen and
almost as large as the house of my slave Kephalos in Nineveh. It
was even divided into an inner and an outer room so that the
Servant of Ashur might preserve his majesty. Except at the entrance, there were no guards posted, for in the midst of his army
what had my father to fear from any man?

That he was my father was impressed upon my mind yet
again when the royal messenger drove the point of his javelin into
the earth and left it there beside the entrance to the king's tent
that all might know the Lord Sennacherib, the sacred king,
wished to be alone with the son of his loins.

The outer room contained only a camp table, behind which
perched a beardless scribe who could hardly bring himself to
glance up from his tablet. The flap to the inner room was held
aside with a cord and the scribe motioned with his stylus that I
was to go through.

"And is it you, lad? Eh?"

The king sat on the edge of his cot, dressed in nothing but a
plain linen tunic, quite as if he had just risen from sleep, although
his eyes said he had not slept in many days. His head was bare
and I could see plainly enough the heavy streak of gray that crept
through his hair. I knelt before him and placed my hands upon
his knees and he took them both in his own, squeezing tightly. I
looked into his face and he tried to smile but then looked away,
dropping my hands.

"Fetch us some wine, eh? You see it? Yes? It's over there on
the table. Bring a cup for each of us, and we'll drink to the
Elamite king, eh? Hah, hah, hah!"

I said nothing but did as he bid. As he took the cup from my
hands I could see that his own were shaking.

"Sit, lad—sit. Come sit beside me."

He was better after the second cup, and his hands were still.

"They are gone, eh?" His glance drifted nervously around the tent, as if he feared that Kudur-Nahhunte might be lurking behind a chair. "They went back across the river, yes?"

"Yes, Lord. They will not return, not for a long time. They have left too many of their best soldiers to lie rotting outside our stockade."

"Did they?" The king clutched my arm with both his hands. "Did they, lad? Eh? You've seen them?"

"Yes, Lord. You have only to step out onto the plain to see the great harvest of corpses."

"Then let's do that, lad. We'll be safe enough, just you and I, yes?"

He rose from his cot, and I helped him into his great silver tunic and with my own hands placed the turban of royalty upon his head. He was like a child being dressed by his mother. When he left the tent one of his courtiers approached, but the king waved him away with an impatient gesture.

"No!" He glared around at the knot of his officers who surrounded us. "None but my son here. A torch!"

One of the guards handed me a torch, and together the king and I walked to the gates of the stockade, men staring at us as we passed as if at the visitation of a god, and then out onto the killing ground at Khalule.

The stink of mortality was heavy in the air. There was no light save from the summer moon and the torch I carried, but that grisly landscape needed no other to reveal its horrors. Blood stained the ground, leaving great black patches where it had dried, and the bodies of dead men lay about in grotesque profusion. One could almost hear the anguished cries of their souls as they floated about aimlessly on the night wind.

"It is true then, eh?"

The king held my arm as we picked our way over the litter of corpses—he limped like an old man.

"It is true, Lord."

"And what of our own army?"

"Badly mauled, but intact."

"Then we will not march south into Elam," he said—for the first time that evening his truly was the king's voice. "We cannot stay here or there will be sickness—phew, what a smell! We will go west, to the Euphrates. With the Elamites gone, that black-

headed rabble will remember soon enough who is Lord of Akkad
and Sumer. We will give my brave men a few months of easy
victories, let them grow rich on booty and gain back their confidence. The Babylonians will pay for this campaign, that they may
learn the price of their treachery to my son and heir.

"Come, Tiglath—you will stand at my side while I issue the
order. They say you fought like a cornered boar and were twice
wounded, and in your first battle, too. Let the lords of Ashur see
how I raise you to glory, eh? Do your wounds hurt you, lad? I
remember how in my first battle I . . ."

And thus did the king my father, in his time of fear, gather
me to him. He made me great, as he had promised when I was but
a smooth-limbed boy, and through him I came to know the ways
and uses of power. I never knew what made him send for me, but
all that I grew to be in the Land of Ashur I owe to that night.

We did march west, and the great men of Sippar threw themselves at the feet of our king, begging that he might spare the city,
for by then all knew that the Elamites would come no more that
year into the lands of Akkad and Sumer. The king in his wisdom
saw the virtues of an easy victory and accepted their tribute, worshiped at the shrines of their gods, and headed south, keeping
always to the shore of the river Euphrates, its waters muddy and
its currents slow as a crippled snake. The cities of Cuthah, Kish,
and Borsippa all made their submission, for the armies of Ashur
were not to be resisted—and would return home soon enough. We
did not move against Babylon, for Mushezib-Marduk, who the
previous year had taken the hands of the god Bel and was king in
that city, had with him a strong army. He had been at Khalule
but like a prudent monarch had suffered his ally to do most of the
fighting and was thus still powerful enough to hold his citadel.
Babylon, as all men know, is a great city, and to take it against a
determined opposition was, for that year, beyond our strength.
We fought no more pitched battles that campaign.

And with the end of summer we turned our faces north toward Nineveh.

Along our route of march his loyal subjects came out to do
honor to their king: Opia, Samarra, Takrit, holy Ashur, Calah, all
the great cities of the land. We traveled the road home with gar-
lands of flowers about our necks, and old women greeted us with

wine and fruit. We had suffered much, and for the god's sake and
theirs, that all might sleep safe in their beds and dream no dreams
of the Elamite. At Takrit they clothed the walls in banners of
green and yellow, and at Calah the people knelt by the roadside to
accept the blessings of the mighty king.

And at Nineveh, which we saw in the distance just as the first
few drops of winter rain were falling, at Nineveh there was joy
close to madness that the Servant of Ashur had once more returned to his capital. Women clutching bread and jars of beer in
their arms danced in ecstasy at the return of their long-absent
husbands and men threw coins in the king's way that they might
be blessed by the touch of his chariot wheels. For three nights no
one slept within the city walls, for it was a time of festival. The
wineshops and brothels were busy places, and women flocked to
the temple of Ishtar to couple their duty to the goddess with the
excitement of the army's return. We were a great nation, trampling our enemies underfoot. We were loved by our god, feared by
all besides, powerful and rich—all believed this and rejoiced in it.
A man in a soldier's tunic wanted for nothing, had he money or
not, and even the meanest soldier's share of booty was no small
thing. Nineveh was far from the plains of Khalule, and here we
could believe in our victory.

As soon as the *quradu* had marched back to the house of
war, I stripped off my armor and joined the lines of men waiting
to steam themselves clean in the baths. Then I put on a clean
uniform and made my way to Esharhamat's apartments in the
king's palace. One of her ladies led me into the enclosed garden,
where Esharhamat was sitting beside her fountain, looking down
into the water.

She glanced up and when she recognized me her face seemed
to come alive. She danced across the tiled floor—this is the only
way to describe how her light little feet flew—and threw herself
into my arms. In an instant I found her lips pressing against mine
with an urgency that nearly took my breath away.

"I knew you would come back," she whispered. "I knew you
would not die, I knew, I knew. . . ."

I kissed her hungrily. I didn't care who saw us—it didn't
seem to matter. I was back in this garden and Esharhamat still
loved me.

It wasn't until we had sat down together, and I held her tiny hands in my own, that I noticed she no longer wore the red tunic of mourning.

"Then you are soon to marry Arad Ninlil," I said, my heart turning to stone in my breast.

"Never! I will never marry him!" The words seemed to choke her.

"He comes here sometimes," she went on at last, her voice lower, colder, as if the memory froze her heart. "He stays for dinner with his mother and looks at me with wide, hungry eyes. Once he . . . I hate him. I will never marry him. I will never marry anyone but you, my Tiglath Ashur, whom the god loves as I do. Never."

I had only to look into her eyes to know that she meant it. She would bring down the king's wrath upon us. We both might perish, but for myself I could not be otherwise than full of joy. This moment seemed worth a thousand deaths.

"But you are out of mourning. . . ."

"Yes. It had gone on long enough. I never cared for him—he was never truly my husband."

"Then nothing has been said of Arad Ninlil?"

"Nothing."

We both smiled, absurdly happy. We were only reprieved, like prisoners given another day before they must face the executioner's knife, but what did that matter? We had this little space of time still left to us. Nothing else seemed important.

I tried to tell her of the campaign, but strangely she seemed to know everything already. Of the slaughter at Khalule, of the march through the cities of the south, everything. She even knew that I was now high in the king's favor. Word of all these things had reached Nineveh long before.

When I spoke of the king, Esharhamat only smiled, watching me out of the corner of her eye. For her all things seemed easy and obvious. It was only after I had gone from her that I realized I had understood nothing, that Esharhamat had grown to be the sort of woman before whom all men are merely children.

It was nearly dark when I left her garden, and at that hour I had no heart for the royal barrack, so I went instead to the house near the Gate of Adad.

"Young master!" Kephalos bellowed as he saw me. He had

grown even stouter in the space of half a year and his green-and-yellow tunic billowed like a sail as he waddled to meet me at the doorway and throw himself on his knees to embrace my feet. "Am I yet the slave of my reckless young lord? The gods of all nations be praised for it!"

He sent Philinna scurrying off to the kitchen to prepare our dinner and the boy Ernos was given three shekels of silver and told to buy the finest wine he could find. Before the stars were out, Kephalos and I, sitting under the vine arbor in his garden, were both most of the way toward being very drunk as he regaled me with stories of how things had stood in Nineveh during my months of absence.

"The gossip among the physicians, Lord, is of course all about the *marsarru* Arad Ninlil's stomach troubles—he has been sorely plagued ever since the army's departure, and many say it is out of jealousy over your exploits. These, Lord, I have paid story-tellers to recount throughout the city and they have rebounded to the profit of us both. My women patients come to hear me speak of you, and of course everyone has confidence in a physician whose master is both a hero and lucky enough to be still alive. By the way, did the ointments prove of benefit?"

"Yes, er . . . ." I was not unhappy to find myself choking on one of Philinna's honeyed locusts, for the red jar was still in my kit, its seal unbroken, and I did not relish another lecture from Kephalos on the depravity and dirtiness of southern women. "My wounds, er . . . Would you like to see how nicely the scars have healed?"

I stood up and lifted my tunic to show him the sword thrust that had danced along my rib cage at Khalule—it was nothing more than a thin white line now, and Kephalos, holding up an oil lamp that he might see the better, inspected it with great interest.

"Were you a vainer man, Lord, you might even wish my art had not done its work so well," he said as I sat down again. "Scars are not unbecoming to a warrior, when they have been honorably sustained, and in a year or two it will require a trained eye to know how close that one came to killing you."

"But, as you say, Kephalos, I am unencumbered with that sort of vanity. Now—tell me. What is said here of the campaign? Do the people have any notion of the real losses at Khalule?"

My slave shrugged his shoulders. "They do not care, Lord. It is to be remembered that Nineveh has the king's charter, and

since none here may be conscripted into the army, one must go to
the houses of the poor to hear the voices of mourning. It was
reported as a glorious campaign, and the merchants have grown
even richer by buying up the spoils. People are disposed to believe
whatever they are told."

When I described to him what the great battle had been like,
and how the king had wept in my arms and had kept his tent for
three days, Kephalos merely nodded, as if it were a story he had
heard many times before.

"You will recall, master, I warned you before you left, so full
of the glory of war. It is an enterprise that profits none but the
crows—and, of course, the shopkeepers and the harlots when
once the army has returned. By the end of the week none of those
soldiers who are this night roaming the streets in search of wine
and amusement will have so much as a copper shekel."

It was no less than the truth. As I walked home through the
crowds of merrymakers, I knew Kephalos was wise. So it was not
in any very happy frame of mind that, upon returning to the royal
barrack, I kicked off my sandals and lay down for my first night's
rest on a real bed in six months. A hundred times I had slept
better on the bare ground.

The next morning I awoke at first light, and my head felt as if
it would split open like a roasted apple. I got up and managed to
wash my face, but I dared not venture out of doors for fear the
light of Holy Ashur's sun would strike me dead. As I buried my
face in my hands I cursed Kephalos and his wisdom and the
abundance of his wine, the taste of which still lingered in my
mouth as if it had died there. I was beginning to learn that the god
had not intended me for a reveler.

"Here—take this."

It was Tabshar Sin. He held a jar of beer to my lips, making
me drink. There must have been something in the beer, for it
smelled like the charcoal ovens outside the city gates, but in a few
minutes my head had contracted back to its usual dimensions.

"What are you doing here?" he asked finally. "I have been
looking for you all over the house of war."

"Why? Where else should I be? This is my room."

I glanced about me, blinking like an owl in the dusty light
from the sole window. Yes, of course there hadn't been any mistake. Esarhaddon and I had lived in this room for five years.

"This is a boy's room," Tabshar Sin said quietly, as if he

were explaining something to a sick child. "Tomorrow I will have another student sleeping in here. You have quarters in the officers' barrack—or has it slipped your mind that you are now a *rab kisir* of the *quradu*? Get up and go to the steam house to sweat your brains supple again. You are to attend the king this evening."

I looked up into his face and saw that he was grinning at me. And then the grin collapsed in an instant.

"You did well, Prince," he said. "Your name is covered in glory, and you have made me proud. Now scour yourself out and then come and tell me of the death of Nargi Adad."

It has always been my observation that the crueler the war and the more ambiguous its outcome, the costlier and more elaborate the victory celebration. We had shed much blood in the south and achieved little beyond inflicting comparable sufferings on our enemy. True, the Elamites had withdrawn back within their own borders and we had accepted the submission of all the great cities of Akkad and Sumer except Babylon—the only one that mattered —but nothing had been settled and next year both armies would take the field again. Our ordeal, it seemed, was only to be the more protracted. Hence the grandeur of the banquet with which the king my father celebrated his triumph.

There was much music that night and much wine, but I was not in the company of men I trusted as well as Kephalos, so I drank but little. The smells of incense and roasted lamb weighed down the heavy air. The wax torches burned in the wall sconces and the women danced—except this year they were naked but for their jewels, and their sweat mingled with the oil on their brown ripe bodies to make them glisten like the stars as they twisted cunningly in what seemed a frenzy of lustful passion.

Yet it was the king who held our eyes, resplendent in a tunic of purple and gold. The turban that covered his graying hair was encrusted with green jewels. When the king laughed, all men laughed with him, and when he told a story, we all listened. The king was glory, power, the divinity of the god himself. The king held us all cradled in his hand like dice ready for the throw.

This evening I was not one of the pages who waited in a doorway. I was one of the king's favorites, gathered around him at the long table. All of his great men were there: the commanders of his army, the Lord Sinahiusur, and the *marsarru* Arad Ninlil—

seated not at his father's right hand, as one might have expected,
but farther down the table, only a little above my own place. The
governor of the city was there, and the *shaknu* of Hindani, glancing about nervously as if he expected that he had been summoned
away from his province to an uncertain destiny. There was even a
woman, though hardly more than a girl, sitting beside the king at
his left hand, pressing her shoulder against his arm.

I thought perhaps she was one of his new concubines, part of
the tribute from our campaign, until, as her eyes wandered about
the room, they happened to come to rest on my face and she
smiled—none of the king's women would have dared to smile at
another man like that.

I did not learn until later that this was Shaditu, his favorite
daughter, the delight of his liver as he called her, for she was
beautiful to look upon and played upon his weakness and fear.
Her mother had been an Egyptian woman who died giving her life
and, it was said, had cursed the child with her last breath. Still,
the king was blind to her wickedness, and she worked much evil
before her life was stopped. She was my own sister, and yet no
woman but a harlot has ever smiled at me as she did that night.

". . . but it was not like the wars of our youth, brother, eh?
Do you remember, in the campaign against the Hittite lands, how
the king of Sidon fled from us into the sea and drowned before the
eyes of the whole city? When Sidka, king of Ashkelon, would not
submit, we took his gods, his women, his daughters and sons. We
burned their bodies in a great fire—do you remember that, eh? *He*
learned to kiss the earth at our feet! And the Egyptians—by
Adad, the Egyptians! How we fought them! How their corpses
covered the battlefield under the walls of Altaku! Would you have
liked to see that, my little honeyed apple, yes? Your old father
when he was not so old . . ."

Shaditu stared up into his face and stroked his hands as they
held her slender young body, and whispered things into his ear
which made him roar with laughter. And the king, who like all
kings had learned to trust no one, trusted in her love.

But the king was drunk with more than his daughter's ca-
resses that night, and finally the lady was sent away that he might
enjoy the dancers' performance all the more. The table rocked
with laughter and soldiers' jokes, and the beating of the drums
became like a fist that struck one between the eyes. The dancers
came closer—a man had only to put out his hand to touch their

gleaming bodies, and more than one man did. At last the king staggered up from the table and two of the women caught him under the arms lest he fall—they moved to his aid with a quickness that must have come from long practice. He laughed, twisting his head from one to the other, and allowed them to help him, and then the rest of us began to rise.

"My Dread Lord, I—"

"No!—Keep away from me! Do not approach me!"

It was Arad Ninlil, his son and heir who had come near him, and the king held up his hands to fend him off as if he had been a leper. In an instant the room was silent.

"Do not approach me," the king repeated, more calmly now. We hardly dared to look at him, and the *marsarru* glanced at us with hatred darting from his eyes. "Come, my pretty little birds. Come—help me to my chamber, for I have drunk too much wine."

The women led him away. We his companions stood about like logs of wood until he was gone, and then Arad Ninlil stalked from the room, looking at no one.

When I could raise my eyes they met those of Sinahiusur. He did not speak. He did not need to speak.

For the days following I found it convenient to forget that I was a son of a king—it was better, I felt, to be just a simple soldier who knows his duty and obeys orders. In war the king was my lord. That was enough. I would follow him through the gates of Arallu; I would lay down my life if he commanded it. I only wished him to forget that he was my father that I might forget it myself. I did not know it yet, but I had lost my faith in kings.

So I returned to the parade grounds at the house of war to drill my men, wringing from their bodies all the bitter humors that had collected there while they reveled through the streets of Nineveh. They did not like it. I worked myself harder than I did them, for I craved the oblivion of weariness, but they did not find that a consolation. Thus I learned that it is harder to keep soldiers under discipline in garrison than it is in battle.

But I drilled them anyway, and soon enough they forgot all about the pleasures of Nineveh. They were good men and forgave me for being in the grip of an idea, for I kept remembering the enemy cavalry at Khalule, how they had cut through our lines like an ax through paper, and I had a notion for stopping them.

"If we could keep our men bunched closer together—make a wall of shields, and then protect that wall with long spears sticking through, the butts firmly planted in the earth and the shafts angled so that their horsemen would have the prospect of riding straight in to be impaled on them . . . I think I might turn aside rather than risk getting spitted like a roasting goose. I think even the Elamites might turn aside, don't you?"

Tabshar Sin listened with great attention, watching as I drew pictures in the dust. He had lost his hand to the sword of a Nairian cavalryman, so my strategy was not without interest to him.

"The spears would have to be of great length," he said finally, shaking his head. "Eight, maybe ten cubits. A rider would have to know he had no chance of reaching your line. How would the shield-bearers carry them?"

"With the javelins. Let them stick straight up in the air to give the enemy warning. Let their horsemen learn to dread the order to charge."

"And once your men break ranks?"

"They would not. Drill them to run without breaking formation. Twenty paces, then drop down on one knee and plant the spear. Then twenty more paces. What will discourage cavalry will have the same effect on foot soldiers. That was something I learned at Khalule—the minute men break ranks, when they no longer fight in concert, the battle ceases and what follows is no more than a brawl."

"Well, you might try it, Prince. But remember, what works on the drill field will not necessarily work in the heat of battle. It becomes a different matter when the men opposing are not your friends from the next barrack but an army of Elamites."

"That is why it is necessary to drill men until they hardly remember the difference between drill and battle, until they follow orders as naturally as breathing."

"Well, it cannot hurt to try. At least it will give them something to do."

And that was how I spent my daylight hours, training men to use a weapon that did not even exist yet.

"No, Prince, bronze drawn to more than four cubits will bend like a tree limb under a load of wet snow."

The head of the royal armorers wiped an eye with the back of his left hand—sparks from his hammer had long since seared away the brows and lashes.

"I could attempt it in iron, perhaps, but I should have to rebuild my furnace. We are not accustomed, you understand, to working metal to such lengths, and iron is as obstinate as my wife."

He smiled shyly, as if he thought I might take offense at his slight joke, but I could see that he was already turning the problem over in his mind.

"What of the weight?" I asked. I did not wish to turn my formations into so many hedgehogs, prickly but sluggish. "I want something that men can carry all day, that they can run with. Will not iron be too heavy for that?"

"No, Prince. It will weigh less even than if I used bronze, for I can draw it thinner. Your soldiers will learn to tolerate the weight quickly enough."

"And by the spring could you produce enough to equip an army?"

"An army?—no. But a few companies certainly. Enough for you to test this new strategy of yours, Prince."

He smiled again. He probably knew more of war than I would after ten campaigns, but if he thought I was a foolish youth he kept his opinion to himself.

"Let us try then."

So I went on drilling my soldiers, making the shield-bearers carry logs that the weight of an iron spear would seem light to them in comparison. The work went on through the months of Marcheswam and Kislef, while the wind turned cold and the leaves began to wither on the trees. Finally the royal armorer had our spears, and when the men grasped that these might protect them from the Elamite horsemen they ceased to complain. By the middle of the winter the men of my company, brought back up to strength with replacements from the northern levies, worked together as easily as the fingers of one hand.

And all of this took place under the careful eye of the king. He came several times to witness the drills and when the spears were ready he kept one of them for himself, carrying it around with him as he paced back and forth to inspect the defensive line of shields.

"But what of your javelin throwers, lad? Eh? They can't do much from behind a leather fence."

"We will only assume this formation when the cavalry are almost upon us, Dread Lord—the element of surprise is important if we hope to panic the horses. And at such close quarters a javelin is not worth much. The archers, as you can see, need only to stand back a few paces and they can still reach the enemy infantry."

"You think it will work, yes? Brother, what do you say?"

The *turtanu* Sinahiusur stroked his beard for a moment and then at last nodded.

"I think it may work, Lord."

"Yes, it may." The king shook the spear he held, as if to test if it would fly to pieces. When it did not he turned his eyes to me and showed his teeth in a fierce smile. "Yes, it may indeed. You are a clever lad, Tiglath Ashur, Son of Sennacherib, Lord of the Earth, King of Kings. Come to me tomorrow evening while I take my meal—tell me if you have any more schemes for conquering the universe with fire and sword, eh? Hah, hah, hah!"

That night, when I was ushered into the king's private chamber, I was surprised to find him alone. He was at a rough wooden table, the sleeves of his tunic rolled back as he ate from golden dishes that glittered in the torchlight. I dropped to one knee, but he seemed impatient of even that much ceremony and beckoned me toward him.

"Come—sit," he said. He poured wine for me with his own hands. "I am sorry I can offer you nothing more—the wine is my own, but the food is the god's. The priests hold it under his eyes and then bring it to me. Did you know that, eh? Thus I eat the god's leavings from his golden dishes, like a dog fed scraps."

I sat uncomfortably, staring at my wine cup. I did not know what to say.

"That is what a king is, my son. He is the god's watchdog, kept on a chain before the door to bark at strangers. Whatever I may appear to the world, that is all I am. Here, drink your wine. The sight of you cheers my heart and I have few enough comforts in my old age. Let us drink to the glory of your name, Tiglath Ashur, Son of Sennacherib."

So we drank to that, and to the glory of Ashur and the confusion of the Elamites, and then to Ishtar, Courtesan of the Gods and Lady of Battles, and then . . . And by then, of course,

I had forgotten all my doubts about the king, who was my father and my friend and whom I loved.

"The god has cursed me in my sons—except for you, lad." He reached across the table to throw his arm over my shoulders. "I blame myself for the death of Ashurnadinshum. I should never have sent him into that dark land—Babylon, may Ashur curse it! And as for Arad Ninlil . . . Well, you have seen him.

"But have you seen my daughter Shaditu?" His eyes glistened. "Is she not a lovely creature—she speaks of you often, so I am glad you are her brother, eh? Hah, hah, hah! She is such a lovely creature and such a comfort, I could not bear to part with her. No, she shall not marry while I live. Is that very selfish of me, Tiglath, eh?"

He did not wait for me to answer, for which I was thankful, but spoke of other things, of his old campaigns, and his women, and the Lady Naq'ia, and his age.

"What will happen when I die, eh, lad? What will happen, I wonder.

"But this new tactic of yours—we shall have to try it in the next campaign. And if it works . . . You are a good lad. You are a good soldier too, and that's all that really matters. I said once I would make you great, but I think, in the end, you will do that for yourself. So all that is left for me is to make you rich. There is a royal estate not two hours' gallop up the river—it is yours, my son. And there will be more in time, much, much more. Is there anything else you would like now, lad? Eh? Speak, and if it lies within my power it is yours."

Since my childhood I had dreamed of this moment. Why else had I sought to cover myself in glory except that I might seek the king's favor for this one thing? And yet the only name that would form itself in my mind was that of Esharhamat. And I might not ask her of the king, lest his eyes darken with anger, for she was the one thing not in his power to give.

And yet the king loved me, and had drunk too much wine . . . He might, even yet—but no. I could not ask it of him. I was the king's servant, loyal to him in all things, and I could not trick him into betraying the god's will.

So while my heart whispered "Esharhamat," I trained my frozen lips to speak another name.

"Dread Lord . . ."

"Yes, my son—speak! Name the thing and it is yours."

"My mother, Lord—that she might be with me again . . ."

In the silence that followed I was truly shamed, first that I had asked such a thing of the king's majesty and second that even in thought, in my secret wishes, I had sacrificed my mother to Esharhamat, whom I was forbidden to love but must love while there was breath in my body.

The king peered into my face, his arm still across my shoulders.

"So small a thing, lad? That is all—just your mother? Then so be it! Eh, lad? Hah, hah, hah!"

And the great king my father, who was perhaps not so drunk as I had thought, was as good as his word, for the next evening, when I returned from drill, I found a closed chair carried by four slaves, a chair such as a queen might use, waiting beside the entrance to the officer's barrack. Down from it stepped my mother, and in her hand was the tablet transferring to me a royal estate of some one hundred *beru* in extent. I set aside my mother's veil that I might see her face, and her blue eyes were wet with tears.

"Oh, my son, my son—and is it really true then?"

"Yes, Mother, it is true."

And thus it was that I fulfilled the promise I had made as a child and by the king's grace led my mother from the house of women.

7

That first night I took my mother to lodge with Kephalos near the Gate of Adad. The following morning, having left my *ekalli* Lushakin in charge of the company's drill, I hired a horse and cart suitable for a court lady to travel in, and Merope and I set out on our journey to my new estate in the north.

It had been some years since I had seen her, but this quiet woman who sat beside me in the cart while we picked our way over the narrow, rutted road was still the mother I remembered from my childhood. There were strands of white mixed in with the copper-colored hair, and the tiny lines around the corners of her mouth spoke the language of a resigned sadness, but she was still, at least in my sight, as beautiful as ever. She hardly spoke on our journey. Instead, she watched me furtively, turning away her eyes if I chanced to look at her.

"I do not know what this place will be like," I said finally—I was beginning to find the silence oppressive. "I do not think, however, the king would have made me a present of a doghole. But if the farmhouse doesn't suit you, we can rebuild it. I have instructed Kephalos to purchase some suitable house slaves and a woman to attend you."

"How can you afford all this, Lathikadas?"

It was the first time she had called me by that childhood name, and I turned and smiled at her. For once she did not glance away like a bride on her wedding journey.

"You needn't worry, Merope. The king is not the only one who conspires to make me a man of substance—that rascal slave of mine already seems to own half of Nineveh, and I appear in his account books for enough silver to keep the likes of you and me for the rest of our lives. He is a rogue but a good friend and robs me, I think, only a little. Never fear, I will build you a house worthy of the king's lady and there, for once, you shall be the mistress."

"I am not the king's lady, my son—only one of his women. And he has not come near my bed in many years."

I did not know what to say, so I said nothing. And as our shadows began to lengthen along the road, we came to the boundary stone marked with the winged disk of Ashur to show that we had crossed onto the king's land.

"No, the king my father had not gifted me with a doghole. As we rode along, the fields, bare now and covered with yellow stubble, stretched to the right hand and to the left as far as the eye would carry. And the farmhouse was not of brick but of mountain stone and built after the Hittite pattern that the rooms might have sunlight during all the hours of the day. My heart rose within me, for I was bringing my mother to a palace.

By the time I had brought the cart to a stop, the farmhands and household slaves had already gathered before the great wooden doors to greet us. As I stepped down they all bowed as one.

"I am Tiglath Ashur," I said, in the voice I used to address soldiers—I was unused to the ways of country people and conscious of my youth, and thus afraid of seeming either raw or weak. "And this is the Lady Merope, my mother."

"Yes, Lord—a rider was here yesterday to bring us word of your coming." A tall man with a black beard and the weathered face of one who has lived out his life within sight of the northern mountains stepped a little apart from the others and bowed once more. There was that in his manner to suggest he was not used to bowing. "I am Tahu Ishtar, overseer on this estate these ten years, in that time the king's servant as he is the god's, as I am now yours. We have prepared the house to receive you, and a woman will see to your lady mother's comfort. If you will follow me, Lord."

We dined that night on roast kid and barley bread washed down with beer—these were not people who had ever tasted wine —and when the meal was finished and my mother and I warmed ourselves against a brazier placed in the center of the room, I enjoyed a sense of comfort and safety such as I had almost forgotten was possible. The smell of woodsmoke was like myrrh.

"Will you be happy here, Merope?" I asked. "I can only stay through the second half of the month, but I will come as often as I can. This will be our home from now on. Will you be happy here?"

"Yes—it is like a dream."

There were tears wetting her cheeks. They glistened in the red light of the fire. I sat down beside her and put my arm across her shoulders, thinking to myself what an empty life she must have led in the house of women that she could think it a dream to find herself here, on an isolated farm, with nothing to sustain her but the occasional visits of her son.

"You must marry, Lathikadas," she said suddenly, letting her hand close on the front of my tunic. "You must bring a wife here, a girl to share your sleeping mat, to bear your children and bring happiness to your life."

"I am young yet, Merope. There is a world of time to think of taking a wife, and for now I am content that you should be mistress here."

I had thought my mother was expressing more a foreboding than a hope, but I was mistaken. I could feel the tension growing as her fingers tightened on my collar—this with her was no womanish fit of baseless possessiveness. Something, some idea or recollection, had frightened her.

"I fear I cannot order your house as you would wish it," she went on—with a hint of panic in her voice. "My son, I have been a slave since childhood, and one does not learn the domestic arts in the king's harems—and I would never be jealous. I would wish you to find love with her, that she might . . ."

"That she might what, Mother?"

She looked up into my face, and I saw something almost like terror in her eyes.

"That she might drive the memory of Esharhamat from your heart, my Lathikadas."

I will not attempt to describe what I felt in that moment. I was too astonished to sort it all out—that word of my harmless meetings with Esharhamat should have reached Merope's ears. Was this business the common gossip of the palace? Could it have reached as high as the king?

No, that it could not have. I was alive and in high favor. But the favor of the mighty is a fragile thing, and all at once I felt that the very ground beneath my feet was no stronger than the crust of stale bread, that it could collapse under my weight from one instant to the next and I would fall to a shameful death. It would take no more than a word.

"But, Mother, how could you have . . ."

"How? You can ask me how?" She made some pretense of laughter, but it was a bitter sound. "How would I, walled up as I was in the house of women, have heard anything of Esharhamat and my son? You forget whom I have there as a companion, and is there a mud turtle from here to the Bitter River who can make a splash that Naq'ia will not hear?"

Naq'ia—yes, of course. And would not Naq'ia delight to torment my mother with such news? I could understand Merope's fear. I could feel it myself.

But I took her face in my hands and kissed her brow, just as I had done as a child.

"It is quite innocent, Mother. I see her from time to time—that is all. Nothing evil can come of it.

"And now I think it would be well if we both found our beds," I continued, as if I had answered all her doubts and could turn her thoughts as easily as I might wheel a chariot about over the broad plain. "Your women wait for you beyond the door. And tomorrow I would rise early to see my property. I would have these people know that their new master is a soldier and does not sleep till noon like some tavern harlot."

Merope showed me her smile, which was a smile I had seen on the lips of other women. A smile that said she knew what all women know, that men are no more than children.

"It would be well, my son, if you were as wise in all things as in this."

The next morning the sun had not risen above the eastern mountains when I opened the door of my new house and stepped outside into the cold light, but Tahu Ishtar, my overseer, was already waiting for me. One hand clutching the shoulder cloth of his rough brown tunic and the other a staff—the mark of his station as the javelin I carried was of mine—he bowed stiffly when he saw me. Standing beside him was a thin little boy who could not have been more than twelve. At a glance from the overseer he too bowed, so low that I could almost see the back of his neck.

"My son Qurdi," Tahu Ishtar said, "who by my lord's grace will succeed to his father's office when I am summoned by the Lady Ereshkigal."

The boy smiled shyly and then dropped his eyes to the ground.

"Will my lord be pleased to inspect his property now?"

I wore the uniform of a *rab kisir* in the *quradu* and my father was the king, but this man, without any show of insolence, had made it plain that he had seen nothing yet to make him tremble with awe. Outside the cities, where they have not learned to be corrupted by foreign manners and the power of wealth, the men of Ashur are just that way—they are not slaves.

"I will be very pleased," I said, smiling at the boy Qurdi. The overseer merely bowed once more.

We spent the first half of the morning looking over the buildings—the threshing floors, the granaries, the barns and stables and cellars—and I was pleased to discover that I seemed to be a most prosperous farmer. I was possessed of sheep, cattle, and horses. I had barley and millet. Flocks of geese patrolled the grounds, looking for the grain that lay scattered for them. In great clay jars kept in the cool earth I had beer and cider enough to drown whole companies of thirsty soldiers. The land had been bountiful to me. And all these things Tahu Ishtar showed me, explaining everything in a calm, detached voice, as if he concerned himself with none of it. He was a proud man and had no wish to appear to boast.

I said little, asking a question now and then, listening to the answers in silence. My overseer would not curry my favor and neither would I his, for I was not a boy now and men must respect each other. The boy Qurdi followed us everywhere, standing close to his father but watching my face.

"There will be snow on the ground soon, Lord. There is little enough to do now, so the people keep to their houses and make ready for winter. You will see their village when you inspect the fields, but for that we must take horses."

We returned to the stables, and I picked myself a great black brute of a horse, bridled him, and threw a blanket over his back. When both Tahu Ishtar and I were mounted, and Qurdi had climbed up behind his father, we set out.

The circuit of my estate occupied more than three hours, through orchards and vineyards and across fields of bare, turned earth and well-cared-for irrigation canals wide enough for barge traffic and brimming with silt-laden water that glistened like polished iron in the cold winter sunshine. Tahu Ishtar explained how each field would be planted against the spring harvest, how the canal locks were managed, and where my tenants worked during each season of the year.

"Will you live among us, Lord?" he asked finally, careful not to look at me as he did so.

"When I can—yes." I could not know whether or not it was the answer he wanted. "I am a soldier and we are at war, but I am leaving my mother here and will come as often as I am able."

He nodded, still without looking at me.

"That is good. It is better for the land when the lord lives on it, and the king, of course, was seldom here. I have not seen the king's face these ten years, although I wrote to his scribes in Nineveh when there was need of advice. I suppose now that will no longer be required."

We pulled up our horses in front of one of the dozens of narrow wooden bridges thrown across the canals, and at last Tahu Ishtar turned his face to me. It seemed that, since I did not intend to hide myself in some great house in Nineveh, living off the revenues of lands I never visited, he had decided I was someone he could bear the sight of.

"No, that will not be required. I prefer to make my mistakes in person."

With the suddenness of spring thunder, Tahu Ishtar opened his mouth and laughed. It was like a soldier's laughter, unforced and fearless. We were not the same men now; we had shared a joke.

He raised his arm and pointed to a wisp of smoke against the mountains.

"Come, then. Yonder is the village where your people wait. You will find yourself an object of curiosity, since there are many among them who have never yet seen the face of their lord."

To enter a village along the flood plains of the Tigris is to venture back into the world of the ancients, for thus the fathers of our race lived before the times of kings and cities, when there was only the land and the god. I had seen many such, circles of mud-brick huts, places too small to have names, but always before I had been the soldier who passed by on the road to somewhere else. I knew nothing of the lives lived before these cooking fires and had never tasted the water drawn from their wells. All who live in the king's mighty shadow are just the same and are thus strangers in their own country, for it was in the villages that we began and it is to them that we return to find the roots of our greatness. We are a race of farmers, for our land is rich, and it is a proverb in every barrack that the best soldiers are born with mud between their toes. The lords in Nineveh liked to forget this, but it was true all the same.

As we rode toward the village I could see that, just as my overseer had promised, a crowd was gathered against our arrival. Already, even at a distance, there was that shouting which comes from many throats, except that these were not for us. These were the cries of lamentation, and this assembly had come together not to welcome their new lord but to bewail some catastrophe unique to themselves. Tahu Ishtar was mistaken—my tenants had forgotten my very existence.

The women in their white wool tunics and their colored shawls over their heads—and they were mostly women, their children clustered around them, and a few old men—threw up their arms and sobbed like the ghosts of the unburied. A few sank to the ground, picking up handfuls of dirt to cast upon their shoulders and heads. The cooking fires had been left to burn themselves out and water jars were scattered about, their contents draining into the earth.

"What is it?" I asked. "What has happened? What distresses them?"

Tahu Ishtar came down from his horse and they gathered about him, all shouting at once. I could understand nothing. At last he stepped over to take my bridle as I dismounted, and his face was hard as ice.

"The lions have come back." His voice was without the least hint of expression, as if he had in that instant lost the power to feel the meanings of words. "When the cold weather comes, hunger drives them down from the mountains. Before this they have stolen only a few goats, but now they have carried off a child."

"My son, my son! My little son!" One of the women fell on her knees before us, seemingly unable to stand under her affliction. "Great Lord, Noble Lord, find my baby for me!"

As she buried her face in the dirt, her hands clutched my

ankles in supplication. She could not even speak now, and hardly weep, so great was the torment of this sorrow.

"That is where the men have gone," Tahu Ishtar said in a low voice. "They have no horses, but it is already too late."

"Still, we must do something."

I knelt and took the woman's hands in my own, and she looked up into my face. I could not tell even whether she was young or old, such was her grief, and the words that had half formed in my mind seemed suddenly paltry things—what could I tell her? That I would bring back her child?

"We must do something," I found myself repeating, this time to her.

I rose and mounted my horse. Tahu Ishtar lifted down his son and put him into the arms of an old man, they exchanged a few words, and the two of us headed out of the circle of mud-brick huts at a gallop. Within minutes we had already passed the knot of men running over the rough earth like a pack of hunting hounds.

We found the dead boy, or what remained of him, just beyond the first set of bluffs that marked where the mountains began their rise.

"They must have sensed pursuit and abandoned their meal," Tahu Istar said—the child's breast had been torn open and one leg was gnawed to the bone. The ground was smeared with blood. He came down from his horse, wrapped the body in his cloak, and handed it up to me. "At least now his mother can bury him."

We rode back to the farmhouse in silence. I cannot speak for my overseer, but my own mind was ringing with the sound of a mother's cries over the mangled body of her son. I kept remembering that these people were now my responsibility, that by ancient custom the tenants of the land had a right to look to their lord for protection. I had not been in possession the length of a single day and already, it seemed, I had failed them.

"How long has this been happening?" I asked finally. Tahu Ishtar was a while answering, as if he too had been deep in thought.

"Last winter and this. The villagers keep fires burning at night to frighten the beasts off, but in the preceding month they have become bolder. A week ago they snatched a goat that had been left tethered behind one of the huts, and now . . ."

"We will need a chariot," I said suddenly—the idea had just

flown into my head. I could only wonder why I hadn't thought of it before. "Have we a chariot? If not, I shall send to Nineveh."

"Lord, there are three great males. They hunt in concert, and their cunning is not to be despised."

"Have we a chariot, Tahu Ishtar—yes or no?"

His little son, his arms clasped around his father's waist as we rode along, watched me through huge black eyes, as if he could not fathom how I could dare to quarrel with the overseer.

"Yes, Lord." Tahu Ishtar stroked the chin of his great beard, doubtless wondering why the great gods had seen fit to visit him with a young fool of a master. "It has not seen use these ten years. The wheels are off and I cannot answer for the condition of the harnesses, but all of that can be seen to."

"It is well, then—have all things readied against the morning, and tell the villagers to organize themselves as beaters. We shall go hunting tomorrow!"

I made a wide circle about the farmyard in the chariot which, between yesterday afternoon and the king's last visit some ten years before, had leaned against a wall in one of the barns like a crippled vagabond waiting for the rain to stop. Tahu Ishtar and his men had worked through the night by the light of torches, and they had worked well. The wheels turned with noiseless ease—my only anxiety concerned the horses, as well matched a set as I could find among the animals in my stables but unused to pulling as a team. More than that, I could only hope that they would not panic at their first sight of our quarry, but in the hunt, as in war, much must be taken upon trust.

My mother stood in the doorway of our house, surrounded by the house servants, watching as I brought the chariot to a sudden halt to test how the platform rocked beneath my feet. As I whipped the horses up again I smiled broadly and waved to her, and she waved back. She had not tried to discourage me from this venture, although I had only to look at her to see that she was afraid of this "sport" in which I was indulging myself.

"It is only a hunt, Merope. I have gone hunting a thousand times, and the king kills lions with a sword for an afternoon's amusement."

What I did not tell her, of course, was that not even the king hunted lions without a retinue of armed men, but perhaps I did not need to. My retainers were only farmers, with nothing but their hand sickles and walking sticks for weapons, and I had never hunted anything more dangerous than the wild pigs that roamed freely over the plains east of Nineveh. Still, I was a warrior skilled with both bow and javelin and could handle a team of horses as well as any man in the royal army. In the pride of my youth I imaged these would be enough.

I waved yet once more and whipped my horses to a gallop.

In the village, Tahu Ishtar and all my tenants were assembled and waiting. They stood in silence as I drew to a stop—like an army before a battle they waited in sullen silence, knowing that all which followed would take its own course, that the time for choices was past. Now all they desired was to believe they were not entrusting their lives to a fool.

"Overseer, have the goats been staked out?"

Tahu Ishtar stepped forward and set his hand to rest on the railing of my chariot. We had settled all these matters between us the day before, but he understood the needs of his people and was therefore content to act the role assigned him in my little pageant.

"Yes, Lord. All is prepared."

I hardly glanced at him. I kept my eyes on the villagers, holding them with my gaze one at a time—it is a trick known to anyone who has held authority over soldiers, as it makes the bond of command somehow a personal matter.

"Then all that remains is to wait," I said, speaking now to all of them together. "There are three of these great cats and they have not dined very well of late, so they will come down yet again from their mountains in search of prey. Let them find it—let them gorge themselves until their bellies are close to bursting and they want nothing more than to lie quietly in the shade by some watering hole and sleep. We have provided the meal, so we will know where to look for them when it it time to close the trap. Tahu Ishtar, see to it that the children and the old people stay behind their doors this day. You know where I will be."

I would have driven away that instant had not one among the men pushed his way forward and grabbed one of the horses by the bridle to keep me from going. He was a small man, no longer young, with eyes that looked as if they had not closed all the night. I raised my whip and he released the bridle instantly, holding up his hands in supplication.

"Lord," he cried, "Lord, allow me to come with you—I have a father's right!"

"Then it was your son yesterday?" I looked first to the man and then to Tahu Ishtar, who nodded in confirmation.

"Yes, Lord—my son." The tears started in his bloodshot eyes and for a moment his voice left him. "My only son, born when my wife and I were already past our best days—there will never be another for us. Take me with you, that I might see them die that tore my boy's life from him!"

"I deny you this, and may the god pardon you for asking it." I allowed my voice to carry an anger I did not feel—for my heart was moved. "You are a farmer, not a wielder of weapons. What would you do, give your wife another corpse to mourn over? More than this, what you wish of me is an impiety. It is our business this day to rid the land of a danger, not to take revenge upon a dumb animal who merely follows the instincts he was born with and is therefore without sin. Tahu Ishtar, keep them all in a straight line—I will await the sound of your beaters!"

I did not tarry then, but turned my wheels toward the wide plains, where I would seek out a hunting ground of my own choice.

A chariot needs space. It is a clumsy affair, difficult to turn and stopped by anything that will not give way before it. A wheel can go over a rock and send the rider flying, or break off and leave him stranded. The only advantages it offers are speed and the fact that, like a boulder rolling down the side of a hill, it strikes terror into the hearts of any who stand before it.

The plains thereabouts were speckled with scrubby little trees, hardly more than bushes but sufficient to entangle a team of horses. It was a long time before I found a place empty enough that my quarry would not simply dart for cover the first instant the ground shook under my charge. There was even an outcropping of rock that I could scramble up for a view of the whole landscape as far as the mountains. I would be able to see the line of beaters, perhaps even before I heard them, and perhaps I would even catch a glimpse of the lions. I tethered my horses, gathered together my weapons, and climbed the rock for a look about me. It would be many hours, I knew, before I saw anything.

The lions had not made much of a meal of that village boy before they were frightened off, and if they had been desperate enough to forage so close to the abodes of men, they couldn't have eaten for many days before that. Tahu Ishtar had seen to it that five of my fattest goats were tethered not far from a watering hole where the great cats would be sure to look for prey—they would feast to their hearts' content and then have no thought for anything except languishing about out of the sun. Doubtless it would come as a disagreeable surprise when they heard the sound of a hundred men and women, strung out in a line and beating the ground with their flails, and when they smelled the smoke from the fires the villagers would set in their path. If Tahu Ishtar managed all according to plan—and Tahu Ishtar was a man to inspire perfect confidence—then his three great males, sluggish and confused, would be panicked straight into my path. With nowhere to run, they would stand and fight, and that I expected to have all my own way.

I had perfect confidence in myself and I felt no fear, only a pleasurable excitement. After all, these were merely animals—not Elamites armed with swords and javelins of their own. Not men like myself. The biggest lion in the world has no more than teeth and claws, and I had no thought of allowing them close enough that I should be in any danger from those. This was merely a day's hunting, no more. I had nothing to fear unless I committed some stupid mistake, and there was little enough danger of that. I was quite cheerful as I sat in the pale winter sunlight, waiting for some sign that the game was afoot.

The sun had declined almost an hour from noon when the first traces of smoke appeared on the horizon. I climbed down from my lookout, untethered the horses, and strung my bow. The chariot was already rolling out over the baked earth when the first of the great cats loped out into the open.

The lions of the east are not quite so large as those found in Egypt, whence the king imports those which he hunts for his private sport, but this one was as big as any I had ever seen, even in the king's preserve. When he saw the chariot he pulled to a dead halt, cocked his head to one side as if surprised and annoyed at this intrusion, and then crouched to wait for what would happen next. I brought the team up to a canter, angling toward him, and when he saw that he was being challenged he broke the air with a mighty roar—it was all I could do to keep the horses from bolting in panic.

In war each chariot is manned by two; one drives that the other is left free to fight with arrow or javelin. It is the same when the king makes war upon the lions of the royal preserve. But I had no one to drive for me, and thus I was compelled to stop before I could attempt a shot.

I drew up some seventy paces from my quarry, who crouched as if to spring and roared out his battle cry. I did not dare step down from the car for fear the horses would simply gallop away without me, so on the rocky platform of the chariot I selected an arrow and took my aim. The lion faced me with fierce, hating eyes. As if sensing his danger, he took a careful step to the left, then another, and then, while he hesitated, I let fly. The arrow pierced him in the chest before, screaming in agony and rage, he tried a last headlong attack.

But it was no good. The rush lasted only a few steps and then he slowed and stood quite still, watching me through eyes already grown clouded with pain, and then collapsed. He lay on his side, panting heavily, and a thin stream of blood spilled from between his great jaws. With my javelin in my hand, I came down from the chariot to give him a quick death.

It was the mistake I had promised myself I would not make. I stood over him, ready to drive the javelin into his heart, when I heard the horses neigh with terror. I whirled around, dropping to one knee, just as the second male began to spring. My weapon was braced against the ground and the lion, intending to fall upon me, fell upon it instead, the copper point tearing open his belly before it broke off.

But before he surrendered to death he managed to sink his great teeth into my left shoulder, tearing at my flesh in his last agony. By the time he dropped lifeless to the ground, he had given me a wound that went to the bone—in an instant I was washed in my own blood and sick with pain. The horses had of course bolted, so there was no retreat. I had only the sword in my belt, I could hardly stand, and already I could hear the last of the great males snarling in the undergrowth.

He took his time—this one would make no mistakes. Perhaps he knew I was bleeding and hoped to wait until I was weakened to the point of helplessness. He wanted me to know he was there, for no wild creature makes so much noise by chance. I had killed his brothers and he was telling me that they would be avenged.

But if I was bleeding, he had the villagers pressing down on him, burning their way ever closer. I could hear them now, the sounds of their shouting and the sticks they beat together. I could smell their fires.

"Come out!" I shouted. "Come out, and may the gods damn you." I stepped away from the bodies of the two lions I had killed to give myself room.

I do not know how long I waited for him to show himself, but it was not long.

Suddenly he was there. I did not see him come, or hear him —he merely appeared. He crouched low and began slinking toward me, every muscle in his great tawny body tensed and ready. He was not afraid—I could see it in his eyes that he meant to kill me. He growled with a low, insinuating sound, almost like a kitten purring. Almost as if he were taunting me with his closeness.

I stood with my sword drawn, feeling the strength ebb from my body, knowing that I must force him to make his rush before I was too weak to have any chance against him.

It was agony to raise my left arm, but I brought the hand up as far as my waist, gesturing with the fingers, inviting him to attack. My knees felt as if they were about to fold under me.

"Come on, damn you. Come and taste death."

But he was not yet ready. He only snarled contemptuously, bringing his shaggy head closer to the ground. He would wait.

It was now or never—I felt quite sure.

As the war cry broke from my lips I charged him, holding my sword low that I could strike up if he sprang. I had the advantage of only a few steps before his great body shot toward me through space and we came together with an impact that seemed to jolt the air.

I remember nothing more. When I came to myself I was lying in my own bed. Tahu Ishtar was using a red-hot knife to sear closed the wounds in my shoulder, and I could hear someone groaning. There was pain somewhere in the room, but I could not be sure if it was mine or someone else's. I remember my mother's face, wet with tears. And then darkness closed over me.

I had taken leave of the house of war for two weeks only, and it was that long before I was strong enough even to venture out of my own bed. To kill the pain I drank wine until I was light-headed, and my mother fed me thick soups that I might recover from the loss of blood—I had the impression that, once she was sure I would live, she rather enjoyed herself. Certainly in those weeks she proved she was a better manager than she had led me to expect.

At the end of the first week Tahu Ishtar paid me a visit, carrying something rolled up under his arm. He spread it out on the floor for me to see and for an instant my heart almost died within me—it was the skin of one of the lions.

"The villagers are tanning all three that you might have them as trophies. This is the first."

He sat down on a stool near my bed, adjusting his tunic around him with an air of great dignity and giving the impression that this was something of an official call.

"They also wish me to tell you, lest you be uneasy in your mind, that they poured libations over the dead animals so that their ghosts will not seek revenge against you."

"What happened?" I asked, pulling myself up a little on the cushions behind my back. "How did they . . . ?"

Tahu Ishtar peered into my face, his eyebrows raised in surprise.

"You mean, you do not know? Then no one does." He laughed and shook his head. "We found them dead and you not far behind. This one had the hilt of your sword sticking out of his mouth—the point had gone straight through to the brain. My people, you know, think you are Gilgamesh come back to life. They are grateful for what you have done."

"I am grateful just to be alive."

We talked for a while after that, of farming matters and the concerns of the villagers, and then, when Tahu Ishtar sensed I was growing weary, he took his leave. After that he visited me often, sometimes bringing his son Qurdi, who would sit upon the lion skin doubled over and staring into its open mouth. Slowly, with the deliberate caution of a country man who is no fool, Tahu Ishtar became my friend.

I had many visitors in that month of convalescence. Kephalos almost moved in with us and had me awash in his ointments.

"You must pay no heed to these Assyrian physicians, Lord, for their whole therapy is based on the foolish notion that illness comes from the gods' anger and they will do nothing but burn incense and pray over you. A little Greek skepticism is all you require."

He would consult endlessly with Merope over my diet—he was worse than any mother—and at last, when I was sick of his fussing, I chased him back to his patients in Nineveh. I think he was glad to go, for country life was not much to his taste.

At the end of the second week, when I was strong enough to walk about a bit without tiring, one of the farmhands came running with word that he had seen the dust from a troop of cavalry that seemed to be coming in our direction, and within two hours the Lord Sinahiusur himself dismounted at my door with an escort of twenty men.

It was a raw day, so after I had sent his soldiers to cheer themselves in my cookhouse I took the *turtanu* into the best room my house had to offer. We sat across from each other on a pair of stools, warming ourselves over a brazier and a jug of Lebanese wine that tasted like honey and stung like a wasp.

"The king has sent me. He only recently heard of your mishap and wished to express his concern. You are recovering, then?"

"Yes, Lord." I smiled and shrugged my shoulders, wondering what had really brought him—the *turtanu* Sinahiusur would not have journeyed all this way from the capital merely to pay a sick call. "In a week or so, when my strength returns, I will have nothing to show for this adventure except a few scars."

He reached across to me and placed his hand upon my arm, as if he would feel that strength for himself. And then he nodded his head.

"Good, then. And since it seems to stand so well with you, my boy, I will exercise my privilege as your uncle and tell you to your face that I believe your mind turns too much upon 'adventures.' You were a young fool to risk your life on so light a pretext —the land of Ashur is filled with villages, but not with princes of the blood. Be not in such a hurry for a glorious name, for it will come soon enough of its own. You will be *rab shaqe* before long— this I know. You should think what it is best to do with such power."

He tasted the wine again, quite as if he had not another thing on his mind, and set the cup down upon the small circular table that separated us.

"This is very good," he said. "Where did you get it?"

"A gift, Lord. You remember the slave Kephalos?"

"Oh, that Ionian rascal! Yes, I have heard that he has done well for you, and I rejoice in it. Perhaps that is what I should have done with him—turn him out of the house to make his own way. He is rich now, is he?"

"And has made me rich, Lord. You put me even deeper into your debt when you gave me that Ionian rascal."

The lord *turtanu* laughed and then, quite suddenly, his eyes grew serious.

"Tiglath, you should know that the king is convinced Arad Ninlil will never succeed him."

He paused for a moment, as if expecting me to speak. He searched my face—I know not what he saw there, but at last he continued.

"He is a weak, foolish boy whom his mother spoilt when she had the care of him, a great disappointment to his father. The omens are all against him, and there is a seer named Kalbi, son of Nergal Etir, who speaks of a reign of darkness over the land. The king dislikes all priests and has since they told him that our mighty father the Lord Sargon fell through his own impiety, for the king loved his father. But these warnings against Arad Ninlil frighten him."

"Is that why he has delayed the *marsarru*'s marriage to the Lady Esharhamat?"

"Yes—that is why."

For a moment the Lord Sinahiusur watched me through narrowed eyes, as if in warning, but he made no remark. He was a wise man and held many secrets within the walls of his skull, and I could not hope that my feelings for Esharhamat had escaped his notice. But perhaps he judged that the time was not ripe to speak of it.

"I myself favor the rightful succession in this matter," he went on. "After Arad Ninlil comes Esarhaddon, as the son of the king's second lawful wife. Do you concur with me in this?"

"Yes—of course." I could not keep the astonishment out of my voice, for why should the Lord Sinahiusur discuss this matter with me?

"Then know that it is the king's hope that you shall follow him on the throne of Ashur."

It was as if someone had clubbed me on the back of the head. I was struck dumb. The *turtanu* sat quietly, seeming to wait for some answer, but I had none.

"Have a sip of wine, Tiglath," he said finally, and with his own hand he brought the cup to my lips. "I wish to know what you will do."

"Do, Lord?"

"Yes, do. Would you fight your brother for the succession, boy?"

"Lord, I love my brother—if the god makes him king, I will serve him with my life."

"You know that whoever succeeds will marry the Lady Esharhamat, do you not?"

"I would not set myself against the god, Lord—not even for the Lady Esharhamat."

"You are a good lad, Tiglath Ashur," he said, and once more he put his hand upon my arm. "I did not think you would disappoint me."

"My lord, as I have said many times, I am in your debt."

"Yes—but it is well to remember that neither you nor I will settle this, nor even the king. This matter will rest with the god."

That night the Lord Sinahiusur was a guest in my house, and the next morning he set out again on the road to Nineveh, leaving me behind with a burdened heart. I did not wish to be king and I loved my brother, yet I loved Esharhamat more than life. I seemed marked out for misery. All this the Lord Sinahiusur understood, for he was a wise man.

"Remember," he said, as we made our farewell, "the king may live many years yet, and Arad Ninlil may yet succeed. Or Esarhaddon may die, or the god may speak against him. We do not know what time will bring in its wake, but for now the Lady Esharhamat is a widow and at her own disposal. The king will wait as long as he may before he puts this question to the god, and you have until then to be happy—that must be your reward, Tiglath. But I promise you that until the god speaks, no one will interfere. That must be enough to content you. Is it?"

"As you say, Lord, it must be."

"Yes—it must be."

"Lord?"

"Yes, Tiglath Ashur?"

"If my brother Esarhaddon is to succeed, then he should be brought home from the west. The king should know his son and, in any case, it would please my brother."

The *turtanu* looked about him for a moment, as if my house and farmyard reminded him of something, and then his eyes settled on my face and he nodded.

"You must give this estate of yours a name," he said. "A name such as befits the seat of a prince. I might suggest the name 'Three Lions,' that your exploit will be remembered forever."

"It shall be as you think best, Lord," I answered, hardly knowing if he mocked me or was in earnest.

"No, it shall be as you think best, Tiglath Ashur. I shall see that Esarhaddon is brought back, although I fancy it will make little difference. Good-bye, nephew. May you recover your strength quickly."

I watched him ride away, and the cold winter wind brought tears to my eyes. Or was it the wind? I knew not.

8

I had not been to see Esharhamat since my return from Three Lions, for during the days of my convalescence I had had little enough to do except to think and I had thought little enough about anything but her. If a man has time to think, his duty always becomes clear enough—he is only betrayed into weakness and sin when circumstances crowd around him. Viewed from a distance, my own sick fancy of love seemed ridiculous enough. I had allowed a childhood infatuation to loom too large in my memory, and my liver had become inflamed because of a foolish abstinence from women. I decided to be a sensible man and a loyal subject of my father and to resume my visits to the temple of Ishtar. I would renounce Esharhamat.

So I did not visit her garden where, in my fancy, she waited by the fountain, her fingertips drifting over the surface of the water as she dreamed of me. There is no limit to the vanity of youth, so while I suffered I took a kind of smug pleasure in the nobility of my sacrifice and the conviction that she must suffer more. I filled my days with drill and hard exercise, and after a time I began to sleep quietly enough. I would forget her presently, I told myself. I even began to believe it.

The illusion was strengthened by the return of my brother. Esarhaddon came back from the west with a black beard that reached to his collarbone and an Ammonite woman who wore a ring through her nose. He brought them both to my room in the officers' barrack, where he waited until a runner could bring me notice of his arrival My throat tightened when I saw him, and even after we had embraced we both could hardly speak. I had not understood how much I had missed him.

"Who is that?" I asked finally, pointing to the woman in the purple-and-white linen robe who was sitting on my bed as if she slept there every night, her arms tinkling with gold bangles as she ran her hands through her hair. I had never seen hair that particular color—it was black but seemed to glow from within with a reddish flame. She smiled at me as though she would have liked to break her fast with me.

"That?" Esarhaddon turned to look, quite as if he could not imagine to whom I was referring. "Oh, that! That, brother, is Leah, whom I won playing at lots with a tavernmaster in the city of Salecah—I think, personally, that he was not sorry to lose her on the account of the vexatiousness of his wife. Would you like to borrow her? She is not good for another thing in the wide world, but she can press the seed out of your loins like juice from a grape. Try her for a night—by the sixty great gods, the things that woman knows to do to a man! It is like having the whole temple of Ishtar all to oneself. Have you wine here, brother, or shall we have to go into the city to get drunk together?"

And drunk we did get—wildly, gloriously drunk. We held riot through the streets of Nineveh, turning over beer pots and tumbling tavern harlots as if we two were a conquering army and had taken the place by storm. We brought the woman Leah with us, Esarhaddon leading her about by a thin silver chain through the ring in her nose—the man who had put it there was wise, for although I could only understand one word in three of her heavily accented Aramaic, it was clear that in that tongue at least she was as fractious a creature as ever drew breath. Finally, out of simple curiosity and when I was drunk enough, I accepted Esarhaddon's oft-repeated invitation and took her aside into a wineshop storeroom and went into her, and never have I known a greedier woman. She would not be content and when I had spent myself she slipped her lips over my member, holding me tightly with her mouth until, faster than I would have thought possible, she had brought me back to full vigor. When I came away my groin ached like an old wound in the cold.

There was not more than an hour to dawn by the time we found our way back to the house of war, so we headed to the steam house to sweat ourselves sober. We sat upon the cedar benches mopping our limbs, and Leah, her fine linens stripped off and tied around her waist as if they were rags, tended the fire for us and poured water on the baking rocks. The sight of her made my head ache.

"How is it her hair is that color?" I asked, for it poured down her naked back and in the dull lantern light seemed almost ready to catch fire of itself.

Esarhaddon, who had not finished with his debauch and was busy breaking the seal on a final jar of Babylonian beer, looked up to see what I was talking about and then grinned and winked at me.

"She soaks it in wine six times in the month and spreads it out over the brim of a wide straw hat with no crown, letting it dry in the sun. Why? Did you think she was born like that? Brother, such women do everything by magic. The west is a land filled with wondrous things—I have been to Judah, where the holy men work such spells that they are more powerful than the kings. And you should see the Egyptian harlots in Damascus—someday I will conquer that land just so I can have my fill of them. But by the sixty great gods, Tiglath Ashur, son of Sennacherib, where within the four corners of the world did you collect all those gaudy scars?"

"I will tell you all my stories for a taste of that beer—my tongue feels as thick and dry as a clay tablet."

In the end I told him all my stories, everything that had happened since his departure for the west, including my conversation with the Lord Sinahiusur.

"Did you believe him, Tiglath?" he asked. For a man who had just been told he stood near to inheriting the mastery of the world, he did not seem greatly pleased. "I mean, do you really imagine it could be possible? One of us, the king?"

"Yes, I imagine it possible. After all, the god could carry a village plowman to the throne of Ashur if it suited his purposes. You and I are the sons of a king, and you by his lawful wife. If the omens are indeed unfavorable for Arad Ninlil—or if he should die —why not?"

I found myself watching Leah with nervous interest. Nothing I had been saying was actually treasonous, but it was not wise to speculate too openly about things touching the succession. She, however, was busy splashing her body from a bucket of cold water and seemed to regard our conversation with the indifference of total incomprehension.

"Calm yourself, brother. She does not understand one Akkadian word in five, and does not care. She is like a cat—if she can groom herself, stretch out in the sun with a full belly, and find a hot male to service her, she is happy. Her mind turns on nothing else. This one is no Naq'ia."

With the mention of his mother's name, Esarhaddon's face darkened.

"It would answer all her prayers, wouldn't it," he went on, his voice taking on a hard edge. "Then she would have the power she has dreamed of all her life."

"You would be king in this land, brother—not she. You could do what you liked with her, send her to some comfortable oblivion where she could content herself with ruling over her women. You are not hiding your face in her skirt now."

"Am I not? You think not?" He laughed, throwing back his head, but it was a bitter sound. "I have not seen her in years, Tiglath, but still I feel her fingers around my neck. No—even as king I would never be strong enough to stand up to her.

"Besides, I do not even want to be king." He stood up and shook himself, making the sweat dance from his body like rain. "You can be king with my blessing. You are the clever one—you would do very well as king. For myself, I am a soldier, not an intriguer."

"But you will have Naq'ia, and she is intriguer enough for the pair of you."

"By Adad's thunder, you speak truth, Tiglath Ashur—but would you want that breasted jackal setting the destiny of the world? No, no more I!"

And then he laughed again, and the cloud lifted from him. We finished the beer and broke the jug against the steam-house wall, and we were gay and carefree once more.

"I have it, brother!" he roared, his arm over my shoulder as naked we walked back to the officer's barrack, Leah carrying our clothes and lighting the way for us with a lamp, for it was still short of dawn. "If I am king, you shall be my *turtanu,* and if you are king you can spend all your royal vigor on the Lady Esharhamat and I shall be master of your house of women—hah, hah, hah!"

* * *

The temple of Ishtar saw a great deal of me in those days. In keeping with my resolution, I wore myself out on the cult priestesses, and on those evenings when I was not paying my devotions to the goddess I was carousing through the city with Esarhaddon, drinking wine until my head throbbed and rutting on tavern harlots. Wherever we went Esarhaddon brought Leah along, leading her by the silver chain that ran through her nose ring—he even took her with him when he visited the sleeping mats of other women, since during his time in the west he had developed a taste for taking his pleasure thus. He once said it was his ambition to buy a pair of identical twins to keep as concubines. "Two women as alike as a pair of hands," he would say. "I wouldn't wish to be able to tell one from the other, like one woman with two bodies— I might even give them both the same name. That would be luxury!" And while he spoke thus, sitting on a bench in the steam house with a cold cloth and a pot of beer, Leah, as silent and practiced as a dairymaid, would kneel between his feet and milk him dry.

And thus the moon dwindled to a sliver and grew fat again as I spent the days in preparation for war and my nights in debauchery. But if I thought that thus occupied with drill and whoring I had escaped from Esharhamat, I was greatly mistaken. I could stumble back to my quarters within two hours of dawn, my brain numb and my manhood wrung out and shriveled like a date husk after pressing, yet I had only to lie down upon my pallet and close my eyes and her unbidden memory would flood into my mind. I had learned how little this torment of love has to do with the body, but I had learned nothing else—nothing that would allow me to find an instant's peace.

And so when the hour came, as I had known it would, that I returned from the parade ground to find an enclosed carrying chair waiting for me beside the entrance to the officers' barrack, I knew that within would be one of Esharhamat's women, shrouded in veils and secrecy. I had only to push the curtain aside and a narrow hand emerged to press into mine a wooden tablet no wider than the span of a lady's fingers and coated on one side with wax. Scratched into the wax was Esharhamat's message: "Why do you never come now? How am I to endure life if my eyes never see your face? Come, or I shall perish of grief that my ghost may haunt you in the darkness. Come, or I shall know you love me not."

Even as I stood staring at the words, there was a knock from within the curtained chair and the bearers scrambled to their feet. There was no need to wait for an answer, for Esharhamat must have known she had won. I went to my room and threw the wooden tablet onto the brazier, and as I listened to the wax hiss as it burned I realized that what I felt most deeply was relief. I would see her again. I could surrender now to what I had always known would be my undoing. I must love Esharhamat while I lived.

The next morning I dismissed my soldiers to a day of rest, put on my best uniform, and walked through the gateway across the dusty patch of ground that divided the house of war from the palace where dwelt my father the king and all the members of his household. All this time, nothing had separated me from her but a few mud-brick walls.

When I was shown into her garden I saw her sitting beside the fountain, dressed as she had been that first morning outside the Great Gate, in the costume of mourning with the red widow's shawl covering her hair. I stood before her and she looked up into my face, and her brilliant black eyes were wet with tears.

"I seem always to be weeping for you, Tiglath," she said, burying her glance in the stone floor at her feet. "For your danger or your unkindness—it is the same, since it seems I must lose you to one or the other."

"Is that why you are in mourning?" I asked. I could not help but smile, since the device was so transparent.

"Have you not made my heart a widow, Tiglath?"

I took my place beside her, but though I was close enough that my arm touched hers she would not look at me again. I covered her hand with mine, but she drew it away. It seemed I was in deep disgrace.

And while she pouted thus, and I struggled with myself to find some word to speak to her, I looked about me and saw with no little shock of surprise that we were completely alone. It had never happened before that Esharhamat had received me without some two or three of her women in discreet attendance at the opposite side of the garden, chattering among themselves like monkeys. It could only be that their mistress had made a point of sending them away.

"I hear you spend almost all your evenings with the harlots at the temple of Ishtar," she said at last. "And when you are not with them, you crawl through the wineshops and brothels with Esarhaddon. I hear the two of you keep your own courtesan, whom you lead about on a leash."

"And who speaks to you of such things, Esharhamat?"

"No one—everyone. It is the common gossip of the palace. I listen as to a thing indifferent, the doings of a stranger."

"Then you have grown indifferent to me?"

I made so bold as to put my arm about her waist and for an instant—merely an instant—she seemed to pull away from me, but then I had no difficulty drawing her into my embrace. We were playing a game, only that. I think we both understood clearly enough who was surrendering to whom.

"Oh, Tiglath," she said, burying her face in my chest, "is the company of these women so much more to your liking than is mine? Do they give you such pleasure then that you would desert me utterly? Oh, Tiglath, how unhappy you make me!"

She wept miserably, shaking in my arms as if the falling sickness were upon her. It was one of the most joyful moments of my life.

At last, when her tears had dried against my tunic, she seemed to rest, holding my free hand in her lap with both of hers. She was quiet, and I could hear her breathing deeply as if in sleep. My bowels were melting in tenderness—what would I not have done or suffered for her sake then? The shawl had slipped down from her head and with my lips I could find the part of her shining hair, black as the waters of death.

"You must not take pleasure with other women," she whispered, almost as one speaking in a dream. "Whatever you would have from them I can give you. You see, Tiglath? I am grown myself into a woman, and I think you would find me fair."

With a quick movement she reached up and undid one of the clasps of her tunic. Then she took my hand and slid it inside so that it rested over her breast, which was firm and tight, and I could feel her heart beating just beneath. The flesh was as smooth as alabaster, and the nipple pressed against my palm with an urgency of its own. When I let my hand slide across it she moaned softly and raised her face to look at me and my lips found hers and kissed them hungrily, for I was stirred to the soul.

"I would spill the blood of my maidenhead for you, Tiglath.

I would do it now if you wished it. I belong to you—my heart and my body are yours, now and always."

Her quick little tongue darted into my mouth and felt nervously along the tip of mine. Her breathing was quick and hot. She meant everything that she said, for her hands carried the same message and they glided up my thighs and cupped around my member, hard as bronze.

Desire closed off my voice and clouded over my eyes. Where had she learned such arts, I wondered in my choking passion. Or perhaps these are things the knowledge of which women have as a birthright. Not even the most skillful of harlots had ever aroused such longing in me.

She undid a second clasp on her tunic and it fell away, sliding down her arms, leaving her exposed from shoulder to navel. Her skin was a pale pink, for she blushed even to her breasts at her own boldness. My hands covered them, as if I would protect her modesty, and I kissed her throat, letting my lips drift down and down. . . .

"This will not do," I said—I found I had just voice enough for that. I lifted her tunic back up to cover her shoulders, wanting her more than ever now. "This is madness, Esharhamat, my love, my—"

"Oh, damn you!" she screamed, and the hot tears started in her eyes. "Damn you, Tiglath, you coward—how dare you speak to me of your love!"

Her little sandaled feet kicked at my shins as if they were a door she meant to break down, and when that did not satisfy her fury she went for my face with her nails and would have raked her claws across my eyes had I not held her back. I took her in my arms and held her to me, pinning her arms so that she could not move—she even tried to bite me, such was her rage.

But at last she was quiet once more. When I was sure I touched her cheek with my lips, but she did not struggle. But if she was overmatched in strength, that was all—and she understood enough to use only weapons of her own choice.

"I would have risked all for you," she whispered tensely, her mouth almost against my ear. "Everything, for just one moment of your love. And you have not even courage enough to push your way in between my legs. Let me go, Tiglath, for I will not hurt you."

Nothing, not the sharpest sword, has the cutting edge of a

woman's scorn. I released her, feeling as if my bowels had been torn away. I would have preferred anything, even to the meanest death, to the cold contempt I saw in her eyes.

"Think what you like," I said, my voice thick, "except that I do not love you."

"Oh, I know you love me, Tiglath—after your fashion."

There seemed no word I could speak that would not make me look a bigger fool, so I turned to go. Esharhamat's garden was no more than twenty paces across, but on that morning it seemed a limitless desert.

"Tiglath!"

I looked back in time to see her push the tunic from her shoulders so that it slid caressingly down her body to leave her naked, the red linen gathered about her feet like a pool of blood. Yes—she had not lied. She had grown to a woman and I found her fair.

"You have eyes at least—use them! And come back to me when your love is strong enough to allow you to take what you want."

For a long moment we stood there like idols of stone. I know not what was in her heart, but for myself I did not understand how I could bear ever to lose the sight of her. But at last, when I could bring myself to look away, I turned once more to go, for there was still no word upon my lips. Surely now, I thought, surely we will now be parted forever.

"Tiglath!"

Even with my back to her, I could hear the quick sound of her sandals against the flagstones. As I turned, she threw herself into my arms and as I lifted her up she wrapped her bare legs around my waist, burying her face in my neck as if she clung to me out of love for her life. And then her hungry mouth covered my face with kisses.

"Only come back to me, Tiglath—my love, my god! I would die if you stayed away."

I was half mad with that mixture of tenderness and lust that can make a man believe the world begins and ends in one beloved body. I knelt there in Esharhamat's garden, her legs still tight about me, as she arched her back and let my lips wander over her breasts. Her little mat of black hair was pressed tight against my belly—I could hear her breath catch each time she moved and the sweet smell of her flesh filled my nostrils. Yes, she had spoken no more than the truth. There could be no price too high for this one moment of passion.

"No—you are right. This is not how it should be."

She pushed herself away, as if struggling against us both, but even as we kneeled together there under Ashur's bright sun I could not keep my arms from her.

"Let me get my tunic," she said in a level voice—all the violence of rapture seemed drained from her. "I begin to feel foolish this way."

When she had covered herself she came back to me and took my hand. Nothing in her look or manner betrayed what had happened between us.

"Come to me again in a few days. By then perhaps I will have thought of something."

She smiled at me, her smile filled with a sense of foreboding. Yes, let the god help all men, for they are but lots held in a woman's hand.

"What is there to think of, Esharhamat? We love each other, but this thing cannot be."

"Can't it?" Her eyes flashed in something like anger. "It can —it must! The god has given us to each other. I feel this in the marrow of my bones. If he has let us find love he will find us a way to happiness. I will not allow myself to be so helpless. I . . . Trust me, Tiglath. You have not a woman's cunning."

A woman's cunning—that was what she called it. Yes, the cunning that is blind to all which it does not wish to look upon. This bright little bird, consumed by the sightless passion of springtime, her heart hammers her breast as she sails on the storm-dark wind, hurrying to build her nest in the brittle, naked branches, stealing straw from everywhere, and she cannot see that the tree is already dead.

And this she called a woman's cunning.

9

As the fates would have it, I did not see Esharamat again for many months. The next morning, even before the sun rose, I found a messenger standing in the doorway of my quarters; he handed me a tablet bearing the king's own seal which commanded me into the royal presence without delay. I had time only to splash a little water in my face and put on my uniform before the messenger and I set out for the palace at a dead run. But we needn't have hurried so—I was left to wait in an outer room, pondering how much the king might know of my offenses and how he would choose to avenge himself.

When the door to the king's sleeping chamber did open, it was not my father or even one of his pages who came out to meet me but the Lady Shaditu, wearing only a thin linen robe that caught the light from behind to show the outline of her body as clearly as if she had been naked. The look on my face only made her smile.

"I have been about my duty. He is pleased that I should help him bathe," she said, not even bothering to hold the robe closed in front as she shrugged her thin shoulders. "He is old—what can he do except look?

"Now, if it were you, Tiglath, brother . . ."

She came near me, put her arms around my neck, and kissed me most wantonly on the mouth.

"Now in Elam," she whispered hoarsely, "in Elam it is a mark of high favor when a royal prince beds with his sister. It means he will—"

But of late I had had quite enough of women who threw

themselves at me and I pushed her roughly away, so roughly that she stumbled and fell to the brick floor.

"We are not in Elam, Lady."

But she merely leaned back on her white arms and giggled like a drunken harlot.

"I could have you impaled upon a stake for that," she said, quite as if it were a matter of no importance—she made no attempt to rise. "You must enjoy putting your life at risk, brother. Either that, or you are wiser than you seem and know that women find a little brutality exciting. Come and help me up, then you may kiss me yet once more."

When I did not move, she found her feet alone.

"Another time will serve as well."

"Come in, Tiglath, my boy—been getting acquainted, eh?"

It was the king. His head was covered with a cloth as he stuck his head out the door. He motioned to me with his arm.

"Come in, come in, my son—now run along, pet, for we two have men's affairs to speak of."

He smiled at Shaditu quite as if she had been a child, and with a glance at me that mocked all men she left the room on her bare feet. The instant she was gone the king seemed to forget her existence. He put his arm over my shoulder and I walked with him into his private apartments.

"I have news that will make you very happy, Tiglath Ashur, Son of Sennacherib, King of Kings. You see, we have this little difficulty in the north . . ."

I was to lead a punitive expedition against a tribe of barbarians who had come down from the eastern mountains and had the effrontery to raise their tent poles within sight of the northern reaches of the Tigris River. The farmers in that area had sent a messenger to Nineveh complaining that their villages were being raided and their women and livestock carried off, and so the king, so he told me, felt that this would be a good chance for me to test my new infantry tactic. I was to leave at once. On three hours' notice my men were to be ready to march. There was no time even to send a message.

And though it tore at my liver to be away from Esharhamat, I could not disguise to myself the fact that mixed with my sorrow was a certain measure of relief, as if I had escaped, at least for the moment, more than one dangerous entanglement.

Besides, I was an officer with his first independent command

—I had three companies of foot soldiers under me and a detachment of cavalry. I did not relish the prospect of another encounter with my all-too-loving sister, and Esharhamat's love was a trap that always stood waiting for me. I could ruin both our lives just as easily one time as another.

After the first day's march we camped almost within sight of Three Lions, but I did not ride over to see my mother. It would not have made a favorable impression on my men had I done so, but I cannot claim duty as my principal reason for staying away. I was quite honestly afraid to look Merope in the face, for she would be certain to ask about Esharhamat and I had no confidence in my talents as a liar.

We were six days reaching the place where the river bent in toward the Taurus Mountains like a drawn bowstring. There was still almost a finger's depth of snow on the ground, but I had no difficulty in finding the traces of my nomad adversaries—I had only to look about me at the burned villages, and to smell the rotting corpses of men and animals, to know they were close at hand.

"Such pointless butchery," I thought to myself, "as if they were boys pulling the wings from flies because they can find no other sport. These are not a people who will stand and fight like soldiers—one glimpse of an army in the field and they will run back to their mountains like deer. I have made this journey for nothing." My heart was black with anger.

But I needn't have worried, for the Uqukadi, although they were savages, were not cowards. The Uqukadi—that was what they called themselves, though doubtless now they have disappeared from the earth or been swallowed up by other peoples; in those times nothing was more ephemeral than the tribal groupings of the mountain nations.

I had no sooner made camp than their delegation was at my tent, come to parley on such insulting terms that it was almost an open challenge to battle.

There were three of them, all of middle years with chocks of gray in their beards, although they seemed to rank themselves by age, and all dressed in the blue tunics and black vests that appeared to be the costume of men of substance among them. But the resemblance went no further. The varieties of human nature are the same among all races, and their leader, a heavy, slow-moving man given to smiling at nothing, I could have met in

Babylon or in Ethiopia, where the tribal elders tie bones into their hair and live in huts made of grass.

The next in precedence was clearly the fire-eater among them, a tall man with a strong face—I noticed that he carried a scar that ran on the left side from his hairline almost to his chin—and fierce black eyes that seemed to pop slightly out of their sockets. I decided then and there that if I should ever take this one in battle I would have his head on a stake before sunset, for he was the sort who by instinct seeks power and, when he has it, causes no end of vexation to his own people and all their neighbors.

The last—and I have often wondered what quirk of social ordering could have raised this one to the eminence of treating of war and peace even for a tribe of mountain bandits—was small and narrow-shouldered and, I gathered, almost an idiot. He never spoke, but nodded vigorously whenever either of the others did—sometimes even when I did. Or perhaps he was not so weak in the head after all, since he was the only one of the three who had sense enough to be frightened. Throughout our brief interview he seemed on the verge of running away like a deer who has seen a snake.

I met them sitting behind a small table in my tent. I did not rise when they entered, nor did I open my lips. I thought it well for them to understand that an officer in command of the soldiers of Ashur does not stand upon forms of courtesy with ragged nomadic raiders who count their wealth in goats. For perhaps as long as two minutes, therefore, the four of us waited in tense silence.

"I wonder what the great king in Nineveh is thinking of that he sets a boy to lead his troops," said the eldest at last, in reasonably fluent Aramaic—the idiot's head bobbed up and down several times in agreement, all the time staring at me with eyes that pleaded like a whipped dog's.

"Perhaps he felt that a boy, as you choose to style me, was all that was required."

I forced myself to grin at him, as unpleasantly as I could manage. Already then I realized we were only probing for weakness—if I did not take their heads back with me to the king, they would probably find some slave to cut my throat as I slept. There was no way this would end except in blood.

"The king in Nineveh is merciful," I went on, still showing

them my teeth. "If you go now, leaving behind your swords, your women, and your livestock, he will allow you to crawl back to your mountains, there to starve to death in your own good time. If you do not, I will take these things from you and you will die here."

"You, boy?"

The one with the fierce eyes took half a step forward, as if prepared to run me through for my insolence. But he would not and we both knew it, so I did not trouble to move.

"Yes, I—Tiglath Ashur, who stood against the Elamites at Khalule and have killed better men than you or any of your tribe, even though any man of Ashur could crush a maggot under his heel and claim as much. Have you come to beg the king's pardon? Have you gathered up your cooking pots?"

"The land here is fertile." The heavy one smiled. It meant nothing; it was as unconscious with him as sweating. "We might choose to stay, on terms. We are a mighty people, and the king in Nineveh might welcome us as allies. . . ."

"The king, who is king here as well as in Nineveh, welcomes you as nothing except food for the crows. Do not speak to me of terms—you have heard his terms. The Land of Ashur can be nothing to you except a place to lay down your bones, so pay your tribute and depart."

I had let my anger rise but not my voice. I must not be a boy now. I must not dishonor land and king by losing my temper in front of wandering thieves who knew no king and thought of land as simply a thing to pick loose from their horses' hoofs. But I was angry. I was angry because I was afraid, and that because I had seen their cooking fires spread out across the plain like flowers after the spring rain. I had come here with less than four hundred men and, judging from the size of their encampment, they could probably field near to a thousand. I was not wrong to be afraid, but I spoke now with my father's voice.

"And if we choose not to depart? What will your king do then, mighty warrior?"

Their mighty warrior grinned back at me, the scar in his face crinkling like old leather.

"Then he will visit upon you death and the miseries of slavery, so that death will seem a blessing to those who survive."

"You threaten eloquently, hero."

"More to the point, I do not threaten idly."

All at once we seemed to have nothing more to say to one another. After a sullen silence lasting perhaps a quarter of a minute I summoned the guard who was stationed outside the tent entrance.

"Yes, Prince?"

My two principal inquisitors exchanged a glance, the heavy one raising his eyebrows in surprise, but this was not the time for formal introductions, so I gave them no notice.

"Provide our guests with safe passage back to their own lines —doubtless they will welcome the chance to kiss their wives and children one last time."

I stood at the edge of the camp with my *ekalli*, who had fought with me at Khalule, watching the three emissaries ride away over the empty plain until even the dust raised by their horses' hoofs had disappeared, and all the time I kept thinking that by this time tomorrow the same earth would be covered with dead and dying men. We turned to each other and he shrugged his shoulders, as if to say, *well, that, at least, is done.*

"They are many," he said, gesturing with his arm toward the horizon as if the Uqukadi were as numerous as a horde of locusts. "And I hear tell the Uqukadi are not cowards either. We will have our bread to earn tomorrow, Prince."

"Let them be beyond counting and each as brave as a lion, but when the time comes each will fight for himself alone. A rabble is never any match for a disciplined army, Lushakin. Never fear—we came here to conquer, not to perish."

I went back to my tent. The day was dying and I wanted to be alone.

In my first great battle I fought as a common soldier, and in my second as sole commander. I must say that my second night before a day of death and suffering was even harder, if such a thing is possible, than the first. I knew that if we lost tomorrow, my corpse would surely be among those left to rot in the sun, but what plagued me was the thought of all the others who would lie around me, whom I would have led to destruction. To die is terrible enough, but to fail . . . If it should fall out that way, then I would count it a blessing that I had found my *simtu* here in the land that bore me.

I did not so much as try to sleep that night. There was no Nargi Adad this time to pour strong Babylonian beer down my throat, so I was defenseless prey to my own thoughts and did not

even trouble to lie down. All night I fought the coming battle over
and over again in my mind, trying to see everything from the
enemy's angle of vision that I might find that spot where my
tactics could be defeated. And all around me slept men who
would never sleep again save in the arms of death. Those hours
were not pleasant for me, and I both feared and hoped that the
dawn would never come.

But it did come. The sun, great Sahur's burning disk, broke
out over the eastern mountains to drive away the mist from the
cold, snow-patched ground, and all around me the camp stirred
into life. I could hear the clink of metal upon metal and the
muffled sound of many low voices even before I left my tent. Men
huddled around cooking fires as they finished their breakfast or,
like good workmen, made ready their tools against the day's toil. I
have heard generals say that they despised their men, but I have
never understood such words, for soldiers, for the most part, are
brave and unpretentious souls with all the simple, straightforward
virtues of humble people who must work and struggle to live. I
loved my men that morning. Even though many or perhaps most
of them were older than I, I loved them with a father's love and
my heart sorrowed for all that they must suffer in the hours
ahead.

My plan was very simple. Two companies of infantry, in
diamond-shaped formations that they could defend themselves
from attack from every side, would march on the enemy camp.
The Uqukadi would attack them with their full force—at least
such was my hope—for if they did not stop us on open ground,
away from their tents, their livestock, and their families, they
would lose all. When the battle was fully joined I would commit
the remaining company of infantry and also my one contingent of
cavalry, these from opposite sides, from the left and from the
right, that they might flank the enemy and harry him from many
directions at once. It was not a plan displaying much strategic
genius. I was not depending on genius. My hopes were pinned on
the new iron spears, that they would stop the Uqukadi horsemen,
that what had seemed to work on the parade ground at Nineveh
would work here, and on the discipline and bravery of my men.

I had drilled these men until they cursed my name, until
their wives and children cursed me. I could only hope now that it
had been enough. We had all fought together before, and I knew
them as soldiers and trusted them. If we failed, the blame would

lie with their commander, not with them. I would have it all to myself.

I went back to my tent to fetch my javelin. I would not fight beside them this time, so I would not need it, but I felt better for holding it in my hand.

As the sun mounted, turning the pink sky white, the companies gathered in battle ranks and my officers came to me for their final orders. We spoke in murmurs among ourselves and then I stood up on the tongue of a supply wagon to address the soldiers. My heart seemed lodged in my throat like an apple swallowed whole.

"You all know what is expected of you," I shouted—there was a low wind that seemed to carry my voice away into nothing. "I will not tell you to fight with courage, for you will do that without any orders from me. But I will tell you to fight with care. They are many and we are few, but they will fight like a mob where we will fight like what we are, the army of Ashur—disciplined, moving and thinking as one man. This battle depends not on any one of us, but on us all. So keep ranks, and tonight it will not be *our* bodies strewn over the fields like fallen leaves. Good hunting!"

I do not know if it was what they wanted to hear, but they cheered me anyway, after the fashion of soldiers. I only know it was not what was in my belly to say, but I could never have said that. I would not have known where to find the words.

It is a strange thing to watch at a distance as the battle you have set in motion unfolds. Strange, and uncomfortable. Men whose names I knew, whose children I had seen playing in the street, were so small and far away that I could not tell one from another. It was all so abstract, like a game of war played on a checkered board with soldiers carved from wood, and yet on this hung so much—my life, the lives of my men; perhaps, someday, even the fate of Ashur's empire. I sat upon a camp stool on a bluff overlooking the field, surrounded by a few officers and the dozen or so runners who would carry my orders to the men below, and I cursed this life I had chosen for myself as I learned what every commander learns soon enough, that the power over life and death does not rest well on the shoulders of mere mortals.

The two diamond-shaped formations trudged across the plain of crushed and yellow grass. I could see the dust raised by their sandals, but at first they hardly seemed to move at all. Their iron spears were invisible to my eye. I watched them as the enemy watched them and tried to imagine how they must look to them. They had crossed almost to the middle of the field before the first Uqukadi horsemen showed themselves, their swords flashing in the sunlight.

The men did well—many a horse pitched over on its side like a pig slipping on ice. They did not waste their arrows, my bowmen, but waited until they could be sure. The Uqukadi had a sea of cavalry, but I doubt if more than half their riders lived even to come near our lines. And those who did had a nasty surprise waiting for them as the bristling iron spears dropped into place. Horses reared in panic at the sight of them, trampling the men they had carried or leaving them behind to die with a javelin between their shoulder blades.

It was working.

Once, twice, three times the infantry raised their spears and ran forward, never breaking formation, then dropped the spears again so that the archers and throwers within could rain down death upon the enemy. I saw a few uniformed bodies lying on the ground, but not many. And the Uqukadi—those who lived—were baffled. Their cavalry was almost useless to them, adding only to the growing numbers of their dead. The plan was working.

"Send in the third company."

"And the cavalry, Prince?"

"No—hold them back. When the time comes, they will make the final assault. They are not needed now."

Suddenly there was nothing left for me to do but watch the ensuing carnage.

By midday, all was over. Those enemy horsemen who could, fled. Those who could not, and would not surrender, were cut down. It was hardly an hour after noon when I mounted my horse and rode into the midst of the Uqukadi encampment.

A few dogs barked, but there was no other sound. I saw no one, but that did not mean they were not there. Women and children and men who had been brave all their lives cowered inside the tents, watching me as I looked about me at the chaos of wrecked cooking fires and abandoned weapons. They knew what awaited a beaten enemy, yet none dared raise a hand against me or any of my soldiers.

"Round them up," I said, leaning over my horse's neck to speak to Lushakin, who looked about him in astonishment—it seemed almost too easy. "Herd them together like cattle. Kill any who resist. Guard them, but do not make a great point of it; we do not want to seem to be afraid of beaten men. Let them wait for a while. Let them have time to wonder what we plan to do with them. Collect their horses, then feed our troops and allow them to rest. They have earned it. But maintain tight discipline—let there be no looting. I will deal with our prisoners after I have eaten."

In the twelfth hour of the day, as the sun began to turn to blood, I rode out to the barren spot where what was left of the Uqukadi huddled in a great circle, packed together like dates in a jug. As I approached, the whole multitude dropped to their knees and pressed their faces into the dirt, for their hour of judgment was upon them and they were filled with fear. I let them wait as I kept my mount, my horse snorting and scratching at the earth with its hoofs as if even a dumb beast could sense what must now come.

There might have been near to two thousand souls there, waiting for me to speak the words that for them would mean life or death. Most of them seemed to be women. Their men were either carrion or had fled—I would guess that something like seven hundred of the Uqukadi warriors had fallen that day, leaving their women and children and the old men to pay the price for their pointless courage.

"Stand up! Hear my sentence."

They rose from their knees, these people, their faces gray and defeated, their eyes on the ground. The women gathered their children behind their full skirts that I might not see them. The men looked as if they could already feel the sword across their necks.

"I want your leaders, your great men—all of them. I want them here at my feet within the tenth part of an hour, or I will burn your bodies with fire and your children will die in chains. You will turn them over to me yourselves, and your time is slipping away!"

They did not make me wait long. Within minutes, twenty men in the blue tunics and black vests that were the badges of their eminence had been forced to the front, cast out from the circle of their followers who wanted only to avoid the full weight of dread Ashur's vengeance. They fell on their faces before me, although they must have guessed that nothing could save their lives. In an instant my soldiers were standing around them, their swords drawn.

"You and you!" I shouted to two men from my old company. "Run into the dog kennel these people call a camp and find an ax and something we can use for a chopping block. Be quick about it —it is impolite to keep such distinguished persons waiting."

My men laughed, but our prisoners must not have found the situation nearly so amusing. Finally, when they understood that they were as good as dead, the elders among the Uqukadi rose to their feet. Among them I recognized none but the seeming idiot who had come to my tent to parley and had never opened his lips. I pointed to him, calling him forward.

"Where are the other two?" I asked. For a moment he looked confused, as if he could not understand me, and then he lowered his eyes again.

"Gone, Mighty Prince," he said—so it seemed that at last he had found his voice. "One of them is fled and the other lies yonder."

He made a gesture toward the battlefield, where the crows were already busy. I did not have to ask myself which was which —I wondered how far into the mountains the heavy one with the empty smile could have ridden by this time.

"Good. And for that piece of information I give you back your life. Go join your people."

His knees nearly buckled under him and he made a move that might have ended in his kissing my foot had I not backed my horse away a pace or two. I was not being generous, no more than when I had allowed the Uqukadi to turn in their own leaders to me for punishment. This one was probably a coward but not, I guessed, quite the fool he appeared. Let him lead his tribe, that they might not pick a stronger man. After the betrayals of today, no chief among them would ever trust the loyalty of these people again, and they would know it. A nation stripped of its illusions about itself will never be strong a second time.

By then the soldiers had returned with a fine broad two-headed ax and a square block of wood someone might have used as a stool. They looked very pleased with themselves.

"Bring us one of the cooks' helpers," I told them. "This is butcher's work."

For a quarter of an hour the air stank with blood. Each man laid his head upon the block, putting his cheek in the clotted gore of his predecessors, and the cooks' helper, a great hairy bulk of a fellow who worked stripped to his loincloth that he might not bloody his clothes, took off their heads as neatly as if he had been cutting turnips for a stew and then, even before its head had rolled to the ground, kicked the twitching corpse aside to make room for the next. I stayed on my horse, though the smell of death made him skittish, and the Uqukadi watched in silent horror—I understood precisely how they must have felt.

When it was over, the cooks' helper gathered up the severed heads and put them in a large leather bag. We would send them to the king, who would rejoice.

"Do not mourn for these," I told the Uqukadi, gesturing down toward the headless trunks that lay at my feet, a few of them still jerking in their limbs like wooden puppets. "They led you to ruin, and I have done you a kindness to rid you of them. Now I will tell you of the terms under which the great king of this land allows you to keep your own wretched lives—no, you will not die here and now, although you deserve it. Let the women stand separate from the men, but let them keep their children with them. Move. Now!"

They did as they were told—they were too cowed to do anything else. In hardly more than a moment they stood in two masses, the women to the left and the men to the right. I called Lushakin to me.

"Take thirty men," I said. "Go through the women and sort out any who speak Akkadian—these will be the wives of farmers hereabouts and must be returned. For the rest, take the young ones between ten years and twenty, provided they have no children, up to the number of one in five."

Lushakin nodded. It was work to his taste. It was quickly done, and the people did not even weep. They were long since past weeping.

"I have taken from you the flower of your young women," I told them. "Your virgins and young wives—I do not interfere between mother and child, but I will have the rest. They will be slaves in the land of Ashur and die there, their hair gray, in the houses of their masters. They are lost to you forever. I will also have from you your horses and half your goats and cattle. Look about you, mighty Uqukadi, and see your dead warriors. Think of the hardships that await you in the months ahead while you struggle to live in the barren mountains. Remember the faces of your women, whom you will never see again, and rejoice in your misery that the breath is still under your ribs. The mighty king of Ashur has let you live this once—remember that as well, and tempt not his wrath a second time.

"Go now, and if the third sunrise finds you on this sacred soil I will slaughter all of you, down to the sucking babes. The king deals mercifully with you now, for you are no more than ignorant savages and do not understand the customs of great nations, but there will be no mercy should you ever return. So depart now. Go!"

While the light held, I set the men to collecting our dead that we might bury them with offerings of food and wine. That night we could see the light from the Uqukadi campfires as they gathered up their possessions and prepared for the long trek back to their mountain home. The best of their men had died in battle, and they had lost their young women, their goods, and their belief in themselves. They could not survive as a nation but would vanish, absorbed by other tribes. They would never threaten the land of Ashur again.

"You did not put them all to the sword," Lushakin said, in a voice that told me he found weakness in what I had done. "Your father the king will not be pleased."

"They will not return. Let them spread the word among the tribes how death and privation wait on the plains of Ashur. The king will be pleased enough."

I wrote a letter to Nineveh that very night.

"To the king my lord, your servant Tiglath Ashur. May it be well with you the king my lord. May Ashur and Shamash be gracious to the king my lord. My lord has won a victory here today—the Uqukadi are as a shadow that sweeps across the land and is gone forever. I send you the heads of their great men, and the plain is strewn with the corpses of their warriors. I have shown mercy in your name that none may say the soldiers of Ashur are cruel through fear. . . ."

I dispatched the messenger at first light. Now I would wait for the king's sentence on me.

For the next several days we waited. I sent out riders to make sure the barbarians really did depart the land. The men rested and rejoiced in the ease of their victory, for we had lost hardly one man in twenty. To keep them busy I ordered a stockade built where we kept the women captives, roped together by the neck.

They were not molested, for the armies of Ashur do not rape and pillage—these are not permitted because they corrupt discipline—but the Akkadian women we had freed from bondage were not so eager to return to their farmer husbands that my men lacked for entertainment. Each night the camp was filled with the sounds of laughter and singing. Each night I slept alone, remembering the sight of Esharhamat's naked body.

We were in the north for three weeks. Word of a great victory over the Uqukadi spread through the countryside and men came to our camp seeking what the marauders had taken from them. I divided cattle and goats as seemed just to me—the horses we would keep against the campaign soon to be waged in the south—and husbands led their wives and daughters from among us, so that day by day the noise of the soldiers' reveling grew quieter. At last there were only ten or twelve peasant women left, a few whom none wanted and more whose men had been killed before their eyes when they were taken captive. To each of these I gave a dowry of livestock and silver from my own pouch, and some married soldiers who had taken their fancy—these would follow us to the south; such women are always of use in an army. The rest simply melted away to try their fortunes elsewhere. The Uqukadi women would have to await the king's pleasure.

At last a rider came, carrying messages and new orders from Nineveh. I took the tablet he handed me, wrapped in leather and sealed with the king's own seal, and retired to my tent, wondering if I was being summoned home in disgrace. I need not have worried.

"To the Lord Tiglath Ashur, mighty prince, beloved son of your father the king, may it be well with you. The heads of your enemies I have ordered spiked outside the Great Gate that the people may know of your glory and the strength of your arms. You have dealt wisely. May the mountain peoples' eyes swell with terror when they hear your name, for a noble enemy is feared more than a cruel one.

"When this reaches you the armies of Ashur will already be on the road south. Proceed quickly by forced march that you may join us where we camp on the Lesser Zab. Give your men no rest, for your father will need your might and your wise counsel and his old eyes hunger for the sight of you. This year you will fight as a *rab abru*, and this no less than your due. Keep the booty of your

victory for your own uses, learning to take pleasure in the tricks
of barbaric women. Come to us quickly."

I was saved, even promoted two levels, for it seemed I had
skipped over the rank of *mu'irru* altogether. Now I would have
under my command not a hundred men but a wing of the king's
army. But what was I to do—and how was I to proceed by forced
march—with more than a hundred female slaves squalling at my
heels?

For every difficulty there is an answer, and finally it hit me
that I should write to Kephalos. Let him bring an escort and let
him take the slaves to market in Nineveh. It was a piece of business he would relish.

I issued orders, and by first light our men were ready to
move. That the women might not slow us down too much, I
bought farm carts at the first village we came to and loaded half of
them aboard that they all could walk and ride in shifts. They were
nomads and therefore good walkers, and for three weeks they had
been locked away in the stockade we had built to contain them.
They seemed to be glad to be on the move and began flirting with
the soldiers assigned to guard them in so outrageous a manner
that I was forced to have a few of them whipped for the sake of
good order.

On the fifth day I met Kephalos on the road two *beru* north
of Nineveh, and his eyes lit up when I led him around to examine
my booty where they rested in the shade of the wagons. The
women hissed at him like geese, jeering and showing off their
bellies to taunt him, but my brave servant was undismayed.

"Master, you have done such a stroke of work here," he
exclaimed, digging his fingers into his heavy brown beard in an
ecstasy of greed. "Look at them—almost children and wild as
animals! Mountain women are notoriously passionate and make
fine whores. I know brothel keepers who will offer—"

"You will not sell them to be harlots, Master Physician—you
will sell them to private persons who wish concubines or house
servants or cheap brides for their sons. After what these women
have known, the meanest dwelling in Nineveh will seem to them a
paradise of luxury, but they will not be sold to the brothels so that
they may be kicked out into the street to starve the minute their
breasts begin to droop. I will not grow rich thus."

Kephalos raged and tore his garments and said I would beggar the both of us with my absurd notions—had he not himself been a prisoner of war, and did he not understand better than I what was right and proper under such circumstances? Was not the market for slaves depressed right now because of the conflict in the south? Where would he find so many fine families willing to marry off their sons to women who spoke gibberish and did not know enough to piss in the street, where it would annoy no one?

"Look at them, Lord—ripe as melons. I may even keep a few of the better ones for my own use. And you would waste these on pottery makers and carters of fish, men who could not command the bride price for a thirty-year-old virgin with bad teeth? Master, I fear you have defied all my advice for preserving your health and have been baking your brains in the sun even to suggest such a crazed idea. But at least the horses, Lord. The king your father has gifted you with *all* the booty, so let me see what can be done—"

"They go to the army, Kephalos—we will need them in the south."

This seemed to drive him wild. He stamped his foot and swore a mighty oath, his white face turning pink as pomegranate oil.

"By all the gods of Naxos and the Western Lands, I am cursed," he shouted. "I am cursed that I must live my days as the slave of a witless boy—pardon me, Lord, but it is no more than the truth. I am cursed above all men."

But in the end, when he saw that I was inflexible, he contented himself with grumbling all through dinner and prophesying that I would die in poverty, such were my mad humors.

"And, of course, my commission will amount to nothing," he went on, eyeing me sidewise as he dipped his jeweled fingers into a bowl of hot water—it was some new elegance he had adopted. "It was not worth the expense of the journey. . . ."

"Two *beru*, Kephalos . . . ?"

"Yes, but one must travel in a certain state, and then there was the price of the escort. But such are the things I do for love of my demented, foolish young master."

He sighed deeply and took a swallow of wine to console himself, but the wine only seemed to deepen his gloom.

"I do not know how the nation will thrive, Lord, if you are to continue in this fashion when you are king. The rich and mighty are not made of—"

I reached across the table and grabbed him by the beard, pulling him toward me, for my heart was all at once full of darkness.

"What do you mean, when I am king? Speak, slave!"

"Master, did you not know?" He blinked at me in astonishment as his fingers settled gently over the hand that seemed about to tear the whiskers from his chin. "I had thought the king your father would have . . . You mean you have heard *nothing*?"

"Not one word—speak."

"Gentle master, please . . ." When I released him he took water from his bowl and rubbed it into the hairs of his face. I was in an agony of suspense, but he hardly seemed to notice.

"There is now no one in your way—except, of course, the Lord Esarhaddon, who all say is a fine soldier but no more," Kephalos went on at last, studying my face as if he had never seen it before. "And even he . . . he was in my house not two days hence and spoke of your elevation to *marsarru* as a settled matter. He has hopes that now you can arrange a command of cavalry for him."

"But what of the *marsarru* who is? What of Arad Ninlil? What of him?"

My canny slave shrugged his thick shoulders like one in the presence of a sad but unavoidable fate.

"Dead, my Lord—dead of an apoplexy, where all thought it would be his stomach troubles that must take him off. Dead this whole week."

10

By nightfall every man in camp had heard the news of Arad
Ninlil's death, and the next morning, while I bid good-bye
to Kephalos and his consignment of women for the slave
markets, I found myself hailed as if I had already been proclaimed
and the throne stood vacant. All soldiers of Ashur hold the king
in great reverence, and these had fought with me in two campaigns—in their eyes I was the *marsarru,* no matter that no *baru*
had probed the entrails of a consecrated goat to understand the
god's will.

I wore a red tunic that day, in token of mourning for my
royal brother, but this did not stop the infantrymen of my old
company from setting up a cheer almost the moment I first
stepped into the sun's light. "Ashur is King, Ashur is King," they
cried, as if they followed me from the temple with the crown
newly fixed upon my head. It was not a thing which could be
permitted. As I mounted my horse I raised my hand with the fist
clenched for silence.

"There is but one king in this land," I bellowed, feigning an
anger I did not feel, for their display of loyalty had softened my
liver. "His name is Sennacherib and he waits for us by the banks
of the Lesser Zab. Why are you not ready to march to his aid? Do
you imagine the Elamites are asleep and the Lord of Ashur has no
use for his army? I go now to stand at his side—whether I have
you behind me or not!"

I turned my face to the south and rode away. I did not hurry,
however, since three hundred men cannot strike camp and prepare to march in an instant. Once out of sight, I let the horse

proceed at his own pace—horses, it has been my experience, will
always idle if they do not feel the prod—and it was no later than
the first hour past noon, and I had not traveled more than a single
beru, when I heard my soldiers shouting after me to wait for
them. At last I turned about and let the reins drop.

I could not help but laugh when, after perhaps a quarter of
an hour, I saw their sweating faces. Lushakin came forward and,
in the men's name, begged my pardon, saying that, nonetheless, it
had been a putrid foreigner's trick of mine to leave them with
their kits unpacked and twelve great jars of perfectly good beer
open and undrunk, which now they had had to leave behind to
cheer no one but the sand fleas. I laughed still more and pardoned
him for his impertinence as well. We lost hardly any marching
time at all that day, and I did not have to hear myself shouted up
as the god's chosen one anymore that campaign.

Yet, though a man may silence others, he may not silence the
voice of his own heart. To be the *marsarru*—it would answer
every ambition I had kept hidden these many years. If it was truly
the king's will, then he would give me Esharhamat for my wife. I
would live in glory and happiness. It would be no mean thing to
dwell in the house of succession.

It was five days before we reached the king's encampment on
the Lesser Zab, for the spring floods were only just beginning to
subside and every little trickle of water was over its banks, leaving
the ground thick with mud. I could only hope the Elamites would
be sensible enough to stay comfortably at home until Ashur's sun
had dried the land enough for gentlemen to fight upon.

On the day of our arrival I found the king preparing himself
for the punishment of a local noble who had tried to bring his city
out against its rightful lord.

"Ah, is it you, Tiglath—*Rab Abru,* Conqueror of the North?
Yes? Come kiss me, my son. I am delighted you have not missed
the day's entertainment. Come, have a cup of this appalling date
wine and tell me all your adventures, eh?"

We sat together in front of his tent, surrounded by soldiers
who stood about watching us from a discreet distance, rather as if
we were dangerous animals, and my royal father poured out with
his own hand some of the contents of the jar that rested on a small
round table at his elbow. He was not precisely drunk, but the wine
—which really did taste like boatman's pitch—had glazed over
his eyes so that they looked as if they were made of polished

marble. I described to him everything that had happened in the north, and he smiled and grunted and nodded his head from time to time but without really seeming to listen. I did not understand this until he pointed to my almost untouched cup and frowned.

"You do not care for the wine, boy? Not to your taste, eh? Drink it anyway, for it is strong and dulls the mind. Have you never seen a man flayed before?"

"No, Lord—never."

"You will today, and that will not be to your taste either. But it is better for a little strong wine. Drink, boy."

We drank in silence until an officer in the uniform of the *quradu* approached and, placing his right hand over his heart, bowed before the king his master.

"It seems the hour has come for me to dispense justice, eh?" The Lord Sennacherib looked at me and grinned uncertainly. "Come, Tiglath, my son—we must not neglect so important a part of your royal education. Hah, hah, hah!"

We rose and, with his arm across my shoulder, my royal father, Lord of the Earth's Four Corners, well and truly drunk now, stumbled toward his chariot.

"You drive, boy," he said. "They say you have a great skill in the direction of horses, and I do not trust myself today—it would not be consonant with my kingly dignity if I were to turn us over into a ditch, eh? Hah!"

The city of Ushnur, or what survived of it, was not ten *ashlu* from the king's encampment—we could have walked the distance in as many minutes, except that kings do not walk when they wish to be seen in their majesty. I had wondered why the army's chief officers were not billeted within its walls until I saw that its walls had been demolished and the city itself almost totally destroyed, its streets clogged with dead bodies.

Three days had passed since the elders had come to Sennacherib on their knees, entreating that they might be allowed to surrender, and still one could see columns of smoke from fires that, by the king's order, had been allowed to continue burning. Even the granaries had been burned, so these people would be without food until the summer harvest—provided they lived until then. I had seen the women begging at the camp gates, some of them, from their clothes and jewelry, the wives of rich men, reduced now to selling their bodies for a handful of millet.

In a siege lasting less than a single day, the armies of Ashur had reduced this place to ashes and barren rubble, swatting it down like a fly, and with almost as little effort. I could not imagine what madness had possessed the citizens to resist.

"I have had some of the survivors driven away with whips that they may wander the land and recount in other cities what has happened here," my father said, smiling at me pleasantly as we drew up before what had once been the city gates. "I mean this campaign to be the last I shall have to fight in the south, so I will leave this land a waste. The black-headed peoples will know that their masters live in Nineveh, not in Susa. See how they cringe before us, my son? They will not soon forget the name of Sennacherib."

We stepped down from the chariot and stools were brought that we might sit in the midst of a wretched crowd whom the soldiers had collected to witness the death of their former lord. Men and women alike, they stared at us with a mixture of fear and that weariness and abject misery which conquers all fear, even of death. I do not think they had will left enough even to hate us.

"Bring him!" the king shouted, his voice loud and vigorous, as befitted a conqueror. There was even that hint of impatience, as if this were a small matter, almost beneath his notice, which is so necessary to royal bearing. "Bring him—let his people see what this oath breaker's witless folly has brought him to."

A line of soldiers opened and the man was brought forward. He was naked and gaunt, less from hunger than from suffering; men who have endured prolonged torture always have that worn look. His wrists and ankles were chained and he seemed hardly able to stand. I wondered at this until I saw that his footprints in the dust were caked with blood—the soles of his feet had been beaten raw with a knotted lash. He could not speak, it seemed; he could not even look the king my father in the face. Plainly this was a broken man.

"Where is Kudur-Nahhunte now, O Marduknasir?" the king asked him, and then waited for the answer he knew would not come. "In Susa, that is where—hiding his head beneath his mother's skirts. Where are your Elamite masters, whose knees you embraced? Not here, Lord. Not here. Only you are here—you and I. And in half an hour you will be a skinless corpse and your hide will be nailed to the wall of that hovel you call a palace—what there is left of it. Yes, let the thing be done!"

The executioners were waiting, their arms crossed over their massive chests. In every army there are always men set aside for such work, and they are always shunned by their fellow soldiers, and they are always just alike—great mute lumps of muscle with tiny eyes, and wearing the smile of an idiot. There were two of them today, and they came forward and one of them took Marduknasir by the chain that ran between his manacles, pulling him to his knees, while the other hammered iron pegs into the ground at the corners of a square perhaps three paces at a side. When he was finished, their victim was dragged to the center and chained by his arms and legs to the four iron pegs, the chains pulled tight so he could hardly move at all. It was time to go to work.

They began with Marduknasir's left hand. One of the executioners took a copper knife from his belt. Its blade was hacked in places, but it looked sharp enough. As he began cutting from the tip of the middle finger and down across the palm, the other poured a trickle of water into the ever-lengthening wound—this, in part, to clear away the blood but principally to intensify the suffering. He then made a second careful incision from the tip of the thumb to the wrist and, this finished, started stripping back the skin so that finally they had peeled it from the whole hand in a single piece, fingernails and all. Then, after removing the manacle for a moment, they started up the arm.

I had never heard anyone scream as did Marduknasir. Perhaps all along he had not believed he would be made to suffer this, for there was in the animal shrieks that rent the air a certain note of panicky incredulity, as if, in addition to everything else, he was experiencing the full terror of the unforeseen, the mortal blow that comes out of the darkness.

But very soon even this was gone, as with his skin they stripped away all that had been human about Marduknasir. It was not long before he was not a man at all, merely a thing that can feel pain and nothing else.

The crowd watched in sullen silence. If any of the man's family were there to witness his ordeal they did not make themselves known, but perhaps they were afraid—that was the purpose of this exercise, to make people afraid. The king and I sat close enough that we could smell the blood that poured down over the exposed, quivering muscles, but our faces revealed nothing. That is what conquerors do. They close their hearts.

It was a slow business, this death—the executioners were in
no hurry. Marduknasir, if one could still call that mass of raw,
bloody flesh by a name, lived at least until the skin was peeled
from his breast and thighs. At least, he still cried out in a soft,
mindless whimper. How long he lived after that only the god
knows; there was only the twitching of his limbs. At last the
executioners stood up. One of them, covered in blood and smiling
—I remember how he smiled—held in his hands, like a garment
he was presenting for sale, the whole skin, even the face with hair
and beard.

"Nail it to the wall of his house," the king said, rising from
his seat. He was sober now, and he did not smile. "Post a guard
that none may take it down for burial. Feed the corpse to the
dogs."

Once more he put his arm across my shoulder, but this time I
think it was to steady me.

"Come, my son. It was just so with me the first time—I do
not envy you the hard lessons of your youth."

The execution of Marduknasir was like a portent of the
whole of that year's campaign, for the king was to show no mercy
to any who resisted him. We burned villages and sacked cities,
sending the survivors into exile after we had impaled their great
men on pointed stakes.

The Elamites crossed to the west bank of the Tigris only once
in defense of their allies. They tried their strength against us at a
place called Lagas—I remember there was a lake nearby where
Esarhaddon and I went swimming the day before the battle,
which was terrible but not so terrible as Khalule had been. After
this one foray, which the annals do not lie in calling a victory for
Great Sennacherib, Kudur-Nahhunte retreated into the mountains of his own land and died soon after at the hands of his
subjects. It would be many years before Elam, weak and demoralized, ventured once more to stir up trouble among her neighbors.

But the seed of rebellion had taken deep root among the
black-headed peoples, and the war we waged against them to kill
it was hard and brutal. It was a war not of pitched battles but of
sieges against fortified cities, a type of war at which the soldiers of
Ashur are more gifted than those of any other nation, but it was a
cruel way to bring the land to submission and we found our one

justification in the hope that this would be the last time we would need to be cruel.

Yet we did not think of justification, only of victory and a return to our homes. A long campaign dries all pity from the hearts of men—we grew to hate the peoples of the south, to hate them for what they made us suffer and for what they made us make them suffer. The butcher learns to hate his victims, and the war turned us into butchers.

And this was the campaign in which Esarhaddon learned the warrior's trade. He was a fine commander of horse, brave, imaginative, and tenacious—so stubborn in battle that his men came to call him "the Donkey"—but I fear he never learned to distinguish the limits of what could be achieved by force. He never grasped that the conquered must be reconciled to defeat or the victory is empty. He never learned to be anything more than a warrior, and for that the Land of Ashur was in time to pay dearly.

The Lord Sennacherib saw this and his mind darkened against my brother, whom he never could bring himself to love— Sinahiusur had said it would be so, and Sinahiusur was a wise man.

Still, he who was the king knew a king's duty and therefore understood that his royal son could not simply be ignored. Thus as he raised me, first to a seat on his military council and then to that inner circle of advisers who helped him rule the world from a war tent in the swamplands of the lower Euphrates, he raised Esarhaddon as well—but always one or two steps behind. I became the king's adviser and emissary, who as the voice of my master treated with sovereign princes as their equal in rank, and Esarhaddon became . . . What did he become—what was he allowed to become—except a soldier whose voice no one heard except his troops?

"When you go to parley with the elders of Umma," the king said to me, "take the Donkey with you." The name made him grin—I do not think he understood it as a compliment. "Perhaps, if he sees how gentlemen are expected to behave, we can make something more of him than a stable hand."

I listened in silence—it was not my place to tell the king he misjudged his son—and went off in search of Esarhaddon.

Did my brother care that he was thus slighted? He said nothing. He seemed not even to notice. But I think he was not such an ox that he did not smart under the king's contemptuous neglect.

Was he not satisfied? Had we not become what we had
dreamed of as boys, terrible in war, the king's two mailed fists to
crush the enemies of Ashur? Yes, we were that. And we loved one
another as of old, with the perfect confidence of children. But
Esarhaddon would not have been human if he had not resented
the manner in which I was preferred over him, and there was little
enough I could do to set the thing right.

So I went to fetch him, that together we might overwhelm
the elders of Umma with the glory of Ashur.

Esarhaddon was indeed good at that sort of diplomacy, for
by the simple expediency of saying nothing he could make common men afraid of him—and I had learned long since that the
nobles of these southern cities were no better than goatherds in
clean clothes. So as I wove together my tapestry of threats and
promises, describing to them the mercy of my king and the terror
of his wrath, Esarhaddon would stand at my back, solid and silent
as any wall, and the great men of Umma would listen as much to
him as to me.

"You are a serpent," Esarhaddon would say. "You hiss like
an adder, and they piss in their loincloths for fear."

"Yes, but only because they can look at you and imagine how
those thick fingers would feel around their necks. No city was
ever taken by bluff, brother."

"Perhaps not. But if one ever is, you will be the one to take
it."

The elders asked for half an hour to consider our demands.
We waited outside the city walls and, half an hour later, the gates
opened and out walked their prince, their sovereign lord whose
house had ruled in Umma for four hundred years, dressed in rags
with the hangman's rope already knotted around his neck.

That campaign saw the destruction of many cities, their walls
torn down, their palaces razed, the wives and daughters of their
kings burned with fire. We would leave famine and death in our
wake, for Sennacherib wished all men to know who was master in
the lands between the rivers. It was his will, and through him the
god found voice, so all must obey.

And yet he spared Umma. He forgave their prince, who
kissed the royal feet, and returned to him his life and honors. It
was not simple caprice, for the king knew that men must not be
made desperate.

"He should have hanged him," Esarhaddon grumbled as we

sat together at the banquet given to the conqueror of Umma by her prince. "He should have left him dangling from the city walls until the rope rotted through—by the sixty gods, this is filthy stuff this traitor serves us for wine!"

"You are in a bad temper because you haven't had a woman in two months, but never fear—I have seen to it you will not be cheated of your rightful pillage. This prince was badly frightened by his brush with death and plans to make us all rich gifts. I have had words with his chamberlain, and yours will be two sisters from his own harem. Egyptian women, very skilled."

"No, I am not in a bad temper over that—sisters, you say? Not, perhaps, twins, you think?"

"No, not twins. A year apart in age. Then what vexes you, brother? Surely even Esarhaddon the Donkey is tired of watching towns burn like cooking fires."

"Yes—no. How would I know what tires me and what does not? The Lady Tashmetum-sharrat is dead, dead of grief for that son of hers, who was a loss to no one, it seems, except her. Did you know? I read it not an hour ago in a letter from my mother."

"No, I did not know."

I glanced up at the head of the table, where the king was in the midst of telling a joke. Everyone around him was already laughing loudly, even though the joke was not finished, and the king laughed with them, interrupting himself that he might share in their pleasure. He did not look like a man who had lost his wife, but perhaps he had not yet heard.

Yet how could he not have heard? I remembered that lady, her eyes vacant, sitting on a couch while her women fanned her, dead to life. Yes, of course, why should she not die of grief, poor neglected creature? And why should the king care if she did?

"What didn't you know—that the Lady Tashmetum-sharrat is dead, or that my mother can write?" Esarhaddon grinned and dug his elbow into my ribs that I might appreciate his witticism. "She had a scribe write it for her. She can do such things now."

"Yes, of course. For now she is . . ."

"Yes—lady of the palace. And you wonder why my heart is bitter. The king should have hung that traitor—look at the way he smirks at him! Sisters, you say, but not twins?"

"No, not twins."

"Are they at least witches? Are they skilled at necromancy? Can either of them do magic?"

"Perhaps not the sort you mean."

"If they are Egyptian they can do magic. All Egyptian women do magic. They learn how from their mothers."

"Then perhaps one of them is a witch. Perhaps they both are."

"Ashur is good to a humble man."

It was not until the month of Ab, when Lord Ashur's sun burns the land until its face is as hard as building bricks, that I returned to Nineveh. The king of Babylon had not taken the field against us all that season, but had kept his army walled up within his city, which vexed Sennacherib most cruelly. No man might claim to be the master of Sumer unless his soldiers controlled the streets of Babylon, and my royal father knew all his victories, all the tribute that had poured into his treasury, all the submissions of lesser kings meant nothing if he could not return home with some one of his loyal servants on the throne of Babylon. He was impatient that the new companies which were forming in the north be brought down with all speed for the final assault. Thus he sent me back to Nineveh to see that his will was done.

I traveled with a bodyguard of twelve men, and we rode without rest during the hours of daylight. By the end of the eighth day we were within sight of the great wall. I entered through the gate that night and in the uniform of a common soldier that my return might give rise to no false rumors—a great city is like a woman and believes every evil whisper it hears.

But if I had any thought of keeping my arrival a secret from the ear of my servant Kephalos I was disappointed. He was there at the door to the officers' barrack when I stepped out into the morning light. So quick was he to make his obeisance that I almost tripped over him.

"Master! May the gods grant you a thousand lives!" he cried as I helped him back up on his feet—it seemed that each time I saw him he grew more massive, and today he was almost beyond my strength. "You must forgive me, for I did not receive word of your return until an hour since."

"I cannot conceive how you heard of it all, considering that I was at some pains to keep that news from the world. If the king's intelligence were as good as yours, his rule would extend by now to the lands beyond the Bitter River."

As we walked through the streets of the city, I noticed that people stepped out of our way and bowed to me as we passed. It was a new experience—almost everyone seemed to know who I was, for even the blue uniform of *rab abru* would not have excited such respect. Kephalos pretended to pay no attention, but I noticed that he had drawn himself up very straight and strode through the crowds with all the dignity of a great prince.

"See, Lord?" he said finally, and out of the corner of his mouth—to acknowledge the thing openly would have been inconsistent with his gravity of deportment. "There is not a dog in Nineveh who does not know the future king."

"And, putting aside the question of your impudence in styling me so, how is it that the dogs of Nineveh recognize this humble soldier as their *marsarru*?"

"Because it is well known that the physician Kephalos is the slave of the great Tiglath Ashur, whom Ishtar, Lady of Battles, loves as her own son."

"And, of course, every dog in Nineveh knows the physician Kephalos by sight."

"Of course."

Of course—probably by now, I thought to myself, most of them owed him money.

It was well that I hadn't broken my fast yet that morning, for Kephalos had laid on something of a banquet at his house near the Gate of Adad. There was bread, beer, wine, cheese, and fruits in varieties I had never seen before, and the servants, I noticed, were all women, all very young, and spoke among themselves a language I did not recognize.

"Uqukadi," Kephalos whispered, glancing about him to suggest his object. "The slave market does not smile on baby girls, so I kept out some twelve or fifteen for myself as a speculation—naturally I discounted their value just a little in my accounts, since I will have the maintenance of them, but you will find, Lord, that I did not rob you beyond the bounds of decency. In a few years, when their charms are a little more obvious, they will fetch a good price."

He smiled, as if he expected me to congratulate him on his sagacity.

"And where have you hidden the fair Philinna, sweet as a fig?"

"Oh—do not speak of her, Lord. She is even at this moment

upstairs in my bed, snoring like a water ox. I have not had a decent day's work from her this year, since she has taken it into her head that I cannot live without her embraces—I can, Lord; I could and do, most of the time. That is half the reason I loaded the house with these tittering children, hoping she would rise to the challenge. But it has all been in vain. By accident, my royal master, you have hit upon the right way—for I know you are too young and thoughtless to have acquired much wisdom. To live the hard life of a soldier, keeping ever to the company of men—that is the only path for him who wishes to enjoy a quiet mind."

I laughed, as delighted at the picture of Kephalos enjoying his quiet mind in the midst of a crowded, stinking war camp as with his pitiful distress as the victim of women—for Kephalos, I knew, would never be anyone's victim very long.

"Nevertheless, we both did very well out of your booty, Lord. Were you not a prince, you would now feel yourself entitled to live like one. For myself, surely nothing keeps me toiling except my concern for your welfare and, of course, that bottomless greed which is the glory and burden of every true Greek—you, doubtless, are less afflicted, since the mother's strain is ever the weaker. I let word be spread that you personally had lain with each of these women—they, naturally, were all too puffed up with pride at the idea to even think of denying it—and such is the credulity of the Assyrians that the story was generally credited. Over a hundred women—think of it! Such fools. The bidding, as a result, was very brisk, for every cur loves to believe he dines on the leavings of royalty. You are very popular in the city, Lord, and since you were absent in the north at the time, no suspicion concerning Arad Ninlil's death has attached itself to you. . . ."

This was the first I had heard of the general report that the *marsarru* had been poisoned. It seemed that when his physicians had attempted to move the body, a thick black fluid had streamed out of his nose and mouth—this, when only a few drops were forced down the throat of a dog, had resulted in the animal's death within the span of a few hours.

There had been no further inquiries, of course. The murder of a prince is the private business of the king—it is not wise even to admit publicly that such a thing could happen—so no one would be summoned to justice. If the lord Sennacherib had his suspicions he would keep them to himself. And he would strike back at a time and in a manner of his own choosing.

It seemed odd to me that in all the time we had been together since my return from the north, my royal father had never once mentioned the death of his son—not even in passing. It was as if Arad Ninlil, whom the gods favored not, had never lived.

I returned to the house of war with a darkened mind, feeling as if a spider's web were closing around me, insubstantial but strong nonetheless.

Whose path was being cleared to the throne, mine or Esarhaddon's? In the last few years there had been a great harvesting of princes, and now, it seemed, someone was doing the Lady Ereshkigal's work for her.

For several days I was busy with the work of the king's new army. It was well, for it left me no time to think. Once only I allowed myself the luxury of a day and a night at Three Lions to visit my mother, who, naturally, had heard nothing and knew nothing and was therefore as content as a woman can be whose only son fights in a great war. It was a day and a night with the only woman I knew whose heart was not filled with plotting. When I mounted my horse to return to Nineveh, I felt as if I were returning to commit some impurity.

And, of course, I did, one single time, go to the king's palace to see Esharhamat, who held my heart in her snare so firmly that I would never free myself.

But I was not her only visitor that day. When I entered her garden I found her sitting by the fountain, and with her was another woman, dressed in a black tunic shot through with silver threads that made her shine like the night sky. Even the shawl drawn over her hair was edged in silver. She turned her head to see who was coming and smiled, as if she had expected me. I recognized at once the Lady Naq'ia.

It was many years since I had seen her, not since the days of my childhood, when she had seemed as fearful as a scorpion. Now she was no longer young, but to my eye younger than the dread beauty who had ruled the house of women like Semiramis of old —smaller too, but that was no more than a trick of memory. She sat there beside Esharhamat, seemingly as close as mother and daughter. And she could smile and smile, and still I would know she and I were destined to be enemies until death. I placed my hand over my heart and bowed to her.

"You have grown, Tiglath—but may I yet call you by that name, Dread Prince?" Her eyes glittered in mocking laughter for an instant, not waiting for an answer. "And yet, though your glory covers the earth now, I think I would still have known you anywhere. Is your mother well?"

"Well, Lady, and happy. I trust it is so with you?"

"Yes—it is so with me."

Time had been kind to the Lady Naq'ia, who was still admired throughout the city as a handsome woman—indeed, since she had only just come out of the seclusion of the house of women, her beauty, newly discovered, struck many with all the force of revelation.

Yet it was a beauty which carried with it the thrill of danger; it was impossible not to sense that this woman was without scruples or affection and understood only the heartless passion of the body. I had no difficulty grasping why my father—such was the story—had paid to the tavernmaster of Borsippa five whole talents of silver that he might have this wild, dark-eyed slave for his bed. But, had he ever learned to love her, I could only pity him.

"Could it be, Tiglath, that you have some word for me of my son?" She smiled again, as if admitting to a ludicrous weakness. "I wrote to him some weeks ago but, of course, have heard nothing. Doubtless you understand that a mother always imagines the worst."

"He suffers from nothing more terrible than boredom, Lady. We fight a war of sieges this campaign—which means that Esarhaddon, as a cavalry officer, leads a dull life. He chafes at his safety and yearns for opportunities to astonish us all with his heroism."

I grinned at her. It cost me nothing, and I did not hate this woman so much that I would torment her about her son, my best and closest friend.

"You have given me the best gift anyone may bestow, and that is a tranquil mind." She rose from her seat and held out her hand to me, which I took without thinking. "And my reward to you will be to leave you alone with this lady, which I know you desire above all glory and wealth. Good-bye, Tiglath Ashur, favorite of the great gods."

And an instant later, when that black shadow had passed

from between us, I turned to Esharhamat, who looked at me out of eyes that seemed deep as death itself.

"Now that she is lady of the palace she comes here often—it seems that already she regards me as her daughter-in-law."

Her eyes, I could have gazed into them forever. I could have become so lost in them that I became empty, until I had no will to be more than merely some small part of her. They spoke to me in the private language of my own heart, and yet they said nothing. Their silence betrayed nothing, except that they hid secrets I could never guess.

What have you done? I heard in the quiet of my mind—the question unspoken but not unasked. *Esharhamat, whom I love more than life, in your passion that makes you deaf even to the god's whispered voice, what have you done—or perhaps only, to what have you consented?*

"Had I asked you why the Lady Naq'ia was here, Esharhamat? I don't recall it."

An instant later she was in my arms, and our mouths sought each other with a hungry tenderness which swept away all doubt. Had some small misgiving stirred in my brain? I had forgotten it as I felt her body pressing against me. I had forgotten—or had ceased to care. I knew only that I must accept her love on any terms on which she chose to offer it.

If there was a sin, then in that moment I took the guilt for it upon myself, making it and Esharhamat my own.

"Do you yet love me?" she whispered, pulling me down to her that I might feel her warm breath against my ear. "Have I lost you forever, Tiglath Ashur, favorite of the great gods, or does some small part of you still remember the name of Esharhamat?"

She did not need to hear my answer—she had it already. As we sat together by the fountain's edge, and my hands wandered over her body, the blood pounded in my head like the war drums of the Elamites and I was lost to all reason and honor. I cared for nothing except her—the smell of her hair, the curve of her breast under my fingers, her little pointed tongue darting between my lips like a hummingbird at the mouth of a flower. I cared only for this moment, while the soul and the body had become one.

And then, abruptly, she pushed me away.

"I have thought," she said. "I have thought of almost nothing else."

"Yes . . . I too . . . At night—your sweet body . . ."

I was almost choked with desire. I tried to press my kiss against her throat, but suddenly she was mine no longer. She belonged only to herself.

"I will go the temple of Ishtar. You will be waiting for me there—you and your sacred silver coin."

It was several seconds before I even understood what she could mean. Looking into her face, so hard set, as if it had been cast in bronze, I did not even know who she was anymore. Was this really Esharhamat? Who was it I had come to love with this ungovernable love? I knew not.

"It is a duty each woman owes, from the lowest to the most high. Why should it not be you who breaks the seal of my virginity, Tiglath Ashur, whom I love even as do the gods themselves, as does the king? You, who shall be king after him, why should it not be you?"

"Because it is forbidden. The Lady Ishtar commands that it shall be a stranger only who . . ."

"The Lady Ishtar is Queen of Battles, too, and has made you her special favorite—what would she not forgive . . . ?"

"This—this she would not forgive."

"This, and all else."

I did not linger in Nineveh. I did not dare. When the king's new army had barely wiped from their eyes the dust of the parade ground, I issued orders that all should be prepared to march with the new sun. I left behind love and passion and faced only a dangerous hardship, but I fled from Nineveh as from death.

Within three days' march a courier reached me with orders to join the main army at the walls of Babylon.

Babylon! So it had come to that already. The greatest city in the world, and our soldiers were camped at her gates.

"We will stay here and watch her starve to death!" the king told me. "We will cut off her food and give her nothing but muddy water to drink. This, Tiglath, this is the city that sold my son to the Elamites. I do not care how long I have to wait. This city owes me a great debt and, by the great gods, I shall make her pay it!"

Babylon, city of Marduk, her walls seventy cubits high and faced with burned brick, her gates the wonder of the world. And we would humble her, and tear her life away. Time would be as nothing. Month would drag into month, the season of flooding would come and go. The king our lord had settled in his heart that he would conquer and avenge his first-born son.

Thus it was that the army I had brought from Nineveh sat down to wait upon the pleasure of the gods.

11

For fifteen months the armies of the Lord Sennacherib kept Babylon sealed shut like a jar of unripe wine. We camped on the plains around her endless walls; we dug canals that the mighty Euphrates which ran in her midst was slowed to a muddy trickle; we gathered in her harvests and slaughtered her animals. It was a boast of that city that even a dog was free in Babylon, but what when Babylon herself was girded about so tight she could not breathe? The dogs then were eaten, as was even the grass between the cobblestones. And while the city died, we waited. Like vultures, we circled round and waited.

And for fifteen months Esarhaddon and I never left the field. The king returned to Nineveh for the winter—there was little enough to occupy the valor even of the common soldiers except, occasionally, a quick strike against some town or other that might have risen in aid of Babylon. But for the most part, and for months together, the Chaldeans kept to their swamps, the Elamites to their mountains, and the great men of Sumer stayed quiet in their homes, waiting to see if the Queen of Cities would really fall. We all waited—the army and the whole world. And Esarhaddon and I stayed in the south.

Yet we were not idle. The siege of a great city is a matter requiring patience, yes, but one does not simply pitch one's tent and wait. The soldiers of Ashur, who were masters at this sort of war, stripped off their tunics and, in their loincloths and their toilsome sweat, dug into the earth like foxes.

Babylon is a city even greater than Nineveh. A man would need long legs to walk around her in the time between noon and sunset, and her wall, which towers over the plains like the face of a mountain, is surrounded by a moat wide as a river. The moat was a simple matter—we only had to divert the Euphrates into a canal and dry it up—but we all learned to hate that wall. I have stood upon the wall of Babylon, and travelers speak no more than the truth when they say that two chariots could ride abreast on the road running along its summit. And its gates were nothing but traps for the unwary, where attacking soldiers could be boxed in by the simple raising of a drawbridge and then slaughtered by archers who stood overhead.

But a wall is not more than one mud brick placed upon another and is no stronger than the ground upon which it stands. We dug tunnels through the earth, starting at a point far enough away that the Babylonians could not reach us with their arrows, and we undermined the wall—all at once a great section of it would just crumble away. This, of course, was the labor of many months.

But long before we brought down her walls, Babylon had begun to die. By the end of winter even the most severe rationing could not prevent famine; the dead were carried away by the Euphrates, and we had only to stand on the shore below the city and count the corpses to know how many were starving from day to day. And when we had changed the course of that great river, so that what flowed under the wall was not more than a brackish trickle, pestilence broke out in the city. Many more starved or succumbed to disease than we killed in our final assault.

And all this can be laid to the cowardly arrogance of one man, for the Lord Sennacherib would have accepted the city's surrender. But her king, Mushezib Marduk, who owed his throne to the Elamites, knew that the full weight of our king's wrath would fall on him and therefore held out as long as he could, unmindful of the suffering of the Babylonians. He saw to it that his troops were kept in bread and beer while he waited vainly for the men of Ashur to go away. In the end he could save neither himself nor his soldiers, nor his people nor even the very walls of their houses. These all perished under the eyes of the gods.

For that day when it would all end, we the armies of Ashur waited, working patiently as ants. For fifteen months we kept our deathwatch.

This time was hardest on Esarhaddon, for the monotony of the siege threw him back upon himself. Esarhaddon understood the business of soldiering, but his life was meant to be a pattern of movement, and inactivity made him fretful. Slowly—so slowly that only one who had known him from childhood would have noticed—he lost his belief in himself. Forced to sit and think, he no longer knew what to think. He preyed upon himself, and his mind, ever turning upon omens and the mighty forces of the unseen, was haunted by dark thoughts.

"Marduk is a powerful god," he would mutter—usually only when he was drunk, but he was drunk a good deal in those days. "He will avenge himself upon us if we destroy his city."

"Perhaps he has deserted his city, for all things happen through the gods' will."

"No—Babylon is a holy place. Mark me, brother. This will be visited upon us one day."

"We do Ashur's will. We are his people; we have nothing to fear from Marduk, who is honored only in Babylon."

He would look at me from beneath his heavy, anxious eyebrows, almost as if I had insulted him.

"Marduk is king of the gods—all men say so."

"Only here, brother."

"All men know the stories of Marduk's power and greatness. Did you not hear them as a child? But, of course—I forget, your mother is an Ionian woman."

His mother, of course, was Naq'ia, a southern woman, bought by the king her husband in Borsippa but born the gods alone guessed where. What rubbish had she stuffed into her son's head? It was possible not even he knew.

There would be whole days when he kept to his tent, speaking to no one but his two Egyptian concubines. Taking advantage of his weakness, they had managed to convince him that they could call up the dead, dispel evil spirits, read a man's fortune in his excrement, and I know not what other foolishness. Esarhaddon held them in such respect that he beat them only rarely and would not permit any of his friends to bed with them. Many times I had thoughts of cutting their throats, for they did great mischief in muddling my brother's head so.

But I believed that Esarhaddon's superstitious melancholies were due as much as anything to lack of exercise, so when the fit was on him I would go to the tent of the *rab shaqe* and arrange that he be sent out to lead a raiding party against some town where they had forgotten the weight of Ashur's hand, and he would return four or five days later carrying a sack crammed with bleeding heads, leading donkeys laden with treasure and enough oxen to feed the army for a month, smiling and laughing and telling tales of his glory not even he believed. Yet afterward he would be his old self again—for a while at least.

My own mind was hardly less dark. I did not live in fear of shadows, but the waiting preyed on my nerves. All we could see over the walls of Babylon was the top of the great ziggurat, which at night—every night—was ablaze with torches as the priests made sacrifice to the divine patron of their city. The people were starving, as much Mushezib Marduk's prisoners as ours, and their piety had taken on the desperation of those who can see no escape save through the power of their great god.

I received Kephalos's letters from Nineveh, in which, because they were written in a language not many in the lands between the rivers could read, he felt emboldened to speak of the dissatisfaction at home. There was division over the king's war against Babylon; many felt with Esarhaddon that the city should be respected. Their reasons were various: fear of Marduk's revenge, a sentimental attachment to Babylon as the mother of our culture and learning. Some even said that Sennarcherib's wits had been turned by grief over his son's death, that he wasted blood and treasure in a blind, senseless rage. It was a dangerous sign that such things could be spoken of Ashur's king. Kephalos, who was not a fool, wrote his letters on sheets of leather which I found neatly folded at the bottom of the boxes of medicines and supplies he sent me. These I always burned.

He wrote me also of my mother, whom at my entreaty he visited regularly, and he would pass on her little messages. He did not write to me of Esharhamat.

Esharhamat—how that name had burned itself into my brain! I saw her in my dreams at night, and, though at times I was half mad with desire of the flesh, I kept my oath to her and took no pleasure in other women.

Perhaps I will yet become the *marsarru,* I thought. I had no yearning to follow my father on the throne, but as his heir I could marry Esharhamat. And if I did not, Esarhaddon would, who did not care for her and would take her like a tavern harlot simply because he could imagine no other way. He would do his duty and father sons by her, and I would grow to hate him for it. I did not wish this—I wished only to possess Esharhamat as my wife in peace. So perhaps it would be best if by Ashur's will I became the next king. These were the ideas with which I entertained myself as an army of five and eighty thousand men waited for the walls of Babylon to crumble.

And when I was not dreaming of the kingship or of Esharhamat and her fair body, I was practicing the arts of provisioner, for my father in his wisdom had settled that we should pay the local peasants for their grain and livestock and not simply take it from them.

"Why should we turn the whole land of Sumer against us?" he reasoned. "The farmers have lost the greater share of their market because Babylon is starving under our blockade. An army eats less than a whole city, and the gold which will pay for our bread is in Mushezib Marduk's treasury—as good as if it were in my own. The city shall pay and we shall eat, and the common people who work the land shall bless us."

This was good policy. And to see that all was honestly done the king appointed his son Tiglath Ashur to treat with the heads of villages concerning the prices for barley, goats, beer, bread, cheese, honey, butter, eggs—the list was endless. I was less than pleased with this work, for the men of Ashur do not admire merchants.

Moreover, the task was one that I and many others did not feel was becoming to an officer of my rank and station, and in the mess I was the object of some mockery.

"The king was wise to choose him," said Arad Malik, my royal brother, now quite a man and fresh from a tour of duty in Lebanon. "The Ionians are well suited to commerce—I know all about the Ionians, who think only of money."

"Pay no attention to him," said Sinqui Adad, a *rab kisir* of my own age who was sitting next to him and did not seem to relish the company. "He is a fool when his skin is full of wine."

I smiled, wishing this ludicrous scene would end.

"Thank you, my friend—I can see that."

But Arad Malik merely shook his head and laughed.

"No," he went on, dismissing all objection with a languid wave. "No, I tell you, the king chose well. Tiglath can sit on his haunches like his ancestors, a bag of copper shekels between his knees as he barters over the price of millet."

"As your mother bargained over the price of her backside?"

It was not I who spoke, but Esarhaddon, who loved nothing so much as an ancient quarrel.

"Is it not true that the king of Hamath found her beside a tavern door, soliciting business for her nether hole? I know not what other part of her men could fancy, a woman with green breasts that hang down to her waist. What a family! At least Tiglath's grandfather never sold anything except sandals."

I have never known anyone bait so easily as Arad Malik, who actually was fool enough to stand up and draw his dagger—I think he would have climbed over the table after Esarhaddon had not Sinqi Adad and a few others pulled him back down to his seat. Esarhaddon, who had been so looking forward to putting a sword through his belly, was understandably disappointed.

All three of us were ejected from the mess to settle this matter among ourselves—the others had no thought except finishing their meal in peace—but Arad Malik by then had considered more carefully and, declining my very civil invitation to mortal combat, went off with a shrug and curse to find his own tent.

"You shouldn't have asked permission. You should simply have taken that rabbit-sticker of yours and killed him," Esarhaddon told me as we walked back to his quarters, where there was at least bread and wine. "No one would have blamed you—the whole world knows that Arad Malik would be vastly improved for having his heart cut out. And duels involve too many risks."

"Perhaps then we should send Leah over to keep him company—she might oblige us by eating him alive."

"Hah, hah, hah! Yes, she would, wouldn't she." Esarhaddon slapped me on the back almost hard enough to break a rib. "By the sixty great gods, she'd leave him shriveled as an Egyptian mummy. Hah, hah, hah! Nevertheless, after you are king I think you would do well to have the impudent dog's throat cut—a reasonable man takes his precautions."

"Perhaps, after I am king, I will give you his mother for your collection, and Arad Malik will oblige us by dying of mortification."

"Hah, hah, hah!"

But for all this I was still left sitting with a bag of copper shekels between my knees. Nor did I murmur against it, for I understood what they, as yet, did not, that the Lord Sennacherib had already decided that I should follow him and was preparing me against that day. A king must know everything about the conduct of war, not merely the leadership of men but even down to the price of barley and the best weight for horse blankets in the winter.

Thus every few days I would take a dozen wagons and an escort of twelve men and head off toward yet another nameless little village to trade in the king's name with farming folk who had probably never heard of Sennacherib, Lord of Ashur. It was on one of those journeys that I renewed the acquaintance of one who seemed to know me better than I did myself.

I was riding out over the vast, trackless plain, flat and almost featureless, which in centuries of flooding the Euphrates had spread out as her bounty, following the great river. There was a grove of palm trees perhaps two *beru* distant—I could see it quite clearly, although my company would not reach it for more than an hour, such is the character of the southern lands—and a grove generally meant a village nearby. At any rate it was a direction, one which I thought I had chosen for myself, although now I am no longer sure.

He was sitting on the trunk of one of the trees, which must have been uprooted during the last inundation, his body covered by yellow priest's robes, faded and almost in rags, his bony, ascetic face tilted up toward the sun, a faint smile upon his lips, although he could have seen nothing to please him—indeed, he could not have seen anything at all through his clouded eyes.

I waved to my men to stay off a little and rode up alone, stopping my horse in front of him, waiting, saying nothing.

"The god still mantles you in his holy light, Prince," he said at last. "You have traveled far."

"No farther than yourself, *Maxxu.*" I smiled and shrugged, hardly knowing whether he could see, or would trouble to notice. That he had known me I found not at all surprising.

"Yes, farther than I. I stay ever in the same place and the world moves. And now you prepare to humble the great city of Marduk."

"Do I do wrong, holy father?"

"You? You do nothing at all, Tiglath Ashur."

"Is it my *sedu,* then?"

I had not meant to mock him, but there must have been some note of disbelief in my voice, for the *maxxu* fastened his blind eyes upon me and his face assumed an expression of contemptuous pity.

"You are alive when many are dead—did you imagine yourself to have survived solely through your own resources? But no, it is not the *sedu* which will bring down mighty Babylon. All is by the god's design."

I leaned forward, and the horse stirred nervously beneath me. Suddenly I was full of fear.

"And is it the god's design that I shall be king, *Maxxu*? Am I to be blessed."

But he shook his head.

"These are different questions, Prince. And I have answered them both already." He looked back up into the sun, blinding and white at that hour of the morning, and the smile returned to his lips. "Go now, Prince. You have the world's business to do—and the god's."

"Will we meet again?"

"Go now, Prince."

When I returned to my men, my *ekalli* Lushakin looked at me with strange eyes.

"Who was that old beggar, *Rab Abru*? Some friend of yours?"

"I hardly know."

A few minutes later, when I glanced back to the palm grove, the *maxxu* was nowhere to be seen.

The month of Tisri was nearly finished, and the nights were already turning cold, when once more the king came down from Nineveh to be with his army. We all knew this meant the final assault on Babylon was about to begin.

"They have brought this upon themselves," he told us. "They have made it plain there can be no peace in Sumer as long as this city clings to its dreams of greatness, so we will wake it from its dreams. We will sack the city. We will carry fire and sword to its holy places—its temples we shall destroy and its gods we shall lead away into slavery. And there shall be such a slaughter here that men will speak of it with horror to the end of the world. When we leave this place, not one house shall stand among the rubble. We shall divert the course of her great river that even the foundations shall be washed away. Babylon will be erased from the minds of men."

We stood around him as he sat in his tent, with a map of the city spread out before him, drawn in charcoal on the hide of a sheep.

"We have collapsed the wall in three points—here, here, and here. It will be at those three points that our soldiers will enter for the assault."

"There is an inner wall, Dread Lord, which has not been breached. Doubtless it will be defended."

The Lord Sennacherib regarded his son Esarhaddon with an expression of astonished contempt.

"What of that, eh? The defenders are so weak from starvation that they can hardly hold their weapons. What we are planning here today, Royal Prince, is not a battle but a massacre."

"Nevertheless, we would be wise to send forces in through the riverbed—here and here." He reached down and pointed at the spots where, north and south, the Euphrates entered and left under the city walls. "The bed is almost dry now."

"These, too, will doubtless be defended."

The men around the table nodded agreement as the king glanced from one to the next. There were officers who had served all their lives under that mighty shadow and knew what was expected of them.

"Yes, but they will not have a wall to defend, only a dry riverbed—a mud bank some eight or ten cubits high. And, as you say, Dread Lord, they will be weak."

"And what would you do, provided you survived?"

"Spread terror."

One had only to look at Esarhaddon's eyes to know what he meant. And, of course, he was right—such a diversion was precisely what the attack required.

"And what do you say to this, Tiglath Ashur?"

I rested my middle finger on a black square in the center of the map, marking the location of the great ziggurat.

"With luck, Great King, we might be able to reach and hold the temple complex, at least for a time. This would draw many of their soldiers from the inner wall, for they will fear for their holy places."

"In other words, you agree with this absurdity?"

"I think my royal brother has spoken wisely, yes."

"So be it." The king rose from his seat and all of us, without thinking, stepped back half a pace. "Then you will lead one prong of this diversionary attack, and Esarhaddon will lead the other. I wish you joy of it."

An hour later I found Esarhaddon sitting on the ground in front of his tent, sulkily drinking a jar of beer. When he saw me he scowled, as if my face called him to painful recollections.

"He would not even have listened to me if you had not agreed. He speaks to me as to an idiot. I am a good soldier, but he will not listen to me."

I sat down next to him and took the jar from his hand, tasted the beer, and gave it back to him.

"He agreed. He gave us the command. If he had not seen that you were right he would not have yielded."

"He yielded only because you agreed with me. You are his darling, his favorite, while I . . ."

"You have never fought with him in a great battle. It will be different after we have taken Babylon."

"I might be dead after we have taken Babylon."

"Then it will not matter."

His brow furrowed for a moment and then he grinned, for he saw the joke. Yet I saw plainly enough how he suffered, who only wished to prove that it was a soldier's heart which beat in his chest.

"We have three days to plan," he said, after each of us had raised the jar to our lips. "How many troops do you think he will give us?"

"A hundred men each would be best—less would invite disaster, but more would only get in the way."

"Then you can have the pleasure of asking him. One company apiece. Swordsmen, with good armor. No archers. It will be close fighting the whole way."

"And we will enter the city one hour before first light."

"Yes—that would be best."

And then, although it was a cold day, Esarhaddon and I went off swimming in one of the canals, playing like children in the gray water, as if we had forgotten the war.

Three days later, an hour before Ashur's sun would rise behind the eastern mountains, I found myself crouched among the dead reeds, sunk to my ankles in mud that clung like pitch, a hundred men waiting at my back. I had only to raise my arm and Babylon's final agony would be upon her.

The outer wall ran around only the eastern half of the city,

encompassing a moat, the main canals leading from the river, and
an inner wall. The western half was protected by the moat and the
inner wall, and the river, over which there was only one bridge,
divided it from the eastern half, where Mushezib Marduk had
concentrated his forces against our assault. In normal times the
river would have been as great a barrier as any work of men—
even in that darkness I could see the gap in the inner wall through
which it was accustomed to run—but we had diverted its flow and
now it was almost dry.

   We wore tunics over our armor so that we would make no
sound, but I couldn't see even a single fire—there was nothing to
show that the riverbed was guarded at all. What would we find
beyond the inner wall? Had they simply abandoned themselves to
death? No, they'd not held out for fifteen months to meet us with
the wide, uncaring eyes of corpses. Somehow it was too easy.

   And then, all at once, the wind changed and I understood.
Yes, that was precisely how they would meet us, for the air was
heavy with the smell of putrefaction. They had been using the
riverbed as their grave pit.

   I could hear my soldiers coughing and gagging behind me—
it was more than men could bear, and there was no relief to be
found in covering one's nose and mouth; nothing could hold back
that filthy stench. I gave the order to light the torches. We would
give up surprise to burn the air clean enough to breathe. It was
either that or give up our advance and go home.

   Of all the horrors of that grim war, nothing could rival what
awaited us once we had filed through the gap in the inner wall.
There must have been ten thousand corpses that had been
dumped onto the muddy riverbed, a great wall of them extending
for perhaps two hundred paces against the eastern bank, their
rotting limbs tangled together like driftwood left after the season
of flooding. Men, women, children—all ages, all conditions of life,
their bellies swollen and their limbs shriveled to stocks. The ones
nearer the bottom of the pile, crushed and rotting, had long since
ceased to be even recognizably human. Rats, huge, bloated with
carrion, made bold by prosperity, stared at the light from our
torches and then, when they had lost interest, returned to their
gruesome feast. Several of my soldiers turned their backs on the
terrible sight, lowered their heads to between their knees, and
retched loudly. I could hear some of them reciting prayers.

   But there were no guards. It was a lapse which I found hard

to condemn in them—what power could compel anyone, even a soldier, to venture near such a place as this? No one interfered with us, even when we reached the bridge.

The bridge at Babylon is famous, its stone pillars—in a land where stone is never found—slender and tapering, reached down into the Euphrates like the legs of storks. The passageway itself was of wood, and with our grappling ropes we would have no trouble reaching it. The great ziggurat towered over us like a mountain.

"What kept you?"

Esarhaddon spoke in a murmur. We stood in the shadow of the bridge, and he looked back over my shoulder in astonished horror.

"No—don't tell me. I can see. But for the sake of our souls, order your men to put out their torches."

We climbed up to the bridge and made our way across to the eastern half of the city. Esarhaddon and I had agreed in advance that I would take the ziggurat while he assaulted the shrine of Marduk—in the heat of battle he forgot his dread even of the gods —but we hadn't even reached the temple precinct when we found ourselves climbing over barricades of rubble and fighting for our lives. The Babylonians had laid a snare for us and we had walked into it.

We were trapped in the narrow streets, and archers fired down on us from windows overhead. We could not fight back. We could not even see our attackers—or, if a man looked up to see, he might end with an arrow buried in his face. Flights of them rained down, their points ricocheting off the mud walls of buildings with a sound like angry wasps.

At every intersection we met attack from both sides. There were confusion and death everywhere. Sometimes stones and bricks fell on us, scattering men's brains. In the darkness and turmoil many died. We could only push forward.

I do not suppose more than three men in five were still alive and able to fight by the time we reached the great plaza of the ziggurat. The first light of the sun was turning the air to a pale gray—we had space at last and could see to regroup. The Babylonians were not so eager to take the offensive. At the base of the ziggurat a group of priests emerged from one of the smaller side temples—the one who seemed to be their leader raised his hand, as if he could force us to stop with the bare prestige of his office.

At a signal from Esarhaddon the soldiers fell upon them and cut them down, leaving them to lie in their own blood. The ziggurat was ours.

At the second tier of that huge structure we sat down to rest and look about us. Everywhere there was the desperation, the confused hopelessness which is the hallmark of a doomed city's final hours. The assault had begun—by now everyone knew it. The citizens of Babylon knew their last day had come.

I could see already fires raging here and there within the city, and the streets were filled with people, many of them expensively dressed—probably most of the others had gold and jewels sewn into their rags, for who else but the rich survive in a starving city?

I have seen wanton boys catch mice in a wicker basket and then, for sport, throw it into a pond. The mice race about, squealing with terror, climbing higher and higher up the walls of the basket as, slowly, it fills with water and sinks. The people I watched from the ziggurat were just such. They clogged every avenue, aimless, confused, trampling one another in their panic. They must have known they were doomed, but that made no difference to them. With nowhere to flee, with no hope, they scurried about, clawing their way through the crowd, driven on by the blind instinct of fear. If anything, they made their own destruction the surer by rendering it impossible for troops to move from one area of the city to another. Only the great processional way to the north was relatively uncrowded—it was from that direction that the armies of my father were mounting their attack. No one wished to flee to the north.

"The king was right. It's all wasted—look at them." Esarhaddon sat beside me, his hands dangling disconsolately between his knees, glaring down at the mobs in the streets. "They're past caring about the defense of their gods. Their gods have deserted them, and they know it. We'll sit here like lumps of dough until the army crashes in through the wall and butchers this herd of cattle."

He was in a black mood. I could not blame him—we had only to look below at the temple courtyard to see the bodies of our soldiers lying where they had fallen, victims of our monstrous miscalculations.

The wall! Suddenly it struck me, almost as though the god had touched my mind. The wall—of course.

"It isn't wasted if we can capture the wall," I said, as if I were speaking to myself. My brother turned his head to look at me, and his eyes were wide with recognition.

"By the sixty great gods . . ."

We had only to follow our line of sight north up the great processional way and we could see the famous Gate of Ishtar. If we could seize that, the city would be ours by noon.

"But how could we do it? They would see us coming."

"A ruse, brother." I grinned at him, showing my teeth like a crocodile. "All soldiers look alike from above, and in a time of general panic . . ."

"And if it doesn't work, we are dead."

But he stood up, for he had already decided—that was what soldiers were for, to die.

The plan was simplicity itself. I would lead a small force of perhaps thirty men and attempt to force my way onto the wall. If I could surprise the Babylonians and gain a foothold, and keep it for even a quarter of an hour, then Esarhaddon would have a chance of both reinforcing me and storming the gate itself. If we could hold the gate open, the rest of the wall was almost beside the point.

I set out with men from my old company, many of whom had been with me since Khalule, and in the cold gray light of morning we headed up the great processional way at a trot. We still wore our tunics, hiding the uniforms that would have betrayed us in an instant. It required less than four minutes to reach the gate.

There were three soldiers on the parapet directly above the great arched entrance. They leaned over, watching us, whether from alarm or mere curiosity it was impossible to say. Their faces will remain in my memory forever.

I had once seen drawings of the gate's plan—every army has such drawings, although no one, I suspect, ever imagined we would need them—and I tried to remember where the stairway was located that led up to the towers. A glance was enough to tell me that it was nowhere on the outside. Where was it? Where?

I drew my sword and raised it in salute, looking up at the soldiers, never breaking stride.

"We are the reliefs," I shouted—in Aramaic. My heart was pounding like a blacksmith's hammer. "Open the trap."

I kept running, straight through the archway, just as if I had done it a thousand times. And suddenly, in an alcove at one of the points where the passageway abruptly widens out to form a room almost twenty paces across, a square of light struck the tiled floor with an impact we could almost hear. Yes, that was where it had been on the drawing. I remembered now. Yes, they had opened the trap for us—and they had fallen into ours.

I went up the stairway first. There was a soldier at the entrance, holding the great wooden door up for me. He smiled. He even extended his free hand. With my sword, which I still carried, I thrust up and under his breastplate, opening his belly like a wineskin. He died with hardly more than a groan. I caught the door as he fell, throwing it back so that its own weight would hold it open. The other two were already upon me.

I killed one, and the other would have taken my head while I did it if Lushakin had not hacked off the man's arm at the elbow. Our soldiers were coming up through the stairway two at a time now, silent, their eyes blazing. Within seconds we commanded the lower parapet. There was another pair of stairways running up through the gate to the upper tower, but this time the doors were already open. I could hear shouting above—they knew they were being overrun.

"Ashur is King!" I shouted, letting the words tear at my lungs—it was the signal that would bring Esarhaddon, and there was nothing to lose now. Suddenly my cry echoed from a hundred throats—"Ashur is King! Ashur is King!" I had no thought of death now. Failure did not exist. I was in a trance of glory. "Ashur is King!"

They met us on the stairs. The first one cut at me with his sword, swinging from right to left in that narrow space—it was his greatest and last mistake. I parried the blow and thrust up, cutting through his leather breastplate as if it had been woven straw. I could feel my men pushing behind me. I was invincible. I could feel the heat of the god's *melammu* radiating about me like a bright cloud of unconquerable power. There were others ahead, but I stepped over the body of the man I had killed, cutting through them as if they were no more than cobwebs. "Ashur is King!" I shouted. "Ashur is King!"

I pushed out into the sunlight, and the man in front of me actually started back, as if he had seen a devil. I struck him upon the temple with the flat of my sword and he fell down like a log— I was no longer killing men; I was clearing them out, trampling them down like river weeds. I must make a path for my soldiers. It was a shining moment.

I know not how many we killed—how many *I* killed—but it was over in the tenth part of an hour. We were spattered with blood and our lungs ached from shouting. Soon, very soon, the Babylonians would counterattack, but that no longer mattered. The gate was ours. The city was ours—the world was ours! What difference could it make if I were dead the next minute? We had won!

From the highest tower of that gate, one of the world's great wonders, we looked down to see the soldiers of Ashur, our brothers, swarming over the broken outer wall. They had to know—they must know. Here, where we stood, was the way. We had opened the city's door to them.

"Ashur is King!" we shouted. We could see their faces as they heard us, as they raised their weapons in salute. We could not stop—we would cry the god's name until our voices died in our throats. "Ashur is King! Ashur is King! Ashur is King!"

When the sun set that night, there was not a single Babylonian soldier still in arms. Most were dead, hacked to pieces by an enemy mad for vengeance, who hunted them down with pitiless efficiency. A few, perhaps, managed to hide, to change into rags and throw aside their weapons, but if they imagined they would find mercy by concealing themselves among the citizens, they erred fatally, for there was no mercy.

Death stalked the streets, waiting for any who dared to show themselves. The lord king kept his word, and the city of Babylon was made to suffer five days of fire, death, and pillage while the army of Ashur roamed about, drunk with victory and the powerlessness of their victims. They were like a pack of wild dogs, these soldiers of the god. They killed for plunder, for revenge, for sport. Whole families were massacred within the walls of their homes. The streets were deep in blood, and there were corpses everywhere. Women were raped before the eyes of their husbands and children—not by one man but ten, or twenty—and then, either in pity or wanton butchery—had their throats cut. Fires started everywhere and were left to burn. There was no clean water except in the camps of the victors and no food, so disease and starvation raged on, for not a grain of millet could be brought within the walls and no Babylonian could leave them alive. It was a mad time.

I did not try to stop the looting and the slaughter—the king, forgetting in his anger that men who run riot like this will be hard to bring to order, had commanded that no officer in his army was to interfere, and I did not. I did not love these people, and felt no pity for them. If they perished and their city with them, I would not regret it—this is what war does to a man's soul. But it did not take long before my heart sickened within me at what my eyes made me witness.

At first I merely thought, this is bad discipline. As an officer, I disapproved of what the king had done. And then, slowly, as I walked the streets and saw what the sack of a great city meant, I ceased to be merely the professional soldier who is concerned that the army should be kept within restraint, and as a man I was appalled by the pointless cruelty of the thing. The corpses of young girls lay in doorways, where their bowels had been searched by the sword; their heads were thrown back and their mouths yawned in voiceless screaming. Children were crumpled in gutters. War was the business of kings and soldiers—if they lost, they died, as was only right. But these were the innocents. None of these had taken part in the murder of the *marsarru* Ashurnadinshum, nor had these taken up arms with the Elamites. Yet these, too, fell victims of the king's wrath. After a few days I stayed in camp, where even from my tent I could see pillars of smoke rising to the sky as Babylon burned. It was not willingly that I ventured again within her gates.

I saw Esarhaddon but once during those days. He suffered no qualms, for the taking of the city and its aftermath, the raw action, had driven away all his doubts and made him happy again. I saw him at night, after the second day of the sack, for he stopped at my tent to display his plunder.

"See? Twins!"

And there they were, led along by the ropes around their necks, two girls, naked, hardly more than children, frightened but glad to be alive, dark-eyed, plump, and pretty—and alike as two petals picked from the same flower. Esarhaddon grinned broadly, well pleased with himself.

"I go now to my quarters to try them out. See, brother, how all good things come to the godly man. Hah, hah, hah!"

I could still hear his laughter, even as he disappeared into the darkness.

And perhaps he was right to believe this blessing was no more than his due for, once again, Esarhaddon had been cheated of the place that was his by right.

He and his men had fought hard to secure the gate entrance, and it had only been because of him that we were able to hold that section of the wall, but it was I whom all had seen upon the tower, shouting the glory of the god. It was my name which was on all men's lips, me whom the king honored for daring, taking me even deeper into his heart.

Then perhaps it really was the god's design to make me king after my father, for he raised me beyond my merits. He seemed to have chosen me to shine over other men, and the Ishtar Gate was where he had seen fit to make his choice known to the eyes of men.

It would seem so. Mine was the glory when an equal share should have fallen to Esarhaddon, whom none called great, mighty, brave.

I would not have blamed him if he had come to think me no better than a thief, though it was not my doing that he was robbed of his fame. But he did not. Or, if he did, it was only in the private places of his own heart that he cursed me, for he never spoke of it. We never spoke of these things, and between us there was ever a brother's love.

For five days the murder and plundering went on, and then even the king, who hated the very ground upon which Babylon stood, had had enough and gave orders that the sack of the city was to end. Soldiers, once they have slipped the leash, are not easily called back to order, and we had to hang a few and whip raw the backs of many more, but at last the army was brought back to ranks. They grumbled, these men of Ashur, but they obeyed.

The spoils of this long siege were great. Babylon was a city of unimaginable riches, and they were now ours. We looted the holy places, the idol of Great Marduk we carried back in slavery to Nineveh, and we found, in his temple, idols of Adad and Shala which had been looted from the temples of Ashur over four hundred years before. We even captured Mushezib Marduk, who called himself king; he had tried to escape but was captured and weighted down with chains.

And when the great buildings had been stripped and gutted, the system of dikes which held back the Euphrates was destroyed so that when the season of flooding came the river would rise and wash away their very foundations. The vengeance of Sennacherib was to be complete.

The last night before we were to turn our faces to the north and find our way home, the king held a banquet. The site he chose was the royal palace, damaged by fire and torn down by the king's order, so we were to dine among its ruins. All of his chief officers were there, and all his sons.

On that desolate piece of rubble, surrounded by a dead city, it was a crazed revel we enjoyed. Our master, the Lord of Ashur, was beside himself with triumph—he even ordered that Mushezib Marduk be brought in that, naked and desperate, chained to a broken pillar in the house where once he had been master, he could witness the festivities of his conquerors. This king of shadow would be taken to Nineveh, there to suffer a death of exquisite cruelty, a death such as only ruined monarchs die, but that night he huddled in a corner like a dog.

And we, the conquerors, drank and ate and laughed, trying not to think or to look too closely about us. And the king my father praised me above all men.

"Look at him!" he bellowed, his face shining. "He is not even twenty and already he carries three great wounds upon his body —and all in the front! What a man, what a warrior he is already— what a king he would make! Is he not a son any man would be proud to own? Is he not?"

He made me stand that all might see the glory of his loins. And they cheered me, these great ones, for they knew the king's will. They cheered me, shouting my name.

I was made to stand and listen, my heart dying within me.

"Do I do wrong, holy father?" I had asked of the *maxxu,* and he had raised his blind eyes to my face and smiled, as if a child questioned him.

"You? You do nothing at all, Tiglath Ashur."

12

After the fall of Babylon the king promoted me to *rab shaqe* and Esarhaddon to *rab abru*—always one step behind. There was little enough else left to do except receive honors, and within a few days the army broke camp and began the long march back to Nineveh. In the Land of Sumer all resistance to the might of Ashur's will was at an end. The city we left behind us as we turned our faces to the north was a ruin in which not even the foxes could have made a home.

But in the Land of Ashur there was no pity. The destruction of Babylon meant only that this long war had at last found its end. The people remembered their sufferings and thought of their present safety and rejoiced to be ruled over by a king who was not afraid to be cruel to his enemies. In the border towns, where hatred of the Elamites and their puppet allies had been greatest, the people gathered by the roads to hail their glorious lord and to hurl curses after Mushezib Marduk as he trudged along behind the conqueror's chariot. We were heroes to those who had not seen the work of our hands in Babylon.

For myself, I tried to close my ears to the shouting. I tried neither to hear nor see nor think, for I heard only the cries of the dying and saw but the corpses of the slain—and I feared they would drive me to madness. My soul was in torment, and at night I could not bear even to close my eyes.

How was this? I felt myself stained with sin, and yet I had done no more than follow what I had always believed—what everyone believed, even the foe—was the path to virtue and honor. Who is nobler, who is more respected in all nations than the warrior? What else was I? A murderer? A thief? Why then this sense of shame?

But I kept such questions locked away in my own heart. Perhaps they were in the hearts of many in that victorious army winding its way home, but I shall never know, for soldiers do not speak of their doubts.

Did Esarhaddon doubt? I think not. Esarhaddon was too busy with his women and the contemplation of his new wealth—the king had showered us both with gold and palaces and great estates, for while he favored me above all others he had come to understand that Esarhaddon was not to be despised.

"But can you not at least make him *rab shaqe*?" I asked. "If I have earned it, so has he. He is the first of your sons and a brave and resourceful fighter."

"You are the first of my sons."

"Yet give him at least a command worthy of him. Let him prove what is in him."

"I know well enough what is in him." The king shook his head. "He is constantly putting before me some new plan to conquer Phrygia, or Egypt, or even Arabia—enlighten me, my son, what is there to conquer in Arabia except sand? And, of course, he would lead each of these campaigns, which I would hesitate to entrust even to my most seasoned officers, as sole commander. He is a boy still, and thinks only of his own glory. He is in love with war, forgetting that it is merely a tool of power, and such as he are a danger to have near the throne. No, I will not give him his own war to fight, not even to please you. Your brother makes my head ache.

"But never fear—after I am dead you may reward him as you see fit."

And, strangely enough, with these views my brother Esarhaddon did not entirely disagree.

"You had best make up your mind that I shall be the greatest of your generals," he said, shrugging his shoulders. "Our father means you to be king after him. And why not? You are a wiser choice than I—everyone would agree with that except, perhaps, my mother—but if I must wait always in your shadow until our father is safe in his tomb, then you had best resign yourself to a quarrelsome reign, for I plan to make up for the slights that are heaped upon me now by conquering all the western lands. I will set up monuments to my glory in Thebes and Memphis, in all the great cities of the Nile, that a thousand years hence, when Tiglath Ashur the king is forgotten, the might of Esarhaddon the soldier will still make men quake in their sandals. You owe me this, brother, for I am neglected that you may be made great."

We had stopped for the night in a village not two days' march from Nineveh, and Esarhaddon, saying he wished to sleep with a real roof over his head, had chased a peasant and his family out of their house and taken it over. He lay on his back on a reed sleeping mat and the twins rubbed warm oil into his thighs, so he was very content with life that night.

"I know as much, brother. I have spoken with the king. . . ."

"Oh, I do not bother with the king." Esarhaddon grinned, pinching one of the twins on the breast to hear her squeal. It did not, however, take a *baru* to see the unhappiness in his eyes. "When you are with him, the king is too deaf with cheering to hear even the name of Esarhaddon. You and half the army could shout my praises to him for a week and he would not notice—not that such a thing could happen, for the army takes its cue from him and sings no one's glory but yours. No, I must wait until you are king. Then, while you stay in your capital with your consort and your eunuch scribes, wondering which of your sons is plotting to have you poisoned, I will fight your wars and become more brilliant than the sun."

"What can I say, my brother? Except that I pray you do not grow bitter against me, for you are wronged through no will of mine."

Yet wronged none the less. Esarhaddon, burdened with his ambition to be great—and why should he not dream of greatness, since we had all been raised to imagine our lives could have no higher purpose than to conquer in the name of our king and his god—what did he not suffer? Was he a block of wood that he felt nothing? No, he was not that. He suffered and knew bitterness. And why should he not hate me, who was the cause of his suffering?

Still, rather than accuse me, he reached out his hand to me and squeezed mine hard in his strong fingers.

"I know this, brother. I know."

And so it appeared that we were all in accord with the future that seemed to stretch before us like the road to Nineveh. Why should I not be king when even my chief rival wished it? The god,

of course, must give his consent, but had he not already marked
me out as the object of his special favor? Who did not wish it,
except Naq'ia—and, perhaps, some part of myself? I had only to
rid my mind of darkness, it seemed, and I would be blessed above
all other men.

So we traveled on to Nineveh, an army of conquerors, having
set all things right in the lands where Ashur was lord. And in
Nineveh the work of our hands was also praised.

"You have accomplished this thing," Esharhamat said to me,
in a soft voice, her mouth almost touching my ear. "The king
loves you, and you appear glorious to the people. You have done
well, Tiglath Ashur, whom I worship with my whole self."

But I was hardly listening. I did not wish to remember my
glory, or the king's love, or how I had come to possess these
things. I wished only to drown myself in the sweet smell of
Esharhamat's body that I might lose all sense of an existence
beyond her. I did not love myself now, so I wished more than ever
to love her.

While she whispered words, I let my hands slide over her
body, finding the wide sleeves of her tunic that I might touch her
breasts. I pressed my lips into the flesh of her neck, hungry for the
taste of her. What were her ambitions or my hopes or the lordship
of the world compared to the passionate demands of the flesh?

And was she less fevered than I? Her breath was hot and
came in quick little gasps as she dug her nails into the backs of my
arms. We were sitting side by side on a marble bench in her garden, the only sound the silvery tinkle of the fountain's waters,
alone—as always, she had seen to that—and I had only to lift the
hem of her robe to spill her virgin blood over the cold stone. I
could feel my manhood, tight, throbbing like a war drum, and I
thought I might choke with desire as she seemed to melt in my
embrace, as if she wished to disappear into my body.

"No . . ." The word was only a constricted little sound, like
a strangled sob. "No, not here—there are too many spies here.
Too many enemies."

"Damn your enemies—I don't care. I can't . . ."

My hands trembled. I tried to undo the clasp of her tunic,
but my fingers would not seem to obey. I would tear it open . . .

"No—not here, Tiglath. Listen to me!"

With calm, efficient strength she pushed me from her, and

when I tried to reach for her again I found my fingers caught in her grip.

"Why do you do this? Why?" I was so angry I stood up from the bench, my hands clenched into fists. I seemed to hate her—I would have done anything, said anything. "If you do not wish me to touch you, then I will go to the temple of Ishtar. I will . . ."

"Good—then go! Tonight! Find a woman who pleases you and drop your silver into her lap!"

I looked into her eyes, seeing once more the blind, greedy rashness of her love, as if she would perish without it, seeing the danger from which she turned her eyes. She should have wept with fear and shame, but she did not. She was laughing.

"If you go tonight, at the last moment of daylight, wait beside the door. The woman who will come to you there, with a widow's veil over her head, will be me."

The remaining hours of that day were the longest I have ever lived through. The prisoner in his cage, waiting for the sun to rise on the morning of his execution, does not suffer more than the lover whose conscience is not easy, and what Esharhamat proposed was a blasphemy against the goddess.

Ishtar grants her blessing to the pure maiden who gives her virginity not with passion but to one who is to her a stranger, a man she will lie with once and see no more. To these the Lady Wrapped in Loveliness gives fertility and a husband with strong loins, but her temple shall not be used as a trysting place. The rites of sacred harlotry have no place for such as Esharhamat and I, and we both understood this. I was filled with darkness. I would meet her, since she would have it so and because I felt myself too covered in sin to resist, but I knew we were damning ourselves.

Esharhamat, it seemed, was easy in her mind, but women are braver than men, who can face death without trembling. She, it seemed, could face even the wrath of heaven. Or perhaps she had merely perfected the art of lying to herself.

I took a horse and rode out from the city, following the river until I could look in every direction without seeing a human figure. Then I dismounted, tethered my horse, and sat down by the rushing waters of the Tigris to listen to its voice until it should wash me clean of foreboding, until I could know what it was I wished for myself.

Did I expect the *maxxu* to come to me yet once more, to tell me the god's will and give me rest? I think not. I hoped for it, to find those blind eyes resting once more on my face, but I did not really expect it. He did not come, but his words haunted my mind, adding to my torment. He had spoken of Nineveh as a dead city. I will find nothing here, neither glory nor happiness nor friendship nor love, he had told me. Yet I had found all these things already. "Listen to the promptings of your heart," he had said. "The sin will not be yours." Yet I was covered in guilt and my heart knew now one direction, now another, as if it would pull me apart. My praises were on all men's lips but my own. I was divided against myself.

No, there was no peace in the muddy waters of that mother of rivers. She rolled past me, heedless. She had been here since the days of the gods and would remain long after I and all the race of men were dust. She nourished us all but was indifferent, as if her bounty were as nothing, as we were ourselves.

I had been sitting by the river's edge a long time. The horse touched my back with its nose, as if to remind me that it had a stall waiting for it back at the house of war. Yes, the point was well taken. I rose and mounted, turning my face toward the city which it was prophesied I would outlive, because there was no escape. Even a horse knew as much, and was therefore wiser than I.

The temple of Ishtar is a vast walled complex of buildings and enclosed gardens, almost a city in itself, and, indeed, it could not be otherwise, for it is home to perhaps two hundred of the sacred harlots and easily twice as many of their servants and followers, most of whom are eunuchs.

The women of this precinct are nothing like the common prostitutes found plying their trade in the wineshops and streets of every city in the world—for there is no degradation in the service of Ishtar, Goddess of Love and Fruitfulness. The temple harlots are women of great beauty and charm—and sometimes of considerable intelligence as well—who are honored wherever they go, surrounded as they are by an aura of inexplicable chastity, as if they had preserved their virginity at the temple door, rather than losing it there like other women. It is not unheard of for them to amass great fortunes and retire, sometimes to marriage with important men—and such a man does not have to feel afraid that anyone might be snickering behind his back, for he is an object of envy rather than the butt of coarse jokes.

Most of the women who come to the temple do not, however, have any thought of staying. They perform their ritual and go home with nothing except their silver coin, which will be sewn into the decoration of their wedding tunic, and perhaps a memory, pleasant or unpleasant as the case might be, and perhaps not even that.

The temple itself is as unlike a brothel as any place on earth, for there is no drunkenness and no shame, everything is pleasant and orderly, and there is not that peculiar sense of mockery which prostitutes generally bring to their work—there is no feigned passion and no sense that the men who come there are merely fools to be teased out of their money and sent away. The virgins who enter only once are too innocent and too apprehensive for that, and the sacred harlots are skilled enough to please themselves as well as their clients.

As the sunlight dwindled to nothing, I waited outside the temple entrance, on the great stairway made of burned brick colored blue and yellow in alternate bands as it rose from the level of the street. The steps were crowded with women, some of them nervously glancing around them—will it be this man who will come for me? or this? or this?—and some merely bored with waiting, and some, the plain ones, who had been there longest, with eyes glazed and hopeless, as if they could see the emptiness of their future stretching out before them.

Esharhamat had not yet arrived, and as I stood there men and women stared at me, as if I must be either hopelessly bashful or some species of idiot who could not bring himself to make a choice. But my uneasiness had for its source something beyond the curious attention of such as these, for I felt as if I were under the eyes of the gods.

Esharhamat did not come. My shadow lengthened across the burned brick steps, covering now one seated figure, now another, and still Esharhamat did not come. Of course—she had seen reason and would save us both from this terrible sin. I tried to hope it might be so, and my eyes darted anxiously up and down the great straight Street of Ishtar. Yes, of course. She would not come. And

fool that I was, I yearned for a glimpse of her that I might know
her love was greater than her prudence.

In the gathering darkness, waiting women lighted little clay
lamps that men might still see their faces. Here and there they
huddled together around a brazier or wrapped their arms about
their knees and slept where they sat. Threads of laughter reached
me through the still air—the temple would still be a busy place
long after the rest of the city slept.

She will not come, I told myself. I understood now that she
had meant this as a punishment upon me, that she was even then
in her own rooms, safe and surrounded by her women, smiling
secretly at the thought of my fool's vigil.

Or, perhaps, not so secretly. Perhaps this was a great joke she
would share with her women, how she had avenged herself upon
the mighty Tiglath Ashur, whose name was glorious but who was
still but a man and, like all men, gulled by a few soft words. Raw
as a schoolboy. A simpleton.

Yet I too could dance to that merry pipe. Esharhamat would
laugh no more when she heard—and she would hear, for she
seemed to hear everything—that Tiglath Ashur, the mighty, the
valiant, whose sinews had the strength of iron and whose heart
was bronze, that her glorious lover on this night, appointed for his
disgrace, had not waited idly but had led another woman—and
more than one, many, and such as otherwise would wait through
many a cold night, poor plain little things—into the temple of
Ishtar, showering their laps with silver and leaving them to dream
all their lives. . . .

But the idea brought me shame almost as soon as it formed
in my mind, for Esharhamat had come after all.

A carrying chair, enclosed, such as only great ladies might
use, stopped at the foot of the temple steps. The little door
opened. A woman covered in the red veil of mourning stepped
down. Yes, of course she had come. I was ashamed of my contem-
plated betrayal, ashamed to have doubted her, glad she had come
and ashamed of that as well. But glad just the same. Esharhamat,
fairest of women, how the desire for her rose in my liver, as if a
green fire consumed me.

I watched as her tiny feet, peeking out with each step from
beneath the hem of her tunic, mounted the great brick stairway to
the temple door. I watched as men and women alike stepped aside
to let her pass, humbled and abashed in the presence of such

radiance. No one could see her face, but no one could doubt her beauty, for it was a thing witnessed by her slightest movement, by the delicacy of her little jeweled hands, by her eyes, large and dark, luminous as the night moon. She had come, to this place, to my arms.

I had only to hold out my hand to her and she touched the palm with the tips of her fingers. We had been born for this moment, she and I. This night, this place, they belonged to us. I had not even to speak her name. She took my arm and we passed through the temple doors.

It was a tiny room where Esharhamat and I became one flesh. The attendant, a eunuch, to whom I gave a gold coin that would feed him until the winter burned to death in the summer sun, provided us with a brazier to keep us warm and with his own hand closed the oxhide curtain across the threshold. I spread my cloak out over the floor—we needed no other sleeping mat—and Esharhamat unfastened her veil and let it fall away from her face. We knelt together there, our bodies touching, my hands on her shoulders as I lowered my mouth to kiss her. It seemed a moment beyond passion, as if we had entered into the presence of a mystery. Our lips brushed—so gently it almost could have been an accident—and then, when I could feel her little pointed tongue searching for mine, I sought her with the hunger of all these empty months of waiting we had known. All my longing for her was in that first kiss. I would gladly have died for this one instant with her.

But I did not die. I had never been so alive as I was then—perhaps I never would be again. Nothing mattered to me, nothing except the taste of her lips and the warm scent of her hair and the feel of her hands on my arms. I lived only in my senses and in my love.

Esharhamat undid the fastenings of her tunic and let it slip to her feet. The dim red light of the brazier played over her legs and belly, but she was hidden in shadow above the waist. I placed my hands upon her shoulders and she covered them with her own and guided them down until they were cupped over her breasts. I could feel the pressure of her quick, shallow breathing against my palms as I kissed her throat, the soft little hollow beneath her ear, the point of her chin.

"Come into me," she whispered, her breath moist and warm

against my cheek. "Come into me—hurt me. I do not care how much you hurt me."

"No, not yet. Not quite yet."

I was hard as new-forged iron, but I wanted to give her some pleasure before I broke her maidenhead. I forced her down with my weight so that her back was against the cloak I had spread over the brick floor, and the tip of my manhood just brushed against her little feathered cleft—I could feel her thighs around me as she tried to encircle me and draw me to her. The tension itself heightened her desire, and soon I was sliding easily back and forth over her tight cleft and she began to moan, softly at first, and then as if she wished to sob with despairing agony. Only it was not agony, but her passionate longing.

Finally, as I thrust forward, I could feel her maidenhead resist and then give way. Esharhamat cried out—but only once, for almost in that instant her pain was swallowed up in a greedy ecstasy as I drove into her, her virgin blood easing my way. I thought I could not bear my own pleasure as suddenly, and in a great rush . . . there were no words, no words.

Afterward, and for a long time, we lay together, locked in silent embrace. I entered her again, and this time there was an even greater feast for the senses but not the same almost unearthly rapture, which perhaps two people may only have once in all their life together. I do not know—my time with Esharhamat was all too brief, and I never knew such joy in the arms of another woman.

"We may not come to this place again," I said at last, when I could bear to break the silence of our perfect concord. "We must never return to this place. But I shall find another—I shall find—"

She stilled me with her kisses. She did not need to hear what, after all, were only words. She knew that now I could never bear to be without her, that she had won, that I would love her always, even at the cost of my life. Yes, of course she knew.

"I will find à house, some quiet place where—"

"You have a house," she murmured, like a mother whispering to her child in the night. "Or, at least, your slave has a house."

"Yes, but the risk—not only to ourselves but to . . ."

"Kephalos? I do not care about Kephalos! It is the same for us as for him, and he is a slave."

I did not say to her what was in my heart, that Kephalos was less my slave than my friend, that it would be cowardly in me to involve him in my own ruin, that she was without pity. I did not say these things. I was silent, for I knew that it was her love for me that made her thus, and I knew that I would do whatever I must, that I cared for no tie on earth, no debt of honor or friendship, so much as I did for the sweet touch of Esharhamat's flesh. Yes, I knew already what I must do.

For the next several days my time was not at my own disposal. The king, ever since our return from the south, had been restless with new energy, as if his conquest of Babylon had awakened him from a trance, and I was now, in fact if not in title, one of the royal companions and was expected to attend him as he followed his rounds of pleasure and duty. I was there at his council meetings and his banquets. I stood behind him when, as Chief Priest of Ashur, he prayed to his god. I listened when he told his stories and laughed when it pleased him to jest. And when he hunted—he hunted now nearly every day, as if he could not bear to part utterly with the pleasures of war—I was at his side. I drove his chariot when we pursued the lions in his private preserve and when we wheeled out onto the great plains around Nineveh to track down the herds of wild asses. When his beaters and his packs of dogs ran deer into his snares so that he could kill them at his leisure with a long spear as, their antlers tangled and their eyes rolling with terror, they struggled in the nets, I carried his weapons and wiped the blood from his hands and face. I was his son and his favorite and these things fell to me as a matter of duty. And even as I came to see that he was after all only a man and not the shining idol of kingship the world took him to be, I grew to love the Lord Sennacherib, whose seed I was, who had taken me to his heart.

The Ruler of the Earth's Four Corners was now old. He had many weaknesses and his mind had grown maggoty with a thousand anxious fears. And, although he still clung to all the symbols of his days of glorious and triumphant youth, his hunting and his revelry, to all the splendor of his power, I suspect he was not blind to the changes in himself. There were but few whom he trusted, but he came to lean on them more and more. The *turtanu*

Sinahiusur—his brother and perhaps his only real friend—the lady Naq'ia, myself, and his daughter, the Lady Shaditu.

I saw much of Shaditu in those days. If I sat at the king's left hand, she sat at his right. When he returned from his almost daily round of slaughter, she was there to meet us at the royal gate, bearing a bowl of water in which he could wash the dust from his face. More than once, as we sat opposite from each other at the banqueting table, her naked foot slipped under the hem of my tunic and she would run her toes over my skin, smiling at me the whole time like the most wanton tavern whore.

And if I did not become her lover, many did. Many a young man cooled his lust on her sleeping pallet, and everyone—except, it seemed, the king—knew. Or perhaps he refused to know. Or perhaps he did know and was past caring.

And, of course, there was always the Lady Naq'ia. She shared his bed almost every night, for if the king went into his other women it was merely for the sake of appearances. Sennacherib had fathered many children, but in the winter of his life he had only passion enough left for her, whom he seemed to need as another man needs air to fill his lungs. The lady Naq'ia was silent and seldom seen, but all knew that in the palace of the king her word had the force of law. I tried, as best I could, not even to remember her existence, but she was part of the atmosphere of those times, like the scent of death on the wind.

And thus, hemmed in by my life as a courtier, with its duties of attendance and the constant pressure of its pale intrigues and nagging, unspoken rivalries, by that world of faint menace which had become the king's inner circle, I had many excuses for putting off my visit to Kephalos's house near the Gate of Adad. I made the most of them, for I did not relish the business.

But at last the thing must be done.

I did not send word to Kephalos that I wanted to see him, for I was afraid that he might guess my errand. Kephalos would know what the whole city knew, and many must have recognized the face of the man who had met a great lady at the steps to the temple of Ishtar—and I would not give him time to frame an excuse for refusing me. It was cowardly of me, for he would need no excuse beyond the claims of simple prudence, but even taken by surprise my slave would be agile enough in his own interest and I had no confidence of being within my rights in this matter.

So I simply appeared before his door one morning, at an hour when I could assume he would be unencumbered with affairs.

The boy Ernos—no longer quite a boy—met me and took my cloak, bowing low and glowering the whole time, as if he suspected some mischief, and when I let it be understood that I wished to see his master without delay he led me to the upper story of the house where, behind a curtained doorway, I found Kephalos lying comfortably in a huge bronze tub, big enough to serve as the sarcophagus of a king, up to his beard in hot, heavily perfumed water. Philinna, naked as dawn, was squatting on the floor behind him, rubbing his fat back with a cloth. They both looked up with surprised annoyance, as if I had caught them at something they would have been as happy to keep to themselves.

"Do not attempt to rise, Worthy Physician, or you will slip and break your head. You see how polite I am? I have not even asked you what you are doing in that thing—what is it, by the way?"

"I am surprised at my young master's ignorance," he announced grandly, taking the cloth from Philinna to wet it and wring it out over his head. "For was it not the king your father's own army which brought this back with them among the spoils from Babylon? It is a most civilized refinement, such as one would expect from the Babylonians—one washes one's body, thus, more effectively and far more agreeably than in a sweating house, where one is also annoyed by the presence of all such common riffraff as care to enter so public a place."

As if to illustrate his point, he raised his foot out of the water and allowed Philinna to polish it with great vigor, as if she imagined it to be a copper cooking pot. While she did so, her great breasts rolled around like waterskins on the deck of a pitching boat.

"Yes," I answered, in Akkadian. "Esarhaddon too thinks it entertaining to take his women to the baths with him. I am not surprised you do not have her in there with you, Kephalos. Would you not find that more convenient?"

"The Lord Tiglath Ashur has a waspish tongue for such an early hour. Can it be that he imagines he has cause to be displeased with his servant?"

He watched me for a moment through narrowed eyes, as if I

were a patient to be treated with salves or hot mustard water, and
then his expression cleared.

"No," he went on finally. "I see it is not with Kephalos that
he is at odds, but with himself. Philinna, hand me a drying cloth
and then be about preparing the prince something to eat. In any
case, leave us."

When the door curtain swung shut, Kephalos, who had already wrapped himself in a sheet of linen the size of a sail, waited
for a few moments, his head cocked to one side as if he were
listening for something, and then padded over to the entranceway
and peeked outside. He left huge wet footprints on the tile floor; I
stared down at them with uncomprehending wonder—I could
hardly understand what I was doing here.

"She is gone. There is no one without," he said, smiling and
nodding. Then, after he had adjusted his linen covering, by now
grown damp straight through and clinging to him like a skin he
was in the process of sloughing off, he raised his hands in a gesture of cynical resignation. "The man is a fool whose trust resides
with his household servants, Lord."

"Am I not to trust you then, Kephalos?"

His hands slowly sank through the air, and as they did my
slave's face seemed to melt like wax, the ends of his mouth col-
lapsing into a frown as his forehead creased and buckled under
the weight of his sorrow.

"Oh, do not speak the thing, master," he said, even as he
sank down onto the rim of his great bronze tub. "Pray, tell me
quickly you have not come about the Lady Esharhamat, for
though all men whisper you will be king one day, you are not yet
safe in the house of succession, and to take that one to your
sleeping mat is to flirt with the executioner's knife."

I did not trouble to ask myself how he could have known
what I wished of him. I did not need to ask, for when I met the
veiled lady at the temple of Ishtar I had announced my intentions
to the world. And, though I felt defeat and ruin crowding about
me, like a farmer who watches a summer flood washing away his
barley harvest, I merely shrugged my shoulders, as if we discussed
a matter of indifference. Doubtless I fooled no one.

"She is a widow, Kephalos, and quite at her own discretion
until she is given again in marriage. Besides, I have been led to
understand by the *turtanu* Sinahiusur that a blind eye . . ."

"The blind eyes will be yours, master, cut out of your head with a dagger should the Lord Esarhaddon become king and discover that you have been rutting on his bride."

"All women are alike to Esarhaddon—he is not fastidious on this point. Besides, my brother loves me."

"Yes, my young fool of a lord, but he does not love *me!*"

Kephalos threw himself to his feet with such violence that the water in his bath nearly cascaded onto the floor. He stamped about like a man distracted, his eyes the whole time fixed imploringly on my face.

"Lord, do not imagine that your brother's forgiving temper can be relied upon to *that* degree—if he finds that you have been using my house as a . . . Oh, by the blessed gods of the west, I cannot bear even to think upon it!"

"Does this mean that in this I am not to trust you, Kephalos?"

"No, master, since it seems I have no hope of dissuading you from this folly—it means nothing of the sort."

My slave, the clever and prosperous physician Kephalos, regarded me with something which in another man might have been mistaken for aggrieved sorrow, as if I were the son who had disappointed a father's fondest hopes, but I knew that look merely meant he was thinking.

"Everyone saw you on the temple steps, master. It was most unwise to meet the lady there."

"But perhaps not everyone is clever enough to guess the lady's name."

"Everyone is that clever, master." He laughed with sudden brevity, as if the joke had only then occurred to him. "This is the price of glory, that all men know your face and are interested in your concerns. If the Lady Esharhamat is spoken of outside your father's palace, it is only because she is loved by the mighty prince, the Lord Tiglath Ashur, whose name is feared to the ends of the earth."

"Do not mock me, Kephalos. It is not wise to mock me in this."

"I do not mock you, Lord—though you have behaved like a great fool and deserve to be mocked. I simply point out what is plain to all men except yourself."

He put his hand upon my shoulder and peered earnestly into my face that I might see he was not in jest. And then he smiled.

"Come, my foolish young master. Let me dress myself that we may both preserve our dignity, and then we will drink more wine than is good for us and discuss how best you may enjoy the Lady Esharhamat's embraces in safety."

13

The year which followed, while I basked in love, glory, and hope, was the happiest of my youth.

Kephalos, who in all practical matters was much wiser than I, saw at once that there was no hope of hiding my intrigue with Esharhamat from the eyes of the palace. At the same time, however, he judged that it was from there we had least to fear, since Esharhamat must marry whoever would be the next king and therefore enjoyed a certain immunity. No one would dare to move against her as long as her conduct escaped becoming a public scandal, and it was on this object that my slave lavished all his cunning.

"At all costs, master," he said, shaking his head vigorously—he had by then become more than a little drunk, which made all his movements more emphatic but seemed somehow to have no effect whatever on his agility of mind—"at all costs we must prevent this affair from descending to the common gossip of the city. The Lady Esharhamat is the prize for which all contend, for with her comes the throne of Assyria, and thus, should some other besides yourself become king, he cannot strike you down for enjoying her bed—at least, he may not do this in public—except if he does not fear to call the legitimacy of his offspring into question. This he will shrink from as long as the common people believe her to be virtuous, and this they will believe as long as you are discreet. She is a widow and commits no offense against decency by pleasing herself with you, but your brother the Lord Esarhaddon, should he rule, will want no hint of suspicion that his sons are not his own. As you say, he is not fastidious in his dealing with women and for himself will not care, but it is best that these matters be kept hidden from view.

"And thus, master, under no circumstances must you bring her here, for all men know whose slave is the physician Kephalos and even the good people of Nineveh are not so blind as not to see what takes place under their very eyes. Besides, there is the small matter of my own safety—Esarhaddon will not scruple to let his wrath fall on me if I too openly assist you to enjoy his future lady of the palace. No, I must make other arrangements."

There are in every city certain quarters where people know it is wisest to pay heed only to their own affairs and leave their neighbors in peace. One's comings and goings are not noted, and if the street is awakened in the middle of the night with sounds of violence, the residents will wait until there is quiet again, then perhaps someone will check to be sure whoever has been left lying in the gutter is actually dead, and then everyone will return to his own blameless rest. In such quarters it is well understood that all men have secrets and that the less these are noised about the better. It was in such a quarter that Kephalos purchased two houses, on different streets, which happened to share a common back wall.

"This is called the Street of Nergal, master." He gestured with his arm as if dismissing a tavern keeper. "Here a young man in a hurry for his inheritance could for about five silver shekels hire a man to cut his father's throat—unless, of course, that young man's name happened to be Tiglath Ashur; the murder of a king is rather too ambitious a crime for such as call this place home. But everything else, from stolen copper cooking pots to the favors of little beardless boys, is for sale here somewhere. One has only to know where to look."

I glanced about me and had no difficulty understanding how the place had come by its name, for that god of plagues, the great patron of the underworld, would have felt quite at home among these leprous-looking walls, these buildings whose upper stories seemed to teeter out toward the street, as if balanced on the edge of collapse. Unlike most of Nineveh, where people in all their noisy, busy self-preoccupation crowded the streets so that one could hardly pass, here there was quiet, and but a few furtive, silent figures—veiled women and men who turned their backs when they felt one's eyes on them—stood about, shuffling their feet, as if waiting for someone they rather wished would never come. Indeed, the place seemed under a kind of curse.

Kephalos peered at me with apparent amusement as we paced over the center of the empty street—anyone might have supposed we were measuring its length.

"I can imagine what you are thinking, master, but I can assure you that no one here will come to you with his hand open. You will be under no threat of exposure, for these people are not much interested in matters of state and have probably never even heard of Tiglath Ashur. Besides, their greed is too cautious for them to think of practicing extortion against a royal prince. You and the lady will be safe enough. Come—let us look at the house."

The place had little enough to recommend it; there was not so much as a three-legged stool on the ground floor, merely an empty cooking grate and a few clay jars with cobwebs stretched over their mouths. Above, in the larger of two rooms, I found a blanket, a sleeping mat rolled up against a wall, and a copper pan for washing oneself in.

"Come in here, Lord, and see my contrivance."

There was a doorway cut in the back wall, covered with a bullhide curtain. Kephalos pushed it aside and then opened a heavy wooden door that had been barred from our side. We walked through to a larger room which took up the entire upper story of a different house. The shuttered windows looked down upon a street I had never seen before.

"The Lady Esharhamat will come to this entrance in a closed chair," he said as we gazed down at the heads of passers-by. "You will wait for her in the other house—why should anyone guess there is any connection between your visits and hers? The man from whom I bought these two buildings claims that they have been the scene of many intrigues, none of which has ever been discovered. You will notice there is a wineshop across the way—it seems a humble enough place, the retreat of men who have nothing to sell but their sweat, but it does a brisk business in rooms taken by the hour and is not unknown to great ladies whose tastes run to muscular porters and boatmen smelling of pitch. The sight of a closed chair is not so uncommon a sight in this street that anyone would pay it special attention."

"It is nothing if not sordid," I answered quietly. "I wonder how she will see these 'arrangements' of ours."

Kephalos shrugged his shoulders, as if at a thing indifferent.

"Probably with far less delicacy than you do, my foolish young master. Women, even those like the Lady Esharhamat, who are hardly more than children, go through the world with their eyes open and have fewer illusions than men. Intrigue is their natural element—you will see, Lord. All will be well."

"All will be well." Kephalos, who could imagine no obstacles but of time and place, did not understand. Or perhaps it was I who did not understand—I do not pretend to know. It was all a confusion and has remained so.

But my slave was right that I would be able to hide nothing from the eyes of my father's court. Within a month, when I went to bid farewell to my brother Esarhaddon before his removal to Borsippa—the king had appointed him *sharnu* of the whole of Sumer, with full martial powers—I had that lesson driven forcibly home.

"I hear you have purchased a house on the Street of Nergal," he told me, as almost his first words. "This, I assume, is for the fair Esharhamat? Come into the garden and tell me all about it that I may know how to chide her when she becomes my lady of the palace. It is always well for a husband to know some little secret which will reduce his wife to silence when she begins scolding about his other women. Come, for I have secrets to unburden as well as you."

His arm was across my shoulder as he spoke, leading me along through the sparsely furnished rooms of his new palace— Esarhaddon had a soldier's dislike of clutter, and his ideas of luxury encompassed none of that grandeur one meets with in the homes of rich merchants.

But for all the intimacy and trust which had become a habit between us, something had altered in his manner toward me. It was difficult to define and I am not even sure if, at the time, I recognized any change had taken place, but somehow my brother had learned to be jealous. He could tease about marrying Esharhamat in my place—why should he care that the lady and I were meeting secretly, since to him women were merely an appetite to be satisfied?—but for all his joking tone there was something almost like a threat in his voice, as if he meant to issue a warning that, in the end, he would make his way in spite of me.

"And just how," I asked, "did you come to hear of these things?"

He turned his head to look into my face, raising his eyebrows in surprise.

"Why? Are they supposed to be so great a secret? My mother told me—how else did you imagine?"

Yes, of course. I should have guessed. For Naq'ia was now living with her son again, and was even to accompany him into Sumer—how she had ever persuaded the king to agree to that I could not imagine, but she had. Yes, what would Naq'ia not know about my doings in the Street of Nergal?

Esarhaddon's garden was merely a bare tiled square beneath the blank sky. It was a place where, after a night spent in the taverns, he could sit alone, huddled in a lion-skin cloak, and breathe in the cold night air until he was sober once more and could stand the sound of women's voices.

His mother, I knew, was driving him to ever more dangerous and mind-numbing debauches as slowly she took over the management of his house and his life, as with the subtle cunning of a spider she tangled him ever more hopelessly in her web. And Esarhaddon, in war as terrible and reckless in his courage as the blind, storming wind, had grown—or perhaps had only grown more—afraid of her. It was almost as if his childhood had never ended.

We sat on a bench of cedarwood and, once a servant girl, one of the Babylonian twins—which one I had no inkling, for truly they were as alike as two halves of the same apple—had brought us wine and a plate of honeyed dates, he waved her away, waiting until she had withdrawn back into the palace, and then turned to me with worried eyes.

"We must be careful, of course," he said, his voice hardly more than a murmur in my ear. "She will wait there by the door and listen, and then run to my mother and tell her everything she has heard. It isn't her fault, poor little weasel; she won't be able to help herself. You see, all of them, all my servants, even my women, they all live in mortal terror of Naq'ia. One can't blame them, but one learns to exercise discretion—not that it matters. In the end, my mother always finds everything out anyway."

He looked at the wine jar in his hand as if he suspected it of containing poison and then took a long swallow.

"Of course, she uses magic—didn't you know that? Her

power is greater even than the king's, for all that he sends me off to amuse myself in the mud of Sumer. Sumer! I ask him for the garrison at Amat, that I may make war against the hill tribes, and he gives me Sumer."

"The king means to honor you, brother." I put my hand on his shoulder and shook it, as if to wake him from a stupor. "You will have rule over the richest province. . . ."

"Rule, but not kingship—I will be *shaknu* of Babylon, but did he not make Ashurnadinshum king?"

"He sees your worth now, brother. He wishes to make you great. And Ashurnadinshum met his death as king of Babylon."

"He wishes me out of the way while he makes you the *marsarru* in my place."

Esarhaddon grinned at me—with ferocity, as if he hated me.

"In my place. That surprises you, doesn't it," he went on. "For I shall reign when our father is dead. All the omens speak of it. Flights of birds spell my name. You don't believe me? Then ask my mother. She has a retinue of sorcerers, and she herself possesses the power to raise the spirits of the dead. I have witnessed this, so I know it to be true. I have seen her in consort with the ghost of our ancestor Ashurnasirpal, whom you know to have been a mighty king. He told her that I should be king and the father of kings. That is what I wished to confide to you, Tiglath my brother—it is destined to be, and neither you nor I can alter it."

I could not tell from his expression if he was pleased or not. He showed his teeth in haughty triumph, but his eyes were frightened.

"I hope there is a rebellion in the south," I said suddenly. I took a swallow of wine and made a face, for Esarhaddon cared not what he drank so long as it fogged his mind. "I hope the Chaldeans come hopping out of their swamps as numberless as frogs in summer, and that you and your armies have not a moment's rest. It would be the best thing for you, brother. In peacetime you spend too much time drinking bad wine and listening to women—especially Naq'ia. You should keep away from women, because you are a credulous fool and believe everything they tell you."

"Probably you are right—yes, most certainly you are right." Esarhaddon slapped me on the knee for emphasis, nearly breaking my leg. "However, a man needs women from time to time, for the sake of his health."

"Your health is not improved in that way by living under the same roof as your mother. And for the rest you should keep none but foreigners, Elamites and black Ethiopian women, since you are not gifted in learning strange speech."

"What of my twins? And the Egyptian sisters?"

"Have their tongues split with a white-hot knife that they may no longer continue to vex you."

"This is wisdom—this is good."

We were both laughing now, leaning against each other for support, speechless with this delicious jest. One of us would try to say something, but before he could our eyes would meet and we would both start to giggle like chattering birds. Esarhaddon seemed to have forgotten all about being king.

"So you do not believe in my mother's omens?" he asked finally, careful not to look at me lest we should begin laughing again.

"I believe that your mother wishes you to believe in them— why? Does the prospect of becoming king appeal to you?"

"No." He shook his head emphatically, taking another long swallow from his wine jar. He was already beginning to act a little drunk, and my brother always saw the world clearer for being a little drunk. "No—*I* do not want to be forever shaving my beard off when the priests say the god demands atonement. *I* have no taste for dressing by ritual and fasting like a *maxxu* on all the evil days. A king cannot call one minute of his life his own. Who would be king if he could avoid it? You, perhaps—but I do not put so high a value on the Lady Esharhamat's charms."

"Still, what of my mother's omens?"

"Esarhaddon, your head must have been chipped out of a block of red granite."

I got up to stretch my legs and walk about a bit, for it was growing cold in that bare little garden. My brother joined me, and we paced off the distance to the far wall, which faced into the Street of Enlil, where he hoisted up his tunic and relieved himself noisily before once more taking the wine jar from my hands that he might continue to drown his thirst.

"So you think I am stupid, do you?" he asked—not at all offended but merely as if it were a point that interested him.

"Yes. Have you any idea how many reports reach me every

week that some baby was born in Calah with the first character of
my name etched on his belly? Or that a blood star like the one on
the palm of my right hand was found on the entrails of a goat
sacrificed in holy Ashur? It is the same with every important man
in the land—people wish to curry favor, so they carry tales of
miracles or prodigies or signs sent from the Lady Ishtar. Only a
fool credits such stuff."

"I am of your opinion." He made an emphatic gesture with
his right arm, as if dismissing all thought of disagreement. "But
what of the ghost of Ashurnasirpal? Surely, brother, you cannot
doubt the truth of what I saw with my own eyes. Do not tell me
you have become so hardened in your Ionian godlessness that you
do not believe in necromancy!"

Poor Esarhaddon, who was well and truly drunk now,
looked shocked at the monstrousness of his own suggestion, and I
was quick to reassure him that in all questions of religious faith I
was as respectable as any man living.

"But tell me—simply as a matter of curiosity—what exactly
was it that you did see?"

Esarhaddon pondered for a moment, his hands dangling between his knees as he sat on the lip of a well that was part of his
garden wall and had probably been dug and abandoned a hundred
years ago—one could look down until the curved brick sides were
lost in an impenetrable blackness. At last he glanced up at me,
puckering his face with concentration.

"Saw? I saw very little—merely some white smoke. One
doesn't *see* anything. But I heard his voice quite clearly. My
mother asked him, will I be king after the Lord Sennacherib, and
he said yes."

"Just yes? Nothing more. Only 'yes'?"

"Yes—what do you want from the ghost of a king, a disputa-
tion? Tiglath, there are times . . ."

"Your mother is hoodwinking you, brother."

By way of experiment, I took the now empty jar and dropped
it into the well, counting slowly as it disappeared into shadow. I
never did hear it strike bottom.

"A wisp of white smoke, and a voice that speaks one word—
I can find half a hundred magicians in Nineveh alone who for two
silver shekels will summon up the ghost of any king you like.
Kings who are dead, kings who never lived. You have merely to
give them a name—even one you make up; *they* will not know the

difference—and if you are gull enough to believe in such tricks you may speak with whomever you choose. Let us go into Nineveh, and I will show you."

"Let us go into my Egyptian sisters instead," Esarhaddon answered, grinning like a dog. "You may have the older one—she likes you, and when she likes a man she . . . No? Alas, brother, you are not as entertaining company since you've grown so besotted with the Lady Esharhamat. But I give you two more months in the house on the Street of Nergal and you will return to yourself and be ready for a change in diet, which is after all the healthiest thing. You will see soon enough that one woman is much like another once she has shown you her backside."

When I tried to punish his impudence by pushing him into the well he laughed and dodged out of the way, tripping me even as he did so. Even sober I was no match for him in wrestling, but I can state to my credit that it was a good quarter of an hour before he had me well and truly pinned, my face in the dirt, screaming for mercy. Then we went back inside and cleaned ourselves off in hot water, changing our tunics before we went in to dinner.

"You have greatly relieved my mind," Esarhaddon announced as he washed the back of my neck for me. "I never had much taste for the idea of being king—I will content myself with power, wealth, pleasure, and everlasting glory."

"Yes, but do not be too relieved. For all that your mother makes up lies about it, you may be king yet. I say nothing more than what is obvious, that when the god wishes his will known in this matter, he will speak clearly enough."

Within the week my brother left Nineveh for the south, and thus he was not present for the Akitu festival, which came in the month of Sebat, after the first snows had fallen on the city.

In all the lands between the rivers there is no holier time. It lasts for eleven days, marking the renewal of the pact between Ashur and his people and the beginning of the new year—which, in fact, really begins in the month of Nisan, with the first of the spring floods. But why the festival is held at one time this year and another the next is a riddle best left to the ingenuity of priests.

During the festival the seventh day is not unlucky, as it is in other months, and all seems happy and prosperous. Had I had

eyes to see, I would have recognized even then that luck had
deserted me, that all my days were filled with evil darkness, but I
had not. I could see nothing except my own glory and happiness.
I thought the god was sealing his bargain with me alone, that I
above all men would be raised to honor, that such was the Lord
Ashur's will, but I was mistaken. I should have seen his warnings,
but I did not. Since they were open to the sight of all, whom may
I blame except myself?

On the first day of Akitu the king may take no food until the
new moon appears, and on that day, after we had witnessed Sin's
pale crescent rising in the eastern sky, the Lord Sennacherib
broke his fast at a banquet in my house, where he dined among
his great lords and I sat at his right hand as if I had been declared
his heir already. I had brought Merope down from Three Lions
that she might be with me and witness this great occasion, and the
king honored us both even further that night by taking his pleasure in my mother's bed—at least, he intended it for an honor;
whether my mother took it as such she did not say, and I did not
think to ask her.

During the day, while his belly still rumbled, my father took
me with him when he went to the Shrine of Shamash, Lord of
Decision, to seek the god's advice on whether Kabtia, king of the
Shubrians, could be trusted in the matter of a treaty concerning
the protection of trade routes in the Northern Sea. It was a routine enough transaction, but I found it not without interest because I had never seen the *baru* at his task and knew that soon
enough the god would have before him the far more significant
question of who was to follow the Lord Sennacherib on the
Throne of Ashur.

The king brought his question written out on a clay tablet,
which he placed before the image of Shamash, as glorious with
gold as his own sun. We waited in silence while the *kalu* performed his office by chanting prayers of supplication and the *ginu,*
the sacrificial goat, tethered to the altar by a silver chain, watched
us with wide, indifferent eyes. The *baru,* a man named Rimani
Ashur, a thin, serious-seeming man in the middle of his life—I
remember how his beard, still black, gleamed with oil—watched
the *ginu,* for the animal's every action, from its arrival in the
temple precincts to its final death agony, was important in inter-
preting the god's will.

At last, when the *kalu* had ceased his chanting, we all looked

up at the image of the deity, vague and majestic behind his cloud
of incense. Shamash, the eyes of Ashur—for every well-educated
person knows that the lesser gods are merely aspects of the one
true god, Ashur, he who gathers all power, all glory, all existence
into his own divinity. Was Shamash ready to give judgment in this
business? The *ginu* gazed first at the sacrificial stone on which it
was about to die, then at me, and then at the king. Then the
animal snorted loudly, as if a piece of straw had caught in its nose,
and the *baru,* taking this as a sign of the god's intention, took the
sacred flint knife from its place on the altar and, after a pair of
novice priests had unhooked the *ginu* from its silver chain and,
grasping it firmly by the legs, hoisted it up to the sacrificial stone,
he severed its throat with a single practiced stroke. The animal
died without a whimper.

Then all except the *baru* and one single assistant left the
sacred precinct of the god, for none but they could be present
when the *ginu*'s entrails were searched. This was ancient custom,
that none might dispute the *baru*'s judgment. He was a holy man,
everyone believed, whose oath to Shamash could be corrupted by
no earthly thing.

"Dread Lord, the organs are normal," Rimani Ashur said,
when he had come out from the sacred precinct and bowed before
my father the king. His arms were red with blood up to the
elbows. "The liver is clear of blemishes and the coils of the entrails follow the usual pattern. There is no disease or deformity.
The god gives you his blessing in this matter."

Already then the *ginu,* now nothing more than the carcass of
a dead goat, lay half consumed on the sacred fire that burned
night and day before the image of Shamash. No man would eat of
this flesh, and its ashes would be fed into the Tigris. Whatever the
baru had seen would live only in his own voice and the record he
would inscribe for the temple archives.

"It is well, priest," the king answered, following the ritual of
acceptance as he raised his hands in thanksgiving to the god. "It
shall be as the Lord of Judgment decrees."

The temple complex formed one wing of the palace, so my
royal father and I walked back to his quarters, where he would
wait out the remaining hours of his fast. It was the first time I had
been alone with him in many weeks. He slowed his pace, as if
relishing these few moments of freedom in a day filled with ceremony.

"It will be just so half a year hence, when I ask the god's blessing on my choice of a successor. You will be king when I am dead, eh? You will do very well."

The Lord Sennacherib put his hand on my shoulder, reaching up to do so since I was almost half a head taller than he. He had told me many times that he loved me ahead of all his other sons, both the living and the dead, and he was my master and king.

"It is Esarhaddon's name you must place before the god," I answered, not certain in my own heart if I spoke out of duty to my father and brother or only because I knew that, once again, I would be pleased to hear myself preferred. "He is the son of your lawful wife."

"The god will withhold his consent. Esarhaddon has a basket of mud where his head should rest. He will do very well in the next reign, but only if he has you set over him to keep him out of mischief. He is a good soldier, your brother, whom you love so fondly, but he is a fool."

The king seemed more and more to lean on me as we walked, as if his hunger were weakening him.

"Esarhaddon would make a bad king," he went on. "The god will withhold his consent—has not Mighty Ashur shown already how he favors you? Has he not granted you a mighty *sedu*? Eh? Esarhaddon . . . paugh!"

We came to the end of a long colonnade, out into the sunlight of an open courtyard. The king dropped his hand from my shoulder and stretched himself as if rising from a dream.

"Do you recognize this place? No?" He laughed, bending at the waist to smite his knee with excess of pleasure. "Look about you, Tiglath Ashur, Son of Sennacherib, Lord of the Earth, King of Kings. Now do you remember?"

Yes, now I remembered. I could feel my throat tightening as I remembered. The block of granite, like a sacrificial altar, still rested in the center of the stone paving—I remembered when I had seen it spattered with blood.

All of this must have shown in my face, for the king nodded, no longer even smiling.

"This is where old Bag Teshub brought you that your manhood might be cut away like his own—by the gods, I wonder if he is still alive. He brought you here, and the priests waited with their knives. But I see you have not forgotten."

"No, I have not forgotten. Nor that you saved me."

"I, and the lord *turtanu,* my brother Sinahiusur. It was more he than I. And he was right. Right—for you have made me proud of you, many times since that day. But the priests . . ."

"Did you know that the *baru* Rimani Ashur is also my brother? Did you, eh?"

"No, Lord."

"But he is. The priests, most of them, favor Esarhaddon over you, but not Rimani Ashur, who favors no one. I trust him, for all that he is a priest. Moreover, the army loves you. And the army counts for more in this land than the priests, who love your brother only because he is known to be a great believer in all manner of omen readers and soothsayers—they hope they will be able to rule through him. Some speak against him—Kalbi, for one; he knows the god's will—but most . . . Still, I trust Rimani Ashur. The god will not make Esarhaddon king—never! And as for his being my son by a lawful wife . . ."

The Lord Sennacherib spread wide his hands in a gesture of helplessness.

"I would put the veil upon your mother's head tomorrow were it not that . . ."

"Were it not that the Lady Naq'ia would object—and that most strenuously."

We both laughed, as if sharing a secret.

"Yes—what a misery she would make of life!" The king put his arm through mine, and we continued our walk. "By the gods, I am almost glad she has taken herself off to Sumer. I miss her already at my couch, but she has a tongue like a scorpion's tail. Women, my son, they are the curse of life. . . ."

That night he ate in my house and lay with my mother, to let all know that Tiglath Ashur, son of Sennacherib, stood higher in his father's favor than any, living or dead.

The next day, the second of the festival of Akitu, was the great procession, when the Lord Ashur is carried through the city to his new year's house, there once more to fight his fight against Tiamat the Chaos Monster and make again the world and the bright sky.

The ceremonies surrounding the festival of Akitu are of great antiquity, and they are much the same throughout all the lands between the rivers. In Sumer, where, through the ancient prestige of Babylon, Marduk is king of the gods, it is his victory which is celebrated, his creative power which men hold in honoring memory. But whether the glory is Marduk's or Ashur's, the myth which is celebrated is precisely the same, and it is not on the names of gods that their divine, life-giving sovereignty rests but on their storied deeds, for it is men who give the gods their names.

This year's Akitu was to be like no other, for it was the first since the long war in the south had ended, and all in the land of Ashur wished to render him thanksgiving for his preserving might. Thus the festival celebrated both our renewal and our deliverance, and all men's hearts were light with joy.

The last minutes before dawn of the great day found the king, his nobles, and all his family in the temple of the god, where he was called to wakefulness by the beating of drums, loud as thunder, echoing through the city like the voice of war. "Let the god awake!" we chanted. "Let Mighty Ashur, Lord of Heaven, King of the Gods, in whose name all things are done, let him rise from his slumbers! Let him shine like his own sun upon the race of his servants!"

And the great golden idol of the god—not Holy Ashur himself but only his image, the god's gift to us that men might approach his glory—looked down upon us with unseeing eyes. What were men that he should notice them? What were their voices that he should hear? Yet in his mercy he did hear, and his bright sun rose over the eastern mountains to give us the light of yet another day. And this day his, who was our strength and our salvation.

And then, in an instant, there was no sound, only the decaying echo of our voices disappearing into silence. The air did not shake, and there was stillness as the multitude, who dared not even breathe, waited upon their king, Sennacherib, Chief Priest and Servant of Ashur.

The king approached his god, in his hands a golden dish weighted down with meat hot from the fire, still steaming in the cold air. The king, too, was a thing of gold, flashing with reflected light as the folds of his tunic moved—a thing of splendor like his god.

"I summon you to eat, Lord Ashur," he cried. "I summon you, Lord of Sky and Earth, to accept this offering from the hand of your servant."

The dish was held before the god that his eyes might behold it and then was passed to a priest in yellow robes, who carried it away. The thing was done.

"I summon you to eat, Lady Ninlil!"

Only this time it was a woman's voice. With everyone else, I turned to see who had been granted the honor this year, and what I saw was my sister Shaditu—naked, her body shining with oil. A murmur ran through the crowd, for it was not a thing anyone had expected.

"I summon you, Consort of the Lord Ashur, Queen of Heaven, to accept this offering from the hand of your servant."

There was such quiet that I could hear quite plainly the soft sound of her tiny naked feet against the stone floor. She was beautiful. Her body was a thing of wonder, and, like all who saw her, I was stirred by the sight of it. I happened to be standing opposite the *baru* Rimani Ashur and I saw how his eyes glowed, as if the brightness of her flesh would blind him. Perhaps I should have realized the truth, even then.

Shaditu held her offering before the image of the goddess— smaller, and at her husband's left hand—and then, when the plate had been taken from her, she glided to her father's side, and he drew her to him in a loving embrace. For the king loved her, and she could commit no folly or disgrace in his eyes.

Merope, to whom these rites were new and strange, was with me and saw all that I saw. As we filed out of the temple and into the bright sunlight she plucked at my sleeve.

"My son, is this—customary? That she be thus naked, like a harlot, without even a veil for her hair? It does not seem a proper thing."

"It is a venerable usage," I said. I smiled and took her arm, for what could she have learned of such things in the house of women? "The Sumerians, all of them, both men and women alike, approached their gods in ritual nakedness—the priests of Elam do to this hour. But such a thing has not been seen in the Land of Ashur for perhaps a hundred years. Perhaps the lady seeks to stamp the day with a gesture of ancient piety, although I would not have suspected Shaditu of being possessed of so profoundly religious a nature."

"I think she is not better than a tavern wench, and wishes only that all men should desire her."

I laughed, not being able to help myself, that my mother was thus shocked.

"Yes," I said. "From what I know of the lady, your opinion is probably not very far from the mark."

But somehow, the image which I could not shake from my mind was not that of my wanton sister Shaditu, glorying in her naked beauty, but that of the *baru,* the king's own brother, Rimani Ashur, his eyes fired with lust.

At last the god, newly clothed in garments of the richest embroidery, the fabric shot through with gold and silver, his lips washed with water from the snows of Mount Epih, was brought forth from his temple, carried upon a litter borne by his priests. The king followed, leading priests, musicians, his nobles, the whole assembled multitude in chants of praise, so that the glory of Ashur sounded through the whole city and echoed in the mountains of the east. Never had I felt it more strongly than at that moment—we were the people of the god, blessed above all men, the servants of heaven's sovereign lord.

We followed the procession through the streets of Nineveh and through the great gate to the Akitu house, which had been built outside the walls as the god's abode during the eleven days of festival. The house was a small structure, standing open on all four sides, its roof supported by pillars of cedarwood. Thus all might see the divine image as he witnessed the ceremonies held in his honor under the open sky. These were many and, on that day, celebrated the god's triumphs over his enemies, both mortal and divine. That was the day on which Mushezib Marduk and his whole family were to meet their *simtu.*

A king, while he prospers, lives in splendor, but when he falls his death is more bitter than the adder's sting. Mushezib Marduk had been cowardly and, in the end, foolish. Because of him the siege of Babylon had been drawn out to tortuous length, until the king my father and all his soldiers lost even the memory of pity. Because of him thousands starved, and thousands more died by the swords of their enemies. And in the end, instead of asking one of his servants to search his breast with a dagger, he had tried to run away, disguised as a one-eyed beggar. He would have been wiser to find himself an easy end while he had the chance.

And where was Mushezib Marduk on this second day of Akitu? He was uniquely favored, for he would view the festivities —such of them as he might survive—from the very porch of the god's own house, where he was chained to one of the cedarwood pillars. There was little enough need of the chain, however, since the Lord of Babylon would not be wandering off, not while his head stuck out through the neck of a bronze jar hardly big enough to hold him. It had been several days since Mushezib Marduk had even seen his legs.

This contrivance, the last refinement of torture, was a wonder of simplicity. The great bronze vessel, which might have held eight or nine *sutu* of oil, had been sawn through at the shoulder so that the whole upper part could be removed and a man stuffed inside like so many measures of dates. Then the upper part had been put back on and bolted in place. This was to be the last home Mushezib Marduk would ever know. The precise means of his death was a secret, even from him, but he would never leave that jar except as offal.

Thus he waited, the neck of the jar coming up to his ears, cursing the gods in a loud voice that cracked from time to time with excess of rage. The people laughed at him—the king laughed with his people. Merope and I stood silently among the other members of the royal family, and she held my hand in a tight grip.

But before he was allowed to die, the Lord of Babylon would lose all that makes life sweet, for his queen and five of his children —only two sons, the rest having perished like soldiers—had been taken from him. My father wished to be very thorough in his revenge.

The children came first. The eldest, a boy, had just a few tufts of beard on his chin, and the youngest girl was hardly more than seven. Their hands were bound behind their backs and, one after the other and before the eyes of their howling father, they were forced to kneel down so that the king's executioner could take them by the hair, pull back their heads, and cut their throats. While Mushezib Marduk raged with grief—for he had not been told this would happen; the Lord Sennacherib wished to keep it as a surprise—the fruit of his loins bled out their lives with hardly a murmur. When the last was dead, their corpses were piled atop a waiting mound of brushwood and logs and left there to be burned later.

And while Mushezib Marduk choked on his sobs and workmen spread straw over the blood-soaked ground, we waited for the next item of entertainment, the high point of the festival—the duel between Lord Ashur and the Chaos Monster.

This is how the world was born: In the beginning were Apsu and Tiamat, gods of the sweet and the bitter oceans. These begot Lahmu and Lahamu, brother and sister, husband and wife, and Anshar and Kishar, who surpassed their parents in strength, beauty, and cunning. Anshar and Kishar, besides many other gods, brought forth Anu, God of the Sky, who sired Ea, God of Wisdom and Magic, who was far greater than his father.

But the young gods were noisy and disturbed the rest of old Apsu, who went to his wife and said, "I will destroy them, that we may sleep." Tiamat was dismayed and cried out in rage, "Let us not destroy what we have ourselves created," but Apsu would have his way and set out to avenge himself upon his children and grandchildren. Ea, however, the wisest of gods, bound him with magic and killed him, turning his body into a mountain where he dwelt in majesty with his wife Damikina. It was there that Ashur was born to them, the most glorious of gods.

Meanwhile, Tiamat had pondered the fate of her husband Apsu and her heart was moved to rage. She decided to attack the gods and destroy them, and even Ea was filled with fear. At last only Ashur dared to meet Tiamat in open combat and, with the aid of a great wind which blew into her mouth so that she could not close it, Ashur fired an arrow down her throat, which found her heart. When she was dead, Ashur cut her body in two, creating with one half the sky and with the other the solid earth. For these great feats of courage and wisdom he was exalted even over his father as king of the gods.

It is this battle which every year the men of Ashur recall to life before the god's eyes. He who plays the god's part is called the *limmu,* and in all the chronicles the year takes its name from him. In the first year of his reign it is the king who is *limmu,* and thereafter his court officers follow in strict order of precedence. In this year it was Enlilbani, a good-hearted, easy, soldierly sort of man, to whom fell the role of Ashur; he was master of the king's table and had also been *rab shaqe* of the army which took Babylon —this last coincidence was felt to be a particularly felicitous omen.

The role of Tiamat was to be filled by none other than the Lady Ahushina, lately the queen of Babylon and wife to Mushezib Marduk, who would witness all from his privileged place in the great bronze jug, for this year the slaughter of the Chaos Monster was to be no mere pantomime.

The lady was led forth naked, her face and body painted yellow and black, the colors of salt and mud, chained by her wrists and ankles. Even under her paint she looked hopeless, already only half alive. She was tethered between a pair of poles and, while she stared at the bodies of her slain children, her eyes blank and uncomprehending, Enlilbani, dressed in the trappings of the god, came forth from the Akitu house, fitted an arrow in his bow, and shot her through the heart. She cried out only for an instant and then was dead.

One of the yellow-robed priests handed Enlilbani a heavy, copper-headed ax, and with it he set about the business of cutting the queen's body in half, hacking it apart from neck to crotch with several mighty strokes that spattered blood like rain. The crowd roared—it was a spectacle very much to their taste.

And what of me and my Greek mother, for whom these things had all the power of novelty? What of us? My mother wept. She turned her eyes away, burying her face in my chest, and wept like a child. I, for my part, had seen many worse things and was moved only to a faint disgust. I had not expected this—the king had not told me of his plans. Of course I, as his son and a member of his inner circle, must be here, but I would have spared my mother had I known.

At last, when the corpses of his queen and children lay together on the pyre, when the whole of life beyond his own poor flesh had been stripped from him, it became Mushezib Marduk's turn to meet death.

Soldiers came and took the great bronze urn from the porch of the Akitu house. They put an iron collar around its neck and pulled it down, dragging it along the ground so that it bobbed and rolled like a float in the running river. Then they set the urn in the center of the pyre and poured water down its neck, pushing Mushezib Marduk's head to one side to make room. He was to be boiled alive. While his family burned to ashes beneath him, he would be cooked like a rabbit in the hunter's pot. As this dawned on him he began to scream. At first words—"No! No! Not this! Mercy! No!"—and then, in the extremity of his fear, only high-pitched cries, like the screaming of a hawk.

They lit the pyre at several points around its base, but the wood was green and filled with pitch so that it burned slowly and with very little smoke. Mushezib Marduk would not have the blessing of choking to death before the fire reached him. The only sounds were the crackle of the flames and the wail of terror that never stopped, never stopped, until one wanted to cover one's ears. The Lord of Babylon did not die until the water in his urn had already begun to boil and spill out over the neck—first white, and then pink with frothing blood. In time, after the urn had been heated red-hot, his head, coming loose of its own accord, tumbled off and fell into the fire. Thus was his end.

When the fire had cooled, its ashes would be gathered and thrown into the Tigris River. There would be no burial for Mushezib Marduk and his seed, no offerings of wine and food. They would have no life in the next world and would be forgotten utterly.

I took my mother away. We did not speak. There were no words, no words.

14

I remember the taste of her breasts. I remember the way she moved beneath me, the habit she had of twitching her hips a little to one side as she neared her climax. I remember how she liked to bite my ears. I remember the blinding love I felt for her, and the memory is itself no less than love, as glowing embers are still fire. Esharhamat—oh, the passion of that name. Esharhamat.

Once, twice a week, as often as we could, we made love in the house on the Street of Nergal. I would wait, wretched, certain she could never come again, until I heard her little hand tapping lightly at the wooden door that separated one building from another, and then, when I had her in my arms, I would carry her to our bed—for we had a real bed, with a mattress filled with raw wool, for there would be no soldierly scorn of comfort with my lady Esharhamat. For a long time we could hardly speak. We could not bear that our lips be parted. How I loved the whole of her sweet body. How I hungered to learn it all, every morsel, with eyes, hands, lips.

We did not see each other during the eleven days of Akitu. The time was filled with rituals and banquets and great public events, all of which seemed to demand my presence, but now we were together again, and I covered her mouth with my own. I wanted to crawl inside her, to be part of her very self, to die and come alive again. There were no eyes for sight, no breath for words, only the careless need to be one and feel our limbs, our very senses dissolving into each other like honey into wine.

At last, as we lay together quietly in our bed, the urgent passion spent so that we could feel once more the restful pleasure of love, I heard hailstones beating on the roof—tat, tat, tat! like birds picking at seeds that have fallen between the paving bricks. It had thundered all that night, so I was not surprised. It was somehow an agreeable sound, enclosing us in safety.

Esharhamat passed her hand over the hair on my chest, as if to smooth it into place. Her breast just touched my arm. I felt . . . I cannot put into words what I felt. It seemed that all happiness must now slip away into nothingness, that all the rest of my life must be in mourning for the end of this one moment. I would not grieve, however, since I had this moment.

"Did you miss me?" she asked, letting her hand come to rest upon my belly and curling her fingers so that I could feel the faint tracery of her nails.

"When?"

"All these last days—when you were with the king, and your mother."

"Are you jealous of my mother?" I turned my head to look at her, smiling. "Are you?"

"No—not of her. Of the king sometimes."

"Why? Why would you be jealous of the king?"

"Because you would lay down your life for him."

I laughed, gathering her to me, for it seemed such a foolish thing for anyone to say. I told her so.

"You only think it is foolish because you are a man," she answered. She pretended to be angry but did not turn her face away when I moved to kiss her.

"Come—why are you jealous of the king? Are you jealous?"

"Yes."

"Then why? I would lay down my life for you just as quickly as for him."

"Then because you would give me up for his sake."

"If he ordered it, how could I not?"

"Not if he ordered it, but if he asked it."

"He is the king. How could I refuse? That would be duty."

"And love? What is love?"

"Love is what I want—or need, to live. Duty is life. It is more than life. It is the same with every soldier. If you were a man you would understand."

"But I am not a man," she said, touching my face with her lips, letting me feel her hungry hot breath, teasing me with the point of her tongue as I tried once more to kiss her. "I am not a man—did you know it? Prove to me that you knew all along I was not a man."

Even as she laughed, a sound like the tinkling of little brass bells, she reached under the blanket and curled her fingers around my manhood, by then once more hard as iron, guiding it into her. As she melted against me, and as she shuddered with longing and a tiny sob broke from her throat, I cared nothing for kings or gods or duty—only for her.

Later, while she slept, I stole out of bed and went to the window, unhooking the shutters that I might see the street below, still glittering with fallen hail.

What had she meant to tell me? Had it been a joke, a mere freak of womanly petulance? What did she want?

As it had from time to time over the past several days, my memory flooded with the look on my mother's face as she watched the butchery before the Akitu house. Had the king meant to inspire fear? He had only displayed his own—the whole spectacle had been grotesque and stupid.

If I became king I could prevent such things. I could have Esharhamat—not in secret but openly, as my wife.

And as my wife she would be forever safe. I knew she was blind and heedless—what would become of her if I could not make her my wife? She refused to see that she could ever become anything else and she imagined, as the rising wind carried her, that it was her own strength that made her soar so high. She might destroy herself by her own rashness if the world did not answer to her wishes. Thus, as I loved her, I was afraid for her.

She was still asleep when I drew the shutter closed again. I sat down on the bed beside her, and I thought, "You are all that matters to me—you, this place, this moment." Was I wrong to love her like that? Yes. I knew it, and did not care.

And as if she had heard, her eyes fluttered open and she smiled at me.

"I would be king for your sake," I said suddenly, having planned to say nothing. "For you sake, and to change the world."

"Would you, my love? But the world will not allow itself to be changed."

* * *

My walk home took me through some of the poorer sections
of the city, where the streets were slippery with ice, mud, and
garbage and men smelled of weariness and stale beer. These were
the houses of day laborers, who rented space for their sleeping
mats one night at a time, who would never have enough money to
buy themselves wives, and whose bodies, when they were dead,
would lie in unremembered graves, their souls without offerings to
ease the pangs of hunger and thirst. Such men, if they had the
stomach and the strength for either, might become soldiers or
thieves, risking death to better themselves a little, but otherwise
the grim course of their lives had been set for them on their
whelping day.

I passed a wineshop—even here there were wineshops, for all
human creatures must have their little luxuries—and noticed that,
on the other side of the street, there was a carrying chair of rich
design, its sides covered with black leather. Around it were squatted
four discontented-looking slaves, casting their eyes about them as
if they wondered how they would ever avoid the contagion of
such a place. They were slaves, yes, they seemed to imply, but still
better than any free man who might find himself here. It was a
slight shock that I realized they wore the dress of royal slaves.

All at once a torrent of laughter reached me from within the
wineshop. I was curious—I almost could not help myself. I went
inside.

It was a crowded, fetid little room with walls of unpainted
mud brick. Men in the cheapest dun-colored tunics sat about, at
tables and even on the floor, playing at lots or talking in loud
voices or merely watching whatever amusement might be going
forward. There was a slight stir just as I came in, for these were
not people used to rubbing shoulders with ranking officers of the
king's army, but I was by no means the focus of interest.

On top of a table at the other end of the room, a great hairy
naked beast of a man was bent over on his elbows and knees,
grunting like a pig as he rutted on a woman whose white legs
stuck out from beneath him like the feelers of some strange insect.
While everyone watched, some cheered the huge beast on as others, some two or three I saw, made bets, dropping little packets of
coins tied up in pieces of oily rag into the lap of an elderly crone
who sat on a high stool and looked as if she might own the place.

Of the woman who was the source of all this entertainment I

could tell little, except that she seemed to be young. I must do something, however—she most probably was here against her will, for who . . . ?

And then, as if to snatch a breath of air from beneath her loathsome, sweating burden, she happened to turn her head enough for me to see something of her face. Yes, of course—I was a great fool—the carrying chair. It was Shaditu!

The king's own daughter—it was intolerable. A few quick steps and I had crossed the room. I grasped the lout by his ankle, yanking him over so that he pulled loose from my sister and landed on the floor backside-first, with a loud smack.

For a moment he was merely stunned. Then he was angry. But even as he gained his feet the copper tip of my javelin was balanced delicately against his throat.

"Out!" I bellowed. "Out, every one of you, out—if you value your lives, out!"

It was more than an instant before my adversary realized that I really was prepared to kill him, that I wore the uniform of a *rab shaqe,* and that he had better do as he was told. He picked his discarded tunic up from the floor and started backing away.

"Want her all for yourself then, my young lord?" the old crone chirped behind me. There was a general laughter, muted and uneasy.

"Everyone—I said, go!"

I had only to make a single pass through the air with my javelin, and they ran for the door like rabbits. In an instant, Shaditu and I were alone.

Shaditu did not at first realize this. She rose on one elbow, drawing her knees up as she did so, and looked around her, blinking like an owl.

"What the . . . ? Oh, it's you, Tiglath—brother. Care to take your turn in the wine press?"

With a slurred laugh—she showed all the signs of being very drunk—she let her thighs fall open to reveal the cleft, worn, glowing red with use and streaming with seed.

"I've been entertaining—what do you think . . . ?"

"You are disgusting," I said, turning my face away as I removed my cloak for her to wear. "Here, cover yourself."

"Oh, Tiglath, don't be cross. Here—give me a kiss, my sweet brother. We never seem to meet except when I am at less than my best."

She gathered my cloak around her shoulders and leaned forward, holding her head in her hands. For a moment I thought she was about to be sick, but this impression was dispelled soon enough as she reached out to take hold of my arm, resting her temple against it.

"Oh, Tiglath, my beautiful brother, if you could but love me," she murmured. "I am driven to this by your rejection."

"You must have your little joke, I suppose."

I pulled away my arm, wondering why I had ever let her take it in the first place. Shaditu could fill any man with uneasiness, and I was a man. I picked up her tunic from the floor; it was a flimsy thing of the thinnest linen, and someone had torn it into shreds—one could easily imagine the circumstances. No, she would never wear this again. I could not find her sandals anywhere.

"Here now, wrap yourself in my cloak. It is cold out, and you are going outside to your chair and then home."

"Not yet, I think," she answered, leaning back on the table and letting the cloak fall open. "Let us tarry here a moment first —just the two of us."

"Shaditu, if you will not go to your chair on your own two legs I will drag you, by the hair if I must."

"I do not think you would, brother."

"And why would I not, sister?"

"Because you know how very much I would enjoy it." She smiled at me, like a cat. "Now give me but a sip of wine and try a little to be nice to me, Tiglath, for I know you do not find it a misery to look at me."

She was right. I could not help myself, for Shaditu was beautiful. Her mouth had been made for kissing, and her eyes were wanton, full of wickedness, but tilted up at the corners as if to smile, as if the sight of you consumed her with pleasure. The flesh of her body was as smooth as water. That body seemed to beckon: Come, taste me, hold these breasts in your hands, push your way between these thighs and know the joy of me. I was but a man, and I felt this. And Shaditu was not blind.

She lay naked upon my cloak, her arms thrown back, her belly rising and falling as she breathed. I went to fetch her a cup of wine and sat down to wait until she drank it and had done with tormenting me.

She sat up and took the wine cup from my hand, smiling to herself as if at some private jest.

"You do not love me, you love another—everyone knows this." She shrugged her shoulders. "I do not care. If you desire me, this is enough; I would not interfere between you and Esharhamat, who must be a poor thing for a man to pleasure himself with.

"But I see that, once again, I have shocked you. Yes, I see I have." The smile on her lips faded quietly away. "You think I am wicked and unfeeling, worse even than the tavern harlots, who at least sell themselves for money with which to live. Perhaps you are right—perhaps also this is not the life I would have chosen for myself, had I been free to choose. But, you see, I was not. I have a father who is old and foolish and thinks to keep me for himself alone."

"You speak unwisely, sister—I would . . ."

"You would what, brother? Do not imagine you can threaten me as you did that crowd of ruffians." She made a faint dismissing gesture, as if her late paramour and his friends were ghosts she would wave away. "I will say whatever I like."

"Were you a man, even my brother in blood, I would kill you for your impertinence."

"But I am not a man, and you are my brother, O mighty Tiglath Ashur—I think myself safe enough from your wrath."

She laughed, throwing her head back, and I began to wish I were someone else that I might slap her face hard enough to make those mocking lips bleed. I desired her—I could not lie to myself —but at the same time I longed to break her body like a rotten twig. There are some women who thus mingle in us yearning and hatred, and Shaditu was one of them.

"What do I say that is not the truth?" she went on, laughing still, but bitterly. "Shaditu is the king's darling and may not have a husband to rule over her while her father lives. Had I been given a man of my own, and been allowed to live in the manner of other women, I might have been content with that and never strayed into the beds of common soldiers and the wineshops of the poor and despised. But perhaps—who can say?—I might have anyway, for perhaps it is simply my nature to be wicked.

"Come into me, Tiglath. You will someday, as we both well understand. Let us take pleasure together." She looked up at me through smoldering eyes. "No? Not today? Or perhaps you have wrung yourself dry in another's arms?"

"Get up, Shaditu—it is time you left this place. Get up, or I will drag you and we will see how you enjoy it."

When she saw the time for teasing was over, she rose from the table like a queen from her throne, drawing my cloak around her so that it covered her up to the tips of her ears. Her slaves scrambled to their feet when they saw us.

I watched her carrying chair disappear down the street, the slaves trotting like dogs in their haste.

But for me this was not only a season of sighing women. I did not have to trifle with forbidden passions to feel myself loved, for I was the darling of the world.

The king, who had settled with himself that I should have the favor of gods and men, sent me to the holy city of Ashur that I might pray in his name at all the ancient shrines and, while I had the opportunity, inspect the garrison there that the priests might see in what esteem I was held by the army.

In this he was not without cunning, for under the surface the sources of power within the nation were struggling among themselves, divided by the late war in the south and the king's siege and sack of Babylon. The priests and others who looked to the old culture of Sumer as to a mother believed that a sacrilege had been committed, that the great gods would avenge themselves upon us for the destruction of Marduk's city. The soldiers and those who, like the merchants and tradesmen, looked to the caravan routes of the west for their prosperity, thought the king had done well to crush Babylon and break forever its alliance with Elam before these two overwhelmed us. These, because the king favored me and because I had seemed so to distinguish myself in that action —thus we blind ourselves to the truth, for how, except in men's eyes, was Esarhaddon's glory less than mine?—these wished me exalted as the *marsarru*. The Babylonian party saw Esarhaddon as their savior—he would turn aside Marduk's wrath and rebuild his city. Thus I was to go to Ashur to ingratiate myself with the gods and overawe their priests. Such devices, so my father gave me to understand, were the skilled workmanship of kings.

But since he did not trust perfectly my hand in statecraft, he sent the Lord Sinahiusur with me lest, for want of wisdom, I disgrace myself utterly.

Except as a soldier marching by beneath her walls, I had never seen the city of Ashur, sacred to the god and seat of our ancient kings. Ashur had been a city when Nineveh and Calah were empty even of their names. Before kings, before cities, before one mud brick stood upon another, the first of our race had come here from the empty wastes of the western deserts, delivered from a life of wandering by the mercy of Great Ashur, who said, "This shall be your place, where the seed of the nation shall grow and scatter across the wide world. I give you my name, that all may know you are servants of the god." No man born between rivers and mountains may see that city of the fathers without his heart rising within him.

Sinahiusur and I rode on horseback, taking with us an escort of fifty men. It was a journey of less than two days if one traveled by water, but our object—at least in part—was to make an impression, and there is no dignity in a reed raft that delivers one up sick and soaking and unsteady on one's legs. I had no taste for being laughed at, so we went by road, as a soldier should. We arrived at the gates of Ashur after four days.

If I had had any doubts that the god meant me to be king, they fled like shadows as we approached the city. Somehow, I knew not how, the garrison had received word of our coming. Four thousand men lined the road—and behind them the common people, the shopkeepers and bakers, the tanners of hides and workers of metal, the farmers and the brickmakers, they and their wives and their children, in numbers beyond counting they had come. And they had but one voice and one song. "Ashur is King!" they shouted. "Ashur is King! Ashur is King! Ashur is King!"

I rode alone at the head of my escort—even the *turtanu* had fallen back that this triumph might be mine alone—and as my horse made its nervous way over the brick highway the people threw flowers in my path, and coins that the touch of my horse's hoofs might bless them, as if I were already their chosen lord. "Ashur is King! Ashur is King!" they shouted, and then, first the soldiers and finally everyone, "Tig-LATH! Tig-LATH! Tig-LATH! Tig-LATH!"

How much may a man thus hear his name on men's lips before he believes himself to be exalted, chosen of the gods, precious in the sight of heaven? How much, before he becomes a fool in his own heart?

That night we were feasted by the city governor, an old soldier whose eyes shone like pools of oil as we talked about past campaigns and the glory of war. He was the second son of the old *turtanu*, who had been a brother of Great Sargon, and called Sinahiusur "cousin," although he could not be brought to call me anything except *"gugallu,"* a word meaning something between "hero" and "commander." At first I thought his intention was merely to tease me, a young man in danger of growing too full of himself, but gradually it became plain that he was in earnest and meant only to show respect. It was an embarrassment coming from one of his rank and age and, I felt, almost an insult to him whom I had always regarded as my patron, but the Lord Sinahiusur, who only smiled and told stories and drank wine, gave no sign that he took it as such, seeming to regard my elevation over him as right and natural.

But by then, of course, I had grasped something which even a few hours earlier, while I was kept blind by borrowed radiance, had eluded me. This spectacle had been arranged.

The skilled workmanship of kings. The report would soon reach Nineveh that I had been received in triumph. That I was popular with the army was well known, but now all would credit me with the favor of the city mob, which is not so negligible a thing that great men might ignore it. The priests would be silenced.

And had I not myself begun to believe? And was that not an object too? The cunning old fox my father would gull me with everyone else. And all this the Lord Sinahiusur had understood from the beginning.

So the next day, keeping to the role assigned me, I abased myself at the shrines of Ashur, Ishtar, Adad, Ea, Nergal, Shamash, Sin, Nabu, and—simply as a precaution—Marduk. I offered wine and fruit, I burned cuttings from my beard to atone for past sins, and I donated gold, silver, copper, and precious stones to the gods' adornment. I listened, humble and silent, to priestly admonitions. I saw my *simtu* read in oil-streaked water. I consulted the *baru*s. I would prosper, they told me, I would be great in the Land of Ashur.

In the evening I went to dine at the barrack, where most were veterans of the southern wars and I was greeted as an old comrade. Among the common soldiers there were many who wished merely to touch my hands—such is the power of myth, for had not many of them suffered more and put their lives at greater hazard than I? Men create their heroes and their kings to reflect what is most noble in themselves, for what was I but their image of all they had done themselves? I felt myself humbled as I sat in the officers' mess, drinking wine with braver men than I who for the rest of their lives would speak of how once they had breached a jar with Tiglath Ashur.

In the morning we set out again for Nineveh. Once more the soldiers and common people lined the road, and once more they called my name as if invoking the power of the great gods, but this time the wine did not set my head spinning and I was able to wave and smile and know that it was merely emptiness, an illusion like the blue water one sees beyond the baking desert.

And the Lord Sinahiusur, who rode beside me, was once more the king's *turtanu,* to whom all in the land save one must bow.

"You did well," he said, his eyes idly searching the horizon—it is a habit which is common enough in old commanders. "There will be other journeys, and these, I think, the king can trust you to make on your own. The nation is like a bride and must accustom herself to the sight of the husband her father has chosen for her."

"But Ashur has not chosen, has he? Not yet?"

"No, but the king has chosen."

"I thought you favored Esarhaddon and the orderly succession."

"I favor the king's will, Tiglath." He turned to me and showed his teeth in a weary smile—the lines about his eyes and mouth were like scars. "And, on reflection, I agree with him that you will sit easier on the throne than your brother. But the god will have his way in this, for all that the king or I may ponder it, and, as you say, the god has not chosen. Not yet."

He glanced back over his shoulder, but the soldiers of our escort were riding some twenty paces behind us, so we might as well have been alone.

"The king listens to women," he went on at last. "Women, when they wish a thing, sometimes cause a man to imagine he has the power to make all happen according to his will."

"But the woman in this case—and I assume you refer to the Lady Naq'ia—wishes by all means that I not succeed my father."

"Yes, what you say is true. But the effect is nonetheless the same, for she fosters in him the belief that this will be resolved, one way or the other, by some choice of his. That is the danger. And, of course, there are other voices besides that of the Lady Naq'ia. The Lady Shaditu, you have no doubt observed, strives with all her considerable power to ingratiate herself with those of the blood."

From the tone of his voice, and the rather pointed way in which he seemed to look at nothing, I was left in no doubt about his meaning. What had he heard? What rumor could have reached him? The *turtanu* saw into everything, so what chance had Shaditu of hiding her conduct from his eyes? Still, of my own involvement . . .

"Lord, I have had no such commerce with my sister."

He turned to face me, twisting about on his mount, and his expression registered genuine surprise.

"No, Tiglath," he said, "it was not of you I . . . It is perhaps best if you forget I spoke at all."

"As you will, Lord."

We rode in silence for several minutes. There was no sound save that of stone-hardened hoofs against the bare ground. And then, all at once, as if to announce the conclusion of some inner dialogue, the Lord Sinahiusur cleared his throat.

"Nevertheless," he said, reaching across to put his hand upon my arm—his eyes were dark and serious, like those of a man who has discarded his illusions one by one. "Nevertheless, it would be well, I think, if in the next reign the Lady Shaditu were put to death."

The Lord Sinahiusur was right when he said there would be other journeys. I went to Calah, to Arbela, to Arrapha, and Balawat. I worshiped at their shrines and ate at the tables of their great men. I visited the garrisons at Zakho and Aqra and Hajiya. I listened to soldiers' stories and told lies of my own. And everywhere I was treated as the king's heir and favorite and men loved me because they saw it was my father's will that they should.

And the envoys of foreign kings came to me and I spoke to them such words as they desired most to hear, how I would protect them from their enemies, how I held their masters to my heart as I might my own brother. These, of course, they did not believe, so I bribed them with gold and silver, and they sent letters home speaking of me as one who must be accorded honor.

Nor did I neglect Lord Sennacherib's great capital of Nineveh, my home since boyhood, though it had become little more than a place where I stopped, now and then, to wash my face in cold water. In Nineveh there was wealth, which was a power I had learned not to despise, so I courted the great merchants, who lived like lords, and the traders and the lenders of money—though not directly, for that would have been unseemly in a prince of the blood.

Thus I sent for my slave Kephalos, saying, "The men of substance in all the Lands of Ashur, the men of other lands who dwell here in the city and deal in metal and wood and all precious things, to these you are no stranger. Speak to them for me. Say I wish them well, for they make the land flourish. Tell them I mean to bring peace and order with me when I come to the throne."

But Kephalos pulled at his beard and frowned.

"Master, what if you do not come to the throne after all? Will not then your brother the Lord Esarhaddon remember that my voice spoke for you in the bazaars? He loves you, as you say, but he does not love me!"

"Then would it not be safer to help me to be king?"

At last he agreed, and he did not stop at a few words in the ears of rich foreigners but sent out storytellers, hired with his own money, to make the common people marvel at the glory of my deeds. For Kephalos understood his own interests and was ever my friend.

Thus I worked, and dreamed of becoming *marsarru*—not from the desire to be king but because I loved Esharhamat, who must be the next king's wife. And because I had convinced myself that I followed the god's will.

I hardly saw Esharhamat in those days, but she registered no complaint for she understood what I was about. We loved each other and tried to wait in patience, believing that patience was all that was required to make us happy. Many times it entered my mind that if I were to ask the king for her hand he would very probably not have refused—he would no doubt think it a wise stroke of policy, to make my selection seem all the more inevitable. The king was no obstacle now. Yet I did not ask. I kept remembering the Lord Sinahiusur's words: *"But the god will have his way in this, for all the king and I may ponder it."* Like a pious man, or a coward, I hesitated to tempt the hand of heaven. I did not ask. And Esharhamat and I met furtively when we could at the house on the Street of Nergal, as if in shame, as if already she were another man's wife and we guilty lovers who feared to be taken in adultery.

And all this time the god kept his own counsel—or spoke in riddles. This I learned from the priest Kalbi, an honest fool who had never learned to let his tongue be guided by the times and could thus be trusted. Of course it was his fate that none listened who had a hand to turn aside his unhappy prophecies. This is how the gods jest with us, by dressing truth as folly.

Kalbi visited me only once. I never saw him again, but the impression he left with me has endured from that day to this. He was a strange little man—short, sudden in his movements, with unkempt appearance and eyes that bulged out of their sockets as if they were being pushed from behind. His father had been Nergaletir, chief *baru* in Great Sargon's time, and he was descended from the true line of prophets and seers.

It was in the month of Siwan, when the floods were subsiding and the land was coming to life again under the hot sun. He came to me at my palace in Nineveh, where my servants brought me word of him upon my return from a day of hunting with the king. I was tired and not in patience to listen to the chatter of priests, but it would not have done to send away one to whose family the gods had entrusted their confidences for a thousand years. So I sent him word that I would see him as soon as I had washed myself, and my servants showed him into my presence at the evening meal.

"My apologies for making you wait, Honored Priest. Please —come, sit. Do me the kindness of dining with me."

But Kalbi stood his ground in the center of the floor, bent slightly forward at the waist, his right hand plucking violently at his tunic while his protruding eyes blinked with painful intensity, as if he were warding off a blow.

"I—have not come to dine, Lord. I thank you, no."

"Then at least sit. Take a cup of wine, at least. No? Nothing?"

But he would not move. He seemed rooted to the spot—or perhaps merely determined to be rude. I could not tell.

"I am not accustomed to the usages of princes, Lord."

He waited in silence, expectant, almost tranquil, as if this should be answer enough. But my servants too were waiting, and the meal my house steward had put before me was doubtless growing cold, so I decided I would not starve to death merely on a point of etiquette and began eating.

"Then I wonder what could have enforced this visit upon you," I said at last, smiling none too kindly—the man was beginning to make me feel uneasy.

"I come bearing messages," he said, apparently relieved that the subject should at last have been mentioned. "Strange and contradictory messages—riddles, in fact. I am at a loss to untangle them, Lord, and wondered if you might know . . ."

"I?" I allowed myself to laugh, although I felt very little in a humor for jests. "I have no skill in these things. Why would you have come to me?"

"Perhaps because you are most closely concerned, Lord. It is said by many that you will be the next king."

"By many, but not, I take it, by the god?"

"No, Lord." He shook his head. The blinking had by now achieved a mechanical regularity and seemed to jolt his head, as if his eyelids were boxes being slammed shut and the sound startled him. "I have asked the god many times. I have prayed to him to know, but he keeps your *simtu* hidden."

"But he speaks to you of other matters?"

"Yes—two. The reign of darkness that is to come, and the black bird which circles over the Lord Esarhaddon."

I pushed the plate from me, for suddenly I had lost all hunger.

"Take care, Priest. The Lord Esarhaddon is a fine soldier who is not to be insulted. He is also my brother, whom I love, so take care what you say of him."

"It is not what I say which matters, Lord, but the god. The god does not favor him but puts him under a bad sign. The Lord Esarhaddon will never reign with the god's blessing."

"Then he will never reign." I took a sip of wine, feigning a calm I did not feel.

"Then why, Lord, does the god show me a valley of shadows which is to come? There will be evil times ahead for the Land of Ashur—this I know."

And Kalbi spoke of omens, of children who had been born with the organs of both men and women, of tremors of the earth, of black clouds hiding the peaks of sacred mountains, of the deaths of stars, of sightings, in the west, of the moon dripping blood.

"There is a woman, Lord, in the temple of Ishtar, who falls into a trance that the Sacred Lady may use her tongue. She is an old woman who has lived within those precincts since girlhood, and the goddess has borrowed her voice only four times before. Last night was the fifth.

"But the goddess hides the truth—did I not speak of riddles, Lord? She puts a question: 'Why must the blood star go down beyond the western waters, to rise again, and then to eclipse forever that the land may wither under the sun?' It occurred to me that you might know the answer, Tiglath Ashur, since the god has marked your body with the sign of a blood star."

"I know no answers. Leave me now, Priest—leave me, for you trouble my mind."

"One question more, Lord, and then I will leave you. Is there one known to you who is blind and yet sees?"

"What do you . . . ?" I stood up so quickly that the table before me jumped away, sending my wine cup clattering to the floor. "What do you know of him? I . . ."

"Nothing, Lord. I, nothing. It is said that there is a blind *maxxu* who comes to you. What does he tell you, Lord? Does he speak of a dark time?"

"I know nothing of such a person. He has never spoken to me."

We stared at each other across the empty air. The wine was spattered over the floor like blood—I could not seem to take my eyes from it.

"Then good night to you, Lord."

He was gone. I glanced up to speak to him but he was already gone.

Thus I had many things to occupy my mind while I traveled in the king's name and waited with the whole nation for the god to make known his will. It was in the month of Ab that the oracles were to be read, and as the season approached I received a letter from Esarhaddon announcing that he planned to return to the city for the occasion, bringing his mother with him—I fancy it was rather the other way about, since nothing could have kept Naq'ia from Nineveh at such a time.

The day he arrived was the hottest of that summer—the very bricks of the city wall bubbled in the sun like roasted fat. I did not envy my brother his journey, for in Sumer the heat could only have been worse, but when I visited him at his palace it was not the discomforts of travel which occupied his mind.

I found him sitting in his garden, under such shade as a sickly olive tree might offer, afraid to go inside and, already then, at hardly an hour past noon, too drunk even to remember to cover his head.

"Come into your own rooms," I said, standing over him—he looked up at me with wide, anxious eyes, as if he couldn't remember who I was. "Come, brother. In this heat, and with such a quantity of wine in your belly, you are likely to have a stroke."

He shook his head and then dropped his gaze to his feet.

"By the great gods, Tiglath, I might count it as a blessing if I were to die quietly in my own garden. It is terrible, terrible. The worst of misfortunes. I fear I am doomed to live a blighted life if this *alu* cannot somehow be turned aside."

I took the wine jar from between his hands and sat down beside him.

"What misfortune?"

"Misfortune? Oh—you mean the *alu*. It happened on the journey, almost before the city gates. A mongoose ran under my chariot and was crushed by the wheels."

"Yes? Is that all?"

"Is that *all*?" He grasped me by the shoulder of my tunic as if he would shake me into my senses. "Do you not know that to have a mongoose run between your legs is the worst magic? Even now my mother's *ashipu*s are studying to see if perhaps the *alu* comes only if a man is standing on the ground—I was above ground, in my chariot. Or, if not, then perhaps some ritual . . ."

"You do not have to worry about this day's sun, brother, for your brains have already been baked hard. I never heard any such nonsense about a mongoose."

Esarhaddon drew himself up straight, as if to assert his dignity.

"You have not read as widely as I in the texts, brother. If you had . . ."

"Since when have you become such a scholar?" I asked, in some astonishment. "As far as I am aware, you can hardly read at all."

"I have them read to me."

"Where? In Sumer?"

"Yes, of course." Esarhaddon blinked at me in astonishment. "It is in Sumer that such learning has been brought to its perfection."

"Then perhaps the *alu* comes only if the mongoose is Sumerian."

"You think such might . . . ?"

"By the great gods, brother! Come inside—this instant! Or your *alu* will have little enough work left to do."

With my arm across his shoulder, he went into his own rooms, where his women bathed his head in cool water. At last he slept and was able to forget about the evil magic of a dead mongoose—at least, for a while.

And this is what his mother had made of him, and in only half a year.

On the evening of the sixteenth day of Ab, the god at last would speak. I spent the morning of that day in Esharhamat's arms, in the house on the Street of Nergal. We had to leave the windows open, for that upper room was like a furnace, but somehow Esharhamat's body was always cool.

"This may be the last time for us," I said, and as I spoke the words my heart felt dead within me.

"And if it is not, what then? When you are named *marsarru,* will you ask the king if we may be married?"

"Those will be the first words to come from my mouth. You know that."

"Yes, I know that."

"But if I am not the *marsarru*?"

"You will be."

"But if I am not?"

"Then promise me—one thing only."

"If I can, I will."

"That you will come back here tomorrow." She moved in my embrace, settling her cheek against my heart. "That in the first hour after midday, you will be here. I could not live if I did not see you once more."

"I will be here," I said. "I promise. If I die for it."

And thus we waited through that final day.

15

For two days after the auspices had declared that Esarhaddon must succeed him, the king hesitated. There was no announcement to the people, although they guessed—within hours after the *baru* had announced that the *ginu*'s entrails had been found to be clear of blemishes, a mob went to my brother's palace and pelted his door with garbage. For two days Esarhaddon was not named *marsarru* and was not installed in the house of succession. The nation waited uneasily while her king struggled with his own heart.

There were reports that some among the kings' younger sons were whispering rebellion within the ranks of the army, although nothing ever came of this, and it is well known that a certain beardless scribe was spreading reports that the priests had somehow played a trick with the omens to put a false successor next to the throne.

And for all this I fear I must bear the blame. It was not my brother's fault that so many voices were raised against him, but mine, for I had been too thorough in preparing the people to receive me as the Lord Sennacherib's heir. They had been led to expect it, to regard it as inevitable, as the king's choice and the god's and therefore their own. Of course they felt cheated—and of course they blamed my brother. This was the fault of my presumption. It was my failure, not his.

But finally the king appeared in public with Esarhaddon at his right hand and declared it to be the god's will that the son of Naq'ia, his only living wife, should be his heir. There was no rejoicing, but the people accepted the king's word and there was

peace. It was, however, noted that the next day, the nineteenth
day of Ab and the first in which the sun shone on my brother as
marsarru, was an unlucky day in which men dressed in rags and
ate no cooked food and did not bed with their wives. Thus did
Esarhaddon come into his inheritance and thus, for me, were the
words of the *maxxu* fulfilled: *"Do not think that happiness and
glory await you here, Prince, for the god reserves you to another
way. Here all things will be bitter—love, power, friendship."*

I was not in the city when the king broke his silence. I had
already asked for and received a commission as *shaknu* of Amat
and the northern provinces, where a border war with the mountain peoples of the east seethed continually like a cooking pot over
a low fire. I would be a soldier again, I told myself, and perhaps I
would die, if not a glorious then perhaps at least a useful death,
for I felt that life had scratched the last word on my tablet—and
all this when I was not yet even twenty years old.

But before the king would consent to let me go he had to be
dissuaded from ordering Esarhaddon's arrest, that he could have
him murdered in some dark cellar.

"I am still king," he raged, pacing back and forth, back and
forth across the floor of his private apartments. In the middle of
the night he had summoned me, and he, I, and the Lord Sinahiusur were alone together behind his locked door. "For all of what
Rimani Ashur may or may not have found in the entrails of a
dead goat, I am still king! Eh? Yes? You should have seen his face,
Tiglath: his teeth were chattering, in this heat, and his skin was as
gray as granite. That cursed priest was lying to me. He and your
donkey brother are in a conspiracy, and by the great gods I'll have
them both hanging by their heels before first light. Eh? How will
they like that? The traitors—the traitors!"

Back and forth he paced, his sandaled feet slapping against
the tile floor. I had received his summons expecting that it meant
I had been chosen, and now I watched his tireless, restless wrath
with weary eyes, my mind numb. I would not be *marsarru.* I
would never have Esharhamat as my wife. My brain did not seem
to have space for these two simple facts.

"There are no traitors, Dread Lord," I said finally—my voice
sounded distant, or as if it belonged to someone else. "You yourself have called Rimani Ashur an honest man. . . ."

"Yes, but he is a priest! Priests . . ." The king my father
pronounced the word as if it left a bad taste in his mouth.

"A priest, but an honest man. And my brother Esarhaddon is the last one who would dare to tamper with the god's mysteries. We—*you* must accept this as Ashur's will."

"I will kill Esarhaddon. With the knife in my own hand I will open his belly so that his guts spill onto the ground like a basketful of wet washing."

"If you do, my father, then you must seek another son than me to rule after you."

His head snapped around to look at me and his eyes blazed, but I was not afraid of his anger—it seemed to me that probably in my whole life I would never be afraid of anything again.

"If you kill Esarhaddon, if you do this wickedness, this blasphemy, if you deny him his life and his rights as your heir, then I will leave this land and never return. Dread Lord, you will never look upon my face more."

"Eh? What is the boy . . . ?"

"The boy is wiser than you are, brother," said the Lord Sinahiusur, his voice sad and calm. "Would you invite civil war?"

"We will have that in any case, eh? We will have that in any case, once I am dead—do you imagine the army will accept Esarhaddon, who would rebuild Babylon tomorrow if he could? Do you think they will accept him? Do you? Eh? Do you?"

The king collapsed into a chair and stared down at his feet as if he felt they too had somehow betrayed him.

"They will accept him if you accept him. They will accept him if Tiglath will accept him." The *turtanu* raised his eyes to me. "What say you, Tiglath? Will you accept the god's will, or will you divide the nation by making war upon the brother you have said you love?"

"You know my answer to that, Lord—you have heard it before."

He nodded. He understood.

"I feel pity for you, nephew," he said finally. "This is what comes of men believing they can rule the god, who must have his own will in the end, yet it is hard. You feel this punishment most bitterly, although the sin is not yours."

"The sin will not be yours," the *maxxu* had said. I started at the echo, and the Lord Sinahiusur and I exchanged a glance that made me wonder how much he could have known of that matter.

Yet I had only to remember Arad Ninlil to doubt that I was

so without sin. Had I consented, along with Esharhamat? If it was so, then the god had found a means of punishing us.

"I will kill Esarhaddon—yes, I will have his life."

The king stared at me with dead eyes. He no longer believed his own words and his anger was spent, leaving only grief. I went to him and knelt by his chair, and he put his arms about my neck and wept. As if his heart were broken, he wept.

"And what of you?" he asked finally, when the tears were spent and he was calm again. "What of you, my son—eh? Esarhaddon will never sit easy on his throne as long as you are alive. You know that, don't you?"

"I have nothing to fear from Esarhaddon, nor he from me."

"Yes—the love of brothers is a beautiful thing."

He said it with a certain distaste, as if acknowledging a dangerous weakness. He sat silent, looking at nothing, seeming to brood over the wickedness of love.

"And what of you—here, now?"

"I must leave the city for a time," I answered. "A long time, I think. There must be no focus for dissatisfaction with the god's will. Give Esarhaddon his chance, and he will shine brightly enough."

"Where will you go, my son?"

"Dread Lord, if you love me, send me where you would have blood spilled. I would fight a war—long and hard and terrible. I would have my heart rubbed smooth of all softness."

The king my father looked up at the Lord Sinahiusur, who nodded his agreement.

"I cannot yet say what I will do," he murmured, his eyes shifting nervously, as if he could bear to look at nothing for more than an instant. "Nothing is settled—I will send you word."

I bowed and left his presence. He and his *turtanu*—his brother, as Esarhaddon was mine—would speak together into the small hours of the morning, but there could be only one decision. The king would raise Esarhaddon until he stood next to the throne, and I would have to find some way of bearing my life. I could be happy without being king, but never to see her again . . .

I went out into one of the palace's many gardens, where the black night sky covered me from men's sight, and I leaned against a pillar there in the darkness, trying to understand why I seemed to feel nothing. A hand seemed to press upon me that I might not breathe, but my heart was numb.

"This is what it is to be dead," I thought. "To be a soul fluttering on the night wind—bodiless, without passions, without ties to life."

There was a faint wind stirring, a hot, heavy wind, thick as water. It blew about me as if I were a shadow.

"Esharhamat," I whispered, and in that same instant I felt the sting of hot tears in my eyes and knew I was still a man to suffer over the loss of his beloved. "Esharhamat . . ."

And there, in the darkness, where none might see, the god gave me a time to let this sorrow crack my breast.

In the first hours after dawn a messenger was shown into my presence bearing the king's orders—it was to be Amat. I would leave Nineveh that night, quietly, taking with me an escort of only twenty men. I would travel with all haste; riders had already been dispatched to the north and my arrival would be expected. I would have full military powers, as if in time of war. I had one last day before leaving behind everything which had been, until that moment, my life.

Amat—how that would gall Esarhaddon! And could the king have intended anything less?

I waited one hour, and then another. Still no one came to tell me that Esarhaddon had been proclaimed *marsarru*—he might not even have been told yet. I would have to see him before I left. I would have to make my submission, that later there could never be any question that he did not command his brother's loyalty.

Esarhaddon's palace was on the other side of the house of war, and I walked through the dusty barracks yards past troops of soldiers who stared at me as if at a prodigy of nature. Was I in disgrace and headed for death? Was I to be the next king? They could not guess, and thus knew not if they should raise their hands in salute or be still. Most only stared.

I went straight to my brother's rooms. None of his servants tried to stop me—they cowered away from me as if they suspected I carried a dagger beneath my cloak.

It was Esarhaddon's custom to breakfast late and I found him still at table, in a plain linen tunic, his feet bare, and surrounded by his women. I placed my clenched fist over my heart and bowed to him.

One of the Babylonian twins started to giggle.

"My Lord Tiglath is very formal this morning," she chirped —this witticism was greeted by a wave of girlish laughter.

"Get out."

Esarhaddon glared around him, and the laughter ceased at once.

"Get out. Leave us—now!"

Like a covey of startled quail, they scattered in all directions. Esarhaddon and I were quite suddenly alone.

"Then my mother's oracles were right," he said.

"Yes, Lord. They were right."

Lord. I saw the way my brother's face changed when he heard me call him that—the word seemed to come as a disagreeable shock.

"The king . . . he sent you to tell me?"

I shook my head, struggling to seem blank, a mere messenger. There was now so much I could never say to Esarhaddon, whom I loved, who could never be quite my friend again.

"The king will be brought to see things as they must be seen," I said, not looking my brother too directly in the face. "The summons will come and with his own hand he will lead you to the house of succession, but—and be guided in this—you must give him time. Stay within the walls of your house, seeing no one, until he sends for you."

He watched me through narrowed eyes, as if half suspecting some treachery, but at last Esarhaddon nodded.

"What you say is wise, Tiglath. It shall be as you advise. And now—come, sit down by me and take a cup of wine, like a brother. Or have you learned so quickly how not to love me?"

There was that in his voice to tell me how I would have wounded him had I denied his wish, so I did as he asked, letting him fill my cup, although I thought I might choke on it.

"It cannot be as it was between us," I said finally. "You will be king in the Land of Ashur, and I will be your subject. It is best if we both understand as much, Esarhaddon. And there are other reasons as well."

"You mean, of course, the Lady Esharhamat."

"I will never see her again. She will be your wife and give you sons to follow you."

"Tiglath, my brother, for all I care you may have her and welcome. By the sixty great gods, I give her to you!" He put his hand on my arm, gripping me with strong fingers as if this were something we could settle between us.

"Would that it were so easy, brother."

"Then I will make it up to you—see if I don't. I will give you back like for like, double, triple! You may have Leah, and the Egyptian sisters—the pick of my women. Only leave me the Babylonian twins, I beg you. A man must have some pleasure in his life."

And the touching thing was that he meant it, every word. I knew then I could never make him understand. I could only shake my head.

"I will leave Nineveh tonight," I said. "I go to the north to make war on the mountain tribes. It is better thus."

Esarhaddon withdrew his hand from my arm.

"I think you are jealous, Tiglath—jealous and spiteful. The very command I had asked for. I, who never wanted more. What he withholds from me, he gives to you with an open hand!"

"You had Sumer."

"Sumer!" His face wrinkled with disgust. "I was a herder of sheep in Sumer—a man could die from lack of exercise ruling in Sumer. The king gives you this command only to show his contempt for me."

"He gives me this command because I asked for it."

"Then it is you who despises me."

"You know that is a lie."

For a moment, while he seemed ready to rise from his seat and strike out, I thought all friendship might be over between us. But then, the struggle within him over, Esarhaddon grew calm.

"Yes, I know it."

"Things have not turned out as we would have wished—that is all."

"Yes. That is the way of it." He peered into his wine cup as if looking for something. "Do you suppose this could be the mongoose's *alu* working itself out?"

I did not know what answer to make, so I said nothing.

For a long time we sat together in silence.

"When do you leave? Tonight?" Esarhaddon asked finally, as if of a thing which had slipped his mind.

"Yes, tonight."

"Then you will miss the ceremony of my elevation—I am sorry for that. But perhaps it would give you scant pleasure."

"I would see that, brother, with an easy heart and gladly. But I would not be present at your marriage."

"Women—they are a curse." He shook his head, vexed, it seemed, by this insoluble difficulty. "You are sure you would not take a few of mine? Not even Leah?"

I could not answer him—in such matters my brother's head was filled with mud. I rose from the table. He rose with me and, when I tried once more to bow, took me in his arms and embraced me. He knew as well as I that, in some sense, we were parting forever.

In the hallway that led to the front entrance, that door on which in less than an hour the people of Nineveh would vent their wrath, where now a bustle of ambitious men were already gathering, I met Naq'ia.

"Then you have not come to murder my son, Tiglath Ashur?" she asked, smiling at her own witticism—she was radiant with triumph. I could not help thinking that she looked like a cat playing with a crippled mouse.

"No, Lady. He is my brother and my lord."

"But now, I gather, no longer your friend?"

"May a king have friends, Lady? If he may, then I am still his friend."

"Your behavior is all that it should be, Tiglath," she said, holding out her hand to me. "But that was ever so. I congratulate you on the steady nobility of your character."

I knew she was mocking me, but I took her hand and touched it with my forehead, for she was now the mother of the future king and deserved this show of respect. But in my heart I hated her.

I looked around at the men who watched us from the walls, not daring to venture too close—yes, of course, they all knew. The whole city knew by then. But Naq'ia had always known. I could see that in her face.

"The god's will has been accomplished," she said, as if in answer to the question which had hardly shaped itself in my mind.

Yes, of course. She had always known precisely how it would end. I could not help but ask myself how that could be, but the answer was not something I really desired to know—I had a sense, even then, that such knowledge as this it would be a blessing never to possess.

On my way home, as I passed through the house of war, I stopped by the barrack of the *quradu* and found Lushakin, my old *ekalli.*

"Have you the stomach for another campaign?"

He regarded me for a moment, scratching the chin of his beard absent-mindedly. Like everyone else, he had heard the rumors.

"Against whom do we fight?" he asked—it was not such an impertinent question. "If it be not against the king, I am your man, Prince, even into the mouth of death."

"No, Lushakin, my old comrade, I do not invite you to civil war. My brother Esarhaddon will not lose his chance at the throne by any action of mine."

"Then it is true, Prince, that you will not be *marsarru*?"

"The god has chosen elsewhere."

Lushakin was not a fool, so he said nothing. But the way he wrinkled his face suggested clearly enough that he might favor another explanation just as well.

"What would you have me do?"

"Just this—gather twenty men who are weary of peace. Tell them to make ready to leave tonight, but say nothing of me. The city is uneasy enough—I would slip away and have no man know of it. Tell them we will make war against the tribes of the northern mountains, but nothing else."

"It shall be as you say, Prince."

I had but one more thing to do, and I would be free of all entanglements—as free as if I were dead.

I had not slept since my interview with the king, but I cannot really account for my state of mind on that day by reference to the lack of a night's sleep. Everything had taken on a peculiar air of unreality—this was no longer my life that I was living. It was as if all these things were happening to someone else, and I was merely the helpless witness. Or, perhaps more accurately, it was like one of those nightmares in which one knows, even while it is going on, that one is dreaming, that it is, after all, only a nightmare.

"Presently I will wake up," I kept thinking. "I will wake up and find myself in my own bed. I will be six years old again and safe in my mother's room in the house of women. My life cannot possibly have come to this."

The house on the Street of Nergal looked dead, like a long-neglected tomb. Had it really been only yesterday that I had seen Esharhamat here, had held her in my arms, full of hope? It seemed impossible. No one had entered this dwelling in centuries. The room that held our bed was like the scene of some terrible misfortune, the memory of which hangs over it as a kind of curse so that people shun that spot and allow it to fall into decay.

"I will be here," I had told her, *"even if I die for it."* *"I will never see her again,"* I had told Esarhaddon. Both of these seemed to involve an absolute moral claim—I could not but have made both promises, and yet each seemed to exclude the other. I sat down on the edge of the bed, overwhelmed, my head throbbing, my breast feeling as if it might explode. For some reason I had left my javelin at home, and it was just as well. At that moment, in the extremity of my despair, I might have used it to tear open my heart.

Faintly, as things happening at a great distance, I could hear the noises from the street below my window, from the street beyond that street, from that quarter, from the whole city. The life of Nineveh went on, precisely as if I did not exist—as if it did not matter that Tiglath Ashur must lose the sweetness of his own life. As if that life had never been lived.

I have no notion how long I sat there like that. Or, at least, notions of time did not seem to enter into it. And then, quite unexpectedly, came the sound of a tiny hand rapping on the door in the wall this house shared with the one behind it. Tap, tap, tap. A pause. Tap, tap, tap.

"Tiglath, are you there?" came her voice at last.

I tried to speak. I opened my mouth and then closed it again, unable to utter a sound. I could not even rise from the bed—it was as if all power over my body had left me.

"Tiglath, answer me. I know you are there. Let me in."

Silence. Then the sound of her fist beating on the door, louder this time.

"Tiglath, let me *in*. Tiglath!"

I waited. I could not seem to breathe. "What if she went away?" I kept thinking. I would never hear that voice again. She would be lost to me forever. And yet I could not answer.

Now, as if in a fury, she pounded against the door—as if she wanted to break it down. I could see how it shook on its leather hinges as she kicked at the base with her sandaled feet.

"Tiglath—TigLATH! I know you are there—you would not have stayed away; not when you promised. Can you not see that we have both been tricked? Let me in, let me in, let me in, let-me-in, in, in, in, in!"

The words tumbled together until they were no longer words. She was only sobbing now, and I could tell from the sound that she must have been kneeling in front of the door. She sobbed and sobbed, pounding on the rough wood hard enough to make her hands bleed. Finally, she had discovered her helplessness. Like a captured bird beating its soft wings against the bars of its cage, until the wings break and the heart bursts. . . .

And then she stopped, and the only sound I could hear was that of her weeping, a low wail, like that of an exhausted child. And then nothing—a blank, an emptiness.

In a long life a man does many things the memory of which afflicts him with remorse. All the acts of spite or cruelty or cowardice collect in the soul like the tiny cracks one sees in the glaze of an old pot. I have committed many wicked and craven acts in my time on this earth, but none which fills me with more shame than my silence while Esharhamat cried out to me to be admitted one last time into my embrace. I was simply afraid, and that fear was more terrible than the fear of pain or even death. I could not have borne my life another instant if I had seen her—not when I knew I would never see her again—and I had not the courage to tell her so. The sound of her weeping beyond the door, that was my last link with our love. I could only listen, helpless, and pray she would not leave me in darkness too soon.

At last I could hear her rising from her knees. I could hear the soft sound of her hands against the door as she steadied herself against it. Would she leave now? Could I stop her? Had I even courage enough left to try?

Her voice, when she spoke again, was calm. There was still the rasp of tears in it, but it was calm enough. It was cold, like spring water in winter, filled with ragged ice.

"Tiglath, I know you can hear me," she said, seeming to measure each word. "I know you have turned your back on me now, and I do not forgive you. I know you love me, and I would gladly have died to hear you say it one last time, but now I hope your love is a curse to you. I hope it haunts you until you die, as it will haunt me. I hope it drives you mad."

"Try to understand," I thought. "Try, my love, try to see

that I am without choice or will. Try, try to understand." But she
would not even wish to understand. Why should she? She was
right to hate me for this betrayal.

"I will marry Esarhaddon," she went on. "I will give him the
sons a king must have, and I will try to find pleasure in his bed—
not love, for all love is dead within me, but pleasure if I can.
Remember, all your life, each night, that I will be in Esarhaddon's
bed in the house of succession. It will be his arms around me, not
yours—not yours. It will be . . ."

That was the end, except for the sounds of her footsteps as
she ran away. When I knew she was gone, then—only then—
could I bury my head in my hands and weep.

It was already dark when I began to make my way home. It
had taken a long time before the paralysis of will—if I may be so
kind to myself as to use such an expression to cover my weakness
—before the paralysis of will departed, to be replaced, slowly,
measure by measure, by a terrible, blind, focusless anger. She was
gone, and forever. What I hated was life, the thought of the hours
and days and years that stretched before me, and all without her.
I wanted to kill, to maim, to share this pain out to others that it
might not break me to pieces.

What people might have thought of me as I lurched along
the street I cannot say. It was dark and I was wrapped in a simple
soldier's cloak—no one could have known who I was. But I felt,
even to myself, as if I had gone half mad. Once, twice, I remember, someone would glance at me and move quickly away.

"Are you lonely, Mighty Lord? Do you want to tell me your
troubles and take some comfort?"

Who was it who had spoken? I did not know; the words
seemed to come from nowhere. I turned my head and saw a little
harlot standing beside me, hardly more than a child. She smiled
uncertainly, as if torn between her fear and her need.

The sight of her filled me with rage—her smiling, mocking
face, I wanted to smash it. I hated her, this common prostitute. I
had never seen her before, and yet I have never hated anyone so
much.

"An easy thing to kill her," I thought. "The work of an
instant. Why not?" I actually did put my hands about her throat.

I shook her, lifting her so that her bare feet actually left the ground. My grip tightened. . . .

And then, just as suddenly, I lost interest, letting her drop. I simply could not be bothered.

She was frightened but unhurt. I took a handful of silver coins from a pocket in my cloak—more money, I would guess, than she had ever seen in her life—and scattered them into her lap. She scooped them up and, scrambling to her feet, ran like a rabbit, no doubt thinking herself unutterably lucky. She really was lucky. I had come within a breath of murdering her.

"The great gods preserve me from madness," I whispered. *"I hope it drives you mad,"* she had said. Esharhamat had said those words to me, had pronounced that curse. Perhaps, already . . .

I might almost have welcomed it.

Like Esarhaddon, I owned a palace in the city, but I did not live in it. The king had settled that I should have quarters within the complex of buildings that was the royal residence—he had wished me near him, as if somehow, by remaining inside the radiant circle of his *melammu,* that aura of divine light which is said to hedge those whom Ashur has raised to mastery, he might transfer it to me.

But if that had been his plan, it had not succeeded. I could not but wonder, as I let myself in by the little side entrance that opened from a garden, I could not but wonder who would occupy these rooms tomorrow, when I would be on the dusty road to the north, perhaps never to return.

There was no one about to take my cloak, so I left it on a bench, sitting down there myself because I could not summon the resolve to do more.

In less than two hours I would put on my battle armor, collect my sword and my javelin, and walk the few steps to the house of war. There a horse would be waiting, and Lushakin and his twenty men, and we would depart from the city like shadows. But between then and now the time stretched empty.

I felt thirsty—I would drink a cup of wine. I went into the great hall, being reluctant to shout for a slave to come to me, but there as well I found I was alone.

Now I did shout, but there was no answer. My servants, all of them it seemed, were gone.

In his own house a prince of the blood is never suffered to be alone. From the time I had ceased to be a boy, living with Esarhaddon in a single room in the house of war, I was always attended by the slaves of the royal household. They were always around, so omnipresent that I had learned to notice them no more than I did the furniture or the color of the walls. But now they had fled my presence. What could it mean?

One idea came into my mind. Someone—perhaps the king, perhaps the Lord Sinahiusur, perhaps someone else—someone had decided that the moment had come for my death. If my house was empty, it was merely that there should be no witnesses when the assassins cut me down like summer wheat.

So be it. The idea of dying held no terrors for me—I would welcome it. But I would not sell my life for nothing. I would not stand quietly and let them cut my throat; there would be no dignity in dying thus, and I would at least die with dignity. They would have to pay for the pleasure of killing me.

On the wall, behind the chair where I sat to take my meals, were crossed a pair of javelins, my boast to the world that I was a soldier. I took one of them down, testing the copper point against my thumb. I would go looking for those who looked for me, and we would see how many would die along with Tiglath Ashur. The idea filled me with a cruel pleasure.

I took off my sandals that my feet would make no sound upon the tile floor. I held the javelin in both hands and went hunting for my quarry.

Where would they be waiting? Would they expect me to know? I tried to see the problem from their side. They had not killed me in the garden as I came home, and the reason could only be that they did not wish to take the risk of some chance witness happening by. They might guard the exits, but they would make their attempt somewhere well inside this wing of the palace—they would wish me to die silently.

I would go to my bedroom. I would find them there, if not before.

When he knows his enemies are within reach, a man's every sense grows as keen as the edge of an iron knife. I could hear every whisper of sound on that hot night, when the air was too heavy to bring even a breath of wind in through an open window. I could hear the dust tumbling through empty space. I could hear the faint hiss of an oil lamp burning I knew not where. I could hear the very darkness. If there had been a murderer waiting with his sword drawn, I would have heard the beating of his heart, but there was nothing. I made my cautious way in silence, until I reached the short hallway that led to my bedroom.

There was a glow of flickering yellow light from beneath the door, which had been left open to perhaps the breadth of my thumb. Someone was within—how I knew I could not have said, but the fact was as plain as if whoever it was had shouted out his name.

I balanced my hand against the door, first the tips of the fingers only and then the palm, feeling the weight of its reluctance on its leather hinges. I pushed it open.

A lamp burned on the floor beside where I was used to sleep, casting strange shadows over the ceiling as if the room were filled with the fluttering black wings of evil spirits. I could see almost the whole room—no one was lurking in a corner, waiting to kill me. There was no one there.

And then the blanket on my sleeping mat stirred. An arm came out, pushing the blanket down, and a woman sat up and smiled at me. For a moment, an instant, a single pulse of time, I felt a wild surge of hope, and then I saw that the woman was Shaditu.

"I sent your servants away," she said, letting the blanket fall away to expose her naked breasts. "They are remarkably loyal to their master, so I had to mix in a few threats with the gold I poured into their waiting hands. I wanted us to be alone."

For those few seconds at least, I think I was quite mad. A wild cry of rage broke from my lips, and I balanced the javelin in my hand and threw with every shred of my strength. The weapon buried its point in the wall, not the width of three fingers from Shaditu's head. Had I meant to miss her? I know not. I do not think so.

At first her eyes grew wide with fear, but that did not last long. Her breast was heaving and she trembled, but not because she was afraid.

"Oh, Tiglath," she murmured, her voice thick with excitement, "how you know to make a woman want you!"

And then, with a kind of reckless violence, she threw back her head and began to laugh. The silvery sound of her laughter filled the room, driving away the shadows the way a dog's bark will scatter a flock of roosting birds—there was no space for anything except Shaditu's ringing laughter. It filled my mind until I wanted to clutch the sides of my head to keep it from bursting.

"Is this how you courted the Lady Esharhamat?" she asked, still hardly able to speak for laughing. "Is this how you brought her to love you, Tiglath, by displaying how easily you could pierce her flesh with your lance? Come—you may poke away at me with your other one. You may drive it in as deep as you like."

To show me what she meant she pulled the blanket away from her legs, opening them as wide as she could.

"Come, Tiglath—dear, strong, loving brother. Is that an easy enough target for you? Hah, hah, hah!" Her breasts and belly shook with merriment.

And then, quite suddenly, she stopped. She smiled at me, a cunning, knowing smile, as if she could see straight into my heart.

"You will never have her again, Tiglath," she said. "There will be other women—many women, if I am any judge—but never the Lady Esharhamat, who will be set to breeding kings, hunched under Esarhaddon's weight like any tavern slut. Let him have her, Tiglath Ashur, hero, mighty warrior. Come and let me teach you how little you have really lost."

There is a line beyond which men may not go and remain men. It is a vague thing, this demarcation that sets the limit to rage, lust, sorrow, joy, the frenzy of fear. It is the limit of what we may endure of these things before they overwhelm us, and no one crosses that line of his own will. I crossed it as I listened to my sister Shaditu mocking me. I hated her. I thought that was all I felt, that bitter hatred as she gloated over the corpse of my dead hopes—I thought that was all, but I was wrong.

If she said another word . . .

I took a step toward her, then another, hardly conscious of what I did, hardly knowing why.

"Did you think it could end any other way? Did you think I would let that cold little bitch puppy have you?"

Even as her eyes followed me, even as my shadow fell across her naked body did she speak to me thus in her throaty, wanton voice, the very sound of which seemed to stab at my breast like a dagger with a broken point.

"*You* were never meant for one such as her, Tiglath Ashur, my dear, stupid brother. What can she offer you that I . . ."

As I stood over her she reached up to touch me. I took her arm just above the wrist and pulled her toward me—I could see the expectation in her eyes and it filled me with what I took to be the purest hatred but which was far from pure. I raised my hand

and struck her, hard, straight across the face so that her head snapped back with a violence that seemed enough to have broken her neck. When she turned her eyes to me again they were shining with pain and a thin trickle of blood was running from her mouth. Still, she smiled at me. I could not stand to see her smile. I tightened my hand into a fist and struck her again, making her cry out.

"Taunt me again," I thought. "Go ahead—give me a reason to kill you. I hardly need one."

"Oh, brother," she whispered through her bruised lips. "How I love you! Here—let me lick the blood from your fingers!"

She grasped my arm with her free hand and tried to raise herself. I tried to shake her off, but she hung on with what seemed like the fear of death.

"Let me kiss your cruel hands," she said, with a voice thick and trembling. "Let me . . ."

I could not help myself. Tears of anguish were streaming down my face. My knees seemed to buckle. I knelt beside her, taking her little neck into my two hands. I meant to choke her to death. I would kill her—I would. Then why did I see no fear in her eyes? Why did her fingers caress my arms? I would break her . . .

But I did not. Suddenly I was covering her face with harsh, hating kisses. She moaned softly, and her tongue licked at my lips.

"Damn you!" I whispered. "Damn you!"

"Yes—yes . . . Damn me, yes."

Her hand slipped down, reaching under my tunic to grasp my manhood, which with astonishment I found was swollen and hard. Her fingers moved up and down its length—I could hardly breathe.

"Hurt me, brother—yes. Avenge yourself on my body, Tiglath Ashur, favorite of the gods, true king. Kill me if it pleases you. Who has a better right—why should I care if I die?"

But I did not kill her. I covered her breasts with my hands, letting my fingers close around them until she screamed with the pain of it. Yet mixed with the pain was a raw longing, as if she hoped it would never stop. Even while I hurt her, she began lifting the tunic up over my shoulders.

Tiglath Ashur, favorite of the gods. Of late the gods had shown me their favor in strange ways. But I did not think to ask what she meant—I was beyond thinking, of that or anything else. If I did not take this woman—not Shaditu, not my sister, but merely this body which writhed beneath me—then I felt as if my breast would shatter with rage.

I went into her. With the first thrust she rolled back on the top of her head and began to moan, a low, hollow sound, as if her body were inhabited by a demon struggling to get out. Her hips moved in time with me, at first slowly and then faster. I buried my teeth in her shoulder and she cried out—even as I reached my climax, she cried out.

I did not look at her as I put on my tunic again. I was not ashamed of what I had done. I merely hated her and desired never to see her face again.

"Will you come to me again?" she asked, in the small, meek voice of a child.

"No—tonight I leave for the north. I am leaving now."

She sat up suddenly, pulling the blanket around her. Even in the flickering light of the oil lamp I could see that her face was flushed and angry.

"You cannot leave. I will not allow it. I will tell the king what you have done!"

"Tell him." I turned to her with cold, indifferent eyes—indeed I felt nothing. "Do, tell him. But never seek to see me again, Shaditu, for the next time I really will kill you and you will take no pleasure in the manner of your death."

"Dog! I hate you! The gods damn you, Tiglath . . . !"

Even as I left this dwelling for the last time, I could hear her curses trembling in the air behind me.

16

"*Tiglath Ashur, favorite of the gods, true king.*" "*Did you think I would let that cold little bitch puppy have you?*" As I rode through the night, the lights of Nineveh fading at my back, these words of Shaditu's throbbed in my mind like a bruise someone had made the mistake of touching. What could she have been talking about? Had she even known herself?

"*Can you not see that we have both been tricked?*" What had Esharhamat tried to tell me as I abandoned her? What was this secret that everyone seemed to understand except myself?

"*Tiglath Ashur, favorite of the gods . . .*" The words trembling with desire.

I had raped my own sister, if rape may have so willing a victim. She had wanted it to happen, and just that way, but if she had not wanted it I would have taken her in any case, and I would have killed her if she had resisted. But she had not thought of resisting. It would seem she had been as busy in her seduction as I had been in my rape.

And somehow this crime, for which I felt no remorse, not then nor later, brought peace to my mind—if peace can be the dead, icy, unfeeling calm which had descended on me. But it gave me the leisure to consider many things: the follies of hope, the blank wall that was my own future, and my sister's strange words. And Esharhamat's.

Somehow, I knew not how, she had snatched my life from me. I was not to learn the truth of it for many years.

But at least she did not seek my death. I do not believe that

Shaditu made good on her threat to tell the king about our encounter. At least, I received no summons back to Nineveh. No
armed men were sent to take my head. And after some time, when
I saw my father once more, he did not speak of it or act toward
me as if I had stolen his heart's jewel.

What, after all, could she have told him? The truth, perhaps.
She might have been unwise enough to do that. And perhaps the
king decided to do nothing. As I have said, these are things I will
never know.

What I did know, or came to know—word reached me by
dispatch within a few weeks after the event—was that on the day
after my brother's proclamation as *marsarru,* even before he had
slept through a whole night in the house of succession, the *baru*
Rimani Ashur was found hanging by his neck in the sanctuary of
the god Shamash.

There seemed to be no doubt he had died by his own hand.
He had left no word behind to explain himself, but that his death
had been his own act was clear enough. He had nailed one end of
a leather belt to the lintel of the doorway, made a noose, stuck his
head through it, and kicked away the stool upon which he had
been standing. All this he had done under the very eyes of the
god, the Lord of Decision.

It was a strange thing to happen, and it made a strange impression. Rimani Ashur might have killed himself for many reasons—I believe now that I know the reason, but I could not have
then—and yet the city, by the conjunction of the two events, saw
his suicide as an act of remorse for calling Esarhaddon to be the
marsarru. All through his days, and through no sin of his own,
my brother was to live with the stain of this event upon him. He
was cursed from the beginning.

But as, in the darkness, my way lit by torchbearers, I traveled along the road north, I understood nothing of these matters.
They lay in the future and in the past, both of which were closed
to me.

It was not quite first light when we arrived at Three Lions,
but even at such an hour we passed men on the road, shouldering
their hoes as they made their way to the fields. They stared at me
with astonishment as I rode by, unaccustomed to the sight of
armed men, not recognizing their lord in the darkness. I can only
guess what terrible apprehensions must have risen in their minds.

As I came near my house, one of the kitchen women came

outside to see what the commotion was. She was a huge, sturdy woman and she carried an oil lamp, treading over the bare ground with ridiculous delicacy.

"Well, Shulmunaid," I said, smiling broadly as I dismounted from my horse. "And have I changed so much that you no longer know me?"

She glanced quickly up at my face and let out a shriek, dropping the lamp in the dust as she turned and ran back into the house. Within a quarter of a minute there were twelve or fifteen people come to witness the master's unexpected return. Even my mother came, only a moment later than the others—she must still have been asleep. She rushed into my arms, burying her head in my chest.

"Oh, Lathikadas," she wept, "is it really you? I thought . . . I was afraid . . ."

"No, Merope, they have not killed your son." I let my hand settle on her bronze-colored hair. "The king has not made me pay with my life because I cannot succeed him."

I gave orders that my men were to be fed and that beds were to be found for them. We would stay a day and a night, which would give me just time to settle my affairs. I did not expect to be back for a long time.

A breakfast was prepared for me and I ate it while the fires in the sweating house were lit. I would clean myself and then sleep and then speak with the overseer Tahu Ishtar, but these matters could wait. First it was necessary to explain to my mother all that had happened and how the future would now shape itself. This I did over breakfast, and she listened to my words, saying nothing. Her stillness was that quiet sorrow of one who has seen from the first how all things must work themselves out.

"I do not know what I will find in Amat," I said. "I will send for you as soon as I know I can do so in safety, but garrison towns are wild places, so that may not be soon."

"I can leave here on an hour's notice," she said calmly, and I found it possible to believe her. "I would rather follow you to the earth's end than stay here alone."

"Amat is the earth's end." I smiled at her, knowing what she meant. "Beyond it is only the kingdom of Urartu and the tribes of the eastern mountains—it is the point of the spear with which the Land of Ashur keeps these at bay. I am afraid we will not discover there a very refined society."

"What is that to me?"

"What is that to me?" For Merope it was all very simple—
her son had hurt himself playing with the big boys in Nineveh,
and now she and he were heading off into a mountain exile. Time
and love would bring all right again. This was why she lived.

I went to the sweating house and steamed out the poisons
which collected in a man when he has been vexed in his liver and
then I slept until it was nearly dark again. I was too tired to
dream, which was a blessing.

When I awoke Tahu Ishtar was waiting for me under the
vine arbor in the garden. He rose and bowed when I approached.

"It is well with your son Qurdi?" I asked him, and he nodded.

"He is grown almost to manhood, Lord. I think he will make
a fine overseer when my *sedu* beckons."

"But may the god grant this will not be soon, Tahu Ishtar."

He bowed again, with all the dignity of a great prince before
his king, for this was a man who understood the uses of power.

"I gather you are bound for the north, Lord," he said, as if it
were the most indifferent matter in the world—the god alone
knew what they understood here of how matters stood in Nineveh, but my overseer was neither blind nor a fool. He must have
guessed much.

"Yes. I will be gone for a long time. I may not return for
many years."

"It is a harsh place, the north."

"It is that, Tahu Ishtar, and its links with the world outside
are tenuous. I think it best that you take the management of
Three Lions entirely into your own hands."

"Am I not to write, Lord?" He raised his eyebrows, as if
mildly surprised, but gave no other sign. I could only smile.

"Yes, write—by all means, write. Tell me how the crops do
and if the river floods more or less than last year. A man likes to
receive news of such things. But do not wait for any word from
me before you do what is needful. It may not come in time."

"It shall be as the master of Three Lions declares."

Thus did I order all things against my departure.

The journey to Amat lasted twelve days. There were no
towns of any size along the way and few villages, so for the most

part we pitched our tents wherever the darkness found us and slept on the ground. At first this was no hardship, for the month of Ab is a time when many choose to sleep outside, wrapped in a blanket on their roofs to escape the heat of their houses, but as we climbed higher into the mountains the nights turned cold. By the time we reached our destination I think we were all looking forward to a bed in a warm room.

Amat—we stood on the crest of a hill and looked down at it in the valley where it nestled like something held in a man's hand. Behind it rose the mountains of the Hakkari range, ragged as broken ice. In mountains such as these, in such holy silences, the gods were supposed to have their dwelling places, where they could look down upon the little works of men, smiling with indifference. What must Nineveh seem from such a height? What must Tiglath Ashur and his little sorrows seem to these, which had risen from the foundations of the world and would endure forever? If a man grieves, it is well for him to remember his own insignificance, to remember that his heart can break without shattering the earth as well. If I had been searching for a place in which to lose myself, I had found it.

But a man is not a god and cannot live in the peaks of mountains, so we turned our eyes to the valley.

The town was a poor thing even by the standard of some other garrison towns I had seen. There was the fortress and, outside its walls, grouped around the market square, some twenty or thirty squat little buildings of unpainted brick, mostly wineshops and brothels and the houses of various other small traders who lived off the custom of the soldiers. There was a general atmosphere of slackness—everywhere there were the little telltale symptoms of sagging discipline and hopelessness, as if the men stationed here had long since forgotten that they were part of the army of Ashur.

I was *shaknu* of a vast territory, but, like most frontiers, it was sparsely settled and my capital, it seemed, was no Nineveh. That was just as well, I thought. I had not come here to delight myself in the pleasure palaces of a great city.

When I approached the fortress gate, the guards, who seemed completely occupied in a game of lots, did not even trouble to challenge me—indeed, they hardly seemed to notice my presence. I rode up to one who wore the uniform of an *ekalli* and, as he came up from his crouch and turned to see who addressed him, I caught him across the side of the head with the butt on my whip, knocking him to the ground.

"You and you!" I shouted, pointing at random to two of his company. "Arrest this man and have him put in a cage in your stockade. He is to have neither food nor blankets for three nights; if he is still alive at the end of that time, bring him to me. Now someone go find the commanding officer of this doghole and tell him that the *rab shaqe* Tiglath Ashur has arrived and would be gratified of an audience—run, you scum!"

They ran, but I doubt if it was to find anything except a hiding place.

The fortress compound made a depressing spectacle. The drill fields were muddy and overgrown with weeds, dirty children played on the plank sidewalks outside the headquarters offices, which looked as if they had not seen a daub of whitewash since the reign of Great Sargon, and on the walls there did not seem to be even a proper guard mounted. Boredom hung in the air like the pall of death. It would be many months before these soldiers were ready to face an enemy in battle—I would have no time here for bitter memories. The king my father had done well when he chose Amat as the scene of my exile.

As my escort dismounted and looked around them with as much dismay as I felt in my own heart, I summoned Lushakin to me with a silent gesture.

"See that the men are billeted and fed," I told him. "Then have a look around this pigsty—without drawing attention to yourself—and bring me word of what you find."

"Yes, my prince. We are a long way from home, eh?"

Longer, as it turned out, than either of us could have imagined. As I walked through the mud to the garrison commander's quarters I had the sense of having stepped outside the civilized world—even the Elamites would have been ashamed of this place.

"We had no idea you would arrive so quickly," I was informed as I stepped up onto the porch. The young officer who met me—"young" being entirely a relative term; I was his senior by no more than a year—gave the impression of being torn between his duty to offer the customary welcoming courtesies to the new *shaknu* and a strong desire to bar my way. "Our *rab abru* is gone for the day on province business—I really couldn't say precisely where he might be found. He will be back by evening, so if perhaps you would allow me—"

"I suspect you know precisely where the *rab abru* might be found," I said, fixing my eyes on the bright yellow pennant that hung with the army wing standard over the fortress gate and proclaimed the rank of its senior officer. My own was in my luggage and would be run up before nightfall. I never went anywhere without it, nor would any other commander.

I smiled, not very pleasantly, at this adjutant who, after all, was merely doing what honor required in protecting his superior.

"Find him. Bring him to me within the half hour, or I will send out an arrest party for the two of you. Is that clear?"

"Yes, *Rab Shaqe*—very clear!"

In saluting, the fellow struck his chest so hard that he would probably carry a mark there for half the month. He went scurrying off toward the town as fast as he could work his legs.

The northern frontier was not a desirable posting. Men were sent to places like this because they had made powerful enemies, or because they had somehow disgraced themselves, or perhaps most often because no good commander wanted them and thus they settled here the way a stone will settle in the mud at the bottom of a horsepond. Doubtless the soldiers here, who probably had heard no news from the capital in many months, were already busy wondering what the *rab shaqe* Tiglath Ashur had done to get himself banished to Amat. I would let them think anything they liked, but they would learn soon enough, and to their sorrow, that my crimes had not included laxness of discipline.

I went inside the headquarters building—there was nothing to be gained from standing about outside, and my interview with the garrison commander, when it finally did take place, would be better conducted in private.

The public rooms presented a sorry enough sight. The floors were dirty, dust and not-quite-empty wine cups seemed to be everywhere, and much of the furniture looked as if it would fall to pieces at a hard glance. What the living quarters might be like I did not even care to imagine.

Without much difficulty I had concluded that it would be necessary to make a few examples among the officers—one cannot expect soldiers to be better than the men who lead them—and I had even less trouble deciding where to start. The garrison commander was in for a trying day. I found myself hoping that he would be deserving of the fate I had in mind for him.

And when at last he arrived—half led, half supported by his

adjutant, like a blind man or a cripple—I was not disappointed. Even from halfway across the room I could smell him. His uniform tunic was wrinkled and covered with what looked like food stains, and his beard was a greasy tangle. And already, hardly two hours past noon, he was drunk—so drunk that when he tried to speak he was no more intelligible than a grunting sow. There was nothing to be gained from berating such a man. He would probably not have understood one word in five.

"Clean this vagabond up," I told his adjutant, keeping my voice level, almost indifferent. "Lock him in a sweating house until he remembers how to think, but have him presentable and sober within two hours. Further, you may issue orders for a general assembly."

"And when shall the garrison present itself, *Rab Shaqe*?"

"In two hours. Everything will happen in two hours, *Rab Kisir.*"

The man looked at me as if I had just pronounced a death sentence on him.

I waited inside the headquarters building. I would not show myself again until the entire garrison had assembled for inspection; it would do them no harm to make their new commander's acquaintance under the rigors of parade discipline. None of the officers thought fit to disturb me—doubtless they were engaged elsewhere. My only visitor was Lushakin.

"By the great gods, Prince, this place is more like a brothel than a fortress," he said, sitting down and breaking the seal of a jar he had brought with him. He offered me the first swallow—we had been together a long time, and such, in his view, were all the courtesies to which my rank entitled me—and then tilted back his head to wash his throat with beer. "The place seems to have as many harlots as lice. So far at least five different women have offered me their backsides, and we have been in barracks not yet an hour together. However, if they are as dirty as everything else around here, I would be afraid to touch them. The food, by the way—at least such as the common soldiers eat—isn't fit for anything except mending walls with."

"The beer is no pleasure either," I said, making a face as he offered me another pull from his jar.

"Ah, Prince, we have all been spoiled by the beer in Sumer. The water of the Euphrates makes the best beer in the world— you cannot expect to find anything like it this far north."

And Lushakin, to whom all beer was merely beer, finished his off with a single long swallow.

"I will tell you something else, though," he said, lowering his voice. "You mustn't expect to go into battle with troops like these and come away alive. They have gone to seed. They hate the very idea of war, almost as much as they hate their officers. Mark my words, Prince, the first flash of a tribesman's sword and they will run like rabbits, every one of them."

"Then we shall have to teach them that there are things far more frightful than any enemy."

"Oh, I think they are learning that already," Lushakin answered, showing his teeth in a wide grin. "Like all soldiers, they have a great curiosity about the new commander, and our boys have been telling them stories."

"Good—let them think I eat babies for breakfast." I could not help but laugh. "Lushakin, I am glad you are my friend and not my enemy, for you have no more scruples than an adder."

My *ekalli* merely shrugged his shoulders, as if I had said no more than what would be obvious to a child.

"And what, Prince, have scruples to do with soldiering?"

An hour later I stepped out into the cold white sunlight to inspect my new army. Their commander, looking as if he would have preferred to be dead, but sober and in a clean uniform, stood in front of their ranks, watching me with an expression of sullen hatred on his face.

Even from a distance these men of Ashur made a sorry sight. I saw rusted weapons and bowstrings grown frayed enough to be mistaken for shocks of wheat. I saw dirt and boredom. They were soldiers, but they stood about like prisoners in a labor gang, and indeed for most of them the army probably was a kind of servitude. They had lost their pride—or perhaps, more accurately, they had never had any to begin with.

"I have come here to assume command," I shouted, still standing on the porch of the garrison headquarters. "Let me show you how that is done."

At a nod from me, Lushakin and five of my *quradu* came forward from the ranks and seized the *rab abru,* grabbing him by the arms and legs and carrying him to the front of the parade ground. He was so astonished that at first he did not even protest, but he was loud enough when they put his feet through rope nooses and hung him upside-down from the log railing in front of a horse trough.

He screamed and shouted curses in a high-pitched, cracking voice, but one could hardly hear him over the laughter of his own troops—it was a measure of how low their morale had sunk that they would take such delight in seeing their commander thus humiliated. Indeed, he made a comical sight, lying on his back in the mud, his legs sticking straight up so that his tunic had slipped to his waist, but soldiers must hate their officers before they will laugh at their disgrace—and an officer who is hated by his men is invariably a bad lot.

When the *rab abru* was well secured and his sandals had been removed, Lushakin turned to me, saluted smartly, and stood waiting for his orders. He knew well enough what they would be. We had discussed the whole performance, and the form of punishment had been his own suggestion—a thing he had once seen in Naharina, done to an Arab caught cheating at lots. But before soldiers the appearance was everything, and so Lushakin waited.

"Ten apiece, *Ekalli.* And don't spare your arm."

Lushakin had found a whip, perhaps the length of a man's arm, made of hippopotamus hide. While another of our troop gripped the *rab abru*'s feet by the toes, forcing him to hold them as level as the top of a table, he laid his whip gently across the soles, as if to measure his stroke.

I will not soon forget how the *rab abru* screamed, like a woman in hard labor. The neat little whip whistled through the air and bit into the soles of his feet, and each time he screamed with what seemed a mingling of terror, pain, and something almost like indignation. Lushakin obeyed his orders—each stroke raised a fine spray of blood, stripping away the skin as efficiently as a knife. Ten strokes on each foot, carefully paced that the performance would not end too quickly—the whistling whip, the dull, sickening thud as it found its mark, the *rab abru*'s feral scream. And the whole time, his soldiers laughed at his agony. It was a spectacle they found very much to their taste. They had seen nothing so amusing in months.

When Lushakin was finished, he poured cold water over the man's by-then raw soles and cut him down. The *rab abru* was driven out of the fortress where, until that day, his word had been law. He was driven forth with a lash, his every step leaving a bloody footprint on the muddy ground. If he had friends in the town to succor him, then he might be saved from privation and death, but to this garrison he was less than a shadow. The sentence, should he ever return, was death. Beyond that, his fate was to be a matter of indifference.

I waited until the soldiers had finished with their joke. I stood in silence, watching them disdainfully, until they grew quiet once more.

"In one month, we shall take the field against the mountain nomads. It will be our last chance while the weather holds, and I have no intention of awaiting your convenience. You have but that one month to make yourselves into an army—otherwise your only hope of life is that the barbarians will take pity upon the armies of Ashur and send only their women and young children into battle against you, for I do not know how a rabble such as I see before me could ever hope to prevail against men."

They did not laugh now. Some of them, no doubt, had fought with the Lord Sennacherib against these same mountain tribes, and they felt the truth of my words, realizing, perhaps for the first time, to what a depth they had allowed themselves to sink, and had the decency to feel ashamed. It was a beginning.

"With your commander—with your late commander, whose name shall not be spoken here—I have dealt lightly because I would not stain the day of my arrival with the taking of life. Doubtless he was not alone in his corruption, for no officer fails in his duty if he believes his men will not suffer it, but he shall take the blame for you all. I will make no inquiries into past sins. I will not ask who among you has dealt falsely or been a coward or robbed another of his food and drink—all of this will be allowed to pass into oblivion. But if it happens again, then the next time you are called to witness punishment you will see death. You will see the fortress walls covered with the hides of traitors. Remember this, and tempt not my wrath.

"Tonight, no man will see his bed—not I, and certainly none of you. This den of vermin shall be put in order, if it must be done by torchlight.

"And tomorrow, at one hour after dawn, we will assemble here again, and we will see if you have forgotten utterly what separates men from beasts. If you have, then I can promise you a day such as you will not soon forget. Your officers shall give you your assignments. I dismiss you to them."

I spent the rest of the day going over the account tablets, and

fortune smiled on my predecessor that I had not done so earlier,
otherwise he might have lost the skin from more than just the
soles of his feet. The man had been a thief as well as a drunkard,
and the great gods knew what else besides.

Already, when I sat down to dinner, I could see the blaze of
torches and smell the burning pitch. The meal was quite good—
lamb dressed with okra, bread and cheese, with only the deplor-
able local beer to let me know I was not eating at my own table at
Three Lions. Before such a meal it was easy to forget that common soldiers might have only such food as was fit to mend a wall
with, but no one can fight with his belly full of straw. I decided
that in the morning I would issue orders that officers and men
would be fed the same rations.

Having ordered the entire garrison to work through the
night, I could hardly seek my own bed, but there was no difficulty
in keeping awake—the noise of the work crews, the orders and
curses shouted back and forth, the unearthly play of torchlight
outside my windows would have kept a corpse from sleeping. And
added to all of that was the cold, for which, at this season of the
year, nothing could have prepared me. In Nineveh, doubtless, half
the populace were sleeping on their rooftops, hoping vainly for
the tiniest breath of wind, but in Amat I sat in front of a brazier,
wrapped in an old cloak, my teeth chattering uncontrollably. I
could almost envy the soldiers outside, who had at least each
other and their work to keep them occupied and warm. I had
nothing except solitude and discomfort, and an idleness that left
my mind a prey to painful recollections—for even here, I found, I
could not drive Esharhamat from my thoughts.

*"Remember, all your life, each night, that I will be in Es-
arhaddon's bed. . . ."* They would be married by now, and she
would be asleep beside my brother, her belly filled with his seed.
She would bear his sons—and forget, in time, that there had ever
been such a man as Tiglath Ashur. That was how she would
avenge herself upon her coward lover, by forgetting his existence.

But I would not forget hers. My ears were filled with the soft
sound of her voice, my eyes with the sight of her. Longing and
remorse tore at my breast with their heavy claws, and I knew she
was right to hate me and believed I could not live another night
without her forgiveness and her love and the cool touch of her
little hands. I suffered then as I knew I would suffer every time
that her name sounded in my mind, and that would be every hour

of my life. Esharhamat. Esharhamat. Drive me mad, but do not abandon me. Esharhamat.

Morning's first gray light was like the mercy of the gods, and it found me in a forgiving mood. I stepped outside, and the parade ground was a changed place—the weeds were gone, the dead leaves had been gathered up, even the barrack walls were sparkling with whitewash. And the men themselves? I saw many a haggard face, but at least their uniforms were clean and their equipment in order. The night had worked a kind of miracle.

But I kept my face empty of expression—no first effort can be allowed to seem sufficient.

"This, at least, is a beginning," I said. "I will allow you three hours of rest before the start of drill practice. We will see then if you still remember anything of being soldiers."

Even as I let the door swing shut behind me, I could hear the murmur of a thousand voices. The news had not been sweet to their ears.

An orderly, one of my own *quradu,* took my cloak as I headed toward my bed. He had been the luckiest man in Amat last night, for there had been nothing to prevent him from sleeping straight through till morning.

"Wake me in two hours," I told him. "Remember, two hours."

I pulled a blanket around me and closed my eyes, not even bothering to kick the sandals from my feet.

It was as well the mountain tribes could not witness that afternoon's drill, or they might have commenced pouring over our borders like locusts. We stumbled through routine exercises like sleepwalkers. Partly this was simple fatigue, for everyone was clumsy with exhaustion, but the real blame lay with neglect—one might have supposed these men had been conscripted only that morning. Experienced soldiers fell from their horses or impaled themselves on their own weapons. Our casualties would have done justice to a small battle, and our war was against no enemy except ourselves.

This giddy performance went on all afternoon. My *quradu* formed up a battle square and took on all comers in a mock engagement fought with wooden swords and javelins with padded points. I led the chariot drills myself, since I would not have these men think their new commander was but a mud-scratching soldier. Every man worked until he was ready to drop.

And finally, when the light died, we dragged ourselves back to barracks for a hot meal—a wretched thin, bad-smelling porridge but at least the same meal for all ranks—and a night's sleep.

But we made progress. On the next day and the day after, the quality of drill improved, and on the third day the supply officer himself came to me asking to be returned to line duties—it seemed his brother officers had made him afraid for his life. I granted the request, promoted Lushakin to *rab kisir,* and turned the matter over to him. He was not pleased, saying that the gods had not intended him for a kitchen soldier, but almost from that hour the quality of rations improved—even the beer.

And also on the third day the *ekalli* I had thrashed at the fortress gate was released from stockade and brought to me while I finished my supper. He was a short man with sloping shoulders and long, powerful arms; indeed, there was something nearly apelike about him. His face was haggard and almost gray from his ordeal, but as he waited for me to speak—doubtless expecting the worst, that I would have him flogged to death now, or driven from camp naked and bleeding, like the *rab abru,* or degraded to a garrison slave—his eyes were too proud to beg. He had endured cold and hunger and the terror of an uncertain fate, but he would not lower himself to show his own weakness. He watched me with something like defiance. "Do what more you like with me," he seemed to say. "You will find that I can stand that too." I decided I did not care to waste such a man.

"The next time you lead a watch, watch. I could just as easily have put a javelin between your shoulder blades, and then you would not be alive to cast covetous glances upon your commander's wretched meal. Here—sit down and feed yourself. There is enough for two, and I don't like a man to divide his attention when I speak to him."

He sat and ate, with his fingers, as greedy as an animal. And when he had finished he threw himself back in his chair and sighed with pleasure.

"Did you enjoy that?" I asked, as if only to satisfy my own curiosity.

"No—it was no better than the slop the rest of us get. I thought the officers took better care of themselves."

"Not anymore."

The tone of my answer must have reminded him that this was no social occasion and he rose to his feet, standing not quite at attention.

"Go back to your barracks, *Ekalli*," I went on. "Get a decent night's sleep for a change and have your men ready for drill practice at the first hour after dawn. That is all."

"Then I am to retain my rank, *Rab Shaqe*?" His voice reflected not so much relief as astonishment.

"Yes. But in the months ahead do endeavor to show me that I have not made a mistake. And be sure to tell me if you have any more complaints about the food."

"I will, *Rab Shaqe*."

Even as he walked away into the darkness, I could hear him laughing to himself. His name was Girittu, and after that he proved himself a good soldier. I never had cause to regret that act of clemency.

And there were no further complaints about the food, which perhaps made more difference than anything else. Better food led inevitably to better morale, and that in its turn led to better drill. Everyone, down to the humblest shield carrier, was more cheerful, as if he had rediscovered his purpose in living. Even the camp prostitutes began to look less slovenly. Within ten days the garrison at Amat was actually coming once more to resemble an army. I decided that at the end of the second week I could risk taking a few companies into the mountains for field exercises.

It was on the night before our intended departure that I received a reminder that some in Nineveh still held me in their thoughts.

I had gone to my sleeping mat early, and, knowing that for the next half month I would have no bed but a blanket spread over the cold ground, had ordered the added luxury of a brazier, heaped high with coals so that my room was almost like a sweating house.

A man is generally punished for these little extravagances, and I spent a restless night, visited by nightmares.

Zaqar, that god who presides over the hours of sleep, sends us our dreams as messages, glimpses into the future and our own hearts. He punishes the wicked with visions of terror, but even in this he is a gentle god, a merciful god, for through these are we brought to seek pardon, and through pardon comes peace and rest. That night Zaqar punished me for my brazier, as he punishes the drunkard and the glutton, for my dreams were full of violence and death.

I was in Babylon once more, and the banks of the dry riverbed were piled with corpses. I was tumbling through the air and into that mass of corruption. I was fighting to free myself, climbing over slippery arms and legs that came away in my hands. And somewhere in this tangle was waiting a man with a sword, ready to cut my throat and leave me here among the rotting dead. If I could not free myself he would kill me, or I would suffocate among the dead. I could hear his voice calling me— distant, like the squeaking of mice. I was sinking, sinking. . . .

And then all at once I was awake, and I knew that there was someone there in the room with me who meant me harm, and that the god had sent me a warning.

I did not hesitate. I threw myself from my sleeping mat and rolled away like a log. There was the sound of wood splintering as a copper ax buried its blade in the floorboard, just where my head had rested. In the dim red light from the brazier I could see the outlines of my assailant's legs, bent at the knee as he tried to pull his weapon loose for a second attempt, and I threw myself at these.

The man fell forward, toppling straight over me, and we both scrambled to gain our feet. My javelin was leaning against the wall next to my sleeping mat, but I could not come near it without putting myself within reach of his ax. We both stood up together—the ax was in his hands now and he grinned at me, seeing that I had no weapon. It was a small room. I had no retreat. He had only to step forward, swinging down at me. . . .

I backed up, and my naked heel touched the brazier behind me. I could feel its heat, a sudden, sharp pain, like the blade of a knife against my leg.

The brazier, its coals still red-hot—my one chance to live.

With a quick twist I reached down and grabbed it, holding it between my two hands. It seemed immensely heavy, and my hands hissed against the fiery black metal. It would consume me —I could not hold this terrible weight or my hands would be burned away like dry grass.

Keeping my back bent, I threw it away from me. I threw it at the man with the ax, catching him in the chest and knocking him down. He screamed as the burning red coals showered over him. For a moment he forgot everything except the fact that he was covered with fire. He dropped the ax—he had no time for that now. He did not even remember I was there.

It was the work of an instant. A few steps and I had the javelin in my hands. The assassin was lying on the floor, howling with terror, thrashing about like a madman as he tried to free himself from the fire. I raised the javelin over my head and drove it into his breast—his screams died with him, as if cut off with a knife.

"By the gods, what . . . ?"

I turned, and saw my orderly standing in the doorway. I pushed past him, my hands throbbing with pain, my brain dead. I had no word for him.

I waited on the porch while they put out the fire, sitting on a stool, as unconscious as an idiot. Someone brought a bucket of cold water, and I soaked my hands in it. They were swollen, but not too badly burned. This surprised me—I felt nothing else except this mild, detached surprise. I would be all right, it appeared. At the time the fire had seemed to pierce to the bone, so perhaps my *sedu* had protected me yet again.

At last, as the noise and confusion died away, I began to recover myself and unanswered questions flooded in on me of their own bidding.

"It is all right, *Rab Shaqe*. The fire is out."

I rose and went into my bedroom—a shambles now, half filled with smoke, the walls dripping with water. The man who had meant to kill me was dead himself, lying curled up on the floor like a child asleep, my javelin still sticking up out of his chest as if to mark the spot. I had driven the point most of the way through him, and pulling it loose proved to be no easy matter.

"Drag him out into the light," I said, handing the weapon to an orderly—my voice sounded thick from disuse. "I want to see his face."

A couple of soldiers, doubtless out of consideration for the floors, rolled the corpse onto my scorched and blood-smeared sleeping mat and carried it thus into the room where I was accustomed to take my meals. Several officers had already collected there, some of them still in their night tunics, and together we examined this dead assassin.

He wore the uniform of a common soldier and looked somewhere between twenty and thirty years of age. There was nothing extraordinary about him—he might have been anybody. I had never seen him before.

"Does anyone recognize him?" I asked. There was a general buzz of negatives and shaking of heads. No one knew this man—or would admit to it. I took the dead man's hand and turned it to look at the palm.

"Collect the *rab kisir*s and have them look at him, just to be sure he isn't from the garrison, but I'll wager this one's never been a soldier. Look—not a callus anywhere. His hands are as soft as a baby's."

I asked for a cup of wine and poured it over the dead man's head as an offering to appease his ghost. Then I gave orders that the roll be taken in all companies to see if anyone was missing—this one might never have seen service, but by the look of it his uniform had, and I wanted to know where he had gotten it.

"Check the town. See if there have been any strangers about—he couldn't have appeared out of thin air."

"What shall we do with the corpse, *Rab Shaqe*?"

It was not an idle question. What does one do in such a case, where the stakes are as high as the lordship of the world and the players are of one's own blood? I did not want it known who had sent this man, but I wanted to be sure that another would not be sent in his place.

"Cut off the head and have it packed in salt," I answered, standing up and trying to seem indifferent, although my guts felt as if they had been tied in a knot. "It is going to Nineveh, whence it probably came. There is someone there to whom I would send it as a present."

17

The next morning, in the town, a soldier was found dead in the alley behind a brothel, the hemp cord which had been used to strangle him still around his neck. His uniform had been stripped from his body and, when the one worn by the assassin was shown to the woman who served the dead soldier as a wife, she identified it from a tear she had repaired in the cloak. Thus was one mystery solved. I gave orders that henceforth entry into the fortress would be by watchword, which was to be changed daily, and let the matter drop. My warning to Nineveh would be my best protection against armed men in the night, and there was a limit to what a commander should be seen to do to safeguard his own life.

Moreover, I had other matters to occupy my mind, and for a while, a week perhaps, I would be away from the garrison, surrounded by soldiers whom at least I could depend upon not to cut my throat as I slept. The regular patterns of military life were themselves a kind of refuge.

So it was that, one day after the assassin's corpse had been displayed to the troops at morning assembly, I climbed on my horse—no mean feat, since my hands were still covered with salve and wrapped in linen bandages—and led the third, fourth, and sixth companies into the mountains for field maneuvers.

All the years I was a soldier, I always loved these sorts of exercises. Everything is so straightforward—there is work, there is food, there is sleep. A task may be performed one way and not another; there is no ambiguity, no room for interpretation. There is the skill of the warrior, which has the grace of simplicity, and

there is the company of other men who see the world no differently than one does oneself. I am excellent with the javelin and
bow, a fine charioteer, a fair horseman, indifferent with a sword.
As a soldier, this was everything I was. My men were willing to
take upon faith my talents as a commander, and moreover, my
rank aside, they had decided that I was one like themselves. There
is no greater happiness than that sort of acceptance—at least,
none that was open to me.

The maneuvers went well. As the god would have it, their
old commander had been posted to Amat only the year before and
thus had only that much time to foster sloth and indiscipline. The
men remembered quickly enough how to fight, but we were yet an
army without an enemy. This would not last forever—almost every night, after we had passed beyond our own boundary stones
and into the gray, barren mountains where no man's word was
law, I could feel upon us, upon our cooking fires and our sentry
lines, the eyes of strangers, the eyes of savage men who lived in
leather tents and called no one "king," who knew that one day
they would meet us in battle and were measuring us against that
knowledge. I could but wonder what they made of what they saw.

When we returned to Amat, I found an emissary from the
king of Urartu waiting for me, eager for parley. His subject was
war.

Urartu had been a glorious and powerful nation, brought low
by the might of the Lord Sargon. Within living memory she had
ruled over a league of the northern states that stretched all the
way to the Upper Sea, but the great king, in the fifth year of his
reign, conquered Carchemish, blocking passage over the Euphrates and thus dividing the league in two. Then, the following year,
after bringing the western lands under his yoke, the Lord Sargon
marched into the homeland of King Rusas, who escaped death by
hiding himself inside the walls of Tushpa, his impregnable capital,
bounded on three sides by steep cliffs and on the fourth by the
Shaking Sea. But the Lord of Ashur laid the country waste, cap-
turing the royal treasury and slaughtering Rusas's subjects in
their thousands. Rusas, overcome by grief, died by his own hand,
and in the reign of his son the land of Urartu became a humble
vassal state, sending tribute to Nineveh and setting up images of
Ashur in all her chief temples, beside that of Khaldi, her own
great god.

But time had turned this great victory into something very

much like a defeat, for Urartu had served as a wall to the northern nomads, whom now she was too weak to resist without help.
Thus, save for the garrisons now under my command, the Cimmerians, the Scythians, and the other great tribal confederations
would have come swooping down from their mountains to delight
themselves in the green valleys of the Tigris. Great Sargon, by
freeing us from one enemy, had cleared the path for another.

The emissary was a thin man, perhaps five and thirty years of
age, and shorter than I by perhaps the width of three fingers,
which still made him seem tall among the men of Ashur. He was
as dark as a Sumerian, with the glittering black eyes, the heavy,
fleshy nose, and the short chin which is typical of all his race.
Except for the fur lining of his cloak—a very practical addition in
these altitudes—he dressed after the fashion of Nineveh, as did all
the men of Urartu I ever met, for, although their language was
different, their debt to us for their manners and culture was as
heavy as ours to the Babylonians.

I invited my guest to dinner—let him eat my simple soldier's
fare, I thought, that he may know there has been a change at
Amat—and asked him to wait until I had sweated off the dust of
twenty days and no longer smelled like a pack horse. While he
waited, and while I sponged myself with hot water, my officers
gathered round me in the sweating house to mop their brows and
tell me all they had heard or could guess about why King Argistis
had thought it well to send an ambassador all the way from
Tushpa to share lamb's meat and bread with the new *shaknu* of
the north.

"Perhaps he is not from Argistis, but seeks our help to topple
him from his throne—they say that king has inherited his father's
strain of madness."

"Perhaps the Urartians have hopes of reducing the terms of
tribute imposed on them."

"I do not care what he wants. I only pray he comes prepared
to bribe us liberally."

But, to the great disappointment of all such hopes, the only
bribes the emissary brought were a hundred jars of Nairian wine,
from vines grown on the edge of the Shaking Sea and surprisingly
sweet and heady. He and I—his name was Lutipri—broke the seal
on several that evening and became tolerably drunk together and,
as a natural consequence, the best of friends.

But the friendship of diplomats, like their candor in drunkenness, has its limits. Lutipri's mind was never so fuddled as it seemed, and he never forgot the reason for his visit. As we sat together on a bench on my porch, roasting our knees before a brazier while we sucked the cool, star-streaked, sobering night air into our lungs that we might drink at least a little more before our servants had to carry us to our respective rests, what I heard at last was the voice of Argistis's servant.

"The lord king my master," he told me, leaning his shoulder against my arm, as if about to whisper a great secret, "the mighty one, who is like a god in Tushpa, whose every word is law above the Bohtan River, he wishes his royal brother Sennacherib, whom he loves, to know that the Scythians are growing insolent in the land of Shubria. They have established settlements. They have even presumed to tether their horses by the western banks of the Shaking Sea."

"They must have little enough joy of it, however, for I have heard that the waters there are brackish and undrinkable."

"Nevertheless, they have come. And the king my master lays claim to all lands touched by those waters. He cannot have mountain tribes less than two days' sailing from his capital."

I considered this for a moment, staring at the glowing coals in the brazier—I had taken a great liking to this brazier, since it had saved my life—wishing my head would stop buzzing like a nest of wasps that I might hear myself think. Suddenly I had a great longing for my bed.

"I assume, therefore, that the mighty Argistis, whom all the world knows to be valiant, has sent an expedition against these impudent barbarians, and that even now they are scattered again like chaff."

In silence we sat, and I filled my guest's cup from one of the jars he had brought me, congratulating myself on still having wits enough left to make such a noncommittal reply, since the Lord Lutipri, who squirmed in his seat and seemed to regard with distaste the wine I had poured for him, was so obviously displeased with it.

"This has not proved convenient," he said at last. "As you doubtless know, we have the Cimmerians, the Medes, and even the Mannaeans pressing in on us from the east. Of course all of these together present no challenge for the glory of our arms, but they are persistent. They threaten us—and you—more directly than do the Scythians. These few savages would require no more than a small punitive raid."

"Still, I do not see how this matter concerns us. Doubtless your king will deal with them in his own good time, and as long as they have not crossed south of the Bohtan River . . ."

"Ah—but, you see, this they have done."

Trapped. Yes, I had trapped myself. It would serve as a lesson to me. I was yet neither wise nor old enough to whisper with adders.

"The month of Elul is now nearly half gone," I said, perhaps a trifle too quickly. "In a month the snows will begin to fall over the mountains. There is no time for a campaign—even a small punitive raid."

"The land lies lower on the western shore. Skirting the mountains, an army could march so far in, say, ten days. One lightning strike, and then south again, following the river home. Everyone knows of your daring, Lord Tiglath, of your defeat of the Uqukadi, of how you opened the walls of Babylon by stealth and overthrew the city. For you, this would be such a small thing."

"Lord Lutipri, your mother nursed you on the venom of a scorpion."

The next day we spoke again, and at length, and this time we were both sober. I complained much of the hazard of such a mission, and in the end I extracted a promise that the king in Tushpa would pay to the Lord Sennacherib twenty *mina* of gold toward the cost of driving the Scythians back over the Bohtan River—to more than that I could not commit myself, seeing that the season for campaigning was almost gone. To this the Lord Lutipri agreed quickly enough, since I was content to let the means of payment remain vague. A day later he began his journey home, and I did all I could to create the impression that I thought myself tricked and ill used.

In fact, I was well pleased. The whole plan appealed to my imagination, and it was precisely what the garrison at Amat needed to shake it from its lethargy—precisely, in fact, what I had promised them. Even the morning after that drunken conversation with King Argistis's wily emissary, I issued orders for a general mobilization.

The march into the land of Shupria would be no easy business. We would avoid the mountains where we could, following the course of the upper Tigris until we had reached the end of the Judi Dagh range, when we would strike north, but that was all rough country. The maps I had showed little detail, so I would have to rely on such of my men as had come from those areas. Two things I knew for certain, however: one was that such chariots as I meant to take would have to be disassembled and packed by horse, which would slow us down; and the other was that speed would be everything. Lutipri had said I could reach my destination in ten days, which probably meant he thought I would be lucky to reach it in twelve. I had every intention of sighting the southern shore of the Bohtan River in eight.

"Will you take the third, fourth, and sixth companies, *Rab Shaqe*?"

"Yes, of course. They are, for the time, my only seasoned troops."

"But they need their rest after their maneuvers, *Rab Shaqe*—you need rest yourself."

"We were in the mountains for half a month. What campaign lasts so short a time as half a month? We will not leave until we have seen the back of this Urartian swindler, so there will be time enough for rest. Make your preparations."

My officers stopped raising objections when they saw that I would not listen to objections, that I had set my heart upon a war before the snows fell. I knew what I was about—a garrison in the grip of winter is a dismal place for men who have forgotten there can be anything except peace. Soldiers must see that all is done for a reason, that if they train for war it is because war is their purpose for living. This these pillow warriors of mine would only believe when they had beheld the enemy's swords flashing in the sun. I had not the slightest intention of letting the fortress at Amat fester like a bedsore.

I would leave one third of the garrison behind, for a large army, like a wounded snake, does not cover ground quickly. My *quradu* I would take, and seven companies. If I could not conquer with them, more soldiers would only mean more corpses to glut the crows. I departed from Amat on the morning of the sixteenth day of Elul, leading men whom, for the most part, I had commanded not even a month.

A soldier on campaign lives a life harder than any slave's,

and that march, across nearly forty *beru* of rough, rock-strewn wasteland, was an ordeal as terrible as any battle. On the first day, while the men were still fresh, we covered seven *beru,* and that night, as I toured the camp, the soldiers I saw huddled about their cooking fires had not even strength left to curse me. The second day we came within sight of the Tigris River, a ribbon of light glistening sluggishly in the distance, and that day we had marched six *beru.* On the third and fourth days we maintained a pace of five *beru,* but I heard much muttering, especially on the fourth day, which was an evil day when decent men would have kept to their tents.

In truth, I felt some uneasiness on this point, but I was more afraid of the onset of winter, which, if it found us still in the field, was certain death, than I was of evil spirits, which are a vague and insubstantial menace. So I told the men we were all under the protection of the god Ashur, who could forgive any sin, and of my *sedu,* which was of great power. When we were not attacked by marauders or struck down by plague, many came to believe me—they did not cease to complain, which is no more than a soldier's right, but I heard no more of evil days.

Each day they had to rise from their bed in the dark because I had given orders that the marches would commence at dawn, whether the men had been breakfasted or not. At the height of noon I allowed one hour of rest, and then the march would continue until almost night. That there might be no ill feeling, I walked myself, using my horse as a pack animal, and ordered all officers to do the same.

By noon of the eighth day, while the men rested, outriders returned to report they had seen the Bohtan River over the next line of hills, and that there were encampments with wagons and much livestock on the meadows on both sides. So the Lord Lutipri had not lied—everyone knew that the Scythians, alone among the nomadic peoples, traveled by wagon.

I gave orders that we would make camp where we were. The men were exhausted and would be in no condition to fight for at least two days. I would not have the enemy know of our presence before then. There were to be no fires lit, and no one except lookouts would approach the crest of the hill. We would wait, and rest, and stay quiet.

I could restrain my soldiers easily enough—most of them were quite content to stay in one place and not move—but I could not restrain myself. I would see this new adversary, so much talked of and so little known, for the Scythians were new to these mountains, so long plagued by wandering tribes, each pushing the next before it in successive waves, and all always moving farther west. Where the tribes had come from, and what had set the pattern of their migrations, no man knew, not even they themselves.

Leaving my horse behind, I walked to the crest of the last hill and, for the rest of that afternoon, sat in the shadow of a great rock and watched as they grazed their animals in the heavy meadow grass and went about the routines of their curious existence.

The Scythians, like the Cimmerians, the Mannaeans, the Medes, the Uqukadi, the Sapardai, and all the rest, are a herding nation—their lives are bound up in a ceaseless search for new pastures for their oxen, horses, and sheep. For the rest, they are bandits, preying on the settled people whom they dispossess. They practice no farming and hold in contempt all who do. Any manner of living that obliges them to stay in one place they abhor worse than death, maintaining that it leads to womanish softness, that only among the nomads are there true men. Naturally, since they seek only to plunder other nations and must constantly defend their own grasslands against other tribes, they put the highest value on the martial virtues—higher even than do the men of Ashur, since among the Scythians every man must be a warrior. They are fine horsemen and fight only as cavalry. Their weapon is the bow, with which they are marvelously proficient, and the lance. They carry no swords, only a rather long dagger which they wear in their belts. They prefer to retire before a formidable adversary, but in battle they are courageous to the point of folly, disdaining even to wear body armor. It is the greatest misfortune to fall into their hands as a prisoner, for their cruelty is a matter of legend.

All of this I had heard at one time or another, and from my mountain vantage there was really little more I could learn—except for two things. The first of these was the very curious manner of their dress; above they wore a heavy quilted jacket that came down almost to their knees, but below they covered themselves with a strange garment the like of which I have never seen among any other peoples. This garment was forked at the crotch, and each leg had its own tube of cloth that covered it almost like a second skin all the way down to the foot. It seemed a very practical way of dressing for a horseman, but I cannot imagine anyone could be very comfortable in such an outfit.

The other thing which excited my curiosity was that there seemed to be no women about. Men and boys alone tended to the animals, but even in their camp—the one which was closest to me —I could see no women. They appeared to do their cooking on their wagons, which were large and covered with a kind of tent that was open at the top to let the smoke escape, so perhaps, I concluded, the women stayed in the wagons.

By rough count, there were close to four thousand men in the two encampments on either side of the river. Assuming that half of these would be fit to fight, that gave them a three-to-one advantage over us in numbers.

Already then I had made my plans, and when the light began to fade I returned to camp to a cold meal and a conference with my officers.

"They are not even bothering to put out patrols," I told them. "They do not expect an attack. We can wait until the morning after next, when our men will be fresh again. Then we will march over the crest in seven battle squares, three in front and four behind. The cavalry and the chariots we will hold in reserve. We shall wait until the second hour before giving them any sign of our presence, that they may have dispersed their herds too widely over the plain to be able to collect them quickly—that way they shall be forced to stand and fight. Let the drums wait until we have nearly engaged, since I think there is little enough chance of frightening the men, but the horses may not be accustomed to the noise."

That night I slept like the dead.

All the next day the men reassembled the chariots and otherwise prepared themselves for battle. I did not concern myself with such matters. I had issued my orders, and that would have to be enough. These soldiers must believe that I entertained no doubts about their will or their abilities. I returned to my lookout and studied the ground upon which this battle was to be fought.

The hill sloped too quickly to the plain to allow chariots to be driven straight down, but there was a path, perhaps just wide enough, that followed the slope at an angle. They would have to proceed in single file, and their wheels would have to be damped, but we had brought only ten, so this would present no problem. I

would send them down after the infantry and cavalry had already
reached level ground.

The process by which the Scythians were crossing over from
one side of the river to another seemed a gradual one, and the
Bohtan, while it probably carried less water now than at any other
time of year, was still a formidable obstacle. How long their forces
would remain thus divided I knew not—it would be at most a
momentary advantage—but these men would have no choice but
to offer battle. They would have no retreat.

That was my only fear, that somehow they would slip away
from me. I had no other doubts. This engagement was as clear in
my mind as if it had already been fought. I might die on this
grassy plain—this being no more than the chance taken by every
soldier—but, dead or alive, I would be victorious.

And the thought of death held no terrors for me. If I perished, then my body would be covered in honey and taken back to
Nineveh, where I would be mourned over by those who cared for
me. I would be free of remorse and suffering, having died as a
soldier ought, and in triumph. And the dead do not endure the
pangs of abandoned love. If I died here, tomorrow . . . The idea
appealed to me more than I could say.

I decided, there and then, that I would drive one of the chariots myself. The men, knowing this, would take courage, and they
would not need me after tomorrow. I had no taste for watching
this fight from a safe distance. I would ride into the very mouth of
death, and snatch out her tongue that it might be forced to sing of
my glory to the last days of the world.

That night I did not sleep, but my mind was calm. What
should I know of fear? What terrors should tomorrow hold, when
I had resigned myself to death? I had but to close my eyes, and
Esharhamat was with me. Once I had disentangled myself from
the net of my living flesh, it would be thus forever. We had never
parted, not really. My unhappiness had been nothing but the confusion of things seen and felt—I had been blinded by the nearness
of life. Death was nothing, only the loss of a man's last few illusions. I could see that quite clearly now.

The next morning, the twenty-sixth day of Elul, I ranged the
seven companies of infantry just below the crest of the hill, where
they would not be seen until the last instant. It was a fine, bright
dawn, and a light breeze blew toward us that the sound of our
preparations would not carry nor would the horses of the enemy

smell us. I watched the Scythian riders herd their animals out onto the meadow. I waited until the grass at my feet had lost the last of its dew, and then I raised my arm to signal that the advance might begin.

"Is it not a fine day, *Rab Shaqe*? Is it not?"

It was my driver, Gadi, his eyes beaming his pleasure. The beard on his face was like down, he was such a baby. This would be his first battle.

"Yes—it is a fine day," I answered, forcing myself to smile.

The lines of soldiers poured down the slope, one after the other, walking slowly that the battle squares might remain intact. The only sound was the crunch of their sandals against the stony ground. The sight of them made my heart swell.

From the crest to the river was perhaps fifteen hundred *gar,* the distance a man might walk in an hour if he kept a brisk pace. In a quarter of that time my infantry would be upon the plain, for this hill did not rise to any great height. Unless the enemy would be content to have themselves backed straight up to the water's edge, they would have no more than an hour in which to engage us—and they would need every minute of that to rally themselves from the first shock of surprise. By then, with good fortune, our cavalry and chariots would be on level ground. Mine would be the last chariot down.

I watched—with some admiration—how the Scythians conducted themselves when at last they saw what had been prepared for them. There was no evidence of panic. Riders went back and forth, giving the alarm, and then some hundred men began to herd the animals together to drive as many as they could across the river to safety. By the time we were ready, they were ready, their lines of cavalry formed and waiting. There were more of them than I had expected, very nearly 2,500 mounted men. They were arranged in four ranks and would attack in waves.

I stepped onto my chariot, which was surrounded by the six riders who would carry orders for me, and told my driver to start down the plain. We had hardly reached level ground when the war drums began their booming. The enemy was engaged.

The first waves of the Scythian riders attacked, screaming like hawks and shooting their arrows with greater accuracy than I would have imagined possible from men on horseback. At the last moment our forces halted and let the paling of long iron lances drop into place around all four sides of their formations. It was not something the enemy had expected, that soldiers on the field of battle could convert their ranks into an impenetrable fortress, and those who were not spitted like rabbits, or who were not tumbled to the ground by horses mad with fear, retired in confusion. I saw the corpses of only a few of our own troops, so at least we had won the first skirmish.

What would they do next? What could they do? That was up to them, and I did not care to give them leisure to consider the problem at length.

"Continue the advance!" I shouted, and a rider turned his horse and raced off in the direction of our formations. He reached the front of the first square, ducked down to say a word to the corner man and, as he straightened up, took a Scythian arrow in the neck and toppled over—it had served him right. Only a posturing fool would ride to the front like that, exposing himself to the enemy. Soldiers at the back of a square have as good ears as those in front.

The second wave of enemy cavalry did not even attempt a direct assault on our formations—they had learned the folly of that. Instead, they split into two halves and harried our lines with arrows. It was what I should have expected.

The Scythians wore no armor, but they were moving targets and difficult to hit except with massed clusters of arrow and javelin. We, of course, were almost stationary but better protected, but we were killing them only very little faster than they were killing us. And there were many more of them. Clearly they planned to wear us down with their numbers—they did not seem to care how many of them died. It would not do.

I ordered the chariots forward—my last order of this battle; the time for orders was over—and picked a javelin from one of the wicker holders that lined the sides of my car. From this moment on I was merely a soldier, no different from any other. It was a release from bondage. As the horses gathered speed, I could feel the blood pounding in my veins like a hammer.

A chariot is a terrible weapon, especially when the horses are protected by an armor of copper scales sewn onto leather. It bears down on an enemy like the hand of heaven, striking terror into men's hearts, and its wheels are fitted with blades, slightly longer than the length of one's arm, which turn with the axle and can cut a man or a horse to pieces with the slightest touch. All soldiers, mounted or on foot, fear a chariot above any other force that can be turned against them.

But there are dangers. A man in a chariot is no less exposed than he is on horse; it takes no more than a lucky hit to fell him, and he can be certain enough that many darts will be turned in his direction. Or if a horse is lamed, or the driver hits a stone and breaks a wheel or is thrown—to have that headlong rush stopped is to become helpless, and to become helpless is to die.

Or one's driver can be killed. That is what happened to me.

He was hardly more than a boy, was poor little Gadi, so eager for glory, and an arrow pierced his side, just under the arm, and found his heart. He turned to me as he died—I am unlikely ever to forget the expression on his face, his look of pain and something almost like remorse, as if he imagined he had failed me —and he just had time to put the reins into my hands before he pitched over backward, already dead, and tumbled onto the field.

But I had no time to think of Gadi. I was alone now, the floor of the car shaking beneath my feet as I reined in the fury of two horses half-mad with the frenzy of war. I understood how they felt. I could feel it myself—I could feel nothing else, nothing but that all-consuming mingling of fear and exultation which is a warrior's passion. I was the god himself, Adad the Thunderer. I would deal out death, stripping men of their lives.

"Ashur is King!" I shouted. The cry broke from my lips, as if of its own will. "Ashur is King! Ashur is King!" The pounding hoofs really were like thunder—I felt as if I might kill the world. "Ashur is King!"

A Scythian bowman slowed his horse to take aim at me, but he waited just an instant too long. I turned in on him and ran him down, my wheel blades leaving him and his mount gutted on the field like a brace of pigs. Another, close behind him, drew out from my path. Then, from the side, he began to bear down on me, the arrow already seated in his bow, but to me he too was already a dead man. I took the reins in one hand—I felt strong enough for that, strong enough for anything—lifted my javelin, and threw. My aim was certain, and the man slid out of his saddle, trying with both hands but all in vain to pull the javelin from his breast, even as he died.

Back and forth I tore across the field, raising a plume of dust that might have been fire. The Scythian horsemen could not keep to their formations—soon they were swarming about aimlessly, clumped up together like bees, and then, as the massed arrows from our battle squares began to take their toll, that grassy meadow quickly turned into a killing field.

But they would not give ground. The Scythians, their backs to the river, fighting for their livestock and the safety of their families, charged us over and over, vainly attempting to drive us off. They were foolish in their stubborn valor—what chance had they?—but their valor was still a sight in men's eyes. The ground was covered with their dead, but they would not stop. At close range our javelins killed them, at a distance our flights of arrows that seemed to block out the sun. Over and over again they would charge on our battle squares, and over and over again they would fall like sparks from a grinding wheel, their light dying as they dropped away. As they tried to regroup, our chariots would scatter them—or drive them together in confused masses, entangled like barley husks.

They would not yield. They seemed to disdain yielding—and their disdain brought down upon them a great slaughter.

As the sun rose toward noon, the battle, which was now within two arrow flights of the Scythian camp, changed its character. As a man loses the giddy excitement of youth and enters into his sober, steady middle age, so our fight, no longer a contest of equals, settled into the grim, joyless, dangerous business of dealing out death. To stay alive oneself and to kill the enemy— these were the only thoughts in anyone's mind. And it was a labor, a bitter toil. My horses' sides were lathered with sweat, and my arms ached. "Let this end," I thought to myself. "Let this madness have an end." I drove down on the enemy, knowing no pity, tearing men's lives from them, that they might stop. That they might fall back and let me show them some mercy.

And at last, when we were almost within reach of their wagons and their cooking fires, the Scythians—some of them—withdrew a little that they might begin the work of retreating across the river and saving what they could. The others drove at us all the harder, and the noise of battle grew shrill in our ears. But it was ending—at last it was ending.

It was when I was circling around to make ready for another charge that I chanced to glance down at the ground and saw, lying on his back in the long grass, the corpse of my driver. Gadi, whose mother would never look on him again, stared up at me with glazed, unseeing eyes—I had almost forgotten his existence.

I stopped for an instant, letting the horses stand, their ribs wheezing in and out like the sides of a bellows, and Gadi's eyes seemed to hold me. *"Did you not care at all?"* they seemed to say. *"Did you not even notice? I am dead. I am dust, and you have forgotten me."* I felt such remorse as if I had killed him myself, and then a terrible, wild, mindless anger. They would pay for this, these savages. I would have just a few more die to follow this boy into Arallu. I lashed the horses and the chariot lurched forward, gathering speed as the wheels whined like dogs.

It was then that the arrow struck me in the back.

The battle ended very quickly after that. When I saw that the Scythians were in full retreat, I gave orders that our advance should stop. We stood on the field, which was now ours, and watched them hurry such of their wagons and animals as they could over the Bohtan River to safety. There was no reason to pursue them—they had lost men and horses almost without number, and I had no inclination to preside over a massacre.

As long as the enemy was within sight, no one saw that I was wounded. As soon as I knew I had been hit—there was no pain at first; all I felt was the impact, as if a friend had clapped me on the back—I reached around and broke off the shaft, throwing it away without even looking at it. Now even the finger's length of wood that stuck out from beneath my shoulder blade was hidden underneath my cloak. Surrounded by my officers, my chariot drawn to a halt, I watched as this victory of mine came to completion. I said but little and stood quite still, for I could feel the point of the arrow scraping against bone with almost every breath I drew.

It was an agony to wait there like that—the arrow point burned in my flesh, and I was sweating with pain. I could feel the blood dripping down underneath my corselet. I stood with my knees locked and one hand on the wheel of my chariot to steady me, watching for the last Scythian rider to quit the field. The wounding of a commander can cause panic among his men, and is at the very least a distraction and a danger. I could wait. Let these soldiers of Ashur have their triumph, let them joy in it at least a little, before they knew.

"*Rab Shaqe,* there is blood running down your leg. *Rab Shaqe,* what is . . . ?"

I could hardly hear him, he sounded so far away. I turned to see who had spoken, but the light seemed to die in my eyes.

"I am not—that is . . ."

I supposed I must have fainted, for the next I knew I was lying prone on a makeshift stretcher and being carried back to camp. I did not relish the journey—with every step what was left of the arrow's point seemed to push its way deeper into my back.

In the middle of the afternoon, lying on a cot in my tent, I was trying very hard to become drunk while the cook, who, one presumed, knew more about slicing meat than most men, was heating up his knife in a brazier, preparing to cut the arrowhead out from beneath my shoulder blade, where it seemed to be lodged. I was not looking forward to the operation, and neither was he.

"Just be sure that you are quick," I told him—he looked as if he could have used a little wine himself, but it seemed best to wait until he was finished. "Cut deep, pluck the thing out with your forceps, and scar the wound closed behind you. You needn't worry—no blame will attach to you, no matter what happens. But please, once you begin, do not be timid."

"Yes, *Rab Shaqe,* I will . . . Yes, *Rab Shaqe.*"

We waited quietly, he and I, watching the iron blade, which was half buried in the coals, turn dark red.

"Look what we have found for you, *Rab Shaqe*—is he not a pretty bird?"

The flap of my tent was open, and through it sailed—and I used the word advisedly, for I do not think his feet touched the ground until he fell over on his face—what at first I took to be a dead body. I was very annoyed; I did not appreciate that sort of joke. And then I saw that the man's hands were tied behind his back and that he was struggling to get up.

Three soldiers were standing just outside. I recognized one of them as the *ekalli* Girittu, his face streaked with dust but grinning proudly.

"We found him among the dead. He must have fallen from his horse and knocked his head against a rock, because he came to while we were practically standing on him—we were engaged in a little looting, as you no doubt can understand, *Rab Shaqe.* A man must have something to show for his day's work. Look at all the gold on him! We think he must be some sort of king."

As if to illustrate his point, Girittu stepped inside the tent

and pulled the man upright so that he rested on his knees and I
could see the front of his heavy coat—which was covered with
round gold spangles, each sewn onto the fabric and about the size
of a child's fist. Clearly this was someone of importance.

"Look at the gash in his leg, *Rab Shaqe*. We marched him
straight up here and he never so much as stumbled. You have to
give them that—these Scythians are not women."

Yes, his leg did have a hole in it, just above the knee. He
looked as if a javelin must have found him. Fortunately for him—
or unfortunately, depending on what I decided to do with him—
he had not bled to death, but it must have been a painful wound.
Waiting for the cook's knife to heat up, I could sympathize.

This was the first of the enemy I had seen up close—or, at
least, had the leisure to study, since I had been close enough to
more than just a few that day—and I was interested. I had never
seen a man who looked quite like this one. His face was a reddish
color such as one sees in the faces of those who have been burned
by the wind, only darker. But the extraordinary thing about him
was not the color of his face but its shape—his ckeekbones were
high up and very pronounced, and his eyes were slanted, hardly
more than slits. It struck me at once that he looked like nothing in
the world so much as a cat, an impression heightened by his thin
beard, hardly more than a few long black strands over his lips and
chin, like a cat's whiskers. I wondered where under the sun these
people could have come from that they had such faces—what
place grew men like this?

This one looked as if he might have been between thirty and
forty years old, but it was no easy matter to guess the age of one
who is of another race.

"You did well to bring him to me," I said. "And I will see
you do not lose by it."

The men nodded and left. I glanced at one of my officers who
happened to be standing near the prisoner.

"Cut him loose."

"But, *Rab Shaqe*, is that . . ."

"I said, 'cut him loose'—do not worry, I will not let him bite
you."

After another moment's hesitation the *rab kisir,* a short man
whose eyes were so close together in his broad face that he always
seemed worried, took the dagger from his belt. The Scythian, for
just an instant, let a flicker of something like suspicion show in his

catlike eyes—he might have imagined I had just ordered his throat cut—but he showed us nothing more. As soon as the bowstring about his wrists was severed he brought his hands around to the front as if to inspect the damage.

"*Rab Shaqe,* the knife is ready."

The cook did not seem pleased with his announcement, but this was not something which could be delayed. The wine had begun to wear off—I hoped I would not shame myself before this barbarian.

"Then do your work," I said. "Pretend you are carving a joint for dinner, but hurry."

It took but the third part of a minute to dig the arrowhead out of my back, but I did not notice that the time passed too quickly. I clutched the legs of the cot and clenched my teeth, but I need not have worried that I might scream. It is easy enough to be brave in front of an audience, and besides, I would not have dared to draw the breath to scream, not with a burning knife in my back. So I managed to get through the business with tolerable credit—at least the Scythian, who watched it all with what seemed an almost jealous interest, did not sneer at me.

When the cook was finished and the hole under my shoulder blade had been plastered with salve, he dropped the arrowhead into my open hand.

"This was made in Nineveh," I said, in Aramaic. "I should have known no Scythian arrow could have touched me."

The light seemed to change in our prisoner's narrow eyes, and I knew at once that he understood me.

I sat up. It was not pleasant to move, and I felt weak from pain and loss of blood, but a prince of Ashur does not treat with foreigners lying on his belly.

"What is your name?"

"I am Tabiti, son of Argimpasa," he said finally, having apparently considered the matter and decided that it would not involve a loss of honor to answer. "I am headman of the Sacan tribe of the Scoloti."

"Scoloti." It was close enough to the Akkadian name, which was "Ishkuzai," that I understood to whom he referred.

"Then Tabiti, son of Argimpasa, since you are a man of distinction, get up off your knees and take a seat."

I motioned to an adjutant, who brought a stool and was unwise enough to try helping the headman of the Sacan tribe to his feet—Tabiti shook him off with contempt, but sat down anyway.

"Why did you attack my people?" he asked. There was nothing like an accusation in his question. He merely wanted to know.

"Because the river yonder marks the sovereign territory of the god Ashur—our king was not pleased with your intrusion."

Tabiti, son of Argimpasa, nodded.

"We care nothing for borders," he said.

"You would do well to care for that one."

He did not answer—he seemed almost not to have heard. And then I noticed that he was looking at my chest.

"You have collected many scars for one so young. It is troublesome to be so unlucky."

He smiled, looking even more like a cat. It appeared that now I had my answer.

"I have fought in many battles," I said. "Thus I have many scars. A man is not counted unlucky in battle unless he is killed— or loses. Neither of these fates has been mine, so it is not I who has been unlucky."

There was no reaction, but of course there would not have been. Doubtless this man had traded insults before.

"I have two choices," I went on, smiling thinly, hoping this proud man would not think I either mocked or insulted him. "I can kill you, and then pursue a leaderless people across the Bohtan River until I have exterminated them all—this, surely you realize, is now well within my power—or you and I can come to an understanding which will save much bloodshed."

"I am not afraid of any death you may visit upon me."

"How have I suggested that you are?"

The answer seemed not what he had expected. He sat quietly for a moment, hardly even seeming to breathe, as if turning something over in his soul.

"Of course, there is always the question of whether you can speak for your people—and whether any of your nation can be trusted."

"My word is law among the Sacan," he said, with a kind of cold fury, seeming almost to spit the words at me. "And the word of a Sacan is his blood oath."

"I am delighted to have that point settled."

We sat facing each other, separated, it seemed, by more than a mere few cubits of air. We were on opposite sides of an unbridgeable hostility, each as alien to the other as if we were not both men. Thus it must be—or must it? I found I was unable to suppress a conviction that this was someone whom I could both understand and, within reasonable limits, trust.

"You do grasp, I hope, that if we follow your people as enemies they cannot escape. This has nothing to do with courage—after today no warrior of the Sacan tribe needs to prove to me that he is a man. I am speaking of facts, of war and the way it is waged against a people in flight, of how their animals will be destroyed and their women and children will starve after the husbands and fathers are dead. You are their leader and must be their eyes into the future. Have I made myself plain?"

He said nothing. For a long moment he did not even move, and then, at last, he consented to nod his head.

"Now—will Tabiti, son of Argimpasa, headman of the Sacan tribe of the Scoloti, give his blood oath that he acknowledges the lordship of King Sennacherib, King of the World's Four Corners, King of Kings? Will he pledge himself to aid the Lord Sennacherib against his enemies? Will he forswear war against the Land of Ashur and honor such boundaries as the king chooses to have respected? Will he give his word on this?"

He sat quiet again, listening to that voice which only he could hear, and then his narrow eyes turned to my face.

"Sennacherib is nothing to us," he said. "We have not seen his might or his prowess in war, and the Sacan will not bow to an empty name. How are you called?"

"I am Tiglath Ashur, son of the Lord Sennacherib, a prince in this land."

"Then I will give such a pledge to Tiglath Ashur, who is the son of a king and who has bested the Sacan in honorable combat —to him and to no other. Will this content you?"

"It seems it must."

18

The next day, by agreement, both sides collected their dead. I gave orders that there was to be no further looting, and no hands or heads were to be collected as trophies. Our losses numbered less than a hundred, but among the Scythians Ereshkigal had reaped a rich harvest—their corpses covered the plain like mown barley. Strangely, they seemed to nurse no bitterness toward us for this. Their defeat seemed to have for them the character of a natural disaster, impersonal, a thing to be endured but no man's fault.

It had been settled between the headman Tabiti and myself that our forces would follow his as they retreated back to the western shores of the Shaking Sea. This journey would take some three days, and it was my intention then to march east to Tushpa before racing the snows back to Amat. The lord Lutipri did not know it, but I had every intention of collecting my twenty *mina* of gold. Although I had forbidden them to plunder the enemy, either the living or the dead, my men were not to be denied their booty, and the king's portion would provide against the maintenance of his garrison for perhaps as long as two or three years. This, I decided, would be a good trick to play upon the Urartians and would teach them, in a way they would be likely to remember, not to trifle with the *shaknu* of the north.

But first there was the work of burial to be done. We dug a long trench by the banks of the Bohtan River, that our fallen comrades might have the satisfaction of lying in the ground they had won with their blood, and interred with them offerings of food and wine to quiet their souls. It was a simple business, the work of an afternoon, for the peoples who live beside the swift-flowing Tigris do not entertain very lively hopes concerning the next world. The duties to the dead ensure nothing more than that they will lie quietly and not trouble the living.

Such did not, however, seem to be the prevailing opinion among the Scythians.

The first thing that struck me, as I watched them gathering up the corpses of their dead warriors, was that they had dug no graves, either on this side of the river or the other. Instead, the bodies were sewn into long leather bags, which they seemed to have already at hand—perhaps each man carried one with him on all his journeys, against the day of his death—and then they were loaded aboard their wagons.

That night the survivors conducted a wild ceremony of grief, in which they danced around bonfires which were visible from a great distance, breaching the cold, still air with shrieks that sent shudders down the backs of men hardened to fear. I dispatched spies to watch in secret, and they reported to me that many of the Scythian men, in what seemed a drunken ecstasy of mourning, had been seen driving arrows through their own left hands—indeed, over the next few days I saw several of them bearing precisely such a wound. These sad revels were kept up for several hours, dying off only as the night sky began to lighten with dawn.

And at dawn the Scythian caravan started on its journey north to the waters of the Shaking Sea.

As soon as the last of their wagons had departed camp, we crossed the Bohtan in force. Let them feel us at their heels, I thought—let them be reminded that they return to the mountains a conquered people. I wished to be quite sure Tabiti understood that he had not entirely escaped our hands.

It was a few minutes after noon when one of their riders came back toward us, bearing an invitation from Tabiti, son of Argimpasa, to Tiglath Ashur, son of Sennacherib, to share a meal with him that evening in the midst of his people. He proposed to make camp that evening at the foot of a high place which he called by the name of Surti. I accepted, over the strenuous objections of my officers, who feared I might be going to have my throat cut. The Scythian rider grinned at my answer, quite as if it represented some purely personal victory, and tore away at a wild gallop.

My officers could easily have been correct—these people

seemed capable of anything—but I could not have refused without offering an insult which would have been the ruin of all my plans. Besides, I did not want to refuse. I was, quite frankly, much too curious about what I would find to allow me to do that.

In the late afternoon I goaded my horse into a trot and began making my careful way through the Sacan caravan in search of Tabiti, who, of course, would be traveling with the vanguard. That ride itself revealed many sights to me, and those few hours were among the most interesting in my life.

For the first time I saw some of the Scythian women, following on foot behind the wagons, dressed in heavy, wide skirts that reached to the ground and were dyed in the most violent colors, linen blouses with full sleeves which they wore rolled back almost to the elbow, and vests decorated with embroidery and little gold and silver disks sewn onto the fabric. They covered their hair with their shawls but did not go veiled after the fashion of married women in my own land, so I had no trouble seeing their faces.

I could only conclude that the Scythians took their wives from many lands, either by barter or conquest, for along with the reddish skin, black hair, and catlike eyes that were everywhere in evidence among the men—and, indeed, among the preponderance of the women—I saw light-haired girls with skin like butter, Urartians with their heavy noses and inward-sloping chins, one or two blacks, and several who would have looked at home in Sumer.

But the one thing which was common to them all, and which struck me most forcibly, was the bitterness of their lamentation. All, without exception, wailed as if their livers would burst, the tears running down their cheeks, their hair streaming over their faces. Doubtless these were the new widows—why were none of the survivors' wives in evidence?—and at first I thought that the Scythian men must be fine husbands to inspire such grief. Then it occurred to me that these tears, these sobbing moans were not the expressions of grief but of fear—deadly, hopeless fear. What could they imagine was to become of them? It was a puzzle to me.

The wagons I noticed were all driven by boys. Most looked between the ages of eight and ten, and many gave evidence of their mixed blood. I saw no other children of either sex and no women but the weeping widows. The men either walked beside their wagons, holding one of the horses by the bridle, or rode.

The Sacan showed signs of being a wealthy tribe. Their

horses, although a trifle smaller than ours, were handsome and plentiful—taking the proportion of horses to wagons as a guide, I would guess that every family had six or seven, and many had more. The men as well as the women demonstrated a great love of ornament: Many decorated their tunics with the gold and silver disks I had noted before, and even the poorest among them wore bracelets of copper. I saw a number of men—the men, by the way, were generally more splendid than the women—with shirts and tunics of a cloth that caught the light like polished metal, dyed intense reds and blues and greens. I learned later that the cloth was called "seric," after the people who made it, and that it came from a land many months to the east. I was also told that the thread was woven by worms that nested in trees, but I was not so credulous as to believe such a thing.

People stared at me as I rode by, but only as a strange sight in their midst. None tried to molest me or to offer me any impertinence, nor was there the least sign of hostility toward the commander of the army which only two days earlier had scattered death among them like rain. At the same time I had no impression that they feared me or had been cowed by their defeat. Truly, they were a remarkable people.

"Ah, the Lord Tiglath Ashur, son of Sennacherib. Give the word—we will make camp here for the night."

Tabiti turned his horse to face me and reined it in to a stop. His casual order, uttered in a flat, expressionless voice, sent riders galloping back into the caravan as if they carried warnings of an immediate attack.

He smiled at me, showing white, even teeth. It was impossible to guess what that smile might mean.

"We have made good time," he said cheerfully. From his tone the two of us might have been intimate friends, traveling together for months. Still, he did not offer me his hand. "The day after next we shall rest by the Shaking Sea, by early afternoon I would guess. The grass and water there are very fine, although the sea itself is dead. It is a fine place—would that we had never left it."

"Why did you?"

The headman of the Sacan shrugged his shoulders and smiled once more his unreadable, catlike smile.

"It is not good for us to settle in one place too long—only look at the Urartians. Tushpa is a fine city, many centuries old. I have seen it from a distance. Yet the men who rule there must depend upon the king in Nineveh to make war for them."

"I came to the Bohtan River to defend the Land of Ashur, not that of the Urartians."

"Is this so?" Tabiti, son of Argimpasa, raised his eyebrows in disbelief. "I wonder, then, what other business could have sent their ambassador to Amat?"

"Then you knew of that?"

"Yes—little though I was able to profit from it. I would never have guessed that . . . You moved your army with great speed, Lord Tiglath. One can only hope they paid you well for so much trouble."

"Twenty *mina* of gold."

"Such a sum?"

As if driven to it by his surprise, the headman of the Sacan dismounted from his horse and handed the reins to the boy who had been driving his wagon and who I assumed was probably one of his sons. I did the same, and together we strolled back along the road made by the wheels of his caravan. For a long time he said nothing. He seemed lost in thought, hardly conscious of not being alone.

"I wonder then," he began again at last, "I wonder that you have consented to this return of ours. They will not be pleased in Tushpa. They may even withhold your twenty *mina* of gold if you were not wise enough to collect it in advance."

"They would not have paid so much in advance, but they will pay it now—I do not propose to give them a choice. Besides, it is nothing to me if they are displeased. If they wish to drive you out, let them do so themselves. I think my lord in Nineveh will be just as contented if you tarry forever by the Shaking Sea, keeping King Argistis's head muddled with anxious thoughts."

"Ah, but if this king does come to drive us out . . . ."

"He will not, I think. I doubt he has the strength—else why would he have sent his emissary to me? I think you will die of bedsores before you are troubled from that direction."

"And now, where before he had but one, the lord Sennacherib has two allies, who do not love each other. You are no less wily than a serpent, my Lord Tiglath Ashur—you would have done very well as a Scoloti."

He threw back his head and laughed, enjoying his own joke as he clasped his hands behind his back, as if to restrain himself.

Barbarian that he was, it suddenly occurred to me that this was a man who could easily rule an empire—who might yet, if the great ones of the earth were not careful. I found I liked him enormously, so I hoped it would never prove necessary to have him killed.

"And now, come," he said, taking my arm just above the elbow. "Let us talk and eat and grow a little drunk together. I am told your officers are not pleased to have you so far from the protection of their swords—are they afraid that I shall poison you? Do they actually imagine I could be such a fool as that . . . ?"

The Scythians do not have very elaborate ideas of personal comfort. Tabiti and I shared our feast squatting together beside a campfire, eating chunks of beef mixed up with wild millet in a pottery bowl. Our drink was fermented horse's milk, called *safid atesh*— which means something like "white fire"—evil-tasting but powerful, which I gathered they vastly prefer to wine, considered an effeminate luxury.

The headman of the Sacan served us both out of a single iron pot, using a copper ladle. The *safid atesh* was kept cool in a wet goatskin bag. The one extravagance was our drinking cups, which were basins of heavy silver set in the brain pans of a pair of human skulls, the mouths kept shut with silver wires—Tabiti held his by inserting his thumb and first finger through the empty eye sockets. He explained that these were the remains of men he had killed himself in single combat, and that it was the custom among the Scythians thus to memorialize a notable adversary.

"This one," he said, holding his own up that I could admire the grinning, fleshless face, "was the eldest son of the headman of one of the lesser tribes among the Aryan. I was just sixteen at the time, and I stripped his life from him with a dagger after he had already killed my horse from under me, breaking my ankle. He got down from his own horse, imagining himself safe and at leisure to make a slow job of me, but he admired his handiwork just a moment too long and I opened up his belly, spilling his guts like fish from a net. The other was a man of no consequence who once attempted to contest my position as headman—I did thus with his skull merely to annoy his family, that they might continue to know their place. There are envious people everywhere."

All of which made me wonder how, had the fortunes of battle gone differently at the Bohtan River, I would have looked with the top of my head sawn off and lined with silver.

"Why do the women lament so?" I asked, curious but also hoping to change the subject.

"Ah—does it trouble your conscience?" He laughed and slapped me upon the shoulder, for he was by then rather drunk. "But it is no concern of yours. They lament that they must follow their lords into the next world, that is all."

"What?"

He said it so matter-of-factly that I had trouble believing he was serious, but of course he was.

"You do not have that custom?" he asked, his narrow eyes expanding with astonishment to almost normal size. "Yes, I wondered why your men took so little trouble burying their friends, but there is a strange variety in such practices. We believe that a man may carry his pleasures with him into the life after death, so a great warrior is buried with his wagon and his goods, including horses and women. The horses have their throats cut, but the women are strangled—I do not know the reason for this difference, except that such is our ancient usage. The cattle and sheep are the inheritance of his sons, since it would not be fitting that they be left impoverished, but his wives will follow him to the grave as they follow the wagon which bears his corpse."

I was able to ride back to my own encampment that night, but only just—the *safid atesh,* which after a few cups had ceased to taste so very repulsive, was stronger than I could have imagined. Tabiti, seeing my woeful condition, had offered me a bed by his own fire, but I knew I could not answer for the actions of my soldiers if I did not return and therefore declined. I think I was almost sober by the time I found my own tent, but I slept very soundly that night.

The next morning, even before dawn, the Scythian caravan was on its way north again, and we were not long in following it. My head, for the first hour or so, felt as if it were packed with cinders, but a decent breakfast and the cold fresh air put me right quickly enough. There is a limit to how bad a man may feel while he is on campaign, away from the complicated evils of daily life. On campaign everything is simple, and a man is at liberty to be happy.

And if that was true for me, it was just as true for my troops.

They had now absorbed the terrible shock of battle and it had left them changed men—or rather, perhaps, men now for the first time. They had found confidence in themselves, having learned to understand the limits of fear, and this showed itself in their most insignificant actions, in the way they readied their kits and cared for their weapons, in their commerce with each other and with their officers. They had come to see that their lives were now guided by a purpose, and this discovery had released them from their sloth and self-contempt. They would never be the same again. We had won more at the Bohtan River than merely a victory.

So I was quite content as we traveled through this wild landscape, surely one of the most awesomely beautiful places on earth. I had the leisure, and the peace of mind, to admire the giant fir trees that shadowed us like the walls of a prison, to listen with quite childish delight to the tumbling hiss of the countless fast-moving little rivers we crossed, each so cold that one drew one's hand out of the water numb, to stare in wonder when, quite suddenly, the forest would part before a bare granite mountain that seemed to mock us like an indifferent god. I could understand why the Scythians were so devoted to their life of wandering, for that day, while we wandered with them, it was impossible not to be happy.

Shortly after noon I sent a rider of my own ahead to seek out the headman Tabiti and invite him to dine with me. It was more than a simple return of courtesies—I was eager to renew my conversation with him, for he was a most singular man.

An army on the march carries no luxuries, so I had sent our cook into the Scythian camp to buy as much mutton as could be had for thirty silver shekels, thinking to furnish my little dinner party and provide the troops with perhaps a five- or six-day supply of fresh meat, but either the Scythians put little value on minted coins or my man was a bad trader, for he came back with no more than twelve head of sheep, enough to provide some six hundred soldiers with no more than a single night's treat. Still, we had our banquet that night and Tabiti, sitting on a leather-covered stool, for all the world like a king in his own court, filled his belly as willingly as I could have hoped.

We drank less that evening, and talked more, even until the last embers had died in my campfire. I learned many things about the Scythian tribes, their manner of life and their relations with the other nomadic peoples. I learned why, except for the doomed widows, I had never seen any of their women, who seem to live their whole lives shut up in the wagons of their fathers and husbands. Tabiti grew expansive as the night wore on and told me the whole history of his life and of the wanderings of the Sacan, so far as these were known to him. He described lands far to the east and mighty cities which even his grandfather had only heard spoken of, making me realize that his world was wider than mine, that the Four Corners within which my father Sennacherib claimed in the name of Ashur to be King of Kings must be only a tiny patch—a bull alone in a cornfield might as justly imagine himself lord of creation.

"And you, Lord Tiglath Ashur, why are you taller than the others of your race? And why is your beard a different color, like wet sand instead of black? Is this because your are the son of a king?"

"No. It is because my mother is an Ionian woman, brought to my father's harem from the islands beyond the Upper Sea."

"Ah, an Ionian! This explains much—some of my nation have traded with the Ionians for jewelry and weapons, things such as that. They are a wily people, full of craft and slyness. Their minds are ever turning on some new scheme, and they have been everywhere and seen all that the world holds. That is doubtless how you came to be such a cunning serpent of a man."

"Does a man inherit his race then?"

"Oh, yes!" He looked at me as if I asked the questions of a child. "Where we are born is an accident. What we are inside our skins is all that matters. But perhaps, since it is only your mother who is Ionian, you have grown up to be quite the river dweller, happy only with soft mud between your toes. Mothers count for very little; my own was a peasant girl my father stole from her village on the banks of the Euxine Sea, but look at me—it seems to have done me little enough harm."

Glancing at me sidewise, he appeared worried lest his words might have given offense, but I only smiled.

"Ah—this wine is from Urartu," he went on. "I have tasted it before, once when we raided close to Tushpa. But it is not the worst and, if he washes his throat with enough of it, a man may become drunk on anything."

"You are right—the wine is from Urartu," I answered. "It was part of King Argistis's bribe, one hundred jars in all."

"A mere one hundred jars? Such a paltry bribe is almost an insult."

"I expect to get more in time."

Tabiti's narrow eyes seemed almost to close as he grinned ferociously at the recollection of my twenty *mina*. He reached across and took my arm in his iron fingers, squeezing as if he thought to break the bone.

"Yes, you do well to take your gold, provided you can get it. But put no great faith in this king or any of his nation—a wise man does not build his wagon of rotten wood."

I must have seemed puzzled, for he released my arm and took a long swallow of wine, all the time studying my face.

"You plan to stop at Tushpa on your way home, Lord Tiglath? Then you will see soon enough."

The next day—only an hour or two after noon, as the headman of the Sacan had predicted—we reached the brackish waters of the Shaking Sea. And there, quite unexpectedly, a peculiar and touching ceremony took place before the warriors of two great nations. We had hardly dismounted when Tabiti ordered that one of his skull-cups be brought. He slipped his thumb and first finger into the eye sockets and held it in the air for all to see.

"I declare that from this day the Lord Tiglath Ashur, a man of prowess and a prince in his own land, is my brother," he shouted. "And in token of this I invite him to partake of the blood oath of the Scoloti."

He caused the skull-cup to be filled with wine, and then he took the dagger from his belt, closed his hand around the blade, and then pulled it through, cutting open the palm across its whole width. The blood rushed from his wound, but he made no effort to stanch it—instead, he let it drip freely into the wine.

Then, with great solemnity, he offered the knife to me.

It is the sort of thing one must do quickly, without thinking, before losing one's nerve, for there is nothing so terrible as the hurt one must inflict on oneself. I pulled the knife blade through my fist with a sudden jerk, my heart pounding. When I opened my hand I was relieved to find that the cut, which started at the ball of my thumb, had not gone all the way to the bone. I too let it bleed into the wine before wrapping it in a cloth. By then I had broken out in a clammy sweat and the pain throbbed all the way to my elbow, but the thing was done.

Tabiti, son of Argimpasa, raised the skull-cup to his lips and drank deeply. I did the same. When we were both finished, the Scythians beat the flats of their dagger blades against their chests and screamed their approval like hawks. My own soldiers, not to be outdone, raised their weapons to the cry "Ashur is King!" In the end, we were all very pleased with one another.

"All true men are brothers, and this world is a strange place," said the headman of the Sacan. "Remember this oath when you have need of a brother."

He took my hand in his own and, as I looked into his face, my eyes seemed to cloud. I though of Esarhaddon, now the *marsarru,* one day my king and lord. My brother Esarhaddon, my friend, who slept in the bed of my beloved.

"All true men are brothers." This strange and savage man meant his own words and had made them truth. The world was indeed a strange place.

How shall I describe the Shaking Sea? Until that day, I had never seen so enormous a body of water—it seemed to me that I had reached the farthest limits of the earth, that I must now be standing at the banks of that great river which surrounds the world in an endless embrace. After this there could be nothing. I strained my eyes, but I could make out no farther shore beyond these vast, blue, blank waters.

"You have tricked me," I said to Tabiti—only half joking. "If I take sail from this place I will disappear forever over the edge."

"No. Two days in a boat, provided you keep the shore to your right, will bring you to Tushpa. I would give much to see King Argistis's face when you arrive."

"I will not arrive. I will perish on this watery desert. Why, by the way, is it called the Shaking Sea?"

"We have many earthquakes in these mountains, and when they come the sea dances. But at such times a man is just as dead if he be on land."

"You fill me with confidence. We men of Ashur, you know, are not sailors."

"Here—let me show you something that may ease your terrors." He reached into the pocket of his coat and then opened his hand to display a copper arrowhead. "Watch."

He pitched the arrowhead into the water—we were standing no more than a few strides from its edge—and it broke the surface with a tiny pop, disappearing from sight.

"Go ahead—watch." Tabiti grinned at me, and his catlike eyes seemed to close completely.

I would not have believed such a thing was possible had I not seen it with my own eyes. In a few seconds the arrowhead rose once more to the surface, to float there like a chip of wood.

"How can this happen?" I exclaimed. "Is it magic? Have you cast some spell?"

"If it is magic, it is not mine. Any bit of metal—or a man's body—will float in these waters. Why, I know not."

I waded in to about the middle of my calves and picked up the arrowhead. Some of the water dripped into the wound on my hand, making it sting like a wasp, and I cursed loudly.

"Perhaps it is its bitterness which makes all manner of things float in it," he went on, as if I had just reminded him of the fact. "Although why this should be I do not understand. The great sea to the west is bitter as well, but any piece of metal thrown into it would sink to the bottom like a stone."

"Are you suggesting I float to Tushpa? With an army of six hundred or more men? Horses, gear, everything—bobbing like corks?"

"No. Send your cavalry and supply horses around by land— they will make better time without a mob of foot soldiers dragging along behind them. Then hire some few dozen boats from the salt makers who dwell an hour or so north of here. They will ferry you and a few hundred of your man to Tushpa in less than two days. By the time you have started dunning this king for his twenty *mina* of gold, the rest of your army will have arrived at the gates of his city to reinforce your eloquence."

"Yes—it might do," I answered. My hand still smarted, but somehow it seemed less of a joke on me. "It might do very well. Tabiti, you are a thief and a rascal, but no fool."

He laughed and slapped his thighs, mightily pleased with us both.

"The Lord Tiglath Ashur will someday learn that it is only by being thieves and rascals that rulers grow great. What is the difference between a thief and a mighty king? The thief steals only trifles."

That very afternoon Tabiti and I rode to the village of the salt gatherers and sat in the elder's hut drinking a vile potion that tasted of fish guts and settling the terms of my passage to Tushpa. It was a tedious process—Tabiti, who spoke the language, haggled like a rug dealer, and the elder pulled his white beard and lamented his poverty in words that required no translation. I had only to listen, frown with impatience from time to time, and try to look the part of the ruthless and willful conqueror who could be counted on to massacre the entire settlement if I met with more avarice than I was prepared to tolerate.

In the end the old bandit came to terms quite amicably, showing me black stumps of teeth as he smiled his approval. I had only to pay him and his boatman twenty silver shekels for four days' work, which was doubtless a greater sum than they would earn from a year of selling salt. I would sail the next morning with two companies of infantry and their gear.

Our last night with the Sacan was one of wary celebration. My soldiers had learned to mix freely with these barbaric wanderers, but they were on their guard, drank but little, and stayed clear of their wagons and their women, for I had made it clear that I would put to death any man who gave pretext for the shedding of blood. It was hard to know how far the hospitality of these people extended and, since they were now our allies and might be useful in the future, I wanted no further trouble with them. Tabiti, I suspect, restrained his own men in similar fashion and for the same reasons.

Great as was the friendship and mutual respect that had grown up between us, I had the distinct impression that he would not be sorry to see the last of me, nor of the army I commanded.

In the morning, when the salt gatherers had assembled their vessels and my soldiers, some of them already white-faced with apprehension, were loaded on board, we set sail for Tushpa.

19

It is said that no true man of Ashur is at ease trusting his life to any waters wider than those of his Mother Tigris, that the broad seas are the home of countless demons. And truly these soldiers of mine cursed their fortune in having such a fool for a commander that he believed the sea could be kept out by the wooden sides of a boat, but for myself I enjoyed every hour of this my first voyage. The water was always calm, so there were no dangers. In two days and a half we were never out of sight of shore, and each night we pulled our keels up upon the beach and slept on the solid land.

Still, this was an adventure. Perhaps because I am half Greek, my stomach never troubled me and I felt none of that green giddiness which makes the gentlest rocking of the waves a source of agony for so many and which no charm or incantation seems to drive off. To me everything was new and interesting, and the journey to Tushpa had all the tranquil charms of novelty.

I learned, among other things, that the Shaking Sea is not quite the lifeless desert it seems. Each evening, after we had beached our boats, the salt gatherers would cast their round nets into the waves lapping at the shore and within an hour or less collect enough fish, each no longer than a man's hand, to feed at least themselves. My soldiers without exception refused even to look at these, contenting themselves with bread and dried goat flesh, and in this they were wiser than their commander, for when the leader of our little fleet brought me, as something of a delicacy, a specimen of his catch, nicely cooked and spread out on a bed of savory-smelling pine needles, I was fool enough to eat it. It tasted strongly of mud and was as brackish as the waters that had spawned it. I smiled and smacked my lips appreciatively, but as soon as decency permitted I stepped into the surrounding forest, jammed two fingers down my throat, and relieved my belly of its unpleasant burden.

The salt gatherers themselves seemed to live on a diet of little else. Their wine, as I discovered to my horror, really was concocted of fermented fish guts, and the only vegetable I ever saw them eat was a variety of bulb, like wild garlic, which they dug out of the damp forest earth. The income they derived from the salt they distilled was spent almost exclusively on fresh meat, but their product was not of sufficient purity to command any great price and thus they probably would have starved without their nets.

These people were among the most primitive I have seen anywhere on earth. All their prosperity depended upon the Shaking Sea—indeed, the sea itself was the chief of their gods—and the existence they derived from it was as barren as that acrid waste. The arts of metalworking, masonry, and carpentry were unknown among them so, although they lived in a land where wood and stone were plentiful, their houses were nothing more than woven reeds over frames of bent poles. Their lives were preserved by their poverty for, although they understood nothing of war and were surrounded by marauding tribes, they possessed nothing worth the trouble of taking except their women, which, after the fashion of the Scythians, they kept hidden from the eyes of avarice.

Yet, in spite of the misery of their circumstances, they were conspicuous for an open, generous serenity. They looked upon us, a mob of armed soldiers, with no symptoms of fear and seemed willing enough to share what little they had. This voyage to Tushpa they appeared to regard as a great lark, a holiday, a gift from their open-handed gods. I found it difficult to despise them.

It was just an hour before noon of the third day when we made our first contact with the Urartian war galleys—they sent four to intercept us, although why they required such a number to deal with some twelve or thirteen little fishing boats was a mystery I could not at first puzzle out.

Tabiti had promised the salt gatherers that I was a mighty prince who could sweep away all before him and who lived under the protection of a powerful god, and this assurance had emboldened them to venture beyond their own end of the Shaking Sea and into those waters where King Argistis's war vessels jealously guarded access to Tushpa. As I mounted to the prow of our lead boat to display my uniform—since this would be our only defense —I could only hope that the Urartians would be as impressed.

It was a wind-still morning, and the great ships had furled their sails and were driven forward by oarsmen hidden behind the black wooden walls that towered out of the sea like floating cliffs. I had almost decided that the Urartians were about to bear down on us and smash our little boats to kindling when, at the last instant, all their oars rose out of the water in unison and hung suspended in mid-air. An officer—at least, someone whom I took from his bearing to be an officer—leaned over the deck railing and peered down at me as if at the corpse of some curious and repugnant sea creature that had tangled his anchor rope. He was a square-faced man with heavy eyebrows and a wide black beard, and I took an instant dislike to him.

"You trespass," he said, matter-of-factly, first in his own language and then, when I did not respond, in Aramaic.

"The armies of Ashur do not trespass," I answered, in Akkadian. "They are at home wherever they go in the wide world. I am here at the invitation of the Lord Lutipri, who came to Amat to implore my aid against the Scythians within this very month. The Scythians are conquered, and if you do not show me more civility I will order one of my soldiers to climb aboard your ship and cut the tongue from your head."

He was greatly taken aback, as I had intended he would be, and for a long time said nothing, doubtless not knowing what to say. A moment ago he had believed himself to be all-powerful, and now he was not so sure. This was not a clever man—I could almost watch the ideas turning over in his mind.

At last I decided to spare him the suspense of indecision.

"These good and simple people wish to return to their homes," I said. "I think it would be best if you took me and my soldiers aboard your own vessels and conveyed us the rest of the way."

When this suggestion did not meet with immediate agreement, I waited through perhaps ten heartbeats—which I could feel throbbing quite distinctly in my neck—and then allowed myself the luxury of loosing my temper.

"I said to lower your boarding ladders, you lout! Are the

men of Tushpa such fainting creatures that they fear to be over-come by a force of less than two hundred strong? I'll have your head to go with the tongue if you keep me waiting another half a quarter of a minute!"

At last it sank through even to this muddy intellect that I could not possibly be bluffing—what could I have gained for my-self except a walk to the executioner's block?—and the boarding ladders were indeed lowered. My idyll had reached its end, and I had become once more the soldier and the diplomat. I waved good-bye to the salt gatherers, with whom I had never exchanged a word in any language, and turned my face toward Tushpa.

By the middle of the afternoon we were within sight of that city, which must rank as the most beautiful in the world. Never before had I seen great buildings made entirely of stone and never again would I see any which so dazzled the eye. The temples and palaces of Egypt are vast, cunningly made, and very grand, but one tires of endless rows of sand-colored columns. Thebes and Memphis are places one quickly learns to live in without really noticing; Tushpa, however, is a ceaseless delight, a jewel box of color, a place of wonder. This I could see even from the wharves, behind which rose walls composed of alternating bands of white and black stone, as delicate and majestic as a high-born woman.

The commander of the Urartian ships—for so he turned out to be—had divided my soldiers among his other three ships and kept me aboard his own, doubtless on the theory that even an adder is harmless after its head is off. He needn't have worried, for I was quite content to sit in his cabin and drink his wine, even after we had touched land and he had sent a messenger hurrying off to report my arrival and seek instructions.

In any case, it was not a long wait. Within the hour the cabin door opened and the Lord Lutipri himself entered, looking no less astonished than my unwilling host, whom he dismissed with the curtest possible gesture. He sat down, blinking at me like an owl in that twilight darkness.

"My Lord Tiglath Ashur," he began at last, "it is not twenty days since . . ."

"Since we last dined together in Amat—yes, my lord. I have come to report a great victory. The Scythians are driven back from the banks of the Bohtan River, which are still wet with their blood."

This wily man narrowed his eyes as he regarded me in silence. I grinned at him, like a boy who has just performed some stunt, but I knew what he was thinking. Finally he shrugged his shoulders, as if at a thing indifferent.

"Of course, my prince, it would never occur to me, who knows you so well, to doubt your words, but—you must understand—my king . . . I hesitate to speak of proof . . ."

"What proof could you require beyond the fact that I am here, and alive?" My grin widened just a shade, and then collapsed. "If more is required, go look at the fresh graves by the Bohtan River. Go send emissaries to the Scythians, who now camp on the western shores of the Shaking Sea. Do not speak to me of proof, my lord."

"On the western shores?" The Lord Lutipri actually rose a handspan or two out of his chair. "But that is Urartian land!"

"I have ceded it to them—they must go somewhere, my lord. Or perhaps you thought I would undertake to massacre them all when all I pledged was to drive them back from the Bohtan River—"

"You had no right!"

"I had the right of necessity. And besides, it was my pleasure."

King Argistis's servant had by then regained his seat and his composure, and merely shrugged his shoulders once more—a sign that he was too wise to rail against an accomplished fact.

"And now, my lord," I continued, "there is the matter of twenty *mina* of gold."

That evening all unpleasantness was forgotten. My soldiers were quartered within the palace compound and provided with food, wine, and women, and I was the king's guest at a banquet in my honor. This meant nothing more than that the Urartians wished to move cautiously; they needed more time to consider the altered situation and think of some way to evade paying their debt.

I was just as pleased, however, since it gave me the best of opportunities to study Argistis and his court at close quarters. I sat beside him, at his right hand, this king whose father my grandfather had driven to take his own life, and heard myself called his friend, his partner in the works of glory, but the sight of him made me shudder with an inward dread.

He was, like most of his race, tall and almost womanly slender. He was not many years older than I, but already his beard was notched with patches of silver and his eyes had a haunted look, as if the burden of his office weighed heavily upon him.

What did the coming years hold for him, I wondered. His nation was hedged about with enemies, and his nobles—or so it was said—intrigued against him. Would his mind crack under some great calamity so that he followed his father's example and searched his own breast with a sword, or would some one of his great men save him the trouble? In either case there was that about him, a kind of aura, which suggested he would not die quietly.

But for however long he would live he seemed determined to live in splendor. Even the Lord Sennacherib might have envied him the opulence of this banquet, at which the least among his courtiers were appareled in tunics of the costliest embroidery, and many, including the king himself, wore robes heavy with gold and silver. The hall in which we dined was walled with smooth green stone, almost like glass, and the tables were of sweet-smelling cedar. We were entertained by musicians brought from Lydia and Egypt, and by fair-skinned courtesans who danced with uncanny skill, rolling their breasts and bellies as they kept time to the rhythm of the flutes. Several of the most beautiful sat beside the guests at the king's own table, speaking in many tongues and tempting their patrons with sugared dates and wine and the charms of their own persons; the sound of their laughter was itself a kind of music. My own had hair the color of polished leather and eyes as green as summer figs. Her body smelled of honey and oil and she kept reaching stealthily under the hem of my tunic to caress my manhood, which I must own was as stiff as a dagger blade.

King Argistis seemed to find this amusing. At last he laid his hand upon my arm and, leaning toward me, murmured, "She is a rare one, is she not? My father bought her for my harem while she was still a suckling babe, and she has lived all her life for my pleasure only. I will have her sent around to your room later—a small token of the love I bear you, Prince."

I smiled and nodded—what else was I to do, since one does not spurn the tokens of kings?—but I could not help but wonder if this fool imagined I would value a night in any harlot's arms at twenty *mina* of gold.

"I am grateful for your favor to me, Lord—to me, and to my soldiers. Saving only that of the king our master, we serve no will but your own."

And then it was Argistis's turn to smile and nod. He was not such a fool as to fail to understand my precise meaning.

"And yet the Scythians are still within my borders, Prince—how does that come to be?"

"For your own safety, Lord," I replied, perhaps just a shade too quickly, as if it were an answer I had rehearsed. "Unless you garrison the western shore—and perhaps even if you do, for they do not fight like women—you will have one or another of these tribes there forever. Better you should have the Scythians for neighbors than some others, for they have tasted the might of Ashur, and their headman, Tabiti, son of Argimpasa, has called me his brother and sworn a blood oath of loyalty. As long as the king in Nineveh and the king in Tushpa are friends, you will have no cause for complaint from the Scythians."

The threat may have been wrapped in a promise, but this king saw it clearly enough. He smiled yet once more and turned the conversation to other things.

By even the standards of kings, however, his table talk was empty, boastful, insipid. He talked about the exploits of his generals as if they were his own—which all kings glory to do—but Argistis was alone in his apparent powerlessness to distinguish between himself and his servants, whom he seemed to regard as mere extensions of his own will. He did not even have the cunning to be jealous. He appeared to regard himself as alone in his kingdom, surrounded by mere blocks of wood instead of men.

"I was wise to treat with you for aid," he said casually, "although I little expected such a swift victory. The Scythian barbarians will know now to fear the might of Urartia."

Had he forgotten the Lord Lutipri's existence? Or my own? And one might imagine the Scythians drawing quite a different moral.

The king my father, I knew, wished for no more conquests, but the king my brother, when his turn came, might turn his ambitious eyes to the north. What an easy victory, I thought, what a joke would it be for Esarhaddon to pull the feathers from this peacock's tail.

Having learned long ago the folly of reveling with fools and scoundrels, that night I drank but little of the strong Urartian wine. However, that man was not alone who, having grown drunk enough to attempt mounting one of the courtesans, found himself too drunk to accomplish the act, so, when at last the king withdrew and the rest of us were then free to stay or go, there were not many who could stagger to their rooms without assistance. But I required no help. When I rose from the table, I made my solitary way to a balcony and there breathed in the cold, clear air—a reminder, if I needed one, that the winter snows would not hold off forever—until the fumes were gone from my head and I was as fresh as a spring lamb.

But it is not always a blessing to be sober. I did not feel lonely or low-spirited, only . . . I did not quite know how I felt, except that my soul was empty.

What was I now, when my king's enemies were conquered and my soldiers safe in their beds? What had I of my own? Was there even life left in my body?

But these were no more than the thoughts of a man who has been awake too long and has the taste of stale wine in his mouth. I would go to bed, and tomorrow the world would seem a friendlier place.

King Argistis had lent me quarters not far from his own apartments—the better, no doubt, to keep me under his wakeful, haunted eyes. When I entered these rooms I was glad to see the brazier still red with living coals. I had already undressed and was washing my face in a basin of cold water when I noticed the girl watching me from my sleeping mat. In truth, I had forgotten all about her.

Half-light and shadow lend a charm to all things, and she appeared even more beautiful as she lay there, leaning back on her arms, her breasts, as they rose and fell with their breathing, seeming to possess my eyes. She smiled at me, as if she knew all about me, as if my heart were open to her. Her smile made me think of a cat with a cornered mouse—*this will be an easy kill,* it seemed to say.

"My lord is weary," she said, in a voice as smooth as linen. "Come. Let me touch my lord's brow with my cool hands."

Yes, the smile said. *I understand the weaknesses of men.* It took me no more than that instant to understand that I did not want to feel the touch of those cool hands.

"I have drunk too much wine," I said. "I fear we would both be wasting our time."

Her smooth shoulders moved in a tiny gesture of dismissal. What was her time for, she might have asked, except to be wasted on such as me?

I had sat down on a little wooden stool, and I watched her in silence. And when at last it was obvious even to her that I was merely waiting for her to leave, she rose from the sleeping mat and came near me. She crouched beside me, touching my arm with her hands, and her lips brushed against my skin as if by accident.

Was I not a man? Could I feel nothing, not even desire? Yes. I felt that. I took her by the shoulders and looked at her in the dim light. I looked at her as I might have looked at a map of some unknown country. I pushed her from me—roughly, so that she fell hard against the smooth floor. I did this and buried my face in my hands.

"Leave me," I said, in a choked voice. "I have no wish to hurt you, but . . . Leave me."

I could hear the sound of her naked feet against the floor, and then the sound of a door closing, and then nothing.

". . . *I hope your love is a curse to you,*" she had said. "*I hope it haunts you until you die. . . .*"

The dawn had almost come before I closed my eyes.

The next morning, I received no summons from the king. He was no doubt closeted with his ministers and servants, listening attentively while they settled among themselves what he should decide to do. Thus, after I had visited the barracks where my soldiers were quartered, I felt myself at perfect liberty and decided to walk alone through the great city of Tushpa and see this miracle of beauty with the eyes of an anonymous stranger.

All that day I wandered through her streets, lost in wonder. The temple of the god Khaldi, patron of the Urartians, was built of massive stones raised in alternating layers of black and yellow, its gates framed in red granite. On the inside the walls were painted in the brightest colors to depict the rituals of his worship, along with demons such as made the blood run cold, and scenes of hunting and farming. These people were masters in the art of carving stone—their friezes, executed after the manner of Nineveh, were astonishing enough, but, beyond this, they had found the true pattern of shaping images in the round. The idol of that terrible deity was so lifelike that I half expected to see it move, to blink its eyes in the smoke of its burned offerings and to bare its savage teeth. The temples of the lesser gods, the palaces of the king and his nobles, and armories and garrisons, even the humblest shops and houses were exquisite in their decorations and their perfection of line. If the mighty gods should ever decide to build a city and dwell on earth like men, even they could not hope to surpass the marvel that was Tushpa.

I returned to King Argistis's palace in a state of elation, that curious happiness that comes to us when, for a few hours, we have been taken out of ourselves, have almost forgotten our own existence. A man playing with his children feels it, as does—so I am told—the artist in the practice of his art. As does the patron of that artist. As does the simplest farmer looking at a sunset. This Tushpa gave me, freely, unconscious even that there was something to give, and not for a moment only but for the whole day. And from that day I always loved the city and felt it a great misfortune that she was ruled by a foolish weakling.

The Lord Lutipri was waiting for me in my rooms.

"You sent the woman away last night," he said, after we had taken our seats and had wine poured for us. "The king was surprised and—I must say it—offended."

"Was the king offended because I was not in the mood for rutting, or because he must now pay me twenty *mina* of gold whether I spend my seed in his harlots or do not?"

Lutipri found this such a diverting remark that he was forced to cover a smile with his hand. This, I think, was his diplomatic way of telling me I should not speak rudely of his master.

"My lord prince must realize there is not such a sum in the whole city of Tushpa. What would you have us do? Melt the idols of our gods?"

"Tushpa is rich—your king is rich. Have I not seen every demonstration of this?" I shrugged my shoulder. "However, the rest of my army will arrive tomorrow, or perhaps the day after, and the first snows of winter will not be far behind them. If the Lord Argistis does not object to quartering a foreign army of some seven hundred men until the spring thaw, then I shall be happy to stay in Tushpa. I could not in conscience leave until I have fulfilled the bargain we both made in the names of our royal masters. How could I? How would I explain myself to Ashur's mighty king?"

"You said *seven* hundred men?"

"Yes. With horses and gear. Did you imagine I conquered the Scythians by myself?"

The Lord Lutipri set his wine cup back down on the table, puckering his mouth slightly as if the taste no longer appealed to him.

"As a reward," he began, not quite looking me in the face, "and as a token of his friendship, my king is prepared to offer you ten *mina* of gold."

"And as a right, in fulfillment of a debt, my king is prepared to accept twenty."

"I think it is unwise for us to speak further of this today, my lord."

"This may be so."

"Thus I will leave you now." He rose from his seat, offering me his hand like a friend. "Let us hope that tomorrow all men shall have grown wiser."

I dined alone that night, wondering how much I would finally squeeze from this crafty servant and his fool of a master. I decided that I would settle for fifteen *mina,* which was, after all, a great sum—I did not wish to stay in these mountains for a whole winter. I was *shaknu* of the north, not governor of Tushpa. I had business in my own country. Fifteen *mina* was indeed a great sum. I would settle for that.

And I would be just as pleased, I decided, if the king sent his harlot back to me tonight. I was being wise enough with her master, but last night I had been a great fool.

I had known no woman since leaving Nineveh. Why? What was I attempting to prove to myself? Esharhamat was lost to me, and I must find a way to go on living. And a man who knows no woman is only half alive. If the woman returned, I would do her more than justice.

But she did not return. I spent the night alone, and not well pleased with my own company.

From the landward side, the only approaches into Tushpa are up steep cliffs of rock. The trails are narrow and winding, full of places of ambush, and, at the top, the city walls are high and fashioned from the same stone—thus, while an invading army may ravage the countryside, the capital itself is impregnable. This the Lord Sargon learned ten years before I was born.

But the Lord Sargon had not had a force of one hundred fifty men already inside the walls.

To remind the Urartians of this, the hour I received word that the rest of my army had been sighted I gave orders that the two companies which had come with me were to assemble for parade. We would march straight out into the city's great square, within sight of the walls—which, of course, had not been built to be defended from the rear—and there we would await the arrival of our comrades. We were King Argistis's guests. If he attacked us he would surely bring the Lord Sennacherib's wrath down upon him. I was prepared to let him ponder the difficulties of the situation.

The Lord Lutipri, who was standing on the wall to witness the approach of these not-quite-invaders, invited me to join him. My officers had their orders—they would be watching from the square and I had only to raise my arm to see those orders obeyed, but he knew that as well as I. There was a cold wind blowing by us as he gave me his hand.

"It is, my prince, in any case not a great force," he said, gesturing toward the lines of horses and men that moved across the valley floor so far below us.

"No, it is not a great force—only a part of the great army my Dread Lord Sennacherib has under his command. A small part."

We watched them in silence for perhaps the space of five minutes. The Urartian soldiers on the walls watched them. No one, however, attempted to interfere as they began making their precarious way up the trails cut centuries before in the cliff faces. At last the Lord Lutipri put his hand on my arm.

"My king is generous," he said. "You have won his heart and he will give you fourteen *mina* of gold."

I turned to him, letting my face go as expressionless as stone.

"Seventeen."

"Done."

We shook hands and were friends again.

"But can you leave tomorrow?" he asked, narrowing his eyes as he looked into the wind. "I have no wish to seem inhospitable, but . . ."

I could not help but laugh.

"Nor I, my lord, to die in the snow on my way home. Yes—yes, by all means tomorrow."

And I was as good as my word. The companies who had only just finished their march from the west—and who had expected a few days' rest—were not very pleased, but it was already the fifth day of the month of Tisri and the air was like ice. Winter came early in these mountains.

The march home took us twelve days. At first we struck west, crossing the Toprah mountain range, until we found the sources of the Greater Zab. Then we simply followed the river home. It was a longer way, but we put the mountains behind us early. Snow was already in the air when, a day's march from Amat, we encountered the first of the garrison outriders. He stayed with us for an hour, and then I sent him galloping home with news of our coming.

We camped that evening not two *beru* from our own gates. We might have reached our own beds by darkness, but I did not wish this army to come straggling home in the middle of the night like a pack of vagabonds. These men were conquerors, and I wanted them to feel it. I wanted Amat to feel it. Soldiers need to know they are soldiers and not pack animals so we would sleep through one more night on the cold ground.

So the next morning, with our drums booming and the citizens of Amat standing by the roadside to cheer, we made our return. These were not the same men who had left only a little over a month before—I was not the same. We were the soldiers of our king and the servants of our god, and we had brought home victory. As I rode through the fortress gates, listening to the shouts of "Ashur is King," with what was now truly an army at my back, I was a proud and happy man.

And a weary one. I could hardly wait to return to my own rooms, eat a hot meal, sweat my body clean, and sleep for twelve hours.

But what I found there took away my weariness as if by magic. It was Kephalos.

My old servant had not changed, except to grow a little fatter. His tunic was of the finest embroidery and his brown beard smelled of myrrh, and he fell on his face before his stinking, dirt-streaked owner and embraced my knees.

"Master!—the gods be praised. . . ."

"Worthy Physician, what in Adad's name are you doing here?"

I raised him to his feet and, as he wiped away his tears of thanksgiving—for no man ever wept easier than my slave Kephalos—he accepted from my hand a cup of wine.

"Ah, Lord, your revered brother the *marsarru* seemed not to have liked the little present you sent him. He shook it in my face —that head, Lord, as nasty a piece of work as I have seen— holding it up by the hair with his own hand, and informed me that 'you may tell the Lord Tiglath Ashur, when you see him, that he has nothing to fear from me!' Well, my young master, I required no broader hint—Nineveh was no longer a place of safety for me, so I packed up to follow you to this wild place."

He looked about him, without any enthusiasm.

The head—yes. I had almost forgotten about the head. But it did not matter. I stood up and placed my hands upon Kephalos's broad shoulders, for the sight of him was dear to me.

"And did you bring your entire household?" I asked. "Where in this little town will you find room for them all?"

"Not all, Lord—not Philinna and the boy Ernos." He shrugged his shoulders and groaned, as if recalling some painful memory.

"In the end, Master, when I grew tired of her embraces and her endless nagging both, I allowed her to follow her old trade as a tavern whore, which she did with great success. She amassed wealth sufficient to buy her freedom—which had been my plan from the first—with enough left over for a dowry that even I would have found attractive had I known less about the woman who came with it. Her husband is a leather dealer on the Street of Ishtar, poor devil. As for the boy, I fear he did not turn out very well. Doubtless he flourishes somewhere, and keeps busy cutting throats."

I laughed and embraced him.

"Kephalos, you dog, how I have missed you!"

20

"**Y**our royal brother Esarhaddon is rarely ever seen in Nineveh these days," Kephalos told me—over a supper prepared by his own cook, whom he preferred, with some justification, to mine. "He has set up his own court at Calah and reigns there as if he were king already. It is said that he and the Lord Sennacherib can hardly bear to be in each other's presence."

The esteemed physician belched loudly, for he had dined well and was more than a little drunk. In the week since he had arrived in Amat he had made himself quite a home and developed a great appreciation for my Nairian wine. I found, upon inquiry, that several jars were missing.

"I hardly know how to tell you, Lord—it was rumored when I left that the Lady Esharhamat is expecting a child."

"That is not very surprising." I tried, as I spoke, to keep all expression out of my voice, there was no telling with what success. "Producing children is rather the point of royal marriages, is it not? And I know for a fact that Esarhaddon has already fathered many on the bodies of his concubines."

"It is believed by some—by many, Lord—that you are the real father of this child."

"Only the Lady Esharhamat could know that for certain. And perhaps not even she."

"Yes, Lord. This I acknowledge."

For a long moment he sat quietly with his head cocked to one side, seeming to study my face. I was not such a fool as to fail to understand.

THE ASSYRIAN   333

"I think," he continued, "I think that this belief is itself born of the hope that it might be true, for the Lord Esarhaddon is not popular . . ."

I held up my hand in a gesture of annoyance—these were not things which I wished to hear, which it was even proper for me to hear—and Kephalos fell silent. It was a painful silence, which lasted until I broke it myself.

"Have you seen my mother?" I asked. My slave's face brightened with relief.

"Yes, Lord. I stopped at Three Lions on my journey north. She is well and lives for the day she may join you—although, the gods know, there is little enough beyond your radiant person to tempt anyone to Amat."

I laughed and refilled his wine cup with my own hand, for Kephalos spoke no more than the truth.

"And for that reason, my friend, as well as many others, I am glad you have come, for I have something in mind. Tell me, am I still rich?"

"Yes, Lord, as rich as ever." He nodded appreciatively and wiped his hands on the front of his tunic, as if the mention of wealth made them sweat. "As rich as any man in the Land of Ashur, save only the king, your brother Esarhaddon, and the lord *turtanu*—although I have found it expedient to . . ."

"To what, dog—speak!" I grinned, to show that I was only joking. "What have you done now to beggar me?"

"I have thought it wise, Lord, to place some small share of your riches—my own as well, Lord, for these are unsettled times and a man must be prudent—into the hands of merchants in Tyre and Sidon, even in Egypt. And I have made these investments under other seals, that none might know these so-and-so-many talents of gold and silver are the property of the Lord Tiglath Ashur, son of Sennacherib."

I must have looked puzzled, for Kephalos puckered his brow and frowned.

"I think the day may come, Lord, when both of us will be forced to flee from this land—provided we are still able. And your brother Esarhaddon, when he is king, will have a long reach."

"I have nothing to fear from Esarhaddon, slave, nor he from me."

"Master, you have many virtues to which I do not pretend to aspire, but in these questions you are like a child and must be content to be led by a slave, whose nature is less admirable than your own but who is therefore much wiser in the workings of a world not at all admirable."

And Kephalos, who was of course quite right and served me better than ever I had served myself, stared down into his wine cup as if ashamed to meet my eye. But it was I, and not he, who had reason to feel ashamed.

"I am sorry, my friend," I said, and put my hand upon his arm. "I spoke in haste and anger. Do not be offended with the prattle of a child."

"I am not offended, Lord. What you have said is true—now. The Lord Esarhaddon is your brother and loves you. But what is true now may not be true forever. Things can change mightily when a man with a weak head finds himself master of the world."

He looked up and smiled, and I saw that I was forgiven. And, yes, of course he had been wise to prepare for a day that might never come. And if I did not care to think of such things, that did not make me any the nobler.

It was time, however, to change the subject.

"But I am still rich?" I asked. "You have not sent every last copper shekel to Sidon and Thebes?"

"No, Lord—you are still rich. As befits a prince."

"Good. Then send to Nineveh that some of my wealth may be brought to me here. I have need of it, for I intend to build a mighty palace for my mother's sake. And I will rebuild the garrison, and the town as well—it is my intention to turn poor little Amat into a great city. And not in brick but in stone.

"And for this, if I am not to be robbed and plundered by every rascal who has something to sell, even if it be only the labor of his own muscles, I shall need my rascal of a slave, the great physician Kephalos, whose brain has more coils than a serpent."

My faithful servant stumbled off to bed that night both very drunk and very happy. I had given him a precious commission, a gift of the most astonishing value. He was to have charge of building a great city—and from such a project, he calculated, the bribes alone would keep him in luxury into extreme old age.

But of course, like a good guest, he had come bearing gifts of his own.

"Your mother, the Lady Merope, described to me your state

of mind as she understood it—she said you were like a man riding away to find death. I have made a few inquiries of my own since arriving here, and what do I discover? Everyone tells me the same thing, that you occupy your time with nothing except soldiering. The brothel keepers claim they have done no business with the garrison commander since his arrival, and I find not a single woman worth the name among your household slaves. I warn you, Lord, that you will never retain your respectability if you continue to go on in this fashion. It is neither proper nor rational nor balanced for one still in the first bloom of his youthful power to keep his fist clamped around his manhood as if it were for nothing except pissing through. Have a care for your health and a decent regard for appearances or, mark my words, in the end this behavior will lead to nothing but ugly rumors."

"And as my physician and my friend, Kephalos, what would you recommend?"

Kephalos nodded and touched the side of his nose with his finger—a salute, of sorts, to my wisdom in seeking his advice.

"I have already taken steps, Lord," he answered.

Steps? What steps? An hour later, when I went to my sleeping mat and found her waiting for me there, I could not account for my own surprise. The room was heated by a brazier which had almost flickered out, and that and the oil lamp I held in my hand gave all the light there was. Still, did I need the blaze of the bright sun to see that she was beautiful?

"I am Naiba," she murmured as I crouched beside her to peer into her eyes, which were large and black and reminded me so much of my lost Esharhamat. She pulled aside the blanket that I might see her naked body—she was only a slave girl, the gesture implied, and wished through her submission to find favor with a new master. "I am Naiba, Dread Lord."

"Yes. I can see that," I said.

This made her smile, for her name meant "beautiful" in the language of the nomad tribes. It was a smile worthy of her name, and made me glad I had kept my ears open among the Sacan.

"Do I please you, Dread Lord?"

"Yes. You please me."

"Then come into me, and find your rest."

She was hardly more than a child. I lay beside her and her girl's breast barely filled my hand. And yet, when my mouth sought her own, I found her slippery, pointed little tongue pushing between my lips with an urgency that suggested no small experience of passion. I wrapped my hand around the neck of the lamp and snuffed out its light.

In the darkness I was free to believe whatever I would, and in the darkness this girl became for me another Esharhamat. I was back once more in that tiny room in the temple of Ishtar, and the old force of my love flooded into me like new blood. As I entered her, and she shuddered beneath me, her name was on my lips like a cry of despair, but I could not speak it. The delight, the joy of her became the only tongue I knew. Had I found my voice it would only have been to choke on my own sobs—I had her once more in my arms and now, for a few moments, I did not have to be alone.

I knew her three times that night before we fell asleep in each other's embrace and I think I gave her pleasure, although this is a matter in which no man may quite trust himself. She was not Esharhamat. Of course, I knew that. Even the illusion passed off after the first time, but I do not imagine the girl could ever have grasped all that she meant to me that night. Perhaps, however, she understood a little that I had given something of my secret self into her care, and if she did—and even if she did not, for what right had I to ask for understanding?—I was grateful to her. And my gratitude was to last forever.

"She is one of the captive women whom you took as tribute from the conquered Uqukadi," Kephalos told me at breakfast. "I have kept her as a slave in my own house and did not force my way through her maidenhood until last year, so she is just nicely broken to harness without having lost her bloom. I trust she did not bring shame upon your servant, Lord, and you are pleased?"

All this he said while Naiba, in a thin linen tunic that clung to her breasts like a veil, knelt at my elbow, smiling and serving me my beer and honeyed barley paste. She might have been a block of wood or not even in the room.

"How could I be otherwise than pleased?" I placed my hand on her hair, which smelled of cedar oil, and she twisted her head slightly and kissed me upon the wrist. "How old were you, child, when I robbed your parents of you?"

"I had just turned eleven that winter," she answered. "But my parents did not feel the loss, for my mother was already dead and my father was among those whose heads you had struck from their shoulders."

She smiled as she said it, as if speaking of indifferent things, but I felt a cold thrill in my throat.

"Then truly you must hate me, for I have done you an injury."

"How is that, Dread Lord?" She shrugged her shoulders, as if puzzled at my meaning.

"Because I had your father killed before your eyes."

"Oh! I hid my face, so I did not see it. And, besides, you were the conqueror—you killed only the clan leaders and thus showed mercy. If my father had triumphed . . ."

She hid her face behind her hands and laughed at this amusing notion.

"And since then I have been a house slave in Nineveh, where every cur in the street lives better than the Uqukadi, whose women must walk through the snow behind the horses of the men. And now I am the pillow girl of a great prince."

"You see, my foolish young master?" Kephalos grinned and folded his hands over his broad belly in amusement. "For all the scruples of your delicate conscience, the world is what it is, which even this slip of a girl knows better than you. You need have no fear—*she* will not push a kitchen knife between your ribs while you are sleeping, not to avenge a father who probably treated his hunting dogs with more kindness. To her you are Tiglath Ashur, Dread Lord, the mighty prince and warrior, whose manhood any woman would be honored to take into her belly. This one has made a good bargain with life, and she is wise enough to know it."

"And you have made a good bargain for me, my friend."

"I hope so, Lord," he answered, reaching across the narrow little table to put his hand on my shoulder. "You have doubtless noticed her resemblance to a certain lady whose name we need never mention? I saw it even when she was but a skinny child and have saved her for you, knowing the day would come when you would need such consolation—any but a fool could have seen how that sad business would end. Use her as you will, believing whatever you like until at last it comes to seem true, for it is unhealthy for a man to harbor up his own seed like a miser, letting it turn putrid to poison both his body and mind. Any woman is better than none, and this one is better than many."

Kephalos spoke no more than the truth, for in the months and years that followed the girl Naiba became precious in my sight. She could not have been any older than thirteen that first

night on my sleeping mat, and yet from that time on she filled a
woman's place in my house. She took care of my clothes, scolded
my servants, and looked after the household money. And she
looked after me just as well. When I was away on campaign she
prayed for my safety to both Ashur and to her own gods. When I
returned she would lead me to the sweating house, strip herself
naked, and rub hot oil into my weary, tender muscles. I did not
eat a meal under that roof that she did not place the dishes before
me with her own hands, smiling at me from the sweetness of her
child's heart. She poured the wine for me and my guests and
helped me to bed when I had drunk too much of it. And every
night, drunk or sober, I slept with her arm outstretched across my
waist and her tight little breasts pressing against my back.

And between us subsisted affection and regard and—so I
hope and believe—even passion. But no love. Not, at least, such
love as would ever have driven Esharhamat from my thoughts.
Naiba, I am quite sure, although she never spoke a word of it,
knew that story, and she was too wise to let her feelings for me go
beyond a certain fondness. I was her lord, and she took pleasure
in the touch of my body, but that was all. And I was not discontented that it should be so.

For at that time I was very little occupied with domestic life
—I had not forgotten, nor was I allowed to forget, that I was
shaknu of the north and commander of the garrison at Amat, and
that I faced the enemies of Ashur across a narrow divide of mountains.

I had only to glance at the tablets which awaited me after my
return from Urartu.

Among them was a letter from the king: "Why have you not
sent me any word?" it began. "Have bandits cut your throat and
left you for dead in some rocky gully, or have you forgotten those
who love you? I am an old man, beset with many troubles, and
my eyes hunger for the sight of you. Send me some message that I
may know you live and remember your father's name."

Before my first morning in Amat had ended, I picked up a
stylus and wrote out my reply:

To the King my lord, your servant Tiglath Ashur. May it be
well with you the King my lord. May Ashur and Shamash be
gracious to the King my lord. I have been on campaign north

of the Bohtan River and beg to send you word of a great triumph. . . .

I described to him the battle, the courage of the Scythians, my meetings with their headman Tabiti, and the alliance into which I had entered in his name. And I told him of the seventeen *mina* of gold I had extracted from the Urartians and gave my impression of that place.

This is not a friendship to support us, for their king is a fool and the might of their armies no more than a boulder in the stream, around which, when the moment comes, the vast numbers of the mountain tribesmen will pour quickly enough—one need only look to the example of the Scythians. I think the snow which chokes their valleys and the passes over their mountains for seven months of the year a greater barrier against the nomads than all their might. I think we must look to ourselves for safety.

And I begged the Lord Sennacherib to send reinforcements that I might lead a series of campaigns against the eastern tribes. And I begged his permission to keep the gold and use it to support and strengthen the garrison.

The king's reply, when it came, made almost no reference to my report. The northern borders, it seemed, were too far away to interest him greatly. His concerns were nearer to his own bosom, and it was his pleasure to be querulous.

Your brother the Lord Donkey vexes me almost daily about Babylon. Can you credit that he would rebuild the city we were at such pains to destroy? He claims to fear the wrath of Marduk.

He sits in Calah—out of my reach, or so he seems to imagine—surrounded by his magicians and his priests, and gives himself the airs of a king already. He fancies himself such a favorite of heaven that if he chances to wake up with a headache after a night of drinking, or if his favorite harlots come down with lice, he must be consulting the omen books to read the meaning of such strange and unnatural events. That, at least, is what they tell me. All men should have proper reverence for the gods, but even a king may dare to squat and empty

his bowels without first consulting the soothsayers. I see his
mother's busy hand in all this nonsense. . . .

Yes, very well. Work your own will about the gold, and I
will send you seven new companies of infantry and five of horse
after the spring floods. I wish, my son, that you would return to
Nineveh to fetch them yourself. Would that you could be here
with me once again, for if your exile is bitter, so is mine.

When one's father is a king and one's brother is the heir, one is
wise to tread lightly around such items of family gossip. I did not,
therefore, respond in my next letter to these complaints about
Esarhaddon. Instead, I asked after the Lord Sennacherib's health,
and suggested that if he was low-spirited he should keep his diet
spare and take more exercise, recommending hunting as good for
the liver. Beyond this, I described to him such improvements as I
planned to make in the garrison buildings, and I made it clear
that these improvements would include a palace for myself to be
built within the fortress walls. I wished him to understand that I
regarded myself as fixed in Amat for some time to come and had
no idea of returning to Nineveh. He would have to work out his
difficulties with the *marsarru* without reference to me.

If the king was chastened, however, he gave no sign of it. For
all the years I lived in the north, he kept me regularly informed
about "the Lord Donkey"—I hardly remember him referring to
Esarhaddon under any other name.

The king my father, who claimed to have had but two ambitions for his reign, to destroy forever the power of Babylon and to
hand over the Land of Ashur to one worthy of succeeding him—
and who witnessed in Esarhaddon the frustration of both these
aims—the Lord Sennacherib, Lord of the Earth's Four Corners,
now decayed almost from hour to hour into sulking old age.

All his letters to me he wrote with his own hand, for he
trusted no scribe. And he wrote with most unkingly candor, so his
mind was open to me and I had no difficulty in reading there the
bitterness of one who had wearied of life.

But I told myself that these things no longer concerned me,
that I was a garrison commander and a *shaknu* and no more, that
my share in the management of the state was confined to a stretch
of mountain waste. I was now a prince in nothing except name
and lineage, and it was my business to be the king's soldier. The
name of that king was no longer my affair.

* * *

Kephalos, even before my return, had purchased for himself the largest house Amat had to offer—a cramped little warren by the standards of the palace he had inhabited in Nineveh, but large enough for reasonable comfort. The difficulty, of course, was that my servant's notions of comfort were anything except reasonable.

"I pray you, Lord, to excuse the poverty of my table," he announced the first time I came to dinner there, "but the kitchen in this place is a smoky box. My cook can hardly see for wiping the soot from her eyes and, as no doubt you understand, luxury is not to be expected under such conditions."

I looked at the silver dishes in front of me and beheld as great a variety of foods as even the king in Tushpa had regarded as sufficient against the gluttony of foreign visitors. Duck prepared after the Hittite manner, lamb roasted in spices, honeyed locusts, fried fish, barley, pumpkin, lentils, several varieties of cheese, and an abundance of fruit almost past imagining. The wine, of course, had been looted from my own cellar.

"In such a wilderness, one must accustom oneself to privation," he went on, sighing loudly before washing his fingers in a small bronze bowl and accepting a towel to dry them from one of the four or five serving girls, each more beautiful than the last, who floated in and out of the room as silently as ghosts.

"Perhaps, with effort and a little good fortune, we can make of the place something worthy of you," I said dryly, for his self-pity was comic enough.

"Yes, Lord—riches relentlessly follow at the heels of power, and I have always known that in your service I would contrive to die a wealthy man." He glanced up, his eyes twinkling with what might have been either greed or irony. "Allow me, after we have eaten, to put before you certain plans I have drawn up in accordance with your instructions. I fancy you will not be displeased."

My purposes were nothing if not grandiose. I would extend the fortress's outer wall to encompass an area nearly five times the size of the present compound, and this extension would be carried out in stone, which luckily was to be found in considerable abundance in the mountains only a day's march distant. It threatened to be no small task, but I would need the space because it was also part of my design to raise the strength of the Amat garrison from thirty companies to a hundred, and that within five years.

And from this need for haste proceeded, paradoxical as it

might seem, the intention to use stone. Brickmaking required the heat of the summer sun, but stone could be quarried and cut even in winter. Besides, I had three thousand soldiers to keep occupied until the next campaign season.

Other work must necessarily follow. There would be barracks to build, and the kitchens, offices, workships, and stables would have to be extended. An army such as the one I envisioned would require parade grounds to train on and hordes of craftsmen in leather and metal to keep them outfitted. And since soldiers and craftsmen and scribes must all be paid, and must have somewhere to spend their money, the amusements of the town itself would have to be enhanced—but this, I suspected, was a matter which could be trusted to take care of itself.

There was work enough to last several years, but thanks to Kephalos we made a good start that winter. The quarries were surveyed and within a month the first great blocks of stone had begun to make their way toward Amat on log rollers.

The men of Ashur are great builders. This is the real secret of their success as conquerors—they understand so completely the arts of fortification that almost any city against which they lay siege is doomed, for those who would undermine a wall must first know how it was constructed. Thus, in the armies of the god no man is a soldier only; he will also have abilities as a carpenter, a mason, a joiner, or perhaps even an architect. And thus I had at my command all the skilled workmen I required.

But skill can only do so much. The earth cannot be dug by magic, and stone blocks, no matter how perfectly their corners have been squared, will not move of their own will. To do these things required a vast force of men with no talents beyond strong muscles and a willing pair of hands.

This difficulty, however, did admit of a solution, since my appointment as *shaknu* carried with it the customary powers of impressment. Besides, we found the local farmers, idle enough during the winter months, more than willing to work at the rate of half a copper shekel a day—such a sum, small as it was, could buy a bushel of dates, and among these folk a bushel of dates was wealth almost beyond imagining.

By the month of Tebet, when there was already a finger's depth of snow upon the ground and the quarry workers split away their blocks of stone by pouring water into the cracks they had made with iron axes and letting the water freeze overnight, the

great new wall of our fortress had risen already to the height of a
man's waist, and I was able to hope that it would be finished
within two years' time. My own palace, which would also be the
military headquarters and seat of government for the northern
provinces, was proceeding even faster. I had hopes it would be
ready for occupation by the season of flooding.

The men of Ashur live by farming and war, and these are
occupations which belong to the long hot months of summer,
after the cold has unclenched its fist and the floods have come and
gone. In winter we sharpen our swords and repair our granaries
and wait. It is the season when, for want of anything better to do,
a man turns in upon himself. It is the season for memory and
tormenting dreams. It is the season of the bitter heart.

Hence I was more than eager to keep myself busy. Had I
been posted to the south, where there was no stone, I would have
enjoyed a wretched enough time, but in Amat there was hardly
any interval to indulge a taste for misery. In the mornings I
worked at my desk; I saw my officers, read reports, and attended
to the hundreds of little tasks by which a garrison of three thousand men is kept warm, fed, and orderly. And in the afternoons I
mounted my horse and rode out to see how the work was pro-
gressing. It was only in the evenings that my brain was tempted
by dark shadows, and even then I tried to keep myself busy—and
if I could not find some piece of business I feasted my officers or
went to Kephalos's house to talk nonsense. And there was Naiba.

And it is no small pleasure to watch walls and buildings
slowly rising at one's command. By the time we began to feel the
first hint of warmer weather, the great fortress walls had risen to
the height of a man's head, three of the new barracks were ready
to receive their occupants, and my own palace, except for the roof
and the interiors of the rooms, was nearly finished and I had
hopes of being able to move in within a few months. I took great
delight in all this, and that delight compensated for much.

For I was then still a very young man, and a young man,
whatever his disappointments, cannot remain afflicted forever. I
had a task in life, something to make every day seem important,
and my flesh was not deprived of its comforts. If I had my black
moments to live through—particularly when the oil lamp had
been snuffed out and I had spent my seed and must wait for sleep
to close my eyes—they were only moments, to be measured

against long hours of forgetfulness and an easy mind. I was, if not happy, at least content.

But by the time the snow had started to vanish from the ground and the floodwaters were rising again, I was beginning to feel restless. The work proceeded well and did not depend on my day-to-day supervision, and the reinforcements from Nineveh could not arrive before the end of Iyyar, and that gave me over two months. Amat could not hold me. I was like an animal in a cage, rubbing its sides against the bars to make its place of confinement as large as possible. I decided on a tour of the provinces.

The villages of the north are small and widely separated, for the land is not as fertile as it is in the south. My new subjects would be too poor to entertain their *shaknu* and a large force of his soldiers without considerable hardship, and I would not be seen as a mere plunderer. Besides, it was part of my object to make these people understand that the garrison at Amat, to which they paid their taxes and sent their menfolk impressed as laborers, was there to protect them. What would they think if it appeared that not even I felt safe to travel within my own territories without an army at my back? How secure in his life and his property was then any man? Thus I set off with a bodyguard of only ten men.

It was a cold morning on which we began our journey, the coldest in many days. The frozen breath of our horses made great plumes in the air, and the fields of stubble left over from the autumn harvest were shining with ice. Naiba stood on the porch of my house, a blanket wrapped around her shoulders, watching with that look of doubt that women have when the men go off on their incomprehensible errands. I smiled at her and swung up onto my mount. It seemed a fine time to be alive.

We followed the Upper Zab south until just after noon and then struck out for the east, entering a line of fertile valleys nourished by a river which appeared as no more than a thread on any map I had ever seen and was bounded on either side by ranges of mountains the names of which none among us could even guess. The river, swollen by the melting snow, was already a torrent, and we could hear quite plainly along its bottom the sounds of huge stones being rolled downstream by its violence. The land on the opposite bank was much more level and open, but it was not until almost evening of the second day that we found a spot at which we could risk a crossing. I could not remember when I had ever felt water as cold as that.

On the morning of the third day, only a little more than an hour after breaking camp, we rode into the first village we had seen since leaving Amat. Perhaps sixty or seventy families, living in the collection of mud-brick buildings, made up this one community, which might have existed on the same spot for easily a thousand years.

Following the etiquette which governs such matters—for even the king's *shaknu* must not imagine the men of Ashur will consent to be treated like a conquered race—I stopped my horse some twenty paces from the village perimeter and waited. In his good time, the village elder, a white-haired, leathery old man with a face like a lion, came out to meet me, his staff of office in his right hand. He bowed, just low enough to be polite without implying servility, and stood in silence.

"You have the look of one in authority," I said. "I bring you greetings from our dread lord, the King in Nineveh, the Servant of the God, the Lord of the World. I am his *shaknu,* and my name is Tiglath Ashur."

"It is a name known even here, my Lord Prince. And I welcome you, the mighty son of a mighty father, as if you were the king himself."

That night the village feasted us on fresh-killed lamb. And I was the guest in the elder's house, where I drank beer with him and his sons and his son's sons. Outside I could hear the laughter of my soldiers, most of whom had probably been born in such a place as this and thus doubtless felt very much at home. I too, though raised in the Lord Sennacherib's court, felt the comfortable familiarity of these whitewashed walls, within which, in a sense, all the men of Ashur have been born, for the village is the root of our lives.

All of us, the elder and his progeny and their guest the *shaknu,* sat on reed mats upon the floor, drinking from pottery jars and enjoying the brazier's fire. And the old man told me of the days when he had been a soldier in the army of the great king Tiglath Pileser, who had made war in the western lands.

"I was but a boy then, and had never been more than half a day's journey from my father's threshold. I was privileged to serve under the Lord Sargon, who became king himself in the next reign but one. He was a mighty man—but for your leather-colored hair and your blue eyes, you, Lord, might almost be his ghost."

"I am not fit even to be his shadow, Old Father, but I am flattered if you think my grandfather lives in me a little. I was born in the hour of his death and this, I fear, is the only legacy I have from him."

I opened my hand to show them the birthmark on the palm.

"I remember the blood star which ushered you into the world—and the Lord Sargon out," the old man said gravely, shaking his head. "It is a fearful thing to be thus marked by the god. It makes me thank the might of Ashur that I was born to a humble destiny."

"To be a prince and live in a golden house must not be so punishing a fate."

It was one of the grandsons who spoke, a man of about my own age but very far gone in drink.

"I would not spurn to be a king's son—ask the Lord Tiglath Ashur if he would trade places."

In the silence that followed, he swallowed hard and lowered his eyes to the ground.

"This fool sprung from my own loins meant no disrespect, Prince," the elder said at last. I could only grin, as if at a joke, and touch his beer jar with my own.

"And none was taken, Old Father. You both speak the truth, for a man's life is what he makes it. If he is wretched in a golden house he has no one to blame but himself."

"No, Prince—a man's life is what the god makes it."

In every village we were received with warm hospitality, for the men of Ashur respect their king and his servants and do not disdain the stranger in their midst. I found that my name had preceded me even to these remote places, which gratified my pride but did not make me once again so willing to speak of my father's fathers, nor did I again show anyone the mark on my palm. I had been boasting, after a fashion—for I was proud to be descended of great kings—and I had been punished for it. I did not delight to be reminded that I was nought but the god's plaything.

We proceeded down this line of valleys until we found a pass in the mountains. Then we crossed the pass and headed back toward the Upper Zab, for I wished to cross it before the floodwaters had risen enough to make the pontoon bridges unusable. It was the month of Nisan, on the day when the New Year's festival would be ending in Nineveh and the god's idol returned to his temple, when we entered the western part of the lands under my authority.

These places are little cultivated by men, and it was not unusual for us to go several days without finding a village or a plowed field. But the weather was mild and there was no shortage of game for hunting, so we felt no privation. Because I was curious—and felt no desire to return to Amat before the time—I led my little troop once more into the high country, into places where only the caravans travel, where none are at home except spirits. I would have felt content to wander there forever.

At last, in the middle of the day, after cresting a line of hills, we saw before us a great mountain. It was not part of any range but stood alone, like a proud king who will endure no comparison. It seemed to confront us without warning. The summit was lost in mist, secluded and holy.

We had been traveling more or less at random, following no specific trail and with no goal in sight, and yet, as I looked up at those rocky slopes, all might and grandeur, I could not overcome the impression that somehow I had been brought to this place, that I had found what, without knowing it, I had been seeking all along.

There was one among my soldiers who, having been born in a village not three days' ride away, could make some claim to knowing the country. I summoned him forward and pointed.

"What is that ahead of us?" I asked him.

"That is Mount Epih, *Rab Shaqe,*" he answered, smiling as if the sight of it filled him with pleasure. "It is the dwelling place of Mighty Ashur, as old as the world."

"Then you have been here before?"

"Oh, no, *Rab Shaqe,* for its precincts are forbidden. But it could be no other. The god marks it as his own—see?"

Yes, I could see. Even through the clouds a dull yellow light was just visible, seeming to flicker slightly like an oil lamp left by the window.

"The summit is never without its mantle of clouds," he went on, "but the god declares himself. They say that when the light disappears it will mean that Ashur has deserted his people and consigned them to destruction."

"And the mountain is forbidden?"

"Yes, *Rab Shaqe*. None may venture there save those whom the god summons—at least, none may return. They leave their bones to bleach on the dead stone and their souls will wander forever, with none to make them offerings of wine and food. It is a place best left to itself."

"I come from Mount Epih," the *maxxu* had told me, so long ago. *"Do you know it?"* And I had answered that I did not, saying that few have been there. *"Few have, yes. But you will one day."* It seemed that the day had at last arrived.

"We will camp at the foot tonight," I said, watching his eyes grow wide with pious dread. "And tomorrow I will climb the mountain. Do not fear—I believe that I have been summoned." I smiled at him, for he was afraid.

"We will know, will we not, if I come down again."

"Yes, *Rab Shaqe*. We will know then."

My soldiers were not enthusiastic for this latest of their commander's freaks. My orders were met with a glum silence, and when we had ridden within half a *beru* of the mountain they all stopped their horses together and waited for me to turn and face them. I could see from the expressions on their faces that they meant to go no farther.

The *ekalli*, who had fought at the Bohtan River and was a good man, not easily frightened, swept his hand sidewise through the air in a gesture of apology.

"We would follow you into the jaws of death," he said, as if ashamed to admit it. "There is no enemy with whom we would fear to do battle for your sake, *Rab Shaqe*. You know all this. But we fear to offend the god, and now you would have us profane the ground of his holy place with our footprints. We beg you, *Rab Shaqe* . . ."

"Do not distress yourself, Sinduri," I said, touched by this appeal, which fell just short of mutiny. I could not bring myself to blame them, for they were right to dread this which I would do, and it was not my place to involve them in the god's wrath. "We will stop here, away from Ashur's precinct, and tomorrow I will go on alone. If I do wrong, none will suffer for it save myself alone."

This satisfied them, and we pitched our tents by a spring that gushed from the bare rock like an omen of peace. We set our cooking fires and ate and each man felt safe as he prepared to close his eyes.

I did not sleep that night. I was not afraid but I felt a strange excitement, such as a man might feel on his wedding day. But I felt as if I had come to the verge of that discovery for which each of us searches as long as the life is quick within us. I was then still just young enough not to fear that.

The hour before dawn brought a thunderstorm. There was no rain and the sky was clear of lightning, but the angry, rolling boom of the thunder was enough to shatter a man's skull. We sat around our dead fire, wrapped in our cloaks, terrified, waiting for the light of morning.

"Do not do this thing which is in your heart, *Rab Shaqe*," they pleaded. "The god, who sees through our every thought like water, is angry. No *sedu*, though yours is mighty, can protect you from the wrath of Ashur."

"I will go," I said, for all that my courage was shaken like a reed in the wind. "The god merely announces himself. If I am afraid of a little noise I am not worthy to come into his presence."

But I was afraid. Even after the storm had passed and the sun shone, I could not eat any breakfast. Yet this seemed a thing I must do, although why I could not have said.

After performing the rituals of purification and making offerings of bread and salt and the cuttings from my beard, I said good-bye to my comrades, almost like one going to his death, and put aside all my weapons, save only the sword, which is Ashur's special symbol.

"The day after tomorrow is an evil day," the *ekalli* Sinduri told me, looking like a man about to bury his brother. "Thus you must be down from the mountain by tomorrow night."

"If I am not back by then, you may assume that the god has taken my life."

"We will wait, and offer prayers and sacrifice that Ashur may forgive you this folly."

Thus we parted, while the grass was still wet with dew.

At the foot of the mountain I took off my sandals, knelt, and laid them beside the path that the god might see I wished not to profane his holy place and would not touch it with any flesh but that of my own living body, that I submitted myself to his will. Thus I began the climb that would bring I knew not what.

I was soon out of sight of our camp, for the trail I followed for the first six hours, until well after midday, wound its way about the mountain like a coiled snake. Each step took me only a little higher, and the way was narrow and covered in places with loose rubble, sharp little stones on which I cut my feet many times. It seemed to wander on and on, rising little by little, slowly wearing me down like the wind smoothing a stone. Yet it was still recognizably a trail. I was glad to have it, for it did not last forever.

Eventually I left even that behind and found myself scrambling over crumbled granite, where I held on to cracks in the rock or the odd bush that always threatened to pull loose with the first tug, or faces of smooth stone that had baked in the pale sun until they were as hot as the walls of a potter's kiln. And always I seemed to be pulling myself straight up, a cubit at a time. There was no end to it. Ashur, it seemed, meant to guard his secrets well.

After the third hour past noon I threw myself down to rest in the shade of an overhang, too weary to go on until I could catch my breath. My legs and arms, even my chest, ached with weariness. I could not remember ever having been so spent. And I was still, it seemed, many hours of climbing from the summit.

I would never make it, I decided. So exhausted, I would surely commit some clumsy blunder and scatter my brains on the rocks below. And besides, it would soon be dark. To climb in the dark is to invite death.

I could have turned back, stopping for the night if the light failed me and climbing down the rest of the way the next morning, but it never occurred to me to do so. There would have been no point, since I had already come so far, for no man may flee the god's wrath. There was no possible way except up, where I would live or die by Ashur's will, since I had placed myself in his hands.

After a while I decided it was time to go on again and stood up. There was a narrow ledge of rock that seemed to taper into nothing around the curve of the mountain slope—not a very promising direction but the only one open to me. I pressed my back against the smooth, featureless granite cliff and began making my cautious way forward.

As soon as I was out of sight of my resting place, I could see that the ledge widened into a path rising steeply up the face of the mountain. It seemed to proceed without hindrance, leading straight up. The god, after all, had delivered me from death.

It was an easy path, and one which others had used before me. For a thousand years the holy men of my race had come here to be received into the god's presence and to search his designs for the men of Ashur.

Here and there I found bits of writing scratched onto the rocks—the first lines of prayers, sometimes only the god's name. Sometimes the words were almost worn away.

I had been brought here for a purpose—brought here, for I understood now that I had come not through my own will but because it was the pleasure of one whose instrument I had somehow become. He who had made the earth and sky from the corpse of the slain Tiamat, who had made man from the river clay and revealed to him all skill, all knowledge, all wisdom, this same had set my foot upon this journey.

Even as I followed the rising path, the god gave me notice of his presence. I saw two omens, one of evil and one of good. In the dust at my feet I found spilled water tracing the pattern of a snake, a sign that I would know evil in my life. The water was still beaded upon the earth, as if it had just been laid down. Perhaps a hundred paces farther on, I startled a covey of quail that flew away to the left. How water could have come to be spilled there, where hardly even the rain visits, I do not know. Why birds should nest in such a place, where there is not a blade of grass to feed them, I do not know. I could understand these things only as the will of Ashur, who meant me to grasp that I would taste of both evil and good, first the one and then the other.

Ashur's sun was just turning red over the western horizon when the trail ended in a path of level ground, as bare as if it had been smoothed with a trowel. This was the summit—there was nowhere else to go. I sat down, wrapping my cloak around me, and watched the darkness gather.

I cannot account for the light by which it is said the god declares his presence in that place. It is clearly visible from the ground, seeming to bathe the mountain's peak, hidden by the clouds, in a divine radiance. Yet as I sat there, on the very crown, I was alone in the cold black night. In his sanctuary, Mighty Ashur hides himself. It remains a mystery.

There was a chill wind that blew in fits and starts, like a teasing woman, but I hardly had the strength even to shiver. I was more than weary, since I had eaten nothing that day and felt giddy with weakness, but my cloak was my only protection against the cold, and above a certain level of physical misery sleep becomes impossible. I would keep a vigil through the night, I thought, and perhaps the god would reveal himself to me.

I took my sword from its scabbard and thrust it point-first into the soft earth. It would be my altar in this barren place.

I waited. The wind dropped, but the cold hardened like ice. It sank through my cloak, into my flesh, into my very bones. If the stars shone or the moon had risen, they were hidden from my sight. I could hold a hand up in front of my face and not distinguish the fingers. There was nothing to divide one hour from the next. Even my brain seemed to have stopped.

It must have been a dream, although I was never conscious of having slept. I never started awake—the dream merely faded, leaving me blank, empty, and then the first glimmer of dawn brought with it a return to life. But it could only have been a dream, for the things which happen in dreams never come as a shock, and what was shown to me that dead night, had I been awake to see them with the sensible eye, would have broken my mind like a dry reed. And yet the dream was no less true for having been a dream, and what I saw was no more than what came to pass.

Ashur is the very light of truth. He is the sun that shines everywhere, and he blinds men with his glory. He blinded the *maxxu* that he might reveal to him the things which would be. He blinds other men that they should pass through the world seeing nothing else. If I saw him that night—and I will die believing none else—then I saw him as light and fire.

I saw many things that night, and understood none of them. I was not the *maxxu,* blind to the shadows of things, seeing only the truth. I would return from the mountain still blinded by the world, believing that the truth was a dream and the dream truth.

I saw the great Tigris, mother of rivers, her waters burning. I stood on the bank across from Nineveh and watched the city of men disappear behind a curtain of flames. Did the burning waters consume her? I did not know. I only knew that she was lost to me forever and that I could not enter her gates again.

And then, all at once, I was in the city, and the city was a cage of iron, and my brother Esarhaddon was without, dressed in the uniform of a common soldier, his face twisted with hate as he beat against the bars with his sword. And then the door to the cage opened, and Esarhaddon pointed with his sword out to the trackless wastes and said, "Go!" And the cage disappeared from around me and I was alone in the world.

And I saw my father, Sennacherib, the great king, worshiping before the image of the god. His robes were of gold, but he was an old man and his hair had turned white and his strength had left him. His glory was as nothing, and god crushed him beneath his wooden hand.

And the hand of the god became Esarhaddon's hand, holding my own. I felt his fingers grow slack in my grasp.

And then everything faded away into a clean, white light that filled the world, leaving room for none. That was how the dream ended, in a blinding light.

It ended, and I was alone once more in the darkness. I do not know how long I waited before the dawn came. Time seemed to have stopped forever.

But the dawn did come. Soon I could see the outline of my sword, still stuck in the earth. When I tried, I discovered that I could not pull it free. I pulled until I thought my back would break, but it would not yield. It seemed to have become anchored to the foundations of the world. Finally I left it there.

I hardly remember the journey back down the mountain. I was almost too weary to put one foot in front of another and my mind buzzed like a hornets' nest—over and over again these strange and troubling dreams returned to me, like the ghosts of slaughtered men haunting their murderer. But the god must have protected my every step, for at last, with the approach of night, I reached level ground. I could already see the soldier's campfire.

"*Rab Shaqe,* you have returned! Indeed the god must have blessed you above all men."

"I would hardly call it a blessing," I said in a toneless voice as I sat down before the fire, staring into its flames as the *ekalli* Sinduri threw a blanket over my shoulders, for I must have left my cloak on the mountaintop and I was shivering with cold. My brain felt numb. When at last I could be brought to understand what he wished for me, I accepted a cup of wine from his hands and drank it greedily.

"You have returned alive from a fearful and holy place, *Rab Shaqe.* That is blessing enough."

"Yes, but he has put his curse upon me for my impertinence, Sinduri. He has shown me the future but has kept its meaning from my grasp. I believe I am condemned only to recognize it when at last it comes."

21

◈◈◈◈◈

In ways I would have found difficult to explain, this one encounter with the inexplicable changed me forever. Or perhaps
it might be more honest to say that it changed not me but the
terms in which I understood myself. What I had gained on the
summit of Mount Epih I could not have said—not then, at any
rate—but what I had lost was clear enough. The god had stripped
me of my sense of power. He had made me the witness to events
over which I was to have no control. He had taught me that I was
nothing, that I had no will, that I was merely the instrument of a
future the course of which his contrivance alone would settle.
Man, for all the arrogance of his pitiful strength, has no power.
There is no power under heaven but that of fate, which is no more
than Mighty Ashur's pleasure.

It was enough to learn on one journey. I was weary of the
lesson and desired no more to wander into strange adventures. We
turned our horses into the rising sun and headed home. The ride
back to Amat took us ten more days.

At last we came within sight of the garrison, with the town,
on the other side, closer to the river, hidden behind it. I was
pleased to see that the fortress wall had risen another two cubits
in height since our departure. As we drew near, the soldiers, taken
by surprise in their labors, dropped the tools they had been using
and rushed to greet us with cheers. "Ashur is King! Ashur is
King!" sounded from many throats, and men held out their hands
to touch me as I rode past. Even Kephalos, fat as a brood sow,
came running up the road, his arms held high in the air, shouting
like a caravan driver.

"So!" he panted, slapping my horse's withers as he walked beside me. "You have not left your bones to dry in the wilderness after all. See how the wall goes up? These mongrel dogs of camp soldiers will work even faster now that you are home, Master, for they have made you their heart."

I looked down into his bloated, shining face and felt a rush of joy and gratitude that the gods had granted me youth and life and the loyal love of this thieving foreigner. I almost said as much, but then, laughing loudly, was just able to stop myself.

"It looks as if you too have been sweating, Worthy Physician —although I do not notice it has made you any the leaner."

Then we were both able to laugh. I was home—Amat, it seemed, was now my home, and I was glad of it.

"Dine with he tonight, Kephalos, and tell me all the news."

"No, Lord," he answered, shaking his head. "You dine with me, for your cook is only a soldier who knows how to cook nothing except goat flesh sauced with its own stale fat. I will, however, allow you to drink such of your own wines as I have condescended to steal from you."

The table was spread before us with plates of fruit, honeyed locusts, spiced lamb's meat, and strange, sweet-smelling millet. There was wine in golden cups and a pretty slave girl named Sahish to pour it. Life on the frontiers of empire had done nothing to curb my servant's taste for luxury.

"Did your tour go well, Master?" he inquired, in the polite tone that indicated as clearly as any words that he regarded me as a great fool who had been wasting his time on profitless wandering. "I trust you noticed that while you were gone I raised the garrison wall to twice a man's height."

He puffed out his chest, at the same time allowing his hand to wander down the girl's shoulder until the thumb rested on her breast. As if she understood this as some manner of signal, she refilled his wine cup almost to the rim.

"So high as that, Kephalos?" I said, finding it difficult not to laugh. "And by your own labors, I'll wager, without a soul to help you!"

He merely shrugged, as if no jest could wound such dignity as his.

"It will soon come to that, Master, for, as you know, the

impressed workers will shortly be returning to their fields. Building will proceed slowly enough from now until the end of the warm weather."

"So be it. A great city is not the work of one winter, and we will both be here to push the task on for many years to come."

Kephalos did not look much encouraged by the prospect. He sat in silence for a moment.

"You have received letters in your absence," he told me at last, and in a low voice, leaning back against the cushions that surrounded him on his banqueting chair. "From Nineveh, bearing the king's seal—and another from Calah. The riders came five days ago, within hours of each other."

"And I suppose you have no idea what might be in them?" I asked, wondering at his tone—what should surprise anyone about my receiving letters from the king?

"Ah, Master . . ." Kephalos twisted uncomfortably in his seat. "When would I presume to let my eyes rest upon your private correspondence? And besides, you know I command no more than some few dozen symbols in the dagger-shaped writing."

"Kephalos . . ."

"Lord?" He smiled painfully, since he would have the truth wrung out of him—we both knew perfectly well that my scribes, whom he bribed, were as much in his employ as my own.

"Speak, Kephalos. What is the news of Calah?"

"Nothing, Lord. Only that the Lord Esarhaddon plans to inspect the garrison this summer . . ."

" 'Inspect'?" I repeated—I could hardly believe it. " 'Inspect'? He uses this word to me?"

"Yes, Lord. He uses the word."

"And what else?"

"And he wishes to announce the impending birth of a son. He says that the diviners are quite certain the lady Esharhamat will be brought to the labor of a son, no later than the last ten days of the month of Iyyar."

The same thought, I imagine, was on both our minds. I had last seen Esharhamat on the sixteenth day of Ab, and Kephalos could count to nine as well as anyone.

With an irritation born of that consciousness, he peered into his now empty wine cup and frowned.

"Sahish, you lazy slut," he shouted in Akkadian, "shall your master and his guest be left to perish of thirst? Be about your duties, girl, or you'll find yourself sweeping out the sleeping chambers in a brothel!"

The king's letter contained no word of Esharhamat. If his son and successor was about to be blessed with an heir my father did not see fit to mention it to me—perhaps the prospect was not very much to his taste, since his message consisted principally of abuse of Esarhaddon.

"The Donkey has been in the south, worshiping at the shrines of the old Sumerian gods and collecting sorcerers—one supposes that even the great are entitled to their diversions. I am constantly pestered with warnings that I must rebuild Babylon before the patience of heaven is exhausted, and perhaps some gesture in that direction is necessary before this division between us becomes a focus for dissent. The Donkey is not popular, so I am forced to clear his way to the throne all the more carefully.

"He proposes to make a tour of the north and no doubt thinks to overawe you with his new splendor. As you love him better than I do, I wish you pleasure in his visit. Certainly it will do him no harm to be separated from his mother for the space of a few months. Since I have grown old and lost my pleasure in her fair flesh, I can see clearly the error I committed by covering her with a veil and calling her 'wife,' but the gods punish old men by opening their eyes to follies which cannot be undone.

"Ghosts flutter about my head and I am oppressed in spirit. My son, has it all been wasted . . . ?"

But if my father could hear only the beating wings of death, all the world around him was awakening to the new year. Each day the sun shone a little longer as it melted the last of the winter snows. The Upper Zab, its waters heavy with their burden of silt, was near its crest. Life had ceased to feel such a vexation.

Since the new barracks were almost finished, I sent some ten of my officers south to collect the reinforcements which would begin their march to Amat as soon as the flooding ended. They had orders to stop at Three Lions on their return and to bring my mother and some of her women with them. The first phase of my life in this place had ended, and I now longed for so much of a settled existence as a soldier can expect. I looked forward to her coming, and to the season of campaigning which would begin with the hot weather.

The night of my return was the last I spent in my rooms at the old garrison headquarters, for the next morning saw the beginning of our move to the new palace. The offices and public rooms were still unfinished, but my own wing, where I could live not as *shaknu* but as a private man, was ready to receive me.

My mother's chamber still smelled of wet plaster, but I ordered that the wooden floor be sanded and polished with wax so that all would be ready against her arrival. Naiba worked from dawn to dark in the arrangement of our new household, tiring herself with anxiety that all should be ready to receive the Great Lady Merope, as she called her. Naiba was, after all, still little more than a child and I could not convince her that she had nothing to fear, that the Great Lady was a mild, harmless creature who had herself been a slave in a lord's house.

Naiba was a stranger here—like my mother, like myself. We were an odd enough match, she and I. I could not help wonder what my mother would make of it all when she arrived.

But the spring would bring the answer—to that and many other questions. There was nothing to do except to wait as the river, having bestowed its gift, went back once more into its own banks and the farmers began again to yoke their oxen to the plow. My soldiers, grown cranky with boredom, talked of campaigns and loot, and once more the battle squares of Ashur's army formed upon the parade grounds at Amat. It was the time for new undertakings, when once more anything seemed possible.

It was on the first day of Iyyar that outriders brought back word that wagons, cavalry, and columns of infantry had been seen less than three days' march from the city. I gave orders to make ready to receive the twelve companies of reinforcements the king had promised.

But even before they arrived, when I rode out to count their lines in the distance, I discovered there were only eight, five of foot and three of horse. The dispatches they carried contained no explanation, so it was simply necessary that I content myself with less.

Still, they made a noble show when they marched up to the fortress gates to present their standards. We could hear the throb of their war drums an hour before the first sentry shouted down from the wall that he had seen their dust on the wind.

The citizens lined the roads to cheer and I, mounted on my horse with nearly the whole garrison assembled for parade, waited

to receive them at the gate. The drums grew louder and I had to
keep the reins tight on my horse, made skittish by the gathering
noise. I felt my heart beating within me as if in answer as it
swelled with a soldier's pride, for the armies of the god made a
fine sight.

At a few minutes after noon, the force commander, a *rab
abru* from his uniform, broke away from the lead column and at a
half-gallop came toward me up the road to fulfill the protocol of
presenting his compliments and reporting the numbers and dispo-
sitions of the companies. He was mounted on a fine black charger
and rode as if he was perfectly aware of the glorious spectacle
they made together. He was almost upon me before I recognized
him for Arad Malik, my royal brother, whom I had not seen since
our encounter under the walls of Babylon.

He reined his horse in to an abrupt halt, saluted, and handed
over to me his commander's baton. I could not have missed the
sly smile on his lips as I accepted it and our eyes met.

"I bring the king's greetings to the Lord *Shaknu,* the Royal
Prince, the Mighty Tiglath Ashur, the Scourge of Ashur," he
said, saluting once again. "And may I be allowed to include my
own?"

"I thank you, Royal Prince," I replied, wondering who could
have taught him such a speech. "And you are welcome, for I have
learned to see the past with a blind eye."

He showed his teeth in a grin—he had grasped my meaning
—and we rode back together to greet the troops.

"The Lady Merope and her women are in a wagon just behind the first column of infantry, where the dirt of travel is less of
an inconvenience."

I nodded—perhaps less of an expression of gratitude than he
expected, but I did not know why Arad Malik had come and I
wished not to commit myself.

The troops filed past, and I received and returned their salute. For just a moment I saw my mother's face behind the curtains of her wagon; she smiled and waved, perhaps a little tenta-
tively, as if unsure of her welcome. I could not wave, but I could
smile and that seemed to be enough.

"Most of them are still raw," Arad Malik said suddenly. It
was half a moment before I decided that he must be talking about
the reinforcements. "But there is a good leavening of veterans. Do
you plan to take them on campaign this season?"

"Yes—unless the Medes send an envoy to kiss my feet."

He laughed at this, just a shade louder than the joke had warranted, and we lapsed back into silence as the columns of soldiers passed by in review. I was conscious the whole time that he was watching me in his sidewise fashion, but I was careful not to meet his eye. Why, when we had detested each other from childhood, was he suddenly so ingratiating? And where had he, cloddish even by the standards of a soldiers' mess, learned these new arts of pleasing? I could only assume that time and circumstances would enlighten me.

When the last of the formalities were over and the eight new companies had been dismissed to find their barracks, I helped my mother down from her wagon and, with her women trailing silently behind us, led her to my new palace.

It had been three seasons of the year since I had last seen her and she seemed worn; that, however, might only have been the fatigue of the journey. As we walked she kept her hands clamped tight on my elbow, as if afraid of stumbling.

"I do not think you will find this place too unpleasant," I said, trying to smile as she looked up at me with moist, anxious eyes—she had often looked at me just that way, even when I was a child; it was the look of one who does not trust in the permanence of any happiness. "It is colder in the winter, but less oppressive in the summer. I have found that the climate agrees with me."

She did not answer, but smiled and glanced away, clutching my arm all the tighter.

"Have you eaten, Merope?"

She shook her head. "Not since yesterday morning, my son —I could not. I know it was foolish of me, but I . . ."

"Then you will eat now. We will feast together now, for tonight I must attend a banquet for my officers and those affairs tend to last until long after decent people have found their beds. Still, we have some few hours yet."

"Are you content, Lathikadas? And at peace?"

"Who in this wide world is at peace?" I answered, laughing uncomfortably. "I have learned to live with myself, which is no trifling thing, and I am occupied with work. I am not unhappy. It will be better now that you are here."

"And do you still think of her?"

It was not a question I cared to answer directly. I shrugged my shoulders and smiled again.

"I have a woman—a present from Kephalos, who understands the way of these things. You will meet her when we dine. I hope you will like her."

"If she pleases my son, I will like her."

We walked up the steps and across the stone veranda, and the guards opened the doors for us. For a moment, looking around her, my mother was lost in wonder.

"It is truly a palace," she said at last. "As if for a king."

"I am a king here, Merope—or, at least, I stand in the king's place and must keep up his dignity. But I promise not to lock you away in my house of women."

She laughed softly, and for the first time seemed able to be really happy. It was a beginning.

The walls of the banqueting hall were innocent of carved panels to immortalize my victories in war and my prowess in the hunt. This deficiency was much lamented by Kephalos, who thought it reflected badly on the *shaknu*'s majesty, but otherwise when my officers, new and old, appeared for the welcoming feast, they found nothing lacking that contributed to their comfort and pleasure. My good servant, ever mindful of the importance of appearances, had made that evening's food and entertainment his special concern. For three days his cook and a vast army of helpers had been busy preparing delicacies enough to sate many times the number of my guests and, looking about me as I entered, I had not realized that Amat could boast so many pretty harlots. There were even musicians. Since my arrival I had not heard the warble of so much as a single reed flute, but somewhere Kephalos had found musicians for the harlots to dance to.

"I have had to buy every drop of decent wine to be found in this doghole," he told me nervously, catching at my sleeve as I prepared to sit down. "I only pray, Lord, that it may be enough, but after an hour or two when everyone is sufficiently drunk, I shall begin substituting lesser vintages."

"I beg you not to be anxious, my friend—a soldier drinks only to be riotous and happy. That a wine be potent is the only requirement he knows how to make of it."

Indeed, judging from the din of the cheering that greeted me when I took my place at table, these men of Ashur were already quite drunk enough for present purposes.

I was in a fair way of being drunk myself before I noticed that there was one among my guests who was not a solider—nor ever could be. Sitting near a corner of the hollow square made by the banqueting tables, sober, largely disregarded by the men around him, sat my royal brother the scribe Nabusharusur, looking much the same as he had the last time we had met, on the eve of my first campaign, when we were both really still boys.

Sitting where he was, he might never have attracted my attention at all if one of the harlots, with a woman's spite against one whom she could not charm, had not begun to tease him, calling on her friends to notice his smooth eunuch's face and attempting to sit on his lap. Nabusharusur, as if accustomed to this sort of raillery, merely pushed her away and, for the rest, sat staring glumly at nothing.

I raised a hand to summon one of the guards.

"Chase that naked bitch out," I told him. "And give her a good hard spanking with the flat of your sword before you let her go, since she thinks it proper to annoy my guests. See to it that her backside is too tender to put on any man's lap for the next half month."

"It shall be as you would have it, *Rab Shaqe,*" he said, grinning. The order seemed very much to his taste.

"And ask the prince my brother the learned scribe if he would consent to join me."

When Nabusharusur came to my table I rose and took his hand, and the officers around me made room for him.

"I did not see you among the passing troops this afternoon," I said, simply to be saying something—this silent, unhappy figure was not an easy man to talk to.

"I do not sit a horse well," he answered. "I traveled in a wagon with your mother's women."

He smiled thinly, as if admitting to an obvious infirmity. It was his way of indicating that he was not grateful to me for my interference, that he had accepted his lot, if not with perfect grace, and would thank me to keep my generous impulses for the benefit of others. Somehow—I could not say how—his attitude inspired a certain respect.

"You wonder at my presence here?" he asked, smiling the

same thin, unhappy smile. "At why I would undertake such a journey? I am employed as a scribe by our brother Arad Malik."

"I would imagine he has need of one," I said, remembering the pretty speeches of this afternoon.

"Yes." The smile grew just a shade broader, as if to acknowledge the justice of my remark. "He is a dolt, but he has just wit enough to know it and to depend on me. I find him useful."

"As what? As someone to carry a sword for you?"

"As a counter against Esarhaddon." He shrugged his narrow, feminine shoulder, conscious that he was taking a risk and seemingly indifferent to it. "He is a soldier, a prince, and still a man. People respect him for these things, and when I put words into his mouth they listen."

"Playing at treason is a dangerous game, brother. Esarhaddon has a memory for slights, and he will be king one day."

"Does he? Will he? Who can know? In these matters the will of the god is all."

"The god has made his will plain already."

Nabusharusur said nothing, answering only with another shrug. I did not have the impression he was as concerned with the god's will as he suggested.

It was not a topic I had any strong interest in pursuing, so I joined his silence with my own and turned my eyes toward the performance taking place within the hollow square of tables, where one of the harlots, stripped naked and gleaming with oil, danced like a madwoman, shaking her breasts in time to the frantic drumbeat and moaning in what seemed an ecstasy of lust. My officers cheered her on and kept time by clapping their hands— one might imagine that none of them had ever seen such a dance, although it was like a hundred others I had witnessed on such occasions. I began to suspect that perhaps I was not drunk enough.

"I wonder that even a man untouched by the gelding knife can find these entertainments amusing," Nabusharusur murmured, as if confiding the thought to himself alone. "This woman, who would delight to sell herself to anyone for half a silver shekel, for a moment now she holds the attention of all. It is a strange thing, this power of the flesh. It is beyond the comprehension of a poor eunuch like myself."

"But I think, brother, that you understand other kinds of

power well enough, and they, too, live more in the mind than in the loins."

I had said perhaps more than I meant to. Our eyes met, and Nabusharusur smiled.

"It is well to know that not all the Lord Sennacherib's sons were born fools. We must speak again, Tiglath Ashur."

And we did, more than once in the ten days that my royal brothers stayed in Amat as guests of the garrison. Nabusharusur, with his thin arms and smooth face, was still as quick in his wits as when we were all boys together in Bag Teshub's schoolroom, and to this the years had added the cold cynicism of one for whom life holds no promises. A lump of earth like Arad Malik could be sufficiently brave in battle—judged simply as a soldier he was well enough—but courage in such men is largely lack of imagination. Nabusharusur was a different case entirely. He saw the truth with nerveless clarity; he feared nothing because he cared for nothing. For the working of mischief one Nabusharusur would always be worth a hundred Arad Maliks. The *marsarru* did not know it, but he had made a formidable enemy.

But it was Arad Malik who spent his time stirring up resentment against Esarhaddon among my officers. When whispers of it began to reach me, I sent not for the *rab abru* but for his scribe.

It was a warm day. We drank wine under the vine arbor in my garden. This was not a conversation I cared to have in the presence of any third person.

"It must stop," I told him. "I expect his visit within the next three months, and Esarhaddon knows how to make himself popular with soldiers. Arad Malik is putting himself under the shadow of the executioner's ax."

"Is he? He is safe enough while the king lives, who cares not what evil is whispered of his successor, and I think you overestimate the *marsarru*'s powers of pleasing. Besides, in the next reign, if Esarhaddon chances to be king, Arad Malik knows that his life will not be worth an hour's purchase."

"How does he know that?"

"From me—I have told him so. And he is on familiar enough terms with the hastiness of our good brother's temper to believe it."

"And what of you?" I asked, suspecting I already knew the answer. "Why have you made this alliance for yourself? It can mean nothing to you who is the next king."

"That is true—provided it is not Esarhaddon. Tell me, brother, can you credit simple spitefulness as a motive?"

Nabusharusur looked at me with an inquiring, faintly contemptuous expression on his face, as if he pitied me my lack of intellectual refinement.

"Do you know, Tiglath Ashur, what is the common gossip of Nineveh?" he went on finally. "Have you somehow escaped the rumor that the *baru* Rimani Ashur hanged himself in remorse for having broken faith with Shamas, Lord of Decision, in the matter of Esarhaddon's selection? Do you honestly believe that the god somehow preferred that thickheaded ox, who is fit for nothing except to sacrifice himself in battle, over yourself?"

There was a tree at the end of the garden in which several blackbirds were contending among themselves for roosting rights —for days the sky had been crisscrossed with their returning numbers. I could see their wings flapping heavily among the still bare branches, and their threatening, unmusical cries were probably audible even within the palace walls. I did not think of omens, but the sight of them made me wish for a stone with which to send them all flying.

"Why would Rimani Ashur have done such a thing?" I asked, hardly aware, until I heard the sound of my own voice, of what I intended. "What had he to gain? The priests, I know, wished to see Esarhaddon made heir, but what had the *baru* to fear from them while the king protected him?"

"There were some things from which not even the king could protect him." Nabusharusur's reply sounded as softly as the dripping of water. "It was the king's wrath which he had to fear, or so men say. For Rimani Ashur was subject to a weakness—an appetite, if you prefer—and this he fed on at the king's own table."

"An appetite? What appetite?"

"One in which I can have no share. And which you, Tiglath Ashur—if the stories one hears are to be believed—have already been sated."

22

I did not attempt to understand Nabusharusur's words—I did not wish to understand them. Even if what he said was true, I could not undo the damage of the past. Esarhaddon was accepted as the *marsarru,* and Esharhamat was his wife. Nabusharusur might not shrink from civil war, but I did. To quarrel with my brother's claim would be to soak the Land of Ashur in blood, and who could say that when we were finished the winner would have strength enough to be more than an easy meal for the nations that prowled at our borders like jackals around a wounded lion?

But I could not shut my mind to memory. I could not forget the look on Rimani Ashur's face when he beheld Shaditu's naked flesh as she made sacrifice on the day of the Akitu ceremony. I could not forget her words that last night in Nineveh: *"Tiglath Ashur, favorite of the gods, true king."* *"Did you think I would let that cold little bitch puppy have you?"* I could not will myself to be as witless as that.

Shaditu had seduced the *baru.* She must have threatened him afterwards—"I will tell the king," she must have said. "He is old and loves me blindly. I will tell him you raped me. He will give you such a death as no man would envy." And, Rimani Ashur, frightened of the king's wrath, had declared the omens in favor of my brother Esarhaddon.

The impiety of such an act was incredible, so that I could hardly bring my mind to accept its possibility. How would it have been possible for a man like Rimani Ashur to have committed such a betrayal of the god he had served all his life? Why? Merely to escape death? Such a deed was worse than death itself and, in the end, he had killed himself anyway. I could scarcely believe it. And yet I did believe it. I did not wish to, but I did.

I had less trouble crediting my sister Shaditu with so unholy a crime. Nor did I have to consider long to find the motive—had she not told me so herself? *"Did you think I would let that cold little bitch puppy have you?"* If the woman I loved was safely in Esarhaddon's house of women, would I not then turn to my loving sister? Was that not precisely what I had done? I was not even flattered that she should have taken such risks for my sake, for to Shaditu probably the whole affair had been no more than a game —the sort of game she had been playing ever since she was old enough to be aware of her own power. Men are but clay in the hands of clever women.

But what had Rimani Ashur seen in the goat's entrails that he should have hanged himself in remorse? Perhaps only that Esarhaddon was not the god's choice. Perhaps only that. It seemed unlikely that I would ever find out.

Or perhaps the *baru* had taken his life for some other reason, something that had not occurred to anyone. It hardly mattered, since my own case was not altered by it. Esharhamat was my brother's wife, destined to be mother of a line of kings which would rule until the gods were dust, and I could not be king without bringing the nation to its ruin.

Was the child she carried mine? Was that to be Dread Ashur's final joke on us all, that I, who could not be king, was to be the father of kings? It was all a great muddle, and it made my head ache to think of it.

I was not sorry, at the end of ten days' time, to see my royal brothers return to Nineveh. I stood on the half-finished fortress wall and watched the dust raised by their escort's horses fade into nothing, hoping the two of them would never return to plague me more. I was weary of their mischief; when the time came, they would have to make their rebellion without me.

"I remember them both as children," my mother said.

"They are not children now. When the time comes for the king to die, they will make us all dance."

"What did they want of you, my son?"

"Want?" I could only shake my head and laugh, though the jest was bitter. "What do the likes of Nabusharusur always want? To spread poison and call it nectar. To make the world as empty as their own hearts. Nabusharusur hates Esarhaddon because Esarhaddon was once unwise enough to laugh at him. He hates me because as boys we were friends. But he hates himself most of all because of what the gelder's knife and his own self-disgust have made of him. Of Arad Malik I saw nothing, for he is nothing except the vessel into which Nabusharusur pours a moment's wrath—he will hold no more than that."

To all this my mother made no answer, for she was wise and saw that I spoke as much of my own wrath as another's.

But if my mind grew dark when I considered the evils which lay ahead—and my own sense of helplessness against them—I was content enough with the present. I had the love of Merope, the friendship of Kephalos, and the willing embraces of Naiba. I had perhaps as much of domestic happiness as most men are allowed and this unblemished, for my mother and my concubine dwelled together in peace.

Indeed, it was more than peace, for Merope, who knew all about slavery among foreigners, had taken this slave girl of mine into her heart so that they became almost as mother and daughter. Naiba always deferred to her as mistress, but I could never quite discover which of them was in fact running my house for they seemed to take every decision, even down to what it was fit I should discover on my breakfast tray, in the course of long consultations—I was always finding them huddled together somewhere, talking in low, conspiratorial voices about the outrageous prices charged for lamb in the market square. My servants, most of whom had families of their own, understood all this very well, and among them the word of one was taken as the word of both. If my mother had some little grievance, or a favor to ask, I was always sure to hear of it first from Naiba, and just as my head touched the pillow. And Merope was her advocate in much the same way. I have since learned enough from life to know that this is the way of women, how they make alliance to achieve sovereignty over their menfolk.

Thus life went along smoothly enough—and I had almost forgotten that there was a world beyond Amat—until the month of Tammuz drew close and I began to expect the visit of my brother Esarhaddon.

Once the floodwaters had regained their banks, that spring was unusually hot and dry. The ground, baked hard by Ashur's pitiless sun, cracked and crumbled away, and winds which

scorched like fire swept the dust into great swirling clouds that
blinded men and beast and chocked their watering places. The
crops burned and withered in the fields. It was a cruel season.

A man's nerves fray like old bowstrings in such weather. It is
too hot to work and there is no escape save in drunkenness and
quarreling. I know not how many of my soldiers I ordered flogged
to keep even the appearance of good order. And this was the time
the *marsarru* had chosen to make his "inspection."

I had word of his coming many days before he arrived. The
Lord Esarhaddon traveled with an escort of two hundred soldiers
and thus, for convenience's sake, followed the river course. My
outriders encountered his heralds near the point where the Upper
Zab makes a vast bend, like a man's elbow, and changes its course
from east to west. They hastened home to tell me of the great
pomp of my brother's retinue. I gave orders that twenty picked
men were to be ready to ride by first light, and the next morning
set off with them to meet this mighty host.

A great prince who maintains his state makes slow progress,
for we made and broke three night camps before we crested a hill
and saw the travelers, stretched out and dragging their great
weight along the river road like an army of ants climbing over
fresh.pitch.

Esarhaddon no longer sat a horse as in the old days but
journeyed by chariot, which was more befitting his dignity as a
marsarru on progress. If he had been marching to war I have no
doubt many things would have been different, but this was a state
visit to the provinces. Even from a distance I could see him—or,
rather, I could see the canopies raised over him to keep off the
sun. I rode to the front of the caravan, which had drawn to a halt
at the first sight of our company, and then dismounted and
walked back through their ranks, leaving my weapons behind me.
When I reached my brother, I placed my hand on the wheel of his
chariot and knelt in the dust, bowing my head as I would have
before the king. When I raised my eyes I saw him grinning at me.

He was a splendid figure in his robes of silver and gold, with
his oiled beard and his turban glittering with jewels, but he was
still Esarhaddon. With a loud laugh he reached down his arm to
me and, when I took it, hoisted me into the chariot like a load of
wood. A rude kick sent his driver tumbling out onto the road.

"Here—you drive," he said, thrusting the reins into my
hands. But he retained the whip, and suddenly the horses were at

full gallop as soldiers and courtiers scrambled to the sides of the road to avoid being trampled to death, all the time Esarhaddon laughing to watch them run and lashing out at them with his whip.

It was a wild career as we thundered down the road, our wheels bouncing over every rock, threatening each time to break the axle and kill us both, the horses snorting like devils in their almost panicked flight. We raised a cloud of dust that must have been visible for half a day's ride.

"This is a good place," he shouted finally, his voice nearly drowned in the pounding of hoofs and the rattle of our undercarriage. "Stop here."

When finally I was able to pull the horses to a halt, Esarhaddon leaped from the car and started running like a madman toward the river, tearing off his glorious robes as he went. At last, stripped even of his loincloth, he jumped into the water, disappearing beneath its muddy surface for a long time. When at last he came up he was floating on his back, his hands clasped behind his head, looking mightily pleased with himself as he kicked against the current.

I dived in after him, and very quickly we were splashing each other with silt-laden water and laughing like children.

"By the sixty great gods," he said, after we had climbed out and were sitting on the shore, our backs drying in the sun, "I will tell you one disadvantage to being raised to glory, Tiglath my brother. All that gold and silver they weave into your tunic—you might as well dress up in a furnace. I thought I would roast to death. Oh, the mercy of Ashur—I am glad to be out of that rig for a while!"

He lay back on the stony bank for a moment and closed his eyes, a contented half-smile upon his lips.

"Welcome to the north, O Dread Prince," I said in a solemn voice, and in an instant we were both helpless with laughter.

That evening, in Esarhaddon's tent, we got very drunk together, chased out all the scribes and staff officers, and, for the particular edification of the five favorite concubines my brother had brought with him from Calah, sang all the obscene songs we could remember from our boyhood in the house of war.

We had a glorious time. All either of us could remember was how wonderful it was to be together again—we were more drunk with that than with wine.

It was to be the last such occasion for many years, for in the morning Esarhaddon, grown sober, wary, and perhaps a little frightened, remembered once more that he was the *marsarru,* and that a *marsarru* may love and trust no man, least of all a brother. As I rode beside his chariot along the road to Amat, I did not have to inquire into the meaning of his silence.

"Perhaps you have not yet heard," he said finally. "My wife the Lady Esharhamat has presented me with a son. Whether it is mine or yours she seems reluctant to guess. He is called Sinid-dinapal, but I think we have wasted our breath in naming him. He is a sickly child and will not last long."

He did not look me in the face as he said this but watched for my reaction out of the corner of his eye, all the time smiling a faint, triumphant smile, as if he knew perfectly well the child was mine and rejoiced that it was likely to die soon.

"The little mother is well, however, and she will bear me other sons—many other sons, I think."

It was five more days before we reached the garrison and with each day Esarhaddon's mood seemed to darken. We feasted together and drank wine, but there was none of the old carelessness. After the third cup I said enough. It was only Esarhaddon, with the sullen determination of one seeking oblivion, who made himself drunk. There is truth in wine, and when my brother was flushed with it and began to grow reckless he would look about him, as if each man at the table were his secret enemy, and talk of spies and usurpers. He never accused me directly, but the thread was there to follow.

He kept me with him during that time, as if he could not bear to be parted from me—or, perhaps, was afraid of letting me out of his sight. But we were hardly ever alone.

At last we came within sight of Amat, and for the last *beru* to the fortress gates I once more surrendered my mount and, taking the bridle of Esarhaddon's lead horse in my hand, walked beside his chariot like a common groom, leaving the soldiers and citizens to cheer him alone. He was the *marsarru* and this display of submission and loyalty was no more than his right, but it pleased him just the same.

That night, at the banquet in the officers' new mess, he put his arm across my shoulders as if nothing had changed.

"The king speaks of making you his *turtanu,*" he said, his tone confidential and secretive. "I do not know if he does this merely to vex me or if such a plan is truly in his heart, but he does speak of it. I thought perhaps you should be told."

"But what of the Lord Sinahiusur?" I asked, thinking of my old patron. Esarhaddon shook his head.

"He has been sick in his legs this whole year and now walks about with a staff to support him. Some men, once they are past their prime, age quickly, and our uncle seems to be one of these. How long can he last? Two years? Three? I think very soon the king will need a new *turtanu*."

I was grieved to hear this. What did I not owe to the Lord Sinahiusur, who had saved me from the fate of Nabusharusur and had guided my steps ever since? He had always been an old man in my eyes, but what before had been merely the self-centered prejudice of a child now seemed the very truth—the great man, second voice in the Land of Ashur, had entered his decline. It occurred to me that I would like to see him once more before he died, to thank him for his goodness to me and to ask his blessing, but there seemed little enough chance of that.

"When his bones are in a stone box in the holy city, will you take his place, brother? Will you go back to Nineveh as the king's new *turtanu*?"

"No." I shook my head. I wanted Esarhaddon to talk of something else. I wanted to be alone, to bury my face in my hands and pay my kinsman and friend the tribute of a few tears, but not even that seemed possible. "No. I shall stay here as *shakru* of the northern provinces as long as the god permits me. If I never see Nineveh again I shall count that as a blessing."

"Good—I am glad to hear it."

Esarhaddon lifted his hand from my shoulder and picked up a skewer of honeyed locusts, pulling them off one at a time and eating them in a single bite. Esarhaddon had always been very fond of honeyed locusts.

"Do you remember, when I came back from the west?" he went on, licking his fingers. "That was the first time we either of us gave thought to the possibility that one day one of us would be king, and I said then that if the crown fell to me I would make you my *turtanu*. Do you remember?"

"Yes. Yes, I remember."

"I would not wish you to be *turtanu* before then, Tiglath my brother, for the *turtanu* stands in precedence even before the *mar-*

sarru, and it would not be fitting that I, who will be king, should yield to my brother in anything."

I turned to look at him, keeping my face as empty as a blank wall, although I felt a cold, dangerous anger in my heart.

"I will not be the king's *turtanu,* nor, when you are king, brother, will I be yours. That too would not be fitting."

Although the smile never left my lips, he was not pleased—I could see that, from the way the light changed in his eyes. That was just as well, for now I had no desire left to please him.

"You blame me for that villain dispatched to murder you—is that not so? That is why you sent me his head. He was not from me, brother."

"I knew that. I knew it then."

"Then why . . . ?"

"Because we both know whom he was from, brother. Tell me —did you show my little gift to the Lady Naq'ia?"

Esarhaddon grinned—no, I saw with some small regret, he was not offended. It was beyond his ken why anyone would imagine him offended by the suggestion that his mother trafficked in assassins.

"She is a great and wise women, Tiglath—you would be wise not to underestimate her."

"I think there is little enough chance of my making that mistake."

"But it is true that—well . . ."

He shrugged his shoulders, as if alluding to some inconsequential but ludicrous weakness.

"Let us say that if there was ever any milk in her breasts it has long since been replaced by adder venom. Yes, I did show her the head, and do you know what she said? No—I will not tell you what she said. You would not find it so amusing. She has been made to understand certain things, however, and you need not think there will be any more night visitors from Nineveh."

"Good. I am pleased to have this unfortunate misunderstanding resolved."

But Esarhaddon, it appeared, was immune to irony. From the expression on his face it was obvious he was already thinking about something else.

"Why do you not wish to return to Nineveh?" he asked at last, his brow tight with something between worry and anger. "Is it because of Esharhamat? She is there, you know—the king keeps

her near him, even though she is my wife. Three times in the
month I must travel from Calah, a distance of nearly four *beru*,
merely to rut on her. It is a great inconvenience."

"No. I did not know she was in Nineveh. But, had I need of
no other, that is a very good reason for me to stay away."

This, of all possible answers, seemed to be the one he least
wished to hear. His heavy fingers drummed against the table, and
he glanced about as if looking for some target for his wrath.

"I do not know why you were wont to set such store by her
embraces, brother," he said, his eyes, black and angry, snapping
around to fasten on my face. "Of all the world's women, she . . .
With me she is as cold as pond water."

What had he expected? I do not know. I only know that I
grasped his arm just above the wrist and squeezed down with all
the strength in my fingers, until I thought it just possible that a
little harder and I might break the bone.

"I think it best, brother, if we never speak of this again." The
words were less a whisper than a hiss. "Really, I think it
best . . ."

"Yes—yes!" Esarhaddon, with some difficulty, tore his arm
away from my grasp. "As you will. I did not think, after so
long . . ."

"Then you are a greater fool than even the king imagines."

Suddenly he stood up from the table—as if he had just seen a
snake. Every eye in the hall was upon him, and even the music of
the flute players died away in silence. I had never seen him look
like that before, almost as if I had struck him.

Then he turned on his heel and strode out.

This incident was doubtless the subject of much discussion
within the garrison, and it is not impossible that it formed part of
more than a few of the secret dispatches which I knew perfectly
well found their way to one or another eager reader in Nineveh.
What was made of it there I cannot guess.

For two days afterwards I did not see Esarhaddon. He closeted himself away with members of his own suite—on the pretext
of "official" business—took his meals alone, and disappeared
from sight. I was not surprised. It seemed to be the wisest thing
that we should stay clear of each other for a time. I did not even
think to concern myself with what he might be planning.

"He is not happy, my son"—this was Merope's verdict on the matter. "The gods in their peculiar wisdom have assigned each of you different destinies, and he is as discontented with his as you are with yours. Esarhaddon is by temperament light-hearted and careless. As a simple soldier he would have found the world a place much to his liking, but as *marsarru* he is adrift, not knowing what to do nor whom to trust. That mantle would have suited your shoulders better."

I could only shrug my shoulders, so well suited to the weight of power, for my mother's words were wise.

"Then what am I to do?" I asked.

"Only pity him, and be his friend—no matter what."

Except that it had become no easy matter to be my brother's friend.

On the third day, after Esarhaddon had once more ventured into the daylight, one of his officers called upon me.

"The lord *marsarru* wishes you to arrange some hunting," he announced, precisely as if he were speaking to my cupbearer.

"Hunting?" I repeated. It was not so much the substance of the request that astonished me as its form.

"Hunting—precisely. There is no need for anything elaborate, just a few beaters and the like. What have you in this area that is worth the trouble?"

He smiled faintly. He was tall, slim, well tended, and about thirty, and he seemed to regard everything he saw around him—including me, as if I had spent all my life wiping the dust of Amat out of my eyes—with contemptuous pity. I could not help wondering where my brother had acquired such a specimen, since he was precisely the type of palace officer Esarhaddon had always most detested. But tastes, it seemed, had changed with circumstances.

"I think we can manage a wild pig or two," I answered dryly. "You may tell the lord *marsarru* that all will be ready against the morning."

I had thought in terms of an expedition lasting three or four days—I had thought it would do Esarhaddon good to spend a few nights under the stars, away from his courtiers, living like a soldier again. I was that naïve.

My first mistake was in underestimating my brother's wish for simplicity. When at daybreak he stepped out of his quarters and looked around at the preparations I had made, he grinned and shook his head.

"The Lord Tiglath Ashur has gone to too much trouble," he said—loud enough for everyone to hear. "What do you say, my brother? Shall we just tether a couple of extra horses behind a chariot and go off on our own? Shall we turn our faces upcountry and disappear for a day, as we did when we were boys?"

I answered his grin with one of my own, for I was very pleased, and threw a bag of provisions on the back of my chariot. Within five minutes Esarhaddon and I were driving out through the fortress gates, alone.

The plains east of the city boast fine hunting—gazelle, antelope, and wild boar roam there in great abundance, and as the water holes dried up lions and even the odd panther were driven down from the hills to take their chance near the dwellings of men. If we caught sight of any of the great cats, however, it would only be at a distance, for they are too wary to be taken without the aid of beaters.

We crossed the pontoon bridge over the river while there was still dew on the grass, and Esarhaddon mounted his horse. Our plan was that I would drive around to the south while he rode north, and we would see if we couldn't catch a herd between us.

"Give me the wineskin, Tiglath," he said, reaching out his hand for it. "Forgive my selfishness, but court life has made me soft and I will feel the heat worse than you."

"Do not distress yourself, brother, for, knowing the greatness of your thirst, I brought two."

He laughed as he took the wineskin and rode away, his horse kicking a plume of dust into the air. I did not see him again for several hours.

I envied Esarhaddon, since this was not very good terrain for hunting from a chariot. For all that the fields were scorched by the sun, this was farmland and crisscrossed with irrigation canals narrow enough to present no difficulties to a man on horseback but which forced me to look for the rickety little wooden bridges that the farmers had thrown across here and there for their wagons to use. I managed to flush out a wild boar, but he was clever enough simply to make for the nearest ditch and thus outran me easily. At last I headed toward the foothills, where the game would be thinner but at least I would be able to maneuver better. There I was lucky enough to stumble upon a herd of antelope, which stampeded at the sight of me but which I was able to run down, picking off with my javelin two of the ones that tired quickest. It was good sport and a haunch of fresh-butchered antelope makes a fine supper. By the time the sun was two hours past its zenith I began to think of looking about for my brother.

"Have you had luck?" I shouted, hailing him from across the wide parched plain. He had tied his horse and was sitting under the shade of an outcropping of rock—I could just distinguish his outlines in the shadow.

He waved back, as if he realized the futility of trying to make himself heard at such a distance. I whipped my team back up to a canter.

By the time I had blocked the chariot's wheel I could see that Esarhaddon could have spent but very little time hunting. There was a bag of dates on the ground beside him and the wineskin was cradled on his lap, looking a good deal gaunter than when I had given it to him a few hours before. He didn't say anything, but he didn't have to. His eyes glittered and the expression on his face was intense and concentrated, which meant that he had been drinking heavily.

"You do well to stay out of the sun," I told him. "But if all you wanted was to fuddle yourself we could have tarried in Amat."

"No—it's more private here. Besides, I am not fuddled."

He sounded almost mournful, so I decided not to tease him anymore. I took the water bag from my chariot and poured some into my hands to rinse off my face. I don't know just when it was that I noticed his sword was out of his scabbard and lying on the ground beside him.

"Tiglath," he said suddenly, "why will you not be my *turtanu* when I am king? Is it because you still hope to become king yourself?"

When I looked around at him I could see that he was not merely trying to goad me. He was leaning forward, his hands balanced upon his knees, as if he really wanted to know.

"I cannot be king while you live, Esarhaddon, and this is not a matter I will discuss with you while your brains are putrid with wine."

"Perhaps you still have hopes?" he went on, as if he had not heard me. "Perhaps you think that some one or another of your many friends will put a dagger in my back, and that when I am safely mixed with dust you can then have everything—the throne, Esharhamat, the god's favor, everything."

"Be silent, Esarhaddon, before I forget that I love you."

"But if you love me, Tiglath my brother, then why do you conspire with my enemies?" He had risen to a crouch now, and he was holding the sword. I could see now in his eyes as they held me —he had drunk himself into a black rage. "Why did you entertain Arad Malik and Nabusharusur in your house, when you know that they hate me? Why, Tiglath! Did Arad Malik offer you the throne if you would join them against me?"

I could almost have pitied him. Arad Malik—how typical of Esarhaddon to get it wrong.

"It is not for you to say, brother, whom I shall see in my own house. Nor is it for me to turn away any who are sent there with the king's commission."

"I knew it—the king!" He was so angry that he actually stamped his foot, something I had not seen him do since childhood. "Always the king! He hates me, and why? Simply because I am not you!"

As a swordsman, Esarhaddon had few rivals. He had always been able to best me in close combat, calling the javelin a "coward's weapon"—perhaps he was even right, for I had no trouble acknowledging to myself that I was afraid.

"Do you deny that they have brought you into their conspiracy?" he shouted, standing now, seeming to test the sword's weight in his hand. "Do you deny that you plot with them against me?"

I could see quite clearly now that it had been his design from the first to bring me out here to this isolated place and to kill me. His mistrust and jealousy had reached such a pitch as that. But still, there was enough left of his old habit of love that he could not do the thing in cold blood—he had to heat his liver with wine before he had the strength to draw his sword on me.

My poor brother—I found I could not but pity him, even now. It was as my mother had said, ". . . *he is adrift, not knowing what to do nor whom to trust.*" Except that now he seemed to think the thing to do was to strip me of my life.

I could have ended the matter quickly enough. Nothing more would have been required than to raise my javelin and put it through his heart, but we both knew I would not do that. Esarhaddon wanted a duel, a fair fight between equals—he was not a coward or a villain, and it was not his way to murder a man when he is defenseless. Nor was it mine. He would have what he wanted.

He was swaying slightly as he stood there—he was very drunk, but even drunk he was a formidable enemy. I could only hope that he was even more drunk than he seemed.

"I do not deny that they hate you," I said, smiling slightly, letting my own anger rise. "And I do not deny, brother, that they spoke to me of you—of your unpopularity, of your unfitness to be king. All this is true enough. Can you deny it?"

"I deny it!" The muscles in his face tensed with anger as he shouted his denial. "I deny it—the god chose me over you!"

"Did he? Or was something arranged with the *baru* Rimani Ashur, who then hanged himself out of shame? They told me of rumors about our sister—rumors that must have reached your ears too, brother."

"I am chosen of the god Marduk, King of the Gods! I am chosen, I am chosen, I am chosen!"

So it had come to that. His mother's whisperings all these years—I could hardly believe . . .

"So now you wish to test the favor of heaven, is that it?" I grinned at him, an angry, hating grin, for even as I drew my sword, I could not drive a brother's love from my heart. "Then come—we will see whom the god honors. We will see who lives and who dies."

The sun's heat was punishing, enough to burn away the very air in a man's lungs. As he stepped out into it Esarhaddon wiped his eyes with his fingertips. He walked slowly, with his feet wide apart. No, he did not relish this fight, any more than I did myself. I waited, letting him come to me.

He was now almost close enough to touch me with his sword point. If he was drunk now, it did not show; he looked solid and impenetrable as he balanced on the balls of his feet, looking for an opening.

We circled around one another, each searching for the other's weaknesses. As boys we had done this a thousand times in play, never thinking that someday we would fight in earnest. On its first pass, Esarhaddon's blade cut through the air with a tearing sound —though he wasn't even trying to reach me yet, only testing, sure of himself, seeing how I would react. He was like a cat with a cornered mouse.

I made a rush and he parried it aside with ease, as I had known he would. He did not follow up his advantage, however—he was not such a fool as to fall into a trap. He even dropped his point a few handspans, inviting me to try again. But I knew that trick too.

He reached up with his left hand and wiped his eyes again. He was sweating heavily and squinting in the light. Yes, he had drunk too much wine to be fighting in the bright afternoon sun. It oppressed him, like a shoulder pack filled with stones. A narrow advantage for me—something to balance against his skill.

Finally he lunged, leveling a blow at me that cut from left to right and would have split my chest open like a fig under a cart wheel had I not somehow managed to dance aside. But this time he did press his advantage, slashing at me once, twice, three times, each stroke coming closer until the last one cut through my tunic at the shoulder, bathing my right arm in blood as I scrambled to get away from him. I did not even know how badly he had wounded me. I was too busy trying to stay alive to feel the hurt.

And then, suddenly, he seemed to waver—not long, but long enough for me to regain my balance. He stopped and peered into my face, his eyes blinking, as if all at once he could not remember who I was or how he had come to be there. It lasted only an instant, this remission, and then he swung at me again. But this time I caught the blow on the edge of my sword and turned it aside.

He was tiring—I could see that now. That was my chance, to let him wear himself down.

The sweat popped out on his face and arms now. He was beginning to grow desperate. He had drawn first blood, but he knew he did not have much time to press the advantage. He wanted to finish me off before his strength failed him, so he kept after me, hacking away at my sword blade like a man trying to cut through a bank of reeds. It was becoming easier and easier to fend him off.

At last he made his mistake. He let his swing carry him just a little too far inside my range, and I caught him on the back of the hand with my point.

It was hardly more than a scratch, just enough to slit open the skin, and though it probably hurt like a demon, it was, I think, more than anything the surprise that did it. Esarhaddon cried out, and the sword dropped from his hand. I did not need any more invitation than that.

For some unaccountable reason, it never occurred to me to kill him then and there. I simply charged, yelling at the top of my lungs and catching him in the pit of the stomach with my shoulder. I could hear the wind shoot out of him with a cough as we tumbled down together. Esarhaddon did not even try to fight me off—he was too busy trying to remember how to breathe.

When he came to rest I was on top, my knee planted in the center of his chest and the blade of my sword across his throat while Esarhaddon, making a series of short gasping sounds, tried to fill his lungs again. It was a moment before he even noticed that I was there.

"You were so sure," I whispered between my teeth—I could think of nothing except my anger. I was ready to kill him in that instant. Perhaps all that saved him was that I wished him to know how he had made me hate him. "May the gods damn you forever, you were so sure. You have grown soft, brother. You have turned into a soft, clumsy drunkard, or you would not now be on your back with my sword blade under your chin."

"Then be quick about it," he croaked. "Go ahead—do your will. Kill me."

I could feel his body going rigid as he waited for the blow. I raised my blade. He was already dead. I had made the decision, and his head was as good as off.

Except that my arm would not obey. And then I knew that I could not, that it was not in me to take Esarhaddon's life.

I pressed the edge into the flesh of his throat until a fine red line of blood popped out beneath it.

"And who would avenge you if I did, brother? Who? The army, perhaps? Do you think so? Or the king? No—he would laugh with joy and beg the god to put me in your place. How long do you think it would be before I entered the house of succession, my brother? Then I would have everything, even Esharhamat. Would she mourn for you, do you think? Would I have to guard my sleep against your widow's fury?"

He did not answer. If he tried—if he even understood—the words came not. He only stared at me with wild eyes, expecting death in the next instant.

"Or perhaps you count on your mother to appease your ghost with my blood. Do you, Esarhaddon? I think not. I think

our father, who is wise enough to crush a scorpion when he sees
one, would have her head on the floor within an hour of receiving
word of your death. What do you imagine might stay my hand?"

His lips opened and then moved to shape a word that had no
voice. And all the time his eyes never left mine. Finally he licked
his parched lips and tried once more.

"I will not beg," he whispered. "Kill me, and hear my curse
as I die."

I was almost weeping with rage. I grabbed him by the tunic
and pulled him up. I kicked him away from me, striking a blow
with the flat of my sword that would have broken another man's
ribs.

But Esarhaddon merely grunted, as if in surprise. Finally,
when he had sat up again, he put his head between his knees and
vomited, staining the ground red with sour wine. I went back to
the chariot and fetched him my water bag that he could rinse the
taste from his mouth.

"Why did you not kill me?" he asked finally. "Not even I
would have blamed you."

I was in no temper to answer. I turned away from him, my
bowels still trembling with an emotion compounded of wrath and
horror. For a long time I could not have spoken.

"Why did you not kill me?" he repeated at last. Strangely, he
sounded quite calm.

"You are alive—is that not enough for you?"

He sat there, his elbows resting on his knees, staring at nothing. He looked exhausted, spent.

"I suppose it must be."

I did not reply.

"I will not ask you to forgive me, Tiglath," he said, staring at
his injured hand as he made and unmade a fist. "I would not
deserve it in any case."

He did not have to ask, for, although I could not have
brought myself to say so, I had already forgiven him in my heart.
We both knew, however, that this incident could never be forgotten, that it would stand between us forever. This, as much as
anything, was what choked my voice, that he had brought us to
this final parting.

"How is your shoulder?" he asked.

In truth, I had forgotten all about it. When I looked I could see the cut was clean and not very deep. It hurt a great deal, but that was a good sign.

"It will not kill me," I answered. "How is your hand?"

"Nothing but a scratch, but my ribs pain me."

"I am glad to hear it."

Our eyes met, and Esarhaddon grinned. He really was sorry. I smiled thinly—it was the best I could do. I sat down beside him and took a swallow from the water bag.

"But they are plotting against me, aren't they—Arad Malik and Nabusharusur, I mean."

"Of course. They could hardly speak of anything else."

"You might at least have warned me."

"Would I have been telling you anything you did not already know yourself?"

He shook his head.

"The king encourages them—or at least pretends to be blind and deaf. The king favors anyone who he thinks will weaken me. I will kill Arad Malik, the first day I sit on the throne."

"Arad Malik is as toothless as a newborn babe. Kill Nabusharusur instead."

"What—that eunuch?"

"Yes, that eunuch. You will not last very long as king, my brother, unless you learn to be afraid of men like Nabusharusur. The fact that his scabbard is empty only means that he is hiding the dagger behind his back."

Esarhaddon nodded, as if he understood.

"We had better bind our wounds," he said, "and think of some story to explain them when we return. We can say that the chariot overturned. Tiglath?"

"Yes—what is it?"

"I will never mistrust you again."

I could but laugh. Even in my owns ears it was a bitter sound.

"You think not, do you?"

We drove back to Amat, and Esarhaddon, to the great consternation of his entourage, issued orders that they would leave for Calah in the morning. We embraced at parting, for we were in company with many others, but I think we both knew that the next time we met it would not be as friends.

23

It was some five days after Esarhaddon's departure that word reached me of an incursion on the eastern border. It was not in itself a very important incident—a band of Median raiders had crossed over into our province of Zamua and had attacked a group of villages not far from the headwaters of the Turnat River, the sort of thing which one must expect every so often after years in which men have almost forgotten the sound of fighting. It was, however, the pretext I had been hoping for.

I wrote to the king in Nineveh, asking permission to assume command of the eastern garrisons for a campaign into the Zagros Mountains. I would carry my battle standards to the very doorposts of the barbarians and remind them, since they seemed to need it, that the Lands of Ashur were not a bazaar stall to be looted whenever it pleased them.

The king's reply was not long in coming: "I have learned, my son, that I must indulge your restlessness, and perhaps it is true that we have been too long at peace and the eastern tribes begin to think we have all turned into women. I grant you all power in this matter. Work your will."

But I had not waited. I had already issued orders that the northern garrisons were each to send half their strength to join me in a staging area near the border city of Musasir. I set out with the best companies of the Amat fortress and what was left of my old comrades in the *quradu*— including even Lushakin, who said he had had enough of being a kitchen soldier and would come even if he had to follow behind with the pack mules.

Thus began my two years of war against the Medes.

They are a strange people, in some ways unlike any I have encountered in a life filled with strange turnings. And since the days of my youth, when I did battle against them, they have risen to be a great nation. Even then they believed that the future belonged to them, and it is possible they may be right, for they lack neither virtue nor cunning. It may be they will roll over the world like a plague of locusts, but I hope not to live long enough to see that day—they will make bad masters over the lands of my ancestors.

Even in the reign of Sennacherib we had been fighting the Medes for nearly two hundred years, ever since the days of Raman Ninari, the third king of that name, who led armies into the eastern lands and there encountered a race of horsemen who wore their hair short and fought with spears and called themselves the "Aryan," the "nobles."

The land there is good, although not so well watered as the Tigris plains, and by that time most of the tribes, but by no means all, had ceased their wanderings and settled in towns and villages along the wrinkled slopes of the Zagros Mountains, where they could farm in the valleys and pasture their horses and cattle on the steppes that sloped gently down to the salt deserts of the north. Where they had come from before that I do not know, nor, although the Medes speak of a homeland where the grass is tall, have I ever met anyone who did. I do know, however, that they came as conquerors, each tribe holding its own territory in subjection as masters over the old inhabitants, whom they regarded with the greatest contempt, for they truly believed in themselves as the favored ones of heaven and this made them cruel. Still, their cruelty was limited by their weakness, for although they recognized themselves as one people, they were divided into many tribes, and each warred against the others as fiercely as they did against all other nations. But already this was beginning to change.

Some ten years before my birth, in the reign of Great Sargon, a raiding party attacked our garrison at Kharkhar, surprising the watch and inflicting great slaughter. Their leader, one Ukshatar, styled himself king, or, in their tongue, "shah" of all the Medes, and indeed he had managed to assemble a confederation of tribes that kept the armies of Ashur busy through several seasons of campaigning. In the end Ukshatar was captured and exiled to the west, where he died, but he left behind him a son, a youth called

Daiaukka. It was a name I had heard many times since my arrival in the north.

Tribes will drift together in loose alliances, or will find some common purpose in the will of a strong leader, but such unity lasts only until victory or defeat. If they triumph, if their combined strength is enough to push aside a weaker foe, then the marauders will inevitably begin to bicker over the spoils. And if their strength bleeds away in battle after costly battle—and this was precisely the fate I had decided upon for the Medes—then they will lose their faith in leaders and their great lords will end with their throats cut while common men sue the enemy for mercy. It was not Daiaukka whom I feared, nor any other chief with a few thousand spearmen who presumed to call himself shah of the Aryan. It was not a man who had rendered the Medes suddenly dangerous, but an idea. Daiaukka was merely the chosen vehicle of a new force that had entered the imaginations of simple herdsmen and farmers, making them believe they had become something more, for the Medes had found a new worship and a new god.

The men of the west believe in many gods, and this makes them tolerant of one another. The Egyptians do not care that the Babylonians pay reverence to Marduk, nor the Babylonians that Telepinu is honored among the Hittites. Their precedence is something for the gods to settle among themselves, and it is felt to be only decent that each man pays his homage at the alter of his fathers. The Hebrews in Judah, it is true, worship only one god whom they believe is the lord of the universe, but they are a small, quarrelsome, unimportant people. The Medes were another matter entirely.

Whence this new religion came I know not. The Medes speak of a great teacher, a prophet of their own race whose name was Zarathustra, but who he was or whether he still lived in those days of if he had ever really existed I was never able to discover. But his was the voice of a worship unlike any the world had ever seen, and it was a voice full of menace for its message was of fire and sword and a world washed in the blood of innocence.

It begins harmlessly enough—there is one god who shall be honored over all others, and he is called the Ahura Mazda, the Lord of Wisdom, or simply the Ahura. The Ahura is all purity—the sky is his body and the sun his eye—and he has created all the other noble gods, the Spenta Mainyu or Bountiful Immortals, of

whom there are six. Balanced against these are all the demons of
the world, of whom one Ahriman is the greatest.

The Medes believe that the history of all that is divides itself
into three periods, each enduring for three thousand years. The
first of these was a golden age in which the Ahura and Ahriman
were one and together created the world. Then, since the knowledge of one thing depends upon its opposite, there was no evil.
But finally these two separated, the one becoming "He Who Is All
Life" and the other "He Who Is All Death," and this began the
second age, the time of trouble and the warfare of good and evil.
The third age began with the appearance of the teacher Zarathustra and will end, finally, with the triumph of good and the remak-
ing of the world, which will then last forever.

There is nothing in this that is so different from the beliefs of
other peoples, who revere one god as the lord of all the others and
acknowledge, as ever prudent man must, the existence of evil
spirits. The difference lies in the way these gods and evil spirits
are approached because, whereas the Babylonians, the Egyptians,
the men of Ashur, even the Greeks—indeed, all the civilized nations of the world—believe that it is right to offer prayers and
sacrifice to all the gods, both good and evil, and thus to incline
them to mercy, the Medes offer Ahriman and all his followers
only curses. All wickedness, even that of the gods themselves, is
to be scorned, and it is the object of prayer and sacrifice to
strengthen the Ahura in his war against Ahriman, to fill his mind
with courage and his limbs with death-dealing power. Thus men
become soldiers in this war of the gods, and it is within their
power to hasten the final triumph of light over darkness. Their
faith in their prayers, which they call "Mantra," is so great that
they imagine the words themselves to have a force independent of
the gods, so that they will ward off evil spirits even if spoken by a
foreigner, by one who understands nothing of their meaning. As I
have suggested, it is a strange worship.

Thus everything in life is very clear to the Medes. They live
in a world divided between light and darkness, good and evil,
perfection and corruption, and the differences between the one
and the other are entirely clear. One is either a worshiper of the
Ahura or a worshiper of fiends—no middle way is possible. The
followers of the true path will be rewarded in this life and the
next; all others are consigned to a most terrible damnation.

The very simplicity of their beliefs has done much to make

the Medes a virtuous people, for the whole of their lives is involved with their insistence on purity. They are good farmers because their prophet teaches that to till the soil and redeem wastelands are acts pleasing to the Ahura. They will not lie, not even to an unbeliever, nor violate the smallest particular of any contract because the Ahura disdains all falsehood. They are kind to their animals, particularly the horse, the camel, the dog, the cock, and the cow, which comes first in reverence, because these the Ahura loves. They do not even practice animal sacrifice nor read the future in the entrails of beasts because these too their god has forbidden them.

In fact, the Medes are so concerned with avoiding any sort of pollution, which they identify with Ahriman and the forces of evil, that death is a great problem for them. Since all of the three elements—earth, fire, and water—are sacred to the Ahura, none may be defiled by contact with a corpse and therefore it may be neither buried nor burned nor cast into the sea. How then to dispose of the dead?

The Medes have hit upon the solution of exposing them on the roofs of high stone towers, which they call, fittingly enough, "towers of silence," where their bones are quickly picked clean by carrion-eating birds. All who touch a corpse are likewise defiled and must purify themselves by washing in cow urine.

There is a popular belief among them that the Land of the Dead is presided over by a god named Yama, who sends forth his dogs each day to sniff out those for whom the hour of death has come and herd them like cattle into his presence, there to be judged for all eternity. These dogs are brown, broad-snouted, and possessed of four eyes, and for this reason a white dog with yellow ears—thought to be an adequate substitute—is always set to guard a corpse against evil spirits.

But the teaching attributed to the prophet Zarathustra is somewhat different. At death, so it is written, a man crosses the Bridge of the Gatherer. If he has followed the path of darkness in life, his foot will slip and he will fall down into the House of Lies, but if he has followed the path of the Ahura he will be allowed to enter the House of Praise, the Dwelling of the Pure.

The purity which leads to eternal bliss is not, they believe, without its rewards in this world as well, and these rewards can be passed on from generation to generation. The Ahura protects his followers, granting them cattle and horses, many sons, and a long life. And the virtuous dead become themselves something only a little short of divine and receive offerings from their descendents, who can invoke their aid against the powers of Ahriman and thus procure for themselves all manner of blessings.

And thus these mountain tribesmen, only lately accustomed to cities and a settled life, had become terrible in the eyes of all civilized men. For it is only doubt and the fear of death which makes it possible for one people to live at peace with another, and from these the Medes had been set free by their new worship. Their pride of race made them believe they were set apart from the rest of mankind, and now their prophet had taught them virtue and a contempt for any who did not follow the way of the Ahura, who promises rewards in this world and the next. To war against evil had become their object in living, and they saw evil everywhere outside the magic circle of their own nation. For such as these death is a blessing, conquest a duty, and mercy the most contemptible of weaknesses. With such as these—molded into a disciplined army—a gifted and ambitious king could sweep across the earth.

So it was not Daiaukka I feared. I feared the voice of his prophet.

It was on the fifth day of the month of Tammuz when I turned my eyes to the rising sun and set out for the land of the Medes. I led a force of six thousand men and would find as many again waiting for me in Musasir. From there we would march south and east, following the line of foothills that eventually rises into the Zagros Mountains, until we reached Zamua and the fortress at Hamban.

That drowsy little garrison town was suddenly swollen almost to bursting with starving, dust-stained country folk, who, with such of their possessions as they could carry wrapped in bundles, had come streaming in from the wide eastern plains to seek the protection of mud walls and the soldiers of their god and king. They had fled before the fury of the Medes, and the fear of what they had seen and suffered was still in their faces. Now they were starving because the garrison had not grain enough to feed them all.

"They are like wolves, Lord—they have no pity." So I was told by an old man as he lay on his sleeping mat beside the town wall, waiting for death. "They come. They steal our oxen and burn our fields and houses. They kill all whom they find. I am old, I do not care, but so many . . ." And his eyes grew wet with tears as they saw once more that which he could not bring himself to speak of. "I will die here. I do not wish to return home."

"I will go there for you," I told him. "And all shall be as it was, for the god's justice will not be turned aside."

He turned to look at me, to look into my face, and it was as if he had not understood.

"The god," he said at last. "Yes, the god . . ."

Thus we knew what to expect when we marched east and entered the devastated region known as Dur Tuqe.

"Dur" means "fortress," but if the soldiers of Ashur had ever maintained a garrison there, they had long since withdrawn to the more comfortable and easily defended cities of the river basins, for in this place the eye found no mud walls or watchtowers, no parade grounds, no roads rutted by the wheels of war chariots. This was land where barley grew, where for centuries no man had carried any weapon more deadly than a mattock. Now the Medes had sown slaughter there.

I was a soldier, hardened to cruel sights, but the bile rose in my throat as I looked about me. It was a landscape of horrors. The birds, so gorged on carrion that they could hardly fly, perched beside the banks of irrigation ditches clogged with the corpses of the farmers who had dug them, and the plains were pocked with the cold, blackened skeletons of burned villages. We rode for hours without hearing a sound louder than the wind. There was no one. They had all fled—or been butchered by the Medes. All this the Medes had done. The Aryan. The Nobles. I did not know it then, but as my eyes searched the desecrated earth I was beholding the glory of their Ahura and the truth of his word. All I saw was death.

"I will return this devastation whence it came," I thought. "I will kill them in their thousands, enslaving their women and sons, burning their cities and their fields. They will remember my name to the end of time, for I will close my heart to pity."

That night we camped beside a stone cliff that bore the carved image of Great Sargon, a figure twice the size of living men, left there to record his glory. Beneath his feet he had caused to be written a warning and a curse: "Stranger, you enter the Land of Ashur, Lord of Heaven, Giver of Victory, the Son of

Wisdom and Power. Here the law of kings prevails, who are mighty in war. Ashur will drown his enemies in their own blood." From the king's hand ran the leads to four Median chieftains who knelt before him, their arms raised in supplication and their lips pierced with rings to make them tractable as cattle. Now it was his grandson's task to make good this royal boast.

The senior officers of our hastily assembled army, with some of whom I had fought at the Bohtan River and even in Babylon, while others were almost strangers, formed a circle around the table in my tent as I explained my plans for the campaign. Before us, drawn in charcoal on an oxhide, was a copy of the map used by the Lord Sargon when he had made war against the Medes, ten years before my birth. It showed almost nothing beyond a ragged line of mountains, a river or two, and the names of some ten or twelve settlements that might have been anything from villages with fifty families to great cities.

"We shall have to move carefully," I told them. "We shall have to send our scouts out two or three days ahead to feel the way for us—we make war upon strangers in their own land, and it is best to be cautious."

"The Medes will think we are frightened," said a *rab abru* from the garrison at Arzuhina, a squat, dark, solid little figure whose name was Bel Itir and who had the reputation of a fire-eater. "What is the point of fielding this vast force if it does no more than lumber timidly about like a water buffalo with a bellyful of nettles?"

As he spoke his eyes blazed in the flickering lamplight, as if he could already hear the laughter of his enemies and held me solely responsible for this intolerable humiliation.

"Let the Medes think what they like. If this year we cut off only the tip of one finger, next year we will be back for the whole arm." I smiled, knowing that a man like Bel Itir would be hard pressed to understand.

"I mean to reduce these barbarians to silence," I went on, speaking now more generally. "When we have finished here, the Medes will not venture from their mountains for a generation— perhaps not even then. But this will not be the work of a single campaign. So let the tribes think we come only to burn a few villages and then, honor satisfied, hurry back to the comfort of our great cities. If they imagine that we have grown soft, they will learn their mistake soon enough.

"Now then—I propose that we follow this line of mountains into Ellipi, to about here, where we will divide into three wings and converge upon this point, called Ecbatana . . ."

So we marched east and into the land of the Medes, an army of near twelve thousand men. And every hour we could feel upon us the measuring eyes of our enemies—they were no more than that, a presence that made the air heavy in our lungs. If was full twelve days before we even saw their faces.

I will never forget my first sight of that warrior race. It was not more than an hour after sunrise and we had covered hardly a single *beru* of our day's march. All at once I raised my eyes and saw them. A group of some twenty riders had appeared on the crest of a low hill—they were simply there, as if they had sprung straight from the earth. How they had managed to slip past my scouts I could only guess, for this was their country, where I was but a stranger.

I raised my arm and brought the line of march to a halt.

We had at last reached the steppes of the Zagros Mountains, that great grassland that seemed to roll forward forever. On our left, at the very limit of the horizon, visible only as a thin, pale ribbon of melting light, was a vast salt desert where, it was said, the sun could kill in a single hour, baking a man's brains into syrup. On our right were the mountains, cold, barren, filled with hidden places—little valleys of astonishing lushness, or so I had heard, the secret homes of the Median tribes. And now, it seemed, since so small a party could entertain no hope of attacking us, they must wish to hear what unwelcome business had brought us so far.

Finally, when they understood we were waiting for them, they pricked their horses forward and rode down, eight or nine abreast, to parley. These would be some local headman or other and his clan elders, and they did not hurry.

The party drew to a halt some seventy paces in front of us, on what they probably considered safely neutral ground. I went forward with my principal officers to meet them.

Some among their number were men full of years, whose knowledge of life's hardships seemed etched into their faces. A few might have been old enough to have fought in the wars against my grandfather from the very beginning of his eastern campaigns, and these, after the manner of those who have spent long lives commanding warriors from the back of a horse, were figures of immense dignity—I noticed that two of them, their hair as white as frost, kept glancing at me as they conferred in excited murmurs. Some were younger. A few, as is always the case, were probably fools.

One, a handsome man in the middle of his life and, like most of his race, tall and slender, kept slightly ahead of the rest and waited in expectant silence, studying me with almost disdainful calm, as if he regarded this meeting as entirely a matter between the two of us. His hair, which showed very little gray, was cut short and tied back with a red fillet, and his beard was carefully curled. He wore heavy boots, trousers like the Scythians, and a sheepskin coat lined inside with fleece. There was nothing except his bearing to indicate that he was lord here.

"I am Uksatar, son of Ianzu, whom the Ahura loved, and *parsua* of the Miyaneh," he announced, the way a man does when he assumes his name will be recognized.

"And I am Tiglath Ashur, son of the Lord Sennacherib who is king in the Land of Ashur."

"I know your name, Lord. I wish to know what has brought you here."

"To know one is to know the other, Uksatar, son of Ianzu, for what except the god's call for retribution would bring a prince of the world's masters to such a place as this?"

I swept my hand over the horizon, as if to indicate its contemptible emptiness. Uksatar, *parsua* of the Miyaneh, seemed oblivious to the insult.

"Then you seek to avenge a few mud huts and a handful of stolen cattle?" he asked, raising his eyes in apparent astonishment. "If you wish only to punish a tribe of raiders, you bring with you too large an army—you will never catch them. If you have come to conquer the land of the Aryan, it is not nearly large enough."

"It is large enough. The man who herds sheep needs no more than a few good dogs."

"I see that the son of Sennacherib, king of Nineveh, still has a bitter tongue," came a voice from behind Uksatar's back. We both looked to see who had spoken, and a horse nosed its way forward. The man who rode it no longer wore the blue tunic and black vest of an Uqukadi, but I recognized him nonetheless. The smile on his thick, fleshy face was still there, as if nothing had changed since our last meeting, and perhaps, for him, nothing had. His people were scattered, dead, or in bondage, but to him, perhaps, it made no difference, for this was a leader whose final loyalty was to no one except himself.

"Then you survived," I observed, returning his salute with a slight nod. "And, it would seem, have prospered."

"A wise man, my Lord Tiglath, can always escape with at least part of his wealth, and a wealthy man is never without influence."

His smile broadened, as if he expected me to congratulate him. He seemed actually to be waiting for it to happen.

"But we took each other's measure long ago," he went on at last, shrugging his heavy shoulders. "Did we not, Lord? There seem to be some among these worthies who suspect you of being a mighty spirit come back to punish them for some ancient wrong, but I have assured them that you are—"

"That is enough, Upash," snapped the *parsua* of the Miyaneh—it seemed that the Lord Uksatar did not relish having his counsels opened for my inspection. "You chatter like a woman. All that is needful is to make the foreigner understand that we do not fear his might and that, in any case, those who plundered the lands of his unclean god broke no law which we recognize."

He turned to me, his eyes narrowing as if he thought to kill me with a look.

"Go home, Prince Tiglath Ashur, son and grandson of kings. You will find nothing here but ruin and death."

"One of us will, in any case," I answered, smiling—this was a game I had played before. "And for now I wish you a pleasant morning, willing even to believe that you are as fearless as you claim."

I raised my hand in salute, but the Lord Uksatar recoiled at the gesture, as if I had made to strike him. Nor was he alone— several among his entourage reined back their horses, and I could hear the murmur of low voices pass among them like a thrill of panic.

"Dastesh!" one of them shouted, as if suddenly overtaken by surprise. *"Dastesh—setare-ye-kohn-s-Sargon!"*

As one man, they wheeled their horses about and galloped off, not stopping until they had vanished from sight.

"By the sixty great gods, *Rab Shaqe.*" Lushakin scratched

his beard in bewilderment as we rode back to our own columns. "What do you think got them so upset?"

I couldn't answer him. I could only shake my head and wonder, the same as he.

"I can tell you."

It was the *rab abru* Bel Itir who had spoken. He rode along beside us, his shoulders hunched grimly, staring out at nothing. At last he ventured a thin, cruel smile.

"I know their tongue a little," he said. "A man learns a few words posted out in this wilderness—enough. It is the birthmark the *rab shaqe* carries on the palm of his hand that frightens them, the blood star, as they called it. It is the mark of our late king, Mighty Sargon. They fear that he is not quiet in his grave and returns in his grandson's person to avenge himself. They fear it is a ghost who leads us into battle."

That night I had a dream. The dream was of an eagle, rising effortlessly into the sky, turning in great circles as the wind lifted it higher and higher. At last it came to rest on a barren outcropping of rock. It looked down, and through its eyes I could see the earth spread beneath me like a wrinkled carpet. The next morning I gave orders that we were to abandon the steppes and begin our climb into the Zagros Mountains.

My officers must have thought I had gone mad, for there was no military reason why we should give up the plains, where at least we had less to fear from ambushes. There seemed to be no reason of any kind, none even that I could see. I was listening to some inner voice, and all I knew for certain was that I would do its bidding and follow where it led.

We did not see the Medes again for many days. They were watching our progress—of this I had no doubt; I could almost feel their eyes upon us—but they kept themselves from sight. They did not attack, as I would have expected them to. They held off and waited. We all seemed to be waiting.

The mark of the Lord Sargon. The red star I have carried since the hour of my birth, since the hour in which he met his death, somewhere in these very mountains. His *sedu* protected my steps—this the blind *maxxu* had told me, long ago. Perhaps it was even true. If ever he was with me, if ever he kept me from harm and led me to see with his own eyes, it was then, in the land of the

Medes, while I wandered the ragged spine of the Zagros, listening for the words of the god's voice.

And then, at last, it came to me. Not the sound of some inner speaking, but an understanding that I been to this place before, had climbed these mountain passes and felt this wind upon my face—that none of this was unfamiliar, that I knew what to expect and would know when I found it, the place where it would happen. And then, at last, I lost my fear, for I was cradled in the hand of Ashur.

On the seventh day since we had left the safety of the plains we found a place of shale and limestone cliffs, beneath which the spring waters oozed like fresh blood. A shepherd was there with his dogs and his flock, one man alone. He watched us with wild, fearful eyes, uncertain whether he ran the greater risk to stay or to flee. I had seen all this before, with my soul's eyes, waking and dreaming. I ordered the soldiers to make camp, for here we would stop.

I summoned Bel Itir to me, for he alone among us understood something of the speech of these lands.

"You have questioned the shepherd?" I asked him.

"Yes, *Rab Shaqe*. It seemed a wise precaution, although he claims to know nothing. Shall I order his throat cut?"

"No—let him go, as an offering to the god. Does he say of what tribe he is?"

"Of the Kullumite, *Rab Shaqe*—great once, he says, but now nearly gone from these mountains."

"Does he say what place this is?"

"He calls it the Place of Bones, *Rab Shaqe*. He does not know how it came by that name."

I knew, although I did not say. And I knew then why the *sedu* of my grandfather, glorious in arms, had led me here. The Place of Bones—yes, of course. Great Sargon could have told how it had come by that name. Nargi Adad would have looked about him and remembered. What other name should it have had? The old men of the Miyaneh had been right to feel afraid.

"Set up watchtowers in all the high places," I ordered. "Set the men to digging pit traps against the enemy horses—no man shall rest until the work is done. I wish this place fortified as against a siege. We will all sleep in our armor tonight, and every night if need be. Each soldier will stand his watch through half the hours of darkness, including the officers."

"You expect them here then, *Rab Shaqe*?" he asked, smiling thinly, as if he thought me mad.

"They will come, Bel Itir, and we will be ready for them. And do not fear but that we will paint the ground red with their blood."

"It shall be as you will, *Rab Shaqe*."

No, it would be as the god willed. Mighty Ashur, Lord of Heaven, he whose power may never be subdued, whose light blinds like the sun, it was he who had brought us here, through his chosen instrument, Tiglath, son and grandson of kings, a little man whom he leads as he might a dog that knows its master.

While the day was still with us, I sent out riders to scout every approach. Sentries were posted along the tops of the cliffs, where even in the black of night they would hear the approach of an enemy force, even if their horses' hoofs were wrapped in linen. Our supply carts, those few that had survived the journey, were turned on their sides and left as obstacles to impede the charge of cavalry. The soldiers prepared their weapons against an enemy they had never seen, for whose very existence they were forced to take my word. No man rested. As the sun faded, we worked by torchlight.

And at last, the thing was done. The cooks made our supper, butchering a pair of horses that the soldiers might have a little meat, but we were almost too weary to eat. And there would be no more than a few hours' rest tonight, as we waited.

All day long the riders had come back, and always they reported that they had seen nothing—not a single man under arms, not even a goatherd with a stick for killing snakes. Our enemies eluded us, although I never doubted they were close enough to reach out their hands to us whenever they liked. These mountains were filled with little canyons where five thousand men could conceal themselves for days, even months, and my scouts might pass by twenty times and never notice the narrow stone gully, covered over with brush, that led to their hiding place. The Medes were at home here. Why should we see even their shadows before they were pleased to show themselves? Nevertheless, they were there.

In my tent my officers gathered. I outlined to them my plans and my expectations, assigning each his role in the coming battle. They listened with sullen attention, saying nothing, for they did not half believe me. Some, I think, were ready to relieve me of command and take me back to Nineveh tied to a pole, but it was no small thing to raise one's hand against the king's own son, so they kept their own counsel and, for now, took my orders in silence.

When I stepped outside, the soldiers were waiting. They, too, doubted, but they were simple men for whom the *rab shaqe*'s word was law. And so, their work finished, they waited in patience to hear that word, to weigh for themselves the purposes that had brought them to this place. This they would hear from the Lord Tiglath Ashur, *shaknu* of the northern provinces, son and grandson of kings. This was their right.

I climbed up on the back of a chariot and looked into that sea of faces, a great murmuring crowd in the wavering light of campfires and torches. What could I say that they might understand and believe? I knew not. I opened my lips and let the words come.

"Men of Ashur, you are the servants of a wise god. Like the eagle, he circles wide above us but always comes back to the same nest. He confides in no man but hugs his vengeance to his own bosom and waits, for he is patient. He has brought us here that we may work its fulfillment and see with our own eyes the unconquerable might of his will.

"We stand, at this moment, on ground which he has made holy to receive us, for here, on this high and rocky plain, twenty years ago and more, Sargon the Great, king in the Land of Ashur, whom the god loved above all men, perished at the hands of his enemies. Here he fell. This flint-hard soil drank his blood. And now the King of Heaven and Earth has led us back to this place that the death of our lord may at last be avenged!"

Their cheers broke in upon me like thunder, echoing from the cliff faces, and I was silenced. Would they have believed me in the cold light of morning? Did they truly believe me then, or did they but wish to believe? I know not.

"Ashur is King!" they shouted. "Ashur is King! Ashur is King! Ashur is King!" They made the night tremble with the sound.

Did they believe me? I know not. I know only that they made my will theirs and would die for the god's glory at my word. In the hearts of simple men is the only truth.

I raised my arm, and at last they grew silent.

"You all know the story of the blood star that blazed in the

eastern sky on the night of Mighty Sargon's death—some among
you may even have seen it, since it lit the heavens like a torch.
And you all know the mark I bear on my hand."

I unclenched my fist that they might see, and a murmur rose
among them, for all men fear such things. And rightly so.

"This I have carried since the hour of my birth—the same
hour in which King Sargon, my father's father, found his *simtu*
on this very ground. I was born, and he died, in one instant. And
that night the blood star burned in the sky like a wound in the
god's own flesh—and it was not for nothing that Holy Ashur thus
placed his mark upon me!"

"Ashur is King!" they shouted, their voices like the pounding of drums. "Ashur is King! Ashur is King!"

"The enemies will come for us here!" I cried, when at last
they would hear me. "Perhaps this night, perhaps the next, but
they will come, creeping through the darkness like jackals. You
know them—they are the inheritors of those who slew our king,
who stripped him of his life and held his corpse for ransom that
his son, whose son I am, was forced to buy him back with silver
and gold before he could sleep in the earth of his fathers. They
will return here, as we have returned, thinking yet again to accomplish great slaughter among the men of Ashur, but it is they
who will perish!"

Mighty Sargon, whom the god loved, the pride of his nation.
There was not a soldier in the king's army who did not hold his
name and memory in reverence. Yes—they would fight, these
common men, whether they believed me or not, for they believed
in him, and in the grandeur he had made of their nation. They
would fight, to avenge his death of long ago. Or, if not for that, for
the honor of dying where he had died.

Each man took up his station that night, his heart full. No
man closed his eyes that night—no man could. We all waited, in
silence, as brothers, sons of the same ghostly father. Our minds,
our wills, were one. No word was spoken, for there was no more
place for words. We all understood, without words. In this I was
but one of many.

It was the last cold hours before dawn when I received the
whispered signal that our sentries had heard the approach of
many horses.

Of all the countless horrors of war, the worst is the waiting.
We were to absorb the full force of the enemy's attack—we knew

not their numbers nor even their names; they were only The Enemy, vague, faceless, a black shadow crowding in upon us. And their onslaught would come in the dark of night, which somehow made it more terrible. To die in the broad light of day was bad enough, but at night . . . A man has visions of his soul wandering blind and lost, knowing no rest, in endless torment, a prey to demons. I was a man no different from the poorest soldier, and I felt all these things. As we waited there, in the Place of Bones, I felt sick with dread.

It was almost with relief when at last we heard their war cries and felt the thunder of their horses' hoofs. They were upon us—the waiting was over and we would see the end now.

I gave a silent signal, and in an instant a hundred bonfires blazed into life—we had banished the covering darkness. Let the Medes know our numbers. Let them know they had lost their chance for surprise.

Nevertheless, they came. Their horses bore down upon us across the length of that rocky plain, but we held back. We waited, watching their charge, knowing they had not seen the traps.

Working until their hands were raw, my men had dug a long trench across the entrance to our camp. They had piled up the earth as a rampart, which must have looked to the enemy horsemen like a crude defense perimeter, the sort thrown up by soldiers who do not really expect attack—the sort a horse and rider could climb over in an instant. They did not see the trench, which had been covered over with reed mats and a sprinkling of dirt, not enough to fool anyone in daylight but almost invisible at night. Its bottom, bristling with sharpened stakes, was hidden from them. They would only learn when it was too late.

The Medes galloped toward us. Even now, as they shook the earth, I could hardly see them except as a dark wave. But they were many. They must have had eight or ten thousand riders—this was no single tribe defending its territory. We did not fight merely the Miyaneh or the Sagarians, men loyal to their clan and a bit of grazing land, but a mighty confederation, a nation. This was what I had feared, all along. I could see it as their horsemen sped across the plain, burning the earth like a blaze through dry grass.

On command, and as one, our bowmen let fly their arrows—dipped in pitch and flaming like torches. They lit the air, turning the night into a weird half-daylight, roofing the sky with smoke and lurid, red-black fire. The Medes would not have to die in darkness.

Yet they did die—dropping from their saddles, our arrows still burning in their breasts. The javelin throwers, their targets clear now, let fly, death whistling through the air like a flight of birds. How many fell before they reached the trench, I know not.

And at the trench . . . How can I describe it? When the earth gave way beneath them, and their horses screamed in terror and pain, their backs broken by the fall or their bellies and necks pierced by the cruel stakes, was it not terrible? Even for us, who had planned it, whose lives would be spared by this awful trap, it was unspeakable. We stood upon the rampart and they perished at our feet, falling into that gruesome tangle of the dead and the dying. And those who did not die at once, we killed as they tried to climb out. We killed them with arrows and javelins and spattered their brains with great stones. Sometimes we killed them with swords and cut their throats with the knives we carried in our belts. We made a rich banquet for the Lady Ereshkigal, and our hearts sickened within us.

When the Medes saw that we had stopped their first rush, they withdrew their cavalry—this was not a fight which would be won by horsemen. But a trench would not stop foot soldiers, and these now followed in their numbers beyond counting, swarming at us like angry bees.

Yet we were ready. Our own soldiers poured over the ramparts and the ditch, now nearly filled in with the Median dead. And we were not a mob but a disciplined army. And we had chariots.

At either end of the trench we had left a little pathway clear, just enough for our war chariots, carried over these mountains in pieces and hastily reassembled, to pass out onto the field of battle, there to do their grim work.

I myself rode in the lead chariot, so I saw what happened in the gray light of that last terrible hour before dawn. It was not a battle, but a massacre. The Medes, disorganized, frightened, their plan in ruins, deserted by even the hope of victory, fought with futile courage and fell like grain before the farmer's scythe. Our army butchered them with pitiless efficiency. They had no chance. They were as men condemned.

By the time the sun had risen over the mountains, it was

over. The few who could, or would, had fled that killing ground, and almost none were left except the dying and the dead. A ghastly silence descended over the face of the land.

I ordered my driver to halt and stepped down. I wished to have a better look at the field of battle—I wished to view my handiwork at close range, but I felt a strange mingling of pride and disgust. Perhaps it was not so strange, for I had known the feeling before. Perhaps it is no more than every successful commander experiences, for the end of all a soldier's patient work is no more than death.

"Look here, *Rab Shaqe*—we've found one still alive and kicking," a soldier shouted to me. "Look, hardly a mark on him!"

I went over to see, making my way carefully across the web of sprawled corpses, and it was true. A Median cavalryman, his forehead grazed by an arrow, had probably been no more than stunned by the blow. He was awake now, crouched on the ground, looking around with fierce, frightened eyes at his captors, who surrounded him with drawn swords, grinning, looking forward to the sport of finishing him off.

But, as it happened, I had other plans for him.

He was a handsome man, and as brave in the face of death as anyone had a right to expect of him. He was young, no older than myself, so it was hard for him. Doubtless he had seen how prisoners were treated among his own people and thought he knew what to expect.

"Do you understand me?" I asked, in Aramaic—he looked well-born, so there was the chance that some attention had been paid to his education.

He nodded. Yes, he understood.

"Then look."

I squatted on the ground beside him and held my hand up before his eyes so he could see the birthmark across my palm. He knew then who I was—he recognized the blood star, the mark of Sargon. I could read all that in his expression.

"When you find your way back," I said, "go to your *shah* and ask him why he thought I would fall into the same trap twice."

Never have I seen such fear in a man's eyes. He believed, I think, really believed that he had come face to face with a living ghost. I was not the Lord Tiglath Ashur to him. I was the wrath of the dead.

I rose and looked about me, seeming not to care that I was on a field carpeted with corpses.

"Shall we kill him now, *Rab Shaqe*?" the soldier asked. I felt almost sorry for him, for he was looking forward to it.

"No—find him a horse. He is going home."

24

Thus was born the legend of Sargon's return to the Zagros. We unfurled the banner of the blood star and it waved before us on the standard of the king's army, just below the winged disk of Ashur, striking terror into the hearts of our enemies. I was the old champion reborn. I would avenge him. The Medes believed all this—may the god forgive me, I half believed it myself.

For the next month our march followed the northern slope of the mountains. We accepted the surrender of many hamlets and towns, taking hostages, horses, food, whatever we needed. The village people, who are always the prisoners and main victims of war, sometimes met us with offerings, casting flowers in my chariot's path as if I truly were some angry demon whose wrath could be thus softened. Sometimes their priests tried to drive me off with strange rites and mantras. I had become a figure of myth, and it caused a giddiness in my mind such as a man suffers when he stands at the river's edge in floodtime and feels the dark waters beckoning to him. It was thus with me, this feeling, like a sickness, of having trespassed. I addressed prayers to Ashur and to the *sedu* of my grandfather, begging forgiveness if this ruse of mine offended against the divinity of either, but these afforded me no comfort.

Only twice in that time did the Medes take the field against us, and only then in small surprise attacks easily repulsed. They fought bravely, leaving many dead behind them, but it was as if they were testing us, feeling for some weakness. And the great, decisive battle never came.

But the days were not wasted. Our scouts ranged wide, and with them went the map makers and the scribes, who recorded all they saw and heard. The lands of the Aryan were becoming something more than simply a great blank emptiness, and when I returned another day with yet another army—and this I knew I would do—I would not then be groping my way in the dark.

By the first dawn of the month of Elul we were within ten days' march of the city of Ecbatana, the goal I had set myself, and still the Medes fled before us into the safety of their mountains. I took no comfort in the ease of these conquests.

One cannot conquer the land—only nations can feel the yoke. The land is always the same, no matter who stands on it, and if I held so and so much territory today, it would revert to itself the moment I left. And leave I must, for I had no intention of establishing garrisons where there was nothing to guard except rocks and grass and crooked little riverbeds that were dry two-thirds of the year. I did not want to own this place. I wanted only that its inhabitants should never think to leave it for the rich plains of the Land of Ashur. And to achieve that I had to give them such a taste of defeat that they would never risk another. And to achieve that I had somehow to make them fight, for victory is always a collaboration between the conquered and the conqueror. But in this they would not oblige me.

We had taken over a village that was well placed for watching the approaches of Ecbatana. Its inhabitants had already deserted it by the time we arrived; in a few of the houses the embers from the cooking fires were still warm. Here my officers and I began drawing up the final plans for our assault on the city, the capital of Ellipi, whose "kings" had already made their submission to Sargon in the last reign and who would therefore be regarded as traitors. It would be a costly triumph and by no means a decisive one, for what is a city after all except brick and stone?

It was here that I received the report that a sentry had seen a lone rider approaching the village, and that he carried a banner of truce.

"Let him pass," I ordered. What harm could he do?

Within two hours I found the Uqukadi noble called Upash bowing before me like a carpet peddler.

"Blessings on you, Mighty Conqueror, before whom all the world . . ."

"Yes—very well," I answered, gesturing to him to rise, for

such servility filled me with impatience and a gnawing suspicion that this oily savage was trying to make a fool of me. "What have you come here to say, barbarian?"

If he was discomfited by this reception he gave no sign, but fell back at once into the attitude of amused contempt he had shown me at our first meeting, five years before. His hand went up to secure the leather cap that fitted so tightly over his close-cropped hair, and he smiled.

"I bear a message from Daiaukka, *shah* of all the Medes. He would parley with you, Lord."

"There can be no objection to this. I will grant him safe passage if he wishes to come to me here."

"Alone, Lord—and in some place of safety. He trusts you no more than you do him."

I shrugged my shoulders, having expected nothing less.

"Very well, then. Let him meet me tomorrow, one hour after midday, on the plain half a day's ride north from this village. I will carry no weapon and will bring an escort of twenty men. Let him keep to the same terms, and I will speak to him—alone."

"To this he will agree. And now—if we might have a private word?"

He glanced around at my officers, as if his meaning had not been clear enough, and I dismissed them and then sat down on the room's only chair, drawing my sword from its scabbard and laying it on the table before me lest my visitor harbor any ambitions concerning revenge.

"You misjudge me, Prince," he said, his eyes fastened on the sword as if to measure its length. "I am not your enemy."

"You are my enemy—men like you are every man's enemy."

"Perhaps. I have lived long enough, Young Lord, to have lost most of my illusions and, in any case, men with high ideals are rarely useful to conquerors."

He smiled, as if we had already reached an understanding.

"Then you have come, I take it, to sell me your present protectors like so many baskets of dates?"

"What loyalty could I owe to the Medes, Lord?" He made a gesture with his left hand that seemed to dismiss the very possibility of such an idea. "Please remember that I have seen you make war before and I know that you will be the victor here, not Daiaukku—now or later, it must happen. A man may be allowed to be practical."

"Very well, then. Tell me what you want and what you can offer in exchange."

We struck our bargain, then and there. I did not like this man and had no reason to trust him, but, yes, I would make him great in the lands of the Aryan. And for this he would be my eyes and ears in the councils of Daiaukka's nobles. He would tell me the numbers of horsemen and foot soldiers commanded by each of the *parsua* of the Median tribes, of the limits of their loyalties, of the jealousies among them, and the weaknesses of each. He would play the perfect traitor. He would make himself very useful, for a conqueror rules not through men's virtues but through their defects. Nevertheless, I did not like this man.

"And what of this meeting? What does Daiaukka want? Is it a trap?"

"It is not that, Lord, for Daiaukka has said that it is not and these people never tarnish themselves with lies. Perhaps he hopes for an honorable peace."

That I did not believe. But Daiaukka had been right not to open his mind to this man, so perhaps he was wise. I would know soon enough.

Daiaukka, *shah* of all the Medes, rode a fine black horse that stood at least two spans higher at the shoulder than that of any of his companions. This horse, as I had been told, was his single indulgence, for his was a nature of the most perfect integrity, possessed of neither avarice nor greed nor fear. He never lied but still contrived to be as cunning as an adder. Both cruelty and pity were unknown to him, since both only deflect a man from his purpose, and his will was as unbending as granite. It was his will that the Medes should be a great nation, as his father Ukshatar, who had died in exile, had envisioned them, and that he should be their master. It was his will that the Medes should one day be masters of the world, the inheritors of the race of Ashur, whom he regarded with unconcealed contempt.

As I watched him across those two hundred paces of whispering grass, noting the skill with which he managed his skittish, high-spirited horse and the graceful economy of his every gesture, I began to realize that this was probably the most dangerous enemy a man could have. I respected and admired him, and hoped that he might die here, in his own mountains, and by my hand. It was my prayer to Holy Ashur that he might spare the world from the purity of men like Daiaukka, *shah* of all the Medes.

"It could be a trick," Lushakin murmured—he had insisted on leading my bodyguard, saying that a foolish prince needed a wise rogue to watch his back.

"It is not a trick, for he has given his word."

"Then be not yourself so scrupulous. Take your javelin and, as soon as he comes within range, plant it in his belly like a garden stake. He is all that holds their confederation together— kill him and the Medes will quickly fall to quarreling among themselves again."

"Until another rises to take his place. Besides, Lushakin, I too have given my word."

"All you high-born nobles have mud for brains."

I laughed, and pricked my horse forward, leaving Lushakin and his hand-picked escort of *quradu* behind. Daiaukka met me in the center of the plain.

For a moment neither of us spoke. Our mounts sniffed at each other nervously, as if they understood the antagonism existing between our races, while *shah* and *rab shaqe* took each other's measure. It was an interesting silence.

Daiaukka was then perhaps thirty years old, but for full half his life he had been at war, rebuilding the alliances that had fallen apart after his father's banishment, and every day of that long struggle showed in his face, which was as brown and weathered as his old leather coat. He seemed ageless, almost indifferent. If he had ever laughed, or even smiled, there was no evidence of it. Only the restless black eyes revealed the man behind the mask.

"You are Tiglath Ashur," he said finally, as if the information would be new to me. "You are named for your unclean god, and your father is king in the western lands, where demons are worshiped. You see—I know you are not a spirit but a man like other men."

"And you are Daiaukka, *shah* of the barbarians, whose father my grandfather sent into exile. Perhaps now, if we are finished insulting one another, you will tell me what you wish."

"Peace."

"The price of peace is submission."

"A truce, then."

"Even a truce must be paid for."

"You plan to take the city of Ecbatana," he said, glancing up at the horizon beyond my left shoulder. He seemed almost not to have been listening to our conversation. "It will be defended. Its loss, and the loss of the men who will die trying to hold it, will not cripple me, but such a siege, even if it is successful, would be expensive for an army such as yours—far from home and surrounded by enemies. We must both decide which is cheaper, war or truce."

"I did not come here to sneak away again."

"No, you came here to win a great victory over us—why, I wonder. Not because a few fools raided three or four of your villages."

"No, not because of that."

"Why, then?"

He seemed genuinely interested. The restless black eyes settled on my face, narrowing with attention. And there was no harm in our understanding one another.

"Because, if they go unchecked, it will not be long before the Medes begin to look with longing at the rich lands where Ashur is king."

"Yes—this is so." He nodded, as if we spoke of indifferent things, thus making a deception even of the truth.

"And I would put an end to all such ambitions."

"And to do this you must win your victory. But this I can deny you, by the simple device of refusing your challenge. I can hide in these mountains until the snows drive you out."

"And while you hide, I can lay waste this nation you are making. I can burn villages and fields. I can slaughter cattle. When the snows come your people will face famine, and they will blame you—and rightly, for it is a king's duty to protect his people. If he cannot, he is not a king."

"This too is so. Thus we will both profit from a period of truce."

"For how long?"

He turned inside himself for a moment, considering the matter. "Two years."

"What will have changed by then?"

"By then I will be ready to fight. Then you will have your victory—or I will have mine."

"Still, you must buy this truce."

"Why? It is to the advantage of us both."

"But more to yours than to mine. If I stay, I may break your grand alliance, by so simple a device as starving it to death. No, you must buy this truce, with gold, slaves, and horses. The men of

Ashur do not make war for glory alone, and I will not go back to my father like a beggar."

"It shall be as you say, Tiglath Ashur. I expected no less, since the men of your race are all thieves. Receive my embassy and they will settle terms with you. We will meet again, in two years' time."

With a suddenness that almost took my breath away, he wheeled his horse about and rode back to his own bodyguard. Our meeting was over, and with it my first campaign in the lands of the Aryan.

The instructions Daiaukka gave to his emissaries must have stressed a need for haste, because I was less than five days in coming to terms with them over the payment of tribute. I was to leave the Zagros with four hundred horses, a like number of slaves—provisioned for the journey, that I would not have to feed them at my own expense—and five *mina* of gold, which was not a great amount but would be enough to pay my soldiers. I was content with my plunder, for although Daiaukka did not seem to realize it, he had ceded me a considerable asset. That wise and cunning man had made a mistake in the composition of the slaves.

It is a hard king who will send his own people into bondage, and the *shah* of all the Medes had apparently yielded to sentiment because nearly all of the men and women who made up my prize were Cimmerians from the north, taken in the almost constant warfare between these two peoples who were undistinguishable in appearance and custom, even language, yet who hated one another with such desperate passion. Thus the Cimmerian captives regarded us as their liberators. I found among them many who were willing, indeed eager, to aid my map makers and scribes, and even to fight beside the soldiers of Ashur. It is a mistake to part with an enemy who has long been a prisoner in your own house.

Daiaukka sent me yet one more offering—the persons of Uk-satar, *parsua* of the Miyaneh tribe, and four of his tribal elders as acknowledgment of the fault committed when the villages of Dur Tuqe had been raided. This was the reason given, but I have no doubt the *shah* served his own purposes first. Perhaps he had hit upon the device for ridding himself of some future challenge to his rule; or perhaps the raids had been carried out against his wishes and he wished to set an example. Or perhaps both. In any case, I was to do with these five as I saw fit, which meant that I was to kill them.

This I did. When our army crossed the border back into the Land of Ashur, I had all five strangled with bowstrings—since the manner of their dying could be of consequence to no one except themselves, I saw no reason to make a spectacle of it—and then had the corpses impaled on high stakes and set out so that they faced east, back to their homeland. I left them there as a warning to any others of their nation who might think to plunder the lands where the god's will was law.

These things were done on the sixth day of the month of Tisri in the twenty-first year of the reign of the Lord Sennacherib. On the next day, since it was an unlucky day, the soldiers rested and kept to their tents, but on the next we began our march first to Musasir and then home to Amat, where the citizens met us with thanksgiving on the second day of the month of Marcheswan, when already at those altitudes the first breath of snow whitens the night air.

All the garrison buildings were now completed, remade in stone that would stand to the end of the world, and the fortress wall was nearly finished. Even the town, which I had left nothing but a collection of mud hovels, had increased in size and splendor out of all recognition. The work had gone well, and for this my slave Kephalos was quick to take all the credit. He had grown even fatter in my absence, so since his girth was the one infallible index of his prosperity, I could only assume he had continued to benefit from a brisk traffic in bribes.

"You, my lord, have not fared so well on this campaign," he said, pulling at his great gleaming beard and shaking his head with resigned sadness. "This king of the Medes has cheated you, for such captives as these, unteachable barbarians with clay in their ears, will not fetch much of a price on the—"

"The captives, most of them, will be returning to their homes after the winter. They are Cimmerians and I want friendship with that nation, since they are bitter enemies with the Medes. Some few—and of their own choice—will serve with us when we return to settle all questions with Daiaukka."

We walked in the garden behind his house, which was only less grand than the palace I had had built for myself as *shaknu* of the northern provinces. I could smell the perfume of frankincense trees and hear the tinkling waters of a fountain, pleasant sensations after months on campaign.

Kephalos made no protest beyond a slight groan, as if the silver he would lose in commissions were being cut from his own flesh.

"Ah, well then, Lord, if it must be, then it must. At least there are still the horses."

"The horses go to the army."

"Dread Lord, this is too much!" he shouted, stopping to stamp his foot against the flagstone walkway. "I know that you love to play the *rab shaqe*, the noble soldier who thinks only of his duty, but by the great gods, a man who pays no need to his own interest can be trusted in nothing else. If you must persist, then at least let me *sell* the horses to the army—through such a device we will do almost as well, and your conscience will be clear."

"To the army, Kephalos, as the king's share in the booty."

"Then I almost am afraid to ask what you plan for the five *mina* of gold."

"It has already been divided among the soldiers. Common men will not fight without the hope of plunder."

Strangely, there was no protest. I looked around at him to see if he could be ill, but he was smiling.

"Kephalos, what have you . . . ?"

"Soldiers spend plunder on wine and harlots," he said, as if explaining some principle of nature. "I have an arrangement with all the tavern keepers and brothel owners in Amat whereby I—which is to say, we—receive a fifth part of all the custom that passes through their hands. This in exchange for certain . . . let us speak of them as 'considerations.' Or, better yet, let us not speak of them at all, for a wise man does not stir up the mud at the bottom of his own well. At any rate, Lord, my sagacity has yet saved us something from your foolishness. Be thankful that your slaves loves you and concerns himself with the hard task of preserving you from beggary."

I did not protest. I only laughed, thinking that if I ever changed my mind and decided I must be king in the Land of Ashur, the simplest way would be to have Kephalos buy the throne for me, since no doubt he was already rich enough to manage this.

"Have you answered your father's letters yet?" he asked,

watching me out of the corner of his eye—the question implied, as if there were any doubt of it, that he knew their contents.

"No. But I must, soon."

"And will you go back?"

"It seems I must. He is the king, and it is his will."

"But if you refuse, he will understand."

"No—he is the king and has ordered me home. He knows I would not flout his will, even if I could."

"Then, after all this time, you will be putting your hand back into the lion's mouth."

"I know that."

We walked on in silence. The wind had picked up and it was no longer such a pleasure to be walking out-of-doors.

"Will you go back with me?" I asked. It was not even a request, but I would have liked his company. Kephalos, however, shook his head.

"No, Lord. As long as your father lives you are safe anywhere in the Land of Ashur, but Nineveh is a place where bad things can befall one who has angered the *marsarru*. I will stay here, that the Lord Esarhaddon will not feel tempted to stain his hands with my blood."

"I think you wrong him, my friend."

"Do I?" Kephalos smiled bleakly. "I think not, Lord. I think you are blinded by the habits of affection and see not the truth of what your brother has become. What will happen to both of us when he is king is not a subject I much love to ponder."

The Lord Sennacherib would now accept no excuse. It was no longer a question of father and son—the king commanded the presence of his *shaknu*. On my loyalty as his subject, I must return to Nineveh.

The evening of my conversation with Kephalos, two days after my return to Amat, I wrote and made my submission. I would be in Nineveh to attend upon the king no later than the first day of the month of Kislef. I could not delay longer.

Then I went into the women's quarters and spoke of these things to my mother. She sat quietly, listening, as was her custom, until I had done.

"Will you take me with you, my son, or shall I remain here?"

"You will accompany me at least as far as Three Lions. I

think it best you stay there until I see what awaits me in Nineveh."

"And what awaits you in Nineveh, Lathikados?"

"I do not know. Nothing good, I fear. I would prefer to stay here until the flesh falls from my bones, but the king will not be denied."

"He wishes to see his son." She smiled at me, as if now all doubts were cleared away. "Why should he not? You are the pride of his life, and he loves you."

I did not reply, since there was no reply I could have made.

"I can be ready in two days," she went on at last. "I am an old woman and have little to hold me to one place."

"You are not old, Merope, and you are still beautiful. The king no doubt will think so."

"The king, without doubt, is past thinking of any woman's beauty, my son. But you are not. Shall you take Naiba with you?"

"Yes—I shall take Naiba with me. You need have no fear that your son will twice be guilty of the same folly."

We said no more of the matter, and Esharhamat's name was never mentioned between us.

Esharhamat. I had been away from Nineveh for almost two years. My life had been full of business. I had taken another woman to my sleeping mat. Yet had a day passed when memories of Esharhamat had not stirred in my mind? The thought of her was like a ghost, visiting silent and unbidden. I was never free.

She was with child again—I had received notice of this from my father. The *baru* predicted a son who would wear the crown of a great nation, so the prophecy which had kept her from me seemed fulfilled.

And I was on my way back—if not to Esharhamat, then to the mud-brick walls of Nineveh. Once more would I drink the waters of the Tigris, mother of rivers. Once more would I behold her great temples and hear the noise of many tongues in her streets. I was her son. Yes, I longed to see her again, even if the sight tore the heart from my breast, for a man cannot walk forever on unknown paths and not grow a stranger to himself. Nineveh—how I loved her as I turned my eyes to the road home! How I will love her while I live, though she become but a name.

Such was the bitter sweetness of my journey, for a man easily takes pleasure in his own pain, and memory makes all things precious, even loss.

I left Amat thinking to return within two months. Kephalos was to carry on with his building projects, and Lushakin, whom I had promoted to *rab abru,* commanded the garrison. The civil government was in the hands of my scribes, who would keep me informed by riders dispatched three times each month.

The weather was unusually cold when we set out, but the roads were good and we traveled fast, although our escort numbered forty men. The wagon for my mother and her women was hardly any encumbrance. We arrived at Three Lions by the evening of the twelfth day, in time for us to dine on fresh-killed goat.

"The gods are pleased, Lord. The river has been kind and we have had fine harvests in your absence."

"Perhaps the gods would be most pleased if I stayed away entirely," I said, but it was not the sort of joke Tahu Ishtar was disposed to understand, so he made a solemn bow and held his peace. My overseer had changed hardly at all since our first meeting, years before, but his son, Qurdi, was now quite grown.

I was not the only one struck by this fact. A handsome youth will make an impression anywhere, and the night before, while my mother supervised her women in the ordering of our house, I had observed that Naiba and he kept exchanging glances that could not be misinterpreted. This morning, while he accompanied his father and me on an inspection stroll of the farm buildings, it seemed that nothing could induce him to raise his eyes from the dust, as if he already felt the shame of having dishonored his master's sleeping mat. It was a situation I found highly amusing.

We were in the stable, where Tahu Ishtar had been showing me a fine silver-colored colt born only four days earlier. It stood beside its mother on thin, ungainly legs while my overseer caressed its neck with his broad, knowing hands. He was a proud man, who would never violate the trust I placed in him, and this animal, born for the service of another, was precious in his sight.

"He is fine," I said. "As fine as the horses of the Zagros, of which the Medes are so proud—as fine as the great black brute that bears their king. I will not part with him. I will have him trained up to war and ride him myself."

"What shall we call him, Lord?"

"Ghost," I answered. The name was as much a surprise to

me as to anyone, for it had just that instant come into my head. "The Medes are greatly afraid of ghosts."

"So it shall be, Lord."

He closed the stall behind us and we went back outside into the sunshine. It was a fine cold day and the blood washed through my veins like wine. It was good to be alive and in possession of so many of the earth's good things. In that moment I envied no man.

"You have done well, Tahu Ishtar," I said. "I grow rich by your labor and care. I feel privileged that I can entrust my property to one such as you."

He said nothing, but frowned, and cast a furtive, sidewise glance at his son. He, too, it seemed, had read rightly the message in a pair of dark eyes.

That night, when the lamp beside our sleeping mat had been extinguished, I let my hand slide up over Naiba's hips, carrying her night tunic with me. She settled closer to me, opening her legs that my fingers might caress the downlike hair of her cleft, and her lips searched for mine as I guided my manhood into her. Was there less passion or more in her embrace? Who was I to her in that moment when her body arched and her breath escaped in tortured, whimpering gasps? A woman's pleasure blinds her eyes, and thus her lover becomes whom she pleases.

She fell asleep in my arms, as she had countless times before. She sighed in her sleep and dreamed.

"I have lost her," I thought. "I won her body, but she is no longer mine."

And what of it? I had never been hers. I was not wounded, not even in my pride—I did not even care. It was simply a kind of joke that the gods had played on me.

I would wait. Naiba was my property and thus far my property had not been interfered with—her soul was not my concern. It might all come to nothing, leaving us all the way we were, and if it did not . . . But I had time until then. I would wait.

I was at Three Lions for five more days and that, it seemed, was time enough for something—perhaps only an understanding, the knowledge of another's heart that fills a glance—for something to have developed between my concubine and the son of my overseer. Naiba was still half-savage and, more than that, a woman grown. What had she not learned of men in the house of my servant Kephalos? What would she not risk to gain some object close to her heart? What could she not conceal? She served my bed each night, as if nothing had changed. But Qurdi—poor Qurdi, once that firm-limbed little boy who had straddled the back of the lion skin his father had brought me, peering curiously into its open mouth—he had not yet so completely left his childhood behind him that anyone with eyes could not read this trouble in his face. He was not born to hide anything in his soul.

Thus I knew all.

And yet there was this mystery—that I should be so little touched by the matter. I did not love Naiba, but love is only one small part of the bond between a man and a woman. She was mine, no less so than if I had covered her with the veil and called her "wife." A year ago I would have felt—what? Anger? Yes, at least anger. And my wrath, against this my chattel and her lover both, would have been terrible to behold. Now I only hoped that they would be discreet, that things did not reach such an extreme that I would be forced to act. Above all else, I wished to avoid punishing the injury I did not feel.

But if my heart did not swell with anger, was I empty? No. Then what was there? I searched and found . . . what? Relief. I was secretly pleased, because here at least was one woman who would weep no salt tears when I turned from her. Here was no Esharhamat.

Esharhamat. I had only to speak her name, to whisper it in the privacy of my unquiet mind, and all was made plain to me. I had returned to her, by the simple device of consenting to return to that city of dead hopes, where perhaps, had the god willed it, she might have sat at my side as consort and queen. Each marker stone on the road to Nineveh brought me nearer to her. She filled my breast and left no room for little Naiba, who had held me in the protective circle of her embrace, as if only waiting for this moment.

Such were the thoughts in my mind as I kissed Merope goodbye and prepared to depart for the city where I would once more be the son of a mighty father, covered with favor and glory, the darling of empires, the master of all save my own voiceless passions.

25

❧❧❧❧❧

Once again, he seemed to be waiting for me. He sat in the dust before the last marker stone on the road to Nineveh. I knew who he was as soon as I could distinguish that the shape in the distance was a man and not simply one of those tricks the sun plays with distant objects. I was not even surprised.

He looked unchanged from the first time I had seen him, some seven years before. I stopped my horse before him and my shadow fell across the spot where he crouched on the ground. He glanced up with his blind eyes that focused on nothing, and he smiled.

"The Lord Tiglath Ashur comes home at last," he said. "He is welcome."

I instructed the *ekalli* in charge of my escort to proceed down the road, telling him that I would catch up in a moment. He stared at the *maxxu* with an expression of something almost like horror and obeyed without uttering a sound.

"Who welcomes him, old man?" I asked. "Do you speak for yourself, or for another?"

"Are you not summoned, Prince?"

A blind man may seem to look beyond what he does not see, as if through the obscuring veil of this world. So it was now. His eyes were fixed on mine, but what was revealed to him was the insensible truth behind the mask. His brown, withered lips parted, as if to laugh, but he made no sound. He seemed to mock me in silence.

"I know now you are from the god," I cried, my heart

clenched with apprehension. "Speak—what do you want from me?"

"I, Lord? Nothing." The thin shoulders moved in dismissal beneath the faded yellow robes. "Have you seen so much and learned so little? You, who have climbed Mount Epih to pray there and receive dreams? Did not the god cradle you in his hand at the Place of Bones? And yet you ask what I want of you."

"Then what have you come to tell me? Speak! Have mercy on me, for I am full of darkness!"

"This is better, Lord. Learn to submit, for the god's will is each man's fate. But I have come with his message only—that you must harden your heart, for you enter now the time of partings. In the years to come you will speak 'farewell' until your tongue sickens of the sound."

"This is every man's fate."

"Yes—at the end of life. But you are still young."

"Is this why I am brought to Nineveh? To say 'farewell'?"

"No, but to do the god's will." He raised a thin arm, and seemed to dismiss me even from his thoughts. "Go now, Prince, for your eyes still blind you. Go."

I would have spoken again, for there was much I wished to know, but I saw it would have been in vain and said nothing. An old man sat in the dust by the roadside, sightless and poor before a mighty prince, but the prince had become an object unworthy of notice. I was nothing. He seemed to have forgotten my existence.

I spurred my horse and rode away, not looking back. I would not have dared.

How long may a thing trouble the mind after it has been forgotten, the shadow that darkens all and is thus itself invisible?

The king's riders met us before we were within two *beru* of the city gates and raced away to announce our coming. Nineveh's walls were draped in banners, and we were met with bread, flowers, and wine. I rode up the Street of Ishtar, my head ringing with the people's cheers, and my father met me on the palace steps and embraced me in the sight of all. I had forgotten the blind *maxxu* with his talk of partings. I had driven him from my thoughts.

The king was beside himself with joy.

"My son!" he shouted, his voice cracking with emotion. "My

son, the conqueror of nations! No man is more glorious than my
son, the pride of Ashur!"

And the people cheered, as if I had come back with a hundred foreign princes yoked to my chariot. A mob will cheer any
man if he is raised up before them; the king might have done as
much for the slave who cleaned his sandals. Yet I did not think of
that either, for it was I whom the king loved.

Gathered about him on the steps were all the great men of
the court—or, rather, nearly all. Esarhaddon, I noticed, was absent. And the Lord Sinahiusur as well.

The king had grown into an old man.

"We shall feast tonight, eh?" he said, leading me inside the
great bronze doors, taller than four men. "We shall grow drunk
and merry, chasing away each dark thought. Yes? Shall it not be
so?"

"Yes—it shall be so."

Where was my mind while I spoke? The king, his hand on
my shoulder, clutching at me as if afraid he might fall, followed
my steps. I had almost forgotten him, because for an instant . . .

She might have been no more than a shade in that vast hall
with its painted walls and its columns of cedar, each so huge that
two men could not touch hands about it. I caught sight of her but
for a moment, before she retired quickly back into the shadow
and was gone. Yet not so quickly that I did not know her.

Esharhamat, whose face I saw in every night's darkness. I
knew her. I knew her behind her veil, as I would have known her
had my eyes been torn from their sockets. Just a glance—that was
all she gave me. What was I to read in that look? Perhaps nothing. Perhaps only dead hatred. I did not know.

She was great with child. So that much, at least, had been
true.

"Yes. Tomorrow will be time enough to speak of the business
of state. Yes? Tomorrow I will be the king again."

He squeezed my arm and I awoke from my waking dream.
"Look at me," he seemed to be telling me. *"I am your father, and
I love you. And I am the king this moment."*

Yet I could not help but notice how the jeweled turban no
longer hid the gray in his hair, and that he seemed always short of
breath. His face was full of lines and his cheeks sunken. He was
not what he had been.

We did grow drunk and merry that night, but it was not the

wine that clouded his mind. He would tell a story, breaking off in the middle because he had forgotten what he had wanted to say, wrathful if anyone attempted to remind him. And always, in his wrath, he returned to Esarhaddon.

"That cursed boy! For he will never be anything more than a boy, a puling baby clinging to his mother's skirts. He will never be a man, and may it be the god's will that he never reign as king."

"It is already the god's will that he shall reign," I said, laying my hand upon the Lord Sennacherib's arm—for so small a thing as this touch, which ten years ago he would have scorned as an intolerable impertinence, now had the effect of distracting him into a calmer state of mind. "And he was always a good soldier. You should give him command of an army that he might fight some great war. He would not make you ashamed."

"I am ashamed of him now."

The king, sullen and resentful, clenched his fist and lowered it lightly to the table.

"Where is the Lady Shaditu?" he cried suddenly. "Where is she? Why is she not here to honor her brother?"

His eyes cast about, searching for someone he might punish for this offense. At last they came to rest on a chamberlain, an elderly eunuch whose name was Shupa and who had served him for thirty years.

"Well? Go and fetch her!"

The chamberlain, who knew his master's temper, bowed himself out of the royal presence as quickly as he could, his head ducking all the while like a bird picking up seeds.

I looked about me, at the other faces round the table, at the king's princely brothers and their sons, at my own brothers, whom birth had placed higher or lower than myself, at the men of humble birth whom fortune or virtue had raised to power at the king's side, men who had been great in the Land of Ashur, some of them since before I was born. Some of them could not—or would not—meet my eye. All were afraid. Did they know what had happened between Shaditu and myself that last night? Nabu-sharusur had known, or guessed. Perhaps in all Nineveh only the king did not know.

But did they need that knowledge to make them afraid? Was it not enough to be the king's servant in the deep twilight of his life, when the heir was filled with hatred? They listened to my father as he mocked his successor, and they said nothing—what could they say? How many of these men would find their heads between their feet the day Esarhaddon took the king's mace in his hand? No—they had enough to fear without my little sin weighing on their minds.

And the king? He had already forgotten about Shaditu. An Arab girl with skin pale as wood smoke was dancing, clicking little cymbals between her fingers and thumbs in time to the music of a flute player in the pleated linen tunic of an Egyptian. The king laughed, clapping his hands, and the Arab girl smiled with her eyes. The king had drunk too much and could not count time to the music, but that did not matter. And his wrath was lost in a moment of idle pleasure.

"Is she not fine, Tiglath my son?" He nudged me with his elbow, almost knocking the wine cup from my hand. "Is she not a pretty thing? Yes? And the way the oil glistens on her breasts and belly! Would she not press the seed from a man's loins, eh? I will make you a present of her—do you hear that, you pretty slut! I give you to my son, the mighty Tiglath Ashur, whom the gods love. Ha, ha, ha!"

"Dread Lord, the Lady Shaditu . . ."

"Yes? What is it you want Shupa, eh?" He turned, scowling, but I think he was only startled.

"The Lady Shaditu . . ."

"Yes? What of her?"

"She begs your pardon, Dread Lord, but her head troubles her and she will not come."

"Yes? Well, what of it? Why do you pester me, Shupa? Can you not see that I am with my son?"

And at last, when the late hour and the wine and his own weakness overwhelmed him, I helped the master of the wide world to find his bed. I unlaced his sandals and covered him with a cloak and sat beside him the little time until he fell asleep. The king was old and his life, like spilled wine, was dripping away with hardly a sound.

I had grown to manhood in that great palace, and I needed no lamp to guide my steps as I sought the door that led outside to a courtyard shrouded in darkness. It was empty. No one was there, only the still, quiet night. I sat down on an old stone bench, cradling between my hands the wine cup I had carried away with me, my heart filled with memories.

"*I am Tiglath Ashur! My father is Sennacherib, Lord of the Earth, King of Kings!*"

The words rang in my memory, as if they had just been spoken. And I had looked up and seen the king, shining like the sun—just here, all those years ago.

Lord of the Earth, King of Kings. And now an old man, my father, lay snoring in his room. And Tiglath Ashur—what of him?

A glimpse of her, stepping out from behind a pillar for one quick peek at her old lover. Esharhamat, in whose eyes a man might lose himself. At least she had not forgotten me, although doubtless it would have been best if she had.

I turned the wine and set the cup down between my feet. It had lost its savor for me, and the night had lasted too long.

"My Lord?"

I turned to look but saw nothing. And then someone stepped out of the shadows—a woman. For a moment I thought . . . But no. It was only the Arab girl.

"No one could tell me where my lord slept tonight, so I came looking for you."

What could she be talking about? And then, of course, I remember—my father's little present.

And why not? What difference could it make?

"Come here," I said, gesturing to her. "Come here, and let me look at you."

She approached, moving silently on bare feet. I held out my hand and she took it. She knelt before me. She smelled of sandalwood and sweet oil.

"They tell me you are a great conqueror," she said. "Tonight you can conquer Arabia."

Her laughter was like the music of silver bells. She opened her tunic and let it glide from her shoulders, knowing I would find her beautiful.

"Let us find a place to take our ease," I said, standing up. "We can go to the house of war and kick some sleeping cadet out of his bed."

Perhaps I had drunk more than I thought. Perhaps I stumbled. My foot brushed against the cup I had left resting on the ground, and its wine spilled across the stones like blood.

* * *

"You are not in the house of women now, Prince."

I had been asleep, my nose pressed against a soft breast that smelled sweetly of oil. Before I knew what had happened I felt a hand closing around my ankle and myself being dragged out from beneath the blanket.

It was Tabshar Sin.

"You have missed breakfast, and I will put you to cleaning out the stables until dinner," he said, grinning at me. With the stump of an arm that protruded from his green uniform he gestured toward the sleeping mat.

"Who is your friend?"

I didn't know. It suddenly came to me that I had not the remotest hint of an idea.

"Who are you?" I asked, turning to her. She grinned, as if at a fine joke. "The *rab kisir* wishes to know your name, and so do I, for you are lovely. Who are you?"

"What name you wish, Lord—though I was born Zabibe. My mother named me after a queen."

"And very right she was."

Tabshar Sin held a pan of water for me and I washed my face, awake now and happy to see him.

"Doubtless I have been assigned rooms in my father's house, although I know not where. Go and find them—wait for me there, Zabibe."

She gathered up her robe and left, and I was not sorry. A woman is a fine thing at night, when one feels lonely and wishes to take one's ease, but the daylight belongs to men.

"Come," I said, putting my arm across Tabshar Sin's shoulders—he was smaller than I remembered him. "You must tell me all the news while we empty a jar together, for I have a great thirst for the beer of Nineveh. . . ."

We sat with our backs against the wall of the old cadet quarters, enjoying the sunshine, already a little drunk.

"Do you remember?" he asked finally, his eyes closed and a faint smile playing on his lips. "I gave you your first instruction with the sword, just here. I thought, 'he has tenacity, but the gods help him in a duel.' I hope you have improved since then."

"A little," I said, thinking of Esarhaddon. "Enough to keep every drunken knave from cutting my throat, but it is not my weapon."

"No—it was Esarhaddon's weapon. But that was before he became the *marsarru* and forgot what it is to be a soldier."

I did not reply. I do not think Tabshar Sin expected that I would.

"I have only one cadet left." He sighed, like a man numbering his afflictions. "One more royal prince—and he will be with the army at the start of the next campaign season."

Something in his voice made me look at him, really look at him, for the first time, and I saw what had eluded me before—that Tabshar Sin, like everyone else, had grown old. There was more white than black in his beard now, and his face, when he closed his eyes, was almost that of a corpse.

"What will you do then?" I asked him.

"I do not know, or even care very much. I suppose I will go home to my native village, where I know no one, and water date palms."

"Come back with me to Amat. Train up soldiers I can use to fight the Medes."

"Do you mean it?" He opened his eyes and looked at me, almost as if I had startled him awake.

"Yes—I mean it."

"Then I might have the good fortune to be killed in battle."

"Then you will come?"

"Yes, of course I will come. I thank you, Prince—it will be like old times."

"No. It will be better."

I took the beer jug that he had been cradling in his lap and tipped it back until its contents washed to the very back of my throat. I was very pleased with myself.

"Where is Esarhaddon?" I asked, not precisely sure why.

"In Calah. But he will be here tomorrow, for the king has summoned him. I think the king cannot resist the opportunity to humble Esarhaddon, so he must come to Nineveh while you are here that he may witness the people's love for his brother."

"Am I loved?"

"Yes. But do not preen yourself too much on account of it. It is true that you are praised because you fight the Medes and hate the Babylonians, but you are praised all the more because you are not Esarhaddon."

"And yet he it was who found favor with the gods."

"But with no one else." Tabshar Sin moved his shoulders, as

if he felt the cold. "There will be trouble. I shall be just as happy to be gone from Nineveh when the Lord Esarhaddon begins his reign."

"And yet much may happen before then. The king may yet live many years more."

"Yes, but not reign many more. You have seen him, Prince. How long must it be before your brother becomes king—in fact, if not in name?"

He reclaimed the beer jar, but only to hold it once more in his lap. He closed his hand around its neck and then seemed to forget it entirely.

"So, you see," he went on at last, closing his eyes once more, "I shall not be sorry to be gone. Or if a Median spear finds me; it is all the same."

All the rest of that morning I found myself sought out by officers and soldiers, some of whom I knew from the wars in the south, some of whom I had never met. I seemed always to be at the center of a little knot of men, some of whom asked me questions—about how the Scythian cavalry fought, and if I had found chariots of any use in the mountain campaigns—and some merely stood about and listened. A few even asked if I would accept them for service against the Medes. It seemed that my reports from the north had enjoyed a wide currency within the house of war. My popularity with the army, it seemed, had never stood higher.

But, as Tabshar Sin had pointed out, this was less my doing than my brother's—I was not he, and I did not follow him in loving the Babylonians, so I was loved myself.

Ever since the Lord Sennacherib had sacked Marduk's city and left her a waste, a home for foxes and a nesting place for owls, there had been two parties, two ways of thinking in the Land of Ashur. One held that the king had done a wicked thing in destroying the ancient power of Babylon. These spoke of her as of a mother, and they feared the wrath of her god. These wished to rebuild her walls, cleanse her sanctuaries, and have the king or one of his sons take once more the hands of Marduk and be king himself in Sumer. This was the will of the priests, and of many besides. The other party—and these were strongest within the army and among the common people—wished Babylon to lie in ruins forever. "Why raise up another nation of enemies?" they asked. "Have we not the barbarians in the north and east? Are these not enough?"

While the king lived, one brick of Babylon's great wall would not lie on top of another. Such was his will. But when the king died . . . It was well known that the priests had great influence with Esarhaddon, that he had spoken many times of our great crimes against the old gods. Thus many were afraid.

So the people and the army looked for someone whom they could prefer over Esarhaddon. Thus I was respected where he was scorned, and my name was on all men's lips.

But to set myself up as my brother's rival was to break with the lawful succession and the will of the gods, and this I was not prepared to do. When my mind was at last understood, the people would set up another idol in my place. Hence Tabshar Sin's warning.

And Tabshar Sin was wiser than I, for I was yet young enough to be greatly flattered by the attention of so many. The vanity of soldiers, it is said, is like a hole dug in the sand—it will swallow anything.

Yet the king was old enough to have grown foolish all over again—and to have ceased remembering, or caring, that one day another king must reign in the Land of Ashur—for he encouraged my pride and hated Esarhaddon, whom he might have turned aside to a wiser policy. The king did his part to make me an enemy of my own brother, and for this evil we would each of us one day be made to pay the price.

But, as I have said, I was flattered. It seemed harmless enough to me that I should be made much of. Did I, the conqueror of many nations, deserve any less? Esarhaddon was to have the throne, so why should I not have glory?

Esarhaddon was to have the throne—and did he not, even as *marsarru,* have that which meant more to me than any throne? Did he not have the Lady Esharhamat? It had been a mistake to return to Nineveh—even I could see this clearly enough—but now I had seen her. I could not help it. The poison was already in my blood.

I could do no harm by putting myself in her way. Was this not what she had done? A few moments, a word—that was all I would ask. She was heavy with child, so it must all be perfectly innocent. There could be no scandal. This is what I told myself, and even believed.

But neither could there be any thought of a secret meeting. There are no secrets in a royal palace, and doubtless Esharhamat was surrounded by spies—the Lady Naq'ia, if not her son, would wish to remain well informed. Besides, if Esarhaddon ever changed his mind yet again and decided on my death, it would not be out of jealousy over his wife.

Thus I settled in my heart that I would go that same evening and call at Esharhamat's garden. Perhaps, out of prudence, she would not see me, but I would go just the same.

In the last hour of daylight, I found myself seated on the stone bench beside the fountain with the laughing water. A eunuch slave had shown me in and left me there alone while he sought his mistress—or almost alone, for a cat, stiff-jointed and too fat to jump up into my lap, rubbed her back against my shins. I picked her up, for we were old acquaintances.

"Well, my friend Lamashtu," I murmured, scratching her under the jaw. At once she began to purr, burying her claws in my thigh out of pure contentment. "You have grown quite elderly since last we met. I see your mistress loves you yet."

"Her mistress was always constant in her heart."

I looked up, startled at the nearness of her voice, and saw Esharhamat standing with her hand upon the fountain's rim. She had come without my hearing so much as the whisper of her robes.

"It is not a claim which you can make," she went on—her expressionless face seemed as hard as polished stone. "Why have you come here, Tiglath?"

"I should think that that, at least, would require no explanation." I smiled, feeling that I had made a foolish blunder.

"You feel no scruples now, visiting your brother's wife? But of course—I had forgot. Esarhaddon is in Calah."

She managed to smile. It seemed to require a vast effort of memory, as if she had forgotten how. The effect was not one of gaiety, but I think she had achieved her object.

"Yes, he is in Calah. He will be here tomorrow and we will meet in the presence of the king, but certainly you will see him before then. Tell him, if you like, that I came to see you."

"Do you wish me to believe that you are not afraid?" She sat down beside me, taking the cat from my lap into her own. "Very well—I believe you. I never thought your cowardice included any fear of Esarhaddon."

"Have you been so unhappy then, Esharhamat?"

The look she showed me then, the astonishment and shock I saw in her face—I do not believe I had ever been so ashamed, although to this moment I still am not sure of what. Not that I suffered from any lack of choices.

"Yes. Yes, I have been unhappy," she answered, her voice suddenly quavering with unspilled tears. "I am unhappy now, and shall be so, I've no doubt, until death frees me—either his or mine, I do not really care which. I have been Esarhaddon's wife for nearly two years, and you can think to ask if I have been unhappy?"

She looked down at her belly, round as a melon, and pressed her hands against it, as if trying to hide it from my sight. The cat, perhaps sensing that this season of comfort was past, stole quietly away.

"They named my little son Siniddinapal, but he died after only a few months. I loved him, but he died. 'Do not despair,' they said to me, 'for you will have other sons.' And now my womb is heavy again and I hate this child, even before he is born —he will be a son, you know. Esarhaddon's son. He will be a king, like his father, and I wish I could . . . I wish my lord husband might have a corpse for his heir!"

There is a bitterness which only women may know, a sense of injustice at the tyranny of their own passions, of having been betrayed by the pitiless logic of nature itself. It places them— some of them—outside this charmed circle which we, with such innocence, call the hazards of life, as if they had died even to the possibility of happiness and come back as avenging spirits. All this I learned, in that one moment, only by looking into Esharhamat's hot, hating eyes.

But it was the wisdom only of a moment. It vanished as, at last, the tears stained her burning face. She did not resist as I took her into my arms.

"I am sorry," I whispered, kissing her hair. "I am sorry. I meant but to obey the god's will, and I have reflected misery on us all."

"Oh, do not speak to me of your god!"

She pushed herself away from me, her anger flaming up again like stirred embers.

"Your god—he plays with us! A child pitching stones at a bird's nest could not have less pity. 'The god's will,' you call it.

Ashur's will—for such an empty thing you let me go to Esarhaddon's bed."

I started to speak, but the words died on my lips. I could only hold her shoulders between my two hands, feeling the terrible passion that shook her.

"Do you know what it has been like for me in his bed—do you, Tiglath?" A terrible, mirthless smile pulled at her mouth as she spoke. "On our wedding night he said, 'Let us see your backside, wife, that we may know what my brother has taught you of the arts of pleasing a man.' That was what I learned behind the veil of marriage. I have been schooled in submission. Still, I do not think to this hour my lord husband takes much delight in me —do you know what he does sometimes, when he is drunk enough? He sends his harlots to instruct me. Sometimes he even comes with them. Do these little disclosures of my married life amuse you, Tiglath? Or can it be that you are embarrassed?"

I admit I could not have said what I felt at that moment. I could not have spoken at all. The very air in my lungs seemed to have hardened into ice. I seemed as incapable of sensation as the tiles in the floor beneath my sandals. It was something like that instant in the midst of battle when one receives a great wound and one is suddenly lost in a blinding, paralyzing flash of light—the pain will come, but for the moment it is far away.

Still, it must come. As I found my breath again I wanted to scream with rage. My hands itched for a weapon—an ax, for choice. I wanted to mix Esarhaddon's blood with the dust. I would not merely kill him; I would cut him into tiny pieces and feed them to the dogs. Why had I not killed him when I had had the chance? His throat under the blade of my sword . . .

I rose to my feet, trembling with dumb wrath. I could not look at Esharhamat. I could not.

"Good—I am glad I told you," she said, her voice calm, empty of passion. "See where the will of Ashur has brought us, Tiglath. For it is not pity I want, but shame."

"Then you have your will, for you have shamed me."

"Then I am happy." She reached out her tiny white hand and touched me upon the arm. "For the day will come when I will ask you to turn your back on your god—and return to me."

26

The king expected my presence at his banquet that evening, but there was no room in my belly for the duties of subject and son. I hardly thought of the king's existence. All I knew was that it would have been impossible to stay another hour in the city of Nineveh.

So I made no excuses and left no messages. I simply went to fetch my horse from the stables in the house of war and rode out into the open country. Night was already covering the world with its wings, but this too I hardly noticed. My mind throbbed like a great bruise. I thought it might burst at the sound of another word.

"Have I now grown so degraded by your brother's touch that you cannot love me, Tiglath?" she had asked, mocking me with her question. "Do you wish to hear more of his visits to my bed—you have but to ask, for I shall hold nothing back from you. Who more than you has a right to know all the intimacies that pass between Esarhaddon and myself, all the little ways he has of endearing himself to a woman. Shall I tell you everything, Tiglath?"

She seemed to laugh and weep by turns, or both together. And at last she threw herself into my arms, sobbing like a child.

"Do not leave me in this darkness, Tiglath—I beg you. Do not turn from me again."

There were no more words. I do not even remember how I came away from her. I can only remember her face, stained with tears.

So I rode away into the black night, half mad with rage and blind, helpless grief.

For what seemed hours I kept my horse to a gallop, lashing him on until his flanks were slippery with lather, until at last he could run no farther and simply stopped, gasping for air, his great chest heaving with every breath. I dismounted and we walked on together, the lights of the city watchtowers far behind us.

The wind was laden with ice and slipped through my cloak like a thousand iron needles. It was then so dark I could not even see the ground.

At last, as my brain began to clear, I felt the cold as an annoyance, an unwelcome distraction, and looked about for some shelter. What I found was a ruined hut, no doubt the abode of some long-dead farmer, its roof gone, its mud-brick walls broken and worn down by weather but still solid enough to offer protection from the wind. I tethered the horse and crouched down in a corner, wrapping my cloak about my knees. It was not a place to offer much comfort, but I would not freeze to death there and somehow I could not be troubled to want anything beyond.

No passion lasts forever. By the chill hours of morning mine had subsided into a sullen resentment, black enough but at least no longer tearing at my breast like a weasel trapped in a leather bag. I began to think with some satisfaction of cutting Esarhaddon's throat. The idea charmed me—for a moment I experienced something almost like pleasure. Such a thing would be impossible —the person of the *marsarru* is as sacred as that of the king—but still I could not deny myself the satisfaction of imagining it. This is always the first step the mind takes to heal itself, the illusion that everything can be set right by some single action.

Then I began to consider more practical solutions. If I could not kill Esarhaddon I could ask him to set his wife aside—he did not favor her, and once she had given him a healthy son . . . But this too was impossible. Everyone knew the prophecy that she was to be the mother of kings. Esharhamat was the seal of legitimacy on his claim to the throne. If she had children by another man, and if the omens favored them, no son of Esarhaddon would feel himself safe.

"Turn your back on your god—and return to me," she had said. *"Turn your back on your god."* Could I do such a thing?

I would not be permitted to kill Esarhaddon honorably, in open combat, but I could contrive to have him murdered. Yes. Men died every day—had not there been questions asked about the death of Arad Ninlil? I would have no shortage of willing accomplices, should I choose to employ them, for rarely had a royal heir stood in lower favor than did my brother. A poisoned cup of wine perhaps . . .

But could I do it? Could *I?* No. I had grown to hate Esarhaddon, but he was safe from me. I was not brave enough for such treachery.

What was left? Furtive meetings with Esharhamat? Nothing more than that? Perhaps not even that.

Not every knot might be untied, it seemed.

Dawn was coming. Ashur's sun was rising behind the eastern mountains. At first it only traced their ragged outline as the sky, with painful slowness, turned a pale gray. Then, finally, the god kindled his fire and rose once more to chase away the dark ghosts of night. The world had his gift of life for one more day.

I cannot claim to have been very appreciative. My legs were stiff from the cold, I was hungry, and a dull, stubborn resentment clouded my mind like the fumes of wine after a night's debauchery. I was in a filthy, poisonous temper that made everything, even the morning sunshine, into a grievance.

I was many *beru* from the nearest dwelling—there was not even a plowed field within sight—and yet, looking about me, I had a vague sense of where I was. Possibly I had passed this way once or twice while hunting; at any rate, it seemed familiar.

Within three hours I reached a village—I had not been looking for one, but I found it. The peasants gathered around my horse shouting "Lord, Lord! The Lord Tiglath!" and almost as soon as I had dismounted I was besieged by women offering me beer from huge clay jars and baskets of fruit and roasted lamb.

There were men here, it seemed, who had fought at Khalule. We sat down together around the cooking fires—the whole population it seemed, some sixty or seventy villagers, including children and old people—and held an impromptu feast.

In the face of such insistent hospitality, one is hard pressed to concentrate on one's private misery and, thus distracted, it was some time before I thought of the fact that I was the most wretched of men. I felt ashamed to have forgotten, but by then, of course, it was too late since, even against my will, I had grown quite cheerful, and I thanked the great gods for having blessed men with childish and inconstant hearts, that their griefs might know such narrow limits. I was not too proud for that.

"Stay among us," the elders told me. "Bring us good fortune and the blessings of the gods."

Why not? I thought. Yes, I will stay here for a time. I will hide myself here.

But there was nowhere for the Lord Tiglath Ashur to hide. The next morning one of the king's heralds, the silver ribbons hanging from his staff of office, rode into the village.

"The Lord Sennacherib, King of the World's Four Corners, greets the Royal Prince, the Lord Tiglath Ashur," he announced, precisely as if he were addressing a multitude instead of one man. He was tall and smooth-faced, really a very grand figure—they always are, these court warriors with their jewel-encrusted swords. "I am one of many sent to discover the reason for the Lord Tiglath Ashur's sudden removal."

It was what I should have expected. My father, who in old age was prey to sudden fears, had probably sent envoys in every direction with orders to find me or not return. It was possible his guards were still turning over each square cubit of the city, seeking me alive or dead. It was a cruel thing I had done. I should have left word.

"You may tell the king you have found me," I said. "I am here and will remain here for a time."

"The Lord Sennacherib bids you return at once." He drew himself up very straight—he really was a pompous donkey.

"That is not possible."

He smiled. And why should he not smile? Did he not speak with the king's voice?

"And why is it not possible?"

"It is not possible because it is not my will!" I shouted—I had simply lost patience. "Go! Tell the king my father that I will come when I will come. Be gone!"

I stamped my foot out of pure vexation, and the man actually started with alarm. They are such heroes, these palace eunuchs. Within the minute he was on his horse and raising clouds of dust on his way back to Nineveh.

Each day while I dwelt among the villagers I went out hunting alone. I brought home deer and wild boar, and my simple hosts rejoiced to be feasting on such abundance of fresh meat, but I took little pleasure in the sport.

I simply wanted to be by myself and thus spent the better part of every afternoon sitting in the shade of an acacia tree, puzzling over the strange shape that life had taken for Esharhamat and Esarhaddon, and for me. My musings led me to no solutions—there could be no solutions; the god had seen to that—but the character of the problem gradually revealed itself with disheartening clarity.

We were all trapped—Esharhamat in a marriage founded upon bitterness and contempt, Esarhaddon in an eminence as little suited to his wishes as to his talents, and I . . . I wanted a woman I could not have, which was a common enough fate, and I could live without the glory of kingship. Why then did I feel so estranged from myself? I did not know. That was my burden, not to know.

And each night I sat among the village men, and we discussed war and farming—the only two fit subjects. We drank beer until sleep came, and then my dreams did not torment me. Thus I lived for five days.

On the third day the king sent another of his heralds and I dismissed him too, although with greater courtesy than the first. And on the night of the fifth day, long after the inmates of the village had found their beds, yet another came, and this one I told I would return to Nineveh. He said his orders were to accompany me back, but I told him that this I would not permit. I was not a truant schoolboy to be hauled back by the ear. I would return as I had left, alone.

The next morning, as I mounted my horse, a village woman gave me a pottery water flask and a small reed bag filled with bread and dried meat.

I rode away without looking back. I heard no sound except the beating of my horse's hoofs.

The Gate of Nergal, which opens onto the road to Tarbisu, was still unlocked when I arrived, so I did not have to shout up to the watchman and identify myself in order to be let in. I simply rode through, one more man on horseback, among so many on foot, hardly noticed at all. A prince who leaves his escort behind him becomes like other men—he has no special majesty and no one recognizes him. Of this it is wise sometimes to be reminded.

I had hardly arrived in my rooms to take off my cloak and

wash the dust of travel from my eyes before a page burst in upon me and, directly behind him, the king himself.

"I ought to have your feet chopped off for wandering away in such a manner," he said, embracing me nevertheless. "And it is a crime punishable by death to refuse a royal summons. My son, much as I love you, I would have your life for this insolence were it not for your brother Esarhaddon. Your absence has obliged the Donkey to remain waiting here in Nineveh longer than pleases him, and I have been kept vastly amused by his impatience and anger. It is always a pleasure to see him annoyed, but he has been almost beside himself—he talks of nothing but your 'unconscionable impudence' and how he would have you flayed if he were king. You are fortunate finally to have accepted him as an enemy. Come —I have kept the banqueters waiting in your honor."

Our entry together into the great hall caused something of a sensation, for no one knew why I had left the city or how I would stand in the king's favor when I returned—palaces do a lively custom in rumors, and possibly half the men who dined with us that night had expected some great change, like a movement of the earth itself, that would sweep them in or out of favor.

And then there was the matter of Esarhaddon's all-too-obvious reaction at the sight of the king leaning on my arm. His face went black with rage.

So my father's banquet was an occasion for great disquiet and, as happened so often in the last years of his reign, it declined rather quickly into a drunken orgy. It took hardly more than an hour before courtiers of otherwise blameless dignity, their faces flushed from wine, were pelting each other with pieces of roast meat. I saw at least three of the dancing girls lifted up to the table, placed on their backs, and rutted on by men who waited their turns in strict order of precedence. It was a scene worthy of a provincial army barrack after two months' campaign.

But the king enjoyed it all. He laughed and made rude jokes, encouraging those who held back to join in the general merriment. Baiting Esarhaddon and watching the depravity of his nobles—his pleasures in life seemed to have dwindled down to these. Finally he got up from his chair, walked to a corner, vomited loudly, and allowed himself to be led off to bed.

And all the while my brother and I, as if by compact, drank little, spoke hardly at all to those around us, and zealously avoided one another's eye. For either of us, one might have imagined, so much as to acknowledge the other's existence would have been insupportable.

But when the king had finally left I went to find my own rest, abandoning the field to Esarhaddon. I was weary of Nineveh. I wanted only to return to the safe forgetfulness of my garrison at Amat, where the only enemy was found in battle. I would most happily abandon all this glittering corruption to my brother, who doubtless had no more taste for it than I did. Let this be his punishment, I thought, to reign in this dog kennel until disgust gnaws straight through his vitals and he dies of it. As soon as the king would release me, I would fly like a bird from his golden net. The Medes would pay me back a thousandfold as I piled up their corpses as monuments to my immortal glory.

Thus simple does the tangled web of life seem to a young man, for I was young then, although I felt myself to be old and full of cynical wisdom.

In my rooms the Arab girl Zabibe helped me off with my robes and rubbed my limbs with hot scented oil. I almost fell asleep under her cunning hands. Almost, but not quite.

"My lord has been absent many days," she murmured as she bathed my face in water mixed with flower petals. "I thought my lord had forgotten his servant."

I had forgotten her—the thought of her had never once entered my head—but it seemed impolite to say so, and I merely smiled.

"Zabibe lives only to find favor with my lord," she went on, her voice as gentle as the flutter of a bird's wings. The tips of her fingers brushed against my manhood, which by then was as stiff as bronze. Her pale skin caught the light from the oil lamp beside my bed, making her seem the only real object in the room. "My lord must learn to put all care behind him, to let it fall away like a soiled garment. My lord must permit Zabibe to ease his heart."

I listened to her voice, feeling like a child whose ear is captured by a cradle song, knowing and not caring that I heard only the skillful chatter of a harlot. What did it matter what was real and what not? Why should I care? I had only now—this moment was all I could call my own. Happiness was a shadow, but pleasure at least was real.

* * *

I awoke the next morning with a headache. The brazier, cold for hours, had left a faint taste of smoke in the air, and Zabibe was snoring like a water buffalo. This was the end of passion—a winter morning, a pounding head, and a woman who, as soon as she opened her eyes, would expect to hear that she was the god's first blessing. I put on my tunic and slipped quietly out of the room. Tonight I might desire this woman's consolation again, but I could not face her now. I escaped to the house of war, where I could steam my soul clean again in the sweating house and enjoy a soldier's breakfast of beer and boiled millet.

"The Dread Lord Sennacherib, King of the Earth's Four Corners, salutes the Royal Prince Tiglath Ashur!"

Within the narrow confines of the officers' mess, his voice boomed like a warm drum. I was sitting at a table with my back to the door, and I could not have been more startled if someone had jabbed me between the shoulder blades with a sword point. I turned and saw the herald with the silver ribbons hanging from his staff, and my heart sank.

"The Dread Lord Sennacherib requests . . ."

"Yes—yes, yes. Just tell me where," I snapped. I was growing weary of this little ritual.

"If you will follow me, Lord—now."

He made a grand, sweeping gesture with his hand to indicate the way out, and I rose meekly to go after him.

There was a litter waiting for me—in all my life I had never ridden in one, since I held my own legs to be as sound as another man's, and this did not seem the moment to start behaving like a pampered concubine, so I dismissed it and followed the herald on foot. We passed back through the palace grounds and out the Gate of Igisigsig and into the royal gardens, which occupied the corner between the river and the city's northern wall, a place my father loved and where I found him sitting under a vine arbor with a cup of wine in his hand. Esarhaddon was with him, looking no more cheerful than he had last night.

"The hero has at last found a moment for us," my brother cried, glaring at me as he rose from his seat. "I am astonished he can be bothered."

The king laughed and pitched the contents of his wine cup onto the ground beneath a flowering bush.

"The *marsarru* here has been telling me that your campaign

against the Medes is a profitless waste. He says our only real safety lies in avoiding the anger of the gods."

He laughed again, stamping his sandaled foot to emphasize the delicious nature of the joke, and Esarhaddon scowled and snorted like a bull beset by flies. It was obvious that this quarrel was of long standing.

"My Lord *Marsarru* is, as always, correct," I answered. "Only a fool risks the wrath of Great Ashur, but I think he will not be displeased if we remind the Medes that he and not their Ahura is lord in the Western Lands."

"I was speaking with reference to the temple of Marduk in Babylon."

Esarhaddon sat down again as I came near him. I think he was afraid I might have offered him my hand.

"That place is in ruins—do you not recall, brother, how you and I labored at its destruction?—and Marduk has abandoned his city and now does honor to Ashur in our temple here in Nineveh. Were you by chance suggesting it should be otherwise?"

I smiled at him. I hated him, at that moment, more utterly than ever I had anyone in my life. And it was not the Medes I was thinking of—or the ruined temples of Babylon, or the honor of the deathless gods—but Esharhamat.

"Yes, my Lord *Marsarru*," the king interposed. "Were you by chance suggesting it should be otherwise?"

He sat with his hands on his knees, turning his head from one of us to the other. His eyes glittered with malicious pleasure, but the sun shining down on his gray old head pitilessly revealed his weary age.

Esarhaddon picked up a pebble and threw it at a bird which had perched on a tree limb some twenty paces away. It was a near miss, and the bird fluttered into the air.

"The Medes are no more danger than that," he said. I could read in his eyes a consciousness of having evaded a direct answer.

"Than what, my beloved son—that bird, or the unerring accuracy of your arm?"

"The god of Babylon must be restored," Esarhaddon replied, seeming to close his mind to the king's mockery. "Marduk, who leaves no insult unanswered, has conceived a great wrath against the Land of Ashur. We cannot prosper until the city is rebuilt. If we neglect this duty, our royal house is doomed."

"I was not born in the Land of Sumer," I said. "I am a man of the north and put my trust in the mercy of Ashur."

"No one needs to remind us that you are half a foreigner, my Lord Tiglath."

"Just as all men remember, my Lord *Marsarru,* that your mother used to sell her backside in the wineshops of Borsippa."

Esarhaddon rose in terrible anger, his hand already on the hilt of his sword. I believe, save for the presence of the king, we might have ended our quarrel there and then, but my father also rose and pushed us apart.

"How dare you!" he shouted. "How dare either of you! Am I a plowman, born with mud between his toes, to watch my sons goad each other to deadly fight? I forbid this! Sit down, Esarhaddon, since you are most to blame. We were speaking of the Medes."

And, as quickly as it had arisen, the crisis passed. Esarhaddon resumed his seat, but from that moment on he might as well have been struck deaf for all the impact my words had on him.

"Then may I now speak of the Medes?" I asked—it seemed we had done justice to every other topic.

"Yes, my son. Speak of the Medes."

"They are a little people. They are not important." My brother did not even look at me as he spoke.

"The Sagarians, the Miyaneh, and the Iranzu—these are only tribes. Yes, they are little people, each in turn, and not important. But if they combine, and think of themselves as one nation, then they are important. And this they are beginning to do, under a man called Daiaukka, who calls himself their king. I have met this king, and he is all that one would most fear in an enemy. Added to this, the Medes have found a new god . . ."

I spoke for some time, telling all I had learned in the eastern mountains, and the king listened with great attention. He would stop me now and then to ask a question—a name, perhaps, or the meaning of some strange foreign word—but for the rest he preserved an impenetrable silence.

"And it is your belief they will march west?" he asked at last, folding his hands in his lap.

"Yes, Dread Lord. Unless we stop them, and soon, they will come down from their mountains like wolves. We must teach them the cost of their ambitions, and if the lesson is terrible enough perhaps then they will leave us in peace for a generation."

"And for this, I have no doubt, you will need a great army," Esarhaddon said suddenly. "Greater by far than that which is presently under your command."

"I will need more men, yes. Perhaps sixty companies more."

My brother nodded, as if this was the answer he had expected. The tight smile on his lips was that of a man whose worst suspicions had been confirmed.

"My Lord King," he asked, "have you considered to what end my brother raises such a force? Surely not to fight the Medes. It cannot be that a few mountain barbarians, who are a threat only in the eastern provinces, justify so massive a response. I think the Lord Tiglath Ashur wishes to strengthen his northern army for reasons which have precious little to do with the Medes."

"And what would those reasons be, my Lord *Marsarru*?"

The king waited for an answer, watching his heir through narrow, speculative eyes.

"I think he prepares for the day when a new king will reign in Nineveh. I think he plans himself to be that king."

Esarhaddon folded his arms over his chest and turned his gaze to me. *I have found you out,* his eyes said. *You think you have been so clever, but your intrigues have been known to me from the start.*

"If that is what my brother believes, I have a very simple answer." I smiled at him—in that moment my love for him was dead. "Let him take command of this army himself. Let it be his weapon, and not mine—he is an able soldier and no doubt will win his victory. Let the glory of conquest be his and not mine."

"So that you may remain behind in the capital and plot with my enemies? Tiglath, do you think I am such a fool?"

"I prepare an army in the north to rob you of your inheritance," I said, shaking my head in derision. "I also wish to stay in Nineveh and rob you of your inheritance. Make up your mind, Esarhaddon—which is it to be? You must settle for yourself what form my treachery is to take."

The king laughed, and when my brother tried to make some response, he waved him into silence.

"Now, let us speak of serious matters," the king said. "You say, Tiglath, that you can stop the Medes for a generation. And then they will return again?"

"Yes, Dread Lord. When they have found another king to make them forget the might of Ashur."

"Yes—it is just so." He shook his head in sadness. "I have been to the edge of the Northern Sea, in the days of my youth, when I made war upon the Hebrews and the cities of Tyre and Sidon. I have seen the waves of that sea lapping the shore—they advance and fall back, just so. And each wave is mightier than the one before, until the ninth and last. This Daiaukka, who calls himself a king, he is not then the ninth wave?"

"No, Lord. His father was perhaps the first, and he is only the second."

"Then purchase for us what time you can, Tiglath my son. I am glad that I am an old man, that I will not be troubled again."

At these words Esarhaddon rose and walked off, not looking at either of us. The king did not even try to stop him.

"Would you do such a thing?" he asked at last. "Would you make war on the Lord Donkey to reign in his place?"

"No."

"It is a great pity. You would have been the better king, but we cannot always see into the god's plans for us. I hate to think what will happen after I am dead."

He passed his hand over his beard, now more than half gray, and stared out at his garden, but with eyes that seemed to see nothing. Or did he see the times that would follow his own? I know not.

"You will have your great war against the Medes," he said at last. "But I think it will be the last gift you will receive from my hands. I am old and tired. My strength leaves me, almost from day to day, and I cannot stand against Esarhaddon alone."

"Alone, Dread Lord?"

"Yes." He looked at me, and suddenly his expression changed. "Or didn't you know? My brother, the Lord Sinahiusur, is dying."

"No—I did not know. I knew he was ill, but . . ."

"Yes, dying. Go and see him, boy, for he was always your friend."

As I waited in the reception hall of my uncle's palace, I was impressed by the quiet. There were many persons come to pay their respects to the *turtanu*—most, no doubt, hoping to beg a final favor—but no one spoke. It was as if they all were expecting someone to arrive at any time and wished to be sure that they did not miss his entrance.

"May it not come for me like this," I thought. "May I find my *simtu* in the heat of war. May it come when I expect it least."

"The Lord Sinahiusur wishes to see you now," his chamberlain said, almost whispering the words into my ear. "If you will but come with me, Prince."

Men followed me with their eyes as we left the great hall. How many of them, I wonder, were foolish enough to envy me?

The bedroom was remarkably small and sparse, with no furniture beyond a few cedar chests. Even as he waited for his final rest, the Lord Sinahiusur, the king's *turtanu,* lay on the floor on an ordinary sleeping mat. I sat down beside him and he took my hand in his—I was astonished by the weakness of his grasp. His illness, it seemed, had worn him away, for the bones in his face showed quite clearly under the skin.

But his voice, when he spoke, was still strong.

"You have seen the king," he said. "Does he give his approval to your war against the Medes?"

"Yes, Lord—it seems I am to be a conqueror."

He did not return my smile, but perhaps he saw beyond my poor joke.

"Yes. A conqueror." He closed his eyes for a moment, and then, seeming to focus all his will on the task, reopened them. "Esarhaddon, too, in his time, will be a conqueror. I wonder how that will bode for the Land of Ashur."

"Do you think I do wrong, Lord?"

"Wrong? No. But it no longer matters what I think—neither I nor the king is important now. Even he knows that. Esarhaddon and you must settle the future between yourselves."

I made ready to speak, to say that he would doubtless recover and live many years yet, but I did not. What would be gained by lying to him when he would know it was a lie? The consciousness of death was in his face. He did not even seem to care.

"The physicians, when I am dead, will open me up to satisfy themselves that I have not been poisoned." He smiled, as if at the foolishness of children. "They will find my belly full of corruption, for it is not by the hand of any mortal enemy I die. I wonder how I have offended against the god that he visits this end upon me."

"You are a pious man, Lord—there can be no sin on your head."

"You think not?" he asked, squeezing my hand. "Perhaps, but I am not easy. We have all gone very wrong somewhere, Tiglath. Yet I cannot seem to discover where. I think it possible the diviners fill us with false hope. Perhaps we sin to imagine we can know the god's will."

We sat in silence for a long moment while, it seemed, the lord *turtanu* reviewed the twisting course of his life. He still held my hand, but I had the impression that he had forgotten I was there with him. It was as if he had taken a moment out of our visit to continue his long dying, and that this was a thing he was obliged to do alone.

"I had thought to see you sooner," he said finally, almost startling me awake. "But then you left the city so suddenly—no, you need not explain. Like everyone else, I have my spies and know the reason. What will you do, Tiglath my boy? What will you do?"

"Do, Lord? What can I do?"

"The god alone knows that."

"Yet he is silent." I shook my head, wondering how we had come to this subject. "He keeps his purposes hidden, that we must grope in the darkness of our own wills."

"Yes—hidden. In this, in so much. But is it not all one, Tiglath? Is not life a seamless garment? You must come again."

"Yes, Lord. Whenever you wish it."

I pitied him—yet only because he was dying. I did not understand then what perhaps he had come to see, that the world was more wicked and the god's designs more twisted than even that wise and pious man could ever hope to grasp. Perhaps he had at last understood that he understood nothing. Perhaps that is the god's last gift to those who are his servants.

He smiled—in a way that concealed the reason for it.

But I did not come again. It was already dark by the time I left him, and the Lord Sinahiusur was to die at sundown of the day following. But I knew nothing of this as I returned to my own rooms. I knew only that I was oppressed in spirit. Zabibe was waiting for me.

"Someone has been here, Lord," she said. There was an unnatural tension in her voice, as if something restrained her from speaking more. "A woman—a household slave, I think, but very elegant in her manners. She asked to see you, but would not wait. She left something for you. It is there, on the table."

I picked up a small bundle wrapped in a linen scarf. I did not open it at once, although Zabibe seemed to be waiting for me to do just that. I found I had no wish to satisfy her curiosity.

"Did she not give her name?" I asked.

"No, Lord."

"Very well, then. Tell them I will have my dinner now."

"It shall be as you command, Lord."

She bowed and left.

Standing there, thinking of nothing, I picked open the tiny knot and found beneath it a lapis brooch, such as women use to pin back their veils. It was carved, decorated with figures of cats. It had come from Tyre—at least, that was what the merchant had told me that morning in the bazaar when I bought it as a present for Esharhamat. It seemed so long ago.

27

All that winter Nineveh was like an old dog biting itself in its sleep. There were disturbances—tavern quarrels that quickly turned into riots, fires in the poor quarters. There was talk of omens and the births of monsters. Men were restless without understanding quite why. They were waiting for something to happen. But what? They could not have said what. There was no peace.

For me it began with the death of the Lord Sinahiusur. His will named me as sole heir, since he had left no sons. I came into possession of his palaces, his vast estates along the upper Euphrates, and gold and silver beyond reckoning. This, added to what the king had already given, made me, after my father and brother, certainly the richest man in the Land of Ashur.

But wealth, it appeared, was not all I had been meant to inherit, for the king appointed no successor as *turtanu*. The rumors—and the city was full of rumors—said he was only waiting for me to ask. So, in all likelihood, was Esarhaddon. So, possibly, was I.

Even as the Lord Sinahiusur's body was being prepared for burial beside the dust of his ancestors, a delegation of senior officers from the *quradu* came to wait upon me in my rooms.

"The king is too old to rule alone," they said. "If you do not take up your late uncle's office, much—perhaps most—of its power will go by default to Esarhaddon."

"Would that be so terrible? Esarhaddon must be king himself

one day—it will do no harm if he learns the uses of authority. Besides, the king may choose someone else as *turtanu.*"

"Who? Who else would be acceptable to Esarhaddon?"

"I would not be acceptable to Esarhaddon. But Esarhaddon is not yet king. Why should the choice lie with him?"

"Because men are afraid."

"Why?"

"Because the *marsarru* has vowed that anyone who thinks to stand above him in this reign will not live an hour into the next."

"Would this not apply to me as well? I am as mortal as another man, and my brother would order my throat cut sooner than most."

"If you are the next *tartanu,* it may be possible to keep Esarhaddon from ever becoming king at all."

"I am not a necromancer, gentlemen. It is not in my power to keep the king my father alive forever."

"The Lord Tiglath Ashur chooses not to understand us."

So it went. But what could I tell them, that I had already pledged my word in this matter? Did I still feel bound by a promise made to Esarhaddon when he was still my friend? I did not even know myself, but, in any case, that was beside the point.

It would have been so easy, as the officers of the *quradu* knew only too well. As *turtanu,* and with the king's full support, I could have bound the army to me, made it the instrument of my will alone so that, when the moment came, I would be able to push Esarhaddon aside and assume the throne in my own right—or, if I preferred, let him stay as a figurehead king and keep the real authority all to myself. In the past, both of these things had happened. I could even have forced him to set Esharhamat aside that I might marry her. As *turtanu* there would be no limits set to my power, provided I had the bowels to use it.

But there was the obstacle. I was not prepared to strip my brother of his birthright. I was not even prepared to threaten it, and if not, what point could there be in my becoming *turtanu*? Esharhamat had said, *"Turn your back upon your god,"* but I could not. The god had set his mark on me, on my soul as well as on my body. I had felt myself in his presence too many times—he had made himself too real for me to set his will at nothing, and his will was that Esarhaddon should be king. In short, I was afraid of this impiety that so many urged upon me. I feared the wrath of

Holy Ashur. Before that, if before nothing else, I was prepared to be a coward.

What was it the *maxxu* had said? *"In the years to come you will speak 'farewell' until your tongue sickens at the sound."* This was to be my unalterable destiny, the god's will. There could be nothing else. Thus it was at the funeral rites for the Lord Sinahiusur, my protector and friend, that I began to speak the word "farewell."

For three days his body lay exposed in his house that all the city might come and see that the great man, the chief minister of the state, was dead. Esarhaddon had already returned to Calah, and the king, by ancient custom, took no part in the mourning—of all our family, I alone kept vigil beside the corpse. During the day strangers came and went, staring at the dead face and then hurrying away. The mighty *turtanu* was merely an object of curiosity now. People did not seem to remember who he was. It was a strange thing, but even before he was consigned to his tomb he seemed forgotten, as if even a life so filled with business as his amounted, in the end, to nothing.

And then, at last, there was the procession, a hushed and strangely awful ceremony, as if to mark the passing of the world's innocence. As his heir I led the mourners, walking behind the plain wooden casket in which his body would be carried to the holy city of Ashur, to a stone sarcophagus in the burial vault of kings. There was no sound—the huge crowds around the royal palace were still, respecting the silence that had descended over the *turtanu* even while he yet lived.

At the city gates, the casket was placed aboard a wagon and, with an honor guard following, we began the five-day journey to Ashur. On the road, each day was like the one before. No one spoke.

The Lord Sinahiusur, his body anointed with fragrant oil, was at last in his tomb. The stone lid was slipped into place and closed with seals of bronze. The light of day would never reach him again. Could this really be farewell?

To die. To be that vague thing, a spirit—or perhaps not even that. Perhaps only sightless dust, blown over the earth by each indifferent wind. It was terrible to contemplate.

As I rode home to Nineveh, I felt as if I could hear the god mocking me—mocking us all.

* * *

But where men die, life does not. Esharhamat, whom I had not seen since first returning to Nineveh, had almost reached her time of quickening. She sent for me.

"Esarhaddon's son shall be named Shamash Shumukin," she said, lying on a couch in her chamber. I sat beside her, and she held my hand tangled in her long, slender fingers. "Do you see how he tries to bribe the Lord of Decision? 'Shamash has created a name.' I fear this child's first act may be to murder his mother. I have had evil dreams, Tiglath. I am filled with fear and I do not even know why. I should be beyond fear, as I am beyond the god's mercy. Why should I be afraid, since I would welcome death?"

"What dreams, Esharhamat?"

"I dream of fire—everywhere fire, red and gold flames like the tongues of serpents. The walls of a great palace are burning around me. And I have set the torch myself. I die by my own hand, yet it is not I. I see it all, as if through the eyes of another."

"Have you consulted a *sha'ilu?*"

"Oh yes—several." She laughed, a little fever of hysterics that was over in a second, and squeezed my hand all the tighter. "In your brother's house there is no shortage of all manner of diviners. I have had my pick, and they all stroke their beards and look grave and promise the truth. One says that the flames are Ashur's anger for some duty in which I have failed. Yet another assures me that I carry the bright sun in my womb—can you credit anyone believing such a thing of Esarhaddon's seed?—and that he will light the world. I have heard endless foolishness from these wise men, enough that it all seems to cancel itself out. Yet I believe the god means to avenge himself, to taunt me with this warning of my own death."

"You shall not die, Esharhamat," I murmured, putting my arm beneath her neck and gathering her to me—I spoke what I knew to be the truth, yet I knew not how I knew. "You and I cannot be finished with each other yet."

She looked into my eyes and smiled, and I found myself wondering, *"Why would the god avenge himself on Esharhamat? What could she have done?"* But then she touched my lips with her fingertips, and I could see the tears starting in her great dark eyes.

"Forgive me—forgive me that I ever left you."

"I forgive you, Tiglath. Could I do less?" Her arms were about my neck now, and I could feel her trembling—or perhaps it was I who trembled. "I forgave you long ago, my love. And did I not curse you? Only love me as you did before, and I will lift the curse from your heart."

"No, do not do that, for your curse was only that I would be haunted by my love, and that is not a curse. I have learned in all this time that when I have not your image before my eyes I am less even than the dead."

We both wept. We held each other and wept, for we had found life again. Nothing mattered except that we belonged each to the other while there was breath beneath our ribs. *"Turn your back on your god,"* she had told me—and had I not at last found the courage? Was she not mine now, in spite of gods and men?

But the Lord Ashur is wise. Wiser than I could know.

The blind man stands in darkness, imagining himself bathed in light. *"Your eyes still blind you,"* the *maxxu* had said. But I must have been deaf as well, for his warning meant nothing to me. I was happy once more, dazzled by Esharhamat's love.

Was she as blind as I? I think not—women are too cunning. She did evil, knowing it to be evil, not caring. She dreaded neither men nor gods. It was a kind of courage that only women can know.

"I have heard of your new Arab woman," she told me. "Ninsunna, my handmaiden, saw her when she went to your rooms."

"A present from the king." I grinned like a fool, being ashamed. "I will send her away."

"No—do not do that. If you do, there will be comment, for a scorned woman will talk, even if she is a slave. Keep her. Sleep with her. Let her imagine herself favored. We will be able to meet but seldom, and I do not care how you spend your seed so long as I have your heart."

Men are but fools when they imagine themselves subtle. Only women and adders are subtle.

Twenty days later Esharhamat was delivered of a healthy son, named Shamash Shumukin in accordance with his father's will, and her fears came to nothing. She did not die. She was alive to bid me farewell when, after the feast of Akitu and the spring floods, I took the road north.

* * *

I went first to Three Lions, thinking to visit my mother and enjoy a few days of rest before joining the companies of fresh soldiers who would accompany me to the garrison at Amat. I would hunt, I thought, and drink beer in the twilight with my peasants. I was quite looking forward to it all, but what awaited me in my own house was yet another intrigue.

At dinner, on that first evening, Naiba was nowhere to be found. I asked after her, but my mother merely lowered her eyes and whispered a few words too indistinct to be heard.

"Merope, is there something you wish to tell me?"

"No, my son." She shook her head, still unwilling to look at me. "There is nothing I wish to tell you."

That one sentence's slight shift of emphasis spoke most eloquently. No—she did not *wish* to tell me anything.

"But if there were something, you would speak. Would you not?"

Silence.

How many possibilities were there? Why did I even trouble to ask, since I could guess easily enough what had been going on while I was absent in Nineveh.

"Send Naiba to me in the morning," I said, rising from the table. There was a half-full pitcher of wine by my place; I decided to take it with me, since I would have no other company at my sleeping mat. "I do not wish to see her before then, but she must attend me while I breakfast."

"Lathikados, I . . ."

"Yes, Mother?"

"Nothing," she answered. And then she looked up at me with dry, hot eyes. "Except—be kind, for my sake."

"Yes, Mother. Tomorrow morning I will decide on the limits of my kindness. See to it that Naiba comes to me then."

I went to bed.

I slept that night as if I had been dead many years. No dreams—nothing. But the next morning I felt much better.

Naiba brought me in my breakfast. She was very quiet and did not look at me directly, but averted her gaze. I did not require an explanation.

"Have you conceived a love for this boy?" I asked suddenly —the instant before, I had intended to say nothing. "You know of whom I speak. Qurdi, the son of my overseer Tahu Ishtar."

"Dread Lord, I . . ." She glanced up, her eyes welling with tears—her eyes, so much like Esharhamat's.

Of course she was afraid, but I had had enough of women's tears.

"Well, if you want him, then I suppose you must have him," I said evenly, tearing the corner from a loaf of bread and dipping it in my beer. "I shall speak to his father this morning and see what he requires in the way of a dowry—no, no, girl, rise. Enough of this."

She had prostrated herself on the floor in front of me and was embracing my ankles, covering my feet with kisses mixed with tears. I almost wanted to laugh, it seemed so simple to make at least this woman happy.

"Stop, Naiba—stop this at once! Yes, that is better. We will speak again, after I have settled the matter. Go—let me have my breakfast in peace."

At last, Naiba dried her eyes and left me. I could hear the patter of her naked feet against the floor tiles, the sound dying away, like wind pushing at fallen leaves.

When one of the house servants came to take away my breakfast things, I ordered that a fire be lit in the sweating house and told her to fetch me a jar of the Nairian wine I had brought with me from Amat—it was now nearly gone but this did not distress me, since King Argistis, I had no doubt, would soon be sending another ambassador seeking yet another favor. I went out to the sweating house and sat for over an hour in the hot, steam-laden air. Then I dressed myself and anointed my hair and beard with oil. I felt quite human again. Then I sent for Tahu Ishtar.

"Overseer, is your son of a mind to take a wife?"

I could see I had taken him by surprise. His face puckered with worry, and he bowed low.

"My Lord, I am shamed," he began. "This matter—this insult to my lord—is a great grief to me . . ."

"I asked only if he wishes to marry, Tahu Ishtar. I make no inquiries. The slave woman Naiba knows her way around a sleeping mat and will bring your son happiness. She is a barbarian, true, and I fancy a few years older than Qurdi, but this is not necessarily such a bad thing—it would not do if they were both children. She knows how to work, too. I will give ten silver shekels that she does not come to her husband a beggar. What say you, overseer?"

I can only guess what Tahu Ishtar might have expected, but in that moment his massive dignity deserted him and he stood before me with his mouth open, unable to say anything. I had to labor to keep from smiling.

"But—forgive me," I went on, when it was clear I was to receive no answer. "Perhaps you object to the girl."

"No, Lord. I . . . She has been your . . . You honor my son to . . . Ten silver shekels—it is a great sum."

"Then may we regard this bargain as struck?"

I held out my hand, and after staring at it as if he could not think what he was expected to do, Tahu Ishtar took it and shook it vigorously.

"My son will be your debtor all his life, Lord," he said, almost shouting the words. "You raise my house to honor when you could have—"

"Let us speak no more of that." I disengaged my hand—no easy thing—and we began walking back to my house. "Let them marry when I return from Amat for the winter. In the meantime, while I stay at Three Lions, I engage not to take the girl to my sleeping mat again and she can live here under the protection of my lady mother, who even now loves her as a daughter."

"As to your sleeping mat, Lord, there is no need that you be inconvenienced," Tahu Ishtar replied, shaking his head—he was a man who understood the proprieties of such a matter. "She remains your property until she takes the veil from my son, and a royal prince is not like other men. My son cannot fault her—"

"Nevertheless, let her be as a daughter of my house. I shall know her no more until Qurdi is prepared to claim her."

And that was where we left the matter. I parted from Tahu Ishtar and sought my own house to tell Naiba and my mother that they must prepare for a wedding. Then, weary of talk, I had my horse saddled and went out with a quiverful of javelins to hunt wild pigs. I did not return until after dark.

A week later, when the dust raised by the columns of my new soldiers was visible from our rooftop, I bade my mother farewell.

"I will be away for only three or four months," I told her. "I will be with the troops almost all the time, so it is better that you stay here."

She said nothing but merely nodded and kissed me. In two hours I was with my army.

At my back as I headed north were three thousand men, the

first payment of my father's pledge for the war against the Medes. They would train through the summer and, after wintering at Amat, would take their place among soldiers hardened by the previous campaign.

But I would not place all my hopes on the forces of Ashur's arms, for it was my intention to make Daiaukka's lot harder than he could ever hope to bear. And to that end I had sent a rider north, over the Kashiari Mountains and across the Bohtan River into the Land of Shubria, whither he was to carry a message:

To the Lord Tabiti, son of Argimpasa, headman of the Sacan tribe of the Scoloti, greetings and all honor from his brother in blood the Lord Tiglath Ashur, son of Sennacherib, who is king in the Land of Ashur. If the Lord Tabiti remembers the love he vowed to the Lord Tiglath Ashur, he will mount his horse no later than the first day of the month of Iyyar and hasten to join him at the garrison at Amat, where they may drink Nairian wine together and plan the conquest of a fruitful land.

He was there, waiting, camped beside the river with fifty of his warriors, when I arrived.

"You have put on flesh," he said, smiling his catlike smile as he held my horse's bridle and waited for me to dismount. I had not even passed beneath the fortress gate but had come directly to his camp. "Did the conspiracies of Nineveh give you no time to take a little wholesome exercise?"

"Why did not you and your riders lodge within the garrison walls? I sent word that you were to be received with honor, and I find you here, squatting by the riverbank. Were my instructions disregarded, or is it simply that the Scoloti hold all comfort in contempt?"

Tabiti laughed and threw his arm across my shoulders as we walked to his leather tent.

"No, your instructions were not disregarded. Your officers have treated us to every kindness, especially that fat Ionian who dresses like a prince—what is his name?"

"Kephalos," I answered, smiling to myself. "He is not a soldier, but he is a cunning fellow and my friend."

"I, too, am a cunning fellow. This Ionian speaks of trading for horses and gold, but since you say he is a friend of yours I will only cheat him a little."

"If you hope to die a rich man, I would advise you to look elsewhere for a victim."

"Doubtless you advise me well, for you must know the proverb: 'Trust a Hebrew before a Phoenician and a Phoenician before an Ionian, but do not trust an Ionian.' However, I am forgetting you are half an Ionian yourself."

We both laughed, but I was not to be so easily deflected.

"You still have not told me," I said, "why you are here, in leather tents, rather than enjoying the garrison's hospitality."

"I have been trying to explain, Prince Tiglath Ashur, but you will not listen." He sat down on a horse blanket spread beneath the shade of his tent flap and gestured for me to follow his example. When we were both comfortable he clapped his hands and a small boy, doubtless another of Tabiti's numberless sons, brought us steaming cloths with which to clean our hands and faces and then a pair of copper cups and a skin of the fermented horse's milk called *safid atesh*—this last was an attention I could easily have forgone.

"Do not expect too much trust," he continued finally, after he had already drained his cup and was refilling both. "My men would think me a great fool if I came so far with so few and then slept surrounded by armed foreigners within the high stone walls of their stockade. I honor you as a soldier, Prince, and could not love you more if you really were my brother, the son by the same woman of my father, Argimpasa. But your soldiers were only lately my enemies in battle, and a man must exercise reasonable prudence. Do not be offended."

I was not offended. In fact he had raised my regard for him even higher, and I was yet more sure of the wisdom of including him in my plans.

We sat drinking together until late into the afternoon and, as before, the *safid atesh* began to taste less disgusting after I had drunk enough of it. Tabiti and I spoke of many things, of the gossip which had reached him from the court of King Argistis—that monarch, it seemed, was indeed slipping into the madness which everyone believed awaited him—of the reputed wealth of Egypt, of the notorious perfidy of the Lydians, of everything, in fact, except any mention of the Medes or my conflict with them. These topics, I noticed, he avoided as scrupulously as I did myself.

But, of course, finally one of us had to speak.

"You are increasing the size of your garrison," he said at last. "You must have brought three thousand soldiers back with you from Nineveh—and I counted twenty chariots. You had not half such a force at the Bohtan River. I have also been struck by the numbers of horses you have pastured in the vicinity."

"You have missed little, it seems."

"A nomad lives by keeping his eyes open." Tabiti, headman of the Sacan, shrugged his shoulders, like a great cat stretching in the hot sun, and grinned. "It is my impression that you prepare for a final reckoning with the Lord Daiaukka—is that not so? I have not been deaf to the stories about your campaign of last summer. I think I am here because you seek allies against the Medes."

"And is that the reason you have come—because such a venture would be to your taste?"

But my barbaric friend, who in sharp trading thought himself a match for my slave Kephalos, only refilled both our cups with his powerful, evil-tasting liquor.

"I am here out of love for you," he said, catching my eye and smiling slightly. "War is another matter—a practical matter, in which a leader must consider the welfare of his people."

"Which means—what?"

"Which means, my brother, that like a good Scoloti, one whom my father would not be ashamed to call his son, I am waiting to hear what bribes you will offer."

It took us but a short time to strike our bargain. By suppertime Tabiti and I had settled between us that the Sacan would attack from the north, forcing the Mannai—a tribe of importance less for their abilities as warriors than for their strategic position, threatening Musasir and the headwaters of the Lower Zab—out of Daiaukka's confederation. My friend's reward for this would be as much of the rich grasslands south and east of Lake Urmia as he could hold, and his presence would be a permanent check on the ambitions of the Medes. The only difficulty we could foresee was from the Urartians.

"We shall have to travel over the northern edge of the Shaking Sea and then south," Tabiti said, dragging his finger through the dust to trace its outline, like a goat stretching to steal grapes from an arbor. "We will keep well away from Tushpa, but King

Argistis still claims all those lands and will be unlikely to let us pass unchallenged."

"He will if he knows you will not stop—why drive you over his borders when you are already on your way thither? This is something which I can arrange for you."

"You think so? You had better be sure, for if I am to make war on the Mannai next summer, I will have to spend all of this summer traveling. I cannot afford to be delayed—the lands of the Urartians are a harsh place when the snows begin."

"Trust me in this. We will come at the Medes from the north and the west, like a pair of hands closing around their throats."

"It is well then, for I am tired of Shubria and my people will be better for a season of fighting. No good Scoloti dies in his bed —it is not dignified."

It was well after dark before I finally rode in through the fortress gates. At first the guards did not even recognize me.

"We were not even sure you had come, *Rab Shaqe*," they shouted down from the barricades, once I had hailed them and they had recognized my voice. "We were beginning to think perhaps you had decided to stay in Nineveh forever."

"Nothing could keep me long from Amat—is it not the garden of the world? Open the gate, dogs, before I have you flogged."

They laughed, and at once I found myself surrounded by soldiers to light the way for me—so many that my horse almost went mad for fear of the torches. In all honesty, I felt I was home once more, for I too was a soldier and a soldier's only true home is his garrison.

The fortress was now virtually completed. Its great wall, the stones still raw from the earth, still glittering with the marks of the cutter's chisel, towered over the rows of mud-brick barracks, the drill fields and stables. Everywhere soldiers and their women sat outside to enjoy the cool, moist night air, and their oil lamps twinkled in the surrounding dark like stars that had fallen from heaven's grace. There was the murmur of numberless conversations, punctuated here and there with laughter, and I could sometimes hear the restless snorting of horses and the sound of their hoofs striking against the hard-packed earth. The cooking fires were almost cold now, but still the smells of meat and millet and boiled onions reached my nostrils. Yes, I really was home. At last I had left Nineveh, with its brick streets and its intrigues, behind me.

The windows of the palace Kephalos had built for me were twinkling with light—my servants, no doubt, were wondering what had kept their master. A groom took my horse and I mounted the great stone staircase even as the tall cedar doors opened to receive me. The house women knelt, and the scribes in their linen tunics bowed from the waist. The *shaknu* had returned, and with him the power of the king. My moment of private homecoming had come and passed.

"My Lord Prince, there is much of business that—"

"And there will be no less tomorrow, Ushnu," I snapped, waving him aside. "So let it wait until then, eh? The road from Nineveh is a long one, and I feel as if I had ridden every *beru* of it in this one day."

My chief scribe bowed again, seeming little pleased with this answer, and I began stripping off my leather breastplate as a slave pulled the sandals from my feet.

"Will the Dread Lord take some supper?" she asked, wiping the dust from my ankles with a damp cloth. She looked up at me and smiled uncertainly, as if afraid I might suddenly decide to strike her. Had I sounded as impatient as that?

"No, Gamelat—I thank you." Gently, I took the cloth from her hand. She was one of my mother's women, purchased when first we had settled at Three Lions. She had known me for years. "Just a little wine perhaps, and then I will find my bed."

She scrambled to her feet, like a dog that has heard its master's voice.

"Yes, my lord. At once."

"And, Gamelat—where is the Lord Kephalos? I had expected to see him here tonight."

"He was here, my lord. He is . . . gone away. Shall I have him summoned back?"

"No—it is not important."

I sat there, in a hallway, drinking the wine that Gamelat had brought me, glad to be alone but for the moment too tired even to stumble off to my sleeping mat. For several minutes my mind would hold to nothing and then, very gradually, the pleasant sadness of memory filled me.

"Esharhamat."

The name seemed to speak itself. Esharhamat. I had only to think of nothing else, and she flooded my soul. Esharhamat.

At any rate, she was safe for the moment. Esarhaddon would

not visit her bed that whole summer, not while she nursed his son, and I was far enough away that the breath of scandal could not touch her. Was she thinking of me? It would be a pleasant thing to believe.

I got up. Enough—I would sleep.

Where was Kephalos, I wondered. It was unlike him not to be there to greet me after a long absence. He had been here— Gamelat had said so. What could have called him away?

But it did not matter. At least, it did not matter tonight. Tomorrow, once more, I would belong to my scribes and my soldiers, my friends and my enemies. Tonight I did not want to be the Lord Tiglath Ashur, *rab shaqe* of the king's army, *shaknu* of the north, son of the Lord Sennacherib, and master of a fat, rascally Greek who treated me as if I were his property instead of the other way about. Tonight I did not want to be anyone. I wanted to be asleep.

There was a flicker of light coming from my chamber. Good —some thoughtful slave had left a lamp burning for me. I was a fortunate man to be surrounded by such attention. I must remember to do something, I thought, to make some gesture of appreciation. But that too could wait until tomorrow.

I swept the curtain aside and my bowels froze. There, waiting beside my sleeping mat, was Zabibe. The flickering, yellow light on her ashen skin gave an almost demonic cast to her beauty, as if she embodied within herself all forbidden pleasure.

"My Lord has not forgotten me?" she asked, smiling teasingly. She crossed her arms in front of her and with the tips of her fingers pushed down the sleeves of her tunic to reveal her breasts. "To have been left behind would have broken your poor slave's heart."

"That woman, Lord, is a devil. Since she arrived here three days ago she has taught your servants to dread her anger—she drove me from your house with her curses on the very night of your return, and now I am afraid to go back there."

Even as he spoke, Kephalos stroked his beard with trembling, agitated fingers. He glanced about as if afraid that even here, in his own house, he was not safe from Zabibe.

"She behaves as if she were already mistress of the *shaknu*'s palace," he went on at last. "As if she stood in Naiba's place—or even that of your Lady Mother—and no one has the courage to contradict her. My lord, I trust, is not such a great fool as to have thought of covering this woman with a veil?"

"No, Kephalos—have no fear. I do not expect ever to take a wife."

"Yes, Lord, but the important question is what *she* expects. Be warned—she is the type who throws things."

"Throws things?"

"Yes, of course. The wine cups will crash against the walls like hail against a tile roof." He shrugged his shoulders, as if astonished that I could be simpleton enough to expect anything else. "Beat her, Lord. Remind her who is master in the palace of a royal prince. That is the wisest thing you can do. Take a whip of hippopotamus hide and beat her until you have flayed the skin from her backside, for if you do not let her know her place she will make of your life such a misery that you will long for the quiet safety of war."

"Yes, I will beat her. If only to please you and restore good order among my house servants, I will beat her."

"See that you do, Lord."

Gradually, consoled by my assurance of retribution, and an abundance of his own wine, Kephalos grew tranquil again. As we waited for his servants to prepare breakfast—knowing that my worthy slave never left his bed until two hours before midday, I had not yet eaten myself—he told me of all that had happened in Amat during my absence, and particularly of his own feats of cunning on my behalf and his own.

"This barbarian who dwells in a leather tent," he confided, in the manner of one with secrets to impart. "This Tabiti—he has many fine horses, and a wealth of gold. I wonder where he gets them."

"By cutting the throats of unwary fools like you," I said, holding out my wine cup to be refilled. "Leave him in prosperity for now—after next summer's campaign he will have a great deal more of which you may rob him."

"This is wise." The learned physician nodded gravely—he was by then too far gone in drink to notice any sarcasm but, as ever, his mind was clear enough to grasp the main point. "You will make this tribe of wandering thieves great—a nation to be feared. And this Tabiti is, I think, your friend. In the years to come, when your brother sits on the throne, you may have need of such friends."

"I am not hatching treason, Kephalos. You sound like the wagging tongues of Nineveh, each one with his own story of how I am plotting to betray Esarhaddon."

"I say nothing of betrayal, Lord, but a man who can claim powerful allies is treated with respect."

I closed my ears to such talk. Ever since my brother had been named *marsarru* I had taught myself how to be deaf to what I did not wish to hear. After a while I left Kephalos's house and returned to my scribes, who were more than eager to bury me with work. By the time the sky had begun to darken I had forgotten all about the wisdom of my alliance with the Scythians, who, in any case, had folded their tents and were already on their way back to the land of Shubria. I rubbed my eyes and thought only of half an hour in the sweating house, dinner, and my bed.

It was in the sweating house, as I watched the steam rise from the glowing brazier, that I remembered Zabibe. The bitch—how dare she follow me from Nineveh without my leave? Even a wife would not think to act in such a fashion.

But, of course, she hadn't followed me. She had arrived in Amat some three days before, carried in a sedan chair like a great lady—one need not wonder that my servants were frightened of her.

Who had provided her escort? A slave woman does not embark on such a journey on her own. Someone had told her to come, had provided her with money and protection. Someone had sent her. I wondered why it had not occurred to me before.

She was a spy.

I did not trouble myself to ask for whom—my movements and intentions were not of interest to that many people.

Had Esharhamat guessed? *"Let her believe she is favored,"* she had advised. Yes, Esharhamat would have understood all these matters better than I. I, who would not even listen when my own slave told me to protect myself with powerful friends.

For a moment or two I considered sending this Arab slut packing back to my father's house of women, but only for a moment or two. After all, what would she learn in Amat that I would not want known in Nineveh? Or, more probably, in Calah?

No—let her stay. Why put Esarhaddon and his mother to

the trouble of finding another to fill her place? I would use her like a tavern harlot and let her pry into whatever secrets she liked.

But tonight, in this at least, I would follow the wise counsel of my friend Kephalos and cut a few notches from her backside that she might remember not to play the fine lady. I had only to recall the fear-filled eyes of my servants and the wrath boiled within me.

"*Ekalli,* go down to the river's bank and cut me a green switch, about the length of my arm. Make sure it is straight and smooth and strip the bark away from all save the thick end."

He grinned, showing me his teeth stained with date sap. He was but a lad, fresh from some peasant village, and he knew it was not his hind parts which would feel the lash. That was all he had learned to care about.

The switch cut through the air with a sound like startled bees. The wood, where the bark was peeled away, was still slippery. I smiled as I thought how I would make my little Arab monkey dance.

There was a tiny room off my sleeping chamber which I used when dining alone. She was waiting for me there, she and some two or three of the household women, preparing the table for my meal. She was wearing only a thin white linen tunic that did not even reach her knees and that she sponged so that it clung to her body. When I first saw her she was crouching beside my chair, almost as if claiming it as a possession.

Yes, of course my slaves bowed to her—she was the master's concubine, she who had found favor in his eyes, the woman into whom he pressed his seed. She would be presumed to have power, perhaps even to the power of life and death, and it was a presumption she was at some pains to encourage.

Well, all of that would cease this very evening.

When she saw me she smiled, and then, when she saw the switch in my hand, the smile froze on her lips and her black eyes seemed to thrill with terror.

The other women, as soundlessly as mice, fled the room.

"My Dread Lord, I . . ."

But her voice died as I raised my whip and then allowed the tip to settle gently on her bare shoulder.

"You have overstepped yourself," I said, letting my voice become almost lifeless. "A harlot with a pretty body, who knows to dance to the flute and cymbals, who can kindle a little lust and thus imagine herself mighty."

"If my lord is pleased . . ." She dropped her eyes, which by then had grown shiny—like so many women, she understood the power of meekness. Yes, let the foolish man believe she had grown all submission.

"My lord is not pleased. He is not pleased to have his servants, trusted and faithful these many years, driven from his door like masterless dogs. No—he is not pleased."

I reached out with a sudden movement and grabbed the sleeve of her tunic. Even as I dragged her to her knees the fabric gave way with a frightful tearing sound, leaving her half naked. She huddled by my feet, her face almost touching the floor, but I took a handful of her long black hair and pulled back her head, forcing her to look at me.

"You—are—less—than—nothing," I said, speaking through clenched teeth, letting the whip keep time with the words. "You—are—no—one—in—this—house!"

With each stroke a thin red line appeared on her back, and as she stared up into my face a thin sheen of moisture appeared on her brow, and I could hear her soft moan. At first I thought it was pain, but it was not pain—at least, not only pain.

"Oh . . . my lord—my Lord Master . . ."

Her voice seemed to come from some hidden place deep within. Her hands, braced against my legs, crept under the hem of my tunic and she pushed aside my loincloth. I weighted more heavily the stroke of my whip, until it seemed to cut into her flesh like the edge of a sword, coating it with blood, but she only seemed to grow more urgent.

"My Dread Lord . . ."

The words were indistinct, muffled. She pressed her face against my groin and then, suddenly, took my manhood between her lips. I could hear the gasps of breath as she seemed to devour me, like a starving beggar.

I am not made of stone. My senses were not dead. All wrath left me, to be replaced by something infinitely more savage. My lash dropped unnoticed to the floor.

She drew back for a moment, still clinging to my legs; her eyes, as she looked at me, were swimming with tears—not of pain or fear, but unspent longing.

"My lord—I beg you . . ."

Had I been in a trance? In an instant I came to myself and pushed her away—hard, that she struck the floor. I turned and left the room, my brain burning.

For two hours I sat outside, on a stone bench in my garden, letting the cold night seep into me. The thoughts tumbled through my mind, one after the other, too quickly to be more than a blur. What had I seen inside myself that filled me with such delicious, terrible dread? Was I a beast or a man? I did not know—I did not wish to know. Yet I could not turn away from this knowledge, which only waited to possess me.

I thought of Esharhamat and my brother. Was it like that? Was I no more than that—or was Esarhaddon so much wiser than I?

Yes, of course. Esarhaddon, with his slow, coarse, deliberate lechery—he, at least, understood himself.

At last I grew weary even of my own ecstatic remorse. My head galloped. I would drink myself quiet, and then sleep.

In my chamber I found Zabibe, waiting, still wearing the same thin white tunic, now little more than a handful of rags.

I had not expected this, had not wished it, but she had come nonetheless. A silver vessel of wine, still cold from the cellar, stood at the end of my sleeping mat, with a gold cup beside it.

The whip lay on my pillow, still stained with blood.

Zabibe poured the wine and with her own hands brought the cup to my lips. I drank, although my throat seemed to squeeze shut. I drank, and felt my desire awaken all over again. Still, I had come to hate her.

This she understood—and welcomed.

"Show me your backside," I said.

She crouched down on her knees and elbows, her head to the wall. The welts on her shoulders looked almost black in the lamplight. I could hear her breathing, in quick little starts, as if some violent passion cut each breath into a hundred ragged fragments.

I placed my hands on her buttocks and pushed them apart. As I thrust into her, the only sound that escaped her lips was a whimper of blissful, welcome pain.

This woman, it seemed, had found that which she sought. It was a thing I must not try to understand.

28

Zabibe kept the whip, and each night she would leave it, along with a vessel of wine and a single cup, at the foot of my sleeping mat. It was mine to use, and if I did not use it she became at first restless and then cold and unresponding, but it was hers to keep, to hide away, to treasure. It was her focus for an intense hunger of the senses, an excitement that was almost like religious frenzy, as if that limber wand had become her idol, the symbol for her god, to whom she prayed for release through submission and pain.

At first I covered her back and buttocks with angry stripes, marks she carried sometimes for days, but in time I had but to touch her gently on the back, to let her feel the whip's hard smooth surface on her skin, and this alone would set her sobbing with desire. She would beg me, but not to spare her—never that. She wanted me to threaten her, with pain, even with death. She wanted me to hurt her. I sometimes took a fold of her breast and squeezed it between thumb and first finger until I left a bruise. I did worse things as well, things it shames me to remember. Once or twice I forgot myself and nearly killed her, and she almost seemed to wish that I had, as if that would have stamped her happiness with perfection. It was an unaccountable yearning.

And it was much the same for me. We played this cruel game almost every night for months, and there was no surfeit, but rather the appetite fed on itself. She was becoming an obsession.

The bonds between men and women are as varied as the patterns the sun makes on rippling water, and as quick to change. I do not speak of love, for love has not often entered my life and I did not love Zabibe, nor she me. Passion was all we shared, and passion, which can exist side by side with contempt and even hatred, is not the same as love. I took a cold, exquisite pleasure in this woman, in her flesh and in her pain-mingled craving. But that was all.

And what of Esharhamat? Had I forgotten her? Had I become so busy with feeding my new appetite for cruelty that she had passed from my thoughts? Hardly that. Indeed, it seemed that the more I became entangled in Zabibe's net, the more I longed for Esharhamat.

"I do not care how you spend your seed," she had told me, *"so long as I have your heart."* I have learned to stand in awe before the wisdom of women, and in this Esharhamat was wise. She knew she had no rivals. Whom could I love but Esharhamat? I wrung out my loins into Zabibe in an ever-rising frenzy of desire and yet, day by day, I grew to loathe the sight of her.

And I do not think it was any different for her. I think we learned a mutual hatred as we toiled in our mutual lust.

But Zabibe was not all that Amat contained. I had not been sent there to entertain myself with a harlot, but to fight my father's battles. I had an army to prepare for war, and for hours, sometimes days at a time, I would hardly think of her as I lost myself in the honest, happy hardship of drill.

I promoted men out of the companies that had fought in the campaigns of the last two years and put them in command of the recruits who had just come up from Nineveh. Tabshar Sin was now in charge of training at the garrison, and when he could vouch for his little boys as decent parade-ground soldiers I would take four or five companies at a time up into the mountains for field maneuvers, going out on forced marches lasting sometimes twelve, sometimes fifteen or twenty days.

We would return to Amat with sunburned faces and bleeding feet, for I knew what these men would face in the lands of the Medes and therefore spared them from no travail, but the farm boys who had left returned as soldiers.

And always my old instructor in arms begged that he might be allowed to accompany us, and always I returned to him the same answer: "Tabshar Sin, would you shame me in front of these puling infants? As their commander and the veteran of many battles I enjoy some credit with them now, but what if they were

to see me worn to nothing beside one old enough to have lost a
hand in the wars of my grandfather?"

"I understand you well enough, Prince," he would answer,
looking at me through narrow, accusing eyes. "You are afraid I
am too old and might hold you back."

"I am more afraid *we* might hold *you* back, my friend."

"Then promise me this—that you will not leave me behind
when next summer you march into the Zagros Mountains. I have
yet a few good battles left in me and I wish to see this rogue
Daiaukka whom you admire so much, to judge for myself if he is
all you have claimed for him."

"It shall be as you wish. But next summer, not this."

Did I think perhaps Tabshar Sin would change his mind? I
do not know what I thought, but may the god forgive me that
ever I made such a promise—and that ever I kept it.

Thus did we spend our days, laboring at the soldier's trade,
happy to weary our sword arms and cover our sandals with dust,
dreaming always of the nearness of glory and of death. And thus
did the hot months of that summer burn themselves out, clearing
the way for the approach of the winter rains and my return to
Nineveh.

There was a sense, of course, in which I had never been
allowed to leave.

The king, after the Lord Sinahiusur's death, had not chosen
another *turtanu* and had tried as best he could to rule alone. It
was an experiment which could never have succeeded, for the
god's empire was too vast and my father had grown old. Yet he
tried. I could gauge the concentration of his effort in the letters
which arrived almost daily at my headquarters in Amat.

      I have today received ambassadors from Ashdod. In public
    audience they bring gifts from their king and messages calling
    me a kind father to all their people, but in private they tell me
    they tire of his rule and ask my permission to overthrow him
    and set up the son in his father's place. This boy, who is the
    child of one of my own women, given to Sharru-ludari when I
    established his lordship after the revolt of Zedekiah of Ascalon
    and restored to him the throne of his ancestors, is a wicked
    boy. . . .

      There is pestilence reported in the city of Dilbat, and the
    moon, we are told, has been seen to drip blood for three nights

in succession. The priests say I should fast and shave my beard in token of contrition for my transgressions against Sin and Nergal, but if I have transgressed, why do the gods visit their wrath upon Dilbat, that accused doghole whose citizens, you will remember, joined the Elamites and those sons of harlots the Babylonians in a cruel rebellion which stole from me the life of my eldest boy? I fail to see why I should be inconvenienced. . . .

It is early, I know, but I have had the auspices taken on that new son Esharhamat has whelped for your beloved brother, the Lord Donkey. I thought it a reasonable precaution since, sadly, the little brat gives no sign that he will oblige us by dying, like the last one. He proves as healthy as his father, alas, but the gods, who are wise, have greatly diminished the injury by declaring that this one, at least, will never sit upon my throne. The goat's liver, I was told, was already filled with maggots, and its heart was as black as if it had been burned with fire. . . .

Burned with fire. I remembered Esharhamat's dreams about a fiery death and wondered what it was which the Lords of Decision had revealed to her.

As always, I was careful in my replies and declined to offer advice even when the king my father sought it of me. I would not be *turtanu,* neither in name nor in fact, neither in Nineveh nor in Amat. Esarhaddon was to be king, and I saw no point in attempting to forestall the inevitable.

So in the first day of Kislef, even while the roads were yet muddy from the first winter rains, I set off for the south with a bodyguard of a hundred men. Zabibe traveled with us in a wagon, but she did not enjoy the journey and filled my ears with complaints whenever I was unwary enough to venture near her, which was not often. Even for the hours of rest I joined my soldiers and pitched a tent on the ground, leaving her to the comforts of her wagon. I did not go into her except once, when we stopped for the night in a village near Elkosh and, having drunk more beer than was wise, I pushed her down on a table to unburden myself of a week's abstinence. The next morning she reproached me bitterly, saying that she was up until nearly dawn picking splinters out of her breasts and belly.

"Hold your tongue, woman," I told her, "or I will sell you to a caravan driver who smells worse than his camels."

After ten days, when we approached lands belonging to my estate, I told the *rab kisir* in charge of my escort to take them and the wagon on to Nineveh. I wished to spend a few tranquil days at Three Lions, and I still had enough shame to wish that my mother might know nothing of Zabibe.

After an absence of many months, it is a fine thing to return to one's own place. Since becoming the Lord Sinahiusur's heir I was the master of many fine estates, most of which I had never even seen, but Three Lions was my home. Here I was not *rab shaqe* and *shaknu,* nor the king's son, nor the rival of great princes. Here I was merely a landowner and farmer. Here I ate my own bread and drank my own beer. And here, under the floor of my own house, I hoped one day to lay down my horses.

The last harvest of the year had been gathered in, and the fields were empty and covered with withered stubble. The mud along the canal banks looked like molten granite—there was hardly water enough at the bottom to come up to an ox's belly. The skies were the color of lead and far away I could hear the muffled booming of Adad's thunder, but there would be no rain this night. By the time I rode into the deserted farmyard I could see flashes of lightning behind the eastern mountains.

The house servants stood in a knot on the porch of my house, murmuring among themselves and staring at me as if they could not imagine how I had come there. A boy came from the stable to take my horse.

"Well," I said, grinning broadly and wondering what was the trouble, "and will no one bring her master a cup of beer? Where is my lady mother?"

"I am here, my son," she said, stepping out from the shadow of the doorway. "May the gods be blessed for having spared you to return to me."

I kissed her upon the lips and we went inside, where I washed my face in a basin of heated water. All the while my mother stood beside me, holding her hands clenched together at her waist like a supplicant. I could only wonder what new domestic catastrophe had befallen us—until Naiba came into the room, silent as a cat, and stood penitently beside the hearth. Her eyes were lowered; she seemed to be gazing down at her belly, which had swollen beneath her tunic to the size of a summer melon.

I burst forth with laughter at the sight of her, and she ran away, weeping loudly and hiding her face with her arms.

"Perhaps we had best not tarry any longer about the betrothal ritual," I said at last, when I could control my voice again. "Best marry the hot little bitch off quickly, or young Qurdi will be a father before ever he is a husband."

"Then you are not angry, Lathikadas?"

My mother stared into my face with an expression that struck a nervous balance between gratitude and astonishment, as if she were relieved to have detected me in some weakness.

"No, Merope, I am not angry," I answered, putting my arm over her shoulders. "I have not gone into the girl in almost a year, as you know, for she sleeps in your room and not in mine, so I have no interest in the matter. If Qurdi is not displeased, there is little enough reason why I should be."

The next morning I received Tahu Ishtar and his son into my presence. It was a visit of ceremony, so I met them outside the door of my house. They bowed low and offered presents of embroidered cloth, copper jewelry, bread, date wine, and honeyed fruit. I accepted these in the name of my slave and thus gave my consent to this betrothal. At last, Naiba came out into the sunshine, escorted by my mother, and her future husband poured scented oil over her hair. At first she flushed with pleasure and then, almost at once, burst once more into tears and had to be taken back inside, Merope clucking over her like a brooding hen.

"My wife was much the same when she was with child," Tahu Ishtar said, after the women had gone. "Their livers grow full of demons. To have been born a man is a great blessing."

The three of us then drank beer together, and Tahu Ishtar and I agreed that, considering the circumstances, it would be well if the marriage took place before I was obliged to return to Nineveh. Qurdi stood silent as we talked and ground his toes into the dust. He would have his wife before he was three days older, but until then, it seemed, he was still only a boy.

The next day and the next there was rain from noon to sunset, and a man could not even amuse himself with hunting. I tried to stay out of my mother's way, for there was much to be done in preparation for Naiba's marriage feast, and at last I retreated to

one of the barns to sit on sacks of millet and grow drunk on beer.
I felt out of place and wished I were still in Amat.

But on the third day the sun was out again, and at the third
hour of the morning, when the farmyard was filled with peasants
from the surrounding villages, I led Naiba to the house of Tahu
Ishtar, her new father-in-law, and, as she sat on a bench before
the door, Qurdi covered her with a veil and declared in a loud
voice that she was now his wife. He looked very pleased with
himself and everyone cheered, for the boy was well liked—even
Naiba did not weep as much as I would have expected. At the end
I stepped forward and solemnly paid her dowry into Qurdi's
hands, counting out the ten shekels of silver so that all could see
that the overseer's son was now a man of substance.

There were seven goats roasted to feed the marriage guests,
and we drank down many great jars of beer. Everyone was merry,
and at sundown Qurdi led his new wife into his father's house for
the first time, although whether he was able to go into her when
she was so far gone with child I do not know. Yet I think they
were both very content with their bargain.

I went to my own bed soon after that, taking with me for
company a jar of strong date wine. I was pleased at the day's
work, for I wished Qurdi well and was fond of Naiba, but I cannot say that my pleasure was unmixed.

"I will never put the veil over any woman's head," I thought.
"And if I have sons they will be the children of concubines." I
had only to close my eyes and I saw Esharamat's face—Esharhamat, whom I loved, who was my brother's wife and the mother of
his son.

If a man drinks enough date wine he does not dream. He
snores like a pig and nothing troubles him. This is the mercy of
the great gods.

"My Lord Tiglath Ashur, the mighty *rab shaqe,* does not
care for wine? But, I am always forgetting, he drinks only the
fresh blood of Medes!"

This, followed by much laughter. It was a banquet given by
Nabu Pashir—the son of one of the king's lesser brothers, a man
of no importance then but one who hoped for better in the next
reign. I cannot even remember why I went, since I must have
known that no one there would be quick to call himself my friend.

But the joke went down very well. Esarhaddon, among such, could afford to display his wit.

"In the spring my noble brother will fight a great war," he went on, perhaps encouraged by my silence. "He plans to lead as many as twenty thousand men into the eastern mountains—it will be a kind of horse-catching expedition."

There was more laughter, for the hour was late and everyone was drunk, even the harlots. The flute players sat in a corner, their knees drawn up to their chests, sleeping contentedly. The table was covered with puddles of spilled wine.

I waited, saying nothing. The men who sat on either side of me faced away, watching my brother, trying as best they could to ignore my existence. Everyone else—everyone out of reach of my hands and feeling it thus safe to indulge a taste for mockery— divided their attention between Esarhaddon and myself. It was a game, and in this company no one harmed himself by becoming my enemy.

He was the *marsarru,* I told myself. His person was sacred and no man could insult him in public. If I answered him at all, I would only end by making myself look ridiculous.

Yet this was Esarhaddon, my friend from childhood, my brother whom once I had loved. Now he wiped his greasy fingers on his tunic, shot through with silver, and grinned at me, hating the sight of me. How had it come to this?

"The great warlord—he sits up in that village of mud huts he calls a garrison and plots cattle raids against tribesmen who have never slept twice in the same place since the day they were born. Oh, it is all very glorious!"

"Yes, and his mother is an Ionian tavern girl whom even the king does not . . ."

I did not even know the dog's name. He sat only two or three places from Esarhaddon himself, staring at me through wide, blinking witless eyes—perhaps he was fool enough to have imagined himself within some magic circle of inviolability, but he must have seen his error in my face for the words trailed away to nothing.

The whole assembly fell silent as I rose to my feet. Men scrambled to be out of my way as I kicked aside the section of table that stood between us, for they knew that one among them had signed his death warrant.

"No! NO—I . . ."

No one tried to interfere, and this one was too drunk and frightened even to defend himself. I grabbed him by the beard with my left hand and with my right drew the dagger from my belt. One quick slash did the business, cutting his scrawny throat so deeply that my blade scraped against bone.

Blood spurted forth, covering me, the table, even the wall behind—he did not even cry out. I released his beard, and he fell backward over the bench upon which he had been sitting, as limp as water.

"I have repaid the insult," I shouted, glaring defiance. "If anyone wishes to claim satisfaction for the deed, he will know where to find me."

I turned on my heel and left. As I made my way to the door, which seemed a journey of hours, I could hear Esarhaddon's voice at my back.

"Damn you, Tiglath!" he shouted. "I'll see that you pay for this—damn you, Tiglath!"

But no one attempted to hold me and, as I walked home, people in the streets merely stared—it was not their business to meddle if my clothes, my hands, even my face and beard were stained with blood. I must have looked like a butcher.

I was a butcher. I had killed a man, and for no better cause than that he had started to insult my mother. Had I really killed him for that? No, I had killed him because he was not Esarhaddon—because it was therefore permitted to kill him. The blood which had soaked through my tunic and was now caking like dried mud should have been Esarhaddon's.

My slaves met me at the door. They had been slaves of the Lord Sinahiusur, just as the palace in which I lived had been his, and thus they hardly knew me. They said nothing, but what must they have thought as I stripped myself naked, my bare skin streaked with blood, and called for wine, hot water, and scented oil? I did not then trouble myself to think.

I regretted nothing. I would not be mocked. Let the lord *marsarru*, the Chosen One of Ashur, let him be warned that I would not be mocked. I regretted nothing. Nothing—I . . .

The king, of course, was furious. I received his summons the very next morning and found him in his garden, sitting on a stone bench, with Esarhaddon just behind.

But this, at least, was not a public occasion. Here I owed my brother no special respect.

"I want to know how you dared do such a thing," my father said, his voice level and deadly. "I want to know why you imagine you can cut a man's throat in front of twenty or thirty of my nobles and hope to escape punishment."

Esarhaddon caught my eye and smiled tensely. It seemed that, for reasons of his own, he too wished to know.

"First of all, they are not your nobles, but your son and heir the lord *marsarru*'s. Second, while he may choose to throw mud from the mantle of his office, he should teach his trained monkeys to hold their tongues, for they enjoy not his safety. If I killed a man, let his life be on Esarhaddon's head—it is not my way to listen quietly to the tauntings of slaves."

"Is this true?" The king twisted around to look up at Esarhaddon. "Is this true, eh? Did the dog have the impudence to insult my son?"

"The Lord Tiglath Ashur speaks words of fire, as befits a conqueror, but Girittu Marduk is no less dead."

"Was that his name?" I asked, returning Esarhaddon's tight, contemptuous smile. "I did not realize such vermin aspired to the dignity of names."

"You should cut throats for a livelihood, Tiglath. You would make a great reputation for yourself in the alleyways of Nineveh."

"And my lord *marsarru* could set up as a brothel keeper, since the life seems so very much to his taste."

"I will have no more of this!" the king shouted, springing up from his bench as if it had suddenly turned into a slab of white-hot iron. "I am an old man, and I will have no more of this—my head pounds with the thunder of angry voices. No more, I say!"

The expression on Esarhaddon's lips did not change, except that the object of his contempt was now not me but our father.

"I am sorry to have tried your patience thus, Dread Lord, but since it involved a slight to the royal dignity—"

"Yes—dignity." The king repeated the word, almost as if it were part of an invocation. His eyes kept shifting from Esarhaddon to me, and they were filled with anxious uncertainty. "Yes—dignity. The dignity of our house . . ."

An old man's moods are as changeful as the sky in springtime. In an instant, seemingly from one breath to the next, the whole carriage of his body changed.

"No—I remember now." He took my arm in his hands, squeezing as if to test its strength. "An insult which had to be answered—the dog chose to cast a slur upon my son. What did he say, eh, Tiglath? Well, no matter . . ."

He sat down again, and the anxiety had vanished from his face. He placed his hands upon his knees, seemingly quite content and at peace.

Above the king's head, Esarhaddon and I exchanged a look. My brother raised his eyebrows, as if to say, "You see how he is?"

"But you must protect yourself, my son." The Lord Sennacherib, Lord of the Earth's Four Corners, glanced up at me, his countenance once more puckered with worry. "Go to the house of this man, this Girittu Marduk, and place offerings of bread and wine upon his bier, lest his ghost seek vengeance against you."

"It seems no less than a sensible precaution," Esarhaddon put in, nodding sagely.

"You see? Esarhaddon agrees." The king's gaze skipped back and forth between us. "Do this, Tiglath—do it at once. And now leave me, both of you. I like to feed the birds that stop here in my garden on their way south. They know me and are not afraid, but they will not come if there are strangers about. Leave me."

I left, but I did not visit the house of Girittu Marduk nor offer sacrifice to his ghost, for the wrath of such a one, either quick or dead, caused me little enough disquiet. The shades of those I had killed could safely leave me to my living enemies.

Esarhaddon had learned one or two things since receiving the god's blessing. Somewhere, somehow, he had acquired subtlety—enough, at least, for him to find ways of managing the king. Yes, of course. The king was failing. In a few years' time it would be Esarhaddon who would hold power in the Land of Ashur. It would be as the officers of the *quradu* had said.

But I had grown accustomed to the knowledge that I walked within a nest of scorpions. It no longer made me feel giddy.

When I returned home I saw a carrying chair waiting. The slaves who squatted before my door wore the tunics of the royal household.

In the audience chamber, which in Sinahiusur's time had been crowded with supplicants, I found only the Lady Shaditu.

"You said you would kill me when next we met," she murmured. She sat on a table, showing me the outlines of her legs through her filmy tunic. "But I do not think you will kill me today. I think that, for the moment, you are sated with blood."

She smiled, implying that she understood everything, that my crimes only made me more attractive. I knew that she was wicked, that her body was a path which must lead to disgrace and death, and yet the thought must intrude itself into my mind that she was also beautiful.

"No, I will not kill you. But I will send you home with your backside in strips if you make me wait to know why you have come."

"Will you serve me like the slave woman Zabibe?" The smile on her lips softened, as if the prospect might not be wholly repugnant to her. "She is a spy—did you know that?"

"Yes. For the Lady Naq'ia."

"It would seem my beloved brother has grown wise with the years. Kiss me, Tiglath."

"Why have you come?"

"Kiss me first, and then I will tell you. Kiss me—I know it is in your heart to kiss me."

She spoke no more than the truth, for I was in a strangely reckless mood. I leaned forward and kissed her and she threw her arms about my neck, forcing her way between my lips with her pointed tongue. My hands found her breasts—her nipples were hard beneath the palms and I let my fingers close over them, pinching hard. Her arms dropped away from me and she groaned with pain, but she did not struggle. Only her eyes, swimming with tears, pleaded with me.

"It seems that you and my treacherous little concubine are just alike," I hissed.

"Yes—just alike."

Yes. I could see it in her begging eyes.

Finally I released her, and at once she covered her breasts with her arms.

"Do not toy with me, Shaditu. I am not one of your palace lovers."

"Would that you were, Tiglath, my love. I could wish that you . . . Oh! I think I shall carry the marks of your thumbs to my grave."

"Tell me why you have come, or you will fill it sooner than you imagine."

"I would rather you buried me in your bed," she whispered,

throwing her arms once more around my neck and kissing my mouth. "I love you, Tiglath, for you are the only man in Nineveh who is not afraid of me."

I disentangled myself and stepped back beyond her reach, for indeed she did inflame my liver.

"I am more afraid of you than anyone."

"No, not of me, merely of yourself. Of betraying yourself. And you are fortunate—or perhaps it is true that you are stronger than the rest of us—because you never have."

"And have you, sister?"

"Oh, yes—and therefore I am filled with fear."

I could see that. It was in her eyes, that fear. And yet it was not fear of men or anything that men could do, nor even of death. It was a fear of the soul. It was the fear of abandonment and despair. It was the fear of one who has stepped into the darkness and knows she will never find her way back.

"Now speak," I said, driving pity from my heart—for who was I to pity Shaditu? "What have you come here to tell me?"

At once she drew into herself. She sat on the table, coy and distant, playing with her painted fingernails. It seemed she was determined to make me court her favor.

"What do you want to know?" she asked, not looking at me, still absorbed with her nails.

"Why you have come here."

"I have told you—because I love you. And because I must choose sides, and quickly."

I did not require an explanation. The whole city was choosing sides—or attempting to force me into giving them a side to choose.

"The king will very soon be king no longer," she went on, quite unnecessarily, "for he is old and tired, and a younger man must take his place. All that remains to be settled is who it will be, you or Esarhaddon. I would rather it were you, but for my own sake I must be one of those who move the balance in the winner's favor."

"The question has already been settled. Esarhaddon is the god's choice. He is the *marsarru* and will be king."

"Will he?" She glanced up at me and smiled, as if I had said something amusing. "Perhaps, if you wish it, Esarhaddon will be king. But you could be his *turtanu*. The army will follow where you lead, and the army can have things all their own way. It has happened before that a *turtanu* has held a king in the hollow of his hand. Perhaps that is the god's choice."

"Shaditu—sister—why did the *baru* Rimani Ashur take his own life? Was that too the god's choice?"

She withdrew her gaze and for a moment sat with her hands quiet, staring at nothing. For all her wickedness she was not a coward, and I could not remember a time before today when she had shown fear, real fear. But in that moment she was afraid.

"Why would I know? My interest is in men's bodies, not their hearts." She laughed—a high-pitched silvery laugh, like the joyless laughter of the mad. And still she kept her eyes from me.

"You seduced him, did you not?" I took her face between my hands and made her look at me. "You came to his bed and made him betray his office."

"How do you know . . . ?"

"Everyone knows—me last of all. I heard the story in Amat, from one whose name you perhaps have never even heard."

"It isn't true. It isn't'! The Lady Naq'ia—"

"What? Did she force you? Or did the two of you simply find you had ambitions in common?"

She pulled away from me and then, after a moment, glared into my eyes with the defiant courage of the lost. No, she would not tell me. But she denied nothing.

"What did Rimani Ashur see among the omens, sister? Do you know?"

"If I told you, and this knowledge helped you to steal Esarhaddon's crown from him, would you take his wife with it or would you take me?"

"I would take Esharhamat."

"Then I fear the truth must have died with Rimani Ashur."

Again she laughed, and the sound was just as bitter. For now she had chosen her side.

I struck her—hard and across the face, with the back of my hand. She fell to the floor, and when she turned to look at me there was blood on her mouth. But still she laughed.

That night I went to see Esharhamat in her apartments. I did not care who knew of it. Esarhaddon would remain in Nineveh for another ten days—if he heard, and wished to object, he was welcome.

"Turn your back on your god," she had said. But it seemed that Ashur had turned his back on me. If he chose to hide his purpose, then I must feel free to follow my own.

Let Esarhaddon object. This time I would not stay my hand.

She met me in a room beside her sleeping chamber. She looked drawn, as if her recent delivery had sapped her strength, and her breasts were swollen with milk.

"I will not suckle my husband's child," she said—the thought seemed to give her some pleasure. "He will have nothing from me except his life. They bring in herdsmen's wives to nurse him. What could be more fitting for Esarhaddon's son?"

"Let me take you to my house. We will go to Amat—let Esarhaddon come for us there if he has the courage."

She seemed not to hear me. I was hardly there for her, her own misery absorbed her so.

What had I done to us both?

"Yet he flourishes," she went on—had her mind broken at last? "He is healthy and strong, like his father. But *this* child will never wear the crown of Ashur.

"Do you want me, Tiglath? Still? Then come with me—come. Only into the next room, where I can rest my back. We need not go as far as Amat, for it makes no difference."

And she meant it. She rose, and took my arm with her two hands, pulling me along. The door to her sleeping chamber was half open—why had I not seen that?

"If Esarhaddon takes us together, what can he do?" She smiled, drawing me through the open doorway. "I must bear the son who will rule after him, and that son is yet to find his way into my womb. What can Esarhaddon do?"

It was a small room and two of Esharhamat's servant were there, crouched in a corner, folding and refolding pieces of white linen—women's work, intelligible only to them. They looked up and, seeing me, rose to leave. They did not linger and their eyes were shining with fear, for they knew their mistress was committing a mad act. The door closed behind them with hardly a sound.

With no word, Esharhamat slipped her tunic off over her head to stand naked before me. She was beautiful—to me more beautiful even than life—but her body was no longer young. Her breasts, once so small and tight, were heavy, waiting to burst, and her belly was puckered with the wounds of her childbearing. I knelt before her, pressing my cheek against her poor flesh, my eyes flooding with tears of pity.

"Am I grown so hideous then, Tiglath?" she murmured, her fingers smoothing back my hair. "Is love gone too?"

"Oh no—my love, my love!" Over and over again I sobbed the words, for I could find no others. "Oh my love, my love."

We held each other a long time, alone, with only the flickering light from a single lamp for company. I do not know how long. My mind was lost to any thought but of Esharhamat. I knew no shame nor fear nor duty. I was an empty vessel until she filled me with the love of her.

We were one flesh again that night. I went into her, and we became one. It was not the same with Esharhamat as with other women, for I had no thought of pleasure. My senses ached with dumb joy, but it was not for pleasure that I loved her. I could not bear to be parted from her, for my soul was in her body and without her I wandered in the empty air like a ghost. I knew I was alive only because I was with her. We were one flesh.

"Come away with me," I said, when at last words were possible between us. "Come away, and we will be together until death."

"How soon would that be?"

"What does it matter? I cannot leave you again."

"You must—you know you must."

"I know nothing, save that I love you."

"I will not go with you, Tiglath." She took her arms from about me and sat up on her sleeping mat. "The time for that is past. You speak only of what you wish to be, not of what can be. You have already made your choice—or perhaps your god has made it for you."

"Before you, I care nothing for this god or any other."

"So you say now, and believe. But it will not be the same tomorrow, or the day after. You belong to him, not to me. I understand that now. I do not even resent it. It is simply that which must be so."

"Why?"

"Because it is his will."

I knew what she said was true, that she was stronger than I. I could not bear the thought of parting, of days or years without her. In my heart I cursed the name of god.

"You enter now the time of partings," the *maxxu* had said, *"when your tongue will sicken at the sound of farewell."*

In the darkness, while the world was yet shrouded by the wings of death, I rose and left her.

"I no longer find favor in my lord's eyes?" Zabibe, always cunning, now played the penitent. She knelt before me, dressed in rags, her shoulders bare. "He does not honor me as before. I am banished from his presence and can count on my fingers the nights I have spent on his sleeping mat since our return to Nineveh. If I have sinned against my lord, then let him punish me, even onto death. But let him not turn from me, for that is blacker than any death."

She touched her head to the floor and embraced my ankles, bathing my feet with her tears. She was very convincing, but no woman is so dangerous as when she seems all weakness and submission. I realized that I had made a mistake in neglecting her.

"Then bring me my whip," I said.

But a raw backside and such endearments as are implied in a little hard rutting would not satisfy her forever. Zabibe knew she had a rival, and she would not rest content until she had discovered her. After all, such discoveries were the purpose that had brought her to me. But in truth I was weary of living with her deceptions. And I had plans for Zabibe.

In half a month I would return to Amat, leading the ten companies of soldiers who would man the garrison there while I took my new army into the Zagros Mountains. By then I hoped to have wiped the tablet of my life clean.

"We must wait and see," I told Esharhamat. "Perhaps I shall die on campaign, or perhaps Esarhaddon will get drunk and break his neck on a stairway. Or perhaps the god will tire of this folly and destroy the world. There is nothing for us except waiting."

It was true. I saw her only five times all the months I was in the city, and all the days between were simply waiting. I lived for those few hours with her, for nothing else. Even the thought of my war against the Medes filled me with emptiness—glory and danger were nothing if they carried me so far from her arms. It was no false delicacy which made me neglect Zabibe. It was no more than that, sometimes for many days, I simply forgot she existed.

I heard many voices during these months in Nineveh, and only half listened to any of them. The king was old and would soon vanish forever, but what was death for one was life for many, and the conspiracies hatched out like maggots in the belly of a dead lion. There were whispers everywhere.

I was constantly meeting people, some of whom were known to me and some not. These encounters would seem fortuitous—I would receive an invitation to join a hunt and, in a party of perhaps a hundred, I might find myself paired with a *rab abru* in charge of a garrison in Rasappa, home on leave. The hunt would be slow. We would talk. Certain hints would be dropped concerning the present situation. There would be complaints about Esarhaddon's policy toward Babylon. I would make some answer and, suddenly, the man would be pledging me his support should I choose to contest my brother's right to the throne. This, or the like, happened to me three, four, I know not how many times.

Some meetings were not fortuitous. On the fifth day before the beginning of the festival of Akitu, two hours before morning, the steward of my house awakened me. He said I had a visitor who would not be turned away. The man came in a carrying chair and wore a hooded tunic that concealed his face—my steward could not even be sure it was a man. He suspected an assassin.

I took my javelin from where it leaned against the wall and went to meet this strange visitor. I found him and, when we were alone, he pushed aside his hood. He was my royal brother, the scribe Nabusharusur.

"You are surprised to see me," he said, smiling with his lips only.

"I am surprised by nothing that befalls me in Nineveh," I answered. "If I may ask without rudeness, brother, what do you want of me at this hour?"

Nabusharusur's thin, nervous hand played over the sleeve of his cloak. There were lines around the corners of his eyes, as if he were always peering into the distance. He was a man—if he was a man—whose life danced forever on the point of a knife.

"I come to tell you that you have enemies."

"This does not surprise me, since I have not led a blameless life."

"You mock me, brother."

"No, brother." I shook my head and smiled, no more pleasantly than did Nabusharusur himself. "It is I who am mocked. I am not such a fool as you seem to think me."

"Then know that there are spies in your own house—the woman Zabibe, for one."

"So I have been told before this. What of it? In this city half the inhabitants earn their bread by spying on the other half. Tell me what I do not know."

"That this woman, to earn her bread, has promised the Lady Naq'ia that she will poison you. I would take no wine from her hands, brother—now, I see, I have told you something."

"Yes. And I might ask why you trouble yourself, brother, and how you know."

"I trouble because I still have hopes of you, Tiglath." He shrugged his narrow, feminine shoulders, as if all his hopes had long since ended in despair. "You are a fool whom the past blinds to the future, but it may not always be so. And, as to my knowledge of this matter—as you have suggested, what secrets are not for sale in Nineveh?"

He bowed and left me then and, as always, I was not sorry to see him go. Nabusharusur was an uneasy soul, and his discomfort was an atmosphere that he carried with him everywhere. Anyone who breathed the same air was infected with it. I returned to my chamber, all hope of rest fled, to await the coming of dawn.

And the next night, at my sleeping mat, I found Zabibe and her whip and a silver vessel of wine. She smiled at me, and I knew that Nabusharusur had saved my life.

"I am not thirsty," I said. "But drink yourself, if you wish. Drink, before it loses its chill."

She shook her head.

"No—I do not care for wine."

I had seen her drink this same wine more times than I could number.

"Very well then, if you choose to vex me."

I picked up the whip, and she smiled again. Doubtless she thought I would parch my throat with desire for her, that sometime before morning I would drink the wine and die.

She lifted the hem of my sleeping tunic and took my manhood between her lips. I cut her back with the whip and she moaned, and I could feel the pressure of her tongue. All the while she sucked on me I beat her, until the blood came. I went into her twice that night. But I did not touch the wine.

The next morning, before the sun rose, I left her sleeping and carried the silver vessel with me. The cooks were already awake, so I went into the kitchen and took one of the long, thin loaves of bread that only servants ate. No one saw anything strange in this.

The garden behind my house had fallen into disuse in the last years of the Lord Sinahiusur's life. It was overgrown and wild, and there were rats—bold creatures the size of cats, that feared neither man nor beast nor god. I went outside and sat upon a stone bench, breaking off pieces of the bread, soaking them in the wine and casting them down upon the pathway.

In time a rat came. He stood quite still when he saw me, watching me through tiny, cruel eyes, and then at last, when he was sure I would not interfere, he came and sniffed at a morsel of the bread. He ate it, and then another. I waited. He looked about for more, his long, naked tail dragging behind him.

And then, in an instant, he came up straight on his front paws and then collapsed. I walked over and kicked him with my sandaled foot, just to be sure. He was as lifeless as a block of wood.

So it was true—there was no doubt. I poured the rest of the wine onto the ground.

Zabibe, no doubt, was surprised to see me alive.

"Tell a servant to fetch my breakfast," I told her. "Be quick, for I have an appetite."

And, indeed, I did. All things taste good to the man who is happy to have been spared. This was a debt I owed my brother Nabusharusur.

And Zabibe would pay. She would pay.

In the morning I would leave for Amat. The barracks of the house of war were ablaze with torchlight as soldiers prepared their kits against the long march. They were fresh conscripts and they knew that some of them were going to war. They would sleep but little tonight. I knew everything they felt. I had only to remember the long road to Khalule.

But my brain did not ring with the clash of weapons and the thunder of horses' hoofs. These things had lost their terrifying strangeness and, besides, I was hurrying to the arms of a beloved woman. Parting from her would be more terrible than any death.

Esharhamat waited in her sleeping chamber. Her women, such as she trusted, would guard us against intrusion until perhaps an hour before first light. Esarhaddon had been the whole month in Calah, waiting, it was said, for me to return to the north.

A single oil lamp burned beside her mat. Esharhamat leaned back on one arm as she turned to me, smiling. As I knelt beside her she touched my face, letting her fingertips rest so lightly against the skin, and kissed me upon the mouth. Our kisses became greedy, almost fierce. We did not speak. There was no time for words. We made love the way the starving feast, as if it might all be taken away in the next instant.

"What shall we do all the long time apart?" she asked at last, when our passion was spent and she huddled in my embrace.

"We shall suffer," I told her, since there was no other answer. "We shall persist in hope, and we shall wait."

"For how long?"

"I know not."

"It is in the god's hands."

"Yes."

"Yes."

Outside, in Esharhamat's garden, the crickets sang. Mother Tigris was in full flood, and the world was awake for another year. And I was leaving at dawn to fight the Medes.

"Tiglath . . ."

"Yes?"

"I think it possible I may be with child."

I held her in my arms, not moving, perhaps not even breathing. What did I feel? A kind of cold shock—it was only the surprise.

"Will it be mine?"

"I hope so, yes. It may be Esarhaddon's, for he is nothing if not scrupulous in his royal duties, but I think not. I believe it is yours, if only because I know already I will love this child."

"Then I am glad."

"So am I."

In an hour, I thought—perhaps not so much—we will have to part. How will I bear it? Now, more than ever, how will I bear it?

* * *

But I did bear it. My heart was dead within me, but I bore that too. Ashur's golden dawn saw me with three thousand soldiers at my back, a spectacle for the people of Nineveh to cheer. I now belonged not to Esharhamat, or our child not yet born, or even to myself, but to the king and his army and to the city mob that must have its hero of an hour, to shout themselves hoarse with his name and then forget him. I was once more that dead thing, a Great Man.

I stopped for a single night at Three Lions and said farewell to my mother—the *maxxu* was right, for my tongue had sickened of the word—and then we marched north, following the mountain trails, which were hard but made a shorter journey and, in any case, were good experience for the campaign ahead.

Zabibe was in a wagon somewhere in the baggage train. I did not send for her. I waited.

At last we crested the mountains and could see the Great Zab River, shining in the morning light like a silver snake. When our horses drank from her waters we were not more than two days' march from Amat.

We slept that night near a good-sized village called Adini, where the headman came to my tent, bowed, and sought the king's blessing. I gave it to him and inquired if his village had a worker in metals who could fix a cart axle for us. It had.

"He will need to be a strong man, for it is a heavy cart—it needs four oxen to pull it."

"Oh, he will do very well, Lord, for he has the strength of an ox himself."

"Good. Then send him to me."

The axle could have waited until we reached Amat, but I could not. In about half an hour the metalsmith came, and he was all I had hoped—a giant, with arms as thick as another man's thighs and a face and chest covered with tiny burn scars from his furnace. He was also very ugly and in some misadventure had even lost an eye, the empty socket of which he plugged with a copper shekel. I watched him at his work, and when he was finished invited him to share a jar of beer with me. We sat together perfectly contented, as if we had known each other all our lives, and the metalsmith scratched the matted black hair on his belly as he drank. I was quite pleased with him.

"Tell me, Metalsmith, do you have a wife?" I asked.

"Alas no, Lord," he answered, grinning rather foolishly. "I had one, but she died. Now her children have no mother and I have no one to cook my dinner."

"It must be a great loss to you. Was she beautiful?"

"No, Lord. She was too skinny and her skin was as rough as granite, but a one-eyed rogue cannot expect a queen for his sleeping mat. She had also a bitter tongue."

"Then I assume you beat her."

"Oh yes, Lord, I beat her—as any proper man would. But it did not soften her."

I desired to hear no more. I went into my tent to fetch something I had purchased in Nineveh—a fine whip, not much longer than a man's arm but woven of boar's hide that had been soaked in salt water.

"Come with me, Metalsmith."

We went back to the baggage train, and I found Zabibe's wagon, where she was lying on a carpet naked as dawn, painting her toenails. She smiled when she saw me, but before she could speak I took her by the wrist and pulled her down into the dust. The Metalsmith's one eye burned with delight when he beheld her, as well it might, for I would venture his village did not hold another that was her equal.

"Here is a new wife for you, Metalsmith . . ."

"No, Lord—NO!" Zabibe tried to pull free from my grasp, but I held her tight. "Mercy, Dread Lord . . . Not this! No!"

I did not answer her cries. In this, a matter to be settled by men, I spoke only to the metalsmith.

"Of course, this one too has a bitter tongue, but I promise that if you beat her hard enough, she will learn to love you. I give you the whip as her dowry."

With a sharp pull on her arm I sent her reeling toward her new husband, who caught her dexterously enough. In an instant she went for him with her nails, but he simply laughed and struck her a playful blow that sent her sprawling in the soft spring mud. She sat up, her eyes streaming with tears, with a bruise on her cheek she would carry for many days.

"Master, I beg you . . ." she whimpered, holding out her hand to me.

"Be silent, woman, for you deserve worse than this. Did you really expect me to harbor an assassin in my bed?"

The metalsmith grabbed her wrist and pulled her to her feet.

Zabibe, her bare legs covered in mud, was at last quiet. Her tear-stained eyes beseeched mercy, but she seemed to know there would be none.

"I thank you, Lord—she is fine." The metalsmith ran a hand caressingly over her shoulder and breast, not caring that she shuddered away from him. "She is beautiful enough that I do not care how bitter her tongue may be."

"Yes, but be sure to beat her. Strip the skin from her backside," I said, smiling with grim satisfaction, enjoying the sight they made together. "And—a warning: Unless you have grown weary of life, always make her taste the food first herself before you eat it. She is an Arab woman and employs some strange spices. You would not care to die of indigestion."

There was fire in the look she gave me as I spoke—such fire as almost made me sorry to part with her. Yes, of course she hated me. But what had I ever cared for her hatred?

"Take her, Metalsmith, before I change my mind."

The whole army could hear her cries as he led her away. Her curses rang in the air.

"May the gods desert you, Tiglath Ashur," she screamed. "May you die a bitter death in the land of the Medes, and may the dogs eat your corpse."

So many women had heaped their curses on my head. I wondered if the gods ever thought to listen.

29

The crows had done their work in two years. Except for bones held together with decaying sinews, there was not much left of the corpses of Uksatar and the four elders of the Miyaneh tribe. The very clothes in which they died had rotted away, so that not even those who, like myself, had been present at their execution could have told one from another.

My charger Ghost, a fine stallion now, a war horse raised up to be unafraid of battle or the smell of blood, snorted nervously and dug at the earth with his hoof as I stopped for a moment to look at the ghastly spectacle—five skeletons, men impaled and left as a warning, left to stare back with empty eye sockets at the eastern mountains from which they had dared to make war on the Land of Ashur.

Of course the warning had been to no avail. At intervals over these two years, and particularly during the winter just past, Median raiding parties had crossed this boundary to plunder what they could from the surrounding villages. There was nothing to be surprised about in this, since they knew I would be returning in any case; why should they then curb their natural nomadic greed?

And although it was not something to which I could very well admit, these incursions were not unwelcome to me since they justified the war we were about to unleash on the people of the Ahura. After all, we were not merely cruel predators, come for the pleasure of butchery and whatever we could carry off, but the armed wrath of our god who will not suffer his people to be robbed and murdered. But, more important, they showed the limits of Daiaukka's control over his confederation of tribes.

Daiaukka was very far from a fool, and he knew that burning villages west of the Diyala River and driving off their cattle would hardly blunt the attack that must inevitably come. He knew as well that my policy of war was not without its opponents, that the king my father's mind had still to be won to this undertaking, and he was wise enough to guess that every hut set ablaze, every peasant killed, every measure of stolen barley was reported in Nineveh and only served to reinforce my argument that the Medes were a threat and must be crushed.

So Daiaukka knew that these border provocations were folly, and if he did not stop them it only meant that he could not. His word was yet something short of law among the tribes of the Zagros, for all that he styled himself *shah-ye-shah,* king of all the kings of the Aryan. So much the worse for him.

So as I gazed up at these five of the Miyaneh, strangled at my command, their skulls covered only here and there with a few remaining strips of dry, curling, sun-blackened flesh, grinning like demons now as they had leisure to reconsider the laughable folly of their crimes, I was not sorry that their warning had gone un-heeded. I promised Ashur that the Medes would not require an-other such for many years to come.

I rode back to camp, a city of tents upon the broad plain, where the northern army was enjoying one final long afternoon of peace before we wet our sandals in the Diyala for the last time and crossed into the lands of the Medes.

Ghost strained at his bridle, eager to break into a run. His long silver-white mane waved in the wind, and the muscles of his mighty body bunched and rippled beneath the skin. He was a fine horse, powerful and swift. I was sure he would bring me luck.

Even as I entered camp, men cheered me, waving and shout-ing my name. When I saw a man whose face I knew, I smiled and waved back, for soldiers must believe their commander cares about them. These had entrusted their lives to me, even as I led them against an enemy famous for courage and ferocity, and as they wished to live and triumph they created an idol and called him the Lord Tiglath Ashur. It is always so. One man is made great only to serve the purposes and hopes of many.

And this year again we would carry the banner of the blood star, waving on our standards beneath the winged disk of Ashur, so I hoped it would not be only my own men who believed in the myth of Mighty Sargon's *sedu.*

I was not, however, trusting solely to the magic of my own reputation. The army I was bringing into the Zagros was twenty thousand strong, well-trained and disciplined men who knew what was expected of them. Many had campaigned before and knew the terror of battle. If we did not prevail, the failure would be not theirs but mine alone. But we would prevail—I was very sure.

"When shall we break camp, *Rab Shaqe*?" Lushakin asked as he held Ghost's bridle while I dismounted.

"An hour before dawn," I answered. "And see to it that every soldier is ready to march at first light. I wish the Medes to see that though we are many we know how to move."

"You think they are watching already?"

"I know it." I looked at him, letting my eyes go wide as if I hardly credited he could be such a simpleton. "Their outriders have been about five hours ahead of us even since our third day out of Amat. You should ride in the vanguard with me, where you could have seen the droppings left by their horses."

Tabshar Sin laughed.

"You had best be careful, Prince, or this simpleton will grow to believe you."

Lushakin, when he saw he had been gulled, laughed too. I had known both men since the days of my greenest youth, so a joke was permitted.

"Nevertheless," I said, "they are there. They are not fools enough to reveal themselves, but they are there. I can feel their eyes on us."

In my tent were maps, certainly the best maps ever made of the lands east of the Diyala, drawn on goatskin by the Cimmerian slaves we had rescued from bondage on our last campaign. There was not a rock on the Zagros Steppes they did not show. At least we would not have to stumble forward like blind men.

"We must keep to the broad plains," I told my officers. "An army of this size cannot maneuver to advantage in the mountains and, besides, why should we give Daiaukka the chance to ambush us? We have size in our favor—no matter how many riders the Medes can field, they cannot hope to overwhelm us—and a giant should not pick the inside of a beer jug for a battleground."

"They might decide simply to ignore us, to wait in their mountains until winter comes and we are forced to withdraw."

"Daiaukka will fight. A king is not a king unless he can

protect his people—he knows that. We shall bring such devastation to the Zagros that he will be forced to fight."

When the meeting was over, Lushakin and Tabshar Sin stayed behind, and the three of us drank wine and talked about the glory of vanished times until well past the blackest part of the night. We all three despaired of sleep, and it is better on such occasions not to be alone.

By the hour the sun first showed itself in the pale-gray sky, the armies of Ashur's vengeance were already on the move. By midday we had crossed the river and were treading the earth our enemies called their own.

By twilight of the second day, outriders reported having sighted the first Median village. I gave my orders against the morning.

"Take one company of men. Destroy everything. Every wall, every farmer's hut—everything. Burn what you find of the harvest and drive as many of their animals back as you can—there is no reason why our soldiers should not have meat for their dinner tomorrow. Slaughter the rest and throw the carcasses down the wells. Kill any man you find in arms or who attempts to resist. Spare all the rest. Use your whips, if you must, to drive them out. We will fill this land with wandering beggars for Daiaukka to feed, if he can. Let no one molest the women, for we are not barbarians."

The Medes build their houses of stone, but the roofs are of wood. They were still burning the next night, turning the southern sky an evil black-red. My soldiers rejoiced—and why should they not, since our enemies served us no better?—but the sight made my bowels turn to ice.

For many days it was the same. Companies of men would fan out from the main body of the army to raid and pillage. Our grain wagons were filled to bursting, and we had horses, cattle, and goats enough to provide for a force ten times our own number. We found silver and gold, and these I divided out among the raiders as booty, keeping, as was the custom, a fifth part for my own share.

It was not long before the village elders began coming to us, as they had on our last campaign, meeting us on our way to offer tribute if we would spare them. But I was without mercy.

"You have given allegiance to a wicked king," I told them. "He has visited this vengeance upon you by warring against the

Land of Ashur. That which you suffer, my own people have suffered before you—this and worse. All those following Daiaukka
must learn what price my god exacts from any who mock his
power."

At my words the elders lamented in cracking voices and tore
their beards.

"Yet, Dread Lord, we are but farmers and herdsmen. We are
not warriors to carry arms into the Land of Ashur. Spare us."

"Are not my own people farmers and herdsmen? Do not
your sons ride with Daiaukka's army? Yet I will grant you a little
pity—more, indeed, than was shown to those I have come to
avenge. I will give you one day's grace. Gather together what you
can and turn your faces to the mountains. You must leave your
wagons, but what you are able to carry on your backs I will spare
you. Take it, and find Daiaukka. Tell him of your sufferings and
demand his protection as a right. Tell him that the Lord Tiglath
Ashur, a king's son and prince in the Western Lands, will not
cease his devastation until he is driven away by force or van-
quishes his enemies in open battle."

I raised my hand in salute, that they might see the blood star
across my palm and know to whom they listened.

And this, as my words were whispered about from one village to another, was how the Steppes of the Zagros grew filled
with the sounds of sorrow, how the footpaths and trails became
clogged with pilgrims. As water breaks before the prow of a ship,
the people who called themselves the Aryan scattered before our
advancing columns. Always, just in the distance, we could see the
clouds of dust raised by their unsandaled feet as they set out on
their hopeless flight from destruction.

And always we found their settlements empty of men, the
goats still tethered in their yards, the grain stores intact, for they
knew that if they broke this covenant we would ride them down
and leave their corpses to feed the dogs. What we could not carry
away as loot we burned and slaughtered.

More than a few times they even left some few of their
women behind, or the women simply stayed of their own accord.
Once I found two sisters in the hut of the village elder—his wives,
they told me, and he a man in his seventies. They were weary of
their lot and begged me to find them young husbands among the
soldiers of Ashur. They would do well by any man worthy of the
name, they said, and to prove it invited me to go into them. I had

been many days alone and thus was glad to oblige them both. Afterward, I gave each two shekels of silver and told them they were at liberty to go with the army as camp followers but that when peace returned they could make their choice from whoever had most pleased them and take the veil after the custom of my country. With this they were well satisfied.

But for most in the lands of the Medes this was a bitter season. Slowly, the land grew waste. There would be famine that winter, and many who had fled would never live to return but would die in the hills—would welcome death as an end to their sufferings. It was an evil thing, but it rested with Daiaukka to end it. He knew this as well as I.

So I was not surprised when his messenger arrived, carrying a token of truce.

The Medes, when they wish to parley, send a rider who bears a spear with white ribbons streaming down from its point. He waves the spear above his head as he approaches, and the ribbons flash in the sun. One man on horseback is not enough to frighten an army, and we would have allowed him through our lines without the elaborate display of his intentions.

He dismounted as soon as he was inside the camp, and without a word spoken on either side, a sentry took him straight to my tent.

"Have you come from Daiaukka?" I asked him.

"I bring a message from the *shah-ye-shah,*" he answered, as if correcting my impertinence for referring to that exalted person by the name he was born with. "He would meet with you—alone. He guarantees your safety."

He was a handsome, tall youth with eyes as large as a woman's and a fine, shining black beard, elaborately curled. He smiled, showing his teeth, as if perfectly conscious of the impression he must be making.

"Why should we trust the life of our prince to such 'guarantees'?" Lushakin asked him. The question almost amounted to an open challenge. "Why should we believe the words of Daiaukka?"

"Because I believe them," the messenger announced—yes, he was a peacock. "I am Tanus, eldest son of Rameteia, *parsua* of the Upasha tribe. I will remain behind here until the Lord Tiglath Ashur returns to you unharmed."

He glanced about him, as if waiting to be congratulated on his heroism.

"Where am I to meet the *shah-ye-shah*?" I asked. "Or is that to be a surprise?"

"He awaits you not two hours' ride from here, near where the foothills begin their rise—there."

I could see them beyond the steppes, a barren, fissured wall. Against the green grasslands they were hard edges of rock which looked as if they had broken through from so great a depth that they could have been the ghosts of some ancient creation come back to haunt the green world. And beyond these the Zagros Mountains, shadowed in blue-black mist the color of burned iron. Daiaukka would meet me there, alone, in some hidden place of his own choosing, out of sight, far from the possibility of help.

"Very well," I said, without giving myself time to hesitate, "the foothills. How will I find him?"

"Do not be anxious on that point, my lord. The *shah-ye-shah* will find you."

He smiled at me, narrowing his eyes. He had all the arrogance one finds in primitive men who have seen little of the world beyond their own village. I did not like him.

"Then I will not be anxious—on that or any other point." I mimicked his smile. "Lushakin, take the Lord Tanus to my tent. See that he is fed and made comfortable against my return."

Tabshar Sin stamped along behind me as I went to fetch my horse, his anger etched in every movement of his hard old body— but at least he had the grace to wait until our hostage was out of earshot.

"Have your brains baked dry, Prince?" he hissed, casting his eyes about to be certain his disrespect was not overheard. "Have you lost all sense of what is due these men you have led to the edge of the world? This *shah-ye-shah* of theirs, this barbarian who was born under a saddle blanket, surely has twenty good men with him and waits only to cut your throat for you."

"Would you have the Medes imagine that the *sedu* of Great Sargon is afraid of them?" I asked, throwing my arm across his shoulders.

"Yes—I would have them know that the men of Ashur are not commanded by a fool who tosses his life away like a broken sandal strap."

"Oh, I have no intention of doing that." I laughed, for I loved my old *rab kisir,* the terror of all the Lord Sennacherib's soldier sons, no less than if he had been my own father. "And if I err in this, you can send me back to clean stables in the house of war."

"I will send you back in a leather bag," he answered, almost shouting between his clenched teeth. "At least take an escort—a few men only."

"No. Daiaukka said 'alone.' "

"Who are we to listen to what Daiaukka says and does not say? Let me come. He cannot object to the presence of an old man with only one hand."

"If he sees you he will certainly think I have come intending to massacre him. No, he said 'alone.' I am not afraid of him, for the *shah-ye-shah* has given his word."

"What trust can any man put in the word of a barbarian?"

"In the word of this barbarian, a great deal."

The sun had declined perhaps an hour in its westward flight when the long grass of the steppes stopped brushing against my horse's knees and we began our climb into the rocky foothills of the Zagros Mountains. Ghost picked his careful way among the sharp, flinty stones. He seemed to sense the danger of these narrow paths, full of twists and sudden inclines, where every bluff could conceal twenty men waiting in ambush and both our lives might stretch no farther than the next few paces of clear ground, and his long ears twisted this way and that, straining for the least whisper of sound. But there was no sound. Daiukka was waiting somewhere ahead, as silent as death. I put my faith in his word and in my protecting *sedu,* but my heart was not easy.

"You have consented to come. Then at least we may speak as men who understand one another."

He was simply there. I had not heard his approach. I merely lifted my eyes and saw him in front of me. He still rode his fine black horse, and on another that might have been its twin was mounted a handsome, well-knit lad of eight or nine years, a son obviously, and one who, for all his smooth face, had already lost the girlish prettiness of childhood. I suspected—even feared—that he would grow up to resemble his father in every particular.

Daiaukka had brought no other companion, and he carried no weapon beyond the short sword thrust into his belt. I had been right about him—he was not a man who would stoop to treachery.

"My eldest," he said, without even glancing at the boy. "His name is Khshathrita, and I have brought him that he may look upon your face and learn something of men's characters."

I did not require this explanation. The boy Khshathrita was searching me with his eyes as if he wished to carry every detail of my appearance with him to the grave. His father had brought him that I might understand that this struggle would not end with one battle or ten but would be carried on onto the next generation and the next, as long as the seed of Ukshatar lived, and perhaps beyond that. Daiaukka wished to show me that my enemy was not one man only but a nation, and that nations are always being reborn. The point was not lost on me.

"I have seen your army," he went on, after a short pause. "It is a fine sight and strikes terror into the hearts of simple villagers. It will perish here in the grasslands of Media."

"One or another army will perish—of that we can both be reasonably sure. I do not, however, think it will be the men of Ashur who leave their bones to dry in the sun."

I smiled at the boy, who for just an instant forgot himself enough to smile back. I could not help but wonder what he made of these preliminary taunts I was exchanging with his father. Did he understand that they were meaningless, a kind of incantation to summon up ghosts in which no one believed? It seemed unlikely.

"The men who follow me number three times the strength of your army," Daiaukka answered. "We have horses beyond counting. Leave now if you ever hope to see your home again. How can you imagine you will prevail?"

"But I have prevailed—and more than once—against forces far larger than my own. Have as many warriors at your back as you care to, and you will still be vanquished. We are not a rabble, Daiaukka. We are the soldiers of Ashur, and we have conquered a world wider than you can dream. A dagger's blade may be no longer than your finger, yet it will cut to the heart where a sword made of clay will crumble under its own weight."

He did not speak, for he had no need of words to give his answer. I could see everything in his proud black eyes—this was not a man who would be made afraid by the sound of a few threats. Yes, I would have my great battle, since it would serve Daiaukka's purposes as well as my own. He merely wished me to understand that he expected it to end with my head on his spear.

"Being so careless of death, you will bring your great army

down from the mountains?" I asked. It was not this question which mattered, but the next—not if, but when.

The *shah-ye-shah*, master of the Aryan, merely nodded.

"Yes," he said at last. "The time and the place will be of my choosing, but we will meet once more. We will measure our virtue against yours and see whom the Ahura favors."

"War has little enough to do with virtue, Daiaukka. He triumphs who makes the fewest mistakes."

He smiled at me, as if he pitied the littleness of my soul.

"I leave you with a gift," he said finally. Without looking, he reached behind him and his son put a leather bag into his hand. "As you say, he triumphs who makes the fewest mistakes."

He dropped the leather bag to the ground and, without a word, turned his horse upon the stony path. I waited until he and his son were out of sight and then dismounted, picked up the bag, and opened it. Inside was the head of Upash, the Uqukadi noble who had thought he could sell me his new lord like so many bushels of millet. I pulled it out by the hair and looked at it. It had not been off his shoulders long, for it still stank of fresh blood. His eyes, clouded by death, looked startled, as if he had been caught by surprise. Perhaps he had. It seemed that this time he had not been able to ride away from his *simtu*.

I made my way back down to the grassy steppes and returned to camp. There was only an hour left before dark when the sentries' drums sounded to announce my return.

It was Tanus of the Upasha who rode out to meet me.

"You have come back alive, then," he said, as if to taunt me for having doubted his king's word.

"Yes, I have come back. We will not meet again until the day we stain the grass red with blood."

He laughed at this. He was filled with triumph, and he laughed. All his eyes could see was the approach of a great battle —perhaps it would be his first, and so the victory would belong to no one except himself. He was young enough to believe that. Lashing his horse, he galloped away, back to his mountains and his own people and his mighty lord.

"The poor fool," I thought. "He understands nothing."

The soldiers cheered as I rode through camp to my own tent. They cheered out of relief that I was not dead in some rocky gorge but had returned to lead them safely home again when we had killed the last Mede—this is how every soldier thinks, and the commander who does not know it is a lost man. They shouted my name and bellowed themselves hoarse, pounding their shields with the flats of their swords when I raised my hand to show the blood star on the palm. They were like children frightened of the dark and I, and the *sedu* of Great Sargon, had become their only light.

"Tabshar Sin," I said, when the old man met me with a cup of wine, "there shall be such slaughter as has not been known since Khalule. It shall be worse, perhaps, for the Medes will fight until we have broken them under the wheels of our chariots."

"Have we come on a fool's errand then, Prince?" he asked— I could see by the look in his eye he was merely testing my nerve, for no man feared death less than my old *rab kisir*. I could only laugh.

"No. We have no choice," I said, when my laughter died. "We must fight them here, or a year from now under the walls of Nineveh. That is not a choice."

"Then we shall defeat them," he said, as if stating the obvious. "The god shall not desert us."

"Yes, we shall defeat them."

I went to my bed that night remembering the smile on Daiaukka's lips when he parted from me. He too believed in the favor of his god.

Over the next ten days our progress was slow and cautious. I had no intention of being surprised by the sudden appearance of Daiaukka's army, so our scouts fanned out to all points of the compass, even into the mountains, to bring back reports of everything that moved within twenty *beru* of our columns. We never saw them—they were as invisible as the wind—yet I had no doubt the Medes were close by and massing for battle.

It was on the afternoon of the tenth day, in the middle of a dust storm that blew in from the northern desert to choke men and horses and bring the sky down around us until it seemed like a vault of earth, that a lone rider came into our camp. He wore the costume of a Mede and his mouth and nose were swathed in a long scarf with small silver coins sewn around the fringe, so that only his eyes were visible. When the sentries challenged him he requested to be brought to me.

"Well, what is it?" I asked impatiently, little pleased to be

standing in the raw, gritty wind—no man who could help himself
ventured out of his tent on such a day. "What would you have of
me?"

It was only when he took a step nearer me, and I could see
his eyes, that I understood. Wary and intelligent, they reminded
one of a cat. This man was no Mede. I dismissed the guard.

"Come inside," I said, as soon as we were alone. "You bring
word from the Lord Tabiti?"

"Brother, I am the Lord Tabiti."

With a single deft movement he removed the scarf, and all at
once it was the headman of the Sacan who stood before me. He
laughed at my surprise, and we fell into each other's arms.

"I hope the Lord Tiglath carried wine with him when he
came into this forbidding place," he said, wiping the dust from his
arms and shoulders. "My throat is parched, and even that filthy
stuff you had from the Urartians would be welcome. By the gods,
are those the rich grasslands where you promised the Scoloti
would win an empire fit for princes of the earth?"

"It makes a better impression when the wind is still and, yes,
there is wine."

I gave orders for a goat to be roasted, and while we waited
for it Tabiti and I broke open a jar and grew drunk together. He
was very weary, having departed his own encampment twenty
days before to see how the ground lay and to find the army of
Ashur.

"We have left the wagons and the women and children behind on the shore of Lake Urmia," he told me. "I have ten thousand good men, and we were traveling fast. They are perhaps no
more than eight days behind me and are staying close to the
foothills of the Elburz Mountains. I had to cross the desert which
lies between here and there—it is a wretched place where only
scorpions can live in comfort. I have seen where the Medes are
gathering. They have chosen well for themselves if they mean to
fight there, for they occupy rising ground some eight days from
here. Daiaukka must have five and fifty thousand men with him."

"He says sixty."

"Sixty then. I believe him. You have what, thirty thousand?"

"Twenty."

"Thirty against sixty—so be it." Tabiti shrugged his shoulders, as if dismissing a trifle. "You defeated my Sacan at the

Bohtan River, where our advantage in numbers was even greater."

"Do the Medes know of your coming yet?"

"No, I think not. The people of the northern mountains are all Cimmerians and hate the Medes. As soon as we draw near, they cut the throats of the headmen Daiaukka has put over them and invite us to a feast of celebration. I doubt if any word of us has found its way south. It is a pleasant thing to invade lands where one is welcomed as a liberator."

I said nothing, since my experience had been different. But neither did I, like Tabiti, have any thought of settling in this place.

"Is it important?" Tabiti asked suddenly. "Do your plans depend upon surprise?"

I almost laughed.

"No, my lord. I entertain a doubt that anything will ever be likely to surprise Daiaukka—even his own defeat."

"Then he must have powerful necromancers in his service." The headman of the Sacan frowned, shaking his head. "Magic is a great advantage in war. Perhaps we should . . ."

"No—it is not that." I did laugh now, unable to help myself, but Tabiti was by then too drunk to take offense. "It is simply that the *shah-ye-shah* has a habit of looking far into the future. His plans do not depend on success in this battle, or the next, or even on his own survival. He prepares the foundations of a house in which he will never dwell, but the design is clear in his mind. One day, long after he is dead, the Medes will be a great nation, rulers of the wide world. He works for this. He knows it will all come to pass, and this knowledge, it seems, is enough for him."

"Then he is mad—but a madman of the most dangerous sort, for he infects others with his own madness."

"Yes, my friend." I filled our cups again and took a long swallow of the wine, which seemed to clear my mind even as I felt the fumes rising in my brain. "Yes, he is very dangerous."

Tabiti remained with us through the next day and night, and in that time he told me of all he had seen since entering the lands where the Medes are called "master." He was a clever man and had kept his eyes open. With more ambition he might have been as great a threat as Daiaukka, but his dreams did not encompass empires and neither did he long to serve the avarice of strange gods. He merely wanted a little well-watered grassland for his people and, of course, some share of a soldier's glory. Perhaps in this he was wise enough to be envied. And, for the moment at least, he was my friend and he opened his mind to me.

"The Cimmerians have not the will to fight," he told me. "I tried to draw them into alliance, but they are too afraid and would not be of much use anyway—they have hearts like dogs and might run off to lick the ground at Daiaukka's feet the first time he whistles for them. If we do not triumph in this great battle of yours, they will turn on us quickly enough."

"Tell me of what you saw of Daiaukka's army."

"What is there to tell?" He spat on the ground to show that he held his enemies in contempt, but we both knew the truth. "They are many, and they have many horses—I lay on a bluff an hour's ride from their camp, and I have not the eyes of a sparrow hawk to count the feathers on their arrows. Besides, there were patrols. I did not dare stay long."

"I know that. Prudence is the first virtue of a commander. I only ask what you did see."

Satisfied with this, Tabiti, son of Argimpasa, gazed through narrowed eyes at the hazy, shadowed line of mountains that lay to the south. We were outside the earthworks that served as a defense against surprise attack, and the sun was far to our backs.

"I was struck by one thing," he said at last. "They had built enclosures for their horses, one at each end of the camp. It was not what I would have expected—perhaps Daiaukka studies to make war like the men of Ashur."

He smiled, thinking he had made a joke. I felt my bowels turning to ice. If the Medes were dividing their cavalry into wings, with their infantry in the center, it could only mean that they had made a start at organizing themselves by fighting units instead of by tribes, as had always been their custom. It meant that indeed Daiaukka had learned something from the campaign of two years ago. It meant that he would no longer send his men down on us in shapeless waves, to fight as barbarians, each with no thought in his head but glory and perhaps the chance of a little plunder, relying on nothing beyond his horse, his own courage, and the favor of his gods, but would now engage us, however clumsily, as a disciplined force. It meant that Daiaukka had discovered tactics.

30

It was three days after Tabiti left us to rejoin his own men that my outriders first made contact with Daiaukka's forces. I received reports of sightings and even skirmishes, and I ordered that henceforth patrols would be conducted in force.

The Medes began a series of raids—trivial annoyances rather than battles, intended merely to test our defenses. In response, I sent out two companies of cavalry on a night attack and they overran one of the enemy's forward positions and returned with forty fresh-cut heads. After this the raids ceased.

Two days later I rode out with one of the patrols and had my first look at Daiaukka's camp.

We stopped at the top of a bluff, perhaps the same one on which Tabiti had hidden himself for his first view of our common enemy. But I did not hide—there was nothing courageous in this, since I was neither alone nor more than three hours' hard gallop from my own sentry lines. Besides, I wanted to be seen. By now the Medes knew the great silver stallion and his rider, and I wanted them to understand that I had come and that the hour of reckoning was at hand.

A party of cavalry crossed the valley to within perhaps half a *beru* of us, but there were only five of them and it was clear they had no intention of engaging us. Finally they stopped. They made no further move; they simply waited to see what we would do while they had their own look at the intruders. One of them was mounted on a fine black horse—the distance was too great to be sure, but I believe this was Daiaukka himself.

Tabiti had been right. The *shah-ye-shah* had chosen his site well. His camp occupied the highest point on slowly rising ground that would give his horsemen a wide area in which to maneuver, while the thick, dry grass might conceal all manner of obstacles for my chariots. To be near water, we would have to establish ourselves at the valley floor, a narrow place to which, if it came to that, we would be forced to retreat in some confusion. And then there was the wind, which blew as hot as a demon's breath all day and changed direction abruptly as soon as the sun approached its highest point. From noon on, when we would engage the Medes most closely, when our arrows and javelins would need it the most, we would have the wind against us.

"The time and the place will be of my choosing," he had told me. *"We will measure our virtue against yours and see whom the Ahura favors."*

He had chosen this place—he had chosen well. But I swore that it would be mine to choose the time of battle, for all the little good it would do me.

"I have seen enough," I said. "Let us return and break camp. It seems we have an appointment."

On the way back, wishing to avoid all inquiries while I tried to sort out what must be done, I rode at the rear of the column. But at last, having grown weary of my own thoughts, I began listening to the conversation between the two soldiers directly in front of me, a pair of farm lads still fresh enough from home to think the rest of the world but a poor place compared to their own village. Yet I found them beguiling enough, since they did not speak of war and strategy and the folly of their commander—my mind was already too full of these things.

"Look at this patch of waste," one of them said, gesturing contemptuously at the valley where, in a few days, he would perhaps lie dead. "I wonder the Medes bother to fight for such land —full of stones and dried to powder. A man could break a hundred copper plowshares just plowing a field big enough to feed his wife."

"Only if she is a dainty eater." The other soldier laughed, poking his fellow in the ribs. "And a prodigious pisser—I know not how else anyone would water this land. By the sixty great gods, look at that grass! In this wind, the first lightning storm will burn the ground black as far as you can see. . . ."

I stopped listening—I had heard enough. The heart in my breast pounded like an ironsmith's hammer.

By the next evening we had dug our earthworks on the valley floor and were as safe there as we could hope to be. Daiaukka made no attempt to interfere. Why should he, while we were closing the trap on ourselves?

When the officers of the northern army met in my tent that night, they were in no very pleasant frame of mind.

"This is madness," they said. "We should withdraw and force a battle on more favorable ground."

"We cannot withdraw," I told them. "We have issued this challenge and Daiaukka has accepted it. If we withdraw he has won his point—he has proved that we are afraid of him. These are the best terms for battle we can hope for, since to decline a fight now will allow him to return to his mountains claiming a kind of victory. There he can only grow stronger while we grow weaker. No, we must fight now."

"We will have no room to maneuver, and the wind will be against us in the afternoon."

"Then we must engage the Medes on their own ground, and we must conquer before the wind can change. Besides, by the afternoon our Scythian allies will have joined the attack—from the Medes' rear."

"You put too much faith in that bandit Tabiti. Probably by now he has already sold us to Daiaukka."

I made no answer beyond a cold silence, in the face of which men who had been my brothers in arms since the beginning could only stare at the ground, clearing their throats in embarrassment.

"The grass here is too high," they continued at last. "We could lose half our chariots before they even reach the enemy lines."

"I have a thought or two about the grass. Issue orders that the campfires are to be kept burning all night and that every man should be with his company and ready to march three hours before dawn. Tell the cooks to have their breakfast ready by then. We are all in for a long day.

"And—remember—if we have victory tomorrow, and if it is at all possible, I want Daiaukka taken alive. We make war less against a man than an idea, and this king of the Medes will be more dangerous dead than he ever was alive."

At two hours after midnight the last reconnaissance patrol came in, five men who had taken the ghastly risk of approaching the enemy lines on foot and in the dark; had they been discovered, nothing could have saved them from the terrible death the Medes visit upon their prisoners.

"What did you see?" I asked them.

"Not much, *Rab Shaqe*. They are dancing."

"Dancing?"

"Yes—dancing. And howling like devils. They take turns running through great bonfires. I would say they are all crazy drunk, except no wine I know of makes a man act like that."

"We shall have to see if we can contrive a day as entertaining for them as the night," I said, smiling thinly. The man looked at me as if he imagined I had lost my mind.

"Yes, *Rab Shaqe*—as you say."

I sent him off to the hour or so of sleep he would be able to enjoy before the entire army began marshaling for battle. Yes, of course he had thought I was mad. Perhaps he was even right. The idea which had shaped in my brain sounded mad enough, even to me. A mad commander leading his soldiers against a mad enemy —not a happy prospect to carry to his sleeping roll.

"My soul is heavy with dread, Prince. What do you plan to do?"

It was Tabshar Sin. He had come up behind me so quietly that I had not even known he was there.

"Do?" I turned and smiled. "I will do as you taught me, *Rab Kisir*—triumph or die. I may perhaps even achieve both."

"Do not jest with me, Prince. I hear the beating of heavy black wings above our heads."

One had only to look at him to see that this was so. I felt ashamed, for death is not a fit matter for a young man's idle jokes.

"Did you hear the patrol's report?"

He nodded.

"Then if the Medes like running through fire so much, they will have a fine time of it tomorrow. In the first hour before dawn, when the winds will have begun in earnest, I will cause the grass beyond our earthworks to be torched. I will make a line of flames, as wide as the valley itself, and within two hours the wind will carry it straight up to Daiaukka's camp. We will not be far behind."

"And the fire will clear the ground for our chariots." Tabshar Sin's gray old head bobbed up and down as he considered the matter. "And the Medes, on the high ground and with the wind in their faces, will have two enemies to fight."

"And when they break through—if they break through—their horses will be panicked and their battle lines in ruins. That is the way I see it in my mind. But in my mind my plans are always perfect and always work. I wish I could fight this engagement there instead of here in this valley."

"And what of the heat? Most of our soldiers are barefoot, and to walk across scorched ground . . ."

"We will follow one quarter hour behind the flames. If those advance as quickly as I hope, the ground will have had time to cool."

"And if the wind should change?"

I put my arm across his shoulders, for I loved him. Yet I could still wish he would not give words to the very dread of my heart.

"Then," I said, looking out into the darkness, where the campfires of the Medes were only tiny points of light, like dying stars, "then I will know what a fool I have been, and that the god has at last turned his back on me."

In the blackest part of the night, in the eerie, flickering light of a thousand campfires, the northern army assembled for the attack. I could read men's fear in their faces—they would not even be allowed the grace of meeting their enemy in the daylight but must perhaps die before the sun could rise, their souls escaping to wander in this terrible darkness. It was a dreadful thing to prepare for battle in the dark.

I had already chosen some fifty of the *quradu* under Lushakin's command, men sworn to silence, who, at my signal, would jump across our earthworks and with their torches begin this awful conflagration. They would be the first to die if things went against us—in this they might be lucky.

No one else, save these and Tabshar Sin, knew of my mad plan. I had not even told my officers. I did not wish to give men time to think, to weigh the risk to which I was putting all our lives. They would all know soon enough.

In the last hour before dawn, just as I had hoped, the wind found its voice. I mounted my chariot and rode out to face the judgment of my soldiers.

"We have been favored by Ashur," I shouted, my words echoing through the lines as they were repeated to men too far away to hear them, "to stop the Medes here, on the lands they call theirs, and not under the very walls of our own proud cities. This will be a terrible battle, for it will be fought to the death—theirs, or ours. But we do not wage war alone. We have many allies. Perhaps even before the sun reaches its zenith, Daiaukka will find he has the Scythians snarling at his back. And even before then— even before a single man of Ashur will have need to draw his sword—the Medes must fight an enemy more terrible than any man. Behold, the bright fire of Ashur, Lord of Heaven!"

I raised my arm. Lushakin and his men crossed the earth-works and put their pitchy torches to the grass. In an instant we all found ourselves gazing into a curtain of fire, yellow and black-red, hissing like some vast and wrathful serpent, terrible to see.

"Behold how the wind takes it!" I bellowed—I could hardly make myself heard above the fury of the fire. "See how it advances against the god's enemies! Prepare your hearts—make ready to follow it to conquest and to glory!"

Even the fire could not have roared as loud as the army of Ashur. As one man, with twenty thousand voices, they shouted, "Ashur is King! Ashur is King! Ashur is King!" I think, in that moment, when at last they had found themselves, they would have followed me into the very flames.

The fire swept forward, faster than I would have thought possible, turning the night into a ghastly daylight. It was fine to see—I could not help but wonder what was in Daiaukka's breast as he watched it coming.

"Slowly now, at walking pace—advance!"

We surged forward, the horses whinnying in barely controlled terror, across the earthworks and onto the blackened ground, grown cool already beneath our feet. The fire surged farther and farther ahead of us, beaten forward by the unrelenting wind. Ashur, in his mercy, had not failed us.

I rode in one of the great war chariots, pulled by a team of four horses covered in glittering copper armor. Even from beneath the pall of smoke I could see that the night sky was beginning to lighten. Dawn was coming.

"Let Tabiti keep his word," I thought to myself. "Let him bring his horsemen down on Daiaukka's back—if only to avenge us if we fail."

I had not driven far, not two hundred cubits across the scorched grasslands, before I found the first dead Mede, his corpse twisted and blackened by the fire, his eyes open but the balls melted from their sockets, his lips pulled back in a grotesque grin. He must have been a spy, caught by the sudden wall of flames, unable to escape. It must have been a fearful death.

There were others—I know not how many others, horses and men, their dying cries muffled for us by the fire's roar. Had Daiaukka been preparing some surprise of his own? Who would ever know now?

We had crossed half the valley floor before we saw any other sign of our enemy. The fire was moving in fits and starts now, seeming to sink to nothing and then thundering back to life. In one of these lulls the Medes broke through—two, perhaps three thousand men on horses that had been blindfolded for the charge but were still half mad from panic. With a cry that was like the barking of dogs wild with the scent of blood, they ripped the bandages off their horses' eyes and came galloping down on us. One flight of arrows and a quarter of them fell dead from their mounts, but still they came. The fire behind them and certain death ahead, they came, their god's name on their lips as they died. A man may take pride in his enemies, and surely these were fine, brave men whom it was an honor to kill in battle.

And kill them we did. The blind confusion born of the fire had scattered the Medes' cavalry formations, so these men could only attack in swarms, like angry bees. They had no chance of breaking up our battle squares—they could only harry us, and then fall before our arrows and javelins and under the wheels of our chariots. Fighting with magnificent courage, they threw their lives away. They died, seeming to hold death itself in contempt.

I wheeled back and forth across the field, scattering the Median horsemen as they tried to regroup for a charge. The black earth was now carpeted with dead and dying men, lying about like fallen leaves after a rainstorm, and my heavy armored chariot, which eight men could hardly lift as high as their knees, bounced over them as if they were rocks in the road. I could hear the screams as my wheels, by now slippery with blood, came down with a sudden shock to crush a man's chest. One, his legs mangled, tried to avenge himself against my horses, slashing wildly at their bellies with his sword. I pulled away, just beyond his reach, and, as I passed, buried the point of my javelin in his neck. He pitched over into the arms of death.

Thus the Median horsemen fought and perished. They

slowed our advance but a little—but that little, it seemed, was reason enough for the fury of their hopeless onslaught.

By this time the fire had achieved the summit of the long upward slope, reaching as far as the earthworks around Daiaukka's camp, and, with the wind dying but still strong, these did not stop its advance. It leaped across, and soon the very tents were burning. As the last Medes on the field turned to flee, I halted my chariot to give the horse a chance to rest and watched. In a few moments the fire laid everything waste, as if no one had ever dwelt there.

But where were the Medes?

Of course—why hadn't I seen it before? They had slipped away behind the wall of flames and smoke and were regrouping farther on, out of reach of both us and the fire. That was why their cavalry had charged us with such reckless courage, to purchase a few extra moments in case the wind changed.

And it was changing—our luck would not hold forever. Having driven the fire up the valley wall to the very summit, the wind began to fade. The fire seemed trapped inside Daiaukka's camp, where slowly it would sputter out. That was where we would meet our enemy, amidst the ashes of his stronghold. And it would not be long before the battle was joined.

The sun was within an hour of noon when we first reached the outskirts of Daiaukka's burned-out campsite. Within minutes teams of laborers had dug out sections of the earth ramparts and pushed them into the surrounding ditch so that our chariots could cross. We took possession, having conquered nothing, not even the scorched earth itself. We had merely arrived at the scene of our ordeal by combat—even as the smoke drifted away we could see the Medes marshaling themselves for the counterattack.

Thus the two great armies faced each other across not even half a *beru* of flat, fire-blackened land. We would fight on level ground now—Daiaukka had lost that tactical advantage—but he had withdrawn his men in good order and his force was still greatly superior in numbers. And now we were all, the Medes and us alike, weary, hardened to fear, and sick of the smell of blood, which meant that the coming battle would be waged with the desperate cruelty of men who have already learned to despair of their lives.

The Medes had their lines drawn up after the pattern they had learned from us: foot soldiers in the center with horsemen at both wings. They had no chariots, an instrument of warfare with which the mountain nations had yet to grow familiar, but our battlefield was so constricted that I feared we would not be able to use our own to very great advantage—the time had come for close fighting, the hardest and most pitiless kind of war. It but wanted a beginning.

There was silence. It was that terrible calm just before the storm breaks as each side waits upon the other. I could hear the rattle of my horses' harness. Everyone, even the Medes, seemed to be waiting for my signal to begin.

At last, when I could stand it no longer, I raised my arm and shouted, "Ashur is King!" Instantly that shout was echoed by twenty thousand voices. I cracked my whip, the chariot lurched forward, and I found myself hurtling down on the Median lines.

I could feel a thousand spears leveled at my breast, but they did not matter—the battle had begun and as I collided with what seemed a wall of enemy horsemen I felt myself as deathless as the very gods.

Words are but poor things to describe what the next hour was like. They passed in a blood-streaked blur as the ecstasy of battle was upon me. I hit a boulder with my chariot wheel and broke an axle, so I cut one of the lead horses free from its traces and, even before I could scramble on its back, armed with nothing but my short sword and a single javelin, I saw a Mede galloping down on me, his lance point already swinging around to impale me like an apple. He was no more than forty or fifty paces from me when I first noticed him, and riding hard, but I seemed to have an infinity of time. In one fluid motion, uncoiling like a snake, I turned and threw, knowing before the javelin left my hand that it would strike home. The Mede horseman pitched over the hindquarters of his mount and fell dead almost at my feet, the point of my javelin sticking a handspan out of his back.

"Good," I thought, "then I have it again." I put my foot on the man's chest and pulled my javelin free with one quick yank. Of such things is a man capable when the blood frenzy is upon him.

For that day I seemed to bear a charmed life. Nothing could touch me. A hundred swords and lances and arrows beyond counting drew me for their mark, but always they fell short, or their aim was wanting, or I seemed able to deflect them. Sometimes I seemed surrounded by the Medes, on foot and on horseback, yet I cut them down like summer barley. I was not afraid—what was there for me to fear when Death was a god who lived in my right arm?

But at last I broke free from this enchantment. All at once I found myself alone. There was no enemy within the reach of my hand, and as I looked about for one I saw how the field was thickly strewn with dead and dying men—Medes and my own soldiers both, having sealed that truce which subsists among the corpses of all nations. It had been a bloody day, and the sun had not yet descended two hours from noon.

We had reached a terrible standoff, in which both armies could only butcher one another, each man hoping to inflict the deadly blow before it fell on his own shoulders. For the most part, the battle squares of my foot soldiers still held, but the Medes, in their vast numbers and their astonishing, reckless courage, were pressing down hard upon them. The cavalry on both sides had abandoned even the pretense of a cohesive strategy, and their horses weaved in and out of the mobs of soldiers to strike at what targets they could find.

Nothing could be worse than this, I thought. The gods made war to punish men's iniquity. And then: We must break free. We must . . .

But what? I was not the *rab shaqe* now—I was only one more soldier among so many. The time for grand strategies was long past, and these men, locked in an embrace of the most sickening carnage, would only fall away from each other when, on one side or both, they grew too weary to hold on any longer.

And before then . . .

I could hear something—a shrill war cry that seemed to come from nowhere, like the screams of a hunting hawk as it falls upon its prey. It was an oddly familiar sound, yet I could not remember where I had heard it before. . . .

And then I knew. I turned my head, knowing what I would see—the Scythian riders, streaming down from a nearby bluff, an avalanche of men and horses. Tabiti had kept his bargain.

My men heard it too—and so did the Medes—and at once it seemed to turn the fortune of battle. Suddenly, as if they had found new hearts, even before the shock of that first charge made itself felt, the soldiers of Ashur surged forward. The Medes began to buckle, and then, from one instant to the next, like a rotting plank under a man's foot, their lines simply broke.

These things happen quickly. What a few minutes before had been a battle all at once became a rout. The Scythians, like scavenging birds, merely finished off an enemy already wounded to the death. Daiaukka's brave warriors, those who did not take to their heels, were simply trampled under the wild rush of our victory. The slaughter which followed was terrible to witness.

And it went on until the merciful darkness forced it to a halt. As long as the sun's light held, the Medes suffered death and mutilation. Those who were wounded or had been left without a horse or found themselves trapped behind the swift current of our advance perished like sheep at the butcher's block as the victors took their revenge and collected trophies: heads, hands—in one case I recall the skin from a man's arm, peeled off even to the fingernails, red with blood. It would make a quiver cover when it dried.

My own soldiers soon grew weary of the business. They had fought since the hours before dawn and were sick of blood, so their officers had little difficulty in bringing them to good order. But the Scythians were fresh and, having been cheated of their proper share of the battle, felt disposed, after the fashion of barbarians, to make the most of whatever was left. They were not my men. I could not have restrained them.

Did I even wish to? I know not. At first the necessity of taking any kind of action did not even enter my brain. I was stupid with exhaustion and for several minutes could only gaze out over the developing carnage with the mute incomprehension of an animal. As soon as the Medes had begun their flight, however, my principal officers began gathering about me on the field to await my commands. It was time to return to life.

"Lushakin!" I shouted—suddenly I was filled with alarm. "Lushakin, take as many men as you need and find Daiaukka. If he is still on the field, find him! Find him alive, if you can—he will be far less use to us with his throat cut by some Scythian bandit— but alive or dead, find him!"

"*Rab Shaqe,* no one except yourself has ever seen him," was his highly sensible answer. "How are we to know one blood-smeared Mede from another?"

"Take prisoners then—find a few willing to sell their lord for a chance to live. Hurry!"

As Lushakin climbed on his horse to do my bidding, I tried to force myself to think. There were orders which at this moment should have sprung naturally to my lips—what were they? My mind seemed unable to hold any idea except that of Daiaukka's hacked and bloody corpse.

He could not be allowed to cheat me. Now now—not after all this.

"Think!" I told myself. "Today, you are the victor here. Act the part!"

"Give the men one hour," I said, "and then I want this brought to an end. And send out patrols to look for whatever has escaped of Daiaukka's cavalry. Do not interfere with them; simply report on their numbers."

"What of the Scythians, *Rab Shaqe*?"

"Yes, what of the Scythians, *Rab Shaqe*?"

I looked up and saw Tabiti leaning over his horse's neck to grin down at me pityingly. He looked as fresh as if he had just risen from his bed.

"We will leave them to their robber chief," I said. "How are you, brother? We would have carried the day without you, but perhaps men will say that you helped a little."

The headman of the Sacan threw his head back and laughed like a jackal. Then, as if he had remembered something, he swung his horse around and scanned the field.

"Not many of the foot soldiers have escaped," he said. "But the riders were more fortunate. It is a thing to be regretted, for the Medes are possessed of fine horses. Yet a robber must take his booty where he finds it, brother."

He laughed again. Tabiti was wise enough to know he had no reason to be displeased with this day's work.

"But I tarry," he went on, gathering up his reins. "My men require me as the companion of their sport."

"Tabiti . . ."

"Yes, brother—what is it?" His catlike eyes widened inquisitively.

"The *shah* Daiaukka, if you find him alive . . ."

"Then I shall kill him. What of it, brother."

"I need him alive, if that is convenient."

"You wish to kill him yourself—yes, I understand perfectly." He flashed his white teeth in an amused smile. "If he falls in my way, I will save him for you. Farewell, brother."

He rode away, like a boy eager to chase rabbits. His was an uncomplicated view of the world and I envied him.

The silence that he left behind was broken by the hurried sounds of voices and the screams of dying men. The real horrors always come at the ends of battles and perhaps it is better so, lest men forget that fighting is a serious matter, not to be entered into lightly. I saw soldiers, their tunics soaked in blood, sitting down among the corpses of their enemies, clearing the dust from their throats with water from goatskin bags filled by women who did not yet know that their sons and husbands were dead. Already my men were starting to quarrel over their loot—it would not be long, if they were left to themselves, before they began cutting each other's throats. Such is ever the glorious conclusion of war.

"I weary of this," I said, to no one in particular. "Someone fetch me a horse that I may return to camp. See that everything I have ordered is done."

It was almost dark before I found my own tent again. With the smell of carnage finally out of my nostrils, I was looking forward to my dinner and then, perhaps, the unimaginable luxury of a full night's sleep, but it was not to be.

A small knot of men was waiting for me and, lying on the ground in front of them, was some object wrapped in a blanket. No one spoke.

At last, in the imperfect way of one whose eyes have seen more than his mind can hold, I understood that what the blanket concealed was yet another corpse—there were so many, why trouble me about one more?

And then I felt my bowels grow cold with apprehension. I knelt down beside the body and uncovered its face. It was Tabshar Sin, staring at me with wide, cloudy eyes that still registered the shock of death.

I had been in many battles, but never, I think, until that moment had I known what it was to hate my enemy.

There are times when it seems impossible to grow drunk. I tried, but it was hopeless. Each swallow merely sharpened the hard edge on things, so that my mind, like a small child playing with a dagger, seemed to cut itself with every fumbling movement.

So I was in no very happy frame of mind as I sat by the campfire in front of my tent, the corpse of Tabshar Sin at my feet, wrapped and ready for burial. A spear had caught him under the arm, breaking off at the shaft only when its point had crossed straight through the center of his chest. They say that such a massive wound brings no pain, that a man is dead before he feels more than the impact of the blow which kills him. I can only hope it is true.

He had met his *simtu* as an ordinary soldier and had lain unnoticed until someone remembered that this was the old man who had taught Prince Tiglath his first lessons in the warrior's craft and enjoyed the *rab shaqe*'s love almost as a second father. I indeed had loved him, yet I could not even weep for him. What was missing in me that I could not shed tears over the body of Tabshar Sin? Why could grief find no outlet except in dark hate?

The wine tasted bitter—life was bitter, and death merely the last of the god's cruel jests. In the morning I would bury my old *rab kisir,* and I promised myself that many Median prisoners would pacify his ghost by emptying their heart's blood onto his grave. They would pay, although it was my fault more than theirs —I should have left him back in Amat, where he would have lived to die in bed. That did not matter, however. The Medes would still pay. I would find an ax and hack off their heads myself as they knelt over his burial mound, and thus they would make my amends for me. Lack of sleep, the strain of battle, grief, and my own uncomfortable conscience all combined to make me cruel.

Or perhaps I was drunk. Perhaps it is best to assume that I must have been. Otherwise it becomes difficult to explain what happened when they brought Daiaukka to me.

The process had been going on throughout the afternoon and evening—Lushakin and his spies had been rounding up every man of importance they could find among the surviving Medes, those fortunate enough to have been taken prisoner and those simply discovered somewhere on the battlefield with enough life left in them to make it worth the trouble of fetching them in. Perhaps twenty or thirty of them, bound hand and foot, waited on their knees before my tent, waited for the conqueror to decide their fates. Most, doubtless, expected to die, but I had settled nothing with myself. Indeed, I had not even considered the matter. A new man would be brought to me, I would glance at him long enough to confirm that he was not Daiaukka, and then dismiss him from my mind, returning to my own morose reflections.

But at last there he was, alive and in my hands. I stood up and turned to Lushakin, who grinned at me.

"Yes, *Rab Shaqe*," he said. "I thought this would be the one. These slaves will try to sell you as many Daiaukkas as there are seeds in a barley field, but this time I had a bit more confidence in their word. He stayed behind, did our hero here. He was still trying to fight off a crowd of those Scythian rascals with nothing but a half-burned piece of tent pole. They weren't very pleased to have their quarry stolen from them, I can tell you—you may even hear of it from your friend the Lord Tabiti, because we had to cut one of them a little before they would mind their manners."

"Take the rest away and leave me alone with him," I said, which made Lushakin frown.

"You don't mean alone, *Rab Shaqe*—he's . . ."

"He's harmless enough." I smiled, trying to be patient. "You needn't worry about me, Lushakin. I can still defend myself against an unarmed man who has his hands tied behind his back."

Reluctantly, he did as he was told, and soon the *shah-ye-shah* was sitting on a log on the other side of the fire, watching me through wary black eyes.

"I will cut your hands free if you give me your word not to violate my hospitality," I said. Daiaukka seemed to consider for a moment and then nodded.

I took the dagger from my belt and severed the leather cords around his wrists. Then I filled a wine cup and set it down beside his right foot. Daiaukka picked up the cup and drank it off in what could have been a single swallow. I filled it again and he emptied it again, so I simply left the jar for him. It was possible he had not tasted so much as a sip of water since that morning. I sat down again.

"How much of your army is still intact somewhere?" I asked. "A third, do you think?"

"I doubt so many—and the best are all dead."

Neither his face nor his toneless voice reflected the slightest emotion. We might have been discussing the fates of strangers for all he revealed of his feelings. It struck me again, as it had at both our previous meetings, that this was a remarkable man.

"And you know what will happen next," I continued. "In the morning I will begin receiving offers of submission from your surviving nobles. There will be a race to see who can most quickly throw himself at my feet, and one tribe will blame the next for initiating this war—and all will blame you. You have lost your gamble, Daiaukka, and the nation you dreamed of making from these goatherds is dead."

"For the moment, yes. But you must finally leave here, my lord, and men will dream again."

He lifted the wine cup to his lips once more and drank slowly, like a man who was at peace with himself. What he said was no more than the truth.

"I have no desire to take your life," I said, feeling uncomfortable, as if somehow I had been the loser today. "I will spare it if you will pledge your submission to the king in Nineveh. It would be better if you could accept the consequences of this defeat and, as you say yourself, wait for better days."

"Better for whom, Lord Tiglath Ashur?" He smiled at me, as if amused by the simplicity of a child.

"Better for your people, whom I intend to see never raise their heads again during my lifetime—who will find themselves with a *shah* of my choosing if you refuse."

"Will they? Yes, of course. Yes, perhaps it would be better for them."

"Then will you submit?"

"I will not submit tonight, my lord." He set the wine cup down beside his foot again and covered his face with his hands, as if to wipe away the exhaustion. "You will have my answer, if you wish it, in the morning, but not before then. My life is in your power and you may take it whenever you wish, but I will not pledge myself to anything simply because I am weary and weak-spirited."

"Then you will have until tomorrow—guard!"

Lushakin came rushing toward us, his sword in his hand, as if he expected to find Daiaukka at my throat and not sitting across the fire while we bargained like caravan drivers. I think he was disappointed.

"You will find the *shah-ye-shah* a bed for the night," I told him. "You will see that he has every comfort."

"Every comfort—yes, *Rab Shaqe*. I have a very comfortable copper chain I will put around his neck."

It was Daiaukka himself who laughed. The man seemed afraid of nothing.

"Post a guard if it eases your heart," I answered. "But bring him to me again in the morning, when I send for him."

Did Daiaukka sleep that night? From what I understood of his nature, it would not have surprised me to find that he did. I never closed my eyes. I remained beside the campfire, keeping my vigil beside the corpse of Tabshar Sin and with no other company except a wine cup, until the broad light of day.

And perhaps, if I really was drunk, the wine fumes clouded my brain enough to allow me to think that I had trapped Daiaukka, for I intended to butcher him myself, to make him the first offering to the ghost of my dead friend, if he did not submit to the might of Ashur. This I would do in full view of his surviving nobles, that they might learn the price of defiance. I would humble their *shah* before their eyes, or I would give him to death, and this too before their eyes. All night I consoled myself with this idea. Yet a man may think himself profoundly clever and be a fool just the same.

The morning came. I ordered that Tabshar Sin's grave should be dug beyond the earthworks of our camp, on ground which he and I and many others had won with our swords for the greater glory of Ashur and our king. I lowered his body into the shallow pit and with my own hands covered him with earth. In a year, when the grass returned, no one would know his resting place. It was to be a day for burials; Tabshar Sin was only the first of many.

On that blackened plain I performed for my old friend the last kindness one man can do another, and there were many to witness the deed. The soldiers of the northern army stood about in silence, knowing that soon they, too, would be called upon to perform the same service for their comrades who lay dead on the field of battle.

The conquered Medes, our prisoners now, only yesterday our foes, watched too, doubtless wondering if they also were about to enter into the long darkness of death. Tabiti, who called me his brother, stood behind me—he smiled slightly, as if already counting his spoils. Daiaukka was there as well, but I had long since abandoned my attempts to see inside his heart.

I rose and wiped the dirt from my hands. I had not slept in two days and nights and my head ached and the taste in my mouth was bitter, but that was only the last dregs of the wine jar and no more than I deserved. Still, I was quiet in my soul and somehow all my wrath had left me. It was clear what must follow.

"If the Medes will have it so," I shouted, that all might hear, "then Ashur's war against them can end at this hour. I invite any who will to kneel and swear his oath of submission to the king my father, the Lord Sennacherib, king in Ashur and Calah and Nineveh, lord of the earth's four corners, master of this place and all the world."

As one man the Median nobles, the great ones of the Aryan, knelt and swore—all of them, save one. For the Lord Daiaukka, the *shah-ye-shah,* he alone whose word I cared about, he stayed on his feet.

"You will not swear, my lord?" I asked him, wondering why I was not disappointed. Why, I wondered, was I glad that he would not submit? Only because he was a great man, whom none would ever humble—yes, perhaps that was the reason.

"No." He shook his head, crossing his arms over his chest. "Others may, but not I. For I have sworn an oath to live as the one *shah* of the Aryan, and to drive my enemies from this my land or die in the attempt."

"You once told me we would have our battle and then see whom the Ahura favored. Can you not accept the judgment of your god?"

At once, the moment the words had passed my lips, I knew I had made a great error.

Daiaukka knew it too, and smiled thinly.

"No, my lord—for you are alive, and so am I. The contest between your god and mine can only be settled between the two of us, no others. You have the power to kill me now, if that is your will, but you will have proved nothing. It must be one against the other and in single combat, to the death."

I could sense the tremor of excitement that passed through all who had heard his challenge. Tabiti stepped forward and put his hand on my arm.

"You must not do this thing," he whispered tensely. "Kill him now—or I will do it for you!"

"None may kill him save I alone," I answered. I was resigned, for I knew that it was not Daiaukka who had fallen into a trap, but I. "He has me. He demands trial by combat, his strength against mine—his magic, if you will, against mine. If I refuse, and slay him like a dog, then he will never die but be king in these mountains forever. He gives me no choice."

Tabiti released his grasp, for he knew I was right.

"There is a condition," I said, speaking for all to hear. "It will be in the gods' hands who lives or dies, but the war must be over. If I conquer, the *parsua* keep their pledge made this day to the king my father. If I die, the Lord Daiaukka must promise that in his lifetime the border between our lands shall not be violated."

"So be it." He nodded—why should he not agree? What had he to lose? "And I ask one favor of the Lord Tiglath Ashur, that I might have three days before we meet to settle this between us. There will be no treachery, but I would see my son once more."

"So be it."

Thus everything was arranged, a duel to the death three days hence.

31

I had treasured the hope that Daiaukka, once he came into my hands, could be persuaded to sue for peace. It was not so very unreasonable a thing to expect, since most men will accept decent terms in exchange for their lives, but once this hope proved vain a commander wiser than myself would have ordered the *shah-ye-shah* quietly put to death, thus preserving the fiction that he had fallen in battle. The Medes would have preferred this, for then he could have taken the blame for a lost war and, in later years, provided a convenient hero, a martyr, to serve as the rallying cry when they felt themselves strong enough to challenge us again. And, for a few years at least, it would have been to my advantage since, being his conqueror, I would have fallen heir to Daiaukka's considerable prestige as a warrior. This would have been a poor substitute for the subservient, humbled, discredited figurehead I could have made of him alive—how, I wonder, could I have imagined that Daiaukka would allow himself to be used for such a purpose?—but it would have been worth something. I should have cut his throat while it was still within my power.

Instead, I made the greatest mistake I could have made and extended to my most implacable enemy the chance for a public challenge which, once issued, could hardly be refused. Once the words were spoken, I could not have ordered his execution without looking like a coward in front of that most important of all audiences, his own defeated and demoralized followers.

Now it would have to be single combat, my protective *sedu* against the renewed magic of his name—and Daiaukka was a man with nothing to lose. The *shah-ye-shah* had trapped me because he saw with painful clarity what I, for one unaccountable moment, had allowed myself to forget: that this was a war which would not end with one battle or one victory; that tactics and the weight of armies, in the end, would matter less than the legends surrounding individual men.

And thus I had presented Daiaukka with his opportunity to create a legend which would be treasured by his race until their final hour.

But there would be three days before our final meeting. I loaned Daiaukka a horse and watched him ride away into the foothills, not knowing where he went nor caring. He would return, which was all that concerned me. He would not oblige me by making good his escape, for he was a man for whom death held no terrors.

I could not say the same. A duel, where one man must die that another may live, is more terrible than any battle, for in battle the danger is less personal—no one of your enemies seeks your life alone—and it is a rare day on which half the men fighting will perish. And I am not ashamed to say that I feared Daiaukka, for he was brave and strong and cunning and since his earliest youth had known no life except that of warrior. The man who would not fear him could have no eyes to see with nor mind to think. I was not so insensible as a block of wood, so I was filled with fear.

But at least, if this was a trouble I had brought upon myself, I alone would suffer from it. By the army it was viewed as a matter of great sport and the betting, so I was told, grew heavy.

In my three days of grace I met with my officers and made plans for our withdrawal. We would establish a garrison at a place called Zakruti, not too far from our own borders, and leave three thousand men there. The rest of us would return to Amat and the garrisons in Zamua and Namri. All this would be the same whether Daiaukka triumphed or I did, for the fortunes of war do not rest with the life of one man.

On the night before Daiaukka's return, the Lord Tabiti, who called himself my brother, came to my tent, carrying his skull-cups and a skin of *safid atesh* under his arm.

"The Medes have their *haoma,* which they drink to make themselves wild with valor, but this is better," he said, filling one of the cups and holding it out to me by the eye sockets. "Here— drink. I know you do not fancy the taste of it, but you need something and wine will leave your senses dull tomorrow. Drink."

"Is it so obvious then, that I am afraid?"

"No. You carry it as well as any man, but I do not need to be told what it is that cuts into your bowels. Who does not fear death?"

"Daiaukka, perhaps." I took a sip of the *safid atesh* and instantly made a face—it was not a taste that improved upon acquaintance. "I think perhaps Daiaukka does not fear death."

"If he does not, then he is not a man. And if he is not a man, then you may kill him by any means without staining your honor, for you will be ridding the world of a demon. Tell me—have you ever known this style of combat before?"

"No."

I thought it prudent not to mention the incident with Esarhaddon and, indeed, the two cases could have nothing in common.

"Then know that Daiaukka will expect you to meet him on horseback, carrying only a spear and a short sword. This is the way with all the tribes, the Cimmerian, the Scoloti, even these dogs the Medes. It will not be understood if you decline this way of fighting—everyone will believe you are a coward. I have seen you on a horse and you are well enough for a man born inside mud walls, but compared to the tribesman you are not much."

"Thank you. You are my friend indeed to speak so kindly of me."

"Do not be insulted, for I say no more than what you yourself know and all for your own good. Daiaukka is a fine rider. As long as he has a horse between his knees he will hold you to a disadvantage—remember that."

I had drunk much by then, for I wished a quiet heart, but I understood clearly enough that Tabiti spoke the truth.

"The Medes hold horses in great respect—remember that as well. Daiaukka will be at great pains to do no injury to your horse, for to cause its death would be a sacrilege for which he would have to answer to his god. You, however, are under no such prohibition."

"What are you suggesting?"

"Kill his horse. As soon as you can, kill his horse. Make him fight you on the ground, where you will at least stand an even chance. If you lose, would it comfort your ghost if I killed this Daiaukka for you?"

"No."

"I may kill him anyway, for my own comfort. I have called you my brother, and the man who strips you of your life has offended against me. Yes, I think I will kill him anyway, that I be spared the reproaches of my conscience. But out of consideration for your fine sense of propriety I will do it with craft, after the custom of the Scoloti—I will invite him to dinner and give him a slow poison that none may know he died at my hand."

"This you must not do, Tabiti my brother. This is not an honorable end for such a man."

"Then, if you have such concern for him, you must kill him yourself, Lord Tiglath Ashur." Tabiti smiled, the cunning smile of a wily, dangerous animal. "I will go now—remember what I said about killing his horse."

Then he rose to depart, leaving the skin of *safid atesh* with me.

I sat up the rest of that night, with only a single oil lamp burning to frighten away ghosts. I drank only enough to dull the edge of my fear and keep me from thinking. No one else came near my tent that night—whether this was because someone had issued orders or because men thought me unlucky and avoided me on that account, I know not. In either case I was content that it should be so, for I wanted no company.

At last, the morning came and Daiaukka with it. He brought a force of his retainers, some three hundred armed men, asking that they might be allowed to witness this duel between us and satisfy themselves that, should he fall, their *shah-ye-shah* had met with no treachery—he did not say so, since he could not without discourtesy, but I think he also wanted to ensure that, should he triumph over me, he would have some means of leaving my camp alive. I did not object, since both were perfectly reasonable precautions.

He also brought his son, Khshathrita. The boy stood beside his father, for all his youth displaying the unselfconscious carriage of a man as he continued to study my face with his large, serious black eyes all the while Daiaukka and I settled the final details.

It was agreed between us that we would fight on the narrow plain beyond the earthworks of my encampment, and that he would take his position at the north side and I at the south side, so neither man would have the advantage of the sun at his back. Daiaukka carried a lance, about five cubits long, and I would have my javelin. Beyond this, we each allowed ourselves a small round shield and a sword no more than a cubit in length, but nothing more.

The horse Daiaukka rode was not the one I had given him but the fine black stallion I had seen twice before, so I can only assume that, for reasons best known to himself, he had not ridden it the day of the battle. I was mounted upon Ghost, who seemed to sense that this morning would see mortal combat and so whinnied and dug at the ground with his hoofs as if consumed with rage.

There might have been forty thousand men, Medes, Scythians, and soldiers of Ashur, assembled there to view the contest, but the only sound was the stirring of the wind over our heads. No man spoke or laughed or even cleared his throat. I could not help but think, it is as if I had already died.

I mounted my horse and rode to my starting point—Daiaukka was already waiting across the field and raised his lance in salute when I came to a halt and faced him. I raised my javelin to signal that I was ready.

One of the Medes came into the center of the field and displayed a white banner. He released it from his grasp, letting it flutter to the earth—this was our signal to begin—and then ran back to join his comrades. It was now solely a matter between the *shah-ye-shah* and me.

For a moment neither of us moved—it was almost possible to hope the thing would never happen—and then Daiaukka urged his horse forward at a canter. I followed his example, resigning myself to the gods. There could be no turning back.

What would he do? How do men fight with spears from the backs of horses? Certainly a throw, under such circumstances, would have little chance of hitting its mark. I had been trained to the useful arts of war, not to this. I would wait upon events.

I did not have to wait long. Quickly Daiaukka gathered speed as he bore down upon me. At the last, when we were separated by perhaps no more than fifty paces, he lowered the point of his spear and aimed it at my chest.

There was no time to dodge out of the way—I had no defense but the shield on my left arm, and Daiaukka's point tore through the layers of its oxhide cover as if they were linen. In a second, as

Daiaukka thundered past me, my shield was tumbling over the ground, rolling like a barrel hoop, and blood was streaming from my shoulder, but by some miracle I had stayed on my horse. I pulled myself up straight and turned to face him, the laughter of the Medes ringing in my ears.

Daiaukka was in no hurry. He galloped well past me and then slowed to a walk before he wheeled around. He was calm, deliberate, perfectly well aware that he had drawn first blood and now had the advantage. There was something almost of contempt in the way he placed the palm of his hand on his thigh as he watched me.

It made me angry—that was good, for I needed anger.

The wound on my shoulder stung badly but showed no signs of stiffening up. I decided it would not kill me before Daiaukka did. I decided also that he would not be given the chance.

This time it was my turn to charge. I balanced my javelin and, when I was within range, threw, pulling Ghost sharply to the right to avoid Daiaukka's spear. It was a bad throw and passed harmlessly over his shoulder to bury itself point-first in the dirt. I rode by and leaned over to pick it up.

But my adversary had no thought of permitting me the chance to recover. Even as the javelin was in my hand I could hear the pounding of hoofs behind me, and it was only by throwing myself to the ground that I could retrieve my life. As soon as he saw that he had missed me, Daiaukka pulled his horse to a stop and reined it around—I had barely time to scramble onto Ghost's back and make good my retreat.

The Medes laughed again, louder this time, and the silence of my own soldiers spoke of their shame in me.

I had torn my wound wider in my fall, and the blood poured thickly over my dust-caked arm. There was no time to bind it, for Daiaukka was already lining himself up, readying for another charge. I felt a shock of pain when I tried to raise my left hand above my shoulder, as if someone were grinding sand into the raw flesh.

Ghost snorted loudly and reared up on his hind legs—he, at least, was prepared to concede nothing.

I circled around, trying to put distance between Daiaukka and me, and then, when I felt I would have room to maneuver— let the clash come if it must—I let Ghost have his head.

Once in range, I threw again, but my aim was no truer and

the javelin fell short. Perhaps it startled the black stallion because Daiaukka also missed his mark, the point of his lance swinging in too late to find me.

Yet it was not men who warred now, but horses. The two great stallions collided almost shoulder to shoulder and we all went down, men and horses both. I scrambled to my feet, drawing my short sword, trying to see through the clouds of dust to discover what had happened. At last I could see Daiaukka, also with his sword drawn. The horses were between us and they were rearing up and striking at each other with their hoofs, seeming to make their masters' fight their own. It was a wild scene—for a moment we both simply watched, struck motionless by awe.

It could not go on. I ran for my javelin and managed to scoop it up before Daiaukka could catch me. When he saw it in my hand he ran back behind the horses—his spear, it seemed, was not for throwing and he would not put himself in my way.

I whistled for Ghost. He came, but not willingly. There was blood on his chest where the black stallion's hoofs had cut him.

I had time now to remount, for Daiaukka had not yet caught his horse, but I waited for a moment, thinking that now it would be an easy thing to kill the great black stallion. A horse is not a man and does not think to dodge out of the way—I had only to raise my javelin and throw . . .

"Kill his horse," Tabiti had said. *"Make him fight you on the ground, where at least you will stand an even chance."*

It was good advice, except then what would I fight with? I would have only my sword, and Daiaukka would have both sword and spear. How was that better?

I scrambled onto Ghost's back, wondering if I was not making a mistake.

We faced each other again. I waited for Daiaukka's charge, wondering how I could hope to escape it this time, but now he appeared to hesitate. Why? What was passing through his mind? I could not begin to guess.

Then I understood—his horse, capering from side to side in that impatient manner one sees in fine stallions, seemed rusty in its movements. And its chest too was marked here and there with crescents of blood, so Ghost, faring better than his master, had at least kept his opponent to an even match.

Daiaukka, sensing his mount's hurt and perhaps its fear as

well, hesitated, allowing the animal to recapture its breath. And all the while his eyes never left the point of my javelin.

He needn't have worried—I was not throwing at all well. I had not yet acquired the knack of it from horseback, but at least I seemed to be improving. Yet if I found my mark within the next two or three attempts, it would only be through pure chance, and that seemed a weak hook upon which to hang one's life. This charge or the next, surely Daiaukka would kill me.

Yet what choice had I? To come down to the ground was to abandon myself to a single throw. My javelin had found the hearts of many horsemen, but always in battle, where many darts may be aimed at a single target. Daiaukka had no opponent save me, so his eyes were on my point alone. He could dodge and weave and parry, and finally tempt me into making the fatal cast. And when that was done, and I had no weapon except my short sword, he would ride me down, trampling me into the dust to kill me at his perfect convenience. No, I did not dare abandon my horse.

He was ready now—I could see it in the set of his shoulders, in the way his hand slid up the shaft of his spear. He would make his charge and I had no choice but to meet it, trying yet once more to catch him on the run.

I let Ghost have his head—he was far more eager than I—and tried to settle into the rhythm of his gallop, that blur of sound, that jolt as his hoofs struck the earth, seemingly altogether. I had to try to time my throw to the instants between, while we seemed to fly together through the empty air.

Daiaukka stormed over the plain, like a blind force of nature that would not be turned aside. His lance was already turning in toward me as the javelin shot from my hand—it was a good throw, dropping down on him like a bird of prey. He saw—he knew. He raised his shield and the javelin caught it on the edge, tearing at it with the bronze point.

But the throw was not good enough, and my dart bounced away to skitter over the ground like a snake.

And I had waited too long. I could not evade Daiaukka's lance—it caught me in the side, and I could feel it ripping me open, burning its way through. I twisted away, and the shaft broke off. I fell to the ground, the impact a sickening shudder, a huge tear in my belly and the point still buried under my ribs.

"He has killed me," I thought. For a moment I could not get

to my feet—my legs would not work. I could feel the blood oozing out between my fingers as I tried to hold myself together. "I am a dead man, even if he leaves the field without a backward look."

Somehow I made it to my knees. Then one foot, then another. I would not die like a slave—where was my javelin?

Twenty paces to my left. It might as well have been in another country. How could I take half so many steps before I bled to death, or Daiaukka trampled me down like a frog in the road?

Daiaukka wheeled around and stopped. For a moment he merely watched, perhaps waiting for me to collapse and die on my own. He had triumphed—he knew it and I knew it. I would die and he would live. I could not see his face at that distance, but I knew what was in his heart.

And Ghost—what of Ghost? He cantered about for a moment, seeming not to know what to do now. He snorted loudly. I called, but he paid no heed. Even my horse knew I was a dead man.

I saw Daiaukka take the sword from his belt. The blade flashed in the sun as he waved it over his head, for he wished me to know what was coming.

No—I would not merely stand and wait for the stroke to fall. I was a king's son. I would not shame my father, the Lord Ashur, and the soldiers who had followed me to this place, not by allowing myself to be cut down like a shock of barley. Twenty paces was not too far if they measured the distance to an honorable and manly death.

My guts felt as if they were stuffed with burning coals, and my knees shook. Yet I could move. I took a step, then another, then another. Daiaukka waited—it seemed to amuse him.

And then he slapped the great black stallion on the haunch with the flat of his sword blade, and man and beast jolted forward. No more than a trot at first, but slowly gathering speed—they bore down on me. This was the moment.

I took another step, and another. I had no chance. I was already dead. What good . . . ?

And then Ghost sprang into life, his great hoofs striking out, tearing at the ground. *His* battle was not over. *He* was not so easily defeated.

I cannot describe the sound he made—never have I heard a horse make such a sound, like the snarling of a great cat. His war cry made the air tremble as he closed on the black stallion.

With a mighty leap that almost carried him onto the horse's
back, he struck out with his hoofs. His neck was stretched
straight and his great square teeth exposed, as if he meant to tear
his enemy to pieces. Once more both horses went down, and
Daiaukka crashed to the ground, rolling over and over.

I did not waste my opportunity. I would die, but not alone. I
paced off the remaining distance at a painful, jerky trot, as fast as
I could bear. I picked up the javelin. It was in my hand—I was a
man once more.

Could I throw it? I did not know. The whole left side of my
body throbbed with pain, and I felt ready to collapse. But I would
try to throw. I had to try.

Daiaukka started to climb to his feet. He was stunned—I
think he had forgotten all about me. He looked about, as if trying
to remember what had happened. He turned to look at me.

It was the last chance I would ever have. Willing myself to
forget my pain, I coiled and threw. Daiaukka could see, but
seemed not to understand. Together we watched the javelin as it
arched through the air.

He might as well have been struck by lightning. He could not
have avoided it, and it fell upon him with seemingly as great a
shock. The point entered his chest, just under the collarbone, and
shot straight through until half its length was buried in his body. I
would have known the moment of impact with my eyes shut, by
the great cry that went up from the Medes. Daiaukka never made
a sound.

He collapsed. He did not stagger and fall like another man—
he simply went limp and crumpled.

I had all the time I wanted now. I walked toward him,
slowly, for it was not in my power to do better. I drew my sword.

But there was no reason. He was lying on the ground, seemingly unable to move. I knelt beside him.

The horses, not twenty paces away, were kicking dust into
the air and neighing savagely, oblivious to us. If someone did not
part them soon, one would kill the other.

But the quiet of mortality had already come to Daiaukka. He
was alive, but only by a little, and lying on his side. He looked
into my face and his mouth shaped a word, but there was no
sound. His tongue came out to moisten his lips and he tried again.

"Do you think . . . ?" His eyes closed. For a moment I

thought he was dead, but at last they opened again. "Do you think it will end now?"

Already I could hear the slap, slap, slap of sandaled feet as the crowds who had come as witnesses surged forward, eager to be present for even the last moments of a man's life. It was the end of privacy. In an instant, living and dead, we would belong to our eager nations.

"It will never end," I said.

He smiled, and then became still. Now, at last, he was dead.

Of what remained of that day, of the next, and of many which were to follow, I remember very little, I hovered close to death and the black bird shadowed my soul with her wings.

"By the sixty great gods, what a gash! You can look straight through and see his liver!"

I recall hearing someone say that as they carried me from the field on a blanket, but nothing more. Daiaukka's face in death, a few sentences—everything else is missing, even the pain.

So what I know of that time, while my life seemed as fragile as a spider's web in the wind, I know it only as it was told me after: of the rumors which swept the camp, even as they carried me back to my tent; of the loud voices among my soldiers, demanding vengeance against the Medes; of the terrible wind, howling like a madwoman, which blew all that night and into the next until the ground was scoured clean where Daiaukka and I had squandered each other's blood—this was taken by both sides as a terrible omen—of these things I knew nothing. For I was not there but in some other place entirely.

As a check on the Medes during this troubled season—for who can tell what desperate and defeated men will think to do if they suspect confusion among their enemies?—the officers I had left in command decided to take the boy Khshathrita as a hostage. It was a reasonable precaution, for after his father's death the heir was the one remaining focus of power among the tribes of the Zagros. Without him they were not a nation, and they knew it. So they would sit quietly and wait, while their *shah-ye-shah*'s son rested by the campfires of his enemies.

My soldiers treated the boy kindly, for the men of Ashur have a great fondness for the young, yet it must have been a fearful ordeal for him. He was, after all, only a child and surrounded by those whom he had been taught to believe monsters of cruelty, and he could not know what fate would befall him were I to die—an event which must have seemed as certain and imminent as the next sunset. But for all this he behaved with the calm dignity of a man, and one who is of the seed of kings. It would not have shamed his father to see him, for Daiaukka lived again in his son.

Once, when for a few minutes the mist cleared from my brain, I opened my eyes to find the boy sitting on the floor beside my cot, his head resting on his hands as if his vigil had been a long one. It seemed odd that he should be there, the son of my slain enemy, but this curious turn did not trouble me. I merely assumed that I must be dreaming. I had had many and far odder dreams in my troubled, deathlike sleep, so what was the presence of an inoffensive boy sitting at my bedside? Perhaps, if this was a dream, he was a messenger from the gods and would reveal if at last I had met my *simtu*—a matter concerning which, in my weakened condition, I had only the mildest curiosity. So I took this visit calmly enough.

"Will you live or die, my Lord Tiglath?" he asked, his voice low, as if it were a private business between only the two of us.

"I know not," I answered. "Have I been a long time deciding?"

He held up three fingers.

"This many days, my lord. When will you know?"

"No sooner than you yourself, boy."

I closed my eyes and drifted back to that twilight sleep that seemed to enclose me like the waters of a bottomless sea.

Later—how much later I could not even have guessed—I woke again and managed to swallow a few sips of beer. The boy was nowhere about.

That was all I remembered until at last, after what my dreams had made into a long and difficult journey through a land filled with monsters, the Lady Ereshkigal was pleased to open her hand and release me.

"Ah, so it seems you will yet live!"

It was Tabiti, squatting like a laundrywoman at the head of my cot. I had to twist my eyes around to see him, and the effort made them throb in their sockets. The wound in my side felt like a nest of scorpions and I seemed to be bathed in sweat.

"Something to drink," I whispered thickly. "Something . . ."

The cup was at my lips before I could finish. It was not beer this time but wine mixed with water. Nothing will ever taste so good again as did those first few sips. Their coolness ran straight through my veins, as if they had been empty until that moment.

"What is this . . . ?"

I reached down to feel what made my side pain me so. I had forgotten all about Daiaukka and his lance until the sharp sting of a fresh wound reminded me. Yes—then I remembered everything.

"He cut a hole in you wide enough to reach inside and pull your bowels out by the coil, brother. They have sewn you closed now, but it was a messy business and there was much blood poured onto the earth. The wound turned putrid, and you have been many days delirious with fever, but it is broken now."

"How many days?"

"Daiaukka has been feeding the crows now for ten days. Until this morning, we thought you would be another course in the banquet. It was a close thing."

"My horse—what of Ghost?"

"A bit torn, but alive and well." Tabiti laughed softly. "Did you know that he killed the big black? He got him down and kicked in his ribs like the walls of a chicken house. He is a fine animal, that horse of yours. Let me have first chance if you decide to sell him."

"I will never sell him. He saved my life."

"I know he did—he and that *sedu* of yours. I do not think you are meant to die for a long time, brother."

He leaned a little closer, like a man with a secret.

"For some days now their sorcerers have been telling the Medes that you would recover. They say that Daiaukka was a fool to do battle with one who cannot die, and no one contradicts them. It is a marvelous thing."

He said no more, for he saw that his words pressed in on me. Instead, he gave me the wine to taste again—perhaps there was something more mixed in with it than water, for soon I fell asleep again, a true sleep this time. It lasted for three or four hours and at its end I felt stronger.

It seemed that, yet again, and for some purpose of their own, the gods had spared me.

In the days which followed I had no visitors except Tabiti,

the boy Khshathrita, and, once or twice, Lushakin. Command of
the northern army was in his hands, and he did not trouble me
with its concerns. A month passed before I was called upon to
remember that I was *rab shaqe*. I had first to remember that I was
alive.

The end of that month saw the arrival of perhaps the last
person I might have expected to find in the wilderness of Media,
for one morning, as a spoonful at a time I was fed the breakfast of
barley gruel that was deemed to be the only food my poor punc-
tured guts could tolerate, I heard someone outside my tent talking
to the guard, begging to be admitted.

Suddenly the voice was a bellow, swearing ferociously—and
in Greek! There was the sound of a scuffle, and the flap came
springing open, letting in the bright sun and my friend and servant Kephalos.

"Master, may the gods of the west, the lords of all true
magic, be praised that I find you alive!" he said as, with great
difficulty, for he was as fat as ever, he knelt by the cot and kissed
my arm, weeping like a woman. His clothes and beard were dusty,
and he smelled of the sweat of many days, yet there was no one
the sight of whom could have been more welcome to my eyes.

"They told me five days ago, in a Cimmerian village near
Heshir, that you still breathed, but I hardly dared to believe it
could be true. I came as soon as the message rider reached Amat,
Dread Lord—I packed my medicine box and came. May Apollo
the Mouse God receive homage forever that he has spared you!"

He could speak no more, for his feelings got the better of him
and tears choked his voice. I wept too, touched by this display of
love and loyalty. We wept together. It was a most affecting scene
and did us both good.

An hour later, quite calm, a cup of wine in his hand, my
slave narrated to me the history of his journey.

"As doubtless you can imagine, the news of your victory in
battle and the defeat and death of the Median king was occasion
for much joy throughout the whole city of Amat. Some dreamed
of glory, some of the end of war and danger and the campaign tax,
and the harlots and shopkeepers dreamed of soldiers' booty—it
went almost as a thing unnoticed that you, Dread Lord, had suffered a grievous wound and even were reported in many quarters
to be dead already, but thus unsteady are the affections of men.

"I went to the *rab abru*, that son of a brothel keeper Marduk

Pashir—you did a foolish thing to leave him in command of the garrison, master, for the wicked little man hates you and plots with your brother the *marsarru* behind your back—and I asked, with that humility of bearing which is only proper in a slave, if I might be allowed an escort for the journey hither, and I found— you will hardly credit it—that I was refused!

"'I cannot spare the men,' he told me, with scant courtesy. 'I have been left short-handed as things are and cannot spare ten or even five able-bodied soldiers to go chasing off into the Zagros on some errand for a fat Ionian slave.'

"'I am physician to the *rab shaqe*,' was my answer. 'He lies gravely wounded and in peril of his life. I must have an escort that I may attend upon him.'

"'From what I hear, he is as good as dead even now. How long will it take you to reach his camp, do you think? Twenty days—provided your throat is not cut along the way. Save yourself the trouble, Physician. He will be bait for crows long before you ever see the outside of his tent.'"

Kephalos drew himself up, filling his chest with air, and thrust out his beard as if daring someone to pull it.

"You may imagine, Lord, what I told him then," he said.

"No, I cannot even begin to imagine—you must tell me."

His eyes narrowed for an instant, as if unsure whether I was perhaps not mocking at him, but then, apparently having decided that, one way or the other, he did not care, he extended his hand in the gesture of a king giving judgment.

"'And if he should not die—what then?' I asked him. 'Or if he should die a month from now through want of proper attention? I might remind you, Marduk Pashir, that the Lord Esarhaddon is not yet king in the Land of Ashur, and that the Lord Sennacherib loves his son and will not be behindhand in punishing any he might suspect of conniving in his death. I leave for the Zagros at sunrise, whether or not you see fit to provide an escort, and if I do not return you may trust that letters reporting this conversation will find their way to Nineveh!'

"And *you* may trust, master, that the escort was waiting outside my door in the morning."

This I believe was true, for Marduk Pashir, whom I knew to be one of my brother's creatures and hence did not care to have at my back in battle, was not the man to risk a king's wrath.

However, what Kephalos narrated of his subsequent adventures was too full of obvious lies to credit. During every hour of the rest of his journey, so he seemed intent upon convincing me, he was beset by marauding bandits and engaged in fierce skirmishes with the remnants of Daiaukka's forces, along with every other variety of nonsense he could think of. And each story, more fantastic than the last, displayed his courage and cunning in much the same way an old soldier might show you his battle scars. A month later, when I inquired of one of the soldiers who had made up his escort, I was assured that nothing had happened, that the journey had been without incident. I had known as much even as, that first day, I lay on my cot and listened.

Yet Kephalos had come. He had made a journey involving hardship and discomfort and, if not actual danger, certainly the threat of it, and all for my sake. Thus I listened to his lies without smiling, for Kephalos, although dishonest in all other things, was my true friend.

And I believe it possible that he did save my life, for I was still not free from attacks of fever and these Kephalos treated with such success that I never relapsed into the deliriums which had so threatened me during the first days after my wounding.

Besides, it was a comfort to have him by. He brought with him news of my mother and all the gossip of Nineveh, and I could speak freely in front of him, for he knew each of my secrets.

It was Kephalos who decided that I was not fit to attempt returning to Amat that summer, and he persuaded me to winter with the garrison at Zakruti. And so by the middle of Tisri—for the snows fall early in those mountains—I was laid out on a cart filled with straw and carried thither. It was a journey of only ten or fifteen *beru,* but it took three days. And when at last we arrived, and I slept within mud walls for the first time in four months, I was weary unto death.

The boy Khshathrita remained with us as a hostage throughout all that late autumn and winter, and between us there slowly developed a strange intimacy. It pleased him to come into my room of an hour and sit on a stool beside my bed for a little talk. He seemed to bear me no ill will for his father's death and, beyond this, to imagine that among his captors I alone, like himself the seed of a king and therefore summoned to greatness, truly understood his position. He expected much of himself, and it is no falsehood to say that he acquitted himself like a man, but, after all, he was still but a child. It did not require the powers of a soothsayer to divine that Daiaukka's son and heir was lonely.

Of his father, whom he held in vast admiration, he spoke much. Also, and with a child's enthusiasm, he described to me the customs and religion of the Medes, whom he regarded as the most virtuous of races. And in his innocence he told me many things about Daiaukka's plans for this new nation, the Aryan, the Beloved of the Ahura, destined to sweep before them the peoples of the world. It was from Khshathrita that I learned of the few years' grace which that dangerous man had been pleased to grant to the Land of Ashur.

"My father spoke of you much the night before his death," the boy told me. "He said that if it was not the Ahura's design to spare his life, then it would only mean that the Lord Tiglath, though an unbeliever, lived under the god's protection—this *sedu* of which your soldiers speak. He told me that I was to abide in peace with you and never to lead the nation against your king so long as you stood at his right hand. To this he bound me by oath. He did not feel I would be greatly hindered therein, for he said you will fall from favor in the reign of your brother."

"Perhaps then, my young friend, you are more to be feared even than was your father." I smiled, speaking in jest, for he was so very serious a child. "Perhaps then I should have you killed lest in later days you bring harm to the Land of Ashur."

"No—this would not be wise," he said, shaking his head. It was as if he had thought long and deeply on all contingencies. "I too have brothers, with whom I live on terms of affection. If I die, one of them will certainly succeed me, and they are bound by no oath."

"Thus it seems I must take what I can get. But can you say truly that it is in your power to enforce this peace upon the tribes?"

"Oh yes, for I am the *shah* now. It will yet be a few years before I am able to make my will felt, but it will be longer before any among the Aryan have much yearning for war."

Green though his years were, the boy had wisdom. He had learned already that understanding of men and power for which there is no word in my native tongue but which the Greeks call "politics."

We became very good friends, Khshathrita and I. When at last I was able to leave my bed and, finally, walk about a bit with

the aid of a stick, we spent much time together exploring the
environs of Zakruti, which otherwise was as forsaken a place as I
ever hope to see. I grew quite fond of him, envying Daiaukka so
fine a son, and I hoped it might never prove necessary to have him
put to death, for it would afflict me to give the order.

Gradually the time of my convalescence passed. Soon I was
able to attend to correspondence for a few hours every afternoon
and to conduct business. There was a hard frost the day I assumed full command of the garrison. I felt the cold bitterly, for it
seemed to settle in my wounds—there has not been a winter since
when that old scar has not troubled me—but I was healed and
gaining strength. By the time the snow began to trickle over the
rocks, I was able to sit a horse once again and could even go
hunting.

But even before I was able to do much more than sit in the
doorway of my house with a blanket over my knees, I was receiving delegations from the tribes, even from those who had taken no
part in the fighting, come to Zakruti to offer their subjection.
They piled the ground with treasure and bowed low, for it appeared that by the bare act of surviving Daiaukka's lance I had
attained something like the status of a god, an evil spirit perhaps,
but one best placated with offerings and homage. As soon as they
left me, of course, they went straight to the boy Khshathrita and
pledged their allegiance to him—he told me of this himself and, of
course, I was having him watched—but I could not blame them
for this. I was the army of Ashur within the Zagros Mountains
and my power of life and death was absolute. But the boy was
their *shah* and they gave their hearts to him.

When the spring came, and with it the time approached for
me to return to Amat, a delegation of the *parsua* arrived to collect
Khshathrita. I gave a banquet, at which these mountain chiefs sat
about uncomfortably, unsure how to behave in the presence both
of their conqueror and their sworn lord, and the next morning, on
what turned out to be his tenth birthday, the *shah-ye-shah* and I
parted as friends.

It was not many days after this that I ordered the garrison at
Zakruti to prepare for the march home. We had stayed in these
eastern lands long enough.

It was neither an eventful journey nor a quick one. Except in
time of war, an army of three thousand men moves at a leisurely
pace, and I was not yet so recovered that I did not find so many

hours of riding a strain. Kephalos complained most bitterly that he had not been raised up to be a caravan driver, and finally he developed such sores on the insides of his thighs that he had to ride in a wagon. We reached Amat in just a few days under one month.

Many clay tablets from Nineveh were waiting on my desk. The first one I read was from the Lord Sennacherib:

> You will be pleased to learn that the Lady Esharhamat has whelped another son, one whom, this time, the Lords of Decision look upon with favor. So our brother the Lord Donkey at last has an heir, although he does not seem greatly pleased. I will say nothing, except that the Lady Esharhamat had honored me with her confidence and that I have caused the child to be given the name Ashurbanipal.

So the child of which Esharhamat had told me was born— our child. And the king knew.

Ashurbanipal. "Ashur has given a son as heir"—that was what the name meant. I would not be surprised if Esarhaddon was displeased.

But I was pleased. My son, who would one day be king of the world. Our son, Esharhamat's and mine.

32

The next summer and autumn were quiet and, if not happy, then at least contented. Each day had its business, but the inner history of my life was largely a blank. My mother returned to Amat and to her place as mistress of the *shaknu*'s palace, and she, Kephalos, and my friends within the garrison were almost my only society. Once in a while some visitor would arrive, but these interruptions were brief. I preferred it thus. I did not return to Nineveh. From time to time rumors would reach us of one intrigue or another, but at such a distance—and in the blindness of my heart—I found it easy to ignore them. I did my work and enjoyed my little pleasures, and the world, for its part, left me largely to myself.

All this was to change, abruptly and forever, on the first day of the month of Sebat, with the arrival of a dispatch rider from the palace garrison commander in Nineveh.

He came late at night—his horse, I heard the next morning, dropped dead from exhaustion as soon as it was inside the fortress walls—and his message, he told the watch officer, could not wait. I was awakened by a frightened housemaid and gave orders that I would receive our visitor in the palace audience chamber.

He was a *rab kisir,* a young man, no doubt the son of some great family whose people had had him appointed to the *quradu* as the first step in a distinguished career. He was handsome, personable, and graceful in his movements, and doubtless he had never been near a real battle. That, however, was probably no fault of his.

"Prince, my message is for yourself alone," he said, glancing with suspicion at the officers who had accompanied me to the meeting. He had already been searched and relieved of his sword, so I was in no danger of assassination. I dismissed my officers, with a caution that they should remain within call.

"Why had he called me 'Prince'?" I found myself wondering. It was a breach of military etiquette not to have addressed me by my army rank.

As soon as we were alone he fell to one knee, as he might have in the presence of the king.

"The Lord Sennacherib is dead," he announced, not lifting his eyes from the floor. Yes, of course.

"When?"

"These ten days ago."

"Why did you wait? A good horseman can make the ride from Nineveh in five days."

"There were disturbances in the city. The garrison commander thought it best . . ."

"To let the situation clarify first? I see. Then the king is dead and there is a 'situation.' " I struggled to keep my face an impassive mask, but what did I really feel? Shock, yes—but what else? I did not know. "There was no warning? Did my father meet with some accident?"

I knew the answer even as he raised his head to speak. I could see it in his face.

"My Lord . . ."

"Yes—speak!"

"The lord king was murdered."

He regained his feet. We stood facing one another for a long moment, both silenced by the awful knowledge that someone—for now, at least, some man with neither face nor name—had dared to raise his hand against the Chosen One of Ashur. The fact itself, the sheer incomprehensibility of it, left room for nothing else. I knew neither grief nor fear nor anger. These emotions were too narrow to hold me, no less than if the earth had rent itself asunder at my very feet.

"How did it happen?" I asked finally, surprised at the sound of my own voice. "Where . . . ? How did it happen?"

"He was at worship in the house of Shamash. Someone—it is not certain who—took one of the idols of the lesser gods and used it to club him to death."

It was as in my dream, I thought. The future which had been

revealed to me upon Ashur's holy mountain—and which I had not understood. My father, crushed beneath the god's wooden hand.

"Unholy act . . ." It was all I could find words for. What manner of man stood in so little fear of heaven that he could do such a thing? "Unholy, wicked deed . . . Who? If you know, tell me—quick!"

I had the messenger by the collar of his tunic and was shaking him as a dog shakes a rat.

"Who, damn you? Speak!"

"My Lord Prince, I know not. I . . . It is not certain . . ."

Yes, of course he knew. I released my grip on him and let the wrath in my liver quiet.

"Who?" I repeated, more calmly now.

"The belief is that your royal brothers Arad Malik and Nabusharusur . . ."

Yes, of course. What an idiot I was not to have guessed. Who else could it have been except Arad Malik, too stupid to see the enormity of the crime, and clever, pitiless Nabusharusur, who feared neither god nor man? Naturally, those two—one could only wonder what had taken them so long to act.

"And there have been disturbances?"

"Yes, Prince. The city is in open insurrection." He nodded quickly, as if confirming his own words. "The garrison commander begs to know your intentions."

"My intentions?"

What was the man talking about? I was nearly thirty *beru* away, and over rough terrain. It would take me a week to reach Nineveh with an army—what could my intentions possibly matter?

But perhaps I was merely being obtuse. The embarrassed look that came into the *rab kisir*'s eyes implied as much.

"Prince, perhaps . . ." He broke off, taking a deep breath. One might have imagined he was preparing himself for judgment. "The fact is, Arad Malik is threatening to proclaim himself king. He may already have done so by now, and if the rebellion is raised in his name . . . Prince, how can you imagine that anyone really wants Arad Malik on the throne of Ashur?"

My intentions. While the *rab kisir* waited for his question to be answered, I considered, for the first time, the importance that must now be attached to my intentions.

Because, of course, the garrison commander was no friend to the *marsarru*—why had it only just occurred to me that Esarhaddon was now the king?—and he was asking me to declare myself. The garrison, it was implied, was remaining neutral, moving neither to support the insurrection nor to suppress it, until he heard from me.

So he had sent this elegant young man, who was too wily to put the thing into so many words but was nonetheless waiting to know if I was prepared to accept the army's support and declare myself king.

I was being invited to lead the rebellion against Esarhaddon.

And, of course, the *rab kisir* was still waiting for an answer to his question.

"You may tell the garrison commander," I began, weighing each word as if many lives might hang on it, which was no less than the case, "you may tell him that my intentions are to write a letter of condolence to the lord *marsarru*—pardon me, to the king —in which I will pledge to him all the obedient loyalty which he has a right to expect from a subject and a member of his own family."

"Then you will not . . . ?"

"No, I will not." I fixed him with a stare that implied astonishment that he could even wonder. "But I will do this—I will advise the garrison commander that he would do well to bring the city of Nineveh to good order and to arrest the traitors Arad Malik and Nabusharusur. Otherwise, the Lord Esarhaddon might draw unfortunate conclusions."

"I see. Have you no other message, Prince?"

"None."

At the word he drew himself to attention and made his salute. Then he turned on his heel and left my presence. What finally became of him I know not, for I never saw him again.

In all likelihood my officers were just outside the door, waiting for me to summon them. But I did not summon them. I was unprepared to speak to anyone, so I returned to my rooms and had a slave bring me a jar of wine. I needed time to think and I needed something to steady me.

Had I been right to answer as I did? And, more important, had I been wise? These questions filled me, yet I kept returning to the same inescapable conclusion—that I had had no choice. The time for rebelling against my brother's succession was during the life of our father, when I could have made my ascendancy so compelling that Esarhaddon would not now dare to question it. Now I would invite nothing except civil war and, possibly, the ruin of the empire. I had made my decision long ago, and it was too late to alter it now.

Yet what would become of me now that the king was dead? I had no illusions about Esarhaddon—the fact that I had not joined in this foolish rebellion against him would not save me. I would not be forgiven. The moment he felt strong enough to act, he would avenge himself for the wrong I had done him by existing, and standing first in our father's eyes.

But perhaps that moment might never come. Perhaps he would think again before challenging the *shaknu* of the north, the *rab shaqe* of a vast army staffed by officers loyal to their commander. In Amat, so far from Nineveh and Calah, so remote from the councils of state, I was not much of an irritant. Perhaps he would prefer not to run the risks involved in satisfying his bad temper. Perhaps he would be content to leave matters as they were.

I would wait. I would write my letter, a letter which contained both my pledge of loyalty and a reminder, if one was needed, that the northern army had not spent the last four years growing soft on barracks food. I would see what answer my brother made and act on that.

And if Esarhaddon should be foolish . . . ? Then, I was not sure what I would do.

The wine was no help. I drank four cups, one straight after the other, and they did nothing except send me to the night pot to empty my bladder. When I returned to the audience chamber I found my officers assembled there, waiting for me.

"The king is dead," I told them. "The Lord Esarhaddon now reigns in his place. There is some unpleasantness in Nineveh, but that is no concern of ours. The next seven days will be a period of mourning—tomorrow, when the announcement is read at parade, it will contain nothing except the fact that the king is dead. Now return to your beds."

They left, without anyone offering to speak. Perhaps they had expected something more, or perhaps they could read the future better than I and did not like to say so.

I went out onto the balcony on the palace's eastern side and saw that the sky was already turning pearly gray. My mother would be up now and should be told.

She wept. Somehow I had not expected it. She covered her face with her hands and wept.

"He was my lord," she said, when at last the tears were spent. "He was my lord, the father of my son. It seems strange that he should be dead."

I sat with her awhile and then went out to the garden, where the only sound was the distant clamor of servants in the kitchen. Merope was right. It did seem strange that the king should be dead. It was the first I had thought of it except as a matter of state —the man who had sired me was at that moment dust in his tomb. I sat on a stone bench, trembling like a plucked bowstring while my overstretched nerves took their revenge.

Over the next several days dispatch riders—and sometimes ordinary officers and men who, for one reason or another, had deserted from their garrisons and found their way to Amat—kept us well informed of events in the south. Arad Malik had indeed proclaimed himself king and, what was more surprising, the Nineveh garrison had taken his side. Esarhaddon had marched to Ashur to assume the throne, and in both that city and Calah the garrisons had pledged their loyalty. Mardin, Tishkhan, and Samsat, along with many other cities in the west, where Esarhaddon's policies toward Babylon were unpopular, had joined the rebels, but the garrisons of the south were all sending detachments to fight with the rightful king. There was to be civil war. I had had no hand in it, but it was to happen just the same. It was even possible—something which was pointed out to me by more than one of my officers—that I could have prevented it had I chosen differently. A man may think and do as he will, and in the end the gods will have all their own way.

Thus I watched events unfolding at a distance. As the first step in claiming his inheritance, Esarhaddon marched on Nineveh with an army of some twenty thousand. The garrison there, seeing themselves outnumbered, abandoned the city and withdrew to a town on the upper Euphrates called Khanirabbat, whither the rebels were collecting their strength. When Esarhaddon once occupied our father's palace, so I was told, a man could almost walk across the Tigris on the waterlogged corpses of those among

Nineveh's citizens whom he had ordered punished for their disloyalty.

My letter to the new king contained all that was proper—praise of the Lord Sennacherib, congratulations, and a pledge of loyalty. I did not mention what I knew of the revolt. I made no offers. If Esarhaddon required help from my armies in this civil war, he only needed to ask. I would wait, I decided, until I was asked. I would not throw myself at my brother's feet.

Yet no word came. The month of Sebat was held over, and still Nineveh was voiceless.

I went hunting nearly every day. There was a hard frost on the ground and precious little game, but it was a way to distract my thoughts from the impending storm and to be alone—I was weary of being watched by men with questions in their eyes: "What will you do, *Rab Shaqe*? What will you do?" The wild deer in the mountains west of the frozen river did not inquire into their future or mine. They also hardly ever showed themselves.

Since my convalescence I had taken to eating a midday meal —a man develops bad habits when he lies about all day being told to conserve his strength, yet it was true that I still needed the extra flesh. On this one day I tethered Ghost and sat down behind a break of stunted, wind-twisted trees to open my leather bag and see what Merope had provided against starvation. I was busy gnawing on a strip of cured and peppered beef when I saw a solitary rider approaching, purposefully but without hurry, his face concealed by the cowl of his tunic.

He reined his horse in some thirty paces distant and seemed ready to wait quietly until I acknowledged his presence. He was carrying no weapon, and there was nothing in his manner which implied a threat. I held up my wineskin for him to see.

"Stranger, if you thirst . . ."

He pushed the cowl away from his face. It was Nabusharu-sur.

Yes, of course I was surprised. He smiled his strange, mirthless smile, as if he had won a victory.

"My spies reported that you came here nearly every day," he said. "I thought it worth the risk to catch you alone."

"Have you 'caught' me then, brother?"

"It is only a manner of speaking, Tiglath. I want nothing but to have a private word or two—will you grant me so much as that?"

"You are the murderer of our father and king, and a traitor to his heir. I should grant you nothing except the length of my sword under your ribs."

"Yet you will hear me, brother."

"Yes, I suppose I will."

He dismounted and let the reins fall to the ground—his horse, I noticed, was a gelding, so perhaps they enjoyed an understanding.

When he sat down beside me I offered him the wineskin once more and he accepted it, drinking deeply. We had, after all, known each other from childhood.

"The cold," he said. "I feel it, perhaps more than you."

"I feel it too. It creeps into my wounds and makes them ache."

"I heard that you almost died in the east."

His smile was at once solicitous and, perhaps without his realizing it, mocking. Yes, he would give the great vain fool this chance to tell his soldier's stories.

It is a mistake to hold other men in such utter contempt. I waited in silence.

"There will be civil war," he began at last, when he saw that I did not mean to speak. "There will be a great battle, perhaps only days from now. Esarhaddon is marching north already. It could have been prevented, if you had listened to me."

"It could have been prevented if you had not murdered the king, Nabusharusur. If you had but stayed your hand we could all now be quiet, and our father would be alive."

"It was necessary. Besides, I did not kill him—I was there, but Arad Malik struck the blow."

"Which he would never have thought to do without you to show him the way. Do not split words with me, brother." I stopped, and took a swallow of wine, telling myself there was no point in losing my temper.

"Why was it 'necessary' to kill the king?" I asked finally, when I was once more in control of my voice.

"Because he had yielded to Esarhaddon. The walls are already going back up around Babylon—they are rebuilding the city."

"Why should you care about that? You, who dread the gods so little that you could murder the king."

"You are right, I do not fear the gods." Nabusharusur made

a gesture with his thin hand, as if dismissing the whole of heaven.
"I do not tremble before idols of wood—why should I? Do you
believe the gods are real, Tiglath? Do you?"

He shrugged his shoulders.

"I believe what I can see. I believe the walls are going up
around Babylon. I believe the king had resigned his power to
Esarhaddon because he was old and no longer cared what happened in the world outside his palace garden. And who is to
blame for that, brother, if not you?"

"I . . . ?"

"Yes, you. The king died in his heart when he saw that Esarhaddon and not you must follow him."

"And now you would make Arad Malik king."

"Yes, if need be. Arad Malik is preferable to Esarhaddon, if
only because he does as I bid. And he is not Esarhaddon—that is
why men follow him, because he is not Esarhaddon."

"And you would have the nation make war on itself to place
one fool on the throne in place of another."

"Yes, if need be. Yet that is up to you, Tiglath."

There was the inevitable pause, during which I had just time
to ask myself, Why am I listening to this? Perhaps because it was
something I wanted to hear.

Nabusharusur, who was nothing if not cunning, gave me just
time to frame the thought, and no more.

"The armies are massing to the west of here," he went on, as
if he had only paused for breath. "They are evenly matched, and
there will be great carnage at the battle—and perhaps after as
well. Do you remember when we were boys, Tiglath, and Esarhaddon, when he could not read the lesson, threw the tablet at
old Bag Teshub's head?"

"Yes. I remember."

"Nothing has changed. What Esarhaddon does not understand, he destroys. He does not understand this rebellion, the
reason for it, and if he triumphs he will destroy half the nation
trying to salve the wound to his pride. Besides, as I said, the
armies are evenly matched, and who knows better than you that
at such times men drive pity from their hearts?"

"There is nothing I can do."

"Is there not?"

As I sat there on the cold ground, the wineskin between my
knees, I tried not to understand. I stared out at nothing, trying to

blank my mind so that this viper would have no power over it. I would not accept the blame he wished to heap on me. I would not . . .

Nabusharusur smiled, as if he knew how it would end.

"There are many who follow Esarhaddon without loving him," he continued, glancing away. "They know not what else to do, since they cannot side with Arad Malik without embracing the man who slew their king. And, as I said, Arad Malik's only claim is that he is not Esarhaddon. But say the word, Tiglath, but proclaim yourself king, even at this hour, and Esarhaddon's strength will melt away like spring frost."

"And what of Arad Malik? Will he 'melt away' too?"

"Leave that fool to me."

"Will you find someone to kill him too?" I asked, turning to look into Nabusharusur's face, allowing myself to smile at him—he could read in it what he would. "Will he go the way of our father the king? And then after him, who else? Me?"

"After him, it is not I who will have power, Tiglath, but only you."

"Yet you would make me responsible for my brother's death—for two brothers, Arad Malik and Esarhaddon both."

Nabusharusur merely shrugged.

"Two must die in any case. You must choose which two, no matter what you decide—Arad Malik and Esarhaddon, or Arad Malik and myself. I do not say the choices are easy, only that they are yours to make. Yours, and no one else's. And you cannot evade them, for to evade is itself a choice. But here is something you might consider—if it is Esarhaddon whom you elect to spare, perhaps you too will at last find your head between your feet. Esarhaddon hates you, or perhaps it had slipped your mind."

He rose, brushing the earth from his tunic with a careless gesture, as if all this mattered not at all.

"I do not expect an answer now, brother," he said. "Think of it, and when I see you in the field I will know which way you have chosen—if you can bring yourself to choose."

He mounted his horse and rode away, vanishing into the distance.

And finally, at what was almost the last possible moment, I received a reply from Nineveh. It was addressed to me not by name but only as the garrison commander at Amat and *shaknu* of the northern provinces, and it was not what I would have expected:

> The king commands that a force numbering 25,000 men shall be assembled from the fortress at Amat, and from those in Zamua and Namri, and that this force shall proceed with all haste toward the town of Khanirabbat in the province of Gozan, there to join with an army under the king's own authority. And this no later than the last day of the present month.

There was nothing else, no acknowledgment of my letter, no word to suggest that I was more than simply another faceless field officer in the king's service. The signature was that of one Sha Nabushu, whose name was unknown to me.

I could hardly credit it. That Esarhaddon had intended the insult was clear enough, but had his only object been to goad me into the arms of his enemies, he could not have hit upon a likelier means. That my brother meant to hold me in contempt was no surprise, but even simple prudence should have made him conceal his purposes a little longer.

Twenty-five thousand men he asked for—rather, demanded. Twenty-five thousand men would deplete the northern garrisons to dangerous levels, but presumably, with a civil war on his hands, Esarhaddon would not worry about that.

I sent off dispatch riders at once, summoning the required forces to proceed by forced march to Amat. What I would do with them when they arrived, I had no idea.

Such matters cannot remain secret very long in a garrison of soldiers, and by nightfall there probably was not a soul in Amat who did not know of Esarhaddon's letter. And as always, and in everyone's eyes, was the same unspoken question: "What will you do, *Rab Shaqe*? What will you do?"

But one voice, however, presumed to make its advice heard, and that belonged, naturally enough, to Kephalos.

"There are now only two possible courses of action open to you," he said, having chased away the slaves who had been serving us our dinner—I had been invited, on two hours' notice, to spend the evening with him, so his intentions had been plain enough.

"The Lord Esarhaddon's order means that you may no

longer remain here in Amat preserving your neutrality. If you do so, then no matter who wins you will be a traitor, and if it is your brother he will doubtless march his army straight to our door as soon as he has dealt with the rebels. I would expect his forces to be in number vastly superior to your own."

"His troops would be exhausted and weakened, where mine would be fresh. Besides, Esarhaddon has little experience of command. I would not be afraid to meet him in the field, no matter if he brought fifty thousand men."

"That is only your wounded pride speaking—you know your words are foolish. Besides, you would never subject the nation to two civil wars, one right after the other. No, you must choose now."

I nodded wearily, staring into my wine cup, sick of life.

"This is so," I said. "Everything you say is truth."

"Then what will you do? You hold the balance in this conflict. Whichever side you favor will triumph. You can make Esarhaddon king, or you can put a ring through his lips and drag him back to Nineveh behind your chariot. Which shall it be?"

Always one returned to the same question: "What will you do, *Rab Shaqe*? What will you do?" And still I had no answer. I could only shrug my shoulders.

"You must remember, master, that you will stand in the greatest peril if you side with Esarhaddon. He will not be grateful."

"Someone else told me that, only a few days ago."

"Then someone else besides your poor slave sees the truth. I know not if Esarhaddon will require the breath from under your ribs, master, but he will surely end all that makes life sweet to you. You and all your friends will be made to suffer."

He pulled at his great brown beard and looked at me with eyes full of supplication—I knew precisely what he meant.

"Besides," he went on, straightening himself and taking a sip of wine, as if these were not matters which touched either of us, "you would make a better king than Esarhaddon. If Esarhaddon is king, it will be the magicians and soothsayers who rule—they and the Lady Naq'ia. You, at least, are half a Greek and therefore less a prey to these superstitious terrors."

"Am I?" I laughed, being unable to help myself. "It is the god's will that Esarhaddon follow the Lord Sennacherib on the throne of Ashur. That is the one fact to which my mind must forever return."

Kephalos reached across the table and put his hand on my arm.

"And if that is so, master, then I despair for us all."

In the gray light of dawn I could watch the companies assembling on the parade ground, eighteen thousand men. I would leave behind only five hundred until reinforcements could arrive from Zamua and Namri, and seven thousand of them would immediately follow my line of march to Khanirabbat. Even Kephalos was coming, although I had given him his release from slavery and arranged for him to travel with a trading caravan which would have carried him well beyond Esarhaddon's reach. But no, he would come.

"My recent adventures have hardened me to campaigning, Dread Lord, and, besides, if you are bent upon committing this folly I cannot leave you bereft of my advice."

He grinned rather halfheartedly, and looked about him like a man saying good-bye to the world. At this moment he was in one of the supply wagons, salving his terror with a wine jug. I would probably be the instrument of his death, yet never had any servant deserved better at the hands of his master.

It was a bitterly cold morning. The ground was encrusted with snow. It was not a good season for campaigning, but in the minds of common soldiers there is no season good for campaigning. And these men were going off to fight not barbarians who lived in tents but their own brothers—I could see it in their faces, that desperation which is born of civil war.

"It is a wicked day which brings this parting," my mother said, standing beside me wrapped in a fur-lined cloak. "I fear you do an evil thing, Lathikadas."

"To fight for Esarhaddon? Yes, Merope, it is an evil thing, but in this affair I do evil no matter what I do, and never more than if I do nothing."

"Can there be no going back?"

There were tears in my mother's eyes as she turned to me with this question to which she knew the answer as well as I. I said nothing, but merely folded her in my arms. Her sobbing was bitter and reminded me of the day when, as a child, I had left the house of women for the last time to stand before the king's judgment. Was it so different now?

"You have been a great man in the Land of Ashur," she said at last. "Your god has fulfilled his pledge. I despair of the days to come."

"Merope, I have gone to war many times before this. Try to be at peace in your mind."

"I cannot be at peace, for there is that inside me which says my eyes will never again be filled with the sight of you."

What was there to say when I knew that within the month my brother Esarhaddon might have my head on the point of his spear? The *maxxu's* words whispered again in my brain, that I had come to the season of partings. Could I tell her that? Hardly that. I could do nothing, except be silent.

I could not even tell her to flee if I should be killed, for she had said already she would not.

"If you die, why should I care what becomes of me?" she had asked. But perhaps Esarhaddon's anger would not reach so low as my mother. That hope would have to be enough.

I kissed her one final time and pulled myself from her embrace. Now I belonged not to her or even to myself, but to the god and a brother who hated me.

"Good-bye," I said.

Until I die my mind will carry the image of her face as she heard me.

I mounted Ghost and rode out through the fortress gates, the northern army, reluctantly, at my back. The crowds that had gathered along the road to see us off were silent. My mother was right—it was a wicked day.

And among the crowds I saw one face, for an instant only, before it disappeared. The brown face of an old man with eyes dead to the sun's light. Yet, in that moment, lost almost before I knew it had come, he seemed to smile, mocking me because I could not see with his eyes.

33

At another season of the year, the area around Khanirab-bat might have been pleasing enough, but in winter it was a picture of ugliness and desolation. The town itself was, of course, empty—and everywhere about, over the low hills and the plain that stretched down to the Euphrates, the grass was withered and yellow and the bare limbs of the few sparse trees trembled in the wind with the palsied motion of an old woman's fingers. The wind was almost the only sound one heard, for even the crows seemed to have departed.

Esarhaddon had established himself not three hours' march from the rebel encampment, yet the terrain was such that the two factions could hardly even see the smoke from each other's campfires. So the appearance of enemy patrols was an almost hourly occurrence and there had been several clashes even before I arrived, which was on the twenty-sixth day of Sebat.

Almost the first news I heard was that the king was in a great fright because the night before the royal star of Marduk had appeared surrounded by a yellow ring. The astrologers offered differing interpretations, but they agreed that this was an evil omen for the Land of Ashur—a safe enough conclusion on the eve of such a calamitous war.

I say "almost" the first news, because the first was that my brother would on no account receive me. I was to establish the northern army as a separate wing to Esarhaddon's left—the unlucky side—and to await his commands.

So be it. My tent was raised on a patch of rising ground, and my standard set before the entrance, but I did not venture out among the soldiers. I posted guards that none might be allowed admittance to me except Esarhaddon's messenger. I took my meals alone. I stayed apart, and my mind hatched out black thoughts like a serpent's eggs left to warm in the sun.

At last the king's herald came, but there were no silver ribbons tied to his staff of office—I was not even to be acknowledged as a member of the royal family. Behind him walked a fat little man with a sparse beard and the blank, protruding eyes of a frog. This, it seemed, was the Sha Nabushu who had presumed to send me orders in the king his master's name.

"You are relieved of your command over the northern army," he told me. "You are to enjoy the freedom of the camp and shall retain your rank of *rab shaqe*—for the present—but you are forbidden to take any part in the coming battle, even as a common soldier. It is a victory which shall belong to the Lord Esarhaddon alone."

I said nothing.

"Do you agree to this?" he asked, his voice challenging but also a trifle uncertain.

"Is my agreement required? I am the king's servant. It is for him to command and for me to obey."

Sha Nabushu's mouth curled into a smile, almost as if he could not help himself.

"Who is to assume command?" I asked.

For a moment the little man hesitated—did he imagine Esarhaddon might intend to keep this a secret? But it is ever so. The servants of foolish and changeable masters are always afraid.

"I have that honor," he replied finally. Yes—perhaps it was not only my brother whom he feared. "You will inform your officers of the king's orders and direct them to meet me here at the fifth hour after midday."

"They are not my officers now, and I am not in a position to give directions to anyone."

It seemed, for the moment, that we had reached an impasse. Sha Nabushu opened his mouth to speak and then, apparently, could not think of the words. I was delighted.

"Yes, of course," I said. "I will see to the matter."

My officers—mine no longer—were not pleased.

"Who is this puppy?" Lushakin asked. "Has anyone ever heard of him? How are we to expect men to risk their lives under the command of such a one?"

"The men will not serve. They recognize no authority except the *rab shaqe*'s. We shall have desertions."

"And we ourselves should be among the first to desert—this is an intolerable insult!"

"It must be tolerated," I said, as calmly as I could, for I was moved by their loyalty but must not show it. "It is the king's will."

"What is your will, *Rab Shaqe*?"

"That you meet with your new commander and obey such orders as proceed from the king's authority. That whatever your feelings may be concerning this business, or whatever is to follow, you will keep them to yourselves and warn your troops to do the same, for it is an easy thing for a man to cut his own throat with his tongue."

"And what of you, *Rab Shaqe*?"

"What of me? I should think my *simtu*, like every man's, is written on the god's tablet. Perhaps I shall learn soon enough what it is to be."

I parted from them then, taking each man's hand, for from this hour I must be as the dead. How else were they to preserve their own lives? And then I left. I put a bridle on Ghost and went for a ride into the surrounding hills. Even as I left the camp I was aware that there were two horsemen following me—I was not trusted out of my brother's sight.

The time of partings. Truly this was the time of partings and, as before, I had not seen it until it was upon me. The king my father, my mother, the army I loved as a man loves his wife, perhaps even my own life.

And, of course, Esharhamat. I had lost her first, yet she it was who filled my heart, even now.

I would never see her again. Now that he was king, Esarhaddon would wall her up in his house of women and I would never see her again. Never would she fill my eyes with her loveliness, as if I were blind or the light had gone out of the world. Then what else mattered, and what was there to fear in death?

I did the god's will, yet in my heart I cursed the god.

Esharhamat, Esharhamat—the name itself had all the sweetness of life. To live was to remember, and to remember to know pain. No, I had no fear of death. And the power of the king my brother became like a shadow. Let him do his will.

I stayed away from the encampment—it is hoped much to

the vexation of my two attendants, who kept five or six hundred paces behind me but did not trouble to conceal themselves—until well after darkness had fallen and the soldiers were settled comfortably around their cooking fires. Then, when I could be sure my tent would be once more my own, I rode back. The soldiers I met greeted me easily enough. They knew nothing of my fall from favor and perhaps would not care if they did, for to such the king was almost as distant as the gods themselves.

I ate a good dinner and kicked off my sandals to go to bed— it is wonderful how easy a man may be in his mind when he has resigned himself to death. I could wonder how Esarhaddon slept and I found I did not envy him.

The additional seven thousand soldiers would not arrive from Amat for two or three more days, but already the next morning I had only to look about me to see that, as if by magic, the king's forces had greatly increased in size. The stretch of open land between our encampment and that occupied by the main army was now filled in with makeshift tents and cooking fires. Perhaps as many as three thousand men had appeared, seemingly from nowhere. They were deserters from the rebels, come to make their peace with Esarhaddon while they still could.

It was the thing reasonable men would do. For the past few days at least, their scouts must have given the rebel commanders notice that the northern army was drawing near, and our intention of siding with the king must have been obvious. The balance was then clearly tipped in Esarhaddon's favor, and this, no matter how they tried, my traitor brothers could not have kept from those who had followed them into treason. And no sane man delights to throw his life away in a lost cause.

The soldiers I saw that morning, camped like beggars at Esarhaddon's door, were simply the first wave of deserters from Arad Malik's cause. There would be more—unless I was most seriously mistaken, there would be many more.

And Esarhaddon was not such a fool as to turn them away. He knew that an enemy, while it grows weaker when confronted by the corrupting hope of mercy, is only strengthened by desperation. Therefore, while they might never stand very high in their king's good opinion, these deserters from the rebel cause would be allowed to live and to serve. Esarhaddon would curse and threaten and then forgive them—most of them—and they knew it. And because they knew it, Arad Malik's army would quietly bleed to death before ever a sword was drawn against them.

So each night the sentries waited for the muffled sounds of men creeping through the darkness, singly or in twos and threes, officers and foot soldiers and cavalrymen on their war horses, and each night these would be made to huddle beyond the camp's earthworks while they waited, squatting apprehensively on the cold earth, for word of the Lord Esarhaddon's clemency. All night they might wait, with nothing behind them but the certainty of ruin and nothing ahead but such of safety as could be purchased by embracing my brother's knees and begging pardon, and finally, in the gray light of morning, they would be admitted, given breakfast, and allowed to sleep wherever they could find a place.

And they were grateful to Esarhaddon—even a dog is grateful to be allowed to live—but as I walked among them, seeing here and there a man whose face or even name was known to me, I saw always the same accusation in their beaten eyes: "Look at us, Prince Tiglath Ashur, favorite son of the Lord Sennacherib, your father who was lord of the world and true king in the Land of Ashur. Look at us, and see that to which we have been brought. Now we must bend our bodies before Esarhaddon— think what future faces us and the nation both. And for this we blame you, no one but you."

But at least these had a future. Some there were who came in the night and found only death, for the king's mercy was not for everyone. My brother had a long memory, as not a few were discovering who had spoken too rashly in the days of the Lord Sennacherib.

With other officers, I was called to witness the execution of one Zakir Nergal, who had been a *rab abru* in the Nineveh garrison and was a man of whom I knew no particular evil. Yet somehow he had offended against the king's majesty and was to pay the price of being roasted in chains, a traditional punishment, honored by custom, but one I had never heard of being employed during my father's lifetime. It did not promise to be a pretty spectacle.

Kephalos accompanied me, declaring his interest to be of a medical character. I warned him, but he would come.

"You need not concern yourself, master," he said, smiling as if at a child's fears, "for a physician is hardened to the sight of pain. I can assure you I have seen far worse things merely attending in my father's consulting room in Naxos—there is no occasion to worry about me."

We took our places around the punishment site, nothing more than a piece of bare earth where a great fire of logs had been burning since yesterday evening—it being a cold morning, we were glad of the warmth, although probably Zakir Nergal would not have agreed—and waited for the king's arrival. His chair was already there for him, and at last he came, glorious in his golden robes and his turban covered with gems. He sat down and looked about him, like the host at a banquet. If he saw me he gave no sign.

It was the first time I had beheld my brother in two years and, since it seemed unlikely that we would meet many more times before he made up his mind what to do with me, I was curious to see the change that kingship had wrought in him. He did not give the impression of a man who knew any great pleasure in glory.

Esarhaddon was even a little younger than I, yet already he wore that look of anxious doubt which I had seen so many times on our father's face. He sat, resting his cheek on the palm of his hand, and all the gold and jewels which were meant to dazzle other men's eyes could not disguise the uneasiness in his own. It would have been better if he had been allowed to live his life as a soldier, in accordance with the childhood ambition we had both shared, and I think he knew as much himself.

The fire had by this time been reduced to a bed of coals, a span or so deep and covered with a skin of ash but glowing red as blood beneath it. This had been raked into a circle and over it was raised a huge iron tripod, its legs wide apart and coming together some fourteen or fifteen cubits above the ground. At this apex there was an iron ring through which ran a long copper chain with a hook at one end.

Esarhaddon nodded. It was time for the entertainment to begin.

A guard of four men brought in the prisoner, who was trailing copper chains from his hands and feet—he kept rubbing his wrists, as if the manacles chafed him. I had known Zakir Nergal for ten years, but had I not been told in advance who was to suffer that morning I doubt I would have recognized him. Such is the change that can come to a man when he has had a whole night in which to contemplate the approach of death—especially such a death as this. Three days ago he had been in glory, a man of high rank around the usurper Arad Malik, and now this.

He looked dead already. His face was thin and haggard, and his eyes, wide, lifeless, and staring, suggested he hardly understood what was about to happen to him. And yet he was afraid. He was half mad with terror—if the guards had released their grip on his arms, I am sure he would have collapsed.

He said nothing. His mouth was open, but he was only panting for breath. He looked as if he had lost the power of speech.

We all drew ourselves up to attention as Esarhaddon rose to speak.

But the king my brother seemed also to have been struck dumb. He looked at the condemned man and his face flushed black with anger, but he could not find the words for this terrible wrath that held him as fast as the copper chains around Zakir Nergal's wrists and ankles. At last he sat down again, defeated, and with a distracted wave of his hand signaled that the thing might now begin.

All this time Zakir Nergal had been staring at the iron tripod, as if he could not comprehend what purpose it might be there to serve. He was marched almost to the foot of the coal bed and then forced down on his knees—it did not require much force. The chains that bound him were linked together behind his back, each end clamped to an iron ring. This ring in turn was hung on the hook at the end of the chain that ran up to the tripod's apex. While Zakir Nergal knelt beside the burning coals, the guards began to pull on the chain so that he was hauled up like a well bucket.

It was then that he found his voice. His screams of panic tortured the very air.

They did not give Zakir Nergal a quick end. At first, as the chain pulled him up, he swung out over the bed of coals, but that was to be no more than a first taste. The guards quickly raised him until, dangling belly-down, he was almost at the top of the tripod, where he could feel the fire's heat only a little more sharply than we who watched.

Slowly, half a cubit at a time, they lowered him down toward the coals. He was so hoarse now that his screams could hardly be heard, but he was still very alive, twisting this way and that, trying to escape—to what, one wondered, when to be free of his chains was to fall straight to the burning death which awaited him? But a man will struggle to escape death, and when there is no escape he will struggle just the same.

Slowly, he came closer and closer to the fire.

He was still alive, still conscious, when the blisters began to rise on his face and neck—huge things, full of water and blood. Then his hair started to smoke, and then burn, and then his clothes. Yet he was still alive, still writhing in his chains, when the guards decided he was close enough and anchored their end of the chain to the ground with an iron pin.

At last he was still. It seemed to take hours, but the spectacle of his agony lasted probably only a few minutes. A man will not die so quickly as that of burns alone, so perhaps he smothered in the thin, white smoke. He dangled there, perhaps the height of a man above the glowing coals, lifeless, burning like a joint of meat left unattended. When the flesh from one foot simply sloughed off, allowing the bone to slip through the manacle, I heard a choking sound beside me. I turned and saw Kephalos, his head between his knees, unburdening himself of breakfast.

Esarhaddon did not stir. He watched, never letting his eyes look away from this horror he had commanded, his face a blank mask. It seemed he had learned that much about being a king— that he was not allowed to feel anything.

When he was satisfied, he rose from his chair and dismissed us. No one was eager to stay. I took Kephalos back to my tent and gave him small sips of wine until he could stop sobbing. It had not been what he had expected.

"By the gods," he said at last, "you are a brutal race, you Assyrians."

I could only smile, although my heart was far from merry.

"I suspect it is the same everywhere," I said. "Esarhaddon is no worse than many. It is the justice of kings."

Yet the justice of kings did not check the nightly pilgrimage of deserters from the rebel army. Each morning found them camped outside the earthworks in still greater numbers, and if Esarhaddon's craving for revenge snatched off some few of these, others lived, and all were willing to try their luck.

The executions continued. The iron tripod was in daily use, and there were times when the smell of roasted flesh hung over

the camp like a pall. I do not fault Esarhaddon for this, since it
was wise policy to offer examples of what the law demands from
traitors. Hedged about by rebellion, he could not afford to seem
weak. Yet I believe the deaths of many could have been traced not
to wisdom but to fear. My brother was trying to kill his own
doubts.

On the last day of Sebat I received a message. A friend, one
Sinqi Adad, who had recanted his allegiance to Arad Malik but
had been denied clemency, was to swing over the coals the following morning—he had asked to see me.

"We were boys together," I told Kephalos. "He fought at
Babylon with us—he was as much Esarhaddon's friend as mine.
It is a cruel thing that he should die like this."

"It is a cruel thing that anyone should die like this," my
servant replied, with admirable clarity of mind.

"Yet I would prevent it if I could."

I looked at him questioningly, and Kephalos puckered his
face with misgivings. At last he nodded.

"It will be a bad thing should it be discovered," he said,
taking a small clay vial from his medicine bag. "Indeed, I had
meant this for you, should you come to grief, but do as you think
best, my foolish master."

I thanked him and left to pay my call.

Sinqi Adad was sitting in the mud, chained to an iron peg.
His hair and beard were matted with filth, and on his arms and
back were long bruises from where the guards had beaten him
with their spears. He looked exhausted and weak. It is not the
custom to waste food on condemned men, but I had brought
bread and wine with me and no one attempted to prevent me from
carrying them into the stockade.

I knelt beside him, holding out the loaf and the wine jar.
With shaking hands he tore off a corner of the round, flat loaf,
stuffed it into his mouth and washed it down with the wine. It was
several minutes before he was very much disposed to conversation, but at last, when the urgency of his hunger had abated a
little, he looked up at me with a sigh and nodded.

"My thanks," he said. "It doesn't atone for your throwing in
your lot with Esarhaddon, but I thank you just the same."

"I had always made it clear that I would honor the lawful
succession. No man has a right to say I misled him."

"Perhaps not, but men will always believe what they wish."

He grinned. Under the circumstances, it was a remarkable act of courage.

"Arad Malik, that gutter dog, you should have seen him when he received word that you had carried your army over to Esarhaddon's side. If the gods honored such a man's curses, what a death you would have died in that moment."

"Is it bad over there?" I asked, hardly knowing why.

"Bad?" He raised his eyebrows as if wondering what I could mean. "It is as bad as this place, only bigger."

With a gesture of his chained arm, he took in the perimeter of the stockade.

"When will Esarhaddon force the battle, do you think? Tomorrow? The next day? Everyone over there knows that there will be no escape if they are caught under that millstone. Already when I left, soldiers were cutting the throats of their officers. Yes, it is very bad."

"Then perhaps there will be no battle. Perhaps, when the moment comes, Esarhaddon will find his enemies on their knees."

"You were not always such a fool, Tiglath." He tore off another corner of the bread and ate it with savage ferocity, all the while looking at me as if he would have liked to tear out my heart as well. "There are some who would prefer an honorable death in battle to a lifetime of serving your brother and his Babylonian gods. I was weak, and stupid enough to believe I could buy my life with submission—you see what an error that was. And now I will die because once I told Esarhaddon to his face that he was not fit to be keeper of the king's pigeons, let alone king. Others, braver than I, will not risk the same fate."

Suddenly he let the bread fall into the mud and covered his face with his hands. He was sobbing.

"Oh, that it should all have come to this!" he said finally, brushing the tears away with his fingers—he smiled, for he was embarrassed. "And for the sake of Arad Malik . . . That is what rankles. Who would wish such a man king? He is no better than Esarhaddon, perhaps not even as good. But Nabusharusur—oh, how I curse the day I first listened to that gelded serpent."

"Why? What of him?" I shrugged my shoulders, understanding nothing. "What has Nabusharusur . . . ?"

Sinqi Adad, clasping my arm with both hands, shook it as if to rouse me from my slumbers.

"He told everyone that Arad Malik was only holding your

place, Tiglath. He made everyone believe that this rebellion was in your name!"

At last he released my arm and let his hands fall into his lap. All the strength seemed to leave him as he acknowledged the enormity of his mistake.

"Have I not said men will always believe what they wish?"

I reached into my pocket of my tunic and took out the vial Kephalos had given to me, keeping it hidden so that only Sinqi Adad could see.

"What is it?" he asked. I think at first he was only surprised.

"Take this before they come for you tomorrow."

"What is it? Poison?"

"No—I am not so brave as that. If I gave you poison to cheat the king of his spectacle I would end by taking your place in the fire. No, it is not poison."

"Then what . . . ?"

"It kills pain and fear. It makes death easy. You will die, but you will not suffer. Take it just before they come to fetch you, or its effects may not last long enough. And bury the empty vial in the mud when you have finished, or someone may guess."

He hid the vial under his ragged clothes and took my arm again.

"You take a dreadful risk, Tiglath—may the gods bless you for it."

"Let it stand as my rebellion against Esarhaddon. I am sorry to have failed you, my friend."

"We have failed each other, you no worse than the rest of us."

And thus we parted. I went back to my tent and hid my face from men. I did not go the next morning to see Sinqi Adad's end, but I was told he died bravely.

That night a messenger arrived from Arad Malik, asking terms for surrender. He came under a standard of truce, and Esarhaddon sent him back in a leather sack, cut by sword thrusts in a hundred places so that his corpse held hardly a drop of blood. Thus the rebels knew what they could expect.

It was clear that the battle, if there was to be one, must be soon—Esarhaddon would have felt himself cheated if there were to be no battle, so plans were rushed ahead. I was not asked to the staff meetings, but even a prince in disgrace is not without his informants, so I knew that orders had been issued to take the field the next morning, which was to be the second day of the month of Adar. And, beyond this, I was given instructions by Sha Nabushu.

"You will take no part," he told me, yet again. "You may not fight, even as a common soldier. The glory of this day shall be entirely the king's."

"So you keep saying. Yet do not fear—I will not make a shadow in the Lord Esarhaddon's sunlight. I shall be present as an observer only, since that is a penance I feel I owe to those who will die tomorrow, but I am just as happy to stay clear of this fight. You see, I have little taste for the butcher's trade."

It was not an answer which pleased, but there was no doubt that Sha Nabushu took my meaning. All the day long one could hear the sound of grindstones. Everyone knew of the wagonload of axes my brother had brought with him from Nineveh. Everyone could guess what they were for.

That night I was invited to Lushakin's tent, where the senior officers of the northern army, who tomorrow would fight under Sha Nabushu, were busy drinking themselves into a stupor. No one was afraid of losing—and, under such circumstances, it hardly occurs to a man that he might be killed, even by accident —but the mood was one of defeat.

"My wife's nephew was in the Nineveh garrison," one of them said. "He has not turned up among the deserters—what am I to say to her when I return to Amat?"

"We shall all have to wash our weapons and make purifying sacrifice. This kind of fighting stinks in the nostrils of the gods."

"They say that the Lord Esarhaddon plans to . . ."

I raised my hand to indicate I would hear no insult offered to the king, and everyone fell silent. I think they, too, in their hearts, blamed me for bringing them to evil days. I stayed only a little longer and then left.

And the next morning, in the gray light before dawn, my head was near split open by the blare of war trumpets.

"Why was I not awakened?" I asked, stumbling out of my tent with my corselet of copper armor plates still only half buckled. "And where in the Lady Ishtar's name is my horse?"

The orderly shook his head, as if ashamed to own it was all his doing.

"Taken away last night, *Rab Shaqe*," he said. "They left you

a brown mare in his place, but you won't find much to praise
about her. She's the next thing to crow bait."

"My horse?" I squinted at him, hardly able to credit it.
"They took my horse?"

"Yes, *Rab Shaqe*—you see, it is known by sight . . ."

Yes, of course. Esarhaddon would have to assure himself
that, even if I should decide to follow the battle from a distance, I
would be as one invisible.

"Then put a bridle on the mare."

She almost was the next thing to crow bait. There was nothing covering her shoulder bones but hide and I suspected she
would probably drop dead if somehow I forced her to a gallop.
Yet, since I had no intention of making such demands on her, she
would do well enough. She was a match for her rider, for it
seemed that neither of us was fit for war.

I kept to a line of low hills, where I would be in no one's way,
staying somewhere between the main body of foot soldiers and the
cavalry companies who rode ahead to seek the initial contacts
with Arad Malik's army. And as the god has made me his witness, I will describe the terrible truth of that day, which saw so
monstrous and pointless a bloodletting. For the battle at
Khanirabbat was far less a battle than a simple massacre.

It was just an hour after sunrise when the first skirmishes
took place. The rebel horsemen were waiting in ambush and
staged a mass attack in Esarhaddon's cavalry. The rebels charged
in a body. Even half a *beru* away I could hear their war cries, and
for a moment they seemed to have plunged deep enough into their
enemy's battle groups perhaps to scatter them and carry their
point. Yet what can three hundred men do—and I wonder if they
had so many—against three or four thousand? And how do bees
overcome the solitary ferret that tries to raid their hive? The
king's horsemen swarmed over the rebels, engulfing them, leaving
them no escape. Within half an hour the fight was over and the
ground was strewn with horses and men, dead and dying, from
both sides. Yet there could be no doubt about the winner. That
was the last cavalry engagement of the day. The rebels had left
their last rider a corpse upon the withered grass.

Two hours later it was the infantry's turn. The rebels had
four or five and twenty battle squares, and these assembled in
haste from companies whose strength had been bled away by the
desertions of the last several days—not even three thousand men,

not a fifth part of their original numbers, proposing to do battle against Esarhaddon's army, perhaps by now seventy or eighty thousand strong.

I will not speak of tactics, for what are tactics when one man stands against twenty or thirty? The rebels were simply crushed—there is no other word. They fought bravely, as men will who know they have no choice except in the manner of their deaths, but they fought without hope.

By midday it was over, except for the killing. Esarhaddon's chosen men went over the field with their axes, hacking to death any of the wounded they could find and taking trophies from the fallen—a wagon rode around to collect the heads. Those few who were unlucky or foolish enough to be taken alive were treated with even less respect. The officers were flayed on the spot; they were pegged down on the first convenient piece of cleared earth and had their skins ripped off like rabbits. I counted at least forty who met this fate, and there were doubtless many I did not see. The common soldiers were spared for the moment. They were rounded up and taken away, but they had not escaped. I heard later that they were marched straight from the battlefield to Calah, a distance of some fifty or sixty *beru,* a distance which fresh and provisioned men could not cross in less than ten days, and these were without food and water. There the few survivors of this ordeal were set to work as slave labor making the mud bricks for Esarhaddon's new temple to the god Marduk. I wonder if one of them lived into the summer.

This is what happened at Khanirabbat. As I honor the gods of my fathers, this is the truth of it.

I saw all this from a distance, happy to be no nearer. Yet I reproached myself bitterly, for was I not the true author of this carnage? The omens had declared it the god's will that Esarhaddon should be king in the Land of Ashur, and I, because I scrupled to defy the god for the sake of a woman's love, had submitted. I do not pretend my motives were nobler—Esharhamat was all I thought of, and I gave her up, a sacrifice to my obedience.

Yet was this the god's will? His sons, the manhood of his nation, left for the feasting of birds and dogs? Had I truly obeyed, or had I so prided myself on the nobility of a gesture that I set all else at nothing? What had I done? I had left the decision of my own fate—of the fates of thousands, perhaps of the nation and the world beyond—to the entrails of a goat.

Some impressions stay with a man for life. I will never forget
the slaughter at Khanirabbat. I will never forget my sense of guilt
and shame. On that day the world became a different place for
me. I lost forever the final illusion of youth—that I could hold
myself free from sin.

The rest of the day, until the light failed utterly as the blood-
stained landscape could at last cover itself in the decency of darkness, patrols crisscrossed the hills looking for fugitives from Esarhaddon's revenge. I do not think that very many of these
escaped, but one did cheat the slave gangs and the executioner's
knife. For my brother Nabusharusur did not die at Khanirabbat,
although it was only the merest chance that I and no other found
him.

It was close to sunset. I had ridden about, almost at random,
more than for any other reason because I could not stomach the
prospect of returning to camp. I did not wish to look into the
guilty faces of murderers whom I had known all my manhood. I
wished to spare both them and myself that final humiliation. So I
let the brown mare wander where she would, only taking care to
keep away from the battlefield.

I passed by a great pile of boulders, stacked on top of one
another like onions on a dish. I stopped for a moment—for no
reason I can remember—and took a sip from the waterskin I
carried by a cord over my shoulder. I was expecting nothing,
looking for nothing, and suddenly I heard a sound. It was faint,
but still recognizable. It was the scrape of metal against stone.

I turned to look—I saw nothing. I listened again and heard
nothing. There was nothing. I was sure of it.

Then I looked again, into one of the deep crevices in that pile
of rock, and there I saw, dimly but unmistakably, the outline of a
human figure, crouched and hiding, still as death.

I drew my sword. Then I looked about, saw that there was
no one near, and put it back in its scabbard, feeling a fool.

"Come out. There is nothing to fear from me."

The figure moved. Gradually, into the dusty twilight, came
Nabusharusur. Whomever I had expected, it had not been he.

He sat down at the mouth of the crevice, still holding a
dagger in his right hand, and looked at me with an expression of
mingled disgust and relief.

"Nothing to fear from you. Brother, whatever it is that makes you say such things, whether in jest or earnest, I marvel at it. Nothing to fear from you—by the gods!"

He looked exhausted, as desolate as a beggar for all the gold bracelets on his arms. His fine wool tunic, which that morning must have seemed almost regal, was crumpled and filthy. Yet he was the same, that perverse pride of his unbroken.

"So, it is all over," he went on. "Give me a sip of your water, Tiglath—like a friend."

He drank greedily and then offered the skin to me again, but I bade him keep it.

"Thank you. And now you can do me another kindness and kill me before you take me back to Esarhaddon. Say to him you found me dead."

"Where is Arad Malik?" I asked, as much to turn the subject as out of any curiosity. Why should I have cared about Arad Malik?

"Gone—ran away yesterday. He did not even wait to hear Esarhaddon's reply to his offer of surrender, the coward. No one needed a gelder's knife to take that one's manhood. Is everyone dead?"

"Yes, almost. Those who are not soon will be, or will wish they were."

"I knew it was hopeless the day we talked in Amat. I knew you would not listen to me, for your ears are always buzzing with the sound of that voice which only you can hear. You think it is the god's, but it is not."

He shook his head, and a spasm of bitter laughter escaped him, like a cry of grief.

"You are a coward, Tiglath, worse even than Arad Malik, who at least had a moment of freedom when somehow he found the will to slay the king our father. Old loyalties fetter you like chains—and the fear that just once you might do a thing not because it is right but because your bowels yearn for it. Ever since you gave up the Lady Esharhamat, you have been in love with self-denial. I knew you would take Esarhaddon's side."

"Then why did you not flee?"

"Like Arad Malik?" He smiled indulgently, as if at a bad joke. "Eunuch though I am, credit me with some dignity, brother. No—I set this thing in motion and I must let it carry me where it would."

The smile died, giving place to something like a weary acceptance.

"And now kill me. I have lost, but I would as soon avoid paying the full price for that and I cannot be sure of having the courage to do myself what needs doing. Kill me, Tiglath."

Instead, I dismounted from the mare and put her reins in Nabusharusur's hands.

"I have enough on my conscience," I said. "Besides, I owe you my life in the matter of the slave girl Zabibe. Take the horse and flee—there is nothing to stay for now, and in the darkness you have a good chance of escape. Do not stop, not even for a day, until you are beyond Esarhaddon's reach."

He did not wait for me to make the offer twice, but climbed on the horse's back, slipping the cord of the waterskin over his shoulder.

"Do not imagine I am grateful, Tiglath my brother," he said —and, indeed, there was no way I could have mistaken the look of loathing hatred in his eyes. "Nor that this settles the account between us, for you are in debt for far more than your wretched little life. We would not all have come to this if you had sided with us. You still owe for what was done here today."

With a slap on the rump, I sent the mare into a canter and watched yet again as Nabusharusur rode away to an uncertain destiny. I could only hope that I would never see him again.

I walked back to camp in the dark, guided by the pale light of the cooking fires. When I reached my tent I found only Kephalos, his face set in the resignation of one who has witnessed every horror.

"It has been an evil day," he said. "My eyes have seen too much."

"Yes, it has been an evil day—even I am sick of war. Shall we depart from this place and go home?"

"Home, master? You mean, to Amat?"

"No, to Three Lions. I would sooner wait there than anywhere else until Esarhaddon decides on my *simtu*. All it requires is to find us horses."

We did not wait for morning. The battle ended, Ghost was tethered beside my standard, and I borrowed another for Kephalos. In the dark we set out, carrying lanterns on the ends of poles. The road south, after all this, was a pleasant place.

34

Inow assumed that I had come to the end of my life, and I wanted to be prepared. As soon as we had arrived at my estate I sent Kephalos on to Nineveh to fetch a scribe that I might put my affairs in order. He returned in three days, by which time I had settled with myself that it would be best to put Three Lions in my mother's name at once, since if I were declared a traitor my property would be forfeit to the king. My other holdings I would leave as they were, for to give a significant share of that vast wealth to anyone I cared for was quite simply to invite confiscation. As matters stood, provided his malice alone did not supply him with a motive, Esarhaddon would not proceed against my mother. I also put into my former slave's hands deeds empowering him to do as he thought best with the gold he had deposited with the merchants in Sidon and Egypt.

"I advise you make haste to be gone," I told him. "It will be a while before my brother remembers his grievances against you, but it will come."

"I could go home to Naxos and live as a rich man," he said, sighing heavily. "The Greek islands are the best places of all for a man to find his comfort and pleasure—the happiness of life, master. Could you not be persuaded to make your escape with me?"

"No. If I cheat Esarhaddon of his vengeance, where do you think the blow will fall?"

"You are thinking of the Lady Merope."

"Yes, of her. There is no time now to fetch her—doubtless I am still being watched at a discreet distance. I must stay."

"Then I too will stay. I will abide here at least until your fate is settled. Perhaps I may be of some use. And afterward there may still be time."

I embraced him and with tears of gratitude in my eyes told him it was my desire that he flee, but he would not listen.

"By my lord's will I am now a free man," he said grandly, "at liberty to go and come as it pleases me, and I have an inclination to see how all this is to be resolved. I will do as I think fit."

"Then think fit to go to Nineveh and see what can be learned there. You will be safe enough if you lose yourself in the crowds—the city is full of foreigners and one more will not be noticed."

This he did, leaving me alone to enjoy as best I could the final days of my liberty.

I would wait at Three Lions until Esarhaddon summoned me —this would be soon, for I knew he would not long be able to resist the temptation to have me beneath his hand, but I decided that until the moment came I would put him from my mind and live for my own pleasure. Thus I hunted every day, though in winter the game was scarce, drank more wine than was good for me, and slept as long and as well as I could. If my servants and tenants had any inkling of my troubles, they gave no sign. Life was almost pleasant.

I discovered, upon my return, that Naiba was the mother of a fine son, a hardy little boy who already walked about on fat little legs, and was with child again. She seemed happy, and so did her husband. It gave me some pleasure to think that not all of my deeds had ended in sorrow.

For, although I might stand blameless before the gods, that no longer seemed enough to wash away the guilt that somehow had stained me at Khanirabbat. Perhaps Nabusharusur had been right: I had believed myself to be hearkening to Ashur's will, and perhaps all this time it had been nothing more than the voice of my own fears.

My eunuch brother had been right in claiming that it began with Esharhamat. I had turned my back on her, imagining myself noble—how was it possible that I should be anything else when my heart bled so? And every year without her had seemed harder, another step farther into the darkness. Yet I had begun the journey and must go wherever it took me.

How could I do otherwise? As Esarhaddon came closer to the throne, his election as *marsarru* had seemed a greater and greater piece of folly, yet it had been proclaimed the will of heaven and all the more stubbornly had I believed it so. Having lost Esharhamat, how could I have admitted to myself that we had both placed so great a sacrifice upon the altar of destiny only to see it so rudely rejected? The more one pays for a thing, the dearer it becomes. That is what greed is, and it blinds one—it burns out one's eyes. I had become blinded by a greed of the spirit, so what price would I not have paid to make Esarhaddon king?

Nabusharusur had been right to call me a coward. I was afraid of everything, it seemed, except death.

Five days passed, and then ten. Esarhaddon's great army had returned from the upper Euphrates—one afternoon, while out riding, I saw, far in the distance, the clouds of dust raised by their columns. By this time my brother was in Nineveh, had celebrated his triumph, and was looking about him. I continued to wait. I was not in a hurry.

At last the king's herald arrived—one man, so at least I was not to be dragged away in chains.

"You are summoned," he said. "The king bids you enter the city alone, and in a manner calculated to cause the least possible disturbance."

"Perhaps I should come disguised as a beggar," I answered. "Or perhaps the king would rather I were brought thither as a common criminal, tied to the tail of a cart."

"You know the king's will."

"Yes—I know it."

He left, the impassive messenger. He had never even come down from his horse, but then I was little inclined to shows of hospitality.

Very well. I would make no great spectacle of my entry into Nineveh—the idea had never so much as crossed my mind, but I would nonetheless dismiss it. I would ride there alone, a man on horseback, carrying no token of rank. I would be as any prosperous farmer come to the capital for business and perhaps a little holiday. Esarhaddon would have nothing to complain of.

In the morning I went out to the stables, accompanied by my overseer Tahu Ishtar, and put a bridle on the dappled gelding I would ride into Nineveh. Ghost, in the next stall, kicked against his gate and snorted nervously, as if he understood everything.

"I may be away some time," I said. "And I desire that the

best possible care be taken of that horse. Once, in Media, he saved
my life."

"It shall be as the master of Three Lions wishes."

My overseer punctuated his answer with a low bow, his hand
over his heart. I wondered how much he might know but decided
that perhaps it would be better not to ask.

"Such I am no longer, for I have made over the estate to my
lady mother. I know you will serve her as faithfully as you have
served me, Tahu Ishtar."

"I and my son both, Lord."

"Good, then—that is settled." I swung up on the horse's
back and held out my hand. Tabu Ishtar took it in both of his.
"And may things prosper with you always, and may the child in
Naiba's belly be another grandson to rejoice your heart."

"Good-bye, Lord. May the god hold you in his hand."

He knew we would never meet again. It was in his voice.

"Good-bye, Overseer."

When he released my hand I let the gelding have a taste of
the spur and left behind this place which had been my home.

I reached the marker stone of my own lands in the first hour
of morning and I did not expect to pass under the Great Gate of
Nineveh until about two hours after midday. With a nimbler pace
I could have been quicker in my journey, but I had had a large
breakfast and was inclined to be lazy and, in any case, nothing so
very pleasant awaited me in Nineveh.

The road ran always within sight of the Tigris River, which
at this season of the year lay within narrow banks. Her cold black
waters raced over her stone bed hissing like an adder—she too
was on her way to Nineveh.

I wondered what would happen there. Would I be confronted
with false witnesses, men paid to testify that I had plotted with
Arad Malik? Would Esarhaddon really stoop to that, since he
better than any would know my innocence?

Yet even as king he would not dare to charge me with my
true crimes, for how could he possibly admit to the world that his
son and heir, the child Ashurbanipal whom the gods favored, was
not his issue but my own? No, if he knew—and I rather suspected
that he did—he would keep silent.

So. What was left? An assassin—a hired dagger hiding in the

shadows? Probably. Everyone would know the truth, but no one would utter it. A king can reign with many scandals behind him, for men—if given a choice—will always believe what they want.

Sinqi Adad had said that before the flesh was burned from his bones. Was this the wisdom that comes to condemned men?

The sun in my face was pleasant. Life was a gift of heaven, even if it lasted but an hour.

Everything was clear on the road to Nineveh.

I met few people on my journey until I had passed the last marker before the city gates—the same spot where I had spoken for the final time to the *maxxu*. There, where the wheel ruts in the mud grew suddenly deeper, I passed a knot of farmers with their wagons, three or four of them, pulled to the side of the road, enjoying a jar of beer and a little conversation on their way to market. One glanced at me as I passed, and the sudden surprise that registered on his face showed that he recognized me. Five minutes later the same wagons passed me at a brisk trot, but the men looked away as they went by.

I stopped on the road and had my midday meal at a spot where I could already see the walls of Nineveh.

How had it all happened? Every step of our downward path was clear to me, and yet I still could not grasp how Esarhaddon and I, friends and brothers, could now be such unforgiving enemies. It seemed strange, and yet inevitable. My life in ruins, his without contentment or ease of spirit—it was bitter. This hatred between us, it was what I regretted most, even more than the loss of Esharhamat, whose love at least I had retained. If it was to be the assassin's blade, striking from some concealed place, I would not grieve to part from my life. Yet I grieved that it would be Esarhaddon whose treasure paid that it might be done.

Having finished my meal, I set out on the last part of my journey. By the time I was within five hundred paces of the Great Gate I could already see the crowds gathering.

By the time I had crossed half that distance they were lining the road, throwing flowers and gold coins in my path, reaching to touch me, or even my horse, cheering.

"Ashur is King! Ashur is King! Ashur is King!" they chanted, their faces flushed, wild with joy. As I passed beneath the Great Gate, the mud walls echoed the shouting. The Street of Ninlil, which led to the king's palace, was clogged with people— foreigners and natives, children and men, women holding out their babies that my shadow might fall across them. I could hardly make my way for the pressure of the mob that surged to come near.

And everywhere the cheering, the same cry from so many thousand throats: "Ashur is King! Ashur is King!" It was almost as if they were pleading with me or their god or both.

"This," I thought, my heart pounding within my breast, "this is the finest hour of my life. Whatever comes now, I will never know another like this."

There is a saying in the east that the three finest things in life are love, power, and revenge. The crowds who came to welcome me home to Nineveh gave me all three, if only for this brief moment. Whatever might come in the hours and days to follow, I was having my revenge on Esarhaddon in advance.

Even on a market day, when the streets are crowded, a man may walk from the Great Gate to the palace of the king in forty-five minutes. That day, on horseback, it took me not less than two hours. The people of Nineveh would not let me go. My head rang with their cheering, and I was drunk with the wine of their adoration. They, at least, had not forgotten me.

The steps of the king's palace were crowded as well. The nobles of my brother's court, perhaps attracted by the commotion, had come in their grandeur and their robes of office to witness what, no doubt, they had never expected and could hardly understand. I saw many faces that were known to me and many that were not. I saw perplexity, alarm, even fear. Yes, of course they were afraid.

And at last even Esarhaddon himself appeared on the palace steps—the king, in robes of gold, come once more to subdue the people of this hated, rebellious city. He raised his hand for silence, but the crowds paid him no heed. They kept up the joyful sound of their cheering—"Ashur is King! Ashur is King! Ashur is King!"—as if I were their king and they followed me from my crowning ceremony.

At last, at the foot of the stairway, I drew my frightened, nervous horse to a stop and dismounted. Esarhaddon was at the top, before the great doors, which stood open on their copper hinges, and I at the bottom, and we faced each other for the first time.

I mounted the steps, one after the other, slowly, the nobles of my brother's court breaking before me and the crowd still cheering at my back. One step at a time—it seemed to take forever.

At last I stood before him. A cold sneer was on his face, as if he had expected this treachery all along. And still they cheered.

I knelt at Esarhaddon's feet.

The crowd went silent. On my knees I held out my hands to him, my king and lord, in token of submission. And then I pressed my brow against the ground in front of him. It was a gesture no one could have misunderstood.

The world seemed to hold its breath. I raised my head and saw hatred in my brother's eyes—yes, for this he hated me more than ever. I regained my legs.

Esarhaddon said nothing. He simply turned and walked back inside through the open doorway.

I was informed it was the king's will that I not dwell in my own residence, the palace I had inherited from the Lord Sinahi-usur, but should abide within the royal palace itself. I was in fact being kept under informal arrest—I had freedom of movement within the palace and the house of war, now garrisoned with troops from the south loyal to Esarhaddon, but the city was forbidden to me.

They feared the mobs, of course. They feared that somehow, even after my public submission to the king, I might snatch the crown from his head—although whether I still had the power was difficult to know.

The mob, I think, was disappointed in me. They had expected that the Prince Tiglath Ashur would be their liberator, their champion. They had hoped for a miracle. As always, I was praised and honored because I was not my brother. And now I had declared myself his servant.

But what it had cost Esarhaddon to be seen receiving this public pledge of my loyalty! One cannot command what is freely given, and how it must have galled him to see me with my face to the ground, honoring him as king because it was my will. The victory had been mine—not his, but mine. I had paid him back for everything in that moment. His pride would never recover. He would remember all his life how I had shamed him. A man may triumph, even on his knees.

And now, again, I waited for his sentence, although now it hardly seemed to matter.

I was alone. Slaves brought me food and tended to my other requirements with silent efficiency but never spoke. For three days my solitude was unbroken.

But on the third night I received a visitor. As I sat before a brazier in what would have been my audience chamber, a door opened, a shadow fell across the floor, and I saw my sister, the Lady Shaditu—at least, I remember thinking, she wasn't an assassin.

Suddenly the slaves were gone. They had simply disappeared.

"I had thought by now you would have chosen your alliances," I said, grateful, in spite of myself, for even such of human warmth as she could provide.

"I have. But our brother does not take his women seriously enough to care where they go or whom they see."

"You are his woman now then?"

"Yes—you were expecting Esarhaddon to be as dainty as yourself?" She smiled at me and sat down beside me on the couch. It was only a smile, nothing more. "A crow steals scraps where it can. Esarhaddon knows my bed, as do other men. I wonder sometimes if he would still recognize me out of it. What happened to the slave girl?"

"The Arab? Zabibe? I gave her to a metalsmith with one eye. If his arm is strong enough—and his stomach—perhaps she is even happy with him."

This made Shaditu laugh. She threw back her head and laughed like a jackal. And then she put her arms about my neck and covered my mouth with her own. I could feel her tongue sliding between my lips. My hands covered her breasts.

"Go ahead," she whispered. "There is nothing to stop you."

Nor was there. Shaditu sighed with passion the moment I went into her.

When it was over, it might never have happened. She smoothed her hair back with her hands and smiled again.

"You perhaps wonder why I came? No—not for that. At least, not only."

"Then what else?"

"To tell you of your danger."

Now it was my turn to laugh.

"My danger . . . ?" I was still almost choking with laughter. "My . . . Shaditu—my sister—do you imagine I do not understand my danger?"

"Esarhaddon is filled with wrath," she said, ignoring this unseemly display of mirth. "When he entered the city, his captives chained to his chariot, an army at his back with which he had won a great victory, the people stood silent. There was no sound but the drums. And then you . . ."

She made a gesture with her hand, as if letting it float in the air.

"That is what you made of his triumph—nothing. Less than nothing. 'He thinks I am king through his grace?' he asks, and men are ashamed to answer him. He will kill you if he dares."

"And does he?"

"You know him. It lies with his dreams and his soothsayers —and his mother."

"If it lies with her, I am already dead."

She did not answer but rose, walking back through the shadowed room to the door, which still stood open.

"Good-bye, Tiglath Ashur," she said. "It is a weakness in me to love you, yet I do. I wonder if we shall ever see one another again."

And she was gone.

I stayed up until dawn and then went to my sleeping mat. A sword lay beside me for company.

The next morning, when a slave brought me my breakfast, there was a bowl of dates on the tray. I had not eaten more than two or three when I found a piece of leather, no larger than the palm of my hand, rolled up and lying among them. The writing on the inside was Greek.

"I, who have been one, understand the art of corrupting slaves. If you have need of me, whisper my name into the ear of the dog who brought this."

Yes, who else but Kephalos could have found his way to me through the walls of my brother's palace? Who else would have tried? But I would have no need of him now.

I had already received my summons to attend upon the king in the third hour after midday.

Esarhaddon was lying down, surrounded by his concubines, his feet dangling over the end of the couch while a black woman, with heavy gold wire woven into her hair but otherwise naked, washed them in a silver basin. I put my right hand over my heart and started to bow.

"Do not dare to do that to me again, Tiglath!" he shouted, kicking the black woman aside and jumping up. "I will not be made mock of twice."

"My Lord . . ."

"Stop it!"

He raised his arm, pointing it at me, and then glared savagely about him. "Get out of here—all of you. Can't you see I have business? Get out!"

For a moment the only sound was the quick patter of bare feet against the floor. It was only when we were alone that Esarhaddon seemed able to relax.

"They can be a nuisance," he said, almost as if to apologize, and then looked at me in a curious, pleading way. Suddenly it was as if nothing had ever changed between us.

"Who is the black one? Is she new?"

"Yes." He smiled, half to himself. "A present from . . . Tiglath, that was a foul trick you played on me."

"If I have offended . . ."

"I said to stop it! Damn you, when you take that tone I know you only mock me."

"You are the king, brother," I said, finding myself almost capable of pitying him.

"Am I? Yes. What of it?" With the petulant discontent of a child, he threw himself back down upon the couch. "I wish by the sixty great gods I wasn't."

"Nevertheless, you are. And there is nothing either of us can do about it."

Suddenly he grinned at me.

"No—there isn't, is there."

"No."

For a long moment he said nothing, but merely lay there on his back staring at the ceiling. I waited, since there was little else I could do.

"You came to Khanirabbat," he said finally, still staring at the ceiling, as if addressing it rather than me. "You could have joined the rebels—perhaps even been king in my place. Yet you came. And when I sent that idiot Sha Nabushu . . ."

"You are the king. If you recall, we have already agreed to that. I am a soldier and the king's servant."

"And if the king demands your life?"

"Then I suppose I will die."

"And when I die, you are thinking, the Lady Esharhamat's little bastard Ashurbanipal will rule in my place. You note I call my son a bastard, Tiglath—he whom the world in its ignorance calls my son. Or perhaps you imagined I would not guess?"

He looked at me now. Had he been a god instead of a man, I would have been burned to ashes under that look. Yet I said nothing.

"*My* son will rule, Tiglath—brother. *My* son, and no other. I bear you no ill will over this—over this, in particular—for I hate her as much as she does me. But my son will have a crown."

"That is for the god to judge. He will choose your successor no less than he chose you. It is vain to imagine otherwise."

The lord king sprang to his feet, trembling with rage as his face grew dark as a thundercloud.

"May the god damn your black soul, Tiglath."

"And may the god grant you all that we both know you deserve—Dread Lord."

There was a moment—only a moment—when I imagined Esarhaddon might be about to speak the words that would have made him my brother again. There was something in his eyes which suggested that pain of recognition a man feels when at last he has seen what he is about to lose. We stood facing each other. Anything might have happened. And then how different might have been the histories of our two lives.

"Guard!"

In an instant I found myself flanked by soldiers. And as I looked once more into Esarhaddon's face I knew that the moment had passed—or that what I had seen there was nothing more than my own last vain hope. Now his eyes showed me implacable hatred, and the despot's freedom from remorse.

"You will conduct the Lord Tiglath Ashur out," he said, his voice half choked with anger. "I believe somewhere we must still have the iron cage in which we accommodated the king of Babylon, the Lord Nergalushezib, during his stay with us. Find it—and place it at my brother's disposal."

One of the soldiers attempted to take me by the arm, but I shook him off and laid my hand across his face hard enough to knock him to the floor.

"Don't you dare!" I whispered through clenched teeth. "I

will go because it is the king's will, but for no reason else. Never dare to put your hands on me again!"

Both soldiers were armed and I had no weapon, not even a dagger, yet the one who was still standing retreated a pace. He looked to the king, his eyes pleading, as if afraid I had the power to strike him dead.

And Esarhaddon too was afraid.

"Yes, of course," he said, forcing out a syllable of feigned laughter. "Remember your manners and behave yourselves—he is, after all, the Lord Tiglath Ashur. A hero, and a prince!"

I could hear his laughter echoing behind me, even as the soldiers conducted me away.

In our family, it seemed, nothing was ever discarded. The cage was in a corner of the palace dungeon, its bars coated with more than ten years' accumulated dust.

The jailer, who was a kindly old man, a former soldier with half his left foot gone, cleaned it up for me as best he could and even gave me a cushion to sit on—the cage was not large enough to allow anyone to stand up inside it. He brought me my meals of bread and water and lightened my spirits with such conversation as was in his power. He remembered Nergalushezib very well and had helped to nail the crown to his head. He told me the cage had not been used since that time.

He had a wife and lived in the city. By his comings and goings I was able to keep some track of time and thus knew the days of my captivity. It was on the twentieth, in what I took to be the middle of the night—although, in that windowless cellar I could not be certain—that I received a visitor.

I certainly had not expected one. I assumed that, the jailer aside, the next person I would be likely to meet down there was the man sent to cut my throat. But it was not he. It was the king's mother, the Lady Naq'ia.

She was at that time between forty and fifty, yet, aside from the gray in her hair, she seemed little changed from the woman I remembered from my childhood. Her tunic and veil of black linen, shot through with silver, were the same. Her beauty was untouched and her smile was still unreadable.

The jailer—not my friend, but the one who relieved him, who never spoke—brought her a stool and she sat down, dis-

missing him with a wave of her hand. For a long moment she said
nothing. She merely peered in through the bars at me, as if the
sight gave her immense pleasure.

"How is your mother, Tiglath?" she asked finally.

"Well, Lady, when last I saw her. That was a month and
some days ago."

"My son has sent a new *shaknu* to Amat, so I assume she
will now go to your estate called Three Lions?"

"Where I hope, Lady, she will be allowed to live in quiet."

"Of course, Tiglath." She smiled. "Your mother is a sweet
soul and I mean her no harm."

"I am relieved to hear it, Lady."

She lapsed into silence again. And then, suddenly, as if something had reminded her of a joke, she laughed. It was a brittle,
silvery laugh, of a kind experience has taught me to mistrust in
women.

"Perhaps you do not remember," she said. "It happened
when you were only a child—I told your mother once that you
would end your days making bricks for the city walls."

"Yes, I remember. Is that to be my fate?"

"That is the difficulty, Tiglath—your fate. As much as it
would please me to see you sweating in a loincloth, in mud up to
your elbows and knees, I think it is not to be." She shook her
head, looking as if she would have liked to reach through the bars
and comfort me.

"There is the city mob to think of," she went on. "A man
who commands their affection as you do is not to be publicly
humiliated—they would not stand for it. And then there is my
son. He wants to kill you but I am not sure he quite dares. And
even if he finds the courage, would it be wise to kill you? How can
we kill you when the mob and the army both hold you in honor,
when you have made so public a submission to our power? Yet
how can we not, when Esarhaddon will never be true king as long
as he stands in your shadow? It is, as I have said, a difficulty. I
have yet to make up my son's mind for him."

The smile, which had never left her face, changed slightly.

"Or perhaps you have been imagining yourself in Esarhaddon's hands? No—in mine, Tiglath. Did you think I would trust
my son with such a decision?"

"He is king, Lady, not you."

"Yes, he is king. Yet I made him so, and without me he will not last as king for very long. He knows this—or soon shall."

"The god made him king, Lady."

"No, Tiglath." She shook her head, gently, like a mother instructing her child. "The god had nothing to do with it. I made him king, and no other."

So it was true. The rumors I had heard from the lips of Nabusharusur—they were true. The omens had been tampered with. It was not simply a wishful fancy of those whom the sudden and unexpected elevation of my brother had disappointed, but the truth. Perhaps—and I shuddered at the thought—perhaps Shaditu had not lied when she called me "true king."

For the first time since my father's murder, I felt the cold grip of fear in my heart—not fear of death, but of what is worse than death. It had all been for nothing, I told myself. Everything, my whole long surrender, for nothing. It was not the god's will I had served, but Naq'ia's.

All this time—Naq'ia's.

"And the death of Arad Ninlil . . . ?"

"Not I, Tiglath—at least not directly." She placed her fingers together before her lips, in what seemed no more than amused pity. "Dare I speak the name of Esharhamat to you, or do you still imagine her so fair, so innocent? Men are just such credulous fools. Yes, Tiglath, she did what I could not, although through means of my contriving. In this, if nothing else, we were allies.

"She poisoned him at dinner, and under the very eyes of his mother. The deed took courage, and a heart as hardened as my own. And her punishment now, as my son's wife, believe me when I tell you it is just."

I had no desire to hear more. I covered my face with my hands.

"Do what you will with me, Lady," I said. "For you have made me the most accursed of men."

"Yes, Tiglath—I know as much."

She rose, for she had achieved her purpose, and was thus willing enough to leave me to my thoughts.

"Esharhamat will not suffer alone," I said at last, my heart full of anguish. "The god will not permit these things to stand unavenged."

She paused for a moment, her hand already on the door, and smiled yet again.

"Perhaps not, Tiglath, although I care little enough for your crude northern god. Yet it seems it is not upon me that he visits his wrath. Look about you. It is I who may leave this dungeon, and you who must stay. Will you ever leave it, I wonder?"

I did leave it, for the god's voice was not stilled. Had I remembered his promise, all that he had revealed to me, I would have understood his design.

But I did not. My heart, in the days which followed, was closed to hope. I lay in darkness, waiting only for death.

And one day I really thought it had come.

But it was not death which came, only Esarhaddon, wearing a soldier's tunic. He came with his bodyguard of *quradu*. He came with a sword in his hand.

"Let him out," he told the jailer. And then, as if his wrath would not be contained, he struck the cage with his sword, making the bars ring. "Let him out, I say!"

It was the dream. Had not the god foretold this? The city a cage, Esarhaddon beating his sword against the bars . . . ?

I could see it in his face. He wanted to kill me, but I did not need Naq'ia to tell me he would not dare. I grinned at him. I knew no fear of him, for I had the god's promise.

The jailer undid the lock and opened the narrow little door. It was the first time in almost a month that I had stood upright, and my knees trembled beneath me.

"Get out of your kennel, dog," my brother growled, his face black with rage.

In the end, two soldiers had to help me. I stood, leaning against the cage that had held me like a fox in a trap, and I mocked Esarhaddon. I had no need to speak. To look him in the face was mockery enough, for it was he who was afraid, not I.

"Go ahead," I murmured. "The sword is in your hand. Nothing stops you. Kill me and be king forever—if you have it in your bowels even to be a man."

"Tiglath, do not . . ."

"Strike!" I shouted, not even caring. "Now or not at all."

We both knew that was the choice.

He was a long time deciding. In his heart, in his face, reigned a conflict plain to all who saw him. Yes, he wanted to kill me. Yes, that was why he had come.

Still, to this hour, I do not know what except the god's will stayed his hand, but at last he threw his sword down to the brick floor.

"Clean him up! The Lord Tiglath Ashur, my royal brother, looks like a dung carter."

He looked about him, smiling, demanding applause for his wit. There was only silence.

"He shall not hear my judgment like a slave," he said, his voice level now, his eyes on me, as if he spoke to myself alone. "Bring him to me in three hours' time."

He turned on his heel and left.

I had three hours. I was taken back to my rooms, hardly able to walk at first but gradually rediscovering that lost art, and there I was fed and bathed by slave women I had never seen before—not my servants, but Esarhaddon's. They did not speak. The solitude of my confinement was preserved, and it was better thus.

"Let him do his will," I told myself. "Let him kill me if he likes, but he will never live down the shame of this day." I took comfort in that, in believing that I had somehow won—that there was something yet to win.

And at the end of the allotted time I was clothed in the silver tunic of a prince and brought before the king in his great hall. He waited there, but not alone.

It was a noble place, the great hall. At its entrance stood the great winged bulls with the heads and beards of men, which are the protective genies of kings. On the walls were carved and painted panels, monuments to the glory of our father's victories. I had seen the Lord Sennacherib here a thousand times, banqueting with his nobles, dispensing justice, receiving tribute from the rulers of lesser nations. All the might and power of Ashur's land found its expression here, no less than in her armies, no less than in the temples of her gods. When foreigners came to this place, they trembled. When we came, we, prince and common folk, for whom the king's voice was as Great Ashur's own, we thrilled with pride.

And now Esarhaddon was here, surrounded by his nobles and the glory of kingship, blazing like the sacred sun in his robes of gold, holding the golden sword, his symbol of office. He stood apart, waiting, his face set and lifeless.

When I entered, all fell silent, turning their eyes to the king. I put my hand over my heart and bowed, for he was the king. I could not change it, and so I must bow to that.

He raised his arm, pointing the sword at my breast.

"This prince is my enemy," he said, his voice filling the hall. "In his heart he honors no king—even in my father the Lord Sennacherib's time he was rebellious. He would hide his rebellion, and yet from me he cannot. For I alone know the twistings of his mind, I, who have been his brother."

He lowered the sword and, with his eyes only, looked about him, judging for himself how men heard his words.

Yet they were not his words, as I understood now, but Naq'ia's. It was her voice I heard, and her wisdom. She had said how it would be—she had made all things between us plain. And thus I could pity Esarhaddon, for he seemed to know it not.

"Thus I banish him."

There was a murmur of voices, many voices, speaking different words to mean the same thing. And while they buzzed like flies over carrion, my brother—he who had been my brother, who had pronounced himself no more my brother—he and I exchanged a silent glance that said all that was needed.

"Let him be gone from this city," he went on, his eyes holding mine. "And let him pass forever out of the Land of Ashur, and all the lands where the might of Ashur's king is felt. In five days I will send out horsemen, that my judgment may be proclaimed. After that, if he is found, let him perish. I will reward the man who brings me his head."

Thus was I given those five days of grace, five days in which to stay ahead of my pursuers. Five days in which to find safety for my life.

"Let him hide himself in the dark lands beyond the sun. Let him fear to return, for his king hates him. Let him be taken from my sight! Go!"

I was led away. I hardly knew where, for my mind was full. Five days. Five days in which to quit the land of my birth. To wander in exile until death. Never would I see . . .

Esarhaddon, pointing with his sword, pointing to a wasteland where no man walked, speaking the one word: "Go!"

In his own time, the god had made all plain.

Thus began my days of wandering. I saw them stretching

before me, filled with sorrow. I thought my life was over. The god, at last, was finished with me. Since the hour of my birth, on the night of the blood star, I had not lived yet five and twenty years.

EPILOGUE

M y youngest grandson has a daughter named Deianira. She is four years old and has a great curiosity about writing, so now she sits on the bench beside me, watching as I scratch my narrative onto the goatskin parchment —I have grown rich in my exile and can afford this extravagance.

Since it is more cumbersome and, in any case, none hereabouts could read it, I have not used the daggerlike script in fifty years. I have not spoken my native Akkadian in nearly as long. I seem to have become almost wholly Greek, so as I form the letters I name them to little Deianira. Sometimes she climbs down from the bench, takes a stick, and draws them in the dust. She will have them all soon.

She is a clever child and a great pleasure to me. I like to think that she may live to be an old woman and will read this story to her own great-grandchildren, and that she will remember with some small affection the old man who wrote it, will remember this moment when we sat together and I filled the parchment with letters, and that thus I will not wholly die. In such vanities do old men comfort themselves.

A man in his first youth asks everything of the gods—wealth, immortal glory, pleasure, love—demands them as a right. Growing old is a process of learning that the gods give but little heed to these petitions. The voice that answers in the wind speaks of other matters, of wisdom and patience, which come of their own with time. Wealth, immortal glory, pleasure—these things are empty. Only love is real. To be happy is to know this, and it is the gods' one gift. When they wish to blind a man, or damn him, they give him the others. In their mercy, sometimes they take them away. They have left me in the shade of my vines teaching the alphabet to my grandson's daughter, and I am not empty of gratitude.

Curious are the destinies of men. A child born in that bitter hour of my banishment would be old now, withered, as I am, ready for death. And I still live. They are all dead—Esarhaddon, Naq'ia, Esharhamat, all the rest. They are ghosts whom I have brought back to live once more in the pages of this my story, my story which is not ended yet. For I was in error—the god was still not finished with me.

I would know exile and obscurity, happiness and sorrow, and something of the hearts of men. And one day I would return to the Land of Ashur. I would learn the secrets which then were hidden, and the will of heaven would stand revealed. My life, which I thought over, was just beginning.

But an old man's strength has its limits, and that story must wait for another day.

NICHOLAS GUILD is the author of several novels, including *The Berlin Warning* and *The Linz Tattoo*. He lives in Connecticut with his wife and son.